JUDGMENT
DAY

JAMES F. DAVID

TOR®

A TOM DOHERTY ASSOCIATES BOOK
NEW YORK

This is a work of fiction. All the characters and events portrayed in this novel are either fictitious or are used fictitiously.

JUDGMENT DAY

Copyright © 2005 by James F. David

A Tor Book
Published by Tom Doherty Associates, LLC
175 Fifth Avenue
New York, NY 10010

www.tor.com

Tor® is a registered trademark of Tom Doherty Associates, LLC.

ISBN-13: 978-0-765-34813-5
ISBN-10: 0-765-34813-6

First Edition: April 2005
First Mass Market Edition: February 2007

Printed in the United States of America

0 9 8 7 6 5 4 3 2 1

ACKNOWLEDGMENTS

I want to thank my wife, Gale, for being the first to read my manuscripts. Seeing the story through the mess in the first version isn't always an easy task. Thanks to my agent, Carol McCleary, for being even more optimistic than I am. Thanks to my editor, Bob Gleason, who never ceases to surprise me with the breadth and depth of his knowledge. Special thanks to those who read earlier versions of this manuscript, including Glenn Moran, Becky Ankeny (even though you didn't finish it), and Beth Molzahn. Your comments were very helpful. Abby, Katie, and Bethany, by now you know your dad has a very odd imagination. Finally, welcome to the family, Drew.

DRAMATIS PERSONAE

SIMON ASH—Trustee of the Crow Foundation, agent of Manuel Crow.

IRA BREITLING—Physical chemist and cofounder of the Fellowship.

RUTH BREITLING—Wife of Ira Breitling, member of the Fellowship since its foundation.

MANUEL CROW—Owner of one of the largest funeral parlor and cemetery companies in the country.

MR. FRY—Part of a CIA splinter group working behind the scenes to secure power.

GRAYSON GOLDWYN—Owner, publisher, editor of the *San Francisco Journal*.

JOHN HENRY—Fellowship pilot, husband of Shelly.

RUSS JACKSON—Assistant editor of the *San Francisco Journal*.

SELMA (GRANDMA) JONES—Resident of Chicago who organizes her community.

WILLIAM LICHTER—Midlevel NASA manager.

COBB MCGRIFF—One of George Proctor's army.

REVEREND CHRISTY MAITLAND—Ordained minister, operates a Christian Mediation Service funded by the Crow Foundation.

WYATT POWDER—Cable news anchor.

GEORGE PROCTOR—Advocate of personal freedom, gun rights, defender of the faith.

ROSA QUIGLY—Social worker, specialist in repressed memories.

FLOYD AND EVELYN REMPLE—Managers of the Sandman Motel, members of the Fellowship.

SALLY ROPER—Financial director of the Fellowship.

JANINE SAMPSON—Metro reporter for the *San Francisco Journal*.

MARK SHEPHERD—Cofounder and leader of the Fellowship.

MEAGHAN SLATER—Nationally recognized leader of the National Womyn's Congress.

EDWARD AND CARIN STAFFORD—Foster parents.

TOBIAS STOOP—Founder and leader of Earth's Avengers.

MICAH STRONG—Fellowship pilot.

SYLVIA SWANSON—Congresswoman.

ROLAND SYMES—Reporter for the *San Francisco Journal*.

KENT THORPE—Physical chemist.

JOSH THROWER—Foster parent.

SANDY WALLACE—Fellowship communications director.

RACHEL WATERS—Aide to Manuel Crow.

CINDI WINSLOW—Associate producer for a cable news network.

CONSTANCE WONG—Graduate student in physical chemistry.

In the last days, God says, I will pour out my Spirit on all people. Your sons and daughters will prophesy, your young men will see visions, your old men will dream dreams.

—ACTS 2:17

SIGNS AND WONDERS

> One day the angels came to present themselves
> before the Lord, and Satan also came with them.
> The Lord said to Satan, "Where have you come
> from?" Satan answered the Lord, "From roaming
> through the earth and going back and forth in it."
>
> —JOB 1:6–7

SAN FRANCISCO, CALIFORNIA

He set the candles in their usual places around the pentagram. That done, he carried the chicken down to the basement—a jet-black rooster, its head darting through the slats of its cage, bright black eyes looking around fearfully. He would sever that head tonight, watching the life fade from its eyes. There was still some joy in that, but sheer repetition had dulled his pleasure.

With ebony hair and eyes to match, a hooked nose and bony frame, Manuel Crow looked like a large featherless raven. Only his voice distinguished him from his avian namesake. Instead of a squawk, it was deep, rich, and melodious. Crow had the voice of a lounge singer but music had never interested him, nothing had, except death.

Growing up in his neighborhood, other boys played Little League or joined Boy Scouts, but not little Manny. He was a loner, shunning the ball games and bike trips to the swimming pool. Instead, he rode his Schwinn along the highways, looking for small animals run over in the night. Opossum were most common, but he also found raccoons, dogs, and cats. Only skunks escaped his attention—his mother would have none of those.

He used a burlap bag to carry his treasures home, the bag bouncing and swinging from his handlebars. Once home he retreated to his "lab," which he had set up in the old woodshed. He opened the animals first, slicing them from sternum to genitals, probing their squashed innards, understanding little of what he saw, but getting a sensual rush from the lifeless graying tissues. Next he skinned them. By puberty he was well practiced at separating the skin from the meat underneath, and like a professional taxidermist, he never cut or tore the fur. With the skin removed, Manny next scraped the muscles—the meat—from the bones. He found little pleasure in that—it was kitchen work. Cleaning the bones was easy compared to the skull, which had many nooks and crannies where the soft brain tissue and fibrous nerves hid. There were eye sockets to be cleaned, too. When he was younger he dug the brains out with a spoon, then used a nut pick to clean the hard-to-reach places. When he was older he used a water pick that he rescued from the trash. Working on his animals absorbed him in the same way putting model cars together did other boys. He spent hours picking out brain tissue, squirting clean the smallest orifices, until the skulls were free of every speck of tissue. Clean skulls were gray, so the final step was bleaching, accomplished by soaking the skulls in buckets of Purex. The finished product was as bright and clean as skulls baked under a desert sun. His best specimens were mounted on boards and by adulthood the walls of his lab were covered with animal skulls. If the skins were in good shape, they were tanned. Bones were stored in shoe boxes.

His parents told their friends their son wanted to be a veterinarian, but it was a face-saving fiction. On the one occasion they brought him an injured bird to heal, he dismembered it while it was still alive. In truth, his parents were afraid of him. They had reason to be.

His fascination with death eventually took him into the mortuary business. It began as an after-school job, his attention to detail and enthusiasm quickly coming to the notice of the owner. Always an energetic employee, he put in extra hours, hanging around, watching others work, and learning the business. The embalming was his favorite and even when he became owner of the mortuary, he kept some of that work for himself. Applying cosmetics to the corpses was difficult for him, since he saw no need to cover the gaping wounds or to putty the crushed skulls. Worst of all was faking compassion for the grieving relatives, but even this he mastered in time. It was a skill that would serve him well later in life.

The death business suited him, but left him with an emptiness—a longing for something more. By young adulthood he began to seek out that something. Sex and pornography bored him but it led him to the darker side of sensuality: sadomasochism. The leather and chains crowd excited him for a time, but when he discovered they too feared death, never willing to fully embrace it, he became disenchanted.

From SM he drifted into satanism, meeting those who worshiped the master of the realm of the dead. Strangely, he found the satanists were mostly women and they welcomed him, eager to teach him their rituals and invite him to their covens. A guest at first, he quickly became a member, then a leader, as he dared to take them to new levels. Before he joined, their worship involved only pentagrams, candles, and ritual. He introduced animal sacrifice.

Now the doorbell announced his guests, and he let them in: ten women and two men. Joking and laughing they made small talk, mostly about jobs and the weather. There was flirtation and contact in anticipation of the sexual free-for-all that would follow the black mass. Donning black hooded robes, they changed mood, solemn now. Crow set the tone, his black eyes and drawn face ready-made for solemn occasions.

The candles were lit, the coven called to worship. The black velvet covering was removed, exposing the statue of the Master. It was a devil, posed on one foot, the other leg held high as if frozen in mid-jump. Its hands reached up as if to catch something falling from the sky. Its head was tilted up; its eyes were closed. Complete with hooved feet and horned head, it was the classic image of Satan—the Devil—the ruler of the underworld Crow's coven worshiped. He had purchased the ceramic statue at a gas station parking lot, painting it red to make it more "satanic."

Crow led the others in worship, calling on the Master to favor them, to empower them through demons. They pledged to do his bidding and cursed the one who had cast him from glory.

As he led the ceremony, his disgust grew. It was nothing but a game to the worshipers, a useless ritual conducted as an act of rebellion, not unlike the tattooing and body piercing the women practiced. It was trick-or-treat for adults, no more real than Sunday morning worship rituals practiced worldwide. No more effective, no less. He had been disenchanted for a long time, and made up his mind then and there that this was his last night as a satanist—time to move on, to continue his search to give his life meaning.

The chanting began, the worship continuing. Candles splattered shadows of the swaying worshipers across the walls and ceiling. Eerie to those who feared darkness, watching the shadows comforted Crow. He found the shadows seductive, arousing him like few women could. Dark places had always been special to him.

Crow swayed with the others, chanting the ancient words, believing none of them. Then it was time for the sacrifice. He picked up the knife from the center of the pentagram, raising it to the dark deity, pledging loyalty, asking the Lord of the Underworld to accept their humble sacrifice. Crow had sacrificed many chickens, but always thought it was a poor sacrifice. If he were a god, he would be insulted by the offering. That was one reason he knew no deity listened to the nonsense they chanted—no deity would tolerate such an insult.

As Crow released the catch, the chicken retreated into

the cage, sensing its doom. Expertly, Crow snagged its neck tight in his fist. The coven's unified voice rose now in anticipation, Crow participating by rote. With the chicken in his right hand, and the knife in his left, he held them high in front of the statue. Then with a last loud supplication he severed the head in one quick stroke. The body flopped to the ground, then was up and running, blood spurting from the stump of its neck—this was the fun part. Then the unexpected happened.

"My time is soon!" a deep voice boomed.

Suddenly silent, the worshipers looked at each other, shaken by the unexpected voice. They turned to Crow, suspecting fakery. He shook his head, denying their silent accusations. The basement room was silent now. Shocked into a few seconds of silence, they began to speak, to explain away what they had clearly heard. Then one of the women pointed in horror. Crow turned to see the devil statue moving. The raised arms came down, the raised leg lowered until the cloven hooves both rested on the pedestal. Crow felt the others back away, leaving him to face the little horror. Then the head turned slowly until it faced Crow. There was a pause—a long moment of terror. Then the eyes popped open, glowing red as if lit by the fires of hell.

"Prepare the way!" a deep voice demanded.

The others ran, but not Crow. There was no fear in him, only joy. It was true—there was an underworld ruled by a deity of death and it had spoken to him. Now falling to his knees, he worshiped the idol, not from ritual, but from conviction.

CHAPTER 2   **BREITLING**

> Then the Lord said: "I am making a covenant
> with you. Before all your people. I will do
> wonders never before done in any nation
> in all the world."
>
> —EXODUS 34:10

COLUMBUS, OHIO

Her tears angered him, his foot involuntarily pressing the throttle closer to the floor.

"What are you crying for? It was the right thing to do."

"It wasn't right, it was convenient."

His foot pushed harder, the pitch of the engine whine reaching a new level.

"You're still in college, and I've got a year of graduate school left," he argued. "We couldn't take care of a kid."

No answer, only more blubbering.

"Maybe someday we would be ready," he said.

"Someday? You'll never marry me! I'm so stupid. I loved you so much."

He hated it when she talked of love. Maybe he didn't love her, but he did like her, so it wasn't like he had been using her.

"It's not a big deal," he said. "Lots of women have abortions."

"Not in my family. Not in our church."

She was right. In their church abortion was preached as murder. They had known each other since Sunday school but she was three years younger and at that age no boy was interested in a girl that much younger. Only when she showed up at the university did he see her differently. A lithe young woman with shoulder-length brown hair, she dressed conservatively but even so her pretty face set her apart from most of the freshmen that year. Her ready smile and bright personality attracted other boys, and eventually him. He still remembered what she said the day he approached her at the library.

"I know you, Ira Breitling," she said with a slight smile. "Your family sat on the left, next to the organ. We sat by the piano."

"I know you, Ruth Majors," he replied.

"In all the years we went to church together you spoke to me a grand total of—never," she said.

"I'm smarter now," Ira said.

Ruth smiled at that, and they talked about common acquaintances. He'd long since left the church, spending his Sundays hungover in bed, but to his surprise, she brought him back. They became a couple, attending church together, holding hands during prayer, sitting close in the pews, sharing hymnals. He was a prisoner of his feelings then, sure she was the most wonderful creature in all creation. He would have married her, but she'd promised her parents not to marry until she finished college. It was a stupid promise, but she'd made it and would keep it. When it was clear she would honor the promise, his frustration grew and he pressed her to go further, kissing wasn't enough. Wanting him as bad as he wanted her, she finally gave in and they became lovers. She was never comfortable with it, tolerating the intimacy because he wanted it. He tried to assuage her guilt by blaming her parents for forcing on her the promise not to marry.

With his lust satisfied, he saw her in a different light; no longer the unattainable goal, she became ordinary in his eyes. Soon, other girls caught his eye, each as unattainable as she had been, some even prettier. He began to wonder if she was the right woman for him, and doubt weakened his feelings for her. He noticed other girls—sitting next to him in classes, flirting with him in the Student Union. He *was* attractive, after all. At five feet ten, with a husky build, red hair, and blue eyes, he had always been noticed by the girls, and now he realized they wanted him. He was ready to talk to Ruth about giving each other some "space," when she told him she was pregnant.

"I still say it's not a big deal," Ira argued. "In a couple of weeks you'll forget all about it."

"I'll never forget—it was murder," she whispered hoarsely.

His foot hit the floor, the little four-cylinder engine knocking loudly.

"You're just depressed. The counselor said this might happen. You'll get over it. And don't call it murder. There was nothing to murder. You know what they told us. It wasn't a baby yet."

She'd stopped crying now, but her eyes were set in a stare, her mind focused on a single thought.

"God will punish us for this," she said.

"You didn't have to do it," he said defensively. "I didn't make you. We agreed it was best—together."

She wasn't listening, she'd slipped into a prayer.

"God, please forgive me for what I did."

At least she wasn't blaming him in her prayer.

"It was just tissue; that's what they called it, 'fetal tissue.'"

"I have sinned . . ."

"Maybe we should go somewhere and talk about this," Ira said, even knowing it would do no good.

Her prayer softened to a whisper, then she came out of it, looking at him.

"Please slow down," she said.

He lifted his foot from the floor, rpms dropping, the car slowing.

"You're going to be late for your shift at the lab," she said.

"I could get Constance to stay late," he said weakly, hoping to get away from her as soon as possible.

"Don't bother, I have to get home," Ruth said. "I'm bleeding."

"Bad? I mean more than normal?"

"How would I know?" she said angrily. "It's not like I've done this before."

"You want me to take you back to the clinic?"

"Take me home." Then she began praying again, softer now, barely above a whisper. He was relieved he couldn't hear her God talk.

"You'll get through this," he said weakly, doubting it even as he said it. She was taking it much harder than he thought she would.

Her prayers continued. He gave up trying to reason with her, riding in silence to her dormitory. She got out without a word.

"I'll call you later," he said through the window.

She walked away without looking back.

He cursed her as he drove away. He didn't feel guilty and he wouldn't let her push her guilt off on him. She was too old-fashioned—he should have known that and never gotten involved with her. He'd grown up with the same kind of narrow-minded people—his parents were like Ruth. The world they lived in was gone, their religion out-of-date, replaced by new theologies that allowed people to be human, to make mistakes.

No, he wouldn't feel guilty—he refused to feel guilty. They had done nothing that wasn't done a million times a year. It meant nothing—in fact it was a good thing. They weren't ready for a baby. Her family would have disowned her if she had a baby out of wedlock and she couldn't live without them. *It was the right thing to do!* he shouted to himself.

He pulled into the parking lot nearest his building, easily finding a spot. It was late Friday afternoon and most faculty and students were gone, getting an early start on the weekend. He and Constance Wong, however, had long days ahead, working in shifts, layering metal atoms on exotic ceramic surfaces. Dr. Kurtz was working against a grant deadline and his graduate students were paying the price.

Grabbing his lab coat, he was apologizing to Constance before she was within earshot. Constance had delicate features, blond hair, almond-brown eyes, and a ready smile. She was good-natured, generous, and as such popular among the physical chemistry graduate students. Once more Ira had counted on her generous spirit. Now close enough that he could be heard, he began his apology again. He only managed "I'm sorry . . ." when she started the vacuum pump, the noise drowning out his words. She frowned briefly, then smiled, pulling him to one side and leaning close so he could hear what she said.

"Kurtz came by an hour ago," Constance said, referring to their adviser. "I told him you were in the bathroom. You're just lucky he didn't come back. I had a diarrhea story ready to cover for you."

"Diarrhea? That's the best you could do?"

"I could have told him you were off with your girlfriend . . ." she began, then trailed off as if she knew where he had been.

"The bathroom story was fine," he said quickly.

"Anything wrong?" she asked sincerely.

"Just a tough day," he said, quickly changing the subject. "I'll set up the next layer."

"Great. Kent should be here any minute."

Ira turned his head so she wouldn't see his frown. Kent Thorpe was universally disliked by his fellow graduate students while at the same time popular with the faculty. He was brilliant, supremely self-confident to the point of being arrogant, and moved smoothly among the faculty as if he were a peer. He was awarded the Armstrong Fellowship on entry, which was a full ride with no teaching expectations. The fellowship freed Kent to pursue his own interests and not serve as an indentured servant to the faculty like the rest of the graduate students. To the disgust of the other students, Kent became a confidant of the faculty, brainstorming with them about their research. Within a year his name had appeared on two published papers when all he had done was consult. Most irritating to Ira was the fact Dr. Kurtz had become Kent's mentor, and now when Kent came to Kurtz's lab he walked around as if he were Ira's supervisor.

Arrogant and condescending, Kent was hapless with his peers, and Ira suspected he had never experienced a true friendship, let alone had a girlfriend, so everyone including Kent Thorpe was surprised when Constance Wong agreed to date him. When they dated a second time, Ira lost twenty dollars in a bet with another graduate student and Kent Thorpe lost his heart. The relationship mystified everyone in the department and even Constance could not explain the attraction. "I know he's not all that good-looking, or anything," she told Ira one day. Kent was average height, with curly brown hair that was long and unkempt. His head was wide in the back, then narrowed to the front, giving his head the shape of an ax. With little neck and wide shoulders, he looked slightly abnormal.

"He's kind to me, and he does something to me no one else does," Constance continued. Ira didn't know what "does something to me" meant, but it explained their relationship as well as anything could. Kent was smart enough to know he wasn't lovable and the miracle Constance represented, so Kent treated her like a queen, becoming protective and jealous. He wouldn't be happy to see Ira alone with Constance.

Constance worked at the computer updating the lab report while Ira reviewed the night's work. Kent arrived a few minutes later, staring coldly at Ira and then smiling warmly at Constance. They left for a break, Kent's arm around her waist.

The matrices they were synthesizing for Kurtz could be constructed out of a variety of metals and glass and they were in the midst of creating twenty-five experimental composites under a Defense Department grant. Setting up a run was complex. The metalo-ceramics they were melding were layered molecule by molecule, but to assure purity the bonding took place in a near perfect vacuum. To align polarity the particle guns were fired under an intense magnetic field. Each piece of equipment had to be recalibrated between runs and the chamber thoroughly cleaned.

Ira removed the metalo-ceramic alloy Constance had just finished, transferring it to a nitrogen chamber to prevent it from reacting with free elements in the atmosphere. He then cleaned the chamber, finding his mind drifting back to Ruth, worrying about her. She said she was bleeding. He should have called her. He did care for her, even if he didn't love her. He wouldn't want anything to happen to her.

His mind on autopilot, he found himself loading the particle guns, forgetting if he had finished cleaning the chamber. He couldn't remember doing the nitrogen flush. He cursed himself, doubling back, looking over his checklist. Then his thoughts drifted back to Ruth, her tear-stained face haunting him. He forced his mind back to his work, checking the calibrations on the particle guns and the magnetic field generator. An image of Ruth distracted him again. She was walking out of the women's clinic, through the protesters, held by the arm of one of the escorts. Someone in the crowd shouted at her, holding up a picture of a three-month-old fetus—Ruth had been three months along. Ruth burst into tears when she saw the human features of the fetus. Another escort quickly stepped in front, blocking the sign. He started the car, pulling forward as instructed by the clinic staff. Then they hurried Ruth out the door and into the car. He would never forget the look she gave him then—a mix of anger and hate.

Ira snapped back to the present, finding himself staring at the terminal. He had been working on a subconscious level, but all the parameters appeared nominal and he was ready to trigger the layering. He punched a key and the vacuum pump thumped away as it emptied the chamber. While he waited, Ruth's face came back—the look of hatred. She blamed him, but he wouldn't accept the blame. "*It was the right thing to do,*" he repeated to himself, realizing he had been telling himself that every few minutes since Ruth had come out of the clinic.

Focusing again on the screen, he clicked a key and powered up the magnetic field generator. The vacuum pump turned off before the magnetic field was to full strength. The sound of a door announced that Constance had returned. Ira realized he had been dawdling. She'd taken a break and he didn't even have the next sequence under way. The field was at full strength so he punched return and the particle guns went to work embedding metal molecules in the glass matrix. As his eyes drifted down the screen he saw his mistake, but it was too late.

Suddenly the hairs on his head and skin stood up—his eyes felt as if they had been blasted by a desert wind. Constance froze, her blond hair spraying out around her head. She reached up, pushing the hair away from her face. When she'd cleared her face she shouted to Ira.

"Shut it down!"

Ira hit the interrupt key—nothing happened. Constance pushed at her static-charged hair, struggling to keep her face clear. Suddenly her hair fell to her shoulders and with a swing of her head she swept the hair from her face. They had only a second to look at each other before they were suddenly slammed to the ground. Ira was smashed into his chair and over backward. One leg of the console collapsed, cables were ripped loose, and the computer crashed to the floor, the monitor imploding.

Ira found himself on the floor, an invisible hand pinning him, threatening to crush his chest. There was no give to the concrete floor and his ribs compressed. Breathing was impossible and even gasps were beyond him. His chest ached as his ribs bowed, his abdomen felt as if tons of brick were being piled on him. Just when he felt he could stand it no more, suddenly he could breathe.

He sucked in desperately, then when the panic of suffocation subsided, he could think again—he thought of Constance. Calling out he got no answer. He stood slowly, fearful of internal injuries, leaning on the end of the console that hadn't collapsed. Constance was lying facedown, a pool of blood spreading around her face.

"Constance? Are you all right?" Ira called.

He stepped toward her but then stopped. Suddenly his stomach felt as if it were in an elevator. Then he felt lightheaded. As he watched, the cables that had been ripped from the instruments began to float. The ghostly fiber-optic cables mesmerized him. Then the blood surrounding Constance formed into globules and lifted into the air. Ira's skin prickled and his stomach churned. He felt as if he were falling. Equipment around him began to float and then to his horror, Constance lifted from the ground, floating limply in the air, slowly rotating as if on a spit. Her nose had been smashed and her face was covered with blood. The horror in front of him masked his own sensations and he was off the floor before he realized it. As he looked down, seeing his feet six inches from the lab floor, he suddenly shot into the air, slamming against the ceiling. The ceiling tiles collapsed, the aluminum brackets bucking as the invisible force pressed him into the air ducts above. The sheet metal crumpled and sharp edges cut into his back. Again he felt his chest compressed and the terrifying feeling of suffocation returned. Constance was there too, he could see her body pressed into the wiring. Suddenly the rest of the false ceiling collapsed, hiding Constance. He wanted to protect his face but his arms were pinned to the ceiling. Then the room brightened. Like a white dwarf star, the vacuum chamber was glowing—white-hot, or electromagnetic radiation, he didn't know. The light was painful, but Ira stared, mesmerized. Then it exploded, the chamber becoming shrapnel, spraying the room with jagged pieces of steel. A piece slammed into Ira's face, burying in his left eye. He found he could scream, but he was also falling, reaching for his punctured eye at the same time. When he hit the floor the pain left him, replaced by darkness.

Slowly Ira became aware again. He felt no pain, no sensation at all; there was only darkness. Then slowly he could see again, even from his damaged eye—but there was little to see. All was blackness, except a pinpoint of light. With no reference point, Ira floated in the blackness, oblivious to up and down. The pinpoint grew, yellowing as it did. Now the size of a golf ball, it was joined by more pinpoints—six white dots that circled the bright center. As these new pinpoints grew they changed colors, only one remaining white. The closest to the core became silver, the next green, and the third red. The three outer dots grew until they outshone the inner dot, and they turned the green of sea foam.

Floating in the blackness Ira struggled to make sense of it. Then he floated nearer the circling dots, drifting in toward the center. The green dot grew, filling his visual field. Then he saw two more pinpoints circling the green dot, the larger chasing the smaller. Captivated by his vision, he was caught unprepared for the return of the pain.

Suddenly he was conscious, lying on the lab floor, his hand pressing on his ruined eye to stop the bleeding. Only then in his pain did the meaning come to him. Ruth's

baby—their baby—God had punished him. An eye for an
eye, that's what the Bible said. But he had taken more than
just the baby's eye. Was this just the beginning? Even in
agony, he knew the fires of hell would be much worse and
he found his lips begging for forgiveness.

CHAPTER 3 **GEORGE PROCTOR**

> Set me free from my prison, that I may praise
> your name. Then the righteous will gather about
> me because of your goodness to me.
>
> —PSALM 142:7

SWEET HOME, IDAHO

He'd never been in a cell that didn't stink of human
waste. Even the holding cells like this one smelled of it.
Sick of the stink, he pressed his face between the bars,
searching for fresh air. He found only the stink of hundreds of men packed together like animals. He wanted
out of there more than he had wanted anything in his life.
Twenty-eight months was the longest stretch he had done
and he vowed it was his last. He wouldn't give up his
guns, that was his constitutional right, but he would go
underground. He'd give up his newsletter and cable
show—become less visible. That way the FBI and ATF
agents wouldn't target him.

He gave up on getting a clean breath and flopped down
on the bench. He knew the guards were doing this
deliberately—he had given them trouble every day of the
twenty-eight months. Always a smooth talker, and a natural leader, he had stirred up trouble among the other prisoners. A word here about the food, a word there about the
amount of exercise time, and soon you have discontent. He

stirred up two riots that way. No guards died, but five were badly beaten. The guards knew he was behind the trouble and paid him back every chance they got.

He should have been released an hour ago, but instead they kept him stewing in the holding cell. He wanted away from the stink and away from the rigidity of prison life. Once out that door he would beeline for his cabin in the Idaho panhandle. There were supplies buried there, some money, and guns. Assault rifles mostly, converted to full automatic. That's how he made his living—a master machinist, he had the skills to machine the parts for the conversion. He could be back in business within a week, supplying survivalists with weapons of independence, but the government would be watching. He would have to be careful.

Now he stared at the ceiling—cracked concrete painted institutional green. Obscenities were scratched in the paint—that was the other common denominator in jail cells. He closed his eyes, trying to relax. When he did he could still see the ceiling.

Startled, he opened his eyes—the faded green paint was as before. With his eyes open, he traced a crack from one wall to the other. Closing his eyes, he could see the same crack just as clearly. Opening and closing his eyes made no difference. It was as if his eyelids had become transparent. Frightened, he squeezed them tightly closed, but the ceiling was as clear and bright as before.

He touched his eyelids; they felt normal, although he could see his fingers touching his closed eyes. They had been ordinary eyes until a few seconds ago; bright blue eyes complementing his blond hair. He pictured his oval face, with his closely cropped hair and small ears. There was nothing unusual about him—until today.

Opening and closing his eyes, he experimented, finding no way to dim his vision. Closing them tightly, he looked around the cell, his fear diminishing but his puzzlement growing. Then, in the middle of a string of obscenities scratched in the wall, he saw a glowing cross. Someone had etched it into the green paint. He opened his eyes and the cross remained, but the glow was gone. Eyes closed, the glow returned. He stepped closer and saw words scratched below the cross in block letters. "GOD SEES ALL." The words glowed as bright as the cross. Opening his eyes the glow was gone, the words ordinary. Through his eyelids they shone with an unearthly light. Now he understood.

His eyes were still closed when the guards came. They always came in twos when dealing with him. He had never assaulted a guard, but he was six feet four, with a barrel chest and beefy arms, and they never took chances.

"Finally found your release papers," one of the guards explained. "They got stuck under the wrong stack. I don't have any idea how that happened."

The second guard snorted, stifling a giggle.

He watched the guards through his closed eyes, seeing them just as clearly as if his eyes were open.

"Wake up! We're talking to you," the first guard prodded.

With his eyes closed he stood and walked to the door.

"What's with him?" the second guard asked. "He sleepwalking or something?"

The first guard inserted his club through the bars, prodding him in the stomach.

"Wake up. Time to go."

Proctor smiled, then opened his eyes, although it made no difference. He could see as clearly with his eyes closed.

The guards opened the cell door, motioning him out. He walked in front of them, eyes closed, negotiating the corners and stairs to the property room. His eyes were still closed when the manila envelope holding his personal effects was dumped on the counter.

"Check the contents against the manifest and then sign here," the clerk said.

He pushed the contents around, interested only in his new ability.

"You gonna open your eyes?" the clerk asked. "At least count the cash. Eighty-seven bucks, right?"

Ignoring the guard he pushed the contents back into the envelope with the edge of his hand and then signed the receipt. The clerk was staring at his eyes, trying to see if he was peeking. Snapping them open he startled the clerk.

"Creep! Get him out of here."

The guards jerked him around and took him to the exit and down the road to the chain-link fence surrounding the prison. Opening the gate they pushed him through.

"Oh, yeah," the first guard said. "The prison bus couldn't wait so you don't got no ride. There's a pay phone down that way so you can call a friend to come get you."

The guards chuckled, knowing he didn't have a friend within a hundred miles. No family either. They were still joking as they slammed the gate, leaving him staring through closed eyes at highway traffic. He didn't mind. He'd been given a gift—that's what his old Bible-thumping grandma would call it—a spiritual gift. He'd never been religious, but he knew this new ability came from God. But there were no instructions with the gift. It wasn't like the gift of healing, a person knew what to do with that—he needed a Bible.

George Proctor turned toward town, opening and closing his eyes, playing with his new gift and wondering what to do with it.

CHAPTER 4 **SHEPHERD**

> "Be strong and courageous, because you will lead
> these people to inherit the land I swore to their
> forefathers to give them."
>
> —JOSHUA 1:6

COLUMBUS, OHIO

Mark Shepherd knelt alone in the hospital chapel thinking, not praying—he was thinking he'd made a mistake. Four years ago he decided to leave the military and enter the ministry. Trained as a weapons technician, he was a specialist in maintenance and repair of nuclear weapons.

But he'd never been comfortable with his special skill. Walking away from the first weapon he repaired, he felt a twinge of guilt. After a year he wasn't sleeping well at night. When it came time to reenlist he'd declined the signing bonus and moved to San Francisco, enrolling in seminary. Too liberal for the conservative seminary he had chosen, he had been a theological misfit from the first day, arguing endlessly with faculty and other students over the role of sacraments in worship, whether baptism was by water or spirit, and whether the Bible was supposed to be taken seriously and literally, or just seriously. He left with a master of divinity degree and no sense of direction.

Still feeling called to minister, he looked for a congregation to pastor but found the doors of the church closed to him. Like his experience at the seminary, the Evangelical churches found him too liberal and the mainstream denominations lost membership every year, closing more churches than they opened. He applied for every opening but wasn't interviewed for any.

Mark moved back to Columbus, where he had grown up, renting an apartment near the university. To pay his bills he took a night clerk job at a Holiday Inn, then volunteered to assist as a hospital chaplain. The dying and the grieving welcomed him but only at the end of life. Honest remorse over past sins was rare. More often he prayed with those afraid of the unknown. To the terminally ill it didn't matter if he was selling Christianity or Buddhism; sometimes it didn't matter to him either.

He met Anita while working at the Holiday Inn. She was a college student working the desk to pay her tuition. A marketing major, Anita was outgoing, friendly, and popular with the guests. She struck the perfect balance between efficiency and cordiality, conversing with the guests as they checked in, her hands simultaneously registering the guests. Anita was pretty, not beautiful, with brown eyes and brown hair that she kept cut short. She smiled with slightly crooked teeth and laughed a little too loud. She didn't turn the heads of the men who checked in but they sought her out when they had special requests or problems to solve. Mark enjoyed working with her and quickly came to enjoy her company.

As a coworker, Mark worried about crossing the line into sexual harassment, unsure of her feelings toward him. He thought there were clues to her feelings, but wasn't sure. Didn't her eyes linger when looking at him? Wasn't her smile quicker and more genuine for him than other employees? Afraid to find out he wasn't something special to her, Mark shied away from taking a first step. Anita solved his problem. One morning as they left work, Anita asked him to breakfast. Mark said yes. Three months later they married and a year later Anita was pregnant.

They used the small inheritance Mark received after his mother's death as a down payment on a house. Mark's father had died when Mark was thirteen and his mother was a poor money manager. By the time Mark was old enough to give her financial advice her investments were seriously depleted. If she had lived five more years she would have been penniless.

They purchased a seventeen-hundred-square-foot starter home on a thirty-year mortgage. With three bedrooms, small family room, and a tiny yard, it was modest but more than enough for Mark and Anita.

They painted the baby's room yellow, since they didn't know if Anita was carrying a boy or a girl. They couldn't afford new furniture so they spent their days off shopping garage sales, purchasing a crib, changing table and dresser, then refinishing them in their garage. Two baby showers, one by Anita's college friends and one by employees at the Holiday Inn, provided room decorations, bottles, diapers, and toys. By the middle of Anita's seventh month the room was painted and furnished, baby clothes were washed and waiting in the dresser, and baby powder, wipes, and diapers were lined up on the changing table.

As Anita entered her eighth month they had narrowed their choice of baby names to one boy's name—Austin— and two girls' names—Judith and Melinda. The Shepherds and the little world they had created were ready for their baby.

Since they were short of money, Anita planned to work through her eighth month at the Holiday Inn. She didn't make it to her last day. The first snow of winter came in mid-October, catching motorists unprepared. There were fender-benders throughout the city but the worst accident occurred on the outer belt. Two young men in a pickup lost control as they passed a tractor-trailer. The pickup went into a spin and the truck driver jackknifed his truck as he tried to avoid them. The pickup spun into the guardrail, out of harm's way, while the semi slid sideways across three lanes of traffic. Then the pileup began.

Anita was three cars back, following a Ford Expedition. The Ford rear-ended the Lexus in front of it, just as the Lexus hit the skidding truck. Anita slid to a stop inches from the Expedition. She was safe, but only for a few seconds. Behind her was a semitruck pulling a flatbed stacked high with lumber. The truck was skidding, finding no traction in a thin smear of wet snow.

Anita's Honda was slammed into the Expedition, her car folding like an accordion as the rear bumper collapsed toward the engine compartment. Anita was caught among the crumpling steel.

Anita was brain dead by the time firemen cut her out of the wreck. At the hospital they performed a cesarean section to try to save the baby but it was too late. One of the surgeons told Mark the baby was a boy. He never understood why the doctor thought he would want to know that.

Mark buried his wife and baby together, buying an expensive headstone to mark their passing. He visited the cemetery daily for six months, keeping fresh flowers on the grave, brushing the snow from their tombstone in winter, then in spring, making sure the new grass growing over his family was watered and weeded.

Too depressed to work, Mark quit his job at the Holiday Inn, staying home, staring at the television, watching the bills pile up. The bank eventually took his house and sold it at auction. The collection officer who supervised the repossession told Mark he was sorry for having to take his home away. Mark believed him.

Once the mortgage, penalties, interest, and repossession costs were paid, there was nothing left for Mark. His mother's inheritance was gone. Mark held a garage sale just before the bank evicted him. He sold Anita's clothes and the baby furniture and most of the rest of his household goods. Then he went through the few pictures there were of him and Anita, filling two photo albums, then burning the rest.

After the sale he had enough to rent an apartment. Again, he chose an apartment close to the university, enjoying long walks on the campus and the noise and bustle of the bars and restaurants along High Street. After three months his money was nearly gone and he had to choose to follow Anita and their son into the afterlife or find a way to go on living.

Mark felt no joy in living, had no sense of direction for his life, and refused to be comforted by friends, pastors, or former coworkers. The only thing he felt certain of was that he wasn't ready to die yet. He feared living, because of the painful memories, but part of him insisted it wasn't yet time to let go of his soul.

He got his job back at the Holiday Inn and two months later returned to his volunteer work as a chaplain. He wasn't ready to return to worshiping with a congregation— he couldn't bear their sympathy—but he did feel he could sympathize with others.

Tonight he knelt in the empty hospital chapel, meditating, opening himself to God, looking for something to fill the emptiness inside. He heard nothing from God and felt no presence of His Spirit. He began to wonder if he should return to the military. At least as a nuclear weapons repairman he carried out a useful function. Growing up in a church, he had loved Sunday school and the stories of the great biblical heroes—David, Samson, Joshua. He had listened to the sermons too, while his friends wriggled in their pews. He believed it when the pastor said that God had a plan for everyone, a purpose for everyone's life, and he prayed nightly for God to make it known to him. Now, life had taught him otherwise. Sitting in an empty chapel he found he not only didn't believe God had a plan for everyone, but he doubted God's existence at all.

Mark sighed deeply, saddened by his losses. He had no house in the suburbs, no wife or baby, no money in the bank, no meaningful career. Now, he knew there was no omnipotent being who cared about individuals and set the direction of their lives. With that realization, Mark pressed his hands to his face and began to sob.

Suddenly he was dreaming—in vivid color. He was alone on a great desert, striding across the great emptiness. The sun was bright overhead, but not hot. Effortlessly, he climbed a dune and looked in all directions. There was nothing but golden sculpted sand, even his footprints erased by the wind. He looked into the distance, seeing much farther than his myopic eyes normally allowed. Instead of curving out of sight, the Earth curved toward the sky, as if he were inside a sphere. He turned slowly, seeing every horizon curving toward the sky, but when he looked up there was no sun. The desert hung above him, the sands threatening to pour down as if from an hourglass. Confused, he stepped from the dune, trodding down the other side. When he reached the bottom he heard a great commotion. Turning, he saw a great horde of people coming over the dune. Afraid, he ran to the top of the next dune, but they followed him up and then down the other side. He ran from dune to dune and still they followed. They became a great burden to him, and he pleaded to be left alone, but still they followed.

"Excuse me, are you the chaplain?"

Mark turned with a start to see a nurse leaning in the chapel door. Disorientated, he looked around. He was back in the chapel, kneeling, as if in prayer. Had he fallen asleep? Was he dreaming? He didn't feel sleepy, he felt exhilarated.

"I said, are you the chaplain?" the nurse repeated slowly.

"I'm his assistant."

"The patient in 303 is asking to see a minister or rabbi, or someone. I think he wants to pray or something. Can you do that?"

"Of course," Mark said.

Mark got to his feet while the nurse watched him curiously.

"I don't think I've ever seen anyone in here before," she said as she led him out into the hall.

Stopping at the nurses station, she retrieved a chart.

"His name is Ira Breitling. He seems pretty young to be asking for a minister. I guess he thinks he's dying."

"Is he?"

"He's in serious condition but it's mostly broken bones. They had to remove his left eye and he ruptured his spleen."

"Car accident?"

"No, he was the one that survived the explosion at the university. It was on the news."

Mark remembered hearing about the incident. A young woman had been killed. There was little else he needed to know, so he excused himself and entered the room. Ira Breitling had one leg suspended above the bed. His left arm was in a cast and a thick band of gauze covered the left side of his face. His right eye was closed but opened as Mark approached the bed.

"I'm Chaplain Shepherd," Mark said. "The nurse said you wanted someone to pray with."

"No. I mean sure, but it's more than that. Do you believe?"

Mark hesitated. Only minutes ago he had abandoned his belief in God and wept over the loss. Then he had had a remarkable dream—a vision. He didn't know what to make of it but it was more than a dream.

"Yes, I do believe in God," Mark said.

"I mean really believe!?" Breitling pressed.

Mark had never had anyone question his faith in this way. People frequently wanted to challenge his theology, wanting to know his stand on creation and evolution, and a host of other theological issues. All this young man cared to know was whether he had taken the first, most critical step. Did he believe there was a God? No qualifiers, no theological litmus test, just a simple fundamental belief in a higher being.

"Yes, I honestly believe there is a God," Mark said. "But that's all I can say for certain. Everything else about God, and the worship of God, is a mystery to me."

Ira closed his good eye, relaxing back into his hospital bed. Then he mumbled, "Thank you, God." When Ira spoke again he told an incredible story—it was the story of the explosion but with detail Mark never read in the newspaper. Then Ira shared his vision of the bright dots circling each other. As Mark listened, he knew what he had experienced in the chapel wasn't a dream, it was a vision—a message from God. When Ira Breitling finished, Mark shared his vision with Ira. They talked for hours after that, alternating with prayer. The nurse insisted Mark leave three hours later. He came back every night after that. When Ira was released from the hospital it was Mark who picked him up.

CHAPTER 5   **MIRACLE**

> God is light; in him there is no darkness at all . . .
> if we walk in the light, as he is in the light, we
> have fellowship with one another . . .
>
> — I JOHN 1:5–7

PORTLAND, OREGON
Twenty years later

Reverend Christy Maitland listened to Simon Ash, a neutral expression fixed on her face. It was a well-practiced expression, used daily in her work as a mediator. She could maintain the "I'm listening but not taking sides" look for hours, even under verbal assault. She had been called every name ever invented for women and even some typically reserved for men. She kept her placid expression through it all, always calm, always accepting.

Today was a good day for Christy, since no one had called her names yet. Her visitor, Simon Ash, was angry, but not at her. Simon was a short man, maybe five feet five, thin, nervous, his brown hair well into male pattern baldness. Simon had a penchant for brown clothes, today wearing brown slacks, white shirt, and a plaid bow tie. Simon always wore bow ties and he fiddled with them while he spoke. He fiddled even more when he was nervous.

Simon had recently taken up the cause of a gay couple enrolled at a local Christian college, and played with his bow tie as he described the ensuing fight with the administration. The couple, he explained, had come out of the closet during their junior year, creating an uproar on the campus. The college was owned by a denomination that still hadn't come to terms with gays in its midst. The gay students sought out Simon, asking him to represent them. Now Simon was in her office, describing his efforts. As a trustee of the Crow Foundation, which funded Christy's mediation service, he was always welcome in Christy's office.

"That fundamentalist college has rules against gays having sex and they are threatening to kick them out if they do."

Christy corrected him gently, her face neutral.

"The rule is no sex outside of marriage. It applies to heterosexual students as well."

"Exactly. That's why I had them flown to Hawaii where they got married. Now the college can't stop them from having sex. If the administration expels them we'll take them to court and go after their state and federal funds. If we can choke off their state and federal financial aid, we can shut them down. Without a breeding ground, these religious fanatics might finally be cleaned out."

"Simon, I'm a religious woman," Christy pointed out.

"You're not like them. You don't let your religion run your life."

Christy did not feel complimented. She had known Simon for several years, never understanding his passionate crusade against religion. Was there an issue from his childhood, an unresolved conflict related to his early religious experience? Trauma?

"I really came to see you for another reason," Simon said.

Fumbling in his coat pocket, Simon pulled out a folded piece of yellow paper.

"These were sent to news organizations all over the country. A friend at CBS sent me this."

Unfolding the paper, she read:

WITNESS A MIRACLE

OCTOBER 2O, AT 4 P.M.

THE LIGHT IN THE DARKNESS FELLOWSHIP WILL INAUGURATE THE NEW CHRISTIAN AGE WITH THE LAUNCH OF THE SPACESHIP

Rising Savior

**Light in the Darkness Fellowship
Route 17, Christ's Home, California**

"I've never heard of the Light in the Darkness Fellowship," Christy said.

"Not many have. They moved into the town of Exeter ten years ago. A few years later there was enough of them to outvote the local residents and they took over the city council. They made the news when they changed the name of the town. The locals were pretty unhappy but couldn't stop them. Since then the cult's been quiet. Until this arrived I didn't know they were a saucer cult."

Christy knew saucer cults were Christian offshoots that confounded their religious beliefs with belief in UFOs. The cults first appeared in the 1950s and had popped up regularly ever since. Virtually all of them claimed communication with "higher beings" and predicted world cataclysm. Usually, the groups drifted apart after their predictions failed and the saucers never appeared. Sometimes these cults took drastic action, like the Heaven's Gate mass suicide.

Christy looked at the announcement again.

"This doesn't say anything about flying saucers."

"What else could it be?"

Christy couldn't guess but wasn't as willing as Simon to jump to conclusions. That was an important trait for a mediator.

"I want you to go with me to see the saucer launch," he said.

Christy looked at the amateurish announcement.

"They couldn't even afford to pay for decent printing. They're not worth your time and effort."

"There's money there, they're just not spending it," Simon said.

Simon was holding back something.

"I just want to get a look at the cult," he said. "With you along, I might be able to meet the leaders."

Christy was being used. Simon wanted to use her reputation as a theological bridge builder to get an inside look at the cult. Uncomfortable playing the Judas goat, Christy looked for a way out.

"We'll never make it. It's at least a six-hour drive."

"I've got a plane."

Trapped, Christy assented, embarrassed because she was only doing it to protect her grant.

Christy was a seasoned commercial air traveler and comfortable in jumbo jets. Simon's plane was tiny in comparison and at the mercy of the air currents in a way the jumbos never were. The plane bounced and swayed in alarming ways, Christy's stomach always a second behind with each lurch. She considered it a miracle when they approached the Light in the Darkness Fellowship Ranch and she still hadn't retched.

Using the highways as markers, Simon followed the

long access road to the ranch. As soon as they crossed the perimeter their perception of the cult was shaped. A double row of barbed wire ran out of sight in both directions.

"See the barbed wire? Look, along the road, guard towers and multiple gates. It doesn't make sense," Simon said.

"Why?" Christy asked. "A lot of cults are security conscious and a little paranoid. Jim Jones in Guyana had his people believing the CIA was out to kill them."

"Saucer cults are usually different. I've never seen one that fortified their compound. They don't feel they need to since they've put themselves in the hands of higher beings—protection is extended to them. They don't lock out the world so they are easily penetrated. I joined one myself when I was in graduate school. It was my master's thesis."

"Are you sure this is safe? If they don't want people driving into their compound, they surely won't want people flying in."

"I called ahead. They have a landing strip and we're welcome to use it."

The central compound came into sight. Essentially a small town, it was laid out in an L shape. There were six wood-frame buildings that looked like shops, barns, garages, and other commercial structures. Surrounding the core were many smaller cottages. The road through the middle of the compound was paved but as they flew over the compound the pavement ended leaving two dirt ruts. Simon continued following the ruts. Then large concrete buildings came into sight. This is where the money had been spent. Several large multistory buildings sat in a semicircle next to a large concrete circle. There was a tower covered with antennae and another topped by a radar dome. Grandstands sat on the far side of the circle with cars parked behind; people sprinkled the seats. What Christy didn't see was a runway.

"Where are we supposed to land?"

"Here it is."

Simon banked the plane into a turn and Christy saw a long strip of green grass.

"You can land there?"

"This plane can."

Christy held her breath as Simon throttled back and set the flaps. Then throttling forward and back, he brought the plane in for a bumpy landing. Happy to be on the ground, Christy quickly climbed out expecting someone to be waiting for them—there wasn't.

"Simon, this doesn't fit either. Miles of security fence and guard towers but no one to take charge of us when we land?"

"It's odd, all right," Simon said, nervously playing with his bow tie. "A cult this security conscious should have had guards waiting for us. Let's get a look around while we still can."

Christy followed Simon toward the buildings. The largest was four stories tall with a large airplane hangar door. The others looked to be industrial buildings, made of concrete blocks and corrugated steel. A few people could be seen in windows, but they ignored Simon and Christy. They circled the buildings but saw nothing unusual and no one challenged them. Finally, Simon stopped in front of the grandstands, studying the concrete circle. It was a plain, poured concrete slab.

"Landing pad for the flying saucers," Simon declared.

"It could be a heliport," Christy suggested.

"Not with these cuckoos. It's a saucer pad, all right. I've seen them before. There's two of them in Wyoming, one just outside of Gillette. That one has its own lights and generator."

Christy saw nothing but normal outdoor lighting around the compound. With nothing left to see, they joined the handful of visitors gathered on the grandstands. An empty podium stood in front of the stands. Simon pulled Christy high into the stands directly in front of the podium, toward a black man in sunglasses who stared at Simon.

"I should have known you'd show up here, Simon."

"I never miss a freak show," Simon replied. "This is Christy Maitland. Christy, this is Roland Symes, you might have read some of his columns."

She recognized Symes's name from his byline. He

wrote for the *San Francisco Journal* and was syndicated
nationally. Symes was an attractive man, just under six
feet tall, hair cropped short, his skin dark, but his facial
features reflecting a racial mix with narrow nose but
wide lips.

"That's Reverend Maitland, isn't it? I tried to interview
you after you brought those white supremacists in."

Christy had been inundated with requests for interviews after she talked a group of white supremacists into
surrendering to federal authorities. It had been three grueling days in the Idaho panhandle and afterward she
wanted nothing but a bath and a soft bed. She turned
down all but one interview.

"I did talk to a pool reporter."

"I don't report what every other reporter has. Maybe
when this fiasco is over you could spare me a few minutes?"

Even sitting, Symes was clearly a tall, thin man. His
eyes were intense and Christy squirmed, searching for a
polite way to say no. Simon saved her.

"What brings the great Symes to an event like this?"
Simon asked. "A high school bake-off would be more
newsworthy."

"I'm not here for the show. You see that guy down
there," he said, pointing.

Christy followed his point to see a man reclining on the
front bench. His head was tilted back—eyes closed. He
was balding, with blond hair combed to cover bare scalp.
His face was tan, but soft-looking with rounded features.
His body looked lean and hard.

"He supplies automatic weapons to every religious gun
nut in the country," Roland said.

"George Proctor," Simon said.

"Very good, Simon. Everyone knows he does it but
he's slick and no one can prove it."

"And you can?" Simon asked.

"I just want an interview."

As Simon and Symes talked, Christy noticed George
Proctor's eyes open. Then he turned and stared at them.
Closing his eyes again, he stood and began stepping from
seat to seat, climbing the grandstand. Only after he faced

them did he open his eyes. They were a vibrant blue. He spoke in slow, measured tones.

"My mother taught me it was wrong to talk behind someone's back."

"You've got good hearing," Symes said.

Proctor turned around, sat, reclining and closing his eyes.

"I see more than I hear," Proctor said.

"My name's Roland Symes. I'm a columnist and I'd like to interview you."

"No."

"It's a chance to give your views to a national audience."

"Pick up a Bible and a copy of the Constitution of the United States of America if you want my views."

"I want your spin."

Proctor turned back around, his eyes still closed.

"You don't spin God's word or the Constitution. The Bible speaks directly to your heart and the Constitution to your mind. An honest man can sense the truth in both."

"Where in the Bible does it say you've got a right to own an Uzi?"

"Samson would have used one on the Philistines if he'd had one."

"That's the kind of thing my readers want to hear," Symes said.

"The story today is what's going to happen here," Proctor said, indicating the concrete pad behind him.

"A saucer landing?" Simon cut in.

Proctor turned to face him, his eyes still tightly shut.

"It's not a landing, it's a launch," Proctor said. Then he stood and walked back down the grandstand, his eyes still closed.

"He's as creepy as they come," Simon said.

"He's dangerous," Symes said. "I won't get anything out of him today."

Symes stood to leave when two men and a woman approached the podium. Symes sat down again, staying for the show. A dozen more sect members exited the nearest building and spread out, circling the concrete pad. The cultists faced the grandstands that contained about a dozen spectators. One of the men stepped to the podium and pulled a card out of his pocket. He looked to be in his forties, of average height and build, with brown hair and eyes. His most distinguishing feature was a Roman nose. When he spoke it was with a loud resonant voice that would be well suited to a preacher.

"Ladies and gentlemen, please join me in a word of prayer. Father God, creator and sustainer of life, master of the universe, we thank You for leading us here today and making this great event possible. We thank You for Your continuing love and for opening this door for Your people. Sustain us as we seek to carry out Your vision. Amen."

"Typically egocentric," Simon whispered. "Cultists always think they are the center of the universe. It's as if God doesn't have anything else to do but watch over them."

"My name is Mark Shepherd. We have invited you here to witness the launch of the spaceship *Rising Savior*. Today we will demonstrate our technology by putting a satellite into orbit. Like the Soviet Union's first satellite, *Sputnik,* our satellite will broadcast only a simple message."

Shepherd paused, and looked at the sparse crowd and then continued.

"We know you expect us to fail, so we will proceed with the launch immediately. After the launch we will distribute information about our launch capabilities and our fees."

Without another word Shepherd turned and walked to the pad, signaling toward the airplane hangar. With the sound of metal on metal the doors slid apart, slowly revealing a dark interior.

"They're awfully serious about this," Simon said, snickering.

Christy was puzzled. She had expected a long sermon designed for the nonbelievers drawn by the flyer, followed by an announcement that the launch would have to be delayed for spiritual or technical reasons.

Leaning back, Symes said, "What are they planning? There's no rocket on the pad and that hangar isn't big enough to hold one that could put a payload in orbit."

"Not to mention the blastoff would kill everyone in the stands," Simon added. "They are delusional."

The doors finished opening and a tractor appeared pulling a trailer. Laughter spread through the spectators.

The machine on the trailer was nothing like a rocket. There were two large steel spheres separated by a latticework of steel tubing. In the middle of the latticework was a small satellite, with a dish antenna and folded solar panels. On either side of the satellite were two halves of another sphere. A small electric cart carrying three men followed the bizarre craft. Two of them were wearing space suits. One of the men in suits wore a patch over one eye.

The sparse crowd continued to snicker and point. Simon laughed hardest of all. Symes became serious, leaning forward. Christy watched with interest. The satellite looked real enough, right down to gold foil shielding on some of its parts. The spheres on either end were identical and sat on round bases. There were hatches built into the top of both spheres. "Rising Savior" was stenciled on both spheres and painted below the name were American and Christian flags.

When the *Rising Savior* was in the center of the concrete pad the tractor was unhitched and returned to the hangar. Ladders were placed against the spheres and two assistants opened the hatches in the tops. Then the two men in the silver space suits climbed the ladders and disappeared inside, the hatches securely latched. Then the clamshells were closed over the satellite. Next, the pad was cleared but then nothing happened for several minutes. Then the man called Shepherd returned to the podium.

"There will be a slight delay while they straighten out a communications problem."

"Next will come the announcement that there are technical difficulties," Simon said.

"What do you think those spheres weigh?" Symes asked.

"They're fake—probably wood," Simon said.

"They're steel," Christy corrected. "From the look of the carriage it's riding on I'd say it's a ton."

"Whatever it's made out of," Simon said, "it's not going anywhere."

Christy inched forward on her seat when Shepherd came back to the microphone.

"The technical difficulties have been worked out and we are proceeding with the launch. If you have sunglasses you might want to put them on."

Christy noticed that George Proctor put sunglasses over his closed eyes.

The pad was still ringed by members of the sect who now pulled sunglasses from their pockets and put them on.

A whine came from one of the spheres and then the other. The noise rose quickly in pitch and then passed out of human hearing range. Then the base the spheres sat on began to glow, the light expanding like an inflating balloon, enveloping the entire craft. Christy closed her eyes, then turned her head to protect her eyes. Just as the light became painfully bright it dissipated. Christy blinked away the dots on her retinas, looking back to the strange craft. Particles of dust began to dance around the craft forming a small dust cloud. The cloud expanded, soon reaching the audience, who covered their faces as it passed. When it did, Christy's skin prickled and the hairs on her arm stood erect. When she looked back the *Rising Savior* was three feet off its carriage and still climbing.

"It's a trick," Simon said. "It's a balloon. It's got to be."

The craft continued to rise and then stopped twenty feet off the ground where it hovered. Cameras flashed.

"I told you," Simon said. "They've got it on wires or something."

Then the *Rising Savior* was moving again, picking up speed. Now silent, the crowd gasped in amazement as the craft rose higher than the buildings, then picking up speed, the *Rising Savior* shrank to a dot and disappeared.

The shocked crowd sat in silence, then excited murmuring began. Some bolted for their cars to spread the news. Symes pulled a cellular phone from his pocket but paused in mid-call. Looking at Christy he said, "What can I say?"

"Say you just witnessed a miracle," she said. "It's the truth."

CHAPTER 6   **CHRIST'S HOME, CALIFORNIA**

> Radioactivity, penicillin, microwave cooking,
> even Cool Whip, are all the products of
> serendipity. Never underestimate the role
> of chance in progress.
>
> — *ACCIDENTAL GENIUS,*
> MALCOLM REYNOLDS

CHRIST'S HOME, CALIFORNIA

After the launch, members of the Fellowship passed out information packets. No high-gloss brochures, no color printing, just black and white on both sides, stapled at the corner. At the top was a Scripture verse: "Lift your eyes and look to the heavens . . ." Isaiah 40: 26. Next there was a picture of the spaceship *Rising Savior,* followed by a description of its lift capability. The next page described the satellite just launched, its orbit, and where to tune to pick up its signal. The rest of the pages listed the kind of space services the Light in the Darkness Fellowship was offering and a list of rates—all in the millions of dollars and indexed to the type of orbit desired. Nowhere could Christy find a technical description of how the *Rising Savior* managed to rise.

Protests were loud and long when the Fellowship shooed the visitors out of the compound and then escorted them down the road to the edge of their property. Christy and Simon were accompanied to their plane by two tight-lipped members of the Fellowship. Simon questioned them but they only referred him to the handout they had been given. Once in the air Christy had a change of heart. Shouting over the roar of the engine she said, "I want to stay. Can you put me down somewhere near here."

"I can, but I don't think you'll get any more out of them."

"That ship hasn't come down yet. I'd like to be here when it does."

"They won't let you close."

"They'll have to say more eventually. Besides, it will be dark soon. I don't like flying in these little planes even in the daylight. Why don't you stay over too?"

Christy didn't really want Simon to stay. Tomorrow was Sunday and there wasn't a church in the compound. She was hoping they would come out to worship.

"I can't stay," Simon said. "I have something I need to do."

Simon's face darkened as he spoke and his voice wavered slightly.

Simon found an airstrip on the outskirts of Christ's Home and dropped her off, then flew off to the north just as the sun was setting. Christy rented a car from a gas station and drove into Christ's Home. She hadn't planned on staying over, so she stopped at a Wal-Mart for toiletries, nightgown, jeans, and a sweatshirt.

Christ's Home was strangely quiet, the streets virtually empty. One pass through town revealed only two motels—the Eternal Rest and the Sandman. The Eternal Rest sounded a little too final so she pulled into the Sandman. The lobby was empty. The sound of a TV came from a back room—a sports report. She rang the bell and a middle-aged woman appeared, smiling pleasantly.

"Hello, dear. Would you like a room?"

"Please."

"How many nights will you be staying?" she asked, passing Christy a registration card.

"Just one."

"Did you come to see the launch?"

"Yes. Did you see it?" she asked, looking up from signing the card.

"Just through binoculars. I want to see one up close sometime."

"Are you a member of the Fellowship?" Christy asked, pushing the card to her.

"Yes I am, Miss Maitland," she said, reading the card.

"How many are there in the Fellowship?"

"I don't really know. Most of the town is, and there are branches other places. We had members from San Antonio stay with us once. Nice folks."

"Here comes the report, Evelyn," a man called from the back room.

"Excuse me, will you. It's about the launch." She turned to go, then paused. "You can come too if you want."

Christy followed her into a sitting room furnished with a couch and recliner. Dominating the room was a wall-screen TV. A man sat in the recliner, two children in his lap.

"Floyd, this is our new guest, Miss Maitland," Evelyn said. "That's Daniel, and that's Faith," she said, indicating the children.

Floyd was thin, except for a noticeable potbelly. He had pale blue eyes, and wore a carefully trimmed mustache, his hair and mustache the same reddish brown. The crown of his head was bare, giving him a monkish look.

The boy resembled his father, with pale blue eyes set in deep sockets, his face round, but showing signs of reshaping into the strong angular features of his father. His hair was blond. The little girl took after her mother, brown hair decorated with pink barrettes, brown eyes set in a thin face—pretty, but not with the striking eyes of her brother.

"Nice to meet you," Floyd said. "As soon as the commercials are over they're going to have a report."

A beer commercial followed a car commercial, then the newscast was back. A picture of the *Rising Savior* from the information packet appeared behind the woman newscaster.

"In the believe it or not category we have a report from California that a religious sect called the Light in the Darkness Fellowship claims to have used some sort of spaceship to put a satellite into orbit. We'll let you, our viewers, judge for yourselves."

A poor quality video showed the *Rising Savior* lifting from the ground, hovering, and then continuing. The video ended when the ship shrank to a dot. Then the newscaster was back—smiling.

"Perhaps it's powered by cold fusion," the reporter said. "And so it goes."

Floyd hit the mute button when the reporter turned to national politics.

"She doesn't believe it," Floyd said, disappointed in the coverage.

"They will," Evelyn said.

"NASA should know it's there. They track those things," Floyd complained.

"Come on, Christy. I'll get you a room," Evelyn said.

Evelyn insisted Christy take the room above the office. "It's the quietist," she assured her. Once in her room, Christy flipped through the channels looking for news. She was still channel surfing when someone knocked on the door.

"I'm sorry," Evelyn said when she answered. "I didn't know you were so famous."

"I'm not."

"That's not what Floyd says. Anyway, we wondered if you wouldn't like to go to services with us tonight. There's a special worship on account of the launch."

"Sure. But I'm wearing the best clothes I have."

"You're fine, I'm going like this. We have to leave soon. Floyd likes to get a front pew."

Floyd and Evelyn honked the horn five minutes later and she climbed into the second seat of a white minivan. The kids were buckled into the seat behind her. They turned east at the intersection in the middle of town, then drove through a residential section, mostly small two- and three-bedroom ranch-style houses. New construction was scattered through the area suggesting a modest building boom. Abruptly the homes ended and they climbed a brush-covered hill. It was too dark to see far, but it appeared to be undeveloped land. After a steep climb they leveled off and she could see the church—a simple A-frame with a large fellowship hall attached. Spotlights lit a large cross on the end of the church. The gravel parking lot was half full of cars.

"Dad, do we have to go to service?" Daniel asked, shouting past Christy.

"No. They'll have activity time for you guys."

"Hooray," Daniel yelled.

"Yea!" Faith echoed.

"Get us a good seat, Floyd," Evelyn said. "I'll show Reverend Maitland the view."

Floyd picked Faith up and took Daniel by the hand, then hurried off with the children while Evelyn walked Christy around the outside of the church. The exterior was covered with T-111 siding, the plainest and cheapest siding Christy had ever seen on a church. There were no adornments, the exterior covered by a thin layer of white paint. While the building looked cheap, the view was spectacular. The lights of the town lit the valley below and distant lights shone as far as the horizon.

"The Fellowship bought the land when we first moved out here. The first thing we did was build this church. Funny thing was that by the time we had our first worship it was too small. We've pushed out the walls a couple of times to make more space but it doesn't seem like we can keep up."

"How many worship with you?"

"Fifteen hundred regulars. We have three services Sunday mornings. We better get inside. Floyd doesn't like saving seats. He hates turning people away. He thinks it's unChristian."

The starkness of the church's exterior was matched by the interior. The walls were nothing but painted Sheetrock; there was no stained glass or chandeliers. Three sections of seats were divided by two aisles, and there was a small balcony in the rear. A piano and organ sat on either side at the front and rows of folding chairs were laid out for the choir in an alcove behind the pulpit. A cross on the wall behind the choir was the only adornment. The pews were polished wood with no padding, although a stack of pads were kept inside the door for those who didn't have enough natural padding.

Floyd was three rows from the front and waving frantically. Evelyn scooted in next to him, leaving Christy on the aisle.

"I thought you'd never get here," Floyd complained.

"Oh, Floyd. No one minds if you save seats. Especially if you have a guest like Reverend Maitland."

"It's not like we're waiting for a parade—this is church," Floyd whined.

"This is an unusual congregation," Christy said. "In most churches the back pews fill first."

"That's true enough here, too," Evelyn said. "But tonight's special."

It was twenty minutes before the service started and by then it was standing room only. The crowd was all adult, the children diverted to the fellowship hall where teenagers entertained them. The organist began with a prelude and then two men and a woman took seats on the platform—there was no choir. Christy recognized one of the men as Mark Shepherd, the spokesman at the launch. The service began with praise songs. The congregation stood, singing them all from memory. Christy knew only a few and stumbled over second and third verses. The singing went on much longer than Christy preferred and the hard wooden pew felt good when they finally sat down again. The church bulletin listed Scripture reading as the next item and Mark Shepherd stepped to the pulpit. He had no Bible. Suddenly he ducked behind the pulpit and reappeared a few seconds later wearing earphones with a microphone attached.

"Tonight's Scripture will be read by Ira Breitling," Shepherd said.

The sanctuary broke into thunderous cheers and applause and people shouted "Praise God" and "Hallelujah." Shepherd let them exhaust themselves before he moved on.

"Ira? Can you hear me, Ira?"

Static crackled over the poor-quality speakers hanging from the ceiling beams. Then a man's voice could be heard.

"This is Ira Breitling aboard the spaceship *Rising Savior* in orbit around planet Earth."

Again the congregation erupted. When it was silent

again, Shepherd asked Ira to read the Scripture. Christy recognized the passage from Psalms.

"'Where can I go from your Spirit? Where can I flee from your presence? If I go up to the heavens, you are there; if I make my bed in the depths, you are there. If I rise on the wings of the dawn, if I settle on the far side of the sea, even there your hand will guide me, your right hand will hold me fast. If I say, "Surely the darkness will hide me and the light become night around me," even the darkness will not be dark to you; the night will shine like the day, for darkness is as light to you.'"

No shouting now, only silence as the voice from space finished. Softly someone said, "Praise God." Then Shepherd closed with a prayer thanking God for supporting them on the long road they had traveled and promising the Fellowship would be faithful to His call.

Now Mark stepped away from the podium and spoke into the microphone, communicating with those in space. Then he came around to the front of the podium, the congregation quieting.

"Sandy, we're ready to begin the satellite transmission."

The speakers crackled again and a woman's voice said, "Beginning transmission now."

A tense pause followed, then from the speakers came a deep male voice.

"'In the beginning God created the heavens and the earth. Now the earth was formless and empty, darkness was over the surface of the deep, and the Spirit of God was hovering over the waters.'"

The congregation listened to the entire first chapter of the Bible but the transmission didn't end, the voice went on to the next chapter. Mark signaled someone behind him and the voice faded out.

"Now the entire world will hear the word of God," Mark said.

Again the congregation cheered and praised God. Christy leaned over to Evelyn. "Is the broadcast coming from the satellite you launched?"

"Yes. Isn't it wonderful?"

Smiling politely, Christy didn't ask whether the transmission would be in all the world's languages.

Bubbling with excitement, the congregation chattered and giggled like children. More singing followed but no sermon or collection. When Christy thought the service should be ending, candles were passed out, a paper ring slipped over the candle to protect the hand from dripping wax. Floyd took an extra candle when they came by. Another prayer was offered and then ushers lit candles at the beginning of each row. Christy's candle was lit and then she lit Evelyn's who then lit Floyd's. When all the candles were burning they stood and followed Mark Shepherd and the other leaders out the door. The children were waiting, the older children with their own candles, and they joined the procession. Daniel and Faith found their parents, Daniel carrying his own candle. Floyd lifted Faith to his hip and gave her the extra candle, lighting it with his own. She smiled broadly and looked down to Daniel.

"Looky, Daniel. Daddy got me a candle," Faith said excitedly.

The children were noisy but the adults silent so Christy honored the silence, not asking where they were going. They passed through the parking lot and into the brush on the far side. A trail had been cut, but the ground was uneven. They walked slowly in the dark, the candles providing little light.

It was a long walk, but finally they emerged into a clearing on the far side of the hill. As they spread out along the crest of the hill, Christy realized they were looking toward the launch facility. There were few lights to be seen, but the congregation stared into the dark expectantly. Then Mark Shepherd stepped in front, wearing his headset, speaking into the microphone. Lights appeared in the distance, spreading around the launch compound until there was a bright glow and structures at the launch site could be clearly distinguished. As her eyes adjusted she could see the circle of light that was the landing pad. Excited murmuring spread through the crowd. Next, Shepherd led them in a thank you prayer and a prayer for the safe return of the *Rising Savior* and the "faithful servants piloting it." The crowd murmured with nervous excitement when the prayer was done.

Minutes passed, Shepherd speaking frequently into his microphone. The children became restless, making up games and chasing each other around. The congregation scanned the skies in all directions, as did Christy. Then Shepherd shouted to be heard.

"Look to the west."

Everyone turned. Christy saw nothing, then someone pointed. A dot of light appeared high above them, almost directly above. The light grew brighter, then split into two lights. The two spheres of the dumbbell-shaped *Rising Savior* were lit. The craft dropped toward them until it was clearly visible, the crowd cheered and praised God as the craft floated over the valley in front of them, hovering where they could easily see it. The air crackled as the ship passed. Then the *Rising Savior* banked and rolled completely over and sped off toward the landing site. The crowd cheered until it was safely in the circle of light, then the valley went dark. With a last cheer and another prayer, the service ended.

Christy lagged behind the congregation, letting them enjoy their achievement. She feared there would be fewer joys ahead, doubting the world was ready for a religious cult to be a space power.

> The dialectical process seems woven into the
> fabric of the universe. Light and dark, yin and
> yang, good and evil, male and female, prosecutor
> and defender, Republican and Democrat. For
> every force that emerges, an equally powerful
> force emerges to counter it. This is undoubtedly
> a healthy process, since we all know the conse-
> quences when a natural or political force
> operates unopposed.
>
> — *A HISTORY OF GOOD AND EVIL,*
> ROBERT WINSTON, PH.D.

SAN FRANCISCO, CALIFORNIA

Simon Ash's slight frame couldn't fill the oversized mahogany chair, his feet barely reaching the ground. Like
everything else in the office, it matched Manuel Crow's
desk, a red mahogany so deep it was almost black, and
contrasted sharply with the brilliant red of the carpet.
Crow liked things big and dark, and big and dark intimidated Simon.

The door opened and Manuel Crow entered wearing a
black floor-length robe trimmed in scarlet. An unused
hood hung over his shoulders. Crow was wiping his
hands on a towel, his black eyes sparkling, a slight
smile—a cold smile that made Simon shiver. Crow tossed
the towel onto the desk. It was stained with blood.

"Good evening, sir," Simon began.

"I wasn't expecting you."

Crow ignored Simon as he hung his robe in a closet
and settled behind his desk.

"I'm sorry, sir, but I thought it was important," Simon
said, adjusting his bow tie. "Have you heard the news?"

"I've been occupied."

Crow reclined in his high-backed executive chair.

"Get to it, Ash."

"Yes, sir. I took Reverend Maitland to help me get access to that cult I told you about. The one that sent out the announcements—the Light in the Darkness Fellowship."

Crow nodded noncommittally while he rocked gently in his chair.

"I thought they were a saucer cult so I took Reverend Maitland along since she has a way of getting close to those fundamentalist types. Anyway, I didn't think they could do it, but they did."

Simon paused breathless, heart pounding, voice quavering, terrified of Crow's response.

"Did what?" Crow asked calmly.

"Huh?" Simon said, confused.

"You said you never thought they could do it, but they did. Did what?"

"Oh. They launched a spaceship."

Crow stopped rocking, his black eyes staring curiously at Simon.

"A religious cult successfully launched a rocket?"

"It wasn't a rocket. It was a . . . I don't know what it was. It looked like two diving bells hooked together. Here, I have a picture."

Simon slid the page from the information packet across to Crow who waited until Simon was seated again before he used a single slender finger to slide the page in front of him.

"You say this thing was launched? But there was no rocket?"

"It went straight up into the air and just disappeared."

"A balloon."

"No, sir. Those flying balls were steel."

Now Crow looked incredulous, but instead of the anger Simon expected, he smiled. Leaning back in the chair he put his feet up on the desk. There was blood on the tip of his shoe. Simon waited nervously, playing with his bow tie.

"Mr. Ash, you are to find out everything there is to

know about this cult. I want to know who the leaders are, who the members are, and where they get their money. Most of all I want to know how this spaceship of theirs works. And, Mr. Ash, I want to know it right now. Do you understand?"

"I'll get right on it." Simon stood to leave, then turned back, shifting nervously from foot to foot.

"Mr. Crow, I've already expended much of my budget for the year."

"You have an unlimited budget until further notice."

"Thank you, sir. We'll stop them, sir."

"You can be sure of that, Mr. Ash," Crow rumbled in his deep voice.

Simon left Crow deep in thought, the blood on his shoe browning as it dried.

CHAPTER 8 **NEWSROOM**

> Social concerns function much like fads. Hoola-
> hoops, pet rocks, and bell-bottom pants have
> come and gone much like our concerns about
> drugs, the homeless, the missile gap and AIDs.
> The one common denominator is that preceding
> each of these concerns was extensive media
> attention. As if with one mind the media select
> a cause, then shape the nation's perspective.
>
> —*A SOCIAL HISTORY OF THE UNITED STATES,*
> SONJA BURGER

SAN FRANCISCO, CALIFORNIA

Roland Symes barely had time to drop his package on his desk before Janine snaked her arm around his waist and pulled him through the crowded newsroom. It was nearly midnight but the newsroom was crowded, most clumped around TVs watching cable broadcasts. They all looked enviously at Roland, knowing he had firsthand knowledge.

"Goldwyn's in one of his moods," Janine confided.

Janine Sampson was a metro reporter, covering local news and San Francisco government. She was young, twenty-seven, with short-cropped brown hair and enough ambition for three people.

"He knows you were at that cult's ranch when they launched," Janine said. "You didn't call it in, so you better have a good explanation."

Goldwyn was owner and editor of the *Journal* and congenitally angry. Roland was one of the few who wasn't intimidated by Goldwyn. Syndicated nationally, the paper needed him more than he needed it.

Goldwyn was waiting in the conference room, sitting at the middle of the table, the back of his bald head against the glass wall. Goldwyn always kept his back to the newsroom. He claimed he didn't like reporters reading his lips, but with his volume they seldom had to. Goldwyn wore a blue suit, white shirt, and red tie. The tie alone cost two hundred dollars. Roland was in his usual jeans and cotton shirt. Goldwyn disapproved of the way he dressed, but as long as Roland's columns were syndicated, he wouldn't make an issue of it. The rest of the reporters wore ties or the female equivalent.

Roland entered the conference room, sitting opposite Goldwyn. Goldwyn held an unlit cigar in his teeth. The section editors were all there, as were a half-dozen reporters. Janine leaned against the window behind Roland, blocking part of the San Francisco skyline.

"Well?" Goldwyn demanded.

"What do you want first? The cult? The spaceship? The satellite?"

"The spaceship."

"From the outside it looked too simple to fly. You couldn't call it aerodynamic: just two spheres connected by a latticework of pipe. The satellite sat in the middle. There was a retractable cowling that covered the satellite before the launch. The spheres were entered through hatches in the top. There was one pilot in each sphere. They both wore space suits. That might suggest the spheres can't provide a breathable atmosphere."

"You can pack a breathing system on your back," Harry Chin interrupted from Roland's left. Chin covered science and technology for the paper and was resident expert on technological matters.

Goldwyn silenced him with a finger point and then nodded to Roland.

"The ship lifted off from the trailer they pulled it out on. They parked it in the middle of a concrete launching pad. There wasn't any blast—no flame, no exhaust of any kind. It started with a high-pitched whine and then there was a bright light—very bright. The air was charged with static electricity. Then the ship just floated up. It paused twice, hovering in place, and then it lifted up and out of sight." Roland paused, thinking back over the launch. "That's about it. They did pass out an information packet."

Roland pulled the packet from his pocket and handed it to Russ Jackson, the assistant editor. Jackson was African-American, six feet tall, and completely gray. He had worked for Goldwyn for thirty years, accumulating more abuse than the rest of the newsroom combined. Jackson looked at each page briefly, then set it picture side up in front of Goldwyn. Goldwyn glanced at it briefly.

"Tell me about the satellite."

"It had solar panels, gold foil to protect sensitive parts, a broadcast and receiving dish—and some gizmos I couldn't identify. Everything about it said it was the real thing. They said it would broadcast a message. The frequency is in that information. By the way I picked up a receiver at RadioShack. I charged it to the paper."

Goldwyn didn't flinch.

"So far all I've picked up is Bible verses."

"Tell me about the cult," Goldwyn said.

"They call themselves the Light in the Darkness Fellowship. No one seems to know how many members there are—maybe a few thousand. They took over the town of Exeter a few years back and renamed it Christ's Home—we should have file copy on that. They couldn't buy that much property without a lot of members, or someone with really deep pockets backing them. I'm guessing they've got a network of believers sending tens and twenties."

Goldwyn took the cigar from his mouth and pointed it at Jackson, assigning him the task of investigating the finances of the cult. Then he replaced the cigar and turned back to Roland—his signal to continue.

"The cult owns most of the businesses in town and most of the property. The original residents who stayed behind after the cult took over seem fairly content. Of course they can't buy liquor in the town and there are no bars, but the crime rate fell through the floor."

"They set up a police state, did they?" Russ Jackson asked.

"Not that I could see. They just don't commit crimes."

"If they have teenagers, there will be crime," Jackson argued.

"Not in Christ's Home. One man I talked with told me of an incident from two years ago. A couple of teenage boys set fire to a haystack. The town had a meeting to decide on punishment The community decided the boys would work for the farmer until he was satisfied. After they paid off their debt the farmer ended up hiring one of the boys."

"It sounds like the 1950s," Janine said.

"Stepford town," Jackson said.

"The 1950s weren't like the 1950s," Goldwyn said. "They tell a good story, but just wait until we dig a little deeper."

Again Goldwyn pointed with his cigar and a reporter acknowledged his assignment with a nod.

"Something's not right about this," Goldwyn said. "No cult can build a satellite."

"No cult could put it into orbit either," Roland said. "I called contacts at NASA and Hughes, but they claim they had nothing to do with the satellite. They don't believe the cult did it either, they think it's some kind of hoax."

"Maybe the Russians sold it to them, they're short of cash," Jackson suggested.

"Did the Russians sell them the launch vehicle too?" Roland asked.

"Is that all?" Goldwyn asked.

"I have orbital information," Roland said. "It's in a synchronous orbit, just north of the equator. Depending on the power of the satellite it could broadcast to most of North and South America."

"That's all you have? That's no more work than an hour on the phone. Where have you been for the last six?"

"Working on the Proctor connection."

"George Proctor the gun nut?" Goldwyn asked.

"That's why I was there in the first place. A source put me onto him."

"Is he part of the cult?" Goldwyn asked.

"No one admits to it. In fact, most of the members of the Fellowship seem to have pacifist leanings, normally not Proctor's type."

Goldwyn took his cigar from his mouth and pointed it at Roland.

"Proctor's not the story here, the emergence of a fundamentalist cult as a space power is," Goldwyn said, his voice loud enough to carry through the glass into the newsroom. "Drop the Proctor thing." Then turning to Russ Jackson, "See what you can do with this picture. I want that spaceship on the front page of the sunrise edition. OK, we're done here."

Then he pulled a lighter from his pocket and lit the cigar, signaling the formal end of the meeting. He puffed on the cigar waiting for the others to leave, pointing at Roland so he would stay behind.

"Give me an eyewitness account for the front page."

"How do you want me to play it? Amazing feat? It's the equivalent of someone cracking the law of gravity in a garage."

"True enough, but play the other side. The danger! A

group of religious fanatics have a monopoly on the biggest technological breakthrough of the century."

Goldwyn stubbed out the cigar, signaling he was leaving. He never smoked anywhere but in the conference room and only after meetings. Pausing at the door he said, "I used to worry that the Muslims would get the bomb. I've got a sick feeling this is worse."

CHAPTER 9 **TOUR**

Those who are wise will shine like the brightness
of the heavens, and those who lead man to
righteousness, like the stars forever and ever.

—DANIEL 12:3

CHRIST'S HOME, CALIFORNIA

The squeal of air brakes and the rumble of a diesel engine woke Christy at three A.M. A truck stenciled with "ABC Television" was parked in front of the office. Christy cracked the window and listened as someone bargained for the empty motel rooms. The bargaining soon elevated to shouting and Christy heard: "Four hundred bucks a night for this dump?" Followed by a mix of cursing and blasphemy. Next she could hear the scolding voice of Evelyn, followed by the man shouting: "Five hundred!" Evelyn was making him pay for taking the Lord's name in vain. The arguing ended and soon the truck rumbled off down the street, returning a few minutes later. The Fellowship owned both motels.

Three more trucks woke her that night and in the morning the street was filled with rental cars and vans sporting satellite dishes. The feeding frenzy had begun. Christy turned on the television. Cable, satellite, and broadcast networks were covering the story nonstop. One channel was broadcasting from the church she attended last night and another from in front of her motel. Other stations were interviewing NASA personnel or showing the orbit of the satellite. The same amateur video of the launch was being shown by everyone. She listened to two scientists speculating on how the *Rising Savior* was powered— one claimed it was nuclear fusion and the other high-intensity lasers. The most interesting story was the detainment of reporters at the launch site.

Two circling helicopters had been broadcasting pictures of the launch facility. There was little to be seen, so one of the pilots decided to land despite being waved away as he descended. The other helicopter hovered over the compound, covering what happened next. After the first helicopter landed a tractor drove out of the garage, a group of men in overalls following. A female reporter and a cameraman stepped out of the helicopter, the reporter holding out a microphone asking for an interview. Without a word the men pulled a cable from the tractor, attached it to the helicopter, and winched it tight. When the pilot climbed out to protest he was grabbed and handcuffed. Next the reporter was handcuffed. The cameraman resisted and three men had to wrestle him to the ground to cuff him, the camera dropping in the process. Then they were put into a van and driven away. The hovering helicopter followed the van down a dirt road through patches of woods to an exit where a county sheriff waited. The report ended with an exterior shot of the county jail where the news crew was being held on trespassing charges.

When the reports began to repeat Christy turned off the TV and left the room. Half the motel doors were open and men and women were walking freely from room to room. At the bottom of the stairs she noticed a hand-lettered sign taped to the pop machine saying $5 a can. Evelyn shouted, "No vacancy!" from the back room when Christy entered the lobby.

"It's me, Evelyn," Christy said.

Evelyn was apologizing as she came out of the back room.

"I'm sorry, dear. Those newspeople are rude and crude and they won't take no for an answer."

"And you're making them pay for it. Five hundred dollars a night? That wasn't the rate yesterday."

"Well, it's not like they can't afford it. Don't worry, dear, you pay the regular rate as long as you want to stay."

"Thank you. It's Sunday, aren't you and Floyd going to worship?"

"We couldn't get near the church. Those newspeople have it surrounded. Besides, everyone's supposed to stay away. They're going to be awfully disappointed when no one shows up for Sunday school."

Christy suspected they wouldn't let a Sunday pass without worshiping, but no invitation was forthcoming so she changed the subject.

"Where can I get some breakfast?"

"The Pig and Pancake is the best. It's just around the corner so you don't have to give up your parking spot."

Writing on a piece of motel stationery, Evelyn handed Christy a note.

"Give this to Keri or Josephine. They'll give you the regular rate because you're a friend."

The Pig and Pancake was a pink concrete block building with two large windows that turned the restaurant into a fishbowl. It was crowded inside and more people were standing out front, many smoking. Christy pushed her way inside to get her name on the waiting list. A grim, middle-aged waitress was keeping the list. She wore a pink checked uniform and had a pile of orange-red hair on her head. Her name tag read "JOSEPHINE." She broke into a smile when she saw Christy.

"I saw you at church last night," she boomed in a gravelly voice. "Evelyn called and said you were coming over. I got a table saved for you."

Josephine led her toward the back, those waiting grumbling behind her. Josephine took her to a back room with windows that gave a view of the gravel parking lot behind the building. An empty booth in the corner was set with a single place setting and a menu. Josephine leaned down while she filled Christy's coffee cup and whispered.

"Don't pay any attention to those prices, they're for the news nerds. Just between you and me there won't be any charge for your meal. Don't even bother to leave a tip. These poor dopes have been tipping fifteen percent on the prices we're charging. You just know they're on expense accounts."

Josephine left her to study the menu. The prices were quadruple normal. The meal came quickly and Christy knew her order was given the fast track. She was finishing the last of her toast when Mark Shepherd slid in across from her.

He looked to be in his early forties with brown hair and eyes. The creases around his eyes and mouth told her he was a man who frowned deeply and laughed heartily. Most distinctive of all was his Roman nose, which blended nicely with his features, especially when he smiled—he was smiling now.

"Good morning, Reverend Maitland. How is the food?" he asked.

"Overpriced."

"It's a matter of supply and demand. It's a long way to another restaurant."

"They could buy flour and cook their own pancakes."

"You haven't seen the price of flour."

"I see you've got it covered. I guess the idea is to fleece the media while you can. In a few days they'll move on to the next story."

"This story will last more than a few days," Shepherd said.

"A few weeks then," she countered.

He smiled, turning to watch a minivan pull into the parking lot. When he was facing her, his nose was barely distinguishable, but in profile his nose stood out. Then his face went from deep smile creases to his serious wrinkles.

"It might last a millennium," he said, then his smile creases returned. "Would you like to see the *Rising Savior*?"

"Of course, it's the talk of the world. But why me? I'm not a reporter."

"I don't want you to report, I want you to understand. You know what they will do to us."

She knew "they" referred to the news media.

"They're treating this like a freak show."

"The media isn't out to get you."

"Aren't they? They've never been a friend of religious people."

"Reverend Shepherd . . ."

"Mark."

"Mark . . ." she began, then stopped. If she tried to convince him there was no media conspiracy, he would believe she was a part of it. It was best to go slow. Christy fixed her neutral expression on her face.

"What about the tour you offered?"

"That van is waiting to take us to the compound."

She felt funny about not paying but he assured her they would never bring her a check, so she let him take her by the arm and direct her toward a back exit. As they passed a table she heard someone say, "Isn't that the guy from the launch." Quickly Mark hurried her out the door and into the back of the van. Reporters and cameramen were pouring out of the back of the Pig and Pancake as they drove away, the tires spraying the reporters with gravel.

"Hoodwinked them again, didn't we, Mark?" the driver said.

Christy recognized him—it was Floyd from the motel. Daniel was on the seat next to him and he turned and waved.

"Hello, Floyd," Christy said. "Hello, Daniel. Where's Evelyn?"

"She's minding the store. She told me to tell you that we're not spying on you but that when we told Mark that you were staying with us he asked to meet you."

"Tell her I understand." Christy said it sweetly but was suspicious. They drove down the main street past the Sandman Motel and then the Eternal Rest that also displayed a NO VACANCY sign.

"What's the rate at the Eternal Rest?" she asked.

"Same as ours. Four hundred dollars a night."

"With a hundred-dollar surcharge for blasphemy?"

Floyd chuckled as he drove.

"Evelyn won't stand for taking the Lord's name in vain. Isn't that right, Daniel?"

"Mama would wash my mouth out with soap if I talked like some of those reporters."

Soon they came to the main entrance to the compound. Floyd drove past.

"The media is waiting for us down there," Shepherd explained.

"Aren't you going to talk to them?" Christy said. "Isn't that why you invited them to the launch?"

"These people weren't at the launch. They had their chance to report the story, now they'll have to pay."

"You're going to charge them for the story?"

"We sure are, aren't we, Mark?" Floyd said. Then looking over his shoulder at Christy he said, "Tell them how much you're charging."

Mark looked embarrassed so Floyd answered for him.

"If you want to talk to our leader it's one hundred thousand dollars for ten minutes."

"That's a lot, isn't it, Daddy?" Daniel asked.

"It's a whole lot," Floyd assured the little boy.

"They won't pay you for a story," Christy said. "It violates journalistic principles."

Mark and Floyd broke out laughing, embarrassing Christy.

"You're stereotyping journalists," she said defensively.

"If they can pay serial killers for their stories, they can pay us," Mark said.

"If you don't talk to them, they'll talk to people about you," Christy said. "Disgruntled former members, employees, your barber, anyone who has a story to tell—it doesn't matter if the story is true or not."

"They'll do that anyway," Mark said. "Besides, they're already bargaining with us. The *National Enquirer* offered forty thousand dollars this morning," Mark said.

"What's this going to cost me?" Christy asked.

Mark smiled, but before he could answer Floyd turned down a dirt road and called for Mark's attention.

"Looky here, Mark. It's one of Proctor's people."

A bearded man stood by a pickup, a rifle in his arms. Mark's worry creases returned and the muscles along his jaw tightened. After a short drive they pulled up to a gate, Mark getting out to unlock it. No fancy electronic security system, just a gate with a big Yale padlock.

Soon they passed three large dish antennae, each turned at the same angle and pointed at the sky, then they were at the compound, parking on the concrete launch pad. As soon as they were out of the car Floyd swung Daniel up to his shoulders.

"Follow me," Floyd said, excited like a kid. "I'll show you something."

Floyd led her through a door into the largest structure. The news helicopter was there, being disassembled. Workers swarmed over it, dismantling it into the smallest pieces possible. Bits of the helicopter were strewn around the large enclosure. Boxes were being packed with other pieces.

"It was Mark's idea," Floyd explained. "Those news-people have been demanding we return the helicopter, so we are. We're sending it to them C.O.D."

"Can I sit in it?" Daniel asked, kicking to get down.

"Yes," his father said. "Just stay out of the way."

Daniel ran to the cockpit while Floyd went to talk with the workers.

"You won't make friends this way," Christy said.

"We just want them to respect our rights," Mark explained. "We've got a restraining order against the other helicopters. We can't keep them from flying over, but we can keep them from landing."

"Is that why your followers seldom go outside?"

"They're not my followers," he said firmly. "We stay inside so there is nothing to see. Eventually we'll provide more information, but on our terms, not theirs."

Taking her arm again he led her around the helicopter. The *Rising Savior* was on the other side, sitting on its trailer. Wires ran out of both spheres to a console thick with electronic gear. The pilot with the eye patch was there with another man. A woman's voice could be heard coming from inside one sphere.

"Three eighty-two, three eighty-three . . . that's it, hold it."

Mark let them work, the men concentrating on an oscilloscope, adjusting a wave pattern. When they seemed satisfied Mark interrupted.

"Ira, this is Christy Maitland. Christy, Ira Breitling."

Ira's grip was firm, his hand warm. His good eye watched her warily. Scars extended beyond the eye patch, reminders of a horrific injury.

"I appreciated what you did in Idaho," Ira said flatly. "Some of our people had relatives there."

"I'm just glad I could—"

Before she could finish Ira turned back to his oscilloscope. The man working with Ira looked embarrassed and stepped forward, extending his hand. He was young, halfway to bald, cherubic-looking with red round cheeks and the smile of a child.

"I'm John," he said. "You have to excuse Ira, he's personality challenged. You may not believe this but that's the nicest he's been to someone since I've known him."

"How long has that been?"

"Ten years, but it seems like a decade."

Christy smiled. John was goofy, but likable.

"John, are you working or not?" Ira asked gruffly.

Making a face, John silently mimicked Ira's words, then said, "Yes, boss. Nice meeting you, Christy, but if I don't get back to work Ira will send me to bed without my supper."

"Come on, Christy," Mark said. "You can see the inside."

Following Mark up a stepladder they climbed onto the trailer. Rungs were welded into the side of the sphere and Mark stepped aside so she could climb. Inside was a young woman sitting cross-legged in the bottom, a circuit board on her stomach—she was very pregnant. She looked up and smiled.

"Hello, Reverend Maitland. I'm Shelly. It's pretty amazing, isn't it?"

Christy looked around the interior. It was roomier than it appeared from the outside, and there were two chairs, one in front of the other. Most of the interior surface of the sphere was covered with equipment and devices she could not identify. Small monitors filled the wall in front of the lead chair, and another set sat in a console in front of the second. Each station had a keyboard and joystick.

"It's tightly packed in here because there's three of every system," Shelly said. "It's set up for two pilots now, but we can squeeze another person in if we want. The other capsule is identical."

"What makes it fly?"

Shelly blushed, then she said, "I can't tell you that."

Mark leaned over next to Christy, his cheek almost touching hers.

"It's not that we don't trust you, Christy, but this technology wasn't meant for the world."

Disconcerted by Mark's closeness, Christy pulled out and climbed down the ladder, Mark following.

"You can't keep a monopoly on this technology forever," Christy said. "If it's been discovered once, it can be discovered again."

"It was given to us by God. If He wants to give it to someone else, He can."

"You could patent your technology."

"Only if we provide details on how it works. We're better protected this way."

Suddenly Floyd shouted from the far side of the work floor, out of breath from excitement.

"Something's happened!" Floyd shouted. "You've got to see this!"

Floyd disappeared and others in the hangar quickly followed him. Christy trailed, wondering what could be more exciting than what she had witnessed in the last two days.

> Experiments with the X-15 showed a single
> stage reusable space plane was feasible. How-
> ever, the race to the moon diverted resources to
> disposable space hardware. While we won the
> race to the moon, we delayed development of
> the technology necessary to make access to
> space affordable.
>
> — *ALTERNATE PATHWAYS TO SPACE,*
> EDWARD NORTON

LOS ANGELES, CALIFORNIA

Not since the last earthquake in California had Roland seen a studio this busy. From the technicians to the on-air talent there was a sense of importance. This wasn't just television, this was "news," and these were the people who determined what the world needed to know. Writers sifted through bits and pieces of information, carefully selecting adjectives to create copy with "punch," then fed the words to the mouths of the "talent" who further modified it with the inflection they gave the words. Simultaneously, editors cut and rearranged videotape to tell the story visually, putting their own unique spin on events. In the control room, where Roland watched, producers made the final decisions about sequence, emphasis, and juxtaposition of video, copy, and talent, and this is what the world was fed.

Roland noted parallels with his own newsroom. At their core, they were all reporters but sometimes Roland thought a better name would be "creators." You couldn't take the human out of the news business and as long as people were in the cycle the truth would always be filtered through the eyes of the beholder. Any story could be seen from a dozen perspectives and someone had to take responsibility for determining what was "truth."

The producers in front of him were surrounded by monitors showing video footage of stories they were developing. Most of the monitors were carrying some angle on the Fellowship. There was video of the launch, the now infamous helicopter incident, interviews with two former Fellowship members, one claiming the cult practiced polygamy. A story on price gouging in Christ's Home had just been added to the mix and they were editing video of the junior senator from California calling for an investigation. Someone from the FAA had been tracked down and was talking vaguely about it being illegal to fly the *Rising Savior*. There were minor stories about the church they worshiped in, Exeter—the town the Fellowship had taken over—and about the security around the compound. There were many close-ups of barbed wire. The rest of the stories amounted to newspeople interviewing each other, or experts speculating about the cult's beliefs and technological capabilities.

Cindi Winslow brought Roland a cup of coffee. She was thirty, attractive, and devoted to her profession. She was the only black female associate producer at the network and talented enough to go to the top. Roland and Cindi saw each other when their paths crossed, both unwilling to give up their careers to build a permanent relationship.

"Watch over here, Roland," she said, pointing. "We've just put together a new story. We used footage from that failed Ariane launch this morning."

Roland was only vaguely aware that a European Space Agency Ariane rocket had failed in an attempt to put an Australian communications satellite in orbit. The second stage had malfunctioned and the satellite was now in a useless low orbit. In a few days the satellite would reenter the atmosphere and a 270-million-dollar project would become a shooting star.

When the story came up on the monitor it started with the footage of the Ariane launch from Kourou, French Guiana, while a voice described the tons of liquid hydrogen and oxygen burned to reach orbit. Stock footage of the flames of a rocket engine came next—Roland recognized the engine of a Saturn V. A young Asian-American reporter appeared on camera describing the combustion process, the cost of disposable rockets, and how rocket exhaust polluted the atmosphere. Next they cut to the footage of the *Rising Savior* silently floating into the sky without the roaring flames of the Ariane. The report finished with talk of a "new era," and then turned grim when the reporter asked, "What will a fundamentalist cult do with this new technology?"

Roland realized that one day after the launch of the *Rising Savior* the media was already spinning rockets as antiques.

"Has there been any other signals from their satellite, Cindi?"

"We're monitoring the frequency they've given us but so far nothing but nonstop Bible reading." Looking at her watch she said, "If you hurry you can catch the minor prophets."

After the preview they put the story into the rotation, the first new slant Roland had seen in hours.

"Cindi, have you run across a George Proctor anywhere in this story?"

"The gun nut? Not that I know of. Is he part of this cult?"

"I'm not sure."

"Hey, Cindi, you're not going to believe this," a voice called.

Roland recognized the new arrival as Wyatt Powder, an on-the-air reporter and weekend anchor. His sculptured good looks and resonant reading voice made it not matter that he was a short man with a less than average IQ. He was on the fast track to network stardom. Acknowledging Roland with a nod he spoke to Cindi.

"The cult is going up again. They're going after the Aussie satellite."

"When?"

"I don't know, but I've got a contact with Hughes Space Group. They built the satellite the Europeans sent up this morning. They've been contacted by the Fellowship and a deal's been made."

"They must have planned this," Roland said.

"Sabotage? But how?" Cindi asked.

"It's too convenient," Roland said vaguely.

"Guess how much they're charging?" Wyatt asked. Without waiting for an answer he said, "Twenty million."

It would be a bargain if they could save the satellite, Roland knew, but it would be like pouring gasoline on a fire. With the infusion of cash the cult would grow, attract more followers and more donations.

"Alert our crews," Cindi said. "I want pictures of the launch. And find out what frequency they're using, we want to listen in."

Then Cindi turned to Roland.

"It looks like the story just got bigger."

CHAPTER 11 **MISSION**

> Cults are the most destructive social phenome-
> non, short of war. They tear families apart, drain
> a country's resources, and agitate the members
> of the dominant religions. Occasionally, the
> worst happens, and a cult gets a foothold, grow-
> ing in power before it can be eradicated, adding
> to the religious delusions of the masses.
> The offshoot of Judaism we call Christianity
> is a good example of this.
>
> — *RELIGION, PLAGUES, AND EARTHQUAKES:*
> *NATURAL AND UNNATURAL DISASTERS,*
> MARION WADE

FELLOWSHIP COMPOUND, CALIFORNIA

Once the deal had been struck to save the Australian satellite, Mark called everyone to worship. The hangar became a church and chairs were set up in a circle. Hundreds appeared for the service, although Christy had seen only a few during her tour. It was a simple service, typical of low churches. They sang choruses from memory, then worshiped in silence. Occasionally someone would stand and share how thankful they were for what God had done for them, then someone else would pray. There was a pentecostal fervor at times but no speaking in tongues. Mark closed the service with a prayer, asking God to protect "His people that would soon go in harm's way."

Then like a hive of workers with a collective consciousness, they dispersed, each returning to their respective task. Christy asked to stay, but Mark declined, promising she could return for the launch.

Reporters were waiting for her at the motel, cameras shoved in her face, reporters demanding to know what she knew. No one told her not to speak, but it felt like betraying a trust.

Floyd helped her push through to her room where she stayed, virtually a prisoner. She spent the afternoon watching TV. The broadcast networks finally returned to regular programming, promising to interrupt instantly if anything newsworthy happened. CNN, Fox, and the other cable networks were still giving the cult heavy coverage but were now mixing in other stories. Sports coverage returned, a sure sign of a drift toward normalcy. At suppertime Evelyn brought her dinner from the Pig and Pancake and a can of pop from what was now a seven-dollar machine. There was no charge for either. Late in the evening Christy fell asleep with the TV on. At three A.M. the phone woke her.

"Come downstairs in five minutes," Evelyn said. "Floyd will take you back to the compound."

"Are they going to—"

"Don't say anything else, just in case someone is listening."

She dressed quickly in her Wal-Mart clothes, then stood by the window peeking out the curtains. It was clear. Then she stepped out, pulling the door closed quietly, and walked down the stairs.

Suddenly a match lit the bottom of the landing. A man

was there in the shadows, lighting a cigarette. Christy froze; reaching into her purse she palmed a canister of pepper spray, then she screwed up her courage and went down the last flight. The man stepped into the light as she reached the bottom.

"You're Reverend Maitland," he said. "Bill Towers, with *Cutting Edge*. Just a few questions if you don't mind."

Christy knew of the tabloid TV show but had never seen it.

"Not now, please," Christy said.

"Where are you going in the middle of the night?" Towers asked.

Christy ignored him, walking toward the office.

"We know the Fellowship is going after that satellite, I just need to know when."

The office was dark so she knocked on the door.

"Just tell me when they're going to launch," Towers persisted.

His voice was harsh and when Christy turned to walk away he jerked her around by the arm and pulled her close. She could smell alcohol on his breath.

"You're one of them, aren't you?" Towers accused.

"Get away from me or I'll scream."

"Tell me what I want to know or I'll scream and every reporter in this place will come running. You'll never get to where you're going."

Christy struggled to get free but he held her firm. Then Floyd's van roared into the parking lot. When Towers looked toward the van Christy Maced him. He was cursing and rubbing his eyes when she climbed into the passenger seat. Lights were coming on in the rooms as they drove away. As they passed the Eternal Rest Motel, two cars pulled out and followed them.

"Uh-oh," Floyd said. "I didn't expect this."

He sped up but the cars stayed close behind.

"This may be a problem. Everyone's busy getting ready for the launch and I won't have help at the gate. We can't let them get on the grounds right now."

Christy was disappointed.

"We've picked up another tail," Floyd said.

"Tail" made Christy smile. Floyd was acting like a secret agent on a mission.

"I'm sure they'll respect your property rights. They won't trespass."

"We had two incidents this afternoon. Three reporters and a cameraman are in the county jail right now. Their bosses won't pay our price for an interview and they're getting desperate." Then Floyd stared long and hard in the mirror. "Here comes one now."

Christy looked back seeing the third car in line had pulled into the left lane and was passing the other two. Floyd sped up to keep ahead of the accelerating car but it kept closing. Now feeling like she was in a spy movie, she watched the car pass the other two until it was nearing theirs. Suddenly it swerved in behind Floyd's van, slamming on its brakes as it did. The two trailing cars hit their brakes to avoid a collision. Tires screamed as the last two cars tried vainly to avoid colliding with the first, the last car in line ramming into the trunk of the second. The car that started the chain reaction swerved left out of harm's way, then sped up, leaving the occupants of the other cars to exchange insurance information.

"He must want an exclusive," Christy said.

The third car caught up again, then passed on the left. Floyd waved at the driver as he did.

"It's one of Proctor's people. Just when I decide they're one of the enemy, they do something like this."

"Do they work security for you?"

"Nope. Mark won't have anything to do with them. He's a pacifist and Proctor's not."

They reached the compound without further incident and again the exterior was deserted. They entered the same way, Christy realizing she had seen only a small part of the complex, her tour limited to the central hangar and one side room.

The hangar was buzzing with activity, the *Rising Savior* still the center of attention. Christy stood back from the activity around the ship, letting them work.

The *Rising Savior* had been modified, a set of manipulator arms had been attached to the right sphere. Ira Breitling sat at the console and spoke into a microphone. Occasionally, a voice crackled back over the speakers. Then the arms began to move, stretching out. A steel drum had been tipped on its side and the arms snaked out slowly until they were inches away. Then the pincers opened and arms moved slowly forward, sliding over the rim of the drum on both sides. Slowly they closed until the speaker crackled and Ira barked out a command. Then the pincers released and the arms were retracted. A minute later John popped up out of the sphere. His cheeks were their usual red and his face one big smile. He wore a space suit but no helmet.

"Hey, Christy," John shouted.

Others turned and looked at her, waving or nodding hello.

"Get back in there," Ira said gruffly. "If you damage that satellite I'll take the twenty million out of your hide."

John put one hand in the air and held his nose with the other, then slowly lowered himself into the *Rising Savior*, imitating someone sinking in a pool.

"We'll launch in about an hour," Shepherd said from behind her.

Mark stepped up next to her. He looked happy to see her. She felt the same.

"In an hour? Isn't that pretty imprecise for rendezvousing with a satellite?"

"It would be if the *Rising Savior* was an ordinary space transport. We have the capability to chase down the satellite no matter when we launch but it's less complicated if we wait until it comes to us. Ideally, we'll launch in seventy-three minutes. Does that sound better?"

"Very NASA-like."

"We don't have NASA's resources but we have some advantages. You see the manipulators on the *Rising Savior*? We didn't have to build an underwater simulator to train John because our manipulators work in a one-gee environment. Those manipulators saved us millions too. They were purchased off the shelf from an industrial supply company. We only had to make minor modifications for use on the *Rising Savior*. We'll get the next set of manipulators free."

"Why is that?"

"If they work we've agreed to trade video of them in operation for another set. The manufacturer will add a little cash on top of that."

"Mark, why is there a dollar sign attached to everything you do?"

Mark's cheeks reddened.

"I know it seems that way but I have to do everything I can to keep us going."

"Are the Australians really going to pay twenty million dollars to rescue their satellite?"

"The European Space Agency is kicking in some of it, but that's the total. Let me show you what we're after."

He led her to the room dominated by a projection screen with several smaller monitors mounted on the wall. There were also five work stations with computers and monitors. She joined Mark at one of the stations. Quickly he pulled up specifications on the satellite. It was cylindrical, resembling the steel drum.

"The Hughes Aircraft people sent this over. They built the satellite for the Australians. Aussat VII is 6.5 meters long. It has two extendable solar panels."

Mark punched a key and the picture of the satellite came to life, the two solar panels folding out from the sides of the satellite.

"There's an antenna array that deploys too."

Another keypunch and the top of the satellite opened, three dishes extending on long arms.

"It's carrying twenty-five C-band transponders and ten Ku-band. Most of the transponder space has already been leased. CBN, HBO, Fox, Disney, TBN, many of the big broadcasters have been counting on it."

"Doesn't doing this make you a bit uncomfortable?" Christy asked.

"Why?"

"Won't this satellite broadcast programming you find offensive?"

"We wrestled with this issue, but several of our members work for the post office and they deliver pornography as part of their job. We don't hold the carriers responsible for what their customers subscribe to."

Christy recognized rationalization when she heard it. By rescuing the satellite the Fellowship was enabling the distribution of what they believed was pornography, yet they adjusted their reality so they remained blameless.

"How much does the satellite weigh?"

"Its launch weight is 1,075 kilograms."

"But in orbit it's weightless, right?" Christy asked.

"True, but it still has mass. Even in orbit the inertia of that mass has to be overcome in order to move the satellite—Newton's second law of motion. The *Rising Savior* can handle it."

"Why are you in a hurry to get this satellite? The flight yesterday was history making and today I saw you making tests on the *Rising Savior*. Don't you want to take the time to analyze the results before you risk another flight?"

"The Australian satellite is in a rapidly decaying orbit and we have to get to the satellite before the orbit degrades to a dangerous altitude. We can't chase it into the atmosphere. The sooner we get to the satellite, the less risk to our ship."

"Am I keeping you from helping get the ship ready?" Christy asked.

"No, that's not my gift."

Mark was referring to his spiritual gift, a concept common in fundamentalist theology. Fundamentalists believed when the person was filled with the Holy Spirit they were bestowed with a gift that should be used for the good of the body. For some it was teaching, for others preaching, and for still others the gift of healing.

"You're not good with technical things?"

"Actually I am, but I wasn't called to build the *Rising Savior*," Mark explained. "That's Ira's job."

"So what is your gift?"

Mark's eyes glazed for an instant and he looked sad.

"My gift is a great responsibility," Mark said.

Others came in, asking Mark questions, so Christy didn't get a chance to follow up on what his "responsibility" was. Instead, Christy returned to the hangar, noting that the cannibalization of the helicopter had been suspended. Christy sat in the cockpit of the helicopter, watching the Fellowship work on their technological miracle. That's what it was, she realized, a miracle built by the hand of man—and woman, she reminded herself, although there were few women working in the hangar. And within a couple of hours, the *Rising Savior* would be rising again.

CHAPTER 12   **LAUNCH**

> Even the poorest general understands the importance of controlling the high-ground. Space is the ultimate high-ground.
>
> — *THE HIGH FRONTIER*, WARREN NICHOLS

GILROY RANCH, OUTSIDE OF
CHRIST'S HOME, CALIFORNIA

After his encounter with Christy Maitland, Bill Towers spread the word that the cult would be launching soon. With the rest of the media, Roland made his way to the Gilroy Ranch. The Gilroys owned property east of the Fellowship's compound. The Gilroys had farmed in the county for three generations before the Fellowship moved in, and they deeply resented the cult. They called members of the Fellowship "religionists" and had refused the cult's many offers to purchase their property. The Gilroy's farm included undeveloped land with a hill from which you could see into the cult's compound. The media were gathering there now, the Gilroys offering the use of the land free to their new "allies."

When Roland reached the Gilroy farm, crews were already working feverishly, the hill sprouting cameras, satellite dishes, and vans packed with the electronic tools of the trade. Tents had sprouted too and the reporters gathered under them drinking coffee and sharing stories from the media wars.

Roland circulated among the reporters, asking about George Proctor. Many knew of him but none connected him to the cult. It meant nothing. There was very little anyone knew about the Light in the Darkness Fellowship.

The sun came up at 6:30 A.M., and at 6:45 A.M. shouting sent them all running for their cameras. Through binoculars Roland could see the *Rising Savior* being pulled out to the concrete pad. The video cameras around him whirred and the thirty-five-millimeter cameras clicked incessantly. Like before, the trailer was parked in the middle of the pad. A long delay followed and then the handlers backed away from the ship. Cameramen began to shoot stills, the clicks of the cameras steadily picking up the pace. Then the *Rising Savior* lifted off its trailer. Reporters gasped at the silent lift-off even though they had seen the tape of the first launch many times. Roland watched in awe, knowing it was the first mission of a new space power.

> When I consider your heavens, the work of your
> fingers, the moon and the stars, which you have
> set in place, what is man that you are mindful
> of him?
>
> —PSALM 8:3

FELLOWSHIP COMPOUND, CALIFORNIA

When the *Rising Savior* disappeared above her, Christy
followed the others into the hangar where chairs were set
up in front of a wall-screen TV, the screen blue. A minute
later a picture of the sky appeared with one of the *Rising
Savior*'s two spheres off to one side. Slowly the sky darkened from blue to a deep purple, then to black, and then
stars appeared. The Fellowship cheered. Then the interior
of one of the capsules appeared, showing Ira in full space
suit, his eye patch showing through the visor.

"We are clear of the atmosphere," Ira said.

The view switched, another space-suited figure appeared, waving at the camera.

"Hi, honey, it's me."

Laughter filled the hangar, echoing from distant corners. Floyd leaned over and whispered, "That's John
Henry. His wife Shelly is working in the control room."

Christy remembered the young blond woman working
in one of the spheres.

"Shelly's pregnant, right?"

"It's their first."

John pushed his faceplate up and leaned close to the
camera.

"Watch this."

A little lump of gum appeared between his lips, then
he pushed it out. The blue gob floated free. Suddenly his

tongue shot out snagging the gum and slurping it back in. "Ribbit," he said.

The crowd roared with laughter. Suddenly Ira was back on-screen.

"Are you working or not, John?" Ira said crossly.

"Actually, you're doing all the work, I'm just sitting here."

The crowd giggled at the exchange. Then the screen filled with a picture of the Earth. White clouds were smeared over the mottled blue-brown surface. The silent view continued for a long time, the Earth slowly moving beneath them like the hands of a clock. The crowd grew restless, going for coffee and soft drinks. Popcorn appeared and soon there was a carnival atmosphere in the hangar. Christy passed on the popcorn but accepted a cup of coffee. The picture suddenly changed angle. Then the audio was back.

"Three miles and closing," John said.

"Roger," a voice replied.

Christy recognized the voice as Mark's.

"Zero five five," Ira said.

"Zero five five," Mark echoed.

"Two miles," John said.

Tension filled the room, the group leaning forward, straining to catch sight of the satellite.

"Zero three zero," Ira said.

"Zero three zero," confirmed Mark.

"I can see it," John shouted.

The crowd leaned even closer now.

"There it is," someone shouted.

Then Christy saw it, a shining spot in a sea of blue. The *Rising Savior* was coming in from above the satellite.

"We're too high, Ira," John said.

"Zero two seven," Ira said. "I'll get us there."

"Zero two seven," came the reply.

The satellite grew, features soon becoming distinguishable. It was different from the computer simulation Mark had shown her. The second stage was still attached to the satellite, and the satellite was still covered with a cowling. As they closed, the *Rising Savior* dropped, coming down to level with the satellite. Now the camera clearly showed the engines of the second stage.

"Zero one one."

"Zero one one."

"Get the manipulators ready, John."

"Yes, sir."

The *Rising Savior* slowed as it approached, the end of the rocket now filling the screen.

"I'm deploying now," John said.

"Forward, forward," Ira said. "Say when, John."

"Forward, forward . . . hold it! I'm going to grab her."

Nothing but rocket engine could be seen now, even the manipulator arms were off camera.

"Almost there . . . One is attached. Two is on its way. Closing, closing . . . got it."

"Lock them down," Ira said.

"Locked. I've got green across the board."

"What are you reading, Mark?" Ira asked.

"All green."

"All right," John said. "We've got her by her bottom. Let's give her fanny a little shove."

The crowd laughed. John was clearly a favorite.

"Stand by, John."

The audio went silent except for the occasional crackle of static. Christy could feel the tension in the room build as if they understood this was the most dangerous part of the mission.

"I read eighty percent field extrusion," John said.

"This is an open channel, John," Mark said. "Switch to the line."

"Sorry. I'm switching over."

They were silent again for a few minutes.

"I'm reading it nominal. Mark, what are you reading?"

"Acceptable. Let's move her."

"Oh boy, oh boy, oh boy," John said.

Laughter rippled through the hangar.

All they could see now was the rocket engine and they became restless as the long minutes passed. People left for the bathroom and others prayed softly in small groups.

Finally the audio was back.

"Hughes confirms orbital position and speed. Prepare for separation, John."

Cheering filled the hangar and people hugged each other and shook hands. The excitement was contagious and Christy stood, clapping her hands.

". . . green, green, green, green. Manipulators retracted and locked," John said.

"Back her off, Ira," Mark said over the speaker. "Hughes Control is going to separate the booster."

The crowd watched in amazed silence as the *Rising Savior* drifted back. The rocket engine shrank on the screen, slowly revealing the entire satellite. A flash and then puffs of gas and the booster began drifting toward the *Rising Savior*.

"Let's do it again, John," Ira said.

"Goody, goody, goody."

"Hughes says it's wobbling a bit. Be careful," Mark said.

"I can see it," Ira said. "John, is it going to be a problem?"

"Not with these mitts."

The engine loomed closer again, this time the *Rising Savior* closing much faster. The arms appeared, spreading wide to make another catch. The wobble looked much worse up close but those in the craft seemed calm. The *Rising Savior* slowed as it approached, the end of the rocket now filling the screen.

"Forward, forward," John said. "Forward, forward . . . hold it! I'm grabbing her."

The image rocked gently, then slowly stabilized.

"I've got her again. Let's go."

The image of the rocket engine remained unchanged, and no motion could be detected.

"Stand by for release, John," Ira said.

"Are you sure there isn't some salvage value in this thing?"

"Are you working for me, John?"

"Yes, master," John said.

The crowd laughed.

"Release her, John."

"Your wish is my command." Static crackle filled the

room, then: "She's free. Retracting arms." A minute later. "All green once more."

The image broadened and soon Christy could see the entire booster. The satellite was gone and nowhere to be seen. The Earth was below, closer.

"The Hughes people are ecstatic," Mark reported. "They've got the solar panels deployed and all systems are reading normally."

"Let's go back and take a look," John said.

"No," Ira said. "Now we go home and check every system."

"Spoilsport. I just hope the love of my life is waiting there for me when I get down."

"You know I will be, John," Shelly said to the screen.

They were all there when the *Rising Savior* returned to Earth.

CHAPTER 14   **UPDATE**

> Horror/comedies are a peculiar movie genre. In these movie hybrids, what begins as fear can quickly be turned into mirth and what begins as mirth can just as quickly be transformed into fear, thus demonstrating the fine line between the two emotions. Good and evil have much the same relationship.
>
> — *A HISTORY OF GOOD AND EVIL*,
> ROBERT WINSTON, PH.D.

SAN FRANCISCO, CALIFORNIA

To Simon, Manuel Crow seemed to have only one mood, solemn. The man smiled frequently but it was a practiced smile and empty of good humor. He would frown on occasion, too, but seldom seemed honestly sad. Perhaps it was his eyes that kept him from expressing emotion. Their icy blackness never changed and facial creases and wrinkles that normally accent emotions could do little to mask the piercing coldness of his stare. Crow's eyes were boring through Simon now as he reported on the cult.

"Gathering information on the Fellowship has been difficult," Simon explained. "I've been forced to rely on secondary sources: neighbors, relatives of members, landlords, public records. I've been unable to penetrate their computer network."

Crow rocked forward, stopping Simon with a raised eyebrow.

"You've never failed to hack into a computer network before," Crow said.

"The problem is they don't have a network to break into. There is some Internet traffic between branches, but mostly personal communications, nothing technical. The Fellowship doesn't have a Web site and I couldn't find a personal Web site for any key member. If they have a computer network it's localized within the compound with no Internet connections."

"Tell me what you do know," Crow said.

"Two men began the cult about twenty years ago," Simon said, pulling on his bow tie. "Mark Shepherd and Ira Breitling. I can't be more specific about the date of its foundation without further research. It seems to have been a cult of two for a few years, then grew slowly. They registered themselves as a church fifteen years ago to avoid taxation. When they showed up in San Francisco they had about two hundred members. They never built a church building until they took over Exeter. In San Francisco they leased a warehouse in an industrial park to use as a research facility. I believe they worshiped in the same building. One of their neighbors remembers seeing the place packed with cars on Sundays. I found the owner of the building but he was little help. He only went inside the warehouse twice when they leased it, but he did confirm it was packed with electronic gear. He also said they were running a small foundry. Two years later they moved to a bigger facility: another old warehouse. They don't go in for fancy. Three years later they moved to Exeter."

"What about their finances?" Crow asked.

"Until they began their launch business, they were dependent on donations; however, it seems those that work for the cult don't take salary. The cult owns their homes, their vehicles, and even provides them food through company stores. It's economic slavery, much like how the coal companies operated fifty years ago."

"Have them investigated for labor law violations."

"That's a good idea, sir," Simon said, making a note on his yellow pad.

"I know there are branches of the cult," Simon continued. "One in San Antonio for sure, one in Florida, and at least one overseas—Australia. These might be tracking stations for their satellite operations. That's a lot to support on donations and at the same time develop the kind of technology they have. It suggests the cult is much bigger than it looks."

"How many do you estimate are supporting the cult?"

"Five thousand."

"Five thousand people donating, not to mention the profits of the businesses they own. Add to that the free labor and I would say it amounts to a considerable sum."

"Yes, sir, and now they have external resources. They were paid twenty million for rescuing the Australian satellite and they have two more launches lined up. NASA is screaming about the loss of business but they are undercutting NASA's prices."

Crow glared at Simon with his icy eyes, making Simon squirm in his oversized mahogany chair and fiddle with his bow tie.

"As you know, the stock market has declined sharply because of the cult," Simon said. "There's been a broad decline in technology stocks, even those not related to space industries. I was hoping the Fellowship had anticipated this and invested strategically. I could have convinced the Securities and Exchange Commission to investigate them for manipulating the market but their investments are minimal. They're either spending it as soon as they get it, or they've got their cash stuffed in mattresses."

"Tell me about the leaders," Crow said.

"As I said, two men are at the core. Ira Breitling, who is rarely seen, and Mark Shepherd, who is the public spokesperson. Shepherd is the one selling interviews and he's the one the cult members refer you to if you start asking questions. The brainwashing is the strongest I've seen. The cult is absolutely monolithic in its refusal to talk to the press or anyone."

"Who is the technological genius behind the *Rising Savior*?"

"It's not clear. Mark Shepherd was military trained in electronics repair, specializing in nuclear weapons. He's a technician, not a theoretician, though. It would take an Einstein to make a breakthrough like this. Ira Breitling was a physical chemistry major and did graduate work in materials science, but never finished his degree. He was injured in a laboratory accident where he lost an eye. He's one of the pilots, by the way."

"The man with one eye flies the ship?"

"Yes. He and a younger man named John Henry went up together to rescue the Australian satellite. This Henry fellow has a master's degree in astronomy."

"Did he distinguish himself in school?"

"He was a good student, but no genius. Besides, he's too young to be behind this technology. He's been out of school for only two years. By the way, the cult paid his way through school. They have developed a lot of their own talent this way, paying for children of the members to go to college and graduate school. There is one peculiarity in their education patterns. The children of the cult only educate themselves through a master's degree; none have finished doctoral programs."

Crow leaned back in his chair thinking.

"That's very interesting," Crow said. "They don't care about the doctorate. They stay in graduate school only long enough to learn what their professors can teach them. Once they reach the point of making a creative contribution of their own with doctoral research, they take their creativity home to the cult."

"Those getting graduate degrees are all in the natural sciences," Simon continued. "Physical chemistry, physics, astronomy, mathematics, and quite a few in engineering. Mostly mechanical and electrical engineering, but also environmental and chemical. They've got two agronomists, although their farming operation is limited. For a fundamentalist cult they are pretty well educated, although it looks like a caste system could be developing—those with the degrees running the glamorous space program while the rest do the grunt work."

"We might exploit that angle," Crow said.

"If they open up a little I'll begin sowing seeds of jealousy. You know, asking the toilet cleaners why those at the top never have to dip their hands in the bowl."

Crow laughed, sending chills down Simon's spine.

"Very good, Mr. Ash. You do have a talent for creating discontent."

"Discontent is the agent of change."

"And of destruction," Crow said, smiling. "So you have no idea of who is behind their technology?"

"No single individual stands out as having that much brain power. If I had to guess, I'd say their discovery is the result of serendipity. They stumbled across the discovery of the century."

"Perhaps it was revealed to them," Crow suggested.

"Who would give away such a discovery?"

"Never mind, Mr. Ash. You've done well so far but I want to know more."

"I've got a dozen people researching. In a month I'll know more about the members of that cult than they know themselves."

"Double the number of researchers."

"Yes, sir." Then he nervously added, "I'll need more space."

"Lease a bigger facility," Crow said.

Simon suppressed a smile. He was feeling a growing sense of power.

"I'll bring them down, sir," Simon said.

"If you'll excuse me, I have another meeting," Crow said, dismissing Simon.

Simon jumped to his feet, excusing himself. Once out of the office, he hurried to the bathroom. Crow was his patron, but whenever he was in the man's presence, his sympathetic nervous system went into high gear. It was like the first terrifying drop on a roller coaster, but the fall never ended.

CHAPTER 15 **PLANS**

> The truly righteous man attains life, but he who
> pursues evil goes to his death.
>
> —PROVERBS 11:19

SAN FRANCISCO, CALIFORNIA

Manuel Crow found Simon Ash a useful stooge. His profound ignorance about religion served Crow's needs, although until the launch of the *Rising Savior*, Crow had felt no clear sense of purpose. It had been twenty years since he had been called to serve the master of the underworld, but to what end he never knew. So, he had spent the intervening years in preparation. He built a funeral home empire, buying up competitors or driving them out of business. He also added to his coven. He now had dozens of devoted Luciferians who worshiped with him regularly. Their loyalty was assured by the blood rituals they participated in. He had an organization, he had money and influence, and he had loyal followers. What he had lacked up until the launch of the *Rising Savior* was purpose.

Crow left his office walking down a mahogany-trimmed

hall to the conference room. Rachel Waters was waiting outside the door. Six feet tall, raven-haired with features sharp and clearly defined as if created by a sculptor with sure hands. With skin the color of pearls, ruby red lips, and black eyebrows and hair, Rachel was a woman of sharp contrasts. Beautiful to those with exotic tastes, she was Crow's trusted assistant, serving his every need and whim. She stood next to him at the blood rituals assisting him like a well-trained nurse and served as his executive assistant with power of attorney over most of his business affairs. Her devotion was complete, her compatibility uncanny. Their dark souls were like two sides of the same coin. There was nothing she wouldn't do for him.

"They're all here," she said. "I told them nothing but they've been talking about the cult while waiting," Rachel said.

"Good."

Rachel smiled, her smile as cold as his.

Those gathered quieted as Crow took his place at the head of the table, Rachel at his right hand. Each of those present owed something to Manuel Crow, either through legitimate business connections, his foundation, donations, or under-the-table money. Crow noticed that Grayson Goldwyn, owner and editor of the *San Francisco Journal*, had taken the seat at the other end of the table. Now Grayson stared back as if an equal, an unlit cigar in his mouth. Representative Sylvia Swanson sat to his left, silver-haired and matronly, a four-term member of Congress elected primarily on Crow's money. William Lichter sat next to her, a middle-aged man who had been promoted beyond his abilities at NASA because of Crow's influence. A pudgy man, balding, wearing tan slacks and a white shirt with a pocket protector and sweat-stained armpits, Lichter had no future except what Crow could buy for him.

Across the table sat the least loyal of the group. Meaghan Slater was a nationally recognized leader of the National Womyn's Congress. She was fanatical only about her own political agenda. She was the most difficult to bring under his influence, her hatred of men deafening her to his words. He succeeded only when he sent his assistant, Rachel, to seduce her. Ms. Slater was as severe-looking as Rachel was beautiful. Her hair closely cropped, her clothes dark and utilitarian, no makeup. Ms. Slater's face remained impassive but her eyes brightened when Rachel entered.

The final member of the group was the cofounder of the Earth's Avengers, a radical environmental group. Tobias Stoop had been disinherited by his industrialist father because of his environmental activism and was now fanatical in his commitment to destroying the industries that had built his family's fortune. He was penniless; it was through Crow's generous donations that his ecoterrorists kept globe-hopping and wreaking havoc.

"Thank you all for coming on such short notice," Crow said, sharing his smile with each person in turn. "I hope the travel arrangements were satisfactory and the accommodations acceptable."

Crow had flown them in, first class, put them up at the best hotel in San Francisco, and picked up the tab for food and drinks. It amused him that Tobias accepted the comforts despite the eco-damage behind the luxuries.

"As you know, a cult calling themselves the 'Light in the Darkness Fellowship' has launched a satellite into orbit. In addition it has rescued an Australian satellite and moved it to a stationary geosynchronous orbit. Now they have contracted to put two additional satellites into space."

Crow paused for effect, watching their faces. He could see they each had their own concerns about the cult—all except Tobias Stoop. Tobias saw no significant threat to the environment from the Fellowship and thus had no interest.

"I believe the emergence of a fundamentalist cult as a space-faring power has grave implications. I have called all of you here because I believe you share those concerns."

Goldwyn's head nodded up and down vigorously. Crow had expected no less from Goldwyn since his newspaper was already portraying the members of the cult as either brainwashed or brain dead.

"Fundamentalist cults have come and gone through the centuries and virtually all share one common feature—intolerance for anyone who does not share their beliefs. Essentially powerless in our country because the great majority of freedom-loving Americans do not share their right-wing religious or political views, these cults have had to resort to violence. Women's clinics have been their favorite target and you all know of the bombings and murders there. Congresswoman Swanson, I appreciate your work on the Reproductive Freedom Act that helped protect women seeking medical care."

Crow avoided the use of the word "abortion." The congresswoman smiled and nodded in response to his praise.

"Minorities and people of diverse faiths have also born the brunt of fundamentalist institutionalized bigotry. But the harm these groups have done has been limited because they have had little power and few resources. That has all changed. Now they have a virtual monopoly on the world's most lucrative industry. With financial limits removed, there's no telling how big this cult will grow.

"Since the Enlightenment, civilization has struggled to rid itself of superstition. These gains are being lost as we sit here. Unless the Light in the Darkness Fellowship is stopped, women will once again find themselves subjugated to men. Religion will once again invade our schools and censors will determine what we read and watch on television. If they are allowed to monopolize this technology they will dictate who goes into space and on what terms."

Crow paused, making sure his speech was being received as planned. He'd pushed as many hot buttons as he could and by the look of those around the table, it was working—except with Tobias Stoop who looked bored. Now Crow turned to him.

"You don't seem concerned, Tobias," Crow said.

Tobias was a tall, thin young man, his skin so tightly drawn over the bones of his face the skin would have little opportunity to wrinkle. Rarely did he joke and when he did they were odd and incomprehensible witticisms. His hair was cropped short in a military cut and he wore faded designer jeans and a white polo shirt with an alligator emblem.

"This could be a good thing," Tobias said. "If it really is a nonpolluting launch option, my people are going to favor it."

"As far as we know their propulsion system does not emit any nuclear radiation or exhaust of any kind," Crow said. "But you should ask yourself at what environmental cost such a marvel is produced."

"What are you saying?" Tobias asked, his interest growing.

"There are rumors the by-product of the process to create the drive is more toxic than plutonium. I also heard they've been burying the waste to hide the ugly truth."

"If that gets into the groundwater—" Tobias said.

"My concern exactly. I'm not here to make false accusations, I only want them to come clean. If their process is environmentally safe, then why keep it a secret? Even if they're too mercenary to share, they should care enough about the planet to sell the technology. Everything points to a cover-up of an environmental disaster."

"You're right, they're hiding something," Tobias concluded.

It was just a jumble of half truths and speculation but Tobias would fill in the blanks and make it into something sinister.

"I can tell you NASA is plenty concerned about these religious fanatics," Lichter volunteered. "And it's not just that they've stolen two satellites off the next STS launch. Everyone thinks there's unlimited space in orbit but it isn't true—not in geosynchronous orbit. We can't have just anyone putting satellites into orbit, especially useless ones that only spout religious dogma."

"The Womyn's Congress has already met about the problem of the cult," Ms. Slater said. "The cult is a paternal hierarchy, with few women in positions of responsibility. Inside that cult it's as if the last forty years of the women's movement never happened."

"As soon as I return to Washington I intend to initiate an investigation of their finances," Congresswoman Swanson said. "If they receive any federal money they must meet

Equal Opportunity and Affirmative Action guidelines. Even if they don't receive federal support directly, they certainly receive tax advantages. I've been wanting to push a case like this through the courts. I say a tax break is the same thing as taking federal money and those who get tax breaks should meet the same fair hiring standards."

"Good, that's the kind of thing we need," Crow said.

"I've got my best people on this cult," Grayson volunteered. "We're investigating the leaders. You don't get to the top of any organization without breaking rules. If there are financial irregularities, drug abuse, or past lovers, we'll find it out. If there's anything the public hates it's a hypocrite."

Now Crow turned back to Tobias.

"What can your people do?" Crow asked.

"We'll start with the usual. The first step is to see if they filed an environmental impact statement when they built that launch facility. We'll check zoning and land use laws. That area is primarily ranching. With a little luck the western red mouse will live on their property. We succeeded in getting it listed as threatened last year and with enough money we can push for endangered status. That would prevent expansion and we could shut down operations for at least two years with legal action. This will be expensive."

"Submit a grant request. My Foundation will fund it."

Now Crow nodded to his right, indicating his assistant.

"Rachel, tell our guests about your efforts."

"We've moved on several fronts. The FCC will be looking into their unlicensed radio transmissions and the FAA will be investigating their aircraft. It turned out the Fellowship had a secret member at the FAA and the *Rising Savior* was licensed as an experimental aircraft. We're trying to get that license revoked. We've also got the Nuclear Regulatory Commission investigating their power source. It must be nuclear. Possibly fusion."

"If it is nuclear, we can get a thousand protesters there within a week," Tobias said.

Crow was pleased. This was going as well as he had hoped.

"This will slow them down," Goldwyn pointed out, "but it won't stop them. What's the ultimate goal?"

"We can't put the genie back in the bottle," Crow said. "The technology is here to stay but we can make sure the religious fanatics don't monopolize it. We must discover their technological secret, make sure it is environmentally safe, and regulate it for the benefit of the world. Especially for marginalized people."

Lichter looked up at the mention of technology, as if he were the final word on it. Pulling one of the six pens from his pocket protector, Lichter pointed with it as he spoke. The pocket protector had "NASA" written in blue across the flap.

"NASA is going to approach them about sharing their technology," Lichter said, poking holes in the air with his pen. "The military is going to approach them too."

"If this was wartime we could confiscate the technology," Representative Swanson said.

"Can you introduce legislation to do the same?" Crow said. "Declare the technology vital to our national interests and raid their compound?"

"Not with the current mood in the country," Congresswoman Swanson said. "According to the polls, many considered the members of that cult heroes. Talk radio has been playing it as a David and Goliath story. The conservatives are eating this up. Calls to my office are three to one in support of the cult. If you want government action, you've got to tarnish their image."

The congresswoman was right and he would take pleasure in doing just that. Satisfied with his progress he thanked his guests, promising to bring them together again, then left them to enjoy drinks. Rachel and Ms. Slater were drifting toward each other when he closed the mahogany door.

Crow left in his Mercedes, driving ten miles to a shopping mall where he parked and walked through the mall and out the other side to another parking lot. Counting four rows over from the exit, he walked down fifteen spaces to a Ford Taurus. The keys Rachel had given him fit and he drove to the freeway, heading south. Ten miles later he turned off and parked at a small neighborhood park. He followed the path to the center of the park. It was after ten and the park was deserted. Fear of what was hiding in the dark frightened other people, not Crow. As he approached the rest rooms a man separated from the shadows and fell into step next to him.

"You looking for a mechanic?" the man asked.

He was younger than Crow had expected.

"I expect any repairs to be permanent," Crow replied.

"My specialty."

"Did you get a look at the compound?"

"The security is a joke. I'll go in after dark."

"How long before you can do it?"

"Three weeks minimum, seven weeks maximum. I'll have to special order the weapon I need. Once I get it I'll wait for a night launch."

"If you take the ship out before they put another satellite up I'll throw in a fifty-thousand-dollar bonus."

"I go when I'm ready. If I earn the bonus, so much the better."

Crow expected more deference from employees. This man was arrogant and perfect for sacrifice. No one knew his name, he lived in shadow, and if he disappeared no one would ask questions. Crow pictured him spread-eagled across the altar, his still-beating heart in Crow's hand.

Crow removed an envelope from his pocket and passed it to the man who tucked it away without looking inside.

"As we agreed. If you do this well I will have another job for you."

"Contact me as you did before."

Then the man disappeared into another shadow. Crow returned to the Taurus, then switched to his own car at the mall and drove to his office. The others were gone now. Passing through his office he walked down the hall toward the conference room. The hall was lined with mahogany wainscoting. Halfway down the corridor he stopped, pushing at a hidden silent switch. One panel popped inward and he stepped through, closing the panel behind him. Turning the lights on he went down the stairs to the secret basement. Going directly to the sanctuary he lit a dozen candles, then turned out the lights. At one end of the room was a bloodstained altar where the sacrifices were offered to the one they worshiped. Behind that, high on a pedestal, was the statue he had bought long ago from a gas station parking lot.

The statue had moved only once, putting Crow's life on a new course. But to what destination? Was he to stop the Christians and their spaceship? He stood before the statue praying to his plaster god, asking for direction, begging for a sign. Then for the first time in twenty years the plaster deity's eyes shifted, now looking directly at Crow. Then the eyes began to glow.

Joy welled up in him and he fell prostrate, pledging loyalty.

CHAPTER 16 **MECHANIC**

Try to imagine a world without evil. Do you picture a world without suffering? A world without war? A world without racism? But "suffering," "war," and "racism" have no meaning unless they are contrasted with their opposites. "Good" cannot be imagined, nor even defined, without a reference to evil.

— *A HISTORY OF GOOD AND EVIL*,
ROBERT WINSTON, PH.D:

CHRIST'S HOME, CALIFORNIA

Hiding his truck in a thicket, he hiked out of the gully and over the hill, pausing at the road. The cult's property began on the other side. He listened since it was too dark to see far in either direction, hearing only natural night sounds: soft rustles of animals scurrying, clicks and chirps of insects, the sound of the grass brushed by the wind. He crossed the road, hiding in the bushes by the perimeter fence. Removing his pack he took out an ohm-meter and touched a fence wire with the leads. The needle remained flat. He checked each of the fence wires. None were carrying any current. Next he removed a pair of night goggles that turned the dark of night into a greenish imitation of day. No one was in sight.

He cut a hole large enough to crawl through but small enough to be covered by the brush on either side. Once through he checked his weapon again. The Stinger missile was secure. He set off through the woods, carefully moving from tree to tree and pausing frequently to study what was ahead and behind. A short distance in he heard the sound of an approaching vehicle. The car came slowly but steadily. When the van approached his entry point, his body tensed. The van passed. He relaxed, waiting for it to drive out of sight. Suddenly it stopped, then backed up until it was nearly parallel with his point of entry. Four men with rifles got out of the van. Another man remained by the van. The men spread out in a skirmish line, walking back along the road as if looking for something. They passed his entry point without detecting the hole.

He studied the man waiting by the van. He was larger than the rest. In the greenish glow he could see the man's head was balding. Night-vision goggles normally turned eyes into dark hollows but this man's eyes glowed bright. Pulling back behind a tree to cover his movement, he removed his goggles and pulled a nightscope from the pack.

Leaning around the tree trunk he zoomed in on the man by the van. He was large, middle-aged, and fit-looking. Most striking were his eyes. In the infrared spectrum they were even brighter. He'd never seen anything like it even in the military phase of his life. Then the man with the bright eyes closed his lids and suddenly his eyes glowed like hot coals. Mesmerized, he watched as the man's head turned from side to side, scanning the woods. Then the strange eyes locked on his hiding spot and he shrank back. When he risked another peek, the man with glowing eyes was waving the other men back to the van.

Soon they continued down the road. After the sounds of the van faded, he put his goggles back on and moved toward the launch complex.

After an hour of creeping slowly through the woods he found a good vantage point. The launch facility was straight ahead. A tower with antennae was to his right and the assembly buildings to the left. In between was the concrete pad the *Rising Savior* would lift from for the last time.

Settling in, he prepared his weapon.

CHAPTER 17 **PREPARATION**

> There are different kinds of gifts, but the same Spirit. There are different kinds of service, but the same Lord.
>
> —I CORINTHIANS 12:4–5

FELLOWSHIP COMPOUND, CALIFORNIA

John was saying good-bye to his pregnant wife with a long, slow kiss, while Ira groused behind him.

"John, are you going to work or are you going to smooch all night?" Ira growled.

John finished the kiss with a loud smack, then said, "I'm thinking, I'm thinking."

"Move it," Ira ordered gruffly.

Ira's wife, Ruth, glowered from the side as Ira walked to the *Rising Savior,* pushing John ahead of him. Then as if he could feel her eyes in his back, Ira turned in his silver space suit and shuffled up to her, bending down to kiss her lips.

"Are we working or kissing?" John said playfully.

Ira ignored John, walking to the ship, pausing at the rungs for Mark to offer the prayer.

"Gotta go to work now, honey," John said when Mark finished. "Keep the light on for me."

As they were helped into the capsules, Shelly and Mark headed to the control room. There were only a few members in the hangar tonight, since the novelty of the launches had worn off and requests to visit from distant members of the Fellowship had declined. Virtually every member had visited the hangar at one time or another to see for themselves what they supported.

Shelly and Mark, having settled at their consoles, contacted Omnitech Space Services who had built the Indonesian satellite they were about to orbit. Technicians from Omnitech had flown out from Houston to oversee the modifications of the satellite and attachment to the *Rising Savior*. As soon as the satellite was secure they had been restricted to the one end of the hangar where they could watch the launch. Omnitech sent more technicians than needed and the extras kept snooping around the *Rising Savior*—probably CIA.

The Indonesian satellite was a third larger than Aussat VII. The launch of the Indonesian communications satellite was a testament to the confidence the world was developing in their launch capabilities. A success tonight and a dozen pending contracts would fall into place, cementing a virtual monopoly on orbital services.

Shelly controlled a bank of monitors, most of which displayed interior and exterior camera angles, broadcasts from the *Rising Savior,* and external security cameras. Some of the monitors were tuned to network coverage of the launch.

"Take a look at this," Shelly said, pointing to a monitor she had tuned to CNN. "It's a clip from the House of Representatives."

Cable news was filling time while waiting for the launch. The network was running excerpts from congressional debate over NASA's budget. Representative Coogan from North Dakota was speaking. He had built his reputation as a Republican budget hawk.

". . . while we've spent billions developing and launching the shuttles, a small group of devoted scientists, spending a fraction of that amount, developed a superior delivery system that orbits the same payload at half the cost. So tell me, fellow congressmen, for what reason do we continue to fund NASA? It is a dinosaur whose age has passed."

The shot changed to a woman at the same podium. It was Representative Sylvia Swanson of California.

". . . will this cult share its technology with its fellow citizens for the legitimate needs of its country? A country that educated them, protected them from foreign enemies, and provided the technological base that is the foundation for their space delivery system? Men and women in our armed forces have sacrificed their lives to protect these people so they were free to make their discoveries. Now that same technology could be used to save the lives of our brave servicemen and -women. We're not asking them to give us their discovery without compensation. But are they willing to help their country? You know the answer, and until they are willing I will continue to support funding for NASA and for a new Manhattan project to crack the secret of the *Rising Savior.*"

"Omnitech is ready, Mark," Shelly said, touching her earphone.

It was time and Mark announced the launch over the loudspeaker. The hangar was opened and the *Rising Savior* pulled toward the launch pad.

> The Stinger in its various evolutions in service
> since 1981 has been the most widely procured
> and used man portable air defence system
> (MANPADS). . . . The system has been
> continuously evolved to exploit advances in
> technology and provide greater capability, espe-
> cially in a countermeasure environment. Basic
> Stinger was used extensively in Afghanistan, and
> has been credited with the kill of 250 Russian
> aircraft when used by operators with
> only limited training.
>
> —JANE'S MISSILES AND ROCKETS

FELLOWSHIP COMPOUND, CALIFORNIA

At the emergence of the *Rising Savior,* he readied the Stinger missile, removing the protective cover, then extending the shoulder support and grip. Removing a pistol from his pack, he packed everything else away, ready to make a quick getaway. The launcher would be left behind but free of any fingerprints. Having gotten this far he had little doubt of getting away. Rescue operations after the destruction of the *Rising Savior* would occupy everyone in the compound until long after he was gone.

The tractor pulled the *Rising Savior* to the middle of the concrete launch pad. A man wearing headphones walked behind the ship, a long cord connecting his headphones to the spaceship. When the *Rising Savior* was positioned, the tractor was unhitched and returned to the hangar. The man in the headphones remained, occasionally speaking into his microphone.

He stood, leaning against the tree, ready to shoot. The Stinger was a heat-seeking missile but the guidance system would be of little use here since there was no engine exhaust for the missile to track. It would be a strictly point and shoot kill. The ship would need to be eight hundred meters distant before he could shoot, the missile using the distance to arm itself and reach its Mach two flight speed.

Finally, the man with headphones disconnected himself from the ship, backing away, putting on sunglasses. Then the ship glowed bright and he turned away. When he looked back the ship was floating in a cloud of dust. It was almost time.

Bracing against the tree he steadied himself, sighting on the rising ship. The craft rose slowly, the dust cloud clearing. His sight was unobstructed and he tightened on the trigger, ready to gently squeeze it. The *Rising Savior* cleared the top of the building and he began the countdown. "Four, three, two . . ." Suddenly the tree next to him splintered and he flinched in surprise, shooting the Stinger. Out of the dark came the man with the glowing eyes. The mechanic reached for his pistol but the man was on him, breaking his nose with the heel of his hand. Pain shot to his brain and his eyes teared. Fighting for his life, he reached for his gun, cocking it as he turned. Then his gun hand was locked in an iron grip. The man with glowing eyes was too strong. With his left hand, the mechanic pulled a survival knife from the sheath on his belt. Before he could plunge it home another man appeared, pointing a rifle at his head. The knife still poised to strike he hesitated, deciding between life and death. He chose life—he'd escaped from jail before.

"I surrender," he said, tossing his knife to the side. "I want a lawyer waiting for me when I get to the police station."

More armed men appeared out of the darkness. Now the man with burning eyes stepped forward to stand toe to toe.

"We're not the police," the man with glowing eyes said.

"I demand to be turned over to the police!" he repeated, realizing he had surrendered to the cult.

His captors laughed, triggering a rivulet of sweat that trickled down his back.

"Turn me in, you've got the evidence!"

The men laughed again.

"I'm afraid we've lost confidence in our criminal justice system," the man with the strange eyes said. "It looks like you're going to have to answer to God."

CHAPTER 19   **TRUMPET CALL**

> . . . and with the trumpet call of God, and the
> dead in Christ will rise first.
>
> —I THESSALONIANS 5:23

FELLOWSHIP COMPOUND, CALIFORNIA

Shelly and Mark were monitoring the launch when John's shout exploded in their ears.

"Whoa!" John screamed. "Someone's shooting at us!"

"Say again," Mark said, not believing what he heard.

"Quiet, John," Ira ordered. "Mark, we've been fired on. I think it was a missile. I'm taking us to orbit."

Now the hangar behind them erupted as witnesses came running in. Floyd carried word immediately to the command center.

"Someone fired a missile at the *Rising Savior!*" Floyd said breathlessly.

"Calm down, Floyd," Mark said. "Is the *Rising Savior* safely away?"

"Yes. Ira took her up lickety-split."

"Are you sure only one missile was fired?" Mark asked.

"That's all I saw," Floyd said.

If it had been an all-out attack the compound would be taking incoming rounds by now, Mark knew. Mark guessed the *Rising Savior* was the sole target but Mark couldn't take a chance. Mark turned to Shelly.

"Gabriel's Trumpet," Mark said.

To his surprise Shelly broke into a smile, then she left, hurrying into the hangar as fast as an eight-month-pregnant woman can move.

"Floyd, spread the word, we're clearing out."

"It's done," Floyd said, hurrying after Shelly.

Contingency plans had been made in case they were attacked and Floyd was activating those now.

"Ira, Gabriel's Trumpet," Mark said into his microphone.

"Gabriel's Trumpet," Ira responded, then the radio went dead.

Then Mark contacted their San Antonio compound.

"Gabriel's Trumpet," Mark said when they responded.

"Gabriel's Trumpet," came the reply.

Next Mark activated the "wipe" program. Soon a coded data stream was beamed to their satellite and then relayed to San Antonio. Immediately after, a worm spread through their computer network destroying the operating system and all the files, leaving nothing but ordinary computer hardware for any invaders. If the Fellowship lost the compound, the computers would be an expensive loss, but their technology would be safe. Then Mark hurried into the hangar.

Floyd was at the hangar doors and Mark signaled him to open them. The Fellowship was about to reveal another one of its secrets.

> Religious belief is based on the assumption of
> the supernatural; that every action is guided by
> the hand of God, or a demon, or a spiritual
> force. This belief persists despite the fact that
> no one has ever been able to substantiate the
> existence of a spiritual world.
>
> — *RELIGION, PLAGUES, AND EARTHQUAKES:*
> *NATURAL AND UNNATURAL DISASTERS,*
> MARION WADE

SAN FRANCISCO, CALIFORNIA

Comfortable in his favorite chair, Crow sipped his wine, watching his television expectantly. The chair was leather stretched over a hardwood frame with mahogany trim. The television was the latest in high-definition technology, a thin wall screen, six feet wide. Crystal-clear coverage of the launch filled the wall, shot from a hill outside the cult's compound. There was no sound coming from the speakers built into the walls around the room. Crow had turned the sound off, unable to tolerate the inane babble of the reporters.

Crow put his wine down, picking up his Cuban cigar, sucking in the rich smoke, holding it in his lungs, then expelling the smoke in a long, slow, luxurious blow. Crow studied the woods between the compound and the launch site, wondering if his assassin was hidden there. The mechanic had refused to tell him when he would strike, so watching the launches had become a ritual for Crow, ever hopeful that this would be the night.

Now the telescopic camera focused in on the cult ship. The air around the *Rising Savior* began to glow and it soon became too intense for the camera, the scene switching to a wide shot from the hill. Now the *Rising Savior* appeared to be a glowing ball in the distance. The glow died and the wide shot of the compound was replaced by a tight shot of the *Rising Savior*. A dust cloud was swirling around the ship and Crow leaned forward watching the ship lift. Now the camera angle widened and Crow held his breath in anticipation. When the *Rising Savior* cleared the top of the hangar Crow relaxed, disappointed. Placing his cigar in a crystal ashtray, he picked up his glass. He was running out of patience with the mechanic.

Suddenly a missile streaked across the screen, missing the *Rising Savior,* continuing across the compound and out of camera range. Crow punched the mute button to restore the sound.

"What was that? Was that a missile?" a confused reporter said dumbly.

A muffled booming was heard in the background and the camera jerked up, the picture blurring.

"Over there, a fireball. An explosion!" Then the reporter became serious. "There has been an attack on the spaceship *Rising Savior* by an unknown party or parties."

Crow threw his glass at the screen, shattering the goblet, the wine spilling across the screen and down the wall. Now Crow watched the action through a pink stain. The camera focused on the site of the explosion and the brush fire spreading out from the impact site. Then the camera pointed back into the compound, the reporter declaring, "Something is happening."

Crow stood, approaching the screen, wiping away the wine with the sleeve of his silk shirt. Then he stood dumbfounded as he realized he had underestimated his enemy.

By this sign [the cross] shalt thou conquer him.

—FROM THE VISION OF CONSTANTINE,
A.D. 313

GILROY RANCH, OUTSIDE OF
CHRIST'S HOME, CALIFORNIA

Cameras were rolling as the *Rising Savior* lifted off, reporters providing running commentary along with the video feed to the cable networks carrying the launch live. The broadcast networks were recording, preparing footage for late-night newscasts and the morning network talk shows. Roland was reminded of the Apollo program, before the public was satiated with space spectaculars. The interest in the Fellowship launches was still high but waning, the broadcast networks now selecting which launches to cover live.

Roland's heart still pounded from excitement whenever the *Rising Savior* was rolled to the pad, not because the launches were thrilling—they lacked the explosive beauty of a shuttle launch—but because of the potential they represented. The Fellowship held the key to a permanent presence in space.

Suddenly a missile climbed from the trees, streaking under the *Rising Savior,* continuing across the valley, exploding on contact with the far hill. Roland leapt to his feet. A small fire could be seen in the distance where the missile exploded in the dry hills. All around him excited reporters babbled to their viewers about what they had just witnessed. The reporters built the story, describing what happened with words like "war zone," "battle," and "carnage," despite the fact that only one missile had been fired.

Roland studied the dark compound for signs of attack.

All was quiet—no attackers, no defenders. Then the hangar door slowly opened and the incredible happened.

As the door opened the lights in the compound were turned off. The reporters around Roland quieted, whispering their commentary now, everyone expecting a response from the cult. Suddenly the hangar opening lit up, the white light brighter than day. Then the hangar faded to dark again, followed by another bright glow and another fade to dark. Three more times the hangar glowed briefly. Then a steady dull glow could be seen from the hangar. The reporters continued in whisper mode, describing in great redundancy what they saw below. Another minute passed, the compound dark, then a ship flew out of the opening and shot into the sky.

"Wasn't that the *Rising Savior*?" a reporter asked.

Before he finished another ship flew out and then three more in quick succession, all of them identical to the *Rising Savior*.

Roland was furious with himself for not guessing their scam—the launch schedule was too grueling to be believed. There were a half-dozen *Rising Saviors,* not a single ship as they had been led to believe.

As Roland watched the last of the ships disappear he wondered what other secrets the cult was hiding.

CHAPTER 22

SHEPHERD'S PRAYER

> To test the power of prayer, Sir Francis Galton
> compared the shipwreck rates of slave ships
> with those of ships carrying missionaries. Con-
> gregations routinely prayed for missionaries, but
> not for slavers. Galton found that the oceans
> claimed slavers and missionaries equally often.
>
> — *A HISTORY OF GOOD AND EVIL,*
> ROBERT WINSTON, PH.D.

SAN ANTONIO, TEXAS

Sitting in a chair, hands folded, head down, Mark Shepherd meditated, keeping his mind clear, open so God
could speak to him. He had prayed like this twice daily
since receiving his vision and never once had God spoken
to him—no deep booming voices, no small whisper, no
visions like that night in the hospital chapel, not even a
fleeting image. It was as if God expected that one
vision—one communication—to be sufficient to guide
Mark down the long road God had placed before him.
Coming as it did shortly after Anita's death, Mark had
latched on to that vision like a drowning man would a life
preserver. The vision, and meeting Ira, had given him a
sense of direction and a feeling that he was doing something important. One day he had been a lonely man, de-
spairing in a chapel, his nascent family buried, and the
next a man with a new family—a family of believers.

That family—the Fellowship—started with Mark and
Ira and now thousands of people looked to him for leadership. The companionship was welcomed at first but now
had grown into a burden he would willingly turn over to
others. God asked too much of him, breaking his back
with the load. Mark's days were spent in endless meet-

ings, making dozens of decisions, seldom confident he'd made the right one. Now there was a new distraction—Christy Maitland.

Christy's face, her smell, her words, were pleasant intrusions, welcome distractions from his burden. He felt some guilt when he thought of Anita, long-buried but still loved, but she would want the best for him. He desperately wanted a helpmate but in his vision he had been alone in that desert. Mark had often wondered if the traffic accident that took Anita and their unborn son had been an act of God, designed to prepare him for his task. If God had taken a woman he loved once, would God do it again?

Mark's watch beeped and he left his office in the San Antonio compound, walking the short hall to the conference room. Mark's office was like the rest of the compound, sparsely furnished with a desk chair, side chair for visitors, and a table that he used for a desk. A five-year-old computer hummed on the tabletop and four file cabinets lined one wall. There were no pictures or decorations, not even a cross. The floor was yellowed linoleum, the walls Sheetrock painted white. The conference room was also sparsely furnished. It was the largest office in what used to be a furniture factory. The name of the factory was still painted on the exterior, nearly unreadable, bleached by the relentless Texas sun.

The others were already gathered. They sat on folding metal chairs around an old Sunday school table with a Formica top and folding legs. The stain of finger paints and Magic Markers still marred the surface. Shelly and John Henry sat to his right, and Ira and Floyd Remple to his left. Sally Roper, the financial manager, sat at the far end of the table. Mark presided over the meetings, but Ira set the agenda.

"George Proctor wants to see you, Mark," Ira said.

"Tell him to get lost, Mark. He'll only bring us trouble," Shelly said.

John faked embarrassment, then said in a soft voice, "What my gentle wife is trying to say, Mark, is that Mr. Proctor may not be part of God's plan for the Fellowship."

"I won't meet with him," Mark said. "Associating with George Proctor will just make it harder for us to reach our goal."

"Maybe you should meet with him," Ira said.

Surprised, everyone turned to look at Ira. Ira had always disliked Proctor.

"He gave me this when he asked to see you," Ira said.

Ira handed Marks strange-looking pair of goggles.

"What are these?"

"Night-vision goggles," Ira said. "Proctor said the last owner of those goggles also owned a Stinger missile."

"Proctor knows who fired at the *Rising Savior*?" Shelly asked.

"He'll only talk to Mark," Ira said.

"I'll see him after the meeting," Mark decided.

"Sally, please give us a financial update," Ira said, moving the meeting along.

Sally Roper was a tiny sixty-year-old woman with white hair, skin tanned a deep brown, and soft gray eyes, bright with intelligence. Despite her diminutive size, she controlled the Fellowship's finances and she wielded great power.

"Tithing is steady, donations are up twenty-two percent over last month, and twenty-three members switched to worker status, saving us sixty percent of their salaries. Our cash reserves are down to $5,354,000 but we have a number of contracts lined up that should provide steady revenue until the new space station is operational. We're retrieving the Chinese weather satellite that malfunctioned last week and will return it to orbit later this month. We're repositioning two satellites for Hughes and NASA has finally come through. We've contracted to take up a supply module for space station Freedom and they want us to rescue the Solar IV satellite. They can't get their booster to push it into a usable orbit."

"Why are they still funding the space station when we can do it for less?" Shelly asked.

"Congress has cut back the funding for Freedom, but not cut it off," Sally said.

"They never will," Ira argued. "The space program em-

ploys people in all the key electoral states. If they put
NASA out of business, they lose their jobs and the president loses votes."

"We've received requests from the NSF and three universities for time on board New Hope," Sally continued.
"The University of Hawaii has temporarily halted construction of the new observatory on Mauna Kea. They
want to explore with us the possibility of locating the telescope on New Hope."

"Get deposits from NASA and the others but no one gets
on the station until six months after we're operational."

The others nodded, Ira making a note. The rest of the
business was routine and much of the work was delegated
to deacons. When they were done Ira waited with Mark to
meet with George Proctor.

Proctor came in, eyes closed, walking directly to the
table and sitting down. Mark had seen Proctor's closed-
eyes act before and didn't understand the point.

"What do these goggles mean?" Mark asked.

"I took them from the man who attacked the *Rising
Savior*," Proctor said.

"How did you find him?"

"We were there that night. He won't be shooting any
more missiles at you."

After the attack, the Fellowship's security people had
found a hole in the fence but nothing else. Mark was relieved to know the man wasn't loose, but he was bothered
that Proctor had killed the man.

"Thanks for saving my people," Mark said.

"You're welcome."

Mark had nothing more to say but Proctor remained,
eyes closed.

"Was there something else?" Mark asked.

"We've been providing security for your people but
without access to your properties we can't do a proper job."

"We have a security force," Ira said.

"Where were they when the missile was fired?"

"We can't afford you," Mark said.

"I'm not asking to be paid."

"Then why do it?" Ira asked.

"Because God told me to."

Mark's and Ira's visions had brought them together; was it possible Proctor had experienced his own vision? Why he latched on to the Fellowship wasn't clear but Mark felt his motivations weren't mercenary.

"I don't want anyone hurt," Mark said.

"I don't either," Proctor said.

"You'll follow my orders?"

"If I can't, I'll tell you."

"Fair enough. I'll get you access privileges to our properties."

Proctor smiled now, opening his eyes.

"I'm here to help you succeed, Reverend Shepherd."

Mark wasn't sure what Proctor knew about the Fellowship's goal but Proctor was admired by many in the Fellowship. When he was gone, Mark left for two hours of simulator training. Pilot training was one of the few pleasures Mark took from his job.

On his way to the hangar Christy came to mind again and Mark wondered if there was any place for her in his future? Was it safe for him to be with her? He hoped so, because he was tired of facing the future alone.

> Like a few of the angels, some of Satan's minions
> have names. One of his demons is known as
> Asmodeus and is the guardian of treasure.
>
> — *A HISTORY OF GOOD AND EVIL,*
> ROBERT WINSTON, PH.D.

SAN FRANCISCO, CALIFORNIA

Rachel's slight smile was enough to reassure Crow that she had succeeded. They were sitting in Crow's office, Rachel's six-foot frame curled up in one of the oversized chairs, her long legs folded under her. Rachel wore a white silk blouse over black slacks, her clothes contrasting nearly as much as her black hair against her pale skin.

"Lichter is a worm," Rachel said in a slow, deep voice. "He didn't have the courage to get involved himself. I had to threaten to cut off his payments to get the names I needed."

William Lichter, who worked at NASA, had been easy to corrupt. Through Rachel, Crow had seduced him with money, paying for bits and pieces of harmless information at first, and as Lichter became hooked on Crow's money, he traded NASA's deepest secrets for a few thousand dollars a year. Lichter had no personal convictions to guide him and no religious or even secular value system to lean on. What little personal worth he felt came from his association with NASA and he exploited that association at every opportunity. He bored his neighbors and acquaintances by exaggerating his role at NASA and his wife used the NASA connection too, as if her husband's status were her own. When it became clear to Lichter that he was rising no further in the NASA hierarchy, he faced a crisis, but Crow's money had helped him maintain the fiction that he was growing in importance and influence. Now NASA itself was threatened, by the Fellowship's technology. Lichter could easily see a future where he had no identity, no job, no income, and no respect from his wife. He would be left with only himself and that was nothing.

"It's better that Lichter stays out of it anyway," Crow said. "We may have further use for him."

"The others we needed all had their price—a surprisingly small price."

"Everyone at NASA is threatened by the cult," Crow said. "Their jobs are on the line and they want the cult stopped as much as I do."

"Do you really think one failure will stop them?" Rachel asked.

"It depends on how big the failure is."

"There might be a problem there," Rachel said. "There are too many variables to know the exact outcome. For one thing, we know very little about the design of their ships."

"We'll just have to trust in a higher power to make sure the failure has the desired effect," Crow said.

"Should I prepare a sacrifice?" Rachel asked.

"Yes, something special," Crow said.

Executed properly, an aerodynamic space vehicle
returning to Earth will descend at a shallow
angle, traveling several thousand kilometers
through the upper atmosphere to minimize friction and prevent excessive build-up of thermal
energy. Executed improperly, the aerodynamic
features are rendered useless and the
kinetic energy of the descending vehicle is
rapidly converted to heat. In short,
the space vehicle burns up.

— *ALTERNATE PATHWAYS TO SPACE,*
EDWARD NORTON

PORTLAND, OREGON

Mediating reconciliations was often stressful but this
one had been particularly taxing. Christy was exhausted,
as were the participants, but after an eleven-hour day they
had reached a breakthrough. Management would not restore Mr. Pilson's sales territory but they would let him
choose between one of two expansion territories. In exchange Mr. Pilson agreed to work solely on commissions
and reach mutually agreed upon sales goals within two
years.

Christy worried that George Pilson was overconfident in
his sales ability. After twenty years of average performance, Mr. Pilson's sales had dropped off dramatically.
On paper, the company was justified in firing him but because of his age Mr. Pilson had filed an age discrimination
lawsuit. Three months after he filed his suit, Mr. Pilson had
agreed to divert the case to Christy's reconciliation center.
George Pilson was an overweight, bow tie–wearing,
middle-aged man, who had trouble relating to a new generation of customers who were increasingly diverse. Be-

cause of Christy's mediation, Mr. Pilson had another chance to prove himself and the company had his name on an agreement that specified performance goals he must meet to keep his job. At least for now, they had both won.

Leaving the final details to the staff, Christy excused herself, returning to her office, telling Janine she wanted no calls. Then she reclined in her desk chair, feet on another chair, and closed her eyes. Just as she drifted off the phone buzzed and she hammered the speaker button.

"What?" she said irritably.

"You have a phone call," her secretary said.

"Take a message—"

"It's Mark Shepherd."

Instantly awake, Christy sat up. They hadn't spoken since the rescue of the Australian satellite but she thought of him often.

"I'll take the call."

"I thought you might."

"This is Christy," she said into the receiver.

"Hello, Christy, it's Mark Shepherd."

Her fatigue was suddenly gone. Surprised by how pleased she was to hear from him, she hid her excitement behind a professional tone.

"It's nice of you to call."

"I was wondering if you would be interested in another tour," Mark asked. "The last segment of our space station New Hope is being lifted Saturday. You could come down for the launch and stay over to worship with us on Sunday."

"I'd love to," Christy said.

Christy felt like she had been asked on a date.

"Do I fly into Guadalupe? I heard that's where you're building your space station."

"Come to Christ's Home," Mark said. "Floyd will bring you to the compound. I'd pick you up myself but I get mobbed when I leave."

"You must feel like a movie star," Christy said.

"More like a prisoner."

Christy heard the sadness in his voice. They agreed on times, then said good-bye. Wide awake now, Christy explored her feelings for Mark, trying to understand what it was about him that made her feel like an infatuated teenager.

Christy was disappointed when the last segment of the New Hope was lifted into orbit two days early. Nevertheless, Christy met Floyd as planned Saturday night, just before midnight. He was as affable as ever.

"I guess your space station is complete now," she said as they drove through the empty streets of Christ's Home toward the Fellowship's compound.

"Not by a long shot," Floyd said, keeping his eyes on the road. "What's up there now is just a small start. We'll keep adding to New Hope as we get the money."

"Are Cokes still seven dollars?"

Floyd chuckled.

"Floyd, I'm a little confused. Mark invited me down to see the launch of part of the New Hope but it went up yesterday."

Floyd hummed, ignoring Christy.

"What aren't you telling me?"

Now Floyd whistled.

"You're hiding something, Floyd."

"All I can tell you is that there is a launch tonight. John is going up after one of NASA's duds."

When they reached the entrance to the compound, Christy was surprised to see only a handful of media people staking out the main entrance. When Floyd stopped to let guards open the gate, the media rushed forward, surrounding the van, pressing cameras to the windows, trying to capture images of those inside. Christy kept her head down, preventing a good picture. Floyd smiled and waved at the cameras.

The long road to the launch facilities was dark. Twice Christy spotted armed men hiding in shadows, speaking into walkie-talkies as they passed. When they reached the launch center she found it was dark too, except for light shining from the windows of the assembly building. Floyd parked outside, ushering Christy to the door. Inside was one of the barbell-shaped *Rising Savior*s. Up close she could see the name "Lamb of God" stenciled across one of the twin spheres. Suddenly Mark popped up out of the sphere, smiling.

"It's good to see you," Mark said.

"Nice to see you too," she said, feeling self-conscious.

Then they were out of things to say and stared dumbly at each other. It was Mark who broke the silent stare, climbing out of the sphere.

"I want to show you something," Mark said.

Mark led her to a room in the hangar she had never entered. It was filled with pieces of spaceships like the *Rising Savior*.

"Replacement parts," Mark said. "All of our systems are built with triple redundancy. No mishaps and only two significant system failures and in both of those cases the backup systems kicked in just as designed."

As he explained, Mark led her through the parts hangar to a wide set of stairs and down three flights. Until then she hadn't realized there were lower levels to the hangar. They came out into a noisy three-story assembly plant, filled with busy people. In the distance she could see the sparks of welding. Overhead a crane moved a piece of curved steel toward the back.

"This is where we put the ships together."

"Everything is built here?"

"This is one assembly site. Some of the structural work is done here and certain subassemblies put together. Eighty percent of what we use is bought off the shelf from industrial suppliers, then modified for our needs. The power plant is shipped in whole when the rest of the ship is finished."

Christy knew better than to ask where the power plants were made. Mark led her through the work spaces, keeping between two yellow lines painted on the floor. Those they passed smiled at her or whispered to other workers. They stopped on the far side in front of an elevator that filled most of the wall. Mark pushed a button and a buzzer sounded, then the wire gates pulled open. Inside he closed the gates and they started up. He was smiling now, as if he was hiding something. When they cleared the floor above she saw it— a new spaceship, much larger than the *Lamb of God*.

The two-sphere design had been abandoned and in its place they had built a ship resembling the blocky space shuttle rather than the sleek space plane. It was shaped like a bullet; a rounded nose widening out but with no wings, then ending abruptly with a flat tail. There were windows high in the front, giving it the look of a jet but no engines in the back.

"This is our new class of ship," Mark said. "We're calling it 'God's Love.'"

"All your ship names sound like sermons," Christy said. Mark laughed.

"That's the point," Mark said. "People will look up and say, '*God's Love* is above us.'"

"It's so different from the other ships."

"It has a different purpose than the lifting spheres. Come inside, I'll show you."

The hatch hadn't been installed yet and they walked through the wall into the lower level.

"This is where the power plants will go when we bring them in," Mark said.

The deck was mostly empty space. Then Mark led her up a ladder to another deck, still under construction. It was a two-story empty space. Two men in coveralls were pulling wires through galvanized pipe.

"See what they're doing? That's real pipe and copper wiring. No shuttle could lift all that weight. It's so much cheaper to use steel and copper than the high-tech alternatives they have to use on the space shuttles. This deck will carry cargo—everything will be in sealed containers. The ship is a hatchback and the end opens in two sections so we can slide the cargo containers in or out. There will be a track system and winches to move the containers."

"The ship is huge," Christy said. "It seems larger than you need to supply the New Hope."

"We're building for the future. Come up to the next deck."

Up another ladder and they emerged on the flight deck. Few of the instruments had been installed but she could see the flight deck was configured for four. Two stations looked out the front windows, and the other two stations were along the walls, one on either side.

"I feel like I'm in a 747," Christy said.

"The New Hope will go where no 747 could. Come back this way."

They walked through a tight space where workmen were welding something to the exterior wall and emerged into a space much smaller than the cargo level. Mark was ducking, although he seemed to have an inch or two of clearance. Then he stepped aside and she could see workmen installing seats at the far end.

"You're going to take passengers?" Christy asked.

"At first we'll just shuttle crew up and down but eventually we hope to take passengers."

"Tourists?"

"You'd be surprised what people will pay."

Christy shook her head in amazement. This man and his followers were single-handedly pushing the envelope of the future.

Floyd appeared, coming down the corridor from the flight deck. Floyd spoke loud to be heard over the workers.

"John and Ray are taking off soon."

"Thanks, Floyd," Mark said.

"Did John and Ira have a falling out?" Christy asked.

"Ira's an engineer, not a pilot," Mark said. "He took the first few flights in case anything needed to be repaired during the flight. Now he only flies occasionally. If you've seen enough here, I have something else to show you."

Christy followed him out, wondering what other marvels they had hidden away in this complex. When they reached the hangar Mark walked to the *Lamb of God* and motioned for her to climb aboard. Shelly waved from the control room.

"How's the baby, Shelly?" Christy shouted.

"As obnoxious as John," Shelly shouted back, "but I love him."

Christy climbed down and then stepped aside as Mark climbed in. Sharing a small enclosed space with Mark made her uncomfortable and she moved as far back as the small space allowed. When he closed the hatch her heart started pounding. She felt like a teenager whose boyfriend claimed he had run out of gas.

"What are you doing?" Christy asked.

"We can't go visit the New Hope with the hatch open."

"You don't mean we're going into orbit?" she asked, excited.

"If you want to," Mark said.

"Don't I need a space suit?"

"Sixty-five trips to orbit without a mishap. Tonight we're just going up and down for a quick look. Will you take a ride with me?"

Smiling, she sat down in the backseat and buckled herself in. "Fly me to the moon," she said.

"Just to orbit—today."

Christy put on headphones and listened as Shelly and Mark ran through a checklist. The first motion she felt was the tug of the tractor as they were pulled out of the hangar. The controls in front of her meant nothing but she could see the indicator lights were all green. Then she heard Shelly give approval for liftoff. Having grown up with shuttle launches she couldn't help but brace herself for the gee-forces of the launch and the earsplitting roar of rocket engines. Instead, she felt nothing except a vibration through the hull. Through the small window in front of her she could see the buildings sliding past as if she were going up in an elevator. Then she was above the roof and she could see the lights of Christ's Home in the distance. As they rose, more distant city lights came into view, then wispy clouds obscured her view. They were climbing rapidly with hardly any gee-force. Even Christy's ears were relatively unaffected, feeling only a slight pressure.

"Our first stop is straight up," Mark said. "Our government just parked a satellite over the compound and I thought we'd take a look at it."

"Why would they do that?" Christy asked, still watching the Earth shrink away below them.

"To spy on us. To steal our technology if they can."

"Couldn't it be a coincidence? A weather satellite, or a communications satellite?"

"They don't keep the launch of those satellites secret. This one is a military Keyhole satellite, capable of photographing objects as small as a pager and listening in on radio and telephone communications."

"*Lamb of God,* this is Christ's Home," Shelly said through the earphones.

"I hear you, Shelly," Mark said.

"John and Ray are closing on NASA's bird."

"Thanks, Shelly. We're almost to the Keyhole. I'm activating the cameras."

Christy looked out again, shocked at how high they were now. The Earth curved away below her.

"Christy, there are sunglasses under your seat. You're going to get the sun on your side in a couple of minutes. Pull the screen too."

Christy found a tab and pulled a dark panel across her window. She was reaching for the sunglasses when the sun broke over the horizon brighter than she had ever seen it. Even with the glasses it was uncomfortable and she turned away.

"We're approaching the satellite," Mark said.

"How do you know where you are?"

"We've got five navigational satellites in orbit that send out constant signals and four ground stations. The computer triangulates using the signals giving me an exact position at all times."

Mark tapped on a display. Christy found the identical display in front of her. There were three sets of figures that changed slowly.

"The next monitor over tells us where our target is located," Mark said.

Christy found the second display, which did not change. She could see the numbers on the two displays were getting close.

"Christy, get ready for weightlessness. I've been accelerating at one gee, but now we'll be slowing and I'm bringing the ship around so you'll see the satellite out your window."

Her stomach fluttered as she felt gravity evaporate. Then the ship rotated and she pushed open the screen and removed her sunglasses. Free from the atmosphere the stars were bright white dots that had lost their twinkle. Their naked appearance was disconcerting but fascinating. Now gravity was all but gone and the sunglasses floated up from her lap. She tapped them into a spin, laughing at the amazing sight. When the glasses drifted behind her she turned her head, discovering her hair was floating free around her head. She pulled her hair back but with no way to tie it the hair continued to have a mind of its own.

"Here, use this," Mark said.

A rubber band floated past her face and she snagged it. Untangling her hair from the headphones she tied her hair into a ponytail. As she finished the satellite came into view. It resembled a canister with solar panels and two large dish antennae. Other objects protruded from the satellite but she couldn't identify them.

"That's a Keyhole satellite, all right," Mark said. "It's state of the art in surveillance technology and it's pointed right at our compound. I suppose you know they've set up ground surveillance at each of our properties? Even in Mexico. Why are they so afraid of us?"

"Your technology. I suppose they think the same force that makes your ships fly could be used as a weapon. You know conservative religious groups have a history of violence."

"Jonestown? They were a cult, not fundamentalists."

"Also the Branch Davidians and various anti-abortion groups," Christy said.

"That's a small sliver of Christianity," Mark said.

. "But a dangerous part," Christy said.

Mark pushed a button marked "VID 1," and the satellite appeared on a monitor. Then Mark orbited the satellite twice.

"We've got enough video, let's go see the New Hope," Mark said.

When they accelerated away Christy realized she was feeling queasy. Closing her eyes, she breathed deep and slow trying to lose the nausea. Mark rotated the ship to keep one side from overheating and she could see the Earth again. Mottled green and blue and covered with white clouds, it was beautiful. Seeing it from space made it look like a work of art, not a planet hanging in an infinite void. Then the ship was rotated again and she could see the New Hope ahead of them.

The space station was made up of six cylinders linked together end to end, with antennae extending in various places. It looked like a centipede floating in space. Two more of the twin-sphere ships were docked at one end and a third was moving along the length of the station. Looking closer she realized the moving ship was only one sphere, not twin pods like the others.

"Mark, that looks like half a ship."

"Spheres are designed to operate independently. John and Ray took the other half to rescue the NASA satellite. We started out using them in pairs until the ships could prove themselves. We also get added lift in tandem. Since we don't have EVA capability it's more efficient to use them separately whenever possible."

"What is EVA?"

"Extra vehicular activity. We don't have environment suits that allow us to operate in space. They are very expensive, so we do everything from the pods with remote manipulators. We won't need space suits inside the space station since the modules lock together and once they are pressurized we weld them together permanently."

"Floyd said you would be adding more to the station."

"Floyd talks too much, but he's right. The modules can be cross-connected to create a row of parallel modules. We can expand the original six modules to twelve that way and then expand them endlessly. That's not our first priority, though. First, we need more communications platforms, so the next twelve modules we build will be positioned in sets of three around the Earth. With these platforms we can provide whatever transponder capacity broadcasters need, not to mention telephone and weather services, all at a lower cost than throw-away satellites."

"More money for the Fellowship?"

"We give good value."

"I can see two rows of windows along the New Hope. Are there two decks?"

"Three. The equipment and storage deck doesn't have windows. The two decks on top of that—wait, it doesn't make any sense this way."

Suddenly she was weightless again as Mark stopped their forward motion. Then their ship rotated and top and bottom reversed—her stomach fluttered again.

"That's better. Now when I say top it will mean top."

Christy's stomach gurgled, rejecting this new orientation.

"*Lamb of God,* this is Shelly," a voice interrupted.

"We hear you, Shelly."

"John and Ray are about to hook up with NASA's wayward satellite."

"Thanks, Shelly," Mark said. "We've got to get back."

Mark punched a button and the video being transmitted by John and Ray from the *Rising Savior* appeared on her monitor. It showed the end of a rocket engine while Ray exchanged numbers with Shelly at the compound control center.

"Hold it there," John said over the earphones. "I'm extending the manipulators. She's wobbling a little, but it shouldn't be a problem. Ray, get ready to compensate for the vibration. Hey, Shelly, remember that magic fingers bed in Walla Walla. We got our quarter's worth then, didn't we?"

"John, everyone's listening to this," Shelly responded, embarrassed.

"That's one," John said a few seconds later. "Stand by while I grab on with the other."

Christy looked out the window, preferring the stars to the tail end of a rocket. Mark was pulling them away from New Hope and the acceleration of the *Lamb of God* helped settle her stomach. Feeling better now, she found she was in love with space, finding the visual simplicity seductive.

"I want to hear more about the magic fingers bed," Ray said.

"You'll pay for this when you get home, John," Shelly said.

Christy smiled, enjoying Shelly's embarrassment.

"All right, I've got it," John said. "I'm locking everything down. I've got all greens. What do you show, Shelly?"

"All green."

"Let's move it, Ray—what's that?" John said sharply.

Christy looked back to the monitor, drawn by the tone of John's voice. Just as she turned back the rocket engine roared to life. Instantly, the screen flashed like a strobe light and then went blank. Now Christy's earphones were filled with confused shouting, some of it John, some of it Ray. Then there was an earsplitting scream, cut off abruptly, leaving nothing but the hiss of static.

"John!" Shelly screamed. "John, can you hear me?"

Again Christy's earphones filled with confused shouting. Mark's voice was there demanding information, as was Shelly's, begging John to answer. Finally Ira ordered the others to quiet down.

"*Rising Savior,* this is Christ's Home," Ira said. "Can you hear me, John?"

After a period of silence, Mark asked, "Cynthia? What happened?"

"NASA won't confirm it but it appears the PAM booster fired while the *Rising Savior* was attached," Cynthia said.

"How?" Mark demanded.

"They won't even admit it happened, Mark, but it did."

"What about John and Ray?"

"We've lost contact. The *Rising Savior*'s dropping from orbit. It looks like it's broken free from the booster."

"Give me the coordinates and I'll go after them," Mark said.

"It's too late, Mark, they are coming down fast."

"Give me the coordinates!" Mark shouted.

"Sending them now," Cynthia said.

Without waiting, Mark spun the *Lamb of God* and Christy was slammed into her contoured seat, hit with multiple gees from the acceleration. Mark concentrated on the controls, forgetting she was there. Through the window she could see they were dropping rapidly. Mark's back was rigid, only his hands moving across the panel in front of him and occasionally working the stick. Mark's descent was reckless and Christy was afraid, her stomach knotting as they raced into the atmosphere. Soon Christy began to sweat—it was getting hot.

"Mark, it's too late," Cynthia said over the earphones.

"Is the *Rising Savior* still generating a field?" Mark asked.

"We've lost all contact. Mark, your hull is heating. You'll burn up before you can reach them."

A bead of sweat rolled down Christy's forehead.

"Mark, this is Ira. It's too late. You can't help them."

Rigid in his seat, Mark kept the *Lamb of God* in its steep descent. A warning buzzer sounded and an indicator light in front of Shelly began to flash red.

"Mark?" Ira said. "Listen to me. God's not through with you yet."

Mark didn't respond, keeping the ship streaking through the atmosphere, the interior now unbearably hot. Christy could see three red lights flashing now.

Christy released her harness, then pushed herself forward against the invisible hand of acceleration. Leaning out she grabbed Mark's shoulder, gripping him tight before she collapsed back. The touch broke through to him and he looked back briefly, then gently slowed the ship. He was ready to sacrifice himself but not Christy.

"Keep tracking the *Rising Savior,* Cynthia," Mark said. "We'll need to know if they burned up on entry."

"They're over the Pacific," Cynthia said. "NASA's worried they're going to hit the coast near San Diego."

Now the sphere was silent as Mark and Christy waited for the final word. Long minutes passed.

"They're down, Mark," Cynthia said. "They went into the Pacific fifty miles from the California coast."

"They didn't burn up?"

"It's not clear," Ira cut in. "Mark, there's no point in doing a flyby. There is nothing to see."

"I know," Mark said. "We're returning to Christ's Home."

Mark turned the ship, climbing gently, the gee-force comfortable. When they were above the clouds again, Mark spoke over his shoulder.

"Would you pray for them, Christy?"

"Dear heavenly Father, accept these two souls that have joined you this day . . ."

CHAPTER 25   **SUCCESS**

> There are six things the Lord hates, seven that
> are detestable to him: haughty eyes, a lying
> tongue, hands that shed innocent blood, a heart
> that devises wicked schemes, feet that are quick
> to rush into evil, a false witness who pours out
> lies and a man who stirs up dissension
> among brothers.
>
> —PROVERBS 6:16–19

SAN FRANCISCO, CALIFORNIA

Crow sat with Rachel relaxed on his red leather couch, watching the report of the space disaster on his new wall screen. Crow wore a blue pin-striped business suit, tie loosened at the neck. Rachel wore her own business suit, navy blue coat over a white blouse, with matching skirt. They sipped coffee from large mugs as they enjoyed the spectacle. The networks had been covering the disaster live since the "accident" occurred last night and had bumped daytime talk shows and soaps to continue the coverage. That would infuriate millions of TV addicts. Crow hoped the disappointed viewers would blame the cult, not the networks for the loss of their daily fix.

At first, NASA had blamed the disaster on the Fellowship, claiming their systems were foolproof. Crow was amused by NASA's response and pleased that it added to the furor. By midmorning the Fellowship had released videotape of the successful capture of the NASA satellite. The few seconds at the end of the tape clearly showed the satellite's booster firing, ending debate on what had destroyed the *Rising Savior* and its two occupants.

NASA spokespeople were panicky now, fearing the accident could be the death knell for the agency. There had already been pressure to cut their funding, since the Fellowship could do NASA's primary job, delivering payloads to orbit, for less money. Now, NASA not only looked like a technological dinosaur, but they looked incompetent and dangerous.

"Too bad they didn't hit San Diego," Rachel said.

"I was hoping it would hit a hospital," Crow said.

"Better yet the local humane society," Rachel said. "There's nothing like pictures of dead puppies and mutilated kittens to turn the mood of the public ugly."

Crow chuckled. Even though he was mildly disappointed, he still counted this as a success. Two of the God worshipers were dead, some of their equipment had been destroyed, their confidence shaken. That was a good day's work. It wasn't a mortal blow but it proved they were vulnerable. It was time to improve his leverage.

"Rachel, I've decided to run for Congress," Crow said. "Begin making the necessary arrangements."

Rachel looked surprised but asked no questions. Instead, she slid down the couch, leaned against him, and rubbed his chest.

"Congressman Crow," Rachel said softly. "I like the sound of that."

FIRST STEPS

> It would be better for him to be thrown into the
> sea with a millstone tied around his neck than
> for him to cause one of these little ones to sin.
>
> —LUKE 17:2

WASHINGTON, D.C.
Two years later

Manuel Crow's Washington office lacked the mahogany that he preferred but the dark walnut hinted at luxury without offending constituents who came seeking favors. Visitors often commented on his office, comparing it favorably to other congressional offices. As a junior congressman, Crow had one of the smaller complexes, made up of an entry with a receptionist desk, small workroom, and two private rooms. Crow's office was on the left and Rachel's on the right. Unlike most congressional offices, Crow's was tidy, looking more like an upscale law office than the office of an underpaid public servant. The furniture and carpet were new, the desks matching, all paid for out of Crow's personal fortune. "Not a dime of taxpayers' money was spent on my office," Crow told every visitor.

Today Crow was meeting with Meaghan Slater, president of the Womyn's Congress. She wore a loose ankle-length dress that resembled burlap with a necklace of large wooden beads.

"The cult continues to grow in power," Crow was saying. "They have a near monopoly on space—even the Russians have begun using their launch services. Nine of the last ten satellites orbited were put up by the Fellowship. All the major networks and telecommunications companies send their signals through the cult's space platforms and they've leased every bit of space in their new space station. Worst of all, support in Congress for NASA is evaporating. My shortsighted colleagues can't see past the savings from using the services of the cult. Once we lose the independent ability to reach orbit, they will have a total monopoly. I know you haven't been a strong supporter of our space program in the past, but can't you see now how important it is for our nation to continue a presence in space?"

Crow watched Slater's brow wrinkle. She was in a quandary. She had long been a vocal critic of any spending that wasn't for social programs and while defense had taken most of her wrath, even the space program's two percent of the budget was too much for her. Now faced with a cult dedicated to traditional gender roles, she was rethinking her position. Crow pushed her a little further.

"That cult is like a runaway brush fire. The only way to stop it is to take away the fuel and that is their launch revenues. NASA must continue to launch its own satellites. I know I don't want my tax dollars going to support a religious cult, especially one that treats its followers the way Shepherd does. I don't have to tell you how they treat women."

She bristled at that and he knew he had her.

"Chattel!" she spat. "That's what women are in that cult, nothing but property. They give sixty percent of the donations but occupy only twenty percent of the management positions."

Crow nodded seriously while wondering where she got her statistics.

"They've turned the glass ceiling into the glass heavens," Slater said.

"That's a cogent way of putting it. Might I use that?"

"Yes, of course," Slater said, flattered.

"If those narrow-minded cultists can break the law of gravity, NASA's scientists—fifty-six percent of which are women—can too," Crow said. "That is, if we continue to give them the support they need."

Crow had created his NASA gender figures up on the spot but experience told him fanatics like Slater seldom cared to check numbers that supported their point of view.

"I'll see to it that the National Womyn's Congress supports continued funding for NASA," Slater said.

"There will be special NSF and military funding too— both just as important," Crow said, pushing her for more.

"Will women be served by these grants?" Slater asked.

"No less than fifty percent of the grants will go to women—more if discrimination can be shown statistically."

Now Slater smiled. She knew women were always less than fifty percent of research scientists, since women continued to prefer careers in the social sciences to careers in hard sciences.

"If women are protected from discrimination, we will support your bill," Slater said.

Meaghan Slater stood, reaching for her coat. Crow stopped her, getting to his real agenda.

"There is another matter," Crow said gently.

Slater's severe features hardened and she sat back down reluctantly.

"I'm looking for advice on a sticky issue," Crow said. "There have been some serious allegations made about members of the Fellowship. It's about the children."

Slater's face softened, her interest piqued.

"Sexual abuse?" Slater suggested.

"I have no proof, only calls from concerned neighbors," Crow said.

"Is it ritual abuse?"

"I have no concrete evidence but I think so. It may be part of their religion."

"Patriarchies inevitably exploit women and children," Slater said. "Sixty-three percent of women in the general population are sexually abused by family members at some time in their lives. The percentage is much higher among conservative Christians."

"Really, I didn't know the situation was that bad," Crow said, again wondering about her numbers.

"Many women and children have buried the abuse so deep it takes months of therapy to uncover," Slater said.

"That may be the case here," Crow said, encouraging her. "The children talk of what they call 'Reverend Shepherd's special hugs.'"

"Shepherd's involved in the abuse?" Slater asked, unable to hide her excitement.

"It looks that way. Ira Breitling too. Breitling likes to take children on what he calls 'field trips.' He checks them out of school like they were x-rated videos."

Now Slater's severe face reddened. Crow had pushed the snowball over the edge and it was picking up speed and mass. Soon the cult would be hit with an avalanche.

"I'll have my people look into this," she said.

"Soon, I hope. I fear for the children."

"I have a friend—Rosa Quigly—she's worked with child protection agencies all over the country," Slater said.

"The author? I've heard of her work with recovered memories—a remarkable woman."

"She helped me remember my own abuse—it was my father."

"It must have been painful," Crow sympathized in the voice he'd used as a funeral director.

"My father still refuses to deal with his issues. He won't admit what he did. We haven't spoken for seven years. My mother's so terrified of him she still defends him."

Her voice was trembling now; Crow feigned concern and then gently changed the subject.

"Is it possible to keep my name out of this? Those that came to me could be identified if I get involved. If I can keep their trust they may continue to feed me information. Of course if you need to use my name, I'll stand behind you."

"I need a place to start the investigation," Slater said.

"I can give you a couple of names to contact. Two families that live in Christ's Home."

"I don't see any need to involve you, but if you do get any more information . . ."

"You'll be the first to know."

When she was gone Rachel came in, curling up on the sofa, her shapely legs tucked under her bottom.

"How did it go?"

"Like the Bible says," Crow said, " 'suffer the little children . . .' "

CHAPTER 27   **LICHTER**

> . . . and so we conclude that the destruction of the *Rising Savior* was the result of a series of human blunders. Rather than the results of a far-fetched government plot as some have alleged, it was nothing more than an unfortunate accident.
>
> —CONGRESSWOMAN SYLVIA SWANSON

CAPE CANAVERAL, FLORIDA

"Good night, Bill," the guard said.

"Good night," Lichter said, closing his car door, disliking the familiarity of the guard. It was bad enough he had to be walked to his car. At least the guards could show proper deference.

Studying the cars in the lot as he had been trained, Lichter drove in circles until he was sure no one was following him. Finally, he took the access road to the highway, nervously studying every passing car. After two of NASA's engineers had mysteriously disappeared, the staff had undergone security training. Lichter had been particularly attentive. The men who had disappeared were on the list of names he had provided Rachel Waters two years ago. The missing engineers had emerged unscathed from the six-month-long internal investigation, then disappeared a year later.

Lichter left the causeway leading from the launch facility, checking his rearview mirror, studying the cars behind him, unsure of what to look for. Was the Fellowship seeking revenge? Congressman Crow cleaning up loose ends?

A family in a minivan with Oregon license plates was behind him, teenagers in a custom-painted orange Mustang next to them. Lichter slowed—both cars passed. Now Lichter sped up, falling in behind the minivan. Now different cars came up behind and he repeated the maneuver, then repeated it twice more. Finally, he reached his exit, confident no one was following.

His payment from Crow was due and his checking account overdrawn again. Parking in the post office lot, Lichter waited, hoping to get to his box when no one was around. The customer flow was sporadic, but there were always two or three coming or going. Finally, he gave up and walked to the entrance, eyeing everyone, observing no unusual behavior. The payment was in his box. He briefly fingered the hundred-dollar bills, feeling the usual thrill, then tucked it into a front pocket.

As he exited he noticed a minivan with Oregon plates. Odd, he thought, seeing two cars from a state that far away in one day. Looking up he recognized the family he'd seen on the highway. The mother was shooing her two children down the sidewalk while her husband walked toward the post office door. Strangely, the children were climbing into another van, one with Florida license plates. The husband was about to pass him when his hand whipped out, punching Lichter in the solar plexus. Lichter's breath exploded from his lungs. Grabbed from behind, Lichter was lifted by his arms and dragged to the van with the Oregon plates. They threw him onto the floor, climbing in after him, holding him down with their feet.

"Put your hands behind you," said one.

"You've got the wrong man," Lichter gasped.

Pain shot through his middle; he'd been punched in the kidney with a metal hard fist. Quickly Lichter put his arms behind his back, where they were taped. When the man bent to tape his mouth a set of brass knuckles dropped onto the floorboard. Crying now, Lichter stared at the brass knuckles, terrified of what other instruments were awaiting him at the end of the ride.

CHAPTER 28 **NEW HOPE**

SETI (Search for Extraterrestrial Intelligence), deep space probes, the Hubble space telescope, and other astronautical advances have brought us more understanding of the universe, but no evidence of another advanced species. Still, it is premature to conclude that we are alone in the universe.

— *ALONE IN THE VOID?*, JAMES LOFF

FELLOWSHIP COMPOUND,
CALIFORNIA

"**H**ow many tons of cargo are you taking up?" Roland asked.

"Sorry, Mr. Symes. I can't really say."

He stepped back while the cargo handler finished attaching hooks to the base of the sealed container. Then the handler signaled someone inside and an electric motor dragged the heavy container into the ship.

"Two tons, at least," Roland suggested.

"If you say so," the man said.

When the last container was loaded, the doors of the hatch were closed, latching electrically. "God's Love" was stenciled on the doors and below it American and Christian flags.

"Better get on board, sir," the cargo handler said.

Roland gave up trying to get information and climbed a ladder to the window level of the ship. The interior resembled an airliner absent of distinctive paint and logos. There were no flight attendants and no pretzels on this flight—champagne was out of the question. Roland wasn't sure there was even safety equipment. The craft certainly wasn't approved for passenger travel, which was why the ship was flying out of the Guadalupe facility.

Representatives of the FAA, the FCC, and OSHA filled the front seats. Next were the Disney executives, three men and a woman, each wearing gold pins in the shape of the world's most famous mouse. Media representatives came next—Wyatt Powder was there with his cameraman. There were others Roland knew and he nodded as he passed. Christy Maitland was sitting by herself and he slid in next to her. Wyatt Powder winked at him when he did. Roland didn't like Powder. He was typical of too many on-air personalities—a good-looking talking head. Of average intelligence at best, Wyatt had a great reading voice—and on that careers in broadcasting were built.

"If you put your hand on my knee I'll scream," Christy said.

"What?" Roland asked, caught off guard.

"I saw Mr. Powder wink. I understand men-speak."

"Don't worry. I know you're involved."

"I am?"

"You and Mark Shepherd? Don't you read the *National Enquirer*?"

"I was mentioned in the *National Enquirer*?" Christy asked, amazed.

"You've been in all the tabloids. So is it true?"

"We're friends," Christy parried.

"You've been into space before, haven't you?" Roland probed.

"I'm not here to be interviewed."

"Sorry," Roland said. "Force of habit." Then with a smile he said, "So, were you in space before?"

Christy sighed.

"Yes. I was with Mark the night the *Rising Savior* was destroyed."

"A terrible accident."

"I wouldn't call it an accident around here," Christy said.

"They still believe NASA sabotaged their launch vehicle?" Roland asked. "Both the NASA investigation and the congressional subcommittee concluded it was an accident, not a plot."

"Mark explained how unlikely it is that the command to fire the engines could be accidentally substituted for one to stabilize the craft."

"It was more complicated than that."

"Yes, and therefore more unlikely," Christy said.

"Unlikely, but not impossible. Besides, why would NASA want to destroy the *Rising Savior*? They knew there was more than one launch vehicle. Not to mention they lost their own satellite."

The entrance of Congressman Crow and Congresswoman Swanson interrupted their conversation. After little more than a year in the House of Representatives, Manuel Crow was already a player, wrangling himself a seat on the new National Technologies Committee. Sylvia Swanson chaired the committee and when the junket into space had been arranged, she had surprised her colleagues by selecting Crow to accompany her.

Roland watched Crow's orchestrated entrance. His shiny black eyes darted left and right as he flashed his well-practiced smile to the other passengers, greeting each by name with a warm handshake and a few friendly words.

"What do you think of the congressman?" Roland asked Christy.

"He's a respected philanthropist."

"Doesn't his foundation support your center?"

"Yes, but I've never met him. As far as I know no one speaks ill of him."

"No one would dare," Roland said.

Crow approached, holding out his hand to Christy.

"Reverend Maitland, I'm glad to finally meet you. I've so admired your work."

"Thanks for your generous support," Christy said.

"It's been a good investment. Next time our country

beats the war drums, I'm going to recommend we resolve the issue at your center."

Crow was still holding her hand and leaning over Roland, ignoring him, so Roland pushed his hand into the congressman's face.

"Roland Symes, *San Francisco Journal.*"

His smile still fixed, Crow leaned back, taking Roland's hand.

"I've enjoyed your columns on the Fellowship," Crow said smoothly.

"I've enjoyed your services, too."

"My services?" Crow asked, puzzled.

"My grandmother is buried in Autumn Rest Cemetery."

"A beautiful place to spend eternity."

Practiced smile still in place, Crow worked back up the aisle.

"Is your grandmother really in one of his cemeteries?" Christy asked.

"No. She wouldn't be caught dead there."

Now smiling, Christy turned to the window and with a jerk the *God's Love* was pulled toward the hangar door.

"How big is this Disney deal?" Roland asked.

"It's the key to their expansion."

"What expansion?"

"New space facilities. Stations, transports, communications platforms."

"They have all that," Roland said. "There must be more to their plans."

"It's all very expensive. Disney has pledged to finance a new station—Space-Disney—plus four passenger shuttles. They'll fly tourists up from all their theme parks. The Fellowship will get a share of the revenue and Disney will sign a long-term agreement to use the Fellowship's orbital facilities for all their cable and network broadcasts."

The loudspeaker crackled.

"Welcome aboard the Space Transportation System *God's Love,*" Mark Shepherd said over a loudspeaker. "Please remain seated until we reach the space station New Hope. We will be experiencing weightlessness during the flight which may result in nausea. For your convenience there are airsickness bags under each seat. Before we begin, I would like to ask God's protection on the trip."

Roland stared at the ceiling while Shepherd prayed. Then they were off, their stomachs dropping as if in an accelerating elevator.

"This is a better ride than I thought," Roland said nervously.

"Since the missile attack they get into orbit as quickly as possible," Christy said.

Roland's stomach fluttered, so he closed his eyes and breathed deeply. Opening his eyes he saw there was nothing but gray outside the window. Closing his eyes and then opening them again, he found they were through the clouds and climbing fast. Quickly the clouds dropped away, becoming a white smear below.

"I think we're safe now, they can slow down," Roland said.

"We're only rising at about five hundred miles an hour. We won't even break the sound barrier. They try to be good neighbors."

"If they were good neighbors they would take some of the money they spend on space hardware and help the people living in the shantytown that's grown up around their Guadalupe launch facility."

"They do spend in the town," Christy said.

"The Mexican government has given them tax breaks— that doesn't help the poor and there are a lot of them in Mexico. They should want to pay taxes."

"Look out the window again, Mr. Symes. I liked you better when you were too sick to talk."

"It's talking that keeps me from getting sick."

"Really," Christy said. Then she turned to the window, ignoring him.

Now the sky was darker but without stars. Roland had no sense of motion, yet his stomach still pushed its contents toward his throat. Wishing he hadn't been so argumentative, he closed his eyes, opening them only occasionally, seeing his arrival in space in flashes. Nearly an hour into the flight the acceleration ended and Roland was introduced to zero gravity. For a few seconds he loved the dreamy feeling of having no body, but then the motion detectors in his ears gave up trying to make sense of conflicting signals and he was hit with a wave of nausea. Soon muscle spasms ejected the contents of his stomach into a plastic airsickness bag. There was still a little juice left for the second heave, but he was dry with the third retch. It was a Ziploc bag and he made sure the yellow and blue halves made green the entire length, then he tucked it back under his seat. Christy held out her bag and he snatched it.

"We're almost there, Roland," Christy said. "If you're ready for it you can see the space station through the window."

Feeling better, Roland leaned over Christy. New Hope space station was ahead, bigger than he had imagined. Twelve cylinders with three connecting segments floated in space. Suddenly the ship rotated, the New Hope spinning in the window. Roland put his head low, dry heaving into the bag. A couple of rows ahead another person regurgitated and then three others joined in.

A soft bump signaled docking. Remaining in their seats as instructed, most of the passengers played with objects, spinning them in the zero gravity. Then Crow unbuckled, launching himself into the aisle, somersaulting in midair. Looking green, Congresswoman Swanson leaned out with a video camera recording Crow's antics. Now Crow floated upside down, his fingers in a "V" sign for the camera.

"It looks like Crow is shooting his next campaign video," Roland said.

Shepherd appeared from the flight deck, pulling himself along the wall, pausing by the hatch, watching a panel of lights. When they were all green he pounded on the hatch with a wrench. After an answering clang, he released the hatch by pulling a long-handled bar. A slight rush of air brought them the smell of the space station.

"Phew," Roland said. "That's stale."

"It's recycled air," Christy explained. "In and out of the lungs of the station's occupants over and over."

"That's slightly disgusting," Roland said.

"Then I better not tell you what they drink up here," Christy said.

"Welcome to New Hope," Shepherd announced. "Release your seat belts and pull yourself forward using the handholds built into the head rests. Move slowly making sure you have a new grip before you release your old one."

Conditioned by a lifetime of living with gravity, the passengers carefully pulled themselves toward the aisle, then single file toward the door. Going his own way, Crow floated above the seats pulling himself hand over hand to the door.

Roland paused in the aisle letting Christy pull herself ahead. Then he mimicked Crow and floated over the seats. His stomach empty, he didn't worry about soiling the cabin. When they were gathered at the door, Shepherd led them into the station. The corridor was lined with handholds and they pulled themselves along, most trying to keep their heads up and their feet down, even though up and down were meaningless. Once through the hatch they gathered in a hexagonal room. A middle-aged couple stood against the far wall, their feet hooked under a rail attached just above the floor. Roland had expected space suits, or fancy coveralls, but instead they were wearing denim overalls and athletic shoes. Both wore their hair short, and wire-rimmed glasses held on with elastic straps.

"Welcome everyone," the woman said. "We hope you enjoyed your trip up."

Roland pulled close to Christy's ear. "They look like a couple of farmers."

"I'm Susan and this is my husband Cal. Would everyone please get a firm grip on a handhold, we have a surprise for you."

Puzzled, Roland tightened his grip, hoping the surprise didn't involve spinning. Cal waited for a sign from Shepherd and then punched a few buttons on a panel and a green light went on—then nothing. Slowly Roland's stomach began churning again. Pressing his knotting stomach, he felt like he was falling—he was. Slowly his feet settled to the deck, his weight returning.

"Artificial gravity!" Crow declared.

The Disney people babbled excitedly, one holding a bag of vomit.

"We're at normal gravity now," Cal announced. "You'll feel better in a few minutes, just walk around. All of the modules have artificial gravity, although two are designed for zero gravity research and manufacturing. One module is being leased by a consortium of universities and will function as a space observatory. The first of three telescopes will be installed next week."

Roland took out a notepad and scribbled.

"Can we get a look at the observatory?" he asked.

"I'm sorry," Cal said. "We're trying to meet a construction deadline and we can't interrupt the workers."

"There's plenty to see, anyway," Susan said, smiling sweetly.

Roland smiled back, mocking her smile.

"While fire is unlikely, every interior surface is coated with fire retardant paint," Cal explained. "When exposed to heat the paint blisters into a thick fire retardant. There's also a halogen extinguishing system in every module."

"You can't breathe halogen," Roland pointed out.

"That's right," Susan said. "That's why each of the red panels you have passed contains breathing masks."

The guide resumed talking but it was more propaganda about the sect's achievements and how they were all "God's blessings." Roland inched closer to a wall. Virtually every surface in the station was covered with compartments, all with closed doors—an irresistible temptation.

"If you will follow me into the next module," Susan said.

Twin steel doors, resembling something from a submarine, connected the compartments. While the guide twisted the wheel releasing the lock, Roland opened a compartment. It was filled with toilet paper.

"Maybe they keep their power plants in the next one," Christy said from behind.

Embarrassed at being caught snooping, Roland followed the others. The tour ended in the last module at an observation deck. Where the door to the next compart-

ment should be was a steel plug. Distinguishing this compartment was a row of windows facing the Earth. The artificial gravity of the station held them to a surface, the
Earth hanging slightly above them. The sun bathed half
the Earth in bright light, spectacularly alien and familiar
at the same time. They all crowded around the windows,
except Crow who hung back, unmoved. They were still
staring when Shepherd entered, hurrying to pull Christy
aside. He looked panicky. Roland inched closer to
Christy and Shepherd, but they stepped out of the compartment. When he tried to follow he was stopped by Cal
at the compartment door.

"I need to talk to Shepherd just for a minute," Roland
said.

"He's busy just now," Cal said firmly.

"He looked worried, any idea what it was about?"

"We'll be serving lunch in a minute."

Frustrated, Roland wandered near a port, listening to
the Disney people talk. They were anxious to deal now
and were speculating on whether the artificial gravity
could be used in the shuttles so that the passengers would
never have to risk space sickness.

Lunch never came and Shepherd didn't return. After
an hour, Susan came back, whispering to Cal. Abruptly
the tour ended.

"I'm sorry, ladies and gentlemen, but we will need to
return to Guadalupe launch facility immediately."

"What's happened?" Powder asked.

"There is no danger."

No one was mollified and worried mumbling continued. Roland hung back but more members of the Fellowship appeared, herding them back to the shuttle. Christy
was still missing. Once back to where they had docked,
the gravity was slowly reduced to zero, then they were
helped back to their seats in the shuttle. Once all were
buckled in, they waited. A few minutes later an unidentified crewman entered going immediately to the flight
deck, saying nothing to the passengers who continued to
worry. Then Christy came in, pulling herself along the
aisle, taking her seat next to Roland. Three other crew en-

tered with Shepherd who pulled himself into the flight deck. The door was sealed and the grim-looking crew members buckled themselves into empty seats, fending off questions from the frightened passengers. When they were away from the station and accelerating, Roland turned to Christy.

"What is going on? Why are they evacuating the station?"

"It's not an evacuation. Those returning with us have families."

"Then what is the hurry?"

"They've taken the children."

"Whose children? The Fellowship's children?"

"Police and caseworkers from Children's Services raided the grade school in Christ's Home. They took all the children away in buses. Seven of the teachers have been arrested and they have warrants for Mark and Ira."

"Christy, they don't take drastic steps like this without cause. What were the charges?"

"Sexual abuse, but I can't believe it. Not Mark, I know him too well."

"Maybe it's for the best," Roland said. "The children need to be protected. If it turns out there's nothing to it, the children will be returned, no harm done."

"They've taken the children away from their homes and their friends," Christy said. "They had to carry some of them out of their classrooms crying—the children thought they were being arrested."

"They're professionals. They know how to minimize trauma."

Roland could see she wouldn't be convinced and left her alone. Mentally, he began writing his next column. His files were loaded with stories about religious people who turned out to be thieves or perverts. He would use those to make it clear that allegations of sexual abuse against the Fellowship fit into a pattern. His files were also full of politicians and community volunteers who had committed similar atrocities, but they would not be mentioned. This editorial would be about hypocrisy. Goldwyn would love it.

CHAPTER 29   **THE INQUISITOR**

> The way to break a man is to start by taking
> away his humanity. First take his freedom, then
> his independence and then his privacy. Without
> these he cannot maintain his dignity. Without
> dignity, a man feels no shame. When a man feels
> no shame, there is nothing he will not do.
>
> — *THE ART OF TORTURE,* COLIN MILLS

PROCTOR'S COMPOUND NEAR
CALDWELL, IDAHO

William Lichter shivered uncontrollably, partly from
cold, mostly from fear. Naked, tied to a chair, and wet
from his own urine, he was miserable and terrified. He'd
been in darkness since the tape was torn from his eyes
and his clothes were cut off. As the hours dragged on he
found the fear of torture was torture itself.

His teeth chattering loudly, he almost missed the sound
of the door lock. With a creak the door was opened and
someone came into his room, closing the door behind.
There was no light when the door opened, and no lights
were turned on. Forcing his jaw to hold still, he listened
as someone moved around the room. Then he heard
something dragged closer.

"Please, can you turn on a light?" he begged.

The sound came closer and then stopped. He could see
nothing but he felt the presence of the other man.

"Mr. Lichter, you don't smell very good," the man said.

"Who are you?" he stammered.

"Just a humble servant of God."

Now Lichter knew the Fellowship had taken him.

"I've done nothing to you people," Lichter said through
chattering teeth.

"What people are you referring to?" the voice asked.

"The Fellowship. You're from that religious group, aren't you?"

"No. We serve the same boss but in different capacities."

"What do you mean?" he asked, terrified of the answer.

"Do you know the Bible?"

"I never went to Sunday school," Lichter said.

"In the Old Testament there is the story of Moses. He led God's chosen people out of Egypt. Perhaps you've seen the movie version?"

"Yes, I know that story."

"Well, Mark Shepherd is our Moses."

"Maybe you're like Jesus—he would turn the other cheek," Lichter suggested.

"That would be a New Testament morality. God seems to have called us back to the roots of our faith. Old Testament morality is more of the eye for an eye kind of justice."

Lichter wet himself when he heard "eye for an eye." The crew of the *Rising Savior* had been burned alive.

"What I want to know from you is who is playing the role of pharaoh?"

"I don't know anything," Lichter lied.

"Shhh! Not now. I'm not ready to ask, and you're not ready to answer."

Lichter sobbed, "I don't know anything. Please don't hurt me. I have a family."

"Now, now, don't cry. There will be plenty of time for that later. First, let me clean you up a bit."

Then there was a hissing sound and a blast of cold water hit Lichter in the face. Methodically the man used the hose to wash him down from head to foot. He ached from the cold when the man finished and the shivering was more violent than before, his entire body shaking. Then the hose was dragged away and the man left. Alone in the dark again he found he couldn't save his tears for later.

Exhaustion brought Lichter sleep but he dosed fitfully, his head hanging down to his chest. When he woke his neck was sore and no amount of movement would bring relief. His hands and feet were numb, the ache long gone from them—he could hardly move his fingers and toes.

He was dehydrated now, wishing the man would bring the hose back so that he could drink. His shivering and chattering had long since burned up the free sugar in his system and he felt weak and trembly. He slumped exhausted in the chair. Then somewhere in the dark the door opened again.

"Mr. Lichter, are you ready to talk about it?"

"I'm thirsty."

"When you answer my questions I'll give you something to drink."

"I'll tell you anything I can. I . . . just don't know anything."

"I can see you're not ready yet. I'll come back tomorrow."

"No. Please, I'm ready."

The door creaked closed and when he heard the lock turned he began to cry again.

"I won't live until tomorrow," he sobbed.

His lips were cracked when the man came again. Now he had barely enough strength to lift his head. He was too exhausted to panic but his fear still knotted his empty stomach.

"Are you ready now, Mr. Lichter?" the man said.

"Yes," Lichter said.

"Who ordered the destruction of the *Rising Savior*?"

"I don't—"

"Do I have to come back tomorrow?"

"It was Congressman Crow."

"Crow?" the man said, surprised.

"Yes," Lichter said, feeling the relief of truth.

"The others said a woman paid them."

"A woman? . . . It might be his assistant," Lichter said.

"What is her name?"

"Could I have something to drink?" Lichter begged.

"When you've answered my questions."

"Waters. Rachel Waters."

"Why would Congressman Crow want to destroy the *Rising Savior*?"

"He never told me."

"Speculate!"

"He doesn't like religious people. He doesn't think a cult should have a monopoly on that technology."

"How are you connected to the congressman?"

"He needed information on NASA's space program. I helped him get it."

"You spied for him?"

"It wasn't like that."

"Why did you do it?"

"He pays me. My family needed the money."

"For what? Your kids aren't sick or crippled, your wife is healthy, you live in a beautiful house, you own two cars—one a Lexus—and you have a boat and RV parked in a storage lot. NASA pays you a good salary, so just what did you need money for?"

He didn't answer because he was afraid of the truth.

"Because without Crow's money your second car would have been a Chevy instead of a Lexus. Without his money you would have had to rent a boat when you went on vacation. Without that blood money you wouldn't have been one step ahead of your neighbors."

"I only wanted the best for my family," Lichter said.

"The men in the *Rising Savior* had families."

"I'm sorry."

"Yes, because you got caught."

The sound of footsteps told him the man was leaving.

"Please. I'm thirsty."

He heard the sound of the hose being dragged. Bracing himself for the blast of the high-pressure hose, he opened his mouth willing to risk drowning for a mouthful of water. When the water came, it was a slow dribble that the man held until he had drunk his fill.

"You'll be moved soon. There will be more questions. Answer them honestly or you will come back here."

"I will," he said, beginning to cry. "I promise."

The hose was dragged away and then he heard the door opening.

"When can I go home?"

"Never," the man said.

The door slammed, leaving him alone again, this time with no hope to sustain him.

> Listen to my cry, for I am in desperate need;
> rescue me from those who pursue me,
> for they are too strong for me.
>
> —PSALM 142:6–7

SAN FRANCISCO, CALIFÓRNIA

Stephen O'Malley was one of the Fellowship's many stealth members. By hiding his association with the Fellowship he was able to advance to full partnership in one of San Francisco's most prestigious law firms. Now that he had stepped forward to defend Mark and Floyd his firm had disowned him. With white hair, expensive suits, manicured hands, Stephen was a distinguished barrel-chested man with a permanent tan.

"You make no statements to the police or to the media!" Stephen O'Malley said. "None! Period!"

"I know, Stephen," Mark replied.

"Don't even say good morning," Stephen said.

"I understand," Mark said.

They were driving toward San Francisco in Stephen's Mercedes.

"The media will bait you," Stephen continued. "They'll say outrageous things to get you to respond. If you answer one question but ignore others, it will look like you are avoiding questions where you might have to lie."

"The media doesn't know where or when I'm going to surrender, Stephen," Mark said. "That was part of the arrangement."

"The media will be there, Mark. These things leak, they always leak."

Stephen was right. Three blocks away they could see a crowd gathered on the steps. Vans with dish antennae were parked on both sides of the street.

"Drop us in front, Floyd, then get my car out of here," Stephen said.

Even before Floyd stopped, the car was surrounded with reporters and cameramen. Blinding electronic flashes lit up the interior.

"Remember, not a word!" Stephen warned. Then he unlocked the car doors, pushing against the faces pressed to the window. "Stand back, please."

Mark slid across the seat, following Stephen who cleared a path with his large body. Questions were shouted and microphones pushed in their faces.

"Is it true you had sex with girls as young as five?"

"Is sex with children part of your religious beliefs?"

"Is it true you fathered seventeen children?"

"Did you ever have sex in orbit?"

Mark's blood boiled, but he kept his eyes fixed on the back of Stephen's head and his mouth shut. As they neared the glass entry, uniformed officers appeared, making a corridor.

Once inside, two police officers sandwiched Mark, taking his arms and pulling him into an elevator. Three more officers pushed into the elevator behind Mark, squeezing out Stephen who protested as the elevator doors closed in his face. Once the doors were closed, the officers laughed.

"Did you see that shyster's face?" asked one.

"Yeah," said another. "His chin nearly hit the floor."

They laughed again. Nervous about surrendering, Mark had counted on Stephen walking him through the process. Now he was scared.

"My lawyer's supposed to be with me," Mark said.

The officers stopped laughing. The officer standing in front of Mark turned, pushing his face inches from Mark's.

"An innocent man doesn't need a lawyer," the big policeman said.

"I didn't do anything—"

"Shut up! If you know what's good for you, you'll keep your mouth shut."

The officer sprayed spittle as he spoke and his face visibly reddened. Instinctively, Mark stepped back against the elevator wall. Mercifully, the door opened and two detectives were waiting to take custody of Mark.

"I'm Detective Harney," the young black detective said. "This is Detective Sitz," Harney said, nodding at his partner, a graying middle-aged man.

Both of the detectives wore gray suits. Harney's fit properly, however, and looked like it cost twice that of Detective Sitz's.

"We'll have some questions but first we're going to process you," Harney said.

Next Harney pulled a card from his pocket.

"I'm sure your lawyer advised you of your rights but just to be sure we're going to do it again. You have the right to remain silent . . ."

Hearing his rights read in a monotone voice crushed Mark's spirit—he was a criminal now.

After he had been sitting in a holding cell for hours, a guard came for him. He was taken to a room furnished with a rectangular table and three folding chairs. A tape recorder sat on the table. A mirror covered one wall—he knew he was being watched from the other side. Mark sat in the chair as directed. An hour passed and his head nodded, his eyes heavy with the need to sleep, his stomach rumbling. He was feeling the effects of the fast. His hunger was terrible, his mind clouded. The hunger would eventually pass and his mind would clear, but it would take hours yet. Then the door opened. Detective Harney came in.

"It's time to talk," Harney said.

Detective Harney sat opposite him, his back to the mirror, a toothpick hanging from the corner of his mouth. He punched the tape recorder.

"You know you don't have to talk to me without your lawyer?"

Mark hesitated. Despite Stephen's admonition to not talk to the detectives, he didn't want to appear guilty.

"So, do you want your lawyer or not?" Harney probed.

"I don't care," Mark said, still unsure.

"Yes or no? It's for the tape."

"No."

"Anything you say can be used against you in a court of law," Harney reminded him.

"I understand," Mark said.

"You still want to talk to me?"

"Yes. The sooner we get this cleared up the sooner I can go home."

"Good man. Do you have anything you want to tell me?"

"I don't understand," Mark said.

"If you confess it will go easier for you," Harney said.

"I don't even know what I'm being charged with."

"We have information that you sexually molested several children."

"Never!" Mark said.

"Maybe you don't think of it as molestation," Harney suggested. "Some religions think it's okay to have sex with children. Do you believe that way?"

"No."

"But maybe some in your church do?"

"No."

"You've got a big church, Reverend Shepherd, with branches all over the country. You can't know everyone in the church, can you?"

"Well, no."

"Then you can't know for sure that some of them might think it's okay to have sex with children?"

"They wouldn't do such a thing."

"But you don't know, do you? Not for sure!" Detective Harney persisted.

"I can't know everyone."

"So you admit it's possible someone in the church molested the children."

"Anything is possible, but I don't believe—"

"Now we're getting somewhere," said Harney, cutting Mark off. "So if you were wrong about your followers, maybe you were wrong about yourself."

"I wasn't wrong—"

"You said it was possible for someone in your church to have molested the children, right?"

"Yes, but—"

"So maybe you are one of those who could have done it?"

"I didn't," Mark said angrily. "I never touched one of the children."

"Okay, calm down," Harney said, taking the toothpick from his mouth and leaning back in his chair. "We'll come back to that. Let's start with the others. Can you give me their names?"

"Who? What are you talking about?" Mark asked, confused.

Groggy from lack of sleep, hunger pangs distracting him, Mark could barely follow the detective's line of questioning.

"The names of those in your church that molested the children. What are their names?"

"I don't know," Mark said.

"Who would know who they are?"

"I mean, I don't know if anyone molested the children."

"But a second ago you said it was possible someone in the Fellowship had molested the children," Harney said. "So who would be the most likely?"

Confused, Mark mumbled more denials.

"Let's try it this way, Reverend. Who has the most contact with the children?"

"Their parents."

"I mean outside the home, like at school?"

"Their teachers, I guess."

"Are any of them male?"

"Well, Roger Forster teaches second grade, and Matthew Simpson teaches sixth."

"It's kind of unusual for a man to teach grade school, isn't it?"

"I don't know."

"Take it from me, it is. Do either of them teach Sunday school?"

"Roger does."

"The little kids?" Harney asked.

"Yes."

"See a pattern here, Reverend?"

"Roger likes children. He's good with them."

"I'll bet. So would you agree that Forster has more contact with the little children than any other man in your church?"

"I suppose."

"Now you've admitted that someone in your group may be molesting your children and that this Forster guy has the opportunity. So, don't you think he might just be the one?"

"He wouldn't."

"But you said someone was."

"I said I didn't know."

"That's right, you didn't know who it was, but he's the one who's most likely—I mean opportunity and all. Wouldn't you say?"

"I guess."

"Yes or no, for the tape."

"Yes."

Harney leaned forward and punched a button on the tape machine again, stopping it. Then he put the toothpick back in his mouth.

"That's a good start. Let's take a break, then we'll try it again. You want a glass of water?"

"I'm tired," Mark said.

"I'll get you some water."

Confused, Mark went over the conversation. He hadn't really said anything but somehow he felt like he'd accused Roger Forster of being a child molester. Unsure, he decided to replay the tape. When he reached for the machine the door opened.

"Hello, Reverend Shepherd. Do you remember me, I'm Detective Sitz."

"Yes."

Detective Sitz had taken off his suit coat, wearing his black tie loose. There was a coffee stain on his white shirt just above the pocket.

"I was watching Detective Harney and you through the

mirror," Sitz said. "He wasn't treating you very well, so I thought I had better take over."

The detective's confirmation of his mistreatment reassured Mark and he found himself warming to the middle-aged man.

"Detective Harney was right about one thing," he said. "It is better to confess. If you do we might get you treatment instead of prison."

"I didn't do anything," Mark protested.

"I believe you, but there have been accusations and even if you are innocent the evidence tells me someone in your flock has been misbehaving."

"I can't believe it," Mark said.

"It's sad, isn't it? You built this great organization and just like that someone can bring it all down. But there may be a way to save what you've built."

"What do you mean?"

"Help us out. If we can clean out the wound before the infection gets any worse, the body might be saved."

"I don't know anything."

"There's something else you might think about. You've never been in prison before, have you? I know you haven't, I've seen your record. You don't want to go there, not for being a child molester. In prison child molesters are at the bottom of the food chain. Even the scum in prison have kids of their own and they're protective—violently so. You don't want to know what they do to molesters. The lucky ones get killed."

Tired and hungry, Mark shook from fear, terrified of prison.

"Like Detective Harney said, if you cooperate we might be able to get you treatment. Some of those mental hospitals are like country clubs—private rooms, lots of exercise time—they'll even let you write your memoirs. Prison makes that holding cell you were in look like a palace. Trust me, you don't want to go to prison, so let me help you."

Punching the tape recorder, the detective said, "When did you first suspect Roger Forster was molesting the children?"

CHAPTER 31   **THE CELL**

> If you want a taste of hell, try prison—more
> scum per square foot you won't find anywhere
> this side of death.
>
> —GEORGE PROCTOR

SAN FRANCISCO, CALIFORNIA

The interrogation lasted hours and Mark stumbled through it, confused, mumbling answers, unsure of what he said or whose name he mentioned. The detectives took turns twisting his words until he began to doubt whether he could trust his own memories. As the hours wore on his fatigue grew, as did his hunger. He realized it was morning when Detective Sitz entered with a box of donuts, sharing them with Detective Harney—they didn't offer him one. When they finished the donuts, they stopped the questioning. Then Harney called another officer who took him by the arm and led him back to the cell block. The officer pulled him past his cell.

"Where are we going?" Mark asked.

"We're moving you," was all the officer would say.

The officer stopped him in front of a large cell, crowded with prisoners, calling to have the door opened. Mark was pushed inside.

The other prisoners ranged from large and hulking to wiry and tough-looking. Most were black or Hispanic and all were battle-scarred.

Mark was out of his element and frightened. This wasn't his world—he didn't know the rules. Standing there Mark felt naked, the men inside sizing him up. He wanted to hide but all four corners were occupied, as were the bunks. He spotted an empty piece of wall and headed toward it. Two steps from the wall a hulking white man with bad teeth stepped in his path.

"Where you going?"

"I was just . . ." Mark stammered.

Mark started to back away, bumping into another man behind him. A powerful arm shoved him forward only to be slammed back by the man in front. Mark tried to step sideways out of harm's way.

Now they backed him toward a set of bunks, the men sitting there scurrying away. A stiff arm in the chest staggered him. Now other prisoners gathered, interested in the show. Another shove and Mark fell against the bunks.

The one with rotten teeth stepped closer. Closing his eyes, Mark prayed for God's protection. A blow to his solar plexus buckled him in half, cutting off his silent prayer. A shove on his head sent him back onto the lower bunk.

"What you doing to the preacher?" a new voice demanded.

Gasping for breath, Mark opened his eyes to see a black man behind his tormentors. He was taller than them by half a head. They turned, sizing him up.

"This ain't your business," the one with bad teeth said.

"I'm making it my business. You got to decide how bad you want him because it's a two-fer. Him and me."

Mark's protector was thick-chested with arms like an NFL lineman and a face deeply creased around the mouth and eyes. After a long stare, the two men gave way, bumping shoulders with his protector as they retreated. On the street Mark doubted the men would have backed down but in this cell the white men were outnumbered two to one.

Mark tried to stand but the black man pushed him back down.

"Bunks are hard to come by. Might as well keep it."

"Thanks," Mark said. "You're an answer to my prayer."

The black man chuckled.

"Me an answer to prayer?"

"Well, I prayed for help and you're the one that helped me," Mark said.

"If you say so, Preacher. I seen you on TV! You're the man that built those spaceships, aren't you? I'm Nick."

"Mark Shepherd," he responded, shaking a big hand.

Grateful to the man, now Mark found himself warming to him. "As far as I'm concerned you're the most important man in the world right now, Nick."

The man chuckled.

"Yeah, I expect I seem that way to you." Then his face turned serious. "Of course out on the street you'd go a different direction if you saw me coming."

"I wouldn't," Mark protested.

"Don't lie to yourself, Preacher. How many black people you got in that church of yours?"

Embarrassed, Mark didn't respond.

"Figures, but it don't bother me none. When I was growing up the only white face in my grandma's church was a picture of Jesus and that got replaced by a black Jesus five years ago."

He laughed then, a deep rumbling chuckle that relieved Mark's guilt. Maybe it was gratitude that made him feel this way, but it mattered to Mark what Nick thought of him.

"Anyone can join the Fellowship," Mark said.

Nick chuckled again.

"That's what people always say but somehow it seems black churches stay black and white churches stay white. Sometimes I think heaven's gonna have a coloreds-only section."

Nick wasn't laughing now; he was somber, thinking. The creases in his face deepened.

"Preacher, you ought to know something. Those two that came after you—they were talking to a guard before you came."

Now Mark frowned. The police were using the prisoners to terrorize him.

"There's more, Preacher," Nick continued. "Most of the men in here are being transferred to the state prison in the morning—me included. Those two are going along, so you'll be all right for a while. But you get your lawyer to get you out of here fast. You ain't cut out for prison life."

Mark nodded, knowing Stephen was somewhere working frantically. When breakfast came, Mark was asleep on the bunk. Nick brought him a tray of runny eggs and burned toast. Mark took a cup of coffee, but passed the tray back, explaining he was fasting.

"Good, more for me," Nick said, scraping Mark's plate onto his. Nick dug into the eggs, eating ravenously. "I've never tried fasting, as you can tell," he said, patting his ample stomach and chuckling. "If I was you, Preacher, I wouldn't fast long. You gotta be strong in prison."

An hour later guards came, removing men one at a time and shackling them. Nick was the sixth shackled and then led off with the first group, smiling through the bars as he shuffled along behind the others. The two men who had terrorized Mark remained against the wall, staring.

Mark kept his head down, avoiding eye contact. The guards came back and took a second group of six men, again his attackers remained. Only four men remained, including the man with rotten teeth and his friend.

Mark's hands began trembling and he shrank back on the bunk, pulling his knees to his chest. He stole a glance at the men. They were watching him. Suddenly the bunk felt claustrophobic and he stepped to the bars, vainly looking for the returning guards. When he turned around the men were behind him.

"Looking for your friend?" the one with rotten teeth asked, stepping close. "He ain't here."

The remaining prisoners retreated to corners. Mark spun to shout for help but a fist slammed into his lower back and his kidney felt as if it had exploded. Gasping with pain, he grabbed the bars to hold himself up. A blow to his other side doubled his pain and he crumpled. Beefy arms snaked around his chest, holding him up and turning him. Held tight now, the one with bad teeth went to work, punching Mark repeatedly in the solar plexus. Mark's breath exploded from his lungs with the first blow and the next two were pure pain. Now the man with bad teeth took a step back. Mark's hopes rose—maybe it was over. Suddenly he took a half step forward, swinging one

leg up and into Mark's groin. The strength of the kick
lifted Mark off his feet. The agony of that kick brought
tears and soon streams were running down his cheeks. He
hung limp, trying to speak, to beg for mercy. Another
kick and the pain reached a new level. Now his attacker
stepped forward, working over other parts of his body.
The blows came fast, pounding his stomach and chest.
Mark managed a soft plea for mercy. A bone-shattering
fist to his jaw was the reply. He slid into blackness, the
beating continuing long after he lost consciousness.

CHAPTER 32   **AFTERMATH**

Whoever gloats over disaster will not go
unpunished.

—PROVERBS 17:5

WASHINGTON, D.C.

Crow hung up the phone, satisfaction spreading across
his face.

"Good news?" Rachel prodded.

Rachel stood in Crow's congressional office, dressed
in navy blue, her skirt fashionably short.

"Your police friend came through," Crow said, leaning
back in his desk chair, arms folded behind his head.
"Shepherd's in the hospital."

"Will he die?" Rachel asked hopefully.

"No," Crow said, disappointed.

"Pity."

"It's better this way," Crow said. "If he had died his
followers would have made a martyr out of him."

"But without Shepherd they would have lost their rudder," Rachel said. "Members would drift away. The cult would die."

"You overestimate Shepherd," Crow said. "He's the front man but the key is Breitling. He's the brains behind their technology. He's the one to kill."

Crow opened a walnut box on his desktop, removing a Cuban cigar. Crow clipped the end from the cigar with a silver cigar cutter, then lit it with a matching silver lighter. Inhaling deeply, he leaned back, listening to Rachel.

"I disagree," Rachel said. "They already have the technology, Breitling's only refining it now—many people can do that. Breitling's genius gave the cult its technology, but it's Shepherd that keeps them together."

Crow puffed his cigar, thinking, finding he agreed with Rachel. Breitling might have been behind the original breakthrough but once the theoretical leap had been made, less creative underlings could develop the technology. Killing Breitling would be satisfying but to hurt the cult you needed to take out the leader, Shepherd.

"Perhaps you're right, Rachel," Crow said. "Still, we have Shepherd on the run for now. Even if he gets out of jail alive, his reputation is in ruins. Disney won't make a deal with a child molester and that should put off other potential partners. Even so it would be better to have both of them in jail. I would dearly love to know where Breitling is and what he's up to."

Rachel looked thoughtful, running her finger back and forth across her lower lip. The lip moistened with each pass, developing a high-gloss sheen.

"We don't know where he is," she said, "but we do know where his wife is." Rachel pursed her lips, moistening the top one with her tongue, then smiled at Crow. "If we took her, Ira Breitling would surface."

Crow tapped ashes from his cigar into a silver ashtray given to him by a tobacco lobbyist. He was considering Rachel's idea. Rachel was deliciously devious and he knew why the Master had sent her to him.

"Just watch her for now," Crow said. "But begin working on a plan to take her."

> I know prison and it's no place for a good man. A
> sense of fair play will get you killed.
>
> —GEORGE PROCTOR

SAN FRANCISCO, CALIFORNIA

One eye was swollen shut, and the other was thick with
sleep. He forced his sleep-encrusted eye open, looking
around the dimly lit hospital room. He willed his mouth
to open but his jaws were wired shut. He could move his
arms and legs, but found he was handcuffed to the bed.
There was a needle in his arm, attached to an IV drip. He
hurt from so many places, individual injuries were indistinguishable. He found a call button and shortly a nurse
appeared.

"I'll bet you're ready for your pain medication," she
said before he tried to speak.

He nodded vigorously, aggravating his pain. She
smiled, then left and returned with a syringe, injecting
the contents into the IV line. Seconds later the pain ebbed
and he felt a warm rush, followed by a dreamy half-
conscious state. The nurse recorded receipt of his medication on a chart, then lifted a plastic bag at the end of
his bed. He realized they had inserted a catheter. Soon he
fell into a dreamless sleep.

His pain woke him again, the room dark this time. He
rang for the nurse, a different woman responding. There
was no smile this time but she brought the medication. He
was asleep as soon as the warm rush washed out his pain.

The next time he was conscious a doctor visited,
telling him he would live, but they had to remove one of
his kidneys. Before he could absorb that news he learned
it would be four weeks before his jaw would be ready for
soft food. The doctor's manner was brusque and his de-

scriptions of Mark's injuries blunt. It was the doctor's way of telling a child molester he got what he deserved.

Stephen was there when he next woke, dressed impeccably in a gray suit.

"Thank God," Stephen said. "Everyone was worried about you, Mark. The Fellowship has been in continuous prayer."

Mark tried to smile but one of his lips was stitched and it hurt.

"Just lie still," Stephen said, mothering him. "You're going to recover but they hurt you badly."

Mark used his free hand to signal he wanted to write. Stephen dug a pen and legal pad out of his briefcase, then held the pad while Mark wrote "THE POLICE ARRANGED IT."

Stephen frowned. "How do you know this?"

"ONE OF THE OTHER PRISONERS TOLD ME," he wrote.

"Prisoners don't make good defense witnesses, Mark," Stephen said. "Unless we can corroborate his story we don't have a case."

Mark frowned, hurting his lip.

"Some good did come out of this," Stephen said. "Their plan backfired. They wanted to scare you into a confession but because you were beaten so badly I was able to get you designated as a 'prisoner-at-risk.' As long as you're in custody you'll have a cell to yourself."

Mark wasn't reassured. Stephen might have a court order, but once in the system it would be easy for the guards to make another "mistake."

"They've raided all our properties in the state looking for Ira," Stephen said. "Whenever they served a warrant Proctor's people showed up making sure they didn't get into anything they shouldn't. It was pretty tense but Proctor kept his people under control.

"Ira wanted me to tell you that things are going well and they can accelerate the project, if they have the money."

Mark frowned again. They had a cash-flow problem and the legal bills would worsen the problem. He needed to be with the Fellowship, problem solving, but instead he was facing prison.

"Sally and the others knew this would worry you, so they prepared a list of options for increasing revenue," Stephen said. "First, the millionaire's option."

Mark expected this one. Since the first flight of the *Rising Savior,* they had been bombarded with requests from wealthy people to purchase flights into space, some offering millions for a single trip into orbit.

"We could sell twenty-five flights tomorrow and fifty within a year."

Mark disliked the option, since it made the cult look mercenary.

"Option two we call 'Eternal Flight.' Our research indicates there is a strong market for burial in space. The deceased person would be sealed in a capsule—an airtight coffin—and then launched on a trajectory that would take them out of the solar system and into deep space. We could also offer funerals in space on New Hope station."

The idea was bizarre and slightly offensive to Mark, but if Sally said it would be a significant source of revenue, it would be.

"Option three is to begin an airline. If we took a two-year hiatus from our development plans, we could build enough passenger ships to acquire twenty to thirty percent of the passenger air business. With our lift capacity, all weather capability, and safety advantages, it would be a guaranteed success. With the revenue it generated we could be back on schedule in five years."

Mark and the Fellowship's management team had discussed this option in the strategic planning stages. However, passenger carriers were heavily regulated and they didn't want that kind of government entanglement. Besides, the major airlines would fight tooth and nail to stop them, in the courts, in Congress, and through government regulators. As long as the Fellowship limited itself to moving passengers to and from orbit, the airlines would concede them this niche.

"Option four is to return to the moon," Stephen said. "It's been suggested we retrace the route of the *Apollo 11* moon landing and revisit the landing site. We would sell it to a network or cable. At the same time we would shoot digital footage of the moon and put it together for theater showing."

The moon option worried Mark, and he wrote, "WE DON'T WANT TO REVEAL THE EXTENT OF OUR TECHNOLOGY TOO SOON."

"Of course," Stephen said. "But you told us to accelerate the timetable and soon they'll know anyway."

Stephen was right. It was likely anyone who had given it serious thought would know that their vehicles weren't limited to Earth orbit.

"Option five is to incorporate and sell stock to investors."

"NO!" Mark wrote vigorously.

"We would keep fifty-one percent for ourselves," Stephen said.

Mark pointed at the "NO!" he had written and stabbed it with his finger.

Stephen nodded, moving on.

"Sixth," Stephen said, watching Mark closely now, "open the membership."

Mark frowned, his stitched lip hurting. He and Ira had argued over this repeatedly. Ira believed they were to be like Lot, leading all who would follow out of the city of Sodom—no one who would turn from wickedness was to be turned away. Mark believed that God would direct believers to them, much as Mark and Ira were brought together. After the flight of the *Rising Savior* they had been flooded with people wanting to join the Fellowship, some sincere, many others attracted to their technology. Mark's opposition to opening the membership had been tested when Ira had argued there were many who had never had the opportunity to hear of Mark's vision before the launch and thus never been able to choose whether to answer God's call.

"That's the list for now," Stephen said.

Mark knew their financial situation was desperate, and getting worse, and their enemies organizing, becoming more effective in their attacks. His arrest had been a masterful step. Somehow the Fellowship had to recover from this blow.

"EXERCISE ALL THE OPTIONS EXCEPT SELLING STOCK AND BEGINNING AN AIRLINE," Mark wrote.

Stephen nodded. "We thought that might be your response. We've selected deacons to implement each of the options you approved."

"WHY DO YOU NEED A LEADER?" Mark wrote. "YOU ALREADY DECIDED WHAT TO DO."

Stephen smiled.

Mark wrote, "WHAT ABOUT THE CHILDREN?"

"None have been returned, yet, but I can get some of them released if their fathers move out and we agree to regular visits by social workers. Unless you disagree, I think we should consent to those conditions."

Mark thought briefly. He had studiously avoided any government regulation of the Fellowship. Most of his followers had a similar distaste for the secular government, and bringing social workers into contact with his followers was like bringing a match to gasoline. He only hoped the love of their children would help them hold their tempers. Nodding to Stephen he gave him the go-ahead.

"I'm afraid a few of the children may get placed in foster care," Stephen said. "These are children they claim were most severely abused and will be key witnesses against you. Floyd's children are among those."

Mark frowned, ignoring the pain in his lip. Floyd and Evelyn would be heartsick, and there was nothing he could do to help them.

"Mark, you should know the court has ordered that some of the children see a clinical social worker. It's supposed to be for recovery therapy, but they'll use the visits to fish for evidence."

Like most of the Fellowship, Mark distrusted psychotherapists. The psychological solution to most problems was to learn to love yourself, ignoring the immoral behavior that was the source of your guilt. Mark worried about their children being subjected to psychotherapy and what might happen to the way they viewed the world.

Were the Christian values their parents had taught them well enough ingrained to withstand a therapeutic assault? Children were easily confused, and in the hands of a professional therapist they would be as malleable as clay.

CHAPTER 34 **THE CHILDREN**

> . . . we have renounced secret and shameful
> ways; we do not use deception, nor do we distort
> the word of God.
>
> —2 CORINTHIANS 4:2

SAN FRANCISCO, CALIFORNIA

Rosa checked the camera, making sure it was ready to record. Next she tested the switch hidden under the arm of her rocker, making sure it triggered the hidden recorder. Then she replaced the special glass that hid it. It was transparent from the camera's side; the children would see flamingos against a mirrored background. Satisfied all was in order she sat in her rocker, meditating to clear her mind. Her face was deeply tanned and wrinkled, making her look older than her forty years. Her straw-colored hair was pulled away from her face and kept in a tight bun. In her long flowered skirt and peasant blouse she looked like a grandmother to the children.

The meditation failed to clear her mind and she thought about the task ahead. The children coming to her were damaged goods now, damaged as she had been by her own father. It was up to her to help them begin to heal, a process that could last a lifetime, as it seemed it would for her. She knew the pain they would go through—she felt it every day. They would be confused at first, unable to remember what had been done to them. She had been that way. Then as she helped them remember, they would continue to deny that it had happened, but if she persisted, they would remember. Then the real pain would begin, as their repressed memories were pulled from the darkness into the light.

She remembered her own pain as her memories came back. At first she had only positive memories of her father—his smiling face, the broad shoulders she rode on, the piggyback rides, and especially his affection for her mother. One by one her friends suffered the breakup of their parents' marriages but her father and mother had bucked the odds and persisted through good and bad times. Growing up, she had often wondered why they kept the vows when so many others couldn't. Perhaps it was because her father was steady and reliable, leaving for work each day at the same time, lunch box in hand, and arriving home each evening to hugs from his two "little jewels." His paycheck came home with him every other Friday and he had no vices, except beer at ball games. With an intact family, and a stay-at-home mom waiting with cookies when she returned from school, she was the envy of her friends. She should have been happy, and she was, until she was thirty. Then she learned the truth.

After her third live-in relationship broke up, she sought treatment for her depression, blaming herself for her problems with men. The first counselor—a man—questioned her choice in lovers, pointing out they had all exhibited addictive behaviors. He had advised her that she try respecting herself more and choosing men who were conventional achievers. For a while she chose men like her father, but found "safe" men unexciting and soon was dating an entrepreneur in the midst of developing a "900" number phone business. When he borrowed her credit cards and ran them up to their limit, she threw him out and went looking for another counselor. She found Liz Timmons. With Liz's help she was able to trace the roots of her problems with men and see behind the veneer of happiness that covered her true childhood. Then, during one of their sessions, she had remembered the horrible truth—her father had molested her.

From that terrible day until now it all made sense to her. Her father had stayed with her mother not because they were a happy couple but because it gave him access to his daughters. Through hypnosis and regression therapy, Liz had helped her recover memories. Bit by bit they reconstructed her childhood, her image of her father slowly changing from childhood hero to monster. With Liz's help Rosa saw that even innocent memories of good-night hugs and tickling turned out to mask dark secrets.

"Are you sure it was just a hug?" Liz would ask.

"He would lean over and we would hug him," she replied.

"You hugged him? Then where were his hands?"

Confused at first, Rosa slowly realized he had been molesting her then, and on many other occasions. After a year of therapy she developed the courage to confront her father and her mother.

That was the most painful night of her life. He had stonewalled her, while her mother sat dumbfounded. When she criticized her mother for letting it happen, she began to cry. The sight of her mother's tear-stained face hurt, but worst of all was her father's refusal to admit his guilt. Until he did she could never be completely whole. A week later they had met again, this time with her sister present. Still in denial, her father again denied molesting her and accused her therapist of distorting her memories. Then to her horror, her mother had come to his defense, and then her sister did too. Her anger spilled out then, at her father for the abuse, at her mother and sister for not stopping him. All of them were in denial and they would not let her help them.

Cut off from her family, she had turned to Liz, who mentored her into a new life. Rosa went back to school, training in psychology first and then social work. After earning her MSW, she practiced with Liz, then set up her own office specializing in recovered memories. When the mother of a little boy enrolled at the Tiny Tots Daycare Center brought her son to Rosa, her career had taken off.

The Tiny Tots case drew national attention to the problem of child sexual abuse. It began with the little boy, Scotty. He had watched his mother using a rectal thermometer to take the temperature of his little sister and commented, "That's the way the teacher takes our temperature." Scotty's mother had been suspicious of the comment, coming to see Rosa with her concern. Rosa had assured Scotty's mother that she was right to be concerned.

Rosa met regularly with three-year-old Scotty after that, pulling memory after memory from his unconscious mind, uncovering an amazing story of sexual abuse involving twenty children. Rosa had worked with most of the children Scotty named, facilitating their memories, until one by one they remembered the perversions they had been forced to endure. Another therapist had similar success with some of the Tiny Tots children and only those children whose parents refused to let the therapists work with them failed to recover their memories.

Rosa was proud of her work in the Tiny Tots case. Four years after Scotty's comment to his mother, Rosa was still seeing six of the children. Seven others continued in therapy with other therapists. Three of the daycare workers were in jail, still in denial, still appealing their convictions. Their appeals were based on recordings she had made of her therapy sessions with the children. Their lawyers claimed Rosa could be heard "leading" the children in therapy, creating false memories. The lawyers were ignorant and didn't understand regression therapy, nor did the experts they called in to testify against Rosa. People in pain won't poke around in the dark corners of their minds willingly, they needed to be led. "Guiding" was an important part of the process and she wouldn't give it up, for the sake of her patients. But she had learned from her experiences with the Tiny Tots case, and knew what the lawyers were looking for. She always recorded her sessions with the children to review her technique, to refine it, but the lawyers didn't need to see everything.

The police arrived, setting up their own camera, preparing for the sessions with the children. She took the remote control from the officer so she could start and stop the police camera from her rocker. Ten minutes after the police left the first child arrived in the company of a social worker. He wore tennis shoes, jeans, and a red plaid short-sleeved shirt with two breast pockets. His brown hair was cut short and a sprinkling of freckles covered his cheeks and nose. He had intelligent blue eyes and looked like he was about to cry. She triggered the police recorder and then her secret camera. Rosa knew the social worker well, she was another of Liz's circle.

"This is Daniel," the social worker said, introducing the boy.

The sullen little boy stared at his shoes, holding the social worker's hand.

"Hello, Daniel," Rosa said. "How old are you?"

"He's five," his social worker answered.

Liz frowned at her. Speaking for children was a common mistake of adults. It devalued them, told them they could not think for themselves. The social worker looked embarrassed, then excused herself and left. When she let go of Daniel's hand he put two fingers in his mouth and began to suck. Rosa had seen the symptom before and knew what it meant.

"Come over here, Daniel," Rosa said gently. "Not too near my rocker, though, I don't want to rock on you."

The little boy stayed where he was, sucking on his fingers. Rosa waited patiently, letting him warm up at his own pace. After some minutes his fingers came out and he spoke.

"I want to go home."

Reinserting the fingers, he sobbed briefly.

"Let's talk about that," she offered.

The fingers remained in his mouth and he stayed where he was. She waited patiently, and as expected, a few minutes later the fingers came out.

"If I talk to you can I go home?" Daniel asked.

"Let's talk about home," she said noncommittally.

Sucking on his fingers furiously now, he tilted his head slightly so that his eyes could watch Rosa. She sat patiently, waiting. After a few minutes he stepped toward her, then paused, eyes on his shoes again. Another minute passed, then he walked slowly toward her, head down, furtively watching her. When he reached the rug at her feet he plopped down cross-legged, his fingers poised in front of his mouth.

"I want to go home," he said.

"My job is to help you go home," Rosa said.

"Huh?"

"That's what I do. I talk with children and when we're all done talking most of them get to go home."

"Today?" he asked happily.

"No, not today," Rosa said.

He looked glum and put his fingers back in his mouth.

"I hate that place," Daniel said.

"You won't be there long. Soon they'll find a nice family for you to stay with."

"I want to go home," Daniel insisted.

"You can't go home today, Daniel, because of what happened."

"What happened?" Daniel said.

"You know," Rosa said.

"I do? What?"

Daniel looked genuinely perplexed, completely innocent. Many of the children Rosa had worked with started that way, their memories deeply buried. She had been that innocent once herself, but it couldn't last and the sooner she brought the darkness to light, the sooner Daniel would face the realities of life. But she had to be careful, the police camera was running.

"Daniel, I have some dolls, would you like to play with them?"

"Boys don't play with dolls," he said.

Bristling inside, Rosa sighed audibly. Daniel's early sex role rigidity was a powerful indicator of the patriarchical environment he came from. There was much work to be done here.

"Lots of boys play with dolls, Daniel. Besides, you can play with them any way you want. You don't have to play with them like a girl."

Rosa opened a chest next to her rocker and pulled out

two adult dolls and a little boy and girl doll, matching the makeup of Daniel's family.

"See, this is a mommy doll, this is the daddy doll, this is the little boy doll and this is the little girl doll."

Daniel kept his head down but was looking at the dolls. There were no clothes on the anatomically correct dolls and for most of the children she worked with it was the first time the children had seen dolls with genitals. As she expected Daniel picked the daddy doll up first. It was a crude indicator, but many in her specialty felt the fact the boy doll was overlooked meant the boy was ashamed of his own body and that shame came from its being misused.

Rosa let Daniel explore the dolls. When he was comfortable with them he danced them around in front of him. Then he bent the father over and put the little boy doll on his back. To the uninitiated it might look like a harmless horsey ride but Rosa suspected Daniel was re-creating a sexual act he was forced to perform but this time forcing the father into the subservient role. Soon Daniel spied a car in her toy pile and the game devolved into driving the dolls around, the father usually behind the wheel. It was enough for a first session but she needed to prepare him for the next session.

"You can come and play again, Daniel, but right now it's time to leave."

"Can I go home?" he asked, eyes bright.

"Not today," Rosa said.

"But I talked to you."

"You did very well, but we need to talk some more."

The shine went out of his eyes.

"I don't want to go back there," Daniel said.

"It won't be much longer, I promise. We'll get you a family to stay with."

"I want to go home."

"Would you like a cookie to take with you?" she asked, standing to get her tin. As she passed the police camera she turned it off, then retrieved the tin of Oreos. Holding out the tin she said, "You can take two if you want." He took one in each hand.

"Daniel, I know you want to go home, and there is a way you can," Rosa said.

"How?" Daniel said hopefully.

"You've got to remember the bad things," Rosa said.

"What bad things?" Daniel asked.

"The bad things your daddy did to you."

Daniel dropped a cookie and his fingers went into his mouth.

"I know they're hard to remember, Daniel, but if you want to go home you have to. You have to remember the bad things your father did to you."

"He spanked me."

"Good, Daniel. But even badder things."

"Like what?"

"Like touching your private places."

"My privacy?"

"Yes, touching your privacy. He touched you there, didn't he?"

Daniel shrugged. "He helps me zip my pants when I go to the bathroom."

"He touches your penis too, doesn't he?"

Daniel shrugged again.

"Try to remember him touching you, Daniel, and next time when I ask you about it, you tell me and then maybe you can go home."

Daniel looked like he was going to cry now, so she picked up his dropped cookie and put it in his shirt pocket, then took him by the arm to the door. Just before she opened it she knelt and said, "When you remember your father touching you, then you can go home. Do you understand?" When he nodded she smiled and hugged him. "Good boy, Daniel."

Daniel's sister was waiting for her session and when the two saw each other they embraced. Three-year-old Faith had to be pried sobbing from her brother's grasp and Rosa made a mental note not to schedule them back to back in the future. Rosa took a moment to set both recorders up for the next session, then put the toys and cookies away. Then she had the social worker bring in

Faith, who stood where Daniel had, with tear-stained cheeks and a runny nose. Rosa waited for her to calm down, thinking of Daniel and the good start that had been made that morning.

CHAPTER 35 **VISITOR**

> Conservatives are notorious for their paranoia. Delusions of persecution leave them believing there are rooms full of men plotting to do them harm. Of course, in reality, nothing of the kind happens.
>
> — *THE CONSERVATIVE CON*, RON CARTER

SAN FRANCISCO, CALIFORNIA

Autumn Rest Cemetery was the centerpiece of Crow's burial empire. The sprawling cemetery spread over seven hills in suburban San Francisco. Evergreen hedges rimmed his property, screening out the housing developments that had crept to the edge of his land. Sprinkled around the grounds were deciduous trees strategically located to increase the value of certain plots. It amused Crow there were so many willing to pay extra to be buried in the shade.

Near the western edge of the cemetery was the mausoleum and crematorium. Cremations brought only a fraction of the revenue of burial. Crow would have built Autumn Rest without the crematorium, except he needed the furnace for his own purposes. For that same reason his office complex was built next to the crematorium, connected by an underground passage unknown to the employees.

After his election to Congress, Crow preferred working at his Autumn Rest office during recess, unconcerned about potential conflicts of interest. His financial affairs were now handled by a "blind trust" that was run by a woman handpicked by Rachel and directed through her by Crow.

He parked his Mercedes in his reserved space, at the same time noticing a man leaving a van and walking directly toward him. As wary as the bird he shared a name with, Crow tensed, standing by his open car door, ready to spring for a hidden gun. Sensing Crow's wariness, the man spread his arms.

"Good afternoon, Congressman Crow," the man said in a low crisp voice.

Military, Crow thought.

"Congressman Crow, if you have a minute I would like to talk with you about a matter of mutual concern," the man said, stopping five feet away.

"If you want an appointment, call my assistant, Rachel Waters."

The man was tall, at least six feet, broad-shouldered, and well muscled—physically intimidating. His brown hair was thin on top and cut short on the sides. His nose was slightly crooked. His brown eyes were flecked with yellow. His thin lips were pulled into a slight smile. A crooked white scar on his right cheek marked some old wound. He was dressed casually, in jeans and polo shirt, wearing a light jacket, even though the afternoon was warm.

"This is about the Fellowship," the man said.

Even more cautious now, Crow played the part of congressman.

"My committee's investigation of the Light in the Darkness Fellowship is ongoing and I can't comment on it until we've completed our fact-finding."

"You had enough facts to try and shoot down one of their ships," the man said.

Crow's face darkened.

"That's an outrageous accusation!"

Reaching slowly into his coat, the man extracted a photograph, handing it to Crow. Crow recognized the man in the photo as the man he had hired—the man he knew as "the mechanic."

"Do you really want to have this discussion in a parking lot?" the man asked.

Crow nodded toward his office building, leading the man inside. Crow led the way, bypassing the business office, preferring not to be seen with a man he might soon kill. Instead, he used his private entrance and led him straight to his office. The man sat opposite the desk, filling the oversized chair like no one else ever had.

"Who are you?" Crow demanded.

"Call me Mr. Fry," the man said.

"What is it you want, Mr. Fry?" Crow asked, expecting blackmail.

"Before we get to that, I want to know what you did with our man?"

"Your man?"

He tossed the picture he had shown Crow in the parking lot onto the desk. It slid across to stop in front of Crow.

"The man you hired to shoot down the *Rising Savior* worked for us," Mr. Fry said.

"Us?"

"The Company."

Crow kept his face impassive, but his heart was racing. Rachel had made the contact with the assassin, but if the CIA knew about him then the game was over.

"No need to worry, Congressman," Fry said. "The agency isn't aware of your activities."

Crow brightened. If only this man knew about him, the knowledge could be contained.

Then, as if he was reading Crow's mind, Mr. Fry said, "Others in my organization know about your involvement."

"I thought you said the agency didn't know."

"This information hasn't been routed through official channels," Fry said, leaning back in the large leather chair. "Sometimes it is necessary to act outside the restrictions imposed on us."

"Like reporting to Congressional Oversight Committees?" Crow suggested.

178 ⊞ JAMES F. DAVID

"We might as well call the *Washington Post* directly," he said.

Crow knew congressmen privy to intelligence were notorious for leaking information in order to block intelligence activities they disagreed with.

"Don't worry, we're not going to turn you in," Fry assured him. "We let you proceed with your plan because we share your concern about the cult. Religious fanaticism in any form is a threat to the nation."

Crow saw through the rhetoric. The threat Mr. Fry and his associates worried about was the loss of control over a segment of society. The Fellowship's technology gave them unprecedented social and economic freedom.

"For a long time the agency has worked to make sure no Islamic countries obtain nuclear weapons," Mr. Fry continued. "The Islamic bomb has been our greatest fear. As it turned out we were looking the wrong way. We were watching for external threats when the greatest threat of all developed in our own backyard."

Reading between the lines, Crow could see that this was about power. Nuclear weapons in the hands of Islamic fundamentalists would radically shift the distribution of world power. The antigravity drive of the Fellowship threatened to do the same thing.

"At first we thought shooting down their craft was the right move and we were happy to support your efforts. However, the Fellowship's disinformation campaign had successfully hidden the extent of their development efforts. Our goal now is acquiring that technology."

"Can you do that?" Crow asked, intrigued.

"We briefly infiltrated two of their labs but with no success. Our people couldn't get access to the drive technology. The rest of the technology used in their ships isn't any more sophisticated than a Boeing 777 and can be bought off the shelf in a half-dozen countries. Still, we have turned up some interesting clues to the source of their power."

Mr. Fry leaned forward, his voice dropping to a near whisper.

"That's why we've come to you," Mr. Fry said conspiratorially.

Careful not to incriminate himself, Crow remained silent, letting his visitor lead the way.

"We suspect after you failed to shoot down the *Rising Savior,* you arranged for its destruction through contacts at NASA."

"Nonsense," Crow lied.

"That was a good piece of work," Mr. Fry said, ignoring Crow's denial. "If you are still interested in ending the monopoly the cult has on this technology, I have a proposal for you."

"I'm listening," Crow said, trying not to sound interested.

"Since we are working outside the Company, we don't have access to the financial resources we need. We can generate income through various means, but it increases the risk of discovery. However, if we can get the resources to complete our current project we believe we can acquire the cult's technology."

"How?"

The man reached inside his jacket, pulling an envelope out of an inner pocket. When he did Crow spotted a gun in a shoulder holster. The man tossed the envelope to Crow, then settled back in his chair.

There was a blurry photo in the envelope. Crow saw only black, white, grays, and shadows. Turning the photo around he realized it was shot underwater, finally he identified a shape—it was a sphere—the *Rising Savior.*

"Their ship is intact?"

"It was tracked by Norad all the way down. Apparently the drive system cut in and out slowing the descent enough so that it didn't burn up."

"Have you raised the ship yet?"

"No. We've acquired the necessary equipment, but we're short of cash. We can have it up in a month if you can provide the money."

"Why do you need me? Surely the agency would bankroll this project."

"They would, but we aren't prepared to share the technology. Too much risk of leaks. Besides, the president doesn't yet understand the threat this represents. The president actually uses the cult as an example of the free enterprise system at work."

Clearly Mr. Fry and his associates wanted the power that came with the Fellowship's technology for themselves, but that didn't matter to Crow. Destroying the cult was his primary goal and he could use Fry and his group. Besides, Crow had been told to "prepare the way." He hoped the world would soon have bigger problems to deal with than rogues in the CIA.

"I think I can help you," Crow said.

"Good. One thing more. We'd also like you to fund a research project. As you know Ira Breitling is the technical genius behind their antigravity drive. We believe he made the discovery while he was a graduate student at the Ohio State University. There was an accident then—that's how he lost an eye."

"You're talking about the explosion."

Crow knew of Ira's past, but Simon Ash had turned up nothing to suggest that the accident at the university was the root of their technological breakthrough.

"You have evidence there is a link between the explosion and their drive?"

"There was unusual structural damage to the building not typical of an explosion."

"Breitling wasn't working on anything related to a space drive—it was a materials science project, I believe," Crow argued.

"The goal was to develop a metallo-ceramic alloy under a Defense Department grant," Fry said.

Crow tucked that bit of information away. If Breitling had made a discovery while working for the Defense Department, ownership of the technology could be challenged in court.

"DOD killed the project immediately after the accident."

"What was the goal?" Crow asked. His visitor was a wealth of information.

"They wanted to develop an energy resistant material to coat ballistic missiles and stealth aircraft. They wanted a material like that used on the belly of the space shuttle but instead of diffusing heat the surface would disperse a wide range of electromagnetic radiation—specifically radar. The project was abandoned when a separate project developed materials that absorbed electromagnetic energy."

"Do they still have records of the experiment?"

"Everything was destroyed in the lab. All we have are copies of the progress reports filed by Dr. Kurtz. Unfortunately, he died three years after the accident."

Crow knew of Kurtz's death, but without Kurtz who would lead the research project?

"As you probably know, one of Kurtz's graduate students was killed in the lab while working with Breitling—Constance Wong."

Crow nodded. Ash had filled him in on all of this.

"But there was another graduate student privy to Dr. Kurtz's work," Fry said. "He's the one we'd like to recruit. Constance Wong was the love of his life. His name is Dr. Kent Thorpe and he hates Ira Breitling."

> The presenting symptoms of clients can usually
> be ignored. Instead, therapists must begin dig-
> ging immediately, because trauma is usually
> buried deep in the unconscious.
>
> — *HIDDEN TERRORS: WOMEN IN THERAPY,*
> ROSA QUIGLY

SAN FRANCISCO, CALIFORNIA

On his fourth session with Rosa, Daniel went straight to the rug and sat down. Rosa noticed that Daniel had scratches on his face.

"What happened to your face, Daniel?" Rosa asked.

"I got in a fight," Daniel said, head down.

"With who?"

"Marty," Daniel said softly.

Rosa knew Marty was one of the older boys at the center. Daniel had complained about Marty before.

"Why were you and Marty fighting?" Rosa asked.

"He was pinching Faith," Daniel said. "He made her cry. I told him to stop but he wouldn't."

Rosa clucked her tongue.

"You should have let Faith handle it, Daniel."

"But she's little and she's scared of him."

"He's the one that's afraid, Daniel," Rosa explained patiently. "That's why he picks on you and Faith. He doesn't like himself very well and he's afraid you won't like him either."

"I don't like kids who bother other kids," Daniel said.

"Daniel, you should know that hitting people never solves problems," Rosa said.

"Marty didn't pinch Faith after I hit him," Daniel said. "I hit him real good. Right in the stomach."

"You should feel sorry for Marty," Rosa said in a

soothing voice. "Try to understand him. He could be a good friend if you gave him a chance."

"Nobody likes him," Daniel said.

"If you didn't have any friends you might pick on other kids too," Rosa said.

"If he didn't pick on us we'd like him lots better," Daniel countered.

Rosa shook her head. Turning social theory into something children could understand was always difficult. With children brainwashed into traditional thinking, like the Remple children were, it would take years of reeducation.

Rosa triggered her hidden recorder, smiled, and said, "Did you try harder this time, Daniel?"

"Yes," Daniel said. "If I remember something can I go home like you told me?"

"You have to remember first," she said.

Daniel nodded solemnly and looked sad.

"It will be all right, Daniel," Rosa said. "Just try and remember."

Rosa sat back in her rocker, smoothed her ankle-length skirt, and triggered the police camera.

"How are you today, Daniel?"

"I remember something," Daniel said immediately.

Turning her head so the police camera could catch her facial expression, she faked surprise and said, "Would you like to tell me about it?"

"Yes. My daddy touched me on my privacy once."

"Only once?" she said, a slight edge to her voice.

"More than once?"

"You tell me, Daniel."

"Yeah, more than once. Can I go home, now?"

"Where did he touch you?"

"My privacy."

"Get the dolls out, Daniel. Show me how he touched you."

Daniel opened the toy box and took out the little boy doll, pointing at the oversized genitals.

"Get the daddy doll, Daniel. Use the daddy doll to show me what he did."

Daniel retrieved the other doll but held it limp in his

hand, his head down. Rosa waited patiently. They were so close and she knew the memories must be welling up in the little boy's mind. The pain of what his father did to him was rushing back, just as the memories of her own father's crimes did her. In his own way, Daniel knew he was giving evidence against his father and that would be hard for him. It would be harder still when he testified in court. Finally, Daniel took the daddy doll's hand and placed it on the little boy's genitals. Tears in his eyes now, he looked up at Rosa.

"Can I go home please?"

"Not just yet, Daniel. I want to talk to you about Reverend Shepherd."

Tears were streaming down Daniel's face.

"Reverend Mark?"

"Did Reverend Mark ever touch your privacy?"

Daniel broke into tears and Rosa knew the truth. Mark Shepherd had also abused Daniel and probably Faith too. Rosa knew patriarchical religious cults had been known to pass children around for use as sexual toys. However, Daniel was so upset it was clear they could not continue, so she picked up the cookie tin, signaling the end of the session. He couldn't stop crying so she put two cookies in his pocket, then turned off the police recorder.

"Daniel, you were very good today. You remembered some, but you need to remember a little more. Can you remember that Reverend Mark touched your privacy too?"

"But he didn't," Daniel sobbed.

"You just don't remember, Daniel, but if you try really hard I think you can. Maybe it was in Sunday school or maybe it was in a car. Did he ever drive you somewhere without your parents? Maybe he put his hand in your lap?"

"I'm never going home," Daniel said.

"If you remember it all, you can," Rosa assured him, even knowing Daniel would never live with his father again.

"You promised," Daniel said.

"You'll feel better if you remember, Daniel."

"I remembered about Daddy," he said, then broke into sobbing.

"That was good, Daniel, very good. You can't go home yet, but for being so good I think I can get you out of the Children's Center."

Daniel's sobbing came under control.

"I hate it there," Daniel said. "The other kids are mean to me and Faith."

Rosa knew Daniel and his sister Faith had been subject to abuse at the center. Praying before meals and at bedtime set them apart and made them targets. Unfortunately for Daniel he had been indoctrinated by the cult into thinking Faith needed protection and that it was his job. By standing up for his sister he took her beatings and denied her the opportunity to learn assertiveness. Being at the Children's Center had been a good lesson for them and made leaving the center a powerful reward that Rosa could use in the healing process. Daniel would be grateful to Rosa, not realizing it was she that kept him there long after the other Fellowship children had been placed in group homes or returned to their parents. That little bit of power was the lever she could use to remove the blockage that prevented him from remembering his abuse.

"In a couple of days you'll get to move to a real home and have a room to yourself. I'll see to it."

"Faith too?" he asked.

"Yes, but to a different home."

"Faith has bad dreams when I'm not with her."

Daniel's paternalism irritated Rosa but changing his attitude toward women was secondary to recovering his memories of abuse. Instead of rebuking him, she tried comforting him.

"The people she is going to live with will take good care of her."

Rosa crossed to the door, signaling Daniel's social worker it was time for him to go. Daniel's social worker took him by the hand and led him out as he used his other sleeve to wipe his nose and eyes.

Rosa understood the little boy's pain, but they had achieved a breakthrough today. He was starting to remember and soon the memories would flood back.

> Remember those in prison as if you were their
> fellow prisoners, and those who are mistreated
> as if you yourselves were suffering.
>
> —HEBREWS 13:3

SAN FRANCISCO, CALIFORNIA

"Ira said to tell you the advance on the TV special put us back on track," Stephen O'Malley said in his deep voice. "Actually, he won't admit it, but Shelly tells me he's well ahead of schedule."

Stephen was sitting by Mark's bed, a legal pad in his lap. He wore a neatly pressed three-piece suit, silk tie, and gold cuff links. His shoes were freshly shined, still smelling of shoe polish. Until recently, Mark could only write his responses, but yesterday they had removed the wires keeping his jaw shut. Still, Mark restricted himself to nodding, since the smallest motion made his jaw ache.

"We've booked all those we can find willing to pay a million dollars for a trip into space," Stephen continued. "After we've exhausted the pool we'll drop the price to five hundred thousand dollars. We might even offer half-day trips for one hundred thousand dollars when this market is tapped out."

"Good work," Mark whispered.

"Sally wants to raise the lease rates for the transponders. We low-balled the price to get the business originally and she's bothered that the networks are pocketing the savings."

Mark was tempted. Communications was the cornerstone of their business, accounting for sixty percent of income. Even a slight raise in rates would significantly increase revenues.

"We promised we wouldn't raise the rates," Mark said softly.

"There was nothing beyond the three-year commitment," Stephen said.

"No," Mark said.

Stephen nodded.

After another look at his legal pad, Stephen said, "We've begun the burial in space program—five customers are on their way into deep space right now. We're off to a slow start. Disposal of bodies is heavily regulated by the states and the funeral industry didn't appreciate us cutting into their business. The profit margin is huge and the liability risks minimal—their clients are already dead.

"I know you're concerned about getting a reputation of catering to the rich, so we have developed an option for lower-income people. They can have their relatives cremated and then we pack the jars of ashes into one of our star chambers—that's what we call the coffins we launch them in. We can get thirty containers into one chamber and at five thousand dollars a container it's very profitable. We also market other low-cost options—sharing chambers, or sending only body parts—usually just the head."

Mark's mouth opened with surprise, pain streaking through his healing jaw.

"You behead people and shoot them into space?" Mark asked in a raspy voice.

"The customers arrange for the decapitation. We do the packing and shipping."

Stephen studied Mark's face.

"It was a way of making the Eternal Flight program more accessible."

Mark spoke slowly and carefully, his jaw aching.

"I suppose it's all right," he said, uncomfortable with the images in his head.

Stephen noticed Mark grimacing with pain and waited until his face relaxed.

"Donations are up significantly since reopening the membership but the retention rate looks poor. Once the new members find out they aren't going to be flying around in spaceships they tend to drop out. We're up thirteen percent in the last quarter although Sally says we can't count on it continuing at that level."

"Don't proselytize," Mark said softly.

"We don't. They come to us and we try to screen them. We're attracting a lot of New Age types, some claim they've traveled in space before and are offering to be guides."

Stephen paused, looking at his yellow pad. Mark knew he had saved the most difficult for last.

"They finally released Daniel and Ruth from the Children's Center. They were placed in foster homes. Floyd and Evelyn are very upset."

"Can't you get them home?"

"I've tried, Mark, but their social worker claims to have evidence of sexual abuse."

"Impossible," Mark said, collapsing back into the bed.

"Daniel and Ruth claim you molested them."

"What?"

Mark was stunned. How could they remember something that hadn't happened?

"But I never did anything to them."

"I know, Mark," Stephen said quickly. "At trial we'll bring in experts on false memory syndrome and try to show that those memories were created."

"Stephen, we must help Daniel and Ruth and the other children. If you need more money, we can let the schedule slip."

"It's not a question of money, Mark. I won't give up, but filing motions on behalf of the children could slow the progress of your case."

"I've been in custody for six weeks, Stephen. How much longer can it take?"

Stephen frowned.

"Normally, we could demand a speedy trial, but the evidence against you and the others is coming from children the prosecutors claim have been traumatized. The judge is giving the state time to let the therapist work with the children. Psychotherapy takes time."

"So does brainwashing," Mark said.

"I feel the same way, but child sexual abuse cases are the only cases where the victim gets more consideration than the defendant."

"Can't I get released on bail?"

"You're still being held because you are painted as the ringleader, as well as that you have the means of fleeing jurisdiction. I'll get a hearing as soon as I can to force the state to present evidence. If they can't, they will have to let you go."

"How soon?"

"Two weeks, maybe a month."

Mark ground his teeth, the motion making his jaw ache. He was worried about his sanity. Was it possible he had molested children and repressed the memories? But if he couldn't trust his memories, then could he trust his vision? And if the vision was false, then what had he done to the thousands who followed him?

"One thing more," Stephen said, "Christy Maitland wants to see you."

Mark's heart suddenly raced. Mark thought often of Christy, worrying what she must think of him. The papers were filled with false accusations and the TV tabloids broadcast every lurid story they could entice someone to tell.

"George Proctor wants to see you too," Stephen said. "I advise against it. You don't need that kind of association right now."

Mark understood Stephen's concern. The media would use George Proctor's criminal history to finish shredding Mark's reputation. Still, Mark had thought a lot about Proctor while he was in the hospital. He was part of what was happening, a piece of the puzzle just as much as Ira and he were.

"I'd like to see them both," Mark said.

"The media will have a field day with this," Stephen said, shaking his head. "The Fellowship will be linked with the militia movement and the NRA."

"We can't let worry over what the world will think paralyze us," Mark argued.

"It's not the world I'm worried about," Stephen said. "It's the judge and jury."

After Mark was returned to jail, Stephen arranged for Mark to meet Christy in the interview room used by lawyers. She would have to be searched by a matron, but the alternative was to see her through a Plexiglas screen. When she entered he stood, embarrassed to be wearing his prison blues. To his surprise she crossed the room and kissed him lightly on the lips.

"I didn't do what they say, Christy," he whispered.

"I know," she said, tracing the scar on his jaw with her finger. "They almost killed you."

"It wasn't that bad."

"Liar."

She pulled him over to the chairs and they sat knee to knee, holding hands. Mark was pleased by her familiarity, but also frightened. He had been alone in his vision.

"Can I ask a favor, Christy?" Mark asked.

"Of course."

"The Remple's children have been placed in foster care. They are very worried about them."

"I'm sure they are, but the state is very careful about selecting foster parents."

"But the Remples are Christian," Mark explained.

"Many foster parents are Christian," Christy said.

"Conservative Christians?"

"I know it's unlikely the foster parents will share all of the Remples' beliefs, but Ruth and Daniel won't be in foster care for long."

"Daniel's five and Ruth only three. They are separated from their parents for the first time in their lives. They'll be vulnerable."

"They will be looking for substitute attachment figures," Christy conceded.

Now Christy looked away and frowned. Her hands loosened in his and he thought she would let go. Then she squeezed his hands tighter and looked him in the eye, her smile returning.

"Would you like me to check on the children?" she offered.

"Would they let you?"

"They might. I've mediated custody cases before."

"Thanks," Mark said.

They talked about trivial things then, everyday things like the weather, sports, favorite foods, and Mark found it comforting. It seemed like only a minute had passed when the guard banged on the door. Christy hugged him good-bye, then kissed him again. They took him back to his cell then, but for the first time since being arrested he didn't mind being alone.

Three days later, George Proctor visited—unlike Christy's visit, they whispered through slits in a Plexiglas screen. Proctor's well-toned body and tanned face reminded Mark of how long it had been since he had felt the sun.

"Hello, George. You're looking well," Mark said.

"You look terrible, Mark," Proctor said bluntly. "You need to get out of this place. I can arrange it."

Mark stared, incredulous, knowing Proctor was serious.

"It would make me look guilty."

"You've already been convicted by the media. When they convict you in a court of law Satan will have a complete victory."

"I know it looks bleak, but breaking out of jail will only make it worse."

Proctor looked thoughtful, rubbing his chin.

"After your conviction you will be transferred to prison," Proctor said, his bright blue eyes staring intently. "The transfer is the weakest link in the custody chain. They'll keep the day and time a secret but I'll know when it happens. That will be our best opportunity. Once you're in prison it's much more difficult."

It was unreal, sitting in prison and talking of escape. How had Mark gotten to this point? He wanted to be free again, to make his own choices—what to wear, what to eat, when to shower. Proctor's offer was tempting.

"George, I appreciate what you've done for the Fellowship."

Proctor shrugged.

"I feel you have a special role in this, but I don't think breaking me out of jail is what God had in mind."

Proctor smiled.

"Let me ask you this, what is heaviest on your heart right now?" Proctor asked.

"The Remple children," Mark answered immediately. "They have been placed in foster homes."

Proctor bristled, deep furrows appearing in his brow. Mark suddenly feared for the lives of the foster parents.

"I don't want anything to happen to their foster parents," Mark said.

"I may not be able to sit on this one, Mark," Proctor said in a tone so low it was almost a growl.

"Promise me that no harm will come to them?" Mark asked.

"I could rescue the children," Proctor said. "It would be easy."

"No. I've asked Reverend Maitland to look in on them. Promise me you won't do anything?"

"I will wait and see what Reverend Maitland can do."

Quickly Mark searched his mind, looking for some way to occupy Proctor, to keep him from violence.

"There is something you can do for me," Mark said. "Faith and Daniel, and some of the other children, are seeing a therapist by the name of Rosa Quigly. She has the children remembering things that never happened."

"It's brainwashing," Proctor said flatly.

"I'm suspicious too," Mark said, "but how can she get away with it? The sessions are all recorded and reviewed. Stephen has transcripts of the sessions and his experts say she stays within therapeutic boundaries."

"What would you like me to do?"

"Nothing violent," Mark said, afraid of Proctor's reputation. "Can you investigate? Find out why the children are making these claims?"

"I'll see what I can do."

"Thanks, George. It would mean a lot to the Remples."

"Remember, the transfer is the weak link," Proctor said.

"I'll remember," Mark promised.

Mark slept little that night, thinking of soaring over mountains, white clouds, and the joy of flying a sphere. Toward morning he found himself wondering if George Proctor really could break him out of prison.

CHAPTER 38   **HOME VISIT**

> . . . the wicked will not inherit the kingdom
> of God . . .
>
> — I CORINTHIANS 6:9

SAN FRANCISCO, CALIFORNIA

The neighborhood was filled with late summer activity. Winding its way through the narrow streets, Christy's car scattered knots of children playing ball games in the street on nearly every block. Christy liked the neighborhood. It was a rich multicultural brew, the kind of place where people of different races and beliefs could live side by side and out of that common experience would come harmony and tolerance. While Christy could see the social potential of such a neighborhood, she also understood it wasn't perfect—there were two obvious flaws.

The first flaw could be seen in the occasional pockets of young men she passed, standing in yards or around muscle-cars, red handkerchiefs dangling from their back pockets. Christy studiously avoided their eyes as they shouted and whistled at her. Still in their teens, these young men were already aware of the racial prejudice that would keep them from reaching their dreams. Shattered dreams leave an emptiness inside that is akin to loneliness and loneliness can be cured by the company of others just as lonely and just as angry.

The other flaw in the rainbow neighborhood was related to the first. The young aggressive men were willing to impregnate but not be daddies. Christy knew that most of the homes she passed were fatherless, seventy percent of the children born to single mothers. Even when the fathers married the mothers of their children, the young families seldom remained intact for more than a couple of years, the pain of knowing they could never provide more than a mediocre living for their wives and children just too much for the proud young men.

She nearly missed the small yellow house squeezed between two large unkempt homes. Edward Stafford answered the door, his manner accommodating, cool. He wore jeans and a blue short-sleeved cotton shirt. His brown hair was cut above the ears and brushed back along the sides. His arms were thick, his hands large. He looked like a carpenter but worked in the City Planner's office.

Edward welcomed Christy, shaking her hand firmly, inviting her in. The living room was neat, the furniture color-coordinated with the blues of the draperies and rug. The furniture was overstuffed and comfortable-looking. Decorations were sparse, giving the room a stark look. Christy preferred a richer environment of personal mementos, still the room showed the personal touches that meant it was a home. A slight smell of pine-scented household cleaner permeated the room, probably undetectable to the Staffords. Most foster parents cleaned when they knew they were going to be visited.

Carin Stafford was sitting on the couch, Ruth at her side wearing jean shorts and a T-shirt decorated with yellow daisies. Carin wore white shorts and a matching daisy T-shirt. Carin smiled in greeting. Ruth watched Christy with no expression. After introductions, Christy was invited to sit down. Carin was friendly, Edward merely polite.

"It's nice to meet you, Ms. Maitland," Carin began. "I've read about your reconciliation work."

"Call me Christy, please."

"We don't need any reconciliation," Edward said. "We get along fine."

Edward meant it to be a joke but his words had an edge to them.

Embarrassed, Carin quickly said, "That's right, we're a very happy family."

"I came to see how Ruth is getting along," Christy said, looking at Ruth.

"She's a doll," Carin said. "You couldn't ask for a sweeter little girl."

Christy smiled at Carin who exuded genuine warmth. Christy leaned toward Ruth and asked, "How are you today, Ruth?"

Ruth shrugged.

"Do you remember me?" Christy asked.

Another shrug of the little girl's shoulders.

"I went to church with you once," Christy reminded her.

Ruth snuggled close to Carin, hiding half of her face.

"Ruth is shy," Carin explained as if she had known Ruth all her life.

"Does she play with other children?" Christy asked.

"She stays in most of the time. We make cookies, I read her stories, we watch *Sesame Street* together."

"That sounds nice for you," Christy said.

"What do you mean by that?" Edward snapped.

Ignoring Edward, Christy turned to Ruth.

"Can I see your room, Ruth?"

Only after Carin nodded yes did Ruth get up.

"We'll be right back," Christy said so Carin and Edward wouldn't follow.

Ruth led Christy past a bathroom with old-fashioned fixtures and came to two bedrooms. Ruth walked into a room decorated in blue and white. The bedspread was white clouds on a sky-blue background and the theme was carried to the walls and ceiling that were sponge-painted with more clouds. Christy paused, peering into the other bedroom. A queen-size bed dominated the small room. Two dressers and a chair left little walking room in the Staffords' bedroom. Green dominated the room, the rug sea foam–colored, the floral bedspread accented with the same color.

Head down, staring at her feet, Ruth sat on the cloud

bedspread waiting. Christy sat next to her and pushed the bangs out of Ruth's eyes—she didn't seem to notice the touch.

"Are you happy here, Ruth?"

Ruth shrugged.

"Why won't you talk to me?"

"Rosa said I didn't have to talk to you."

"Did she tell you not to talk to me?" Christy asked.

"Not exactly."

"Then why not talk to me?"

"'Cause if I don't do what Rosa says I won't ever go home."

"Did she tell you that?"

Ruth shrugged.

Christy didn't know what to think about Ruth's comments. Three-year-olds' verbal abilities often fooled adults into thinking they understand more than they really do. Christy knew Rosa Quigly's reputation and couldn't imagine why she would tell Ruth not to talk to her. Christy concluded Ruth had misunderstood.

"Ruth, everyone wants you to go home as soon as you can."

"Today? Can I go home with you today?"

Tears dripped from the corners of Ruth's eyes, running down her cheeks. Christy pulled her close, stroking her head.

"I'm sorry, but not today, Ruth."

They rocked together gently for a minute, Ruth crying softly.

"Do you like Carin and Edward?" Christy asked.

After a sniffle, "Carin is nice, I guess."

"What about Edward?"

Ruth shrugged and said no more. Christy thought it a good assessment since she didn't know what to think of Edward either. Then Christy asked Ruth about things in her room and the little girl perked up a bit, showing off her new toys and clothes—Carin liked to shop. Then Christy left Ruth to play and rejoined Carin who hadn't moved from the couch. Edward was pacing the room.

Ignoring Edward's glare, Christy sat near Carin.

"She thinks you're nice," Christy said.

Carin beamed.

"You like Ruth a lot, don't you, Carin?"

Carin nodded, her smile fading slightly. Edward moved closer now.

"Remember, she's not your daughter," Christy said gently.

"I know she's not mine." Then with sadness and resignation she added, "I have children but they live in Texas and I don't get to see them often. I gave them up when I divorced. My husband was . . . difficult."

Edward came to her defense.

"When he found out about our relationship he threw Carin out of the house in front of their children—in her nightgown. I wanted to beat him in court and get the children but Carin didn't want to put her children through it."

Carin was sad, but not crying.

"It was for the best," Carin said. "Heather and Nate weren't ready to accept Edward. The divorce was hard enough on them."

"Do your children come to visit?" Christy asked.

"No," Carin said. "They're both teenagers now and aren't comfortable here." Carin looked nervously at Edward. "I visit them when I can."

"Carin, don't get too attached to Ruth. She will go home someday."

Edward and Carin exchanged looks.

"How could they put her back in that home, after all those terrible things they did to her?" Carin asked.

"They are only allegations," Christy said.

"They did it! There's no doubt," Edward said angrily.

"Edward was abused by his father," Carin explained. "He was a pastor."

Christy nodded, concerned that Edward's hatred of religion could be passed on to Ruth.

"Do you take Ruth to church?" Christy asked.

"What for?" Edward snapped.

"We believe that children aren't ready to be exposed to

religion," Carin quickly explained. "When she's older she can decide for herself."

Christy hid her frown. By not taking Ruth to church, the Staffords were already deciding for Ruth.

Christy chatted a few more minutes about activities the Staffords had included Ruth in—trips to the zoo, a county fair, and many shopping trips with Carin. Most foster homes lacked the resources of the Staffords, many homes taking foster children for the additional income they brought. Carin's motive was different. Ruth was a substitute child for Carin, who was grieving the loss of her biological children. Edward's motive for taking a foster child was even simpler. He was trying to please Carin. Ultimately, the Staffords' motives didn't matter. Ruth was getting good care, better care than most foster children.

Daniel's new neighborhood reminded Christy of her own. Made up of remodeled older homes, it was an upscale haven for young professionals who favored the urban life. Unlike the Staffords' neighborhood, the people on the street were predominantly of one hue—white. However, only a few blocks away the rainbow shades of the city resumed.

Daniel's foster home was a two-story frame house on a well-shaded street. The house looked newly remodeled, the paint fresh, the windows new. There was a little yard in front, the grass as well maintained as a putting green.

Josh Thrower was Daniel's foster parent. Josh's good looks struck Christy immediately. His carefully trimmed Elizabethan beard was perfect for his thin face and his thick black hair was carefully cut and combed. He was six feet tall, with a medium build and fit body. Josh wore casual slacks and a short-sleeved shirt and was well manicured to the point of being called pretty instead of handsome. Shaking her hand warmly, Josh welcomed her.

Josh led Christy into the living room where Daniel waited. Daniel was dressed in khaki shorts and a polo shirt. The living room was furnished in Scandinavian blond woods and light fabrics, all very modern. The house was impeccably clean and ordered, like Josh.

"Do you remember me, Daniel?" Christy asked.

"Yes."

"Would you like a cup of tea?" Josh offered.

She thanked him and he disappeared into the kitchen. An uncomfortable silence followed, Daniel standing, staring at his shoes and fidgeting.

"How are things going for you, Daniel?" Christy probed.

"Fine."

"Have you made any friends in the neighborhood?"

"No," Daniel said.

Josh came back with tea on a tray, including a cup for Daniel who flavored his tea with two heaping teaspoons of sugar. Then he held it like Josh and Christy, waiting for it to cool.

"Have you always liked tea, Daniel?" Christy asked.

Daniel shook his head no.

"I've introduced Daniel to quite a few new things," Josh explained. "He'd never had sushi before, had you, Daniel?"

Another shake of the little boy's head.

"It's bad," Daniel said. "I didn't eat it."

Josh laughed. "I think so too, but the point is to try. You'll never know what you like if you don't try everything at least once."

Josh's words were about food but the lesson was about his philosophy of life.

"Daniel has tried curry, cajun, swordfish, kiwis, oysters—lots of things," Josh said. "What's your favorite, Daniel?"

"Pizza," he said.

Christy and Josh laughed.

"But he tried them all and that's what's important," Josh said.

"Is there anything you wouldn't try, Daniel?" Christy asked.

Daniel shrugged his shoulders.

Josh's lips tightened slightly, but he kept his smile.

"There's nothing I haven't tried," Josh said. "Sometimes you have to try something several times before you get to like it."

Again Christy knew they weren't talking about food.

"It's unusual for a single man to be a foster parent," Christy said. "Who watches Daniel when you are at work?"

"I work at home," Josh explained. "I'm a Web-site designer. If my clients wouldn't insist on seeing me face-to-face on occasion, I wouldn't ever have to leave home."

"I wonder if I could see your bedroom, Daniel?" Christy asked.

Josh read between the lines and let Daniel take her upstairs.

Every room they passed was neat as a pin. One of the upstairs bedrooms had been converted to an office: three computers were spaced around the room along with a scanner, two printers, and other equipment Christy couldn't identify. Daniel's room was as neat as the others and decorated much like the living room. The blond woods were there, the light fabrics in off-white, matched to the drapes. There was a matching desk, bookshelves, and a chest of drawers. The books on the shelves were children's books—*The Chronicles of Narnia*, *Where the Sidewalk Ends*, *The Giving Tree*, *Slobbering Sam and the Devil Cat*. The books were ordered by size and color, held in place by animal bookends—elephants on one shelf, dogs on another, dragons on the third. A combination television and DVD player sat on a small stand. There was a row of movies on the lowest bookshelf— Disney, animal adventures, film versions of some of the children's novels on the shelf above. No dirty clothes littered the floor, no toys were left out of place, no picture books sat next to the bed.

"Did you clean your room just for me?" Christy asked.

"Josh cleans it every day."

"Do you help?"

"He doesn't like me to. I used to make the bed like they

taught us in that other place, but he always redid it, so I quit."

Josh sounded anal retentive to Christy but her own home could use a little of that kind of pathology.

"Your parents miss you, Daniel," Christy said.

"Can I go home?" Daniel asked.

The question came without hope.

"I don't know when you'll go home," she said honestly. "Has Rosa said anything to you about when you might go home?"

Daniel turned to the wall, his hand coming to his mouth, his middle fingers slipping in.

"She says I can't go home until I'm better," Daniel mumbled with a mouth full of fingers.

"Better?" Christy said, puzzled. "What did Rosa say was wrong with you?"

Daniel shrugged, his fingers still in his mouth.

"Are you getting better?" Christy asked.

Daniel shrugged again.

"Did Rosa tell you not to talk to me?" Christy said.

Another shrug.

"What did she tell you?"

"She said I didn't have to talk to you if I didn't feel like it."

That was his right. Christy had long championed children's rights but found herself uncomfortable when a right was used against her.

"What do you and Rosa talk about, Daniel?"

"I'm not supposed to talk about it."

Rosa had made sure Daniel and Ruth knew their rights. It did protect them but it frustrated her. Christy knew if she was clever she might coax Daniel into talking about his therapy but that violated her own ethical principles.

"Do you like living with Josh?" Christy asked.

"I want to go home."

"I know you do, but is he nice to you?"

Daniel turned back to face her, pulling his wet fingers from his mouth.

"Yeah. He buys me things."

"Like what?"

"Toys and stuff."

"Clothes too?"

"Yeah." Now he frowned. "Josh likes buying clothes. You should see his closet."

"Does he do anything that bothers you?"

Daniel looked puzzled, then pulled his fingers from his mouth.

"He cleans a lot," Daniel said.

"That would bother me too," Christy said with a smile.

Christy finished the interview by asking Daniel about the things in his room and where Josh had taken him, then she left him to talk with Josh alone.

Josh was on the couch. She sat across from him, picking up her tea.

"How has Daniel adjusted?" she asked.

"Fine," Josh said. "He sucks his fingers when he's upset, but Ms. Quigly says the habit is the result of his abuse and not a reaction to living here."

Christy didn't question Rosa's interpretation of the behavior, not knowing if Daniel had the habit before he was taken from his parents, although she didn't remember seeing him do it in Christ's Home.

"He's pretty quiet," Josh continued. "He doesn't say much but he's talking more than when he first came to live with me. He'll play games with me now and he seems to enjoy going places."

Now Josh leaned forward.

"I want Daniel to know I didn't take him in for the money so I set up a savings account and the state payments go there. It's his scholarship fund."

Few foster homes had the resources to give up the state subsidy. It was a nice gesture on Josh's part.

"That's very nice of you, but he won't be with you long enough to accumulate much of a fund."

"Really?" Josh said with surprise. "Ms. Quigly doubted Daniel would ever go home. He was badly abused, you know?"

"I know there have been allegations," Christy corrected.

"Ms. Quigly said it's more than just allegations," Josh said.

"Has she shared with you some of the things Daniel told her in therapy?"

"No," Josh said quickly. "Just her feeling that he was severely abused."

Again Rosa was skirting ethical boundaries without clearly crossing the line.

"Daniel comes from a church-going family. How do you meet his spiritual needs?"

"You can be a spiritual person without going to church. In fact, in my experience, church often gets in the way of connecting with the spirit within."

"Did you attend church when you were little?"

"Right up until my father left my mother for one of the deacons in our church."

Edward didn't bother to hide the anger and pain of that memory. Christy realized that Josh and Edward Stafford both had unpleasant childhood experiences associated with church. She knew it had to be a coincidence, but it was unfortunate that the Remple children had ended up in homes with reasons to dislike religion. Still, while laws encouraged the placement of minority children with culturally similar parents, there was no such protection for children of Christians.

Then they talked briefly about Daniel's habits, which except for not having any friends, were typical of five-year-old boys. Then Christy said good-bye to Daniel and left. On the way home she thought about what to tell Mark. The Staffords and Josh Thrower were well meaning, but their worldviews were far different than the Remples'. Given enough time with their foster parents, Ruth and Daniel would take a different path than the one their parents had placed them on. Worst of all, according to Josh, Rosa had uncovered something that meant the children would never go home.

CHAPTER 39

RETURN TO THE MOON

> Houston, this is Tranquility base.
> The Eagle has landed.
>
> —NEIL A. ARMSTRONG

NEW HOPE STATION, EARTH'S ORBIT

"**A**re you working or not, Shelly?" Ira asked gruffly.

Shelly ignored him, then finished kissing and hugging friends. Next, she put her face six inches from the television camera and said, "Be good, John Jr., Mommy will be home soon. I love you!" Those gathered in the docking port of the station applauded loudly. Finally, she turned to Ira who held out his hand. Shelly brushed aside the handshake and hugged him warmly. Ira stiffened. Not knowing what to do with his hands he let them hang limp at his side. When she finally released him he was red-faced and stammered when he spoke.

"You be careful, Shelly," he said sincerely. "I should be going with you."

"No, Ira. They can't know where you are."

"It's not right," Ira insisted. "What if something goes wrong?"

"Then we'll handle it. Besides, you've got something more important to do."

Ira nodded, then took her hand and squeezed it.

"You be careful," Ira repeated.

She knew Ira was thinking of what happened to John. Ira had lost his protégé and Shelly a husband. Their mutual grief had cemented an already strong friendship.

"I'll come back," she said, then turned and entered the *God's Love.*

Her stomach flip-flopped as she moved through the overlapping gravity fields of the station and the ship. Pulling the hatch closed, she sealed it. After a green indi-

cator light came on she climbed to the cockpit where
Micah Strong sat in the pilot's seat. Micah had been preflighting the *God's Love* and had a full board of green
lights. Shelly patted Bob Morton and Gus Sampson on
their shoulders when she passed the engineering stations
that had been specially modified for this trip.

"It's about time," Micah said, imitating Ira's grumble.
"Are you working or not?"

Shelly smiled and took the seat next to Micah's. Flipping on the monitor she was greeted by Sandy Wallace
who would control the video feed to the network. Sandy
was twenty-eight, with a slight frame, short brown hair,
and brown eyes. The cut of her hair, her delicate features,
and her crisp, serious manner combined to create an aura
of competence.

"How is the reception, Sandy?" Shelly asked.

There was a pause while Sandy moved out of focus.

"The network is receiving us," Sandy said. "We go live
in ten minutes so tell the crew to keep their fingers away
from their noses. Give me the rest of the video, Shelly."

Shelly spoke over her shoulder to Gus.

"Sandy wants all the cameras on," Shelly said.

"Can do," Gus said, then flipped the toggles for the other
six cameras mounted around the ship. Green lights lit up
under each toggle. Under every camera a red light was now
glowing. Two cameras were mounted in the cockpit, four
more were spread through the ship, and two were mounted
externally.

When she turned back she saw Micah had his finger up
his nose. She slapped his elbow and he extracted his finger, smiling while he pretended to wipe it on his shirt.
Sandy came back into focus on Shelly's monitor.

"It's looking good. Nice clear signal."

Gus began speaking to Sandy, so Shelly turned to the
preflight checklist. Micah was as fanatic about safety as
Ira—which is why Ira picked him for the trip—and although Micah had completed the preflight, he would insist
she double-check.

"Here comes the lead-in," Gus said.

Shelly turned on a small monitor mounted between her

and Micah. They were only minutes away from the launch now.

The network had been on the air for an hour, running a history of the space program, leading up to the *Apollo 11* landing on the moon. The Fellowship crew also spent a week recording interviews. Their portion of the program would be cut in over the next week as they traveled to the moon and back. In tonight's program, they would be interviewed as part of the segment called "One More Leap for Mankind," which focused on technological advances since the Apollo missions and the declining role of government in space travel. The segment ended with footage of the *Rising Savior*'s first launch. Footage of the other flying spheres and the new class of ships like the *God's Love* followed, plus internal and external footage of the space station New Hope. Then they began the dramatic lead-in to the launch. They were now only a commercial break away from the launch.

The sound of a beer commercial caught Shelly's attention and she called the station.

"Sandy, I thought the networks agreed not to sell advertising time to beer companies."

"They tried, Shelly, but they were undersold by ten minutes. I authorized it only yesterday. Because of the charges . . . you know."

"Mark isn't going to like it," Shelly said.

"If we can't fully subscribe the program, the next one will be a tough sell," Sandy said.

Micah was listening and he looked up from his checklist.

"Did you try the condom companies?"

"This isn't scrambled, Micah," Shelly said. "The network probably has that on tape."

Micah feigned shock.

"Stand by, they'll be coming out of commercial soon," Sandy said.

Shelly looked down at her checklist, but couldn't concentrate. She often felt distracted around Micah. She had refused to acknowledge the feeling at first but knew she was attracted to him. After John's death she never thought she would love again—not that this was love. Micah was gentle like John, but without the cherubic good looks. Micah was average height, with black hair already speckled with gray at twenty-seven. His face was thin, his chin pointed. His eyes sparkled most of the time and the corners of his mouth were usually curled into a grin. With Shelly he was disarming, tender, and attentive, but so subtle that she was perpetually unsure of his feelings.

Sandy began a countdown and Shelly and Micah tucked their check sheets into net bags. Then Micah spoke over his shoulder.

"Bob, cut the gravity. Take it down slow, remember we have visitors on board. I don't want to be dodging barf balls."

"Right, Micah," Bob said. "No barf balls."

Shelly cut off the transmission to Sandy, then spoke to Micah.

"Micah, they might have heard that too."

"Oops!" he said, covering his mouth and winking at her.

Why did she always fall for the comedians? Shelly wondered.

A minute later they broke free from the station, leaving Earth orbit for the moon.

Even though I walk through the valley of the
shadow of death, I will fear no evil for you are
with me in the presence of my enemies.

—PSALM 23:4

SAN FRANCISCO, CALIFORNIA

Mark leaned through the bars of his cell to get a better
look at the TV mounted near the ceiling. Most of the prisoners were in the TV room, watching on a wall screen,
but because of the court order isolating Mark, he had
been left behind.

The commercials ended and Wyatt Powder was back,
talking about the ". . . strange circumstances under which
man, and woman too, would return to the moon." The
word "strange" referred to the Fellowship, although under pressure the network had agreed to avoid the word
"cult." Instead, Powder used "strange," "unusual," "conservative," and "religious," to marginalize the beliefs of
the Fellowship.

Wyatt finished reading his introduction, then turned
over the launch description to a science correspondent
who talked of the "antigravity drive," of the *God's Love*
as if he knew how it operated. Then Wyatt began an unnecessary dramatic countdown, since the Fellowship
launched ships like airports did airplanes. Launches
weren't the complicated matter they were for NASA. It
was simply a matter of releasing the docking clamps and
then venting the airlock that pushed the ship away from
the station. Once free, the drive was engaged.

The network filled the airwaves with dramatic music as
they switched to one of the *God's Love*'s external cameras. When the count reached zero, the lock was vented—

particles sparkled into space. Now they switched to a camera mounted on the station and followed the *God's Love* as it pulled away.

Mark studied the ship—it had been modified. Two lifting spheres were attached to the normally sleek *God's Love,* one on the top, one on the bottom. It looked like a barbell had been driven through the *God's Love*.

Now the *God's Love* turned slowly, the cargo doors of the tail swinging to the camera. Then it picked up speed, moving off, shrinking quickly. The picture changed to one beamed from a camera mounted on the *God's Love*. It was a spectacular shot, the space station a black silhouette against the bright blue field of the Earth. The New Hope station slowly shrank to a dot, the camera lingering on the Earth as its diameter steadily shrank until it was the size of a quarter.

Next, a shot of the full moon filled the screen—it was file footage, spliced in to make the story complete. Wyatt Powder was still talking, now describing the four-day voyage to the moon and how important it was for viewers to be tuned in for every day of the coverage. After a set of commercials Wyatt's face was back, jovial now, introducing the next segment.

"Just who are these intrepid explorers destined to retrace the footsteps of Armstrong, Aldrin, and Collins?" Powder intoned pompously. "Let's meet them now, up close and personal."

Shelly's smiling face appeared. The smile looked forced to Mark.

"Ms. Henry, thank you for joining us when we know you are busy with the technical details of the launch."

"I'm not busy at the moment. The computer has control of the flight, and there are three other crew monitoring the flight path of the ship."

"I see. Can you tell us how it feels to be the only woman on a spaceship traveling to the moon?"

"I'm sure I feel the same way the rest of the crew feels. We are thankful to God for His many blessings that made this possible. It is our hope that what we are doing will glorify Him."

"But as a woman, you must have a unique perspective."

"If I do I'm not aware of it," Shelly said.

Wyatt Powder looked irritated, which tickled Mark. Shelly was trying to prevent Wyatt from creating division among the crew.

"As a mother, you are leaving a child behind to undertake a dangerous mission. Your thoughts on this?"

The corners of Shelly's mouth sagged as she began to lose her smile. Powder was baiting her. He knew members of the Fellowship were under investigation for child abuse.

"Many professional women have their children cared for while they work."

"Is your son being cared for by someone in the Fellowship?" Powder asked.

"I'm confident my son is in good hands," Shelly said firmly.

Sensing he had pushed her far enough, Powder changed the subject to technical details about the flight. Shelly explained that they would closely match the speed and trajectory of the *Apollo 11* flight on the outward trip, but demonstrate the capabilities of the *God's Love* on the return. Then Wyatt had her introduce the rest of the flight crew. Seeing Micah, Gus, and Bob again buoyed Mark; their answers to Powder's questions were shallow platitudes designed for a network TV audience.

Now the monitor switched to an external view, the camera showing the speckled blackness of space. Transfixed by the infinite tapestry of space, Mark lost himself in thought, and suddenly he was back on the desert of his vision, a great crowd of people following every way he turned. Once again he felt a great weight of responsibility, a burden he didn't think he could bear. Suddenly he was back in his tiny cell. Down the corridor a prisoner was screaming obscenities at a guard. Gently pounding his head on the bars, he despaired. Every day since he and Ira had begun the Fellowship, Mark wished he could be free from his responsibilities, but now that he was, he found the separation even harder to bear. Somehow, soon, he had to get free.

CHAPTER 41

REPORTER

> The greatest achievement of the space age was
> the successful delivery and return of a man to
> the moon. The next challenge is to deliver a per-
> son to the moon and leave them there.
>
> — *ALTERNATE PATHWAYS TO SPACE,*
> EDWARD NORTON

BETWEEN THE EARTH
AND THE MOON

Deep in the belly of the *God's Love,* Wyatt Powder's face filled the overhead monitor, the network anchor droning on about the Fellowship's re-creation of *Apollo 11*'s 1969 mission to the moon. Roland Symes frowned, pained by Powder's odd prose. Roland knew the copywriters who wrote Powder's scripts and the limitations Powder put on them. Powder disliked words with "ess" sounds, since he had lisped when he was a kid. So when it came time to explain why "escape velocity" was not an issue for Fellowship ships, the writers had used "breaking the bond of gravity" instead, and in place of "silent blackness" to describe space, Powder insisted on rewriting it to "quiet void." Roland imagined Powder hoping the Fellowship's re-creation of the *Apollo 11* mission would fail so that he wouldn't have to call it a "success."

Roland's report was due soon and Roland switched his monitor to mission control. Sandy Wallace's pixielike face appeared.

"How long until my segment?" Roland asked.

"Five minutes twenty seconds until commercial," Sandy said. "Wyatt will give you a fifteen-second lead-in after the break."

"Thanks," Roland said. "Switch me to the network so I can talk to Cindi."

The picture dissolved into snow and then Cindi was on the screen. Roland positioned himself in front of the camera mounted above the monitor so that Cindi would get a clear image.

"Wyatt has eaten into your time," Cindi said bluntly. "You have to cut your piece by a minute ten."

"What?" Roland exclaimed. "It took me three days to get it just right."

"Cut some of your ruminations on being part of the post-moon-landing generation," Cindi suggested. "It's not that interesting."

"Why didn't you tell me that last night?"

"I knew Wyatt would use some of your time and this way you didn't waste time last night rewriting it."

Cindi finished with a smile.

"I'm not experienced at on-camera work," Roland admitted. "Maybe Wyatt could rewrite his script in five minutes and still be smooth, but I write for a paper."

"We don't let Wyatt write his own scripts," Cindi said, showing no sympathy.

Roland rarely appeared on television, so it was a surprise when the Fellowship picked him to be the media representative to accompany them to the moon. The only rationale the Fellowship gave was that he had been at the original launching of the *Rising Savior*. When Roland was picked the network threatened to pull out of the deal unless one of their own reporters was on board, settling on Roland only after the Fellowship offered an extension on the price guarantees for orbital transponder services. Roland's boss at the *San Francisco Journal* had his own theory about why Roland was selected. "You're the token black man," Goldwyn grumbled, jabbing the air with his cigar.

Christy Maitland came through the hatch, having finished with her on-camera interview. Her inclusion in the moon crew wasn't as surprising, since her relationship with Mark Shepherd was well known, at least the tabloid version of it.

"How did your interview go?" Roland asked.

"The usual. He misunderstood thirty percent of what I said and wasn't really listening to the rest."

Christy leaned in front of the camera to say hello to Cindi.

"Good job, Christy," Cindi said. "You made Wyatt look good."

"Not an easy task," Roland whispered. Then to Cindi, Roland said, "You really didn't like that section on being a post-moon-landing baby?"

"Cut it," she said flatly. "How are you two doing with the Stepford bunch?"

Roland waited for Christy's response.

"They're nice people," she said, then looked at Roland.

"Too nice," he said. "It's like living with Ozzie and Harriet."

"No one can be too nice," Christy said.

"Yes they can," Roland argued. "It's called overcompensation. They're hiding something and I don't mean their technology."

"Then what?" Christy asked.

"I don't know yet, but something is up."

"Accept them for what they are, Roland," Christy said. "A sincere group of people trying to live by their beliefs as best they can."

"Perhaps," he conceded, "but they've already kept many secrets—their antigravity technology, the fact there were more ships like the *Rising Savior,* the New Hope, the *God's Love.* They're a very secretive group."

"Name a high-tech company that tells their competition about its products before they are ready for the market?" Christy countered.

"You're on in thirty seconds," Cindi said over the speaker.

"Great," Roland grumbled. "Christy's put me in the right mood for this."

Christy laughed, then kissed him on the cheek.

"Maybe that will help," she said.

Roland looked up at Cindi's scowling face.

"No, that didn't help at all."

In working with Victorian women in therapy, Sigmund Freud found that many reported childhood sexual memories. Freud interpreted these as sexual fantasies. Rather than fantasies, what these women recalled was sexual abuse at the hands of their fathers and brothers.

— *HIDDEN TERRORS: WOMEN IN THERAPY,*
ROSA QUIGLY

SAN FRANCISCO, CALIFORNIA

Daniel sat cross-legged on the floor in front of the TV. It was the best high-definition television made, Josh had told him. Like the bike and toys Josh bought him, everything was the best. Daniel found it easy to like nice things. At home he only got new toys on his birthday or Christmas. When Josh bought him a new bike he didn't ride it for three days, but it was shiny and new and at last he let Josh teach him to ride. Josh spent a whole day running up and down the street with him, making sure he didn't fall. By the end of the day Daniel could ride all by himself and was so proud he wanted to show his parents, but Josh told him he couldn't. He cried that night.

The first night at Josh's house Daniel had cried in bed. Josh heard his sobs and sat with him, slipping his arm around Daniel's waist. Daniel pushed the arm away, putting his fingers in his mouth and sucking. Daniel wouldn't talk to Josh, but Josh stayed with him until he stopped crying. Finally, taking his fingers from his mouth, Daniel told Josh how much he missed his family and friends. After that, Daniel felt better and he let Josh hold him close. Then Daniel told Josh about the mean kids at the Children's Center. Josh sat beside him patiently, asking questions. When Daniel had it all out, Josh asked him to tell it all again. Daniel felt better after the second telling and had to choke back tears only when he talked about Faith being teased. Josh said he understood that kids could be mean and told him that kids used to pick on him because he was different. It made Daniel feel better, although he couldn't imagine anyone wanting to beat up someone as nice as Josh.

Josh sat with him every night after that, reading him stories, talking to him, listening to him. They were good friends now and Daniel didn't mind staying with Josh. He didn't think about home as much anymore.

When his sixth birthday came Josh bought him a video game player with six games. Daniel had always wanted one but his parents wouldn't buy one. They were too expensive, his parents said, but Daniel knew they thought that playing video games was bad for him. When he told Josh that, Josh laughed and said, "Make believe isn't bad for children. Using your imagination is what children do best. Just try the games, if you don't like them you don't have to play them."

Daniel did try the games. Some of them were scary, but he quickly got used to them, even the karate game that splattered blood across the screen as the hero fought demons and monsters. Soon it was his favorite game.

When Daniel first came to live with Josh he had prayed before eating, just like he did at home. Each night Josh had waited patiently while Daniel prayed, but he never closed his own eyes. One night, Daniel asked Josh why he didn't pray and Josh said, "Because praying never made any difference. Look at it this way, Daniel, your parents prayed all the time and still you were mistreated and taken away, and now your whole family is unhappy. I don't pray and you came to live with me because here you will be safe."

Daniel didn't like hearing that, but the more he thought about it, the more he wondered why the person who didn't pray had good things happen to him but bad things happened to his parents and him and they did pray.

One night Daniel got the courage to skip praying before he went to bed. He was fearful all the next day but nothing bad happened. He then tried not praying for two days and he found that those days were just like the days when he did pray. Then he went a week without praying. He got the bike that week. Shortly after that he stopped praying before meals too. Now he reached for the food as soon as he sat down at the table just like Josh and he didn't miss praying at all.

Watching the television tonight and seeing Shelly on TV made him sad at first because it reminded him of home. Josh offered to turn it off, but he said no. He also recognized Micah but he didn't know the others who were on the trip to the moon. His parents weren't on the show, although he knew they helped build the spaceships. They gave most of their money to the Fellowship, then told him they couldn't afford to buy him things. He felt a little angry when he thought about that.

Josh put a big bowl of popcorn in front of him and patted him on the shoulder.

"If you want to turn the channel, go ahead," Josh said.

Daniel nodded, grabbing a handful of popcorn. Josh sat on the couch with his own bowl. The popcorn was air-popped and lightly salted. Daniel liked lots of butter on his popcorn—that was the way his dad made it—but Josh said the butter wasn't good for him. He understood that Josh only wanted what was best for him and learned to like it the way he cooked it.

Daniel dug out a big handful of popcorn and stuffed it in his mouth, kernels falling into his lap. He chewed noisily, drowning out the sound of the announcer. Shelly's face appeared on the screen again but now he found he wasn't really homesick at all. He liked his new bike, video games, and nice clothes. He didn't have to sleep in a big room with mean kids—he had a room all by himself. Josh's rules weren't as strict as his parents' rules and he didn't have to get up Sunday mornings for church. Instead, he watched cartoons until Josh got up and then they would meet Josh's friends at a restaurant for breakfast. He still missed Faith and his parents some, but day by day, he missed them less and less.

> People who want to get rich fall into temptation
> and a trap and into many foolish and harmful
> desires that plunge men into ruin
> and destruction.
>
> — I TIMOTHY 6:9

SAN FRANCISCO, CALIFORNIA

Fry showed up at Crow's office unannounced, inviting himself in to watch the second night of the televised trip to the moon. Fry wore a blue sports coat with tan slacks, his shirt open at the collar. There was the usual bulge in his coat where his pistol was holstered. Fry's large frame easily filled one of Crow's oversized chairs; he crossed his legs.

Angered by the man's audacity, Crow suppressed his rage. Rachel greeted Fry warmly, hugging him. Crow approved of Rachel's handling of Fry. If Fry could be seduced, so much the better for Crow's purposes. Crow smiled at Rachel, who brought Fry a whiskey, then squeezed into the chair with him.

Tonight's broadcast focused on the crew of the *God's Love,* comparing the experience of those who had traveled to the moon on the Apollo missions with those of the Fellowship. The night's "space spectacular" would be the launching of a satellite that would relay signals from the surface of the moon.

The key difference between the Apollo and Fellowship missions to the moon was artificial gravity, which made life in space Earth-like. There was no need to eat from a tube, and space sickness was limited to periods where it was necessary to turn off the gravity field. Still, a manned ship hadn't traveled out of Earth's orbit since the last Apollo mission and the sense of adventure remained.

Intercutting interviews with Apollo astronauts and the Fellowship, the network tried to create drama and a sense of history in the making, but all Crow felt was irritation. Despite his efforts, Breitling and Shepherd continued down whatever path they were leading their sheep. His Master had told him to "prepare the way," and he had interpreted that as stopping the Fellowship. But if that was his task, he was failing. Fry chuckled at a whispered comment from Rachel, irritating Crow.

"Couldn't you stop the network from buying this?" Crow demanded.

Drink in his hand, Fry waved it at the screen, sloshing it over the side, onto his sports coat and slacks. Fry's face was red from a combination of liquor and Rachel's attention and it made the scar on his right cheek stand out like a streak of lightning against a night sky.

"We've got people inside the network but not high enough up to control programming. The best we could do was make sure the script had some of the right spin. Newspeople are hard to control; they have their own agendas. Still, we managed to use their dislike of religious people."

Fry drained his glass, then looked at Rachel.

"Honey, would you mind?" Fry said.

Rachel smiled sweetly, refilling his glass, then putting the bottle on the coffee table in front of Fry. She settled next to him again, slipping an arm around Fry's shoulders, pressing against him. Fry responded with a sigh, then winked at Crow.

"It's easier to manipulate the press than to silence them, especially when it comes to Christian cults," Fry continued. "The press pretty much prints whatever we feed them. We've never had as much luck with other religions. The FBI tried to use the press to break up a Muslim sect in New York a few years ago, but they wouldn't take the bait. We had an informant that was telling us this sect was plotting a high-profile kidnapping. We kept feeding rumors to the press through the FBI, but not a single newspaper or television station carried our allegations.

"Not only wouldn't they run the story we fed them,

they only made halfhearted attempts to investigate. The only story run about Muslims in New York that month was about a free food program another sect started. The FBI finally gave up and sure enough the sect snatched a federal judge."

"Didn't that judge die in the police raid?" Rachel asked.

"Shot in the back of the head," Fry said, illustrating with a slap to the back of his own head. "Killing that judge guaranteed two of the Muslims a death sentence and the rest are doing twenty to life."

"The Muslims claimed the police shot the judge," Rachel said.

"They couldn't match the slug to any of the Muslim guns or to the police weapons," Fry said, smiling. "They never will either."

"Why is that?" Rachel asked.

Fry opened his sports coat and pointed at the gun in his holster. Then he laughed uproariously. Rachel giggled, then refilled his glass.

Crow knew Fry wouldn't be stupid enough to be carrying a weapon used to kill a federal judge, but understood the judge was murdered to make a better case against the Muslims.

"The revenue from this telecast is significant," Crow said. "The Fellowship will use it to expand their space station."

"We don't think so," Fry said. "We don't think they are building more modules for the space station. There's a change in what they're buying. Wherever the network money is going, it isn't going into the space station."

Rachel was leaning against Fry now, head on his shoulder, hand rubbing his chest. Either the liquor or Rachel's attentions had loosened Fry's tongue.

"More ships then?" Crow suggested.

"Maybe. Judging by the type and quantity of equipment they are buying it would be a very large ship."

Crow was intrigued and frustrated. The molestation charges had been Crow's best effort yet and it hadn't stopped them.

"What kind of equipment are they buying?" Crow asked.

"Some of it is the usual stuff—environmental systems, air-handling equipment, CO_2 scrubbers, water recycling and reclamation systems—it's the kind of equipment they purchased for their ships and space station. None of it is classified technology. It's basically the same equipment used in submarines. They've also bought the usual electronic components, including CPUs. They assemble their own computers and run their own software."

"It sounds like they're building components for another station, to me," Crow said.

Fry shook his head.

"When they built the New Hope they sent the components up to orbit as soon as they were finished. They have enough materials for a station half the size of the New Hope and yet nothing has been launched. There are other differences too. The proportions of their purchases are all wrong. The Fellowship is buying more exotic materials, a lot of titanium and tungsten and more platinum than ever before."

Fry sipped his drink now, apparently aware he was drunk.

"They're buying internationally too, which is new for them," Fry continued. "Sweden is supplying them with industrial lasers and Germany with electric furnaces. They've got an industrial plant somewhere but we can't find it. Parts and materials are shipped either to Mexico or California but those flying balls haul materials all over the planet. They're impossible to track."

Crow realized the Fellowship's space technology was about to take another leap forward and he was powerless to stop it—at least, not without Fry's help.

"How is the project going?" Crow asked.

"No real progress," Fry said. "That Thorpe is a workaholic. He won't leave the lab. He rarely sleeps. His hatred of Breitling keeps him going."

"Have you opened the drive on the sphere you recovered?"

"No," Fry said. "We're not going to open the drive unless we have to."

"Look at the TV screen," Crow said. "Don't you think it's time?"

Fry's thin lips tightened and the yellow flecks in his eyes seemed to glow. He and Crow had disagreed before over how best to proceed with discovering the Fellowship's technological secret.

"I'll decide when it's time," Fry said.

"My money is funding this project," Crow countered. "If I don't see some progress that funding might dry up."

Now Fry leaned forward, staring hard at Crow and speaking in a low gravelly voice.

"You're in this, Crow, and you'll stay in it to the end."

Crow's hatred of Fry was intense but he still needed the man's resources.

"What does Thorpe think? Does he want to leave the drive sealed?"

"Thorpe agrees that opening the drive should be a last resort," Fry said.

Crow knew Fry was lying. Thorpe would do what Fry told him to do.

"Thorpe is reconstructing their control systems. He says he's getting clues to how to control the sphere."

"We need to know how it works," Crow argued.

"One step at a time."

Crow was frustrated, but he let it drop. He felt a sense of urgency that Fry did not share. Crow fumed through the rest of the show. When the broadcast ended, Rachel walked Fry out to his car, giggling at his every remark. A half hour later she came back, getting a mirror from her purse, then fixing her makeup.

"He'll kill us when he thinks we're no more use to him," she said.

"I know," Crow said. "The trick is to know when to kill him first."

> Reaching the Moon by three-man vessels in one
> long bound from Earth is like casting a thin
> thread across space. The main effort, in the
> coming decades, will be to strengthen this
> thread; to make it a cord, a cable, and finally a
> broad highway.

> — *THE BEGINNING AND THE END,*
> ISAAC ASIMOV

BETWEEN THE EARTH AND THE MOON

"**T**he network will be ready for you in three minutes,
Shelly," Sandy said.

"We're ready here."

Shelly switched the monitor to the cargo bay. Paul
Swenson could be seen hand-cranking the inner cargo
door. Paul was barrel-chested, blond, and blue-eyed, but
not a big man, only five feet five. Gravity meant nothing to
him and up and down were interchangeable as far as his inner ear was concerned.

"What's wrong with the hatch, Paul?" Shelly asked.
"Isn't the electric motor working?"

"It is, but I don't trust it."

Paul was another of Ira's favorites. He finished crank-
ing the inner door closed, which was a second door set
inside the outer door. The indicator turned green but Paul
twisted the handle and double-checked the locking mechanism anyway.

"Now I know it's sealed," Paul said.

"The networks will be watching in about two minutes,"
Shelly said.

"Right. So no more scratching where it really itches,"
Paul said.

"Is Glen there?" Shelly asked.

Glen came into view, waving at the camera. Glen Swan was the size of a jockey and flew with the same light touch. Small-boned and fragile-looking, he was actually wiry and rugged. Glen was vain and worked to keep his black hair neatly in place and his clothes neatly pressed. Amiable and easygoing, he and Paul were good friends.

"Glen, the network wants to make it look like I'm releasing the satellite, but I'll leave control with you," Shelly said. "They can't get you on camera but they can me."

Glen looked disappointed, then smiled. "This was my big break," he said.

"He's wearing his designer coveralls," Paul added.

"Just get the satellite out safely," Shelly said. "Ira will be watching."

Paul and Glen mimicked fear, their eyes wide, their mouths open.

Shelly switched back to Sandy's channel to find Wyatt Powder sharing his wisdom.

"Intellectual pabulum," Micah said.

"On your best behavior, Micah," Shelly ordered. "We go live any second now."

Then Sandy came on-line.

"You're on in five, four, three . . ." Sandy said, her voice trailing off.

Shelly waited two more seconds, then began acting for the home audience.

"Paul, Glenn, prepare to release the satellite," Shelly said. "Gus, bring the gravity down to zero."

"Gravity to zero," Gus said.

"Bob, begin depressurizing the airlock."

"Activating pumps now," he said.

The commands and responses were crisp and professional, not like normal interaction.

Shelly's stomach fluttered as the gravity waned, and she worried she might throw up on international TV. Pretending to push buttons, she watched herself on TV repressing a smile, feeling stupid. Then Micah leaned over and flipped two of the toggles that controlled the external landing lights, appearing briefly on camera. A minute later he repeated the performance, getting himself on camera again. Then the view switched to an external shot showing nothing but stars. Then Wyatt Powder's voice explained that the satellite would appear shortly from the rear of the craft. Shelly took the opportunity to slug Micah on the arm.

"Ow!" Micah complained.

"What were you doing flipping the lights on and off?"

"I noticed you forgot to play with those switches. Besides, you were hogging the camera!"

Now he was smiling broadly and rubbing his arm. She was laughing at him when her face appeared on the monitor again. Sobering quickly, she reached over and flipped the same toggles Micah had, stifling a giggle and trying not to look at Micah.

"Gravity is zero," Gus said.

"Pressure is zero PSI," Bob said.

"Opening exterior doors," Shelly said, then switched the monitor from Sandy to Glen, who nodded and then checked his indicator panel before operating the exterior doors. The monitor switched to inside the airlock and a shot of the satellite with the doors opening behind it. Shelly took the opportunity to push a lock of hair back that had floated in front of her face.

"You want to powder your nose too?" Micah asked.

Shelly punched his arm, aiming for the spot she hit before. He yelped.

When the door was fully open she said, "Cargo doors are open and secure," then she waited for Glen to give her a thumbs-up sign. Then, after Glen engaged the winch, Shelly said, "Begin release sequence."

The satellite moved gently toward the field of stars. Wyatt Powder's voice cut in, trying to make the moment more dramatic.

"The satellite they are launching now will serve as a communications relay between the space station and the ship as it attempts a lunar landing." Wyatt's face appeared in a box in the corner, obscuring part of the satellite. "It will take up its lonely vigil, and remain here, delicately balanced between the gravity of the moon and the gravity of Earth forever."

When the satellite had reached the edge of the cargo door, Shelly waited for Glen to start the process and then said, "Extend the cargo arm."

The satellite was pushed outward with an arm clamped to the bottom of the satellite. Now the people on Earth saw an exterior shot and the satellite could be seen behind the tail of the ship. When the satellite was fully extended only the top portion could be seen peeking above the ship.

"Release the satellite," Shelly said needlessly. "Retract the cargo arm."

The boom came away from the satellite, leaving it floating motionless in space. Wyatt began talking again, so Shelly turned to Micah.

"Move us away from the satellite so they can get a full shot of it."

The ship moved with a slight jerk, the full satellite coming into view. There were dish antennae built into both ends of the turnip-shaped satellite. It was ungainly, dark, and ugly, surely not what the audience on Earth had expected. Then Shelly spoke to Paul.

"Are you ready, Paul?"

"Just give the word."

Then for the audience at home she said, "Power up the satellite."

Lights appeared on the satellite, illuminating the dish antennae and every seam and joint. The bulbous shape glowed in the inky blackness like the star on a Christmas tree. The ugly shape was replaced by the glowing splendor.

The lights were for show, built in at the last minute at the request and expense of the network. They had no functional purpose but there was no denying the aesthetic power.

"Paul, what about the satellite's systems?"

"Everything looks good. Let me try an orientation maneuver."

Shelly watched the monitor as the antennae on both ends extended slightly, then changed angles. Then the satellite tilted and rotated 360 degrees. When the satellite ceased rotating Paul announced he was satisfied. Then

Shelly switched her monitor to Sandy, who was standing by on New Hope station.

"Sandy, the satellite is in position and responding to our commands," Shelly said. "We are releasing control to you."

"Roger that, *God's Love*," Sandy replied.

Micah nudged her arm and whispered, "Roger? Sandy actually said 'Roger.' She's really getting into this."

Shelly smiled. They were all acting a bit, trying to sound like astronauts, although on normal flights they used very little technical jargon. The antennae on the satellite retracted and then extended again, and then the satellite rotated, all under Earth control. A few minutes after the test Sandy radioed they had full control on New Hope station. Before Shelly could answer, Micah said, "We roger that, New Hope control. Everything is five by five here, we are resuming ETM trajectory after PIB."

Sandy acknowledged Micah's transmission, and Shelly checked to see that the network had Wyatt Powder narrating while they kept the external cameras on the shrinking dot that was the satellite. Then she turned to Micah.

"What is ETM?" Shelly asked.

"Earth to moon," Micah said.

"And PIB?"

"Pee in Bag. Now if you'll turn your head I'll execute it."

Shelly turned her head, giggling through the entire PIB.

> There is no such thing as justice—
> in or out of court.
>
> —CLARENCE DARROW

SAN FRANCISCO, CALIFORNIA

Stephen stood when the guard brought Mark into the courtroom, directing him to a chair next to Floyd. Floyd greeted him warmly, and they shook hands and hugged. Floyd had been free pending this hearing, while Mark had spent the time in jail or in a hospital. The charges against them both amounted to child molesting, but Mark was considered the greater risk since he was the leader of the Fellowship.

Evelyn was there, seated behind Floyd along with two other women from the Fellowship. She reached out to Mark but the guard held Mark back. Instead, Evelyn said, "God bless you," then sat back with the other women from the Fellowship.

The courtroom was packed with reporters and the hearing would be broadcast. A Court TV camera was mounted high on one wall. The camera followed Mark's every move. Mark knew that somewhere there were reporters doing play-by-play descriptions of the courtroom activities— describing his clothes, his greeting of Floyd and Evelyn, and reading his facial expression. If he showed emotion he would be described as depressed or frightened. If he showed no emotion they would describe him as callous or cold. Every hand motion, scratch, leg crossing, or change in position would be interpreted by legions of experts who specialized in nonverbal communication. Stephen had even warned him to cover his mouth when whispering because lip readers were employed by the media.

This wasn't the trial, only a hearing to determine whether there was enough evidence to take the case to trial. Floyd and Mark were the central targets of the prosecution, which continued to hold out plea-bargain deals to the other members of the Fellowship if they would testify against their leaders—none had opted for the deal. The only witnesses to be heard today would be Floyd's children, Faith and Daniel. If they implicated their father and Mark, they would be held over for trial. Floyd was confident his children would vindicate him. Mark wasn't.

Stephen had been morose since seeing the transcripts of the children's claims. His requests for his own experts to interview the children had all been denied, since the prosecution had argued that introducing new therapists would destroy the trust relationship they had formed with Rosa Quigly. "In the children's best interest" had been the phrase the judge used when she limited Stephen's access to transcripts of the therapy.

The bailiff called the court to their feet; Judge Lana Tucker-Cannon entered the court. She was fifty, married three times—the hyphen coming from her most recent marriage—and childless. Her hair was pulled back in a gray bun, and her lips were thin and tight, giving her a stern demeanor. Stephen had warned Mark she was not to be trifled with.

Judge Tucker-Cannon rapped a gavel and everyone sat. Then she talked with her bailiff, and the case was called. With the formalities over she turned to the assistant district attorney who would make the state's case. Walter Hanson was a thirty-five-year-old African-American on the fast track to higher office. The case had been his for the asking and his plan was to see justice done and his career advanced at the same time. Before he could begin, Stephen stood asking for recognition. Judge Tucker-Cannon's forehead creased, her eyebrows almost touching.

"What is it, Mr. O'Malley?"

"I would like to ask for a continuance. We have not had access to the recordings of the children's therapy so I could not properly prepare."

"Did the state provide you with transcripts per my order?"

"Yes, Your Honor, but—"

"We've been through this, Mr. O'Malley. Therapy is a confidential process, and your possession of the transcripts is as intrusive as I'm going to let you be unless this goes to trial."

"If the therapeutic relationship has been abused, then the charges should be dropped," Stephen argued.

"The accusations about your clients preceded the therapy."

"But, Your Honor, the reputations of these men will be irreparably harmed if the state is allowed to pursue charges that have no foundation."

"This is a preliminary hearing, Mr. O'Malley, and my primary concern is for the children. Now sit down!"

Mark feared Stephen had pushed the judge too far.

Hanson continued.

"Your Honor, the state is prepared to present a limited case in order to spare the children the trauma of facing the men who molested them."

"Objection, Your Honor," Stephen said. "No evidence has been introduced to show the children were molested by my clients or anyone else."

"Alleged molestation," Hanson corrected, then continued. "We would like to call only two witnesses to the stand: Daniel and Faith Remple."

Mark looked at Floyd who smiled confidently. Then Floyd turned and smiled at Evelyn whose head was bowed in prayer.

The assistant district attorney asked for Faith to be brought in and Stephen immediately objected.

"Your Honor, the child has already been traumatized by the forced separation from her parents. Being interrogated in front of a hundred witnesses, not to mention a vast television audience, will exacerbate the trauma. We respectfully request that the courtroom be cleared and the camera turned off."

"I have no objection," Hanson said.

"Well I do," Judge Tucker-Cannon said.

Assistant District Attorney Walter Hanson was as surprised as Stephen. It was common to protect children from unnecessary public exposure, especially in cases like this.

"Mr. Hanson has made it clear that these allegations may be just the tip of a very big iceberg. If these children have the courage to testify, it may empower other children to come forward."

Now Walter Hanson spoke.

"Your Honor, the state recognizes the legitimate concerns of the defense for the welfare of the children and concurs with his request to have the courtroom cleared and the camera turned off."

"No, Mr. Hanson," the judge came back sharply. "However, I will compromise. The courtroom will be cleared but the camera will remain on, operated by remote. The children's faces will not be shown."

"Objection, Your Honor," Stephen said.

"Overruled. Bailiff, clear the court."

"I request that the children's mother, Evelyn Remple, be allowed to remain," Stephen said.

"Request denied, Mr. O'Malley. She is excluded since she may have played a role in the alleged abuse."

Evelyn sobbed noisily as Floyd screamed denials, defending his wife.

"Control your client, Counselor, or I will have him bound and gagged!"

Floyd slapped Stephen's hand from his shoulder.

"She can't say things like that," Floyd shouted. "It's slander."

The camera was focused on Floyd now, taking in his tantrum and broadcasting it to the world. Mark sagged in his chair fully understanding the extent of the worldly forces arrayed against them.

Stephen got Floyd back into his chair and the court was cleared. Only the camera remained, its tiny red eye watching every move.

Hanson asked for Faith to be brought in, the bailiff leaving by a side door to fetch her. Floyd watched the door intensely, waiting for the first glimpse of his daughter in three months. The door opened and Faith was there, holding the hand of Rosa Quigly. Faith was wearing a pink ruffled dress with white tights and white patent leather shoes—all new. A matching pink bow was in her tightly curled hair. Floyd started to rise but Stephen forced him down. Faith started toward her daddy, Rosa Quigly holding her back. Then Rosa knelt and whispered to Faith, whose eyes teared.

"Your Honor, Ms. Quigly is coaching the witness," Stephen objected.

The judge looked over and the therapist whispered a final word, then stood, still holding Faith's hand. Mark looked at Hanson, who was watching the scene with interest—even concern.

"Ms. Quigly, show Faith where to sit."

The therapist led Faith to the witness stand, then stood next to her. Judge Tucker-Cannon leaned over and spoke to Faith.

"Do you know the difference between telling the truth and telling a lie, Faith?"

Faith mumbled, "Yes."

"In court you must always tell the truth. Do you understand?"

"Yes."

"Will you promise to tell the truth?"

"Yes."

"Thank you, Faith."

"That's my daddy," she said, pointing and then waving. Floyd waved back, a tear running from one eye.

"We know he's your daddy, Faith, but don't be afraid," the judge said.

"Your Honor," Stephen protested.

"What?"

"You suggested she had something to fear from my client."

"I did not. I was only reassuring her. I don't want any further interruptions from you, Mr. O'Malley. You are the one frightening the child."

Hanson watched the exchange from his table, now looking puzzled.

"Is Ms. Quigly going to be allowed to stand by the child during the proceedings?" Stephen asked sharply.

"Sit down, Mr. O'Malley," Judge Tucker-Cannon ordered.

"Will you at least instruct her not to coach the witness?"

"You're one step away from a contempt citation, Mr. O'Malley," Judge Tucker-Cannon said sternly. "Ms. Quigly may remain near the child in order to comfort her." Then turning to Rosa she said, "You may not coach the child."

The judge nodded to Hanson, who began by introducing himself.

"Faith, my name is Walt. I need to ask you some questions. Some of the questions are going to be hard."

"I know."

Stephen scribbled: "HOW WOULD SHE KNOW UNLESS SHE HAS BEEN COACHED?" on a yellow pad and showed it to Mark and Floyd.

"Do you know the difference between places where it's okay for people to touch you and places where people shouldn't touch you?"

"Yes."

"Has anyone ever touched your private places?"

Faith looked up at Rosa Quigly who nodded slightly.

"Yes," Faith said.

"Objection, she's coaching the witness," Stephen said, jumping to his feet.

"Quiet, Mr. O'Malley. I won't warn you again. Ms. Quigly, be careful."

"Did your daddy ever touch you in your private places?"

Faith hesitated now, looking up at Rosa, who kept her head still this time. Then Faith looked at her father.

"I want to go home."

"I know you do, Faith, but you have to answer the question," Walter Hanson said. "Did your daddy touch your private places?"

"Yes."

"Faith!" Floyd exclaimed, devastated by the accusation.

"Silence!" the judge said, glaring at Floyd.

Stephen took Floyd's hand, whispering to him, calming him. Faith was crying now, sniffling and wiping her nose on her sleeve.

"Faith," Hanson said softly. "Did your daddy ever show you his private places?"

Faith looked at Rosa and then down at the floor and said, "Yes."

"Did he ever make you touch his private parts?"

"Yes."

Each of Faith's answers was softer than the one before.

"Did he ever touch your private parts with his private parts?"

"Yes."

"Permission to approach Faith, Your Honor?" Hanson requested.

The judge nodded and Hanson walked toward Faith carrying two anatomically correct dolls.

"Can you show me how he touched you with his private parts."

Faith took the dolls and with a well-practiced move laid the male doll on top of the female doll.

"Did anyone else here today do this to you, Faith?"

She nodded but did not speak.

"Yes or no, Faith?" Hanson prodded.

"Yes."

"Who was it?"

Faith pointed at Mark.

"Pastor Mark," Faith said softly.

Mark felt as though his heart had stopped. Reading the transcripts could not prepare him for hearing little Faith accuse him of an unspeakable act.

"Thank you, Faith," Walter Hanson said.

Hanson sat down, giving Stephen a chance to question Faith. Before he could, the judge cautioned him.

"Be very careful, Mr. O'Malley."

Stephen smiled at Faith.

"My name is Stephen, Faith."

She nodded, her eyes peeking over the dolls who remained in the obscene position she had placed them in.

"Have you ever played with dolls like this before?"

"Yes."

"Where?"

"At Rosa's."

"Did she show you how to put the dolls together like this."

"Yes."

Stephen looked at the judge as if to have the case dismissed. The judge doodled on a pad, ignoring Stephen.

"When your daddy touched your private parts, was it after you went to the bathroom?"

"Yes."

"Was he using toilet paper?"

"Yes."

Again Stephen turned to the judge, who kept her eyes down.

"Faith, you said that you knew the questions would be hard. How did you know that?"

"Rosa told me."

"Did Rosa tell you how to answer the questions?"

"No."

Stephen stared at Faith, thinking. The judge noticed the silence and looked up. A few seconds passed, then Stephen asked, "Faith, did you know I was going to ask if Rosa told you how to answer?"

Now Faith looked up at Rosa who stood stone-faced.

"I don't know," Faith answered evasively.

"Did you play court before you came here today?"

"Yes."

"Where did you play court?"

"At Rosa's."

"Was Walter there when you played court?"

"No, just Rosa and me."

"Thank you, Faith," Stephen said.

Stephen wrote on the yellow pad and showed it to Mark and Floyd. "SHE'S BEEN REHEARSED AND THE JUDGE IS GOING TO LET THEM GET AWAY WITH IT!!!"

"I have another question, Your Honor," Hanson said.

"Faith, did your daddy or Pastor Mark ever touch your private places when they didn't have toilet paper?"

"Yes."

The judge thanked Faith then, and she hopped out of the chair expectantly, looking at her father. When Rosa took her hand to lead her away she said, "Am I going home now?" The therapist bent to her ear and whispered. Faith's face fell then and she let herself be pulled out of the courtroom, looking over her shoulder at her daddy the whole way. When the door closed behind her another tear ran from Floyd's eye.

"She's little," Floyd said. "She didn't know what she was saying. Daniel won't say those things about us. Daniel and I have always been close."

Daniel was brought in next, avoiding eye contact with either his father or Mark. This time Rosa Quigly left the little boy in the witness box and went to sit in the spectator's gallery. Mark realized that with Rosa behind them they could not watch Rosa's body language. Daniel was sworn in as Faith had been, his head hanging the whole time.

"Daniel, I know this is difficult for you, but it's important for you to tell the truth," Hanson said. "Did your father ever touch your private parts?"

"Yes, he touched my penis," Daniel said firmly.

Hanson seemed surprised by Daniel's easy use of the word "penis," but immediately adopted it. Mark looked at Floyd, whose face was white.

"Did Pastor Mark ever touch your penis?"

"Yes."

"Did your father ever make you touch his penis?"

"Yes."

"Did Pastor Mark ever make you touch his penis?"

"Yes."

"Did your father and Pastor Mark ever make you do anything else that you thought might be wrong."

Now Daniel's face reddened, and he looked up, past his father to Rosa Quigly. When Mark turned she was sitting like a statue.

"Yes."

"What, Daniel?"

"They put things inside me."

"Do you mean in your anus?"

"Yes."

"What did they put in you?"

"Their fingers."

"What else?"

"Their penises."

"Did they ever do that to other children, Daniel?"

"Yes."

"Who, Daniel?"

"Tommy and Brady."

"What about Faith?"

"Yes."

"It's a lie!" Floyd roared, jumping to his feet. "I never did any of those things to you, Daniel. Why are you doing this to me?"

Judge Tucker-Cannon pounded her gavel and shouted at Floyd and Stephen. When Stephen pulled on Floyd's arm he was pushed away.

"You're hurting your mother too, Daniel. You'll never get to come home now, Daniel. You'll never see your mother again."

Two guards grabbed Floyd and pulled him across the table as he struggled to get free, trying to reach his son. "May God forgive you, Daniel. May God forgive you," he shouted as they dragged him out of the courtroom, the camera tracking him all the way to the door.

Now the courtroom was silent except for the whir of the electric motor as it turned the prying red eye of the camera from the now closed door back to Mark. Daniel sat on the stand, fingers in his mouth, tears running down his cheeks. Then Rosa Quigly moved to stand next to him, holding him and comforting him like a mother would.

> Men visiting the moon would miss the protec-
> tive features of an atmosphere . . . Surface tem-
> peratures where the sun is directly overhead are
> estimated to rise to about 250° Fahrenheit, far
> above the boiling point of water (212°).
>
> — *WE REACH THE MOON,* JOHN N. WILFORD

THE MOON

Paul and Glen checked in from the spheres, ready to separate from the *God's Love* and descend to the lunar surface.

"I've got all green here, Shelly. Pressure's good, all
backups functional," Paul said.

"All my indicators are green too," Glen said.

"Gravity is zeroed out, Shelly," Gus said.

"Bob, release the locks," Shelly ordered.

The *God's Love* gave a shudder as the mechanisms that
held the spheres to the larger ship released.

"Paul, Glen, acknowledge separation, please," Shelly
said.

"The *Jesus Wept* is separated," Glen radioed from his
sphere.

"The *John Henry* is free," Paul echoed.

Shelly checked the monitor. The lag from the Earth
was noticeable now since the signals were sent from lunar
orbit, through the relay satellite, to the space station, to
the ground station, to the network studios, and then
broadcast back again with the network audio added. The
three-second lag allowed Shelly to reexperience what had
already happened in her time. She saw particles blow
away from the docking rings that held the spheres to the
God's Love, and then the spheres drifted away, the high-

contrast surface of the moon serving as a dramatic back-drop. It would play well on the HDTV screens back on Earth.

Shelly lingered on the sphere named for her dead husband, guilty because her thoughts were of Micah. She repeated the "until death do us part" segment of her wedding vows, reminding herself that God had separated her from John.

"The spheres have been released from the mother ship," Powder said after they separated, and "The spheres are now operating under their own power," when the spheres moved away from the *God's Love*.

After a minute of Powder's needless comments, Micah said, "He could work for the department of redundancy department."

Gus's giggle encouraged him and he mocked Wyatt's deep voice.

"The pilot is breathing now. His chest is going up and now it is going down. Here it goes again, his chest coming up and now down again." Now the entire flight crew was laughing. Sandy's face appeared on the monitor and she asked, "What's so funny?" They sobered until Shelly said, "Sandy is now asking the flight crew what is so funny?" It was a full minute before they could speak without chortling.

"The seals are tight," Bob said, bringing them back on task.

Shelly acknowledged Bob's report that was meant to reassure them there were no leaks at the points of separation.

The cameras mounted on the *God's Love* continued to follow the spheres as they dropped toward the moon's surface—a surface so painfully bleak it was beautiful. Sandy appeared on the monitor again.

"The network wants the signals from the spheres."

"Paul, Glen, turn on your cameras," Shelly said.

Shelly looked over her shoulder to see two monitors come on above Bob's head; both showed the moon in detail.

"The network is taking the signal . . . now," Sandy called.

Shelly watched the monitor and listened as Wyatt announced they would be "switching to the video camera in the sphere piloted by Glen Swan." She noticed Powder avoided using the name of the ship—*Jesus Wept*—he avoided all the ship names except for *John Henry*.

Glen's video was still being fed to the network and showed him nearing the surface, coming in at a steep angle. Now he leveled out and the ship shot across the surface of the moon just above the craters and ridges below. The picture was spectacular. Even Powder was quiet, now only uttering an occasional "fantastic" or "breathtaking." Glen slowed, then turned the *Jesus Wept*. The surface disappeared briefly, whited out when the camera caught the sun. As soon as the signal reached Sandy back at New Hope station, she radioed a warning.

"Tell Glen to be careful," Sandy said. "The network camera can't take direct sun."

Shelly acknowledged, passing the warning on to Glen. The video from the *Jesus Wept* was mesmerizing, the bleak but beautiful surface of the moon filling wall screens all across planet Earth. It was fantastic television but there was more to tonight's show. Shelly called to Paul.

"Paul, are you almost there?"

"Yes. I'll circle until you give the word."

"Sandy," Shelly said. "Paul's ready, is the network?"

A minute later she said, "Send him in," and the signal switched to Paul's ship.

Paul raced across the surface like Glen, but then slowed, dropping lower. Soon he was diving below the lip of craters, ridges towering above him. Occasionally climbing to clear obstacles, he gave the viewers a roller-coaster ride across the lunar surface. The ground was rocky and pitted with craters of all sizes. Some sections were nothing but rock, looking like cold lava fields. Other sections appeared smooth with a gray, powdery surface.

Bob spoke to Sandy giving her the distance to the target and soon the network added a musical backdrop to the footage and the sounds of "Thus Spake Zarusthustra" were broadcast into viewers' homes, the timpani booming digitally. Then Paul slowed, coming to a ridge, then climbing and dropping into a plain on the far side. It was less rocky here, with open spaces, littered with pebble-sized rocks. In the distance the sun glistened off an object. The craft slowed again, letting the music build suspense, Wyatt Powder now mercifully silent. The object took on definition—sharp angles appeared marking it as man-made. It was a lunar lander—at least the bottom half that served as the launch platform.

The *John Henry* approached slowly, swinging wide of the lander, revealing an American flag planted in the lunar surface. Closing on the flag, the camera zoomed in until it filled the screen, and then the *John Henry* was past, and turned toward space again, filling the screen with stars. Wyatt Powder said something then, but no one heard—nothing could detract from the power of the moment.

"I guess we're on," Micah said, picking up his checklist.

Reluctantly, Shelly pulled hers from the net bag. They had come to the moon for the money but she had been caught up in the excitement the network created, understanding the heroism of the first men who set foot here. They came in crafts far more fragile than the *God's Love*. Every ounce of the Apollo crafts had to be engineered to save weight and still carry out essential functions. Flying in Apollo capsules, landing on the surface of the moon in delicate crafts, and planting their flag was the work of heroes.

The network switched to shots from Glen's ship that approached another landing site, this time showing a lunar rover parked where men had left it decades before. As the *Jesus Wept* passed over the Lunar Rover, Micah paused in the middle of his checklist.

"Look at that. Parked in the same place for all these years and it still has its hubcaps," Micah said. "Must be a safe neighborhood."

Gus and Bob laughed. Shelly gave him an exaggerated frown.

When the checklist was done, Micah took control of *God's Love*. Shelly switched to the internal speakers. "Prepare for landing," she said as Micah rotated the *God's Love*, then nosed it over so they were plunging toward the surface.

Religious experiences which are as real as life to some may be incomprehensible to others.

—WILLIAM O. DOUGLAS

SAN FRANCISCO, CALIFORNIA

Mark had lived in the high-contrast world of prison so long he could not appreciate the stark beauty of the moon. It was too bleak, reminding him of his surroundings. Still, his eyes never left the screen. Two cells away, another prisoner yelled to the guard to change the channel. Movies packed with violence and nudity were the favorites among the prisoners, who cheered murder, dismemberment, and rape. The guard ignored the prisoner. Mark was barely aware of the exchange.

The *God's Love* was now descending like an airplane, dropping out of orbit at an angle, the heavily cratered lunar surface slowly rising to meet the ship. Mark knew the *God's Love* could rise and fall like an elevator, and the angled descent was for psychological as well as dramatic purposes. The angled descent provided a panorama of the moon's surface that a vertical descent could not.

Mark lost himself in the rush of colorless landscape, briefly forgetting his surroundings. If someone hadn't accused him and Floyd of child abuse, he could have been at the controls of one of the spheres, circling the moon a hundred feet off the surface. The spheres were his favorite because they were all power with little mass to be overcome. They responded to the slightest touch, rotating and swerving on command.

The *Apollo 11* lander appeared again, the *God's Love* slowing to creep across the Sea of Tranquility, angling so both the lander and the flag were seen. Then the *God's Love* hovered, settling onto the surface. Shelly spoke from the cockpit saying, "People of Earth, *God's Love* is on the moon." Then Wyatt Powder broke in. "The Fellowship tends to put everything in religious terms, but what they are saying is that their spacecraft has landed on the surface of the moon. If you remember Neil Armstrong's words at the same moment, they were 'Houston, this is Tranquility base. The Eagle has landed.' "

The camera on the *God's Love* rotated, giving a panorama of the moon's surface. When it came back to the flag it angled down, zooming in on the footprints in the thick dust coating the surface, as perfect as when first impressed.

Wyatt Powder announced a break in the broadcast from the moon, so that the local news would cut in, allowing the crew of the *God's Love* to suit up for an EVA. "That's extra-vehicular activity," Powder explained. Then he told viewers to be sure and return and he signed off.

Mark returned to his bunk, thinking of the dangers Shelly and the others were facing. He was reluctant to let his people leave the safety of *God's Love*, but Shelly and the others sided with the network. They didn't want to travel that far without actually stepping on the surface. When the network agreed to pay the additional costs of the environment suits, the deal was struck. Still, Mark was living with the results of that decision—more anxiety. He slipped into prayer, and prayed through the newsbreak and two dozen commercials.

Religion, in short, is a monumental chapter in
the history of human egotism.

—WILLIAM JAMES

SAN FRANCISCO, CALIFORNIA

Rosa turned off the engine but made no move to get out
of the car. They had spent two hours together after the
court hearing, sitting in her office, most of the time in silence. Then she had taken him to dinner where he had
played with his food, too upset to eat. Now they were at
Josh's.

"Daniel, you did what had to be done today. It was the
right thing to do for you, your father, and Pastor Mark.
Unless they face what they did to you, and deal with
their issues, they will just go on hurting others like they
hurt you."

Daniel thought she was right but his memories were
fuzzy. With Rosa's help the memories had become
firmer, but he was still unsure.

"Do you remember what your father said as they took
him away? He said, 'May God forgive you.' You know
what he meant, don't you?"

Daniel kept his head down, silent. He thought his father was asking God to forgive him for lying but he
waited for Rosa to explain.

"He asked God to forgive you because he won't. He
was saying good-bye to you, Daniel. He thinks you
turned on him, Daniel, betrayed him and his God. But you
didn't. He betrayed you when he stole your childhood.
You took a giant step toward mental health today, Daniel.
You separated yourself from your father and his religion
which he was using to smother you. You'll blossom now,

Daniel, like a flower pushing its way through the dark soil into the bright sun. It's a new day for you. Daniel. You're not completely free yet, but freedom is only a few steps away."

Too confused to respond, Daniel opened the car door and walked up the steps to the porch. He carried his burden into the living room where Josh was lying on the couch, reading. The stereo was playing jazz, Josh's favorite type of music. Josh sat up when he came in, using a remote control to turn off the music.

"Do you want to talk about it?" Josh asked.

Daniel shook his head. Turning on the TV, he sat cross-legged on the floor and stared at the screen. He tried to watch but he kept seeing the look on his father's face—but he did remember it happening that way—he was pretty sure. It was in his parents' bedroom but he couldn't remember what day or what time. He remembered doing it with Pastor Mark too. Somewhere in a field—but he also remembered Rosa saying, "Maybe he took you to a park or somewhere in the woods." He had been crying when she said that. "You must remember, Daniel, if you ever want to go home," she said over and over. "Now remember, was it in a park where he made you do it, or was it in the woods?" "In a park," he said tentatively. "Good, Daniel. But parks can be crowded and he wouldn't want someone to see, so was it really a park?" He thought for a moment, remembering the open land near where the church was built and then said, "Maybe it was a field." She praised him again and from that day he always remembered it as happening in the field near the church.

The commercials ended and the lunar landscape appeared. The parents of his friends were on the moon. His fingers went into his mouth. Every value he had been raised with was being challenged by Rosa and Josh. With anxiety beyond his ability to cope, the value system of his childhood began to crumble—he could no longer live in perpetual conflict. Since he couldn't trust his memories, he suddenly had no past. After his testimony against his father, his hope of going home was gone.

Unconsciously, his mind acted; now free of loyalty to

his parents, his mind reconfigured the past, resolving all conflicts. Suddenly his memories of abuse firmed up, details were added, they became bright and clear, leaving no doubt what had happened, and as a result, his anxiety decreased. Now that he knew his father had lied to him he realized everything his family had taught him was a lie. Belief in God evaporated, the thought of church and Sunday school now repelled him. Free of family and church teachings he was open to alternatives. Josh had been right about his religion, and his mind now unconsciously accepted the values Josh modeled.

The memory of what happened in court still hurt, but a new feeling emerged—anger. How dare his father blame him for telling the truth? How could his mother support his father against him? Anger felt better than guilt and he nursed it. Self-righteousness swelled in him. He pulled his fingers from his mouth, never to return, took a deep breath, and felt better than he had in three months. He looked around at the house where he lived now. It was nicer than his old house. Here he was really loved and Josh didn't make him do things he didn't want to do. Here he didn't have to be afraid and that's the way a home should be. He knew then he never wanted to leave Josh.

Josh left the room and soon came back and handed him a big bowl of mint chocolate chip ice cream—his favorite. It was the expensive kind, which his parents never bought.

"Do you want me to turn the station?" Josh asked.

"No," he said firmly. "I want to watch."

When Josh settled back on the couch, Daniel turned to him and asked, "Can I live with you forever?"

Josh was surprised.

"What about your parents?" he asked.

"I never want to see them again!"

> Every answer given arouses new questions. The
> progress of science is matched by an increase in
> the hidden and mysterious.
>
> — *JUDAISM AND SCIENCE,* LEO BAECK

THE MOON

Nowhere on Earth was there a landscape to match the
dust, craters, and ridges of the moon. The people of Earth
saw all of this on their high-definition televisions, broadcast from the nose of the *Jesus Wept* while it continued
soaring across the surface. Intercut were shots of the
moon walkers being fitted into their PLSS suits—
portable life-support system.

Christy and Roland were climbing into the bottoms of
their suits, assisted by Gus and Bob. Paul had docked the
John Henry on the top of the *God's Love* and was there
too, helping Micah and Shelly. Glen would continue to
entertain the viewers on Earth with lunar landscapes until
the moon walk began. Because his docking ring was on
the bottom of the *God's Love*, he could not dock the *Jesus
Wept* until the shuttle lifted off again.

Christy wore special underwear wired with sensors to
monitor her physiological signs. It fit tight, embarrassing
her at first, but she was past blushing, relying on Gus to
help her into each piece of the cumbersome suit.

The PLSS suits were based on the original NASA design. Essentially pliable spaceships, they performed all
the same functions except propulsion. Technological advances since the sixties had reduced the weight and bulk
of the packs, which were now only about half the size of
the originals. The forty-pound packs were powered by silver zinc batteries about the size of a Sony Walkman and
they contained a half pound of oxygen in reserve that was

tapped to maintain a nitrogen-oxygen mix at a comfortable level of pressurization. Carbon dioxide and other contaminants were scrubbed by charcoal filters in the pack. Body heat was removed by a network of water-filled, quarter-inch tubes. The water was then forced from the suit where it would freeze and vaporize. The suits also contained biomedical data transmitters connected to sensors in their underwear. Data on oxygen reserve, water temperature, suit pressure, and battery charge level were continually transmitted. They had energy and oxygen for only two hours on the surface—half the Apollo design. An oxygen reserve would provide another fifteen minutes. Unlike the Apollo suits, their suits were fully computerized with a heads-up display triggered by a touch on the sleeve.

The original astronauts underwent years of training for their walks on the moon; Christy had trained only three days. Even with minimal training, she had wanted to go, to be one of the few to step on the moon.

With her torso sealed in the bottom of the suit, she put her hands into the gloves that were secured to the arms of the suit with red metal rings that locked together with a firm twist. Now sealed in the suit from neck to foot, she was hot and sweating. Gus wiped the beads on her forehead with a tissue, then he turned on her backpack, the computer measuring the temperature in the suit and beginning the water circulation to lower the temperature.

When the helmet was placed over her head all sound was shut out and she felt like she was alone in a small cave. The helmet was twisted and locked into place and suddenly a tiny green light glowed to her left. Static startled her and then she heard Gus, who stepped in front of her so she could see his face.

"Turn on the heads-up display."

Holding out her arm and bending at the waist so she could see the controls on her sleeve, she pushed the switch and the display was painted across the bottom of her visor. The suit temperature was seventy-eight degrees but declining. The pressure was within the green range, and the power indicator was reading one hundred percent.

The others were ready, helmets locked into place and suits pressurized. Now Sandy could be heard sending instructions from Earth.

"As soon as I sign off the network will get the audio feed, so if you have anything private to say, say it now."

"Would someone scratch my nose?" Micah said, rubbing the glass of his helmet on Shelly's suit.

"Thanks, Micah," Shelly said. "Now my nose itches."

"Does anyone have anything serious to say?" Sandy asked.

"I do," Gus said. "If you hear any warning tones you hurry to the ship. Any peculiar readings and you head to the ship. If you feel light-headed, back to the ship. If you see any defects, especially bubbles in your suit, back to the ship. If you have a premonition of danger, back to the ship. Is that clear?"

They all answered yes, but their simultaneous transmissions cut the audio in and out, making a cacophony of static and human voices.

"All right," Gus said to Sandy. "We're ready."

"The network gets the audio in five, four, three, two, one."

"Seal the hatch, Gus. Depressurize the hold," Shelly said.

Gus and Bob stepped out of the hold and sealed it. Soon Christy felt the vibration of the pumps as they recaptured the atmosphere. She checked the readings in her suit, noticing the heart rate indicator showed her pulse racing. It embarrassed her since her readings were broadcast back to the New Hope. She was excited, not afraid.

Roland stepped in front of her so their helmets touched and shouted, "Unbelievable!" She smiled and nodded, then he stood next to her facing the cargo doors as the pumps stopped.

Micah walked to the back wall and looked at a row of gauges, each lit with a green light.

"Zero psi, Bob," Micah said.

"Zero psi," Bob repeated.

"Opening the cargo doors," Micah said.

"They are now opening the cargo doors," Wyatt Powder said a few seconds later.

More vibrations and then a spear of light split the back of the compartment. One of two sun screens automatically slid into place on Christy's helmet. Now Christy could see the moon as only a few had seen it—at eye level. She was looking across a plain of gray chalk, pockmarked with thousands of small craters and sprinkled with rocks the size of her fist. It was magnificent desolation.

With the doors open wide, Shelly and Micah pulled a ramp to the edge of the deck, then dropped it, fitting three prongs into slots in the floor. Micah shook the ramp to be sure it was secure. Then Shelly led off, followed by Roland and then Christy with Micah trailing behind and carrying a bundle.

"They are leaving the safety of the ship now, just as the *Apollo 11* astronauts did, but this time our intrepid explorers represent all of America, not just European American males."

A sigh came over Christy's suit speaker but it was impossible to tell whose it was. All of them felt the same way about Wyatt Powder's PC commentary.

The suit was cumbersome but manageable in the light gravity. She used exaggerated motions, stretching out her arms and legs as far as she could, and she moved easily, albeit slowly. She stepped out under a speckled black sky above a colorless landscape. Her heart pounding with excitement, she reached the bottom of the ramp and stepped onto the surface, feeling little through her thick boot. She walked a few steps and looked back seeing her footprints on the moon. The surface was like powdered chalk and compressed an inch under her weight. Then she stepped behind a rock shaped like a football and pressed down hard, lifting her foot carefully to leave a perfect footprint. On an airless body that footprint would last for eons unless obliterated by another walker. The others were tucking samples—souvenirs—away, so she looked quickly, picking three rocks the size of eggs. She dropped them in the pouch on her leg and zipped it closed. Then she unzipped the other leg pouch and removed a small doll, a plastic ID card with her picture on it, and a plastic case containing notes friends had written and her own brief biography. She placed these on the football-shaped rock, arranging them carefully since they would remain in that position forever.

"Let's move to the lander," Shelly said.

Shelly led the way using the kangaroo hopping motion perfected by the Apollo astronauts. Christy hopped after the others, finding it an efficient means of moving in the light gravity. Cameras on the ship followed their moves while Wyatt Powder continued to describe the obvious. They lined up on the back side of what was left of the lunar lander for a photo, then circled the lander giving the front side where Neil Armstrong had stepped onto the surface a wide berth. They would not trample the original footprints.

Shelly posed with the *Apollo 11* American flag in the background, Micah taking her picture. Then one by one and in all combinations they had their picture taken. Wyatt broke in when Roland was posing.

"Roland, as the first African-American man to walk on the moon, what are your thoughts right now standing in front of the flag of the nation that has mistreated your people for so long?"

"I may have thoughts on that later, Wyatt," Roland said, a little out of breath. "But now I'm struck by the significance of this moment. I'm standing on a world other than the one humanity evolved on. We've left the nest and taken our destiny into our own hands. If we can learn to live out here, to survive . . . no not just survive, but to thrive—all of this could be ours." Dramatically, he raised his arms to the stars and turned a full circle.

Now Micah opened the bundle he carried. It contained pieces that fit together making a pole and there was a flag attached to one end. Micah pulled a mallet from a suit pocket and hammered a stake into the surface. Then he slid the flagpole over the stake, the pole now upright.

"As you can see, our explorers are preparing to unfurl a second flag near the original *Apollo 11* flag," Wyatt said. "We want to emphasize for our many international viewers that these flags do not represent any claim to the moon. The moon belongs to all nations."

Christy twisted off the metal bands that held the flag tight to the pole. There was no wind to unfurl the flag, so an arm was attached to the top of the pole at a right angle. Then Micah released clips, and pulled the flag up to the cross arm, displaying the flag. It was the Christian flag— white and purple background with a cross in the top left corner. Powder was shocked into silence, but only briefly.

"My apologies to our many viewers of different faiths. I assure you that we at the network did not know that the Fellowship would use this momentous scientific event to push their religious beliefs."

Suddenly Bob was shouting in Christy's helmet.

"Everyone back inside, Glen is in trouble."

Her helmet exploded with sound as everyone demanded to know what had happened. Bob's voice was back briefly but cut up as two or three tried to speak over him. Shelly passed Christy, hopping furiously toward the ramp. Christy tried to keep up but fell face first into the powdered surface. The slow-motion fall did no damage and she struggled to her feet to find herself next to Roland, who set a manageable pace. Christy matched her rhythm to his and they soon reached the ramp, a confusion of voices urging them to hurry. Halfway up the ramp her stomach fluttered and she grabbed the railing to steady herself. She looked up to see the *John Henry* lifting into the air.

Once in the hold Micah turned off the suit transmitters to clear the frequency. While they secured the ramp, Bob explained what had happened from the flight deck.

"There was a fire on the *Jesus Wept*. Glen was screaming." Bob paused, his voice thick with emotion. "He was putting the fire out when he went down. He's using the respirator, but the temperature in his sphere is climbing."

"Is he still transmitting?" Micah asked.

"Intermittently to save power."

"Is he hurt?" Shelly asked.

"Yes," Bob said grimly.

The pumps droned on, slowly pressurizing the hold, taxing everyone's patience. Suddenly their stomachs fluttered. Christy stepped toward the wall but the *God's Love* lifted midstep and she lost her balance, unable to regain it in the clumsy suit. Roland fell too, crashing into her. Then the ship shot forward, tumbling them across the floor toward the rear bulkhead. She hit the wall with enough force to bruise. Roland tumbled into her, sandwiching her against the wall. The force quickly built to at least twice normal gravity and she could not push Roland off. He felt her struggle and managed to slide sideways, flopping against the wall next to her.

Micah and Shelly were hanging on the rail, watching the gauges. The force lessened to near normal gravity, but still pushed them to the rear. Micah helped Shelly out of her helmet, then she did the same for him. Working together they were able to get out of their suits, letting them tumble to the rear wall where Roland and Christy were pinned. Roland stood, leaning out, reaching for Christy's helmet.

"I'll unlatch you," he said over the speaker.

She waited while he fumbled with the releasing mechanism at her neck. She was working on his helmet when electric motors hummed and the doors opened. Micah and Shelly pulled themselves through while it was only a crack, and were gone without a word. Roland and Christy worked together to get her out of her suit, and then Roland from his. When they were free Roland pulled himself to an intercom and called Shelly. Gus answered.

"What's happening, Gus?" Roland asked.

"We've taken off to find Glen. The *Jesus Wept* has crashed onto the surface somewhere. He was supposed to call in every fifteen minutes but he hasn't."

"Can we help?" Christy asked.

"Pray and stay out of the way," Gus said, then with a click was gone.

Roland pulled himself along the wall and out the hatch. Christy watched the reporter go. The story of the century kept getting bigger and she couldn't blame him for wanting to be a part of it. Christy prayed for Glen and his safe return, then put her coveralls on and gathered the others' clothes. She was struggling up the ladder with her load when the acceleration ended, leaving only the moon's gravity. She hung on the ladder a minute letting her stomach settle, then climbed to the top, dragging the bundle behind.

Micah and Shelly were in the pilot's seats, still in their underwear, and Roland was standing between Bob's and Gus's engineering seats. Roland made room for Christy, and smiled when he saw the coveralls, struggling into them while she steadied him. They tucked the other coveralls under Bob's seat, not wanting to disturb Shelly and Micah.

They were high above the surface, moving fast. The radio was active, Paul checking in regularly from the *John Henry* and Sandy requesting updates from the New Hope. A monitor between Micah and Shelly showed the view from the front of the ship. Wyatt Powder's head was cut into the corner, his mouth moving silently. They were still broadcasting. The whole Earth was watching the drama.

"I see him," Paul's voice crackled over the radio.

Christy's stomach churned again as the ship banked into a new direction.

"I've got my camera on it," Paul said.

Bob twisted a dial and the monitor changed. They were looking down into a crater. It was bigger than most, one rim casting a large crescent-shaped shadow. In the shadow she saw the *Jesus Wept*.

"It's heeled over and up against the crater wall," Paul radioed from the *John Henry*. "You'll never get on it at that angle."

Micah and Shelly exchanged worried looks. Then Shelly said, "Paul, can you nudge it over? Maybe away from the wall?"

"I'll try."

The *John Henry* dropped into the crater, then slowed, creeping up to the fallen sphere. The camera lost the image a few feet from contact, and they had only Paul's voice to tell them what was happening.

"I can't get against it," Paul said.

"Careful," Shelly said. "We don't want to lose you too."

Occasional static was the only sound for the next minutes.

"It's not working. If I only had the manipulator arms."

"Get some altitude, Paul," Micah said.

Paul backed off and they could see the *Jesus Wept* sitting against the crater wall, the hatch angled over and pressed against the rock. Micah leaned down studying the image and then he talked with Shelly. She nodded and then he released his shoulder harness and swung out of his seat. Turning to Roland he said, "We can't dock with the *Jesus Wept* unless we get it away from that crater wall. I'm going outside to see what I can do and I could use some help."

Roland nodded and followed him toward the ladder. Christy trailed after. They went to the hold, unbolting the handrail. She kept out of the way as they freed the rail, which was simply a long length of pipe. Then Micah left, returning with a coil of nylon rope. Then Christy helped them into their suits. They were half dressed when the speaker crackled with a warning.

"Hang on to something down there," Shelly said. "We're decelerating."

With no rail on her side, Christy firmly gripped a rail bracket. The gee-force hit, quickly building to double Earth's gravity. Christy barely held on, her hands clawing for a better grip. Suddenly the force diminished, and she was flung back the other way, jerked violently. Only after she felt the vibration of surface contact did she relax her grip.

Quickly they returned to suiting up. When Christy had latched their helmets, she retreated through the hatch, pushing it closed. She cranked the mechanism to seal the hatch and it turned easily. With the satisfying sound of metal gripping metal it was closed, the indicator switching from red to green. Then the pumps went to work. There was nothing left for her to do so she climbed back to the flight deck whispering a prayer for Glen.

The lunar soil could only have formed on the surface of an airless body. It built up over billions of years of continuous bombardment by large and small meteorites, most of which are so small they would have burned up if they had entered the Earth's atmosphere.

— *THE NEW SOLAR SYSTEM*,
J. KELLY BEATTY, BRIAN O'LEARY
AND ANDREW CHAIKIN (EDS.)

THE MOON

Roland waited nervously behind Micah for the hold to depressurize. It was some minutes before the cargo doors opened and they dragged the ramp into place. Then Micah led them out at a fast shuffle hop. Shelly had the ship nose toward the downed craft so the crew inside could watch. Roland and Micah circled around, Micah carrying the length of pipe and Roland the coil of rope. The pipe made hopping difficult for Micah but Roland made good time with only the rope. He stopped by the *Jesus Wept*, examining the hull—it appeared intact. High above him Paul slowly circled in the *John Henry*—all this broadcast over live TV on Earth.

"See if he's alive," Shelly said over his speaker.

Roland picked up a rock and rapped hard on the wall of the sphere three times. Then he pressed his helmet at the same spot and waited—there was no reply. Three more pounds, then he pressed against the hull again. Then came three faint taps.

"I can hear something," Roland reported.

"Thank God," Shelly said.

Micah dropped the pipe and walked around the *Jesus Wept*.

"It hit pretty hard," Micah said. "It's buried a couple of feet into the surface."

Then taking the rope he scrambled up the wall of the crater, trying to reach the top. When Micah slipped on loose rock, sliding back down the edge, Roland climbed halfway up to meet him and then pushed him until he reached the top of the sphere, where he wedged himself between the crater wall and the sphere.

"Paul, bring your sphere down," Micah called. "We'll try and pull Glen's ship away from the wall."

"Got it," Paul said.

The *John Henry* floated down, stirring dust as it landed. Roland instinctively turned, protecting his eyes, forgetting the faceplate of his helmet. Micah tied one end of the rope to the top of the *Jesus Wept,* then tossed the rope to Roland, who tied the other end to a ring welded near the bottom of the *John Henry.*

"Try it, Paul," Micah said. "Back away nice and easy."

Again, halos of dust appeared, above the craft at first, then when the *John Henry* lifted, below the craft. The *John Henry* hovered just a little higher than the *Jesus Wept* and then moved back, the rope pulled to its full length and then stretched taut. The *Jesus Wept* remained stuck.

"Stop, Paul!" Micah's voice came over the radio. "We don't want to break the rope." Then to Roland, "Let's try and loosen it."

Roland helped Micah pull rocks out from beneath the ship and out of the path they intended to pull it along. When they had removed what they could, Micah retrieved the pipe while Roland pounded on the ship again. There was no reply.

"He's not answering," Roland said grimly.

Roland's oxygen indicator suddenly switched from green to yellow.

"Up here, Roland."

Micah was halfway up the crater, wedging the pipe between the ship and the wall. Roland started up, then paused, noticing Micah had no fulcrum. He selected the largest boulder he could manage and carried it up with him. Together they wedged the rock between the pipe and the crater wall.

"We're ready, Paul," Micah said. "Go slow and be ready to stop if I yell."

"Right," Paul said.

The *John Henry* moved off, tightening the rope. When it was taut Micah and Roland heaved on the pipe. Roland pushed with all his might, his grunts broadcast to the world—the sphere moved, slowly at first, then suddenly the ship was dragged away from the wall.

"Hold it, Paul," Micah shouted. "That's far enough."

The *Jesus Wept* rocked slowly, settling into the dusty surface, clear of the crater wall but still tilted.

"Shelly, can you dock it at that angle?" Micah asked.

"It's too steep. The nose would bury into the ground."

Roland hopped to the pipe, carrying it to where the sphere rested. Micah worked a rock toward the sphere. Wedging the pipe under the craft again, they pushed down on the lever, tilting the craft.

"Hold it, Roland, I'll get something to wedge it with."

As Roland held the pipe, a warning beep sounded in his helmet. His suit had switched to the reserve system— he had fifteen minutes of oxygen left.

Micah pushed a rock under the craft to hold it upright. The sphere was close to vertical but slightly tilted, threatening to roll off the rock. Sweating in their suits, they moved the pipe and its rock fulcrum, lifting the craft again and pushing another rock under. This time the ship remained stable. Even with the light gravity, Roland had to fight his suit for every movement, and he was nearing exhaustion, a yellow light blinking furiously in his visor.

"All right, Shelly," Micah said. "You should be able to dock now."

"Get back inside," Shelly ordered.

"We might need to adjust the angle. We'd better stay," Micah said.

"Bob says you're low on oxygen," Shelly said.

"It will be close, but—"

"Micah, Glen may already be dead. I don't want to lose you too."

Micah hesitated, then motioned to Roland and they hopped back to the *God's Love* and up the ramp. Dropping the ramp out the back, the hatch was secured.

"Hang on," Shelly warned. "We're taking the gravity down to zero."

As the gravity faded, they hurried to the remaining rail. Soon the only force holding them to the floor was the vertical lift. Then Roland's stomach flip-flopped and he was pushed toward the rear wall. Weightlessness returned. Micah pulled himself to the interior bulkhead and studied the gauges. Suddenly Roland's oxygen indicator changed to red, a warning buzzer sounding.

"Micah, I've got a problem here."

"I'm out of oxygen too," Micah said, panting.

Trying to stay calm, Roland listened to Shelly talk with Bob and Gus as they brought the ship over the *Jesus Wept*. His breathing deepened with each gasp. Then Micah released his grip and floated off the floor.

"Micah? Micah, are you all right?"

Roland pulled himself forward, snagging Micah's foot.

"Shelly, Micah has passed out."

Bob replied, "Get his helmet off, there's no oxygen left in his suit."

"What about the pressure?" Roland asked.

"There's enough."

Roland pulled Micah down but couldn't hold him and release his helmet at the same time. After three tries he neared panic. He was panting now and light-headed. He reached for Micah's helmet again but the light began to fade from his eyes—he was suffocating. Now he clawed at his own helmet, reaching behind for the release. Suddenly he was blown back, sailing across the hold, smacking into the back wall. He bounced, drifting toward the middle. Then he saw a bright spear of light—the door was opening. Christy shot through the door, hitting him in the chest. They floated to the corner, Roland barely conscious, hyperventilating, only dimly aware of her legs wrapped around him, riding him like a horse. Then there was a gush of air and the sweet taste of oxygen.

When he opened his eyes Christy was there, looking

concerned. He smiled at her and she smiled back. He tried to sit up.

"Hold still a minute," she said.

"What about Micah?"

"Gus is with him. He's sitting up."

Now Roland relaxed. After a minute Christy released him and helped him out of his suit. Micah was getting out of his, Gus doing most of the work.

"What happened to the moon's gravity?" Roland asked.

Gus answered as he worked with Micah. "They have to be particularly careful with the *Jesus Wept* on the surface. The docking mechanism isn't designed for the potential stress, so Shelly is trying to duplicate zero gravity conditions."

Micah was holding his head now, clearly in agony. Then he looked at Gus.

"Let's get to the docking ring," Micah said.

Gus helped Micah from handhold to handhold toward the door. Christy steadied Roland, who was dizzy. The docking ring was welded into the floor of the lowest deck. Once there, Micah turned on a monitor. Roland was surprised to see the ships weren't docked yet—the sphere approaching at a snail's pace.

"Shouldn't we be hurrying?" Roland asked.

"We don't have an automated docking system," Gus said. "Shelly is flying the ship by hand and if she hits it wrong she could damage the docking mechanism. We'd never get Glen out then."

"Gus, I don't trust the video," Shelly said over the speaker. "Can you see the alignment through the viewer?"

Gus pulled himself to the floor and unscrewed a metal cap exposing an eyepiece. After a minute he said, "Looks good, Shelly. Almost there, almost there . . ."

With a metallic vibration the ships were mated. Quickly Gus cranked the locking mechanism. A green light lit.

"We've got a green, Shelly. Pressurizing."

The pump worked at an agonizing pace, but then the pressure indicator turned green. Gus released the hatch and pulled it open. He dove headfirst down the tunnel, working the hatch on the *Jesus Wept*.

"I've got it," Gus shouted. "I'm opening the hatch."

Gus yelped as smoke billowed out of the tunnel. Micah grabbed Gus's feet and pulled him back out. Gus's face was black with soot and his eyes runny.

Now Roland pulled himself down the tunnel into the black hole that was the sphere. The smoke was still thick, but dissipating, spreading through the *God's Love*. His eyes teared and his throat burned. Holding his breath he felt around the interior, contacting a chair—empty. He pulled himself fully into the sphere. Pressing his face to the floor, he breathed through the fabric of his sleeve. It made a poor filter and his lungs burned. After a racking cough he held his breath again and looked around. The air was cleaner at the bottom and he could see through the gloom. Glen lay on one side of the sphere wearing an oxygen mask. The skin on one side of Gus's face was blistered and black.

Roland wedged his feet under a chair, then lifted Glen. Weightless, the limp form moved slowly at first, then picked up momentum. Roland had to breathe again, sucking in the foul air of the sphere. Coughing uncontrollably, he pushed Glen as high as he could. Suddenly arms appeared, pulling Glen into the *God's Love*. Roland sank to the floor, searching for cleaner air—he continued to cough. Body racked by coughing, he managed to stand and he was grabbed and dragged up the tunnel. The hatch was slammed behind him and sealed. He hung on to the wall clearing his lungs with deep, painful coughs.

"We've got him, Shelly," Gus yelled. "He's alive."

"Thank God," Shelly said. "Hang on, we're taking off."

The ship lifted and they were pressed to the floor. Glen's face mask was removed, revealing the extent of his burns. His right ear was nearly gone, and the burn spread down his neck into his suit. Piece by piece they removed his clothes, finding the burn down his shoulder and onto his back. In places the charred clothes and skin were melded together in one indistinguishable mass. Christy worked tenderly, peeling off the clothes, exposing the wound. A doctor was contacted on Earth and directed the exam over a video link. Christy used a stetho-scope and blood pressure cuff with some expertise. Glen's respiration was shallow, his blood pressure dangerously low. The doctor warned against medicating for pain until he woke, since it would further depress his breathing and blood pressure.

Roland watched from a perch high on the wall, impressed with Christy's tenderness and fortitude. Nothing is as horrifying as third-degree burns. The burns were washed with pads soaked in sterile water but left uncovered since the gauze would only mat into the wound. The doctor ordered intravenous fluids but they needed gravity for that. Roland helped move Glen to the next compartment, then found a monitor showing the *John Henry* closing on the other docking ring. Once again the ships came together at a painfully slow rate. Only when Paul was out of the ship did gravity return.

Under the doctor's direction, Christy established an intravenous line and they hung a bottle of saline solution. There was nothing else to be done then. The others fell to prayer, sometimes praying silently, sometimes out loud. The prayers were for Glen's healing and for his wife and children back on Earth. Praying did nothing for Roland and he knew it couldn't help Glen.

Christy left to change clothes while the others continued praying. When she was gone Micah repeated the medical exam, checking pulse and blood pressure and recording the time and result. Then he pulled a small flashlight from his pocket and checked pupil response. Then he prayed with the others until Christy returned.

Soon Micah left for the bridge, stopping for two pain pills from the medical kit on the way. Roland followed Micah. Bob was at his station and Shelly was talking with Sandy on New Hope station when Micah slid into the seat next to her. Micah buckled in, so Roland gripped the back of Bob's chair expecting something to happen immediately—it didn't. Shelly called Gus to the bridge.

The *God's Love* was leaving orbit early and they needed to update orbital positions and feed these to the computer. Once the relative positions of the moon and

Earth were established they were ready to plot a course
and leave orbit. When Bob asked for the speed to complete the calculations for return to Earth, the pilots were
silent. After Micah and Shelly exchanged glances, Paul
was called to the bridge. Then Shelly turned to Roland.

"Roland, would you go down and check on Glen? We
need a little privacy before we leave orbit."

"I'd be willing to keep anything I heard off the record,"
he offered.

"It will only be a few minutes."

Reluctantly, Roland left, passing Paul on the way out.
He rejoined Christy, who was listening to Wyatt Powder
on a monitor.

"We've momentarily lost the picture from the spacecraft." Then after pressing on his earpiece, "We will return to live coverage of the drama unfolding in orbit
around the moon as soon as possible. To recap, there has
been a fire aboard one of the spheres and the pilot of the
ship has been injured. They were able to locate the damaged craft and after the heroic efforts of two men, one an
African-American, they were able to right the sphere,
making it possible to rejoin the mother ship."

Shelly turned down the sound when Roland came in.

"How is Glen doing?" he asked.

"The burns are severe and there could be infection. We
don't know if he has internal injuries but his abdomen is
swollen and purplish."

"It doesn't sound good," Roland said.

"If we could get him to a hospital they might save him,
but we're a quarter million miles away."

Christy wiped Glen's brow with a wet cloth. The man
was pasty white and sweating.

"They kicked me off the flight deck," Roland said.

"They're trying to save Glen's life and we only get in
the way," she said.

"I'm not so sure Glen's life is their primary concern."

"That's a terrible thing to say," Christy said sharply.
"He's a friend and a member of their congregation."

"I was asked to leave the flight deck when Bob asked
for the speed on the return flight."

"The Fellowship has always been secretive about their ships and their capabilities. You knew they were going to return faster than the flight out to demonstrate their technology."

"So why not let me hear it now? Soon the whole world will know."

Christy didn't respond but her eyes told him she thought he was paranoid.

"Right now they are up there deciding whether Glen will live or die."

"What do you mean?"

"Christy, what if this ship is capable of much more speed than they've let on? What if it can make the return to Earth in half the time—say fifty hours—but they don't want the world to know, so they decide they would rather let Glen die than reveal their secret."

"Keeping that secret isn't worth a man's life."

"What if they could get us back in a quarter of the time? A tenth?"

"Impossible."

"If this ship could travel to the Earth in ten hours would that secret be worth a man's life?"

"They wouldn't risk Glen's life just to keep a secret."

There was no point in arguing with Christy, but Roland felt she had been taken in by the Fellowship, blinded by her feelings for Mark. He would never marry her, Roland was sure of that. To marry someone outside their narrow definition of the faith was to be "unequally yoked." While the foot soldiers might marry with the hopes of redeeming the spouse, Mark Shepherd never could without splintering the Fellowship.

Excusing himself, Roland left for the cargo hold, where he found a flashlight in an emergency kit. While there he fished in Christy's environment suit for her moon samples. She smiled when he handed her the rocks, but he suddenly felt guilty.

"Sorry, it never occurred to me that you might want to be the first to touch them. I left my samples in my suit if you'd like to switch."

"I'm just happy to have been here," Christy said.

"Those will be worth a lot of money back on Earth."

"I would never sell mine, would you?"

"Never."

He had four rocks in his suit, a person in mind for each—Cindi Winslow was one. Now he handed Christy the flashlight.

"I saw Micah check Glen's pupillary response when you were changing."

Christy lifted Glen's eyelids and flashed the light in the comatose man's eyes.

"Both pupils are responding," Christy said.

"What does that mean, Christy?"

"It can mean many things—"

"What does it usually indicate?"

"He's not brain dead."

"He could be saved if we got to Earth in a hurry?"

"Maybe. I'm not a doctor."

He didn't say any more. He hadn't changed her mind about the cult, but he had started her thinking. Once started down that road, Roland was sure she would find her way to his point of view.

> If you plant petunias, but among them grows a
> marigold, we call the unwanted flower a weed.
> Evil can be thought of as the unwanted vegeta-
> tion in our garden. Put the marigold with other
> marigolds and it ceases to be a weed. Similarly,
> no one is evil among their own kind.
>
> — *A HISTORY OF GOOD AND EVIL,*
> ROBERT WINSTON, PH.D.

SAN FRANCISCO, CALIFORNIA

Grayson Goldwyn sat in his usual place at the end of
Crow's table, an unlit cigar clamped in his teeth. Goldwyn was listening to Sylvia Swanson attentively, mindful
of her position of power. Her silver hair hid her face, but
Crow had seen it often enough since joining her in the
House of Representatives. She had mentored him at first,
but he quickly learned to work the system, trading votes,
embracing special interest groups, hobnobbing with lob-
byists. Now his power was out of proportion to his se-
niority and she resented him, even hated him. It didn't
matter. He knew many of her secrets.

Crow turned his attention to the newest member of his
council, Archie Cox. After William Lichter's disappearance, Rachel had recruited another NASA employee. Cox
was shy and retiring, cowed by the presence of so many
powerful personalities. His bald head was beaded with
perspiration, his black-rimmed half glasses perched on
the tip of his nose. Cox's gambling addiction made him
easy prey for Rachel. He was hopelessly in debt to book-
ies, and Rachel now fed him enough of Crow's money to
keep the leg breakers at bay, but not enough to get him
off the hook. Like the congresswoman, there was no way

out for Cox. He was Crow's for as long as Crow had use for him.

Cox was an assistant project manager currently assigned to project HeeChee, which was NASA's attempt to duplicate the technology of the cult—so far with no success. Most of project HeeChee amounted to covert surveillance of the cult. Today Cox had something special to share and he nervously thumbed the corner of a pad of yellow paper, waiting for the meeting to begin.

Crow surveyed the rest of those around the table, noticing that Tobias Stoop studiously avoided Crow's eyes. Before the meeting, Crow had taken him to task for his lack of progress. Stoop had explained that the Fellowship hadn't done any significant construction where there were endangered species and no significant pollutants could be found at any of their U.S. sites. Much to Stoop's disappointment they had found no radioactive waste. Worse, the cult launches had actually reduced the use of chemical rockets that were significant polluters. Stoop was ready to move on to new targets, but Crow still had plans for him.

Bleary-eyed, Meaghan Slater dragged into the meeting late, her hand shaking as she poured a cup of coffee. She and Rachel had spent the evening together. Rachel, however, was as neat and attractive as ever. Plopping into her seat, Slater finger-combed her unkempt short hair while staring into the coffee cup. Slater's organization, the Womyn's Congress, had maintained a nonstop assault on the Fellowship, faxing press releases almost daily about its patriarchical practices. The most recent fax pointed out that despite the diversity of the moon landing crew, the cult was heavily dominated by males, with only a few females in key positions. Lawyers for the Womyn's Congress had filed lawsuits to block the use of federal funds to purchase launch and communications services from the Fellowship. The suits were working their way slowly through the courts, but they had lost the early rounds, running into the constitutional right of freedom of religion. The Womyn's Congress's propaganda barrage had thoroughly discredited the cult with liberals—that was the easy part—but had made few inroads into the broad middle class that continued to be blinded by the glitter of the Fellowship's technological breakthrough.

"Thank you all for coming," Crow said in a soothing voice, developed through years in the funeral business. "I wish I had better news for you but as you all know we have failed in our efforts to end the cult's domination of the artificial gravity technology."

Meaghan Slater looked up with bloodshot eyes, her words coming in short bursts as if speaking made her head throb.

"I disagree," she said. "We've been successful in uncovering the sexual abuse the cult had hidden away. As therapy progresses we are likely to uncover ritual abuse, perhaps even Satan worship as well."

Rachel stirred in her chair behind Crow and he suppressed a smile. Ms. Slater didn't realize how close she was to real Satan worshipers.

"The leaders have been bound over for trial and the evidence is damning," Slater continued. "We can use the sexual abuse to drive a wedge into the cult. With some of the fathers out of the homes their wives might be reached. They've been conditioned to be passive housewives but they have also been taught they have a maternal instinct. We can use that to turn them against their husbands. Some will want to hurt their husbands just as their children have been hurt. These women could be the key to acquiring the cult's technology."

Goldwyn pointed at Ms. Slater with his cold cigar.

"She's right. I'd say we have the cult on the ropes. Once the trial is under way the cult's crimes will be exposed by every media outlet in the world. The mothers of those children will be running scared. You might try offering money to some of them to move away and start a new life—in exchange for certain information."

"I'm ready to offer money," Crow said, "but we have a standing offer of one hundred thousand dollars for information on the whereabouts of Ira Breitling and no one has come forward."

"They still have faith," Congresswoman Swanson said.

"Once Shepherd is convicted they'll fight each other to betray Breitling."

"Perhaps," Crow said.

"What about the moon landing fiasco?" Goldwyn asked. "The death of one of their own people took some of the shine off of their success. I understand they have been grounded by the FAA."

The cigar went back into Goldwyn's mouth as he finished speaking.

Now Archie Cox leaned forward, clearing his throat, waiting to be called on.

"Mr. Cox," Crow said.

"The cult did include FAA and NASA representatives on its investigation team and the cause of the fire has been determined," Cox said tentatively. "They will be flying again soon."

Disappointment spread around the table and Cox let the others grumble before continuing.

"Unfortunately, the accident resulted from an easily correctable design flaw. Wiring under the seats in the sphere was compressed by the weight of the pilot, causing it to rub against the seat frame. Eventually the insulation was rubbed off and it shorted, the spark igniting insulation. The high oxygen content of the sphere meant the fire spread quickly. The sphere filled with toxic fumes; at the same time the propulsion system failed and it crashed into the moon."

"Can't they keep the ships grounded and draw out the investigation?" Goldwyn asked.

"The cult has already rewired two of its spheres using protective conduit. Besides, if we keep them shut down they'll fly out of Mexico."

"I know we've made some progress with the cult, but something has happened that makes acquiring the technology urgent," Crow said. "Mr. Cox, would you please share what you've learned."

Now Cox was the center of attention. Sweat beads coalesced on his bald head, then ran down his forehead.

"As you know, on the trip to the moon the cult placed a satellite in orbit between the Earth and the moon. The satellite was balanced between the gravitational fields of the two bodies, which places it nearer the moon than the Earth. No one had seen the cult satellite before the TV broadcast but as soon as we did we knew it was unusual for a relay satellite. Much too large for one thing and it showed similar design characteristics with the spheres, although it was cylindrical. When we later directed a space telescope to take a closer look it was gone."

Expecting something dramatic, those at the table stared blankly.

"You mean you couldn't find it?" Stoop asked.

Looking over the top of his glasses, Cox said, "We knew right where to look for it. The satellite wasn't there."

"I fail to see the significance," Goldwyn said, his cigar firmly in his teeth. "It probably drifted around to the other side of the moon."

"Not possible," Cox said simply. "There is another piece to this puzzle," he said, beginning to enjoy being the center of attention. "Since the satellite wasn't where they left it, we searched lunar and Earth orbits for it but with no luck. We used radar scans, infrared, space telescopes, every technology at our disposal. We finally had to turn the space telescopes back over to civilian use. Two weeks later we got a call from Professor Shrenk at the University of Arizona. He had been using the Hubble telescope to study Venus and turned up something interesting. One of his photos showed an object in orbit. It appears to be the cult's satellite."

Now the group talked over each other, asking questions. Cox continued.

"If we use the day the *God's Love* arrived at Earth as the earliest day the satellite could have departed, and assume the day Shrenk shot the photos was the day it arrived at Venus—which is unlikely—the satellite journeyed to the second planet in our system in thirty-three days."

Those in the room were surprised but lacked the knowledge to understand the significance. Meaghan Slater was the first to admit her ignorance.

"That's fast, isn't it?" Slater asked.

"The Magellan space probe took fifteen months to reach Venus. The cult's satellite did it in a fifteenth of that time. Put it another way, that satellite traveled at a speed in excess of thirty-three thousand miles per hour."

Goldwyn looked properly impressed, but Meaghan Slater and Congresswoman Swanson only mildly interested. Tobias Stoop yawned. Cox tried to ram home the significance.

"The cult's trip to the moon took four days. The craft orbiting Venus could have traveled from the Earth to the moon in eight hours."

Now all except Stoop were impressed, each seeing the implications from their own perspective. Goldwyn struggled between seeing it as an important story and worry over the expanding power of what his paper was calling "techno-religion." Meaghan Slater was frustrated by the continued success of the cult—patriarchies were an anathema to a feminist. Congresswoman Swanson saw opportunity. The cult's success could be used to convince others they had been victimized. She had built her career on pitting groups against each other—minorities against the majority, poor against rich, secular against sacred.

Still disengaged, Stoop watched dispassionately, irritating Crow. Crow had expected more from the poor-rich-boy but he and his ecoterrorists had made only halfhearted efforts at harassing the cult. The lawsuits they had filed had been quickly dismissed. Their most potent weapon was halting new development by forcing endless environmental impact studies, then using those studies to invoke the Endangered Species Act and force more studies. On average they delayed projects nearly four years and only thirty percent of projects had the financial resources for lengthy court battles. Those that did proceed were then sabotaged. Crow needed all his guns firing and wasn't going to let Stoop's Earth's Avengers sit on the sidelines.

"The cult's technological edge seems to be increasing exponentially," Crow said. "The moon is now only a day trip, Venus a month away. What is their intent? What will they do with this technology?"

Crow let his words hang, the tension build. Stoop checked his watch.

"This cult is different from others in several respects. The most obvious difference is their technological expertise. Given the disdain fundamentalists show for education their scientific innovations are particularly surprising. The second difference is their seeming reluctance to proselytize. Normally cults shear as many sheep as they can lay their hands on. Most distressing to me is that they don't invest in facilities. Most cults build churches which are really monuments to themselves. The Fellowship has the money to build, but they don't. Why?"

"They build in space," Goldwyn corrected.

Crow smiled coldly—his impatience clear.

"Yes, but only the minimum to meet their needs. Where's the monument?"

Goldwyn pointed with his cigar. "So what's your point?"

"Put the three together. They develop technology that allows them to travel into space efficiently and travel through space with great speed. Second, they limit the number of cult members. Third, they don't put money into earth-bound structures." Pausing again for effect, he then said, "What does that suggest to you?"

Congresswoman Swanson was the first to see it.

"They're planning on leaving the Earth," she said.

Now they all gasped, mumbling to their neighbors. Crow noticed Stoop was interested again.

"Move to where?" Slater asked. "Venus? Is that possible?"

Now Cox leaned across the table so all could see him, waiting for Crow to acknowledge him with a nod.

"No, it's not possible to live on Venus. Venus is nearly a twin of Earth but covered with a thick cloud layer that traps ultraviolet radiation, creating a greenhouse effect. The surface temperature is nine hundred degrees Fahrenheit and the atmospheric pressure is eighty-eight times that on Earth. The atmosphere is almost entirely carbon dioxide, and sulphuric acid clouds circle the planet."

"But that's where they sent their satellite," Goldwyn said.

"It may have been only a test," Cox said. "It's more likely they would move into orbit or possibly to the moon."

"The moon doesn't have an atmosphere," Goldwyn pointed out needlessly.

"They would have to live underground," Cox continued. "Oxygen can be cooked out of the lunar surface and with a few nutrients the lunar soil could grow ample food. A space colony makes more sense, however. Their launch vehicles have dropped the price of delivering payloads to orbit to the point where it is feasible to build a sizable space station."

"In orbit they are vulnerable to attack from Earth, and to a lesser degree that would be true on the moon," Crow pointed out. "This cult may be different than any other in some respects but all cults share one characteristic: paranoia. They believe someone is out to get them—the government, secret organizations, the devil—who the enemy is doesn't matter."

Crow paused, amused because in this case all three were out to stop the cult.

"Earth orbit and the moon are too close for a group this paranoid."

"Mars. It's Mars, isn't it?" Stoop asked, his eyes bright with anger.

Now all turned to Cox.

"Mars is only half the size of Earth and has only about a third of the gravity. The Martian day is almost identical to Earth's—twenty-four hours and thirty-seven minutes. The atmosphere is carbon dioxide, and thin—about one-hundredth the pressure of Earth. Even so winds can reach two hundred miles per hour. And it's cold. Temperatures average minus sixty-four degrees Fahrenheit."

"They couldn't live there either," Goldwyn said, cigar tight in his teeth.

"Not easily, but at the equator, at perihelion—when Mars is closest to the sun—the surface temperature can reach eighty degrees. Colonists could not travel without breathing apparatus, but Mars has potential the other planets don't. The atmosphere could be improved and with enough time the planet could be terraformed into something more Earth-like. It would mean warming the poles to melt the ice cape to release the water."

"Not possible," Goldwyn objected.

"Have we seen the limits of their technology?" Cox asked.

Crow watched Stoop out of the corner of his eye. His bright eyes were now flaming, his fists were clenched and his lips tight.

"They would rape that planet just like this one," Stoop said. "They must be stopped."

Crow nodded seriously, repressing a smile. Once again he had all his guns firing.

CHAPTER 52 **INVESTIGATION**

Have nothing to do with the fruitless deeds of
darkness, but rather expose them. For it is
shameful even to mention what the disobedient
do in secret. But everything exposed by the light
becomes visible . . .

—EPHESIANS 5:11–13

PROCTOR'S COMPOUND,
NEAR CALDWELL, IDAHO

P roctor's followers were a scruffy-looking lot. Weathered by farming or construction, their working-class exteriors distinguished them from educated folk. Rough-looking, red-necked from honest work, and committed to Jesus Christ, they felt called by God to defend the faithful against any and all enemies, whether human or supernatural. They trained with light arms every weekend and were as battle-ready as a National Guard unit—many were still active. Proctor drilled them for full-scale warfare, but so far God had limited his army to security detail for Shepherd's Fellowship—Proctor's wolves were guarding Shepherd's sheep.

Shepherd had asked Proctor to "investigate Rosa Quigly," and Proctor put his best people on it. He looked into her personal life—finances, lovers, health issues—and her professional life—former patients, ethical violations. Shepherd needed the kind of dirt that the government was using against him. Unfortunately, there were few in Proctor's army who could move among professionals. Richard Green was one of the few. Clean-shaven, good-looking with short blond hair, blue eyes, and straight white teeth, he cleaned up well and could pass for a professional in the right clothes.

Rich's father had brought him into Proctor's army when he returned from college to work the farm. Only a dissertation away from a doctorate in psychology, Rich answered an altar call and came to know the Lord. At that moment he realized he had been worshiping at the altar of psychology instead of the altar of the Lord. Unwilling to exchange eternal life for a graduate degree, Rich had returned to the family farm. Three months later he joined Proctor's army.

Rich began his research by accessing databases nationwide from the attic of an eighty-year-old farmhouse. Rich also visited people who knew Rosa and her work, pretending to be a potential client. Now Rich was ready to report. Proctor's compound had a small lake and they were sitting on the dock, dangling their feet in the cool water.

"Our Miss Quigly hasn't published much," Rich was saying. "She's made some money on a handbook for helping patients recover repressed memories. The book is widely used by feminist therapists, but experimental psychologists generally dislike it. I talked with a researcher at the University of Washington who called the techniques in her book manipulative and dangerous. Still, judges continue to refer children to her."

"Including Cannon-Tucker," Proctor said.

"Quigly's name appears in numerous articles about the Tiny Tots Daycare case," Rich continued. "Quigly was one of three therapists assigned to the case and the most successful—successful by her definition. The children under her care remembered more bizarre stuff than other children. There were claims that adults urinated on them and forced them to eat feces. Strange thing is that none of their parents ever noticed their children smelled funny when they were picked up from the center."

Proctor shook his head in disbelief.

"Kids won't eat broccoli without a fuss, how'd they get them to eat feces?"

Rich laughed.

"That daycare center didn't have showers or tubs, only toilets and sinks. There was no way to clean the children up before sending them home. Besides, the facility is an open design. The only rooms with full walls are the bathrooms and the storage rooms, which are jammed with junk. People came and went all day long, dropping kids off and picking them up and no one ever saw anything out of the ordinary. Still, the owners were convicted and three employees plea-bargained to get lighter sentences. After it was over even the prosecutor complained Quigly pushed her children too far. All those bizarre memories made the charges less credible."

"Anything else we can use?" Proctor asked.

"The defense charged she was leading the children in therapy with coercive questions. The transcripts show that she would suggest that an adult did something to them, then scold them if they denied it and praise them if they said they remembered. She gradually shaped their memories. The case was nearly thrown out because of her, but the judge permitted the testimony. To satisfy the defense the judge instructed the jury to consider the effect of the leading questions in their deliberations."

"The judge wanted that conviction," Proctor said. "Tucker-Cannon wants hers too."

"I also met with Quigly's father. She's accused him of sexual abuse. Quigly's father is convinced he's the victim, not his daughter, and blames his daughter's therapist, a woman by the name of Liz Timmons. His wife and Rosa's sister support his version of their childhood. They filed a lawsuit against Timmons, but it was thrown out."

Quigly's father might be useful in defense of Mark and Floyd.

"Are they recording the sessions with the Remple children?"

"Yes. Stephen has seen the transcripts and Quigly's not making the same mistakes that she did before."

"You can't get inflection from a transcript," Proctor said. "Can we get a look at the recordings?"

"They will be made available to O'Malley in three weeks. He's prohibited from letting anyone except a court-approved licensed therapist review them."

Proctor swished his feet in the cool water, enjoying the contrast with the August heat on his head. He didn't trust the therapist to turn over the recordings in good condition—the government had a history of mysterious gaps in tapes, disappearing E-mail, and misplaced documents.

"We need to see those records now," Proctor said.

Rich nodded. Like a good soldier he didn't question orders.

"There's minimal security on her building," Rich said. "Getting in is easy but there's over fifty hours of sessions. That's a lot to go through. We better copy them. Is Guy okay for the third man?"

"Yes. Pick two others as lookouts."

"When do you want to go?" Rich asked.

"Immediately?"

"I'll get busy," Rich said.

Proctor swished his feet in the water. Closing his eyes he looked into the pond, seeing through the glare into the depths. A trout hung motionless near the bottom, unaware he was being watched. Miss Quigly was like that trout, Proctor thought. Now he would see if she was as easily caught.

Two nights later, they were ready. Rich drove the van, Proctor in the passenger seat, the others in the back. It was midnight and few cars were on the street. It was the third trip past the clinic, making sure the coast was clear. The Womyn's Counseling Center was an old mansion remodeled into a professional building. Planned Parenthood had an office there, fortunately their clients' abortions were performed down the block at a women's clinic. Security was tight around abortion clinics, but the counseling center had avoided most of the protests. The largest space was leased by two psychologists and Quigly, who practiced with a Master of Social Work degree.

After the third pass they parked around the block, then cut down an alley lined with Dumpsters. One man remained in the van, a second posted himself in the shadows across from Quigly's building. Carrying packs, Proctor and Rich waited across from Quigly's building while Guy forced an entry. The only security was a simple door and window alarm and Guy quickly bypassed it, opening a window and crawling inside. A few minutes later the back door opened a crack.

Proctor led Rich into the back, closing the door behind. They paused, watching the alley, then Proctor checked in with the others.

"Blue?"

"Clear," came Jim's reply from the van.

"Red?"

"Clear," said Nick from the alley.

Guy and Rich clicked on pencil flashlights. Proctor closed his eyes, seeing better than his men. They moved down the hall to the sparsely furnished waiting room. There was a couch, two chairs, and end tables with magazines, coloring books, and crayons. A receptionist's desk faced the front door and a lone filing cabinet stood in a corner. Rich started toward the filing cabinet.

"Leave it," Proctor ordered. "We're looking for something bulkier."

Quigly's office door was locked but Guy opened it with a sliver of plastic slid between the door and the frame. Once inside the office, they spread out looking for storage spaces. There were two small rooms off the office, one housed a mini-kitchen, the other a storeroom with movable shelves that could be stacked tightly to one side. The shelves were packed with videotapes and disks. The recordings were organized by name and date and they found those for the Remple children on disk.

Unpacking two laptop computers they plugged them into a multiple socket extension, the red power lights glowing. They started with the earliest disks and soon the machines were humming. Guy and Rich could feed the machines, so Proctor wandered around Quigly's office. There was a desk pushed in a corner, the top neat with a single unit TV and DVD player in the corner. He hit the power button and eject, but no disk emerged. Pencils and pens littered the center drawer, and file folders filled the right bottom. The top left drawer was locked. Proctor used a knife to force the drawer open. Inside he found a loaded .38-caliber revolver. The gun had no safety and there was no trigger lock. Proctor put the gun back, relocking the drawer. Now he looked around the rest of the office.

The walls were decorated with macramé. In every corner there were stands holding large plants. The centerpiece of the room was a rocking chair, sitting in front of a rug. A large chest sat next to the chair, a camera on a tripod pointed at the rug. Sitting in the rocker, Proctor imagined terrified children, ripped from their families, at the mercy of the woman in the rocker. How vulnerable they would be, desperate to get home, nothing familiar to comfort them, only the strange woman rocking back and forth.

Proctor studied the room, every decoration organic, or organic-looking. Then he spotted the flamingos on the wall, etched onto a mirrored surface, looking like some cheap carnival prize. The flamingos didn't fit. He closed his eyes and the mirrored surface was gone—he could see another camera behind the flamingos. Walking with his eyes closed he went into the kitchenette. A cupboard covered the wall hiding the camera. Opening the doors he found shelves holding mugs, coffee supplies, and boxes of cookies. Tapping on the wall he could hear the hollow it hid. Returning to the other side he opened his eyes so he could see the flamingos. The frame was screwed to the wall but when he pushed up on the glass it slid up and out. Behind it was the camera. It was empty. Replacing the glass, he returned to the kitchen, opening the cabinet next to the first. It held boxes of paper and stacks of yellow pads. He removed the supplies, then pulled out the shelves. Closing his eyes he studied the edges of the cabinet. A thin line ran around the inside, the shelves mounted only to the sides of the cabinet, not the back. Sliding a knife blade into the crack he pried the back out, revealing stacks of disks, some labeled with the Remple name. He picked the earliest dates he could find and carried them to Guy and Rich.

"Copy these instead," he said.

Once the computers were burning copies, Proctor showed them the hidden trove. Then Proctor returned to Quigly's rocker, thinking of the trout hidden deep in his pond, and of dropping a lure, hooking it, and reeling it in.

CHAPTER 53   **EVIDENCE**

> The therapist must ask herself, how far she is
> willing to go to help her client uncover the
> repressed truth? I'm prepared to go
> as far as is necessary.
>
> — *HIDDEN TERRORS: WOMEN IN THERAPY*,
> ROSA QUIGLY,

SAN FRANCISCO, CALIFORNIA

Walter Hanson finished his objection, then waited for Judge Tucker-Cannon to rule. Stephen had Floyd and Mark back in court, the judge ready to hear his arguments for why the testimony of Faith and Daniel should be excluded. After finally receiving access to the recordings, Stephen had been granted a hearing.

"Mr. O'Malley may proceed," the judge said. "The

more of this we get out of the way before the trial the smoother things will go."

Hanson accepted the ruling, his motion perfunctory.

"Thank you, Your Honor," Stephen said. "After finally getting access to the recordings of the therapy I discovered that there are discrepancies between what the transcripts indicate and what actually took place."

Hanson watched Stephen, curious.

"Before I replay the first session, I would like to call Rosa Quigly to the stand to clarify the intent of the sessions she held with the children," Stephen said.

Hanson did not object and Quigly was brought in and sworn. Dressed in a long flowered skirt with a blouse and vest, hair pulled back in a bun, she looked grandmotherly.

"Permission to approach the witness?" Stephen asked, then showed her a labeled DVD case.

"Do you recognize this disk?"

"It's the recording of Daniel Remple's first therapy session."

"If the bailiff would play this, please," Stephen said, handing it over and then returning to the table.

The bailiff put the disk in the player and soon Daniel appeared on the screen, standing in a doorway holding a woman's hand. He wore jeans and a red plaid shirt, his lips tight, his eyes puffy. Floyd let out a little gasp at the sight of his son. The judge silenced him with a sharp rap of her gavel.

"This is Daniel," said the woman holding Daniel's hand.

Daniel's head dropped, his hair hiding most of his freckled face.

"Hello, Daniel," Quigly said off camera. "How old are you?"

"He's five," the woman holding his hand said.

"Come over here, Daniel," Quigly said. "Not too near my rocker, though, I don't want to rock on you."

Daniel stood still, his fingers going into his mouth. He sucked furiously. Minutes went by and the video showed only Daniel sucking his fingers, then the fingers came out. "I want to go home," he said, the fingers going back into his mouth. Two sobs racked his body.

Mark looked at Floyd who wasn't handling it well. Tears were streaming down his face. Then Floyd glared at Quigly, his gaze pure hatred. Quigly ignored the defense table, her eyes fixed on the video.

"Let's talk about that," Quigly said on tape.

The fingers remained in Daniel's mouth and he stayed where he was. More minutes passed before the fingers came out again.

"If I talk to you can I go home?" Daniel said.

"Let's talk about home."

Now Daniel sucked on his fingers furiously. His head tilted up and he looked past the camera. After a minute he stepped forward and paused, his head down. Another minute passed, then he walked slowly toward the camera, head down, fingers in the mouth. When he reached the rug at her feet he plopped down cross-legged, fingers still deep in his mouth.

"I want to go home," he said.

Floyd sobbed with the pain his son's pleas caused.

"My job is to help you go home," the therapist said.

"Huh?"

"That's what I do, I talk with children and when we're all done talking most of them get to go home."

"Today?" Daniel asked hopefully.

"No, not today."

His fingers went back into his mouth and he mumbled, "I hate that place."

"You won't be there long. Soon they'll find a nice family for you to stay with."

"I want to go home."

"You can't go home today, Daniel, because of what happened."

"What happened?"

"You know."

"I do? What?"

Stephen pushed PAUSE with Daniel's confused look on the screen, his questions hanging in the air. Then Stephen turned to Rosa Quigly who looked confident.

"Daniel doesn't seem to think his father or anyone else did anything bad to him," Stephen pointed out.

282 ✠ JAMES F. DAVID

"He is still in denial at this point," Quigly said calmly. "The memories of what was done to him are so terrible his conscious mind can't cope with the pain. Betrayal by the father is the worst pain a child can experience."

"If the memories are repressed, then there is no way to know whether a person has them or not, is there?" Stephen asked.

"There can be symptoms," Quigly said. "Nightmares, bed wetting, shyness, fear of strangers—all can be indicators."

"Most children have nightmares at times, many wet their beds, most are shy around strangers—parents actually encourage that. Isn't it true that virtually all children exhibit these behaviors at some time or another?"

"Sexual abuse is more common than you are willing to admit," Quigly snapped.

"Is it universal?"

Now Quigly leaned back in the witness chair, as if she were supremely confident in her answer.

"We don't yet know the extent of the problem."

"Except for an occasional nightmare, Daniel showed none of those behaviors you listed. In fact, until he was taken from his home, his teachers and neighbors report he was a happy little boy devoted to his father."

"Not all abused children exhibit these symptoms and many identify with the sexual aggressor in an attempt to reduce the emotional pain of the abuse."

Stephen looked at his yellow pad, then asked, "So, any child, whether they show the symptoms or not, may have been sexually abused?"

"Yes."

"Then how can you tell the children who have been abused from those that have not?"

"Through therapy we can uncover the repressed memories."

"A difficult process?"

"Sometimes."

"Daniel has been in therapy for nearly six months."

"His memories were deeply repressed."

"Are you familiar with 'false memory syndrome'?" Stephen asked abruptly.

Now Quigly's eyes flared, but her tone remained even.

"No psychiatric or psychological association recognizes that as a diagnostic category."

"Isn't it true that memories can be implanted into people through hypnosis?"

"I don't use hypnosis."

"Is it true that memories can be implanted through hypnosis?" Stephen repeated.

"Some believe that," Quigly conceded.

"Isn't it true that if a person is under extreme stress their memory can be altered?"

"No, it's . . ."

Rosa Quigly stopped in midsentence, realizing she was about to undercut her own testimony.

"You can't have it both ways, Ms. Quigly. Either memories can be altered under stress or they can't. Which is it?"

"Memories might be suppressed under stress but that doesn't mean they are altered."

"Really? If I suddenly couldn't remember part of my childhood you wouldn't call that an altered memory?"

"It's an incomplete memory."

"If I suddenly remembered that I had been kidnapped by aliens from outer space would that be an alteration?"

"It would be a hallucination."

"Why?"

"Because you were never kidnapped by aliens."

"How do you know?" Stephen asked in a kindly voice. "Would you believe I was kidnapped by aliens if I could produce confirming witnesses?"

"It's a ridiculous question."

"Then there's no harm in answering it."

Rosa's face was flushed, her answer crisp.

"If enough reliable witnesses supported your claim to being abducted by aliens then I would believe it."

"If a little boy told you he wasn't molested by his father or the pastor of his church, and his friends, family, and the child's teacher told you it never happened would you believe that boy?"

Quigly glared but was spared from answering by Hanson's objection.

"Your Honor, Mr. O'Malley is being argumentative. This hearing was called because of some alleged irregularities with the therapy. Mr. O'Malley seems to have forgotten that."

"I agree," the judge said. "What is the point of this?" Tucker-Cannon asked.

"I'll be returning to the recording in just a minute, Your Honor. I have just a few more questions."

The judge looked unhappy but allowed Stephen to continue, warning him to get to the point.

"Daniel showed none of the symptoms of sexual abuse before therapy—"

"He sucked his fingers," she interrupted.

"That wasn't on your list of symptoms," Stephen said. Then holding up a copy of her book, Stephen said, "Finger sucking isn't listed in your handbook."

"It would be included under the general category of 'anxiety behaviors.'"

"Couldn't every habit?"

"Objection," Hanson shouted.

"I'm about to my limit," the judge said.

"I apologize," Stephen said quickly. "Just a couple of more questions."

The judge thought long and hard but finally nodded and Stephen continued.

"Did you know that Stephen didn't start sucking his fingers until after he was taken from his family?"

"I didn't interview the family."

"Don't you practice family therapy?"

"I know the family through Daniel's memories."

"But you believe his memories were altered through trauma. So, how can you trust his memories?"

"His memories weren't altered, they were lost and then recovered."

"Daniel's memories of abuse weren't constructed in therapy?"

"I don't tell the children what to remember, they remember it on their own."

"So you never suggest to a child they must remember something specific?"

"Never."

"Did you suggest memories to the children in the Tiny Tots Daycare case?"

"I never told those children what to remember—I was assertive in the therapy, but the children needed to break through the stress barriers. Besides, I have refined my technique so there is no question that the Remple children are uncovering real memories."

"Wasn't the concern in the Tiny Tots case that the children were coerced into remembering things that never happened?"

"They weren't coerced."

"Hypothetically. If a child was deliberately stressed by a therapist—say the therapist threatened to never let them see their parents again—might the resulting anxiety be so great that the child's memories could be altered in order to reduce the anxiety?"

Now Quigly glared at Stephen, her jaw working back and forth.

"That didn't happen," she said in slow heavy speech.

"Hypothetically, could it happen?"

More teeth grinding, then, "Some believe that."

"But you were careful not to coerce the children, right?"

"Absolutely."

"Thank you, Ms. Quigly. Let's watch the rest of the session."

When all eyes in the court were on-screen, Stephen turned and winked at Mark, but as the therapy proceeded Mark saw nothing to give him hope. The transcripts appeared accurate. When Daniel used the daddy doll to give the little boy doll a horsey ride, Floyd smiled.

The therapy session ended abruptly, Quigly saying, "You can come and play again, Daniel, but right now it's time to leave."

"Can I go home?" he asked.

"Not today."

"But I talked to you," Daniel protested.

"You did very well, but we need to talk some more."

Daniel's eyes swelled with tears again.

"I don't want to go back there."

"It won't be much longer, I promise. We'll get you a family to stay with."

"I want to go home," Daniel pleaded.

"Would you like a cookie to take with you?" Quigly asked, now coming partly into view, then the image disappeared, the screen turning blue.

Hanson was on his feet almost immediately.

"Your Honor, what's the point of all this? If you followed along with your transcript you'll see that it matched word for word what we've been watching."

"I agree, Mr. Hanson," Judge Tucker-Cannon said. "Mr. O'Malley, you appear to have wasted the court's time."

"One last question, please, then I'll make my point," Stephen begged.

The judge nodded reluctantly, and Stephen stood.

"Ms. Quigly, each of your tapes ends with Daniel getting a cookie. Is that how you end your therapy sessions?"

"Yes. The cookies help the children know when it's time to go and it helps them begin to feel good about themselves again."

"Thank you, Ms. Quigly." When she started to leave the stand he said, "Would you wait one more minute."

Stephen opened his briefcase and pulled out another disk, handing it to the bailiff.

"We're not going to watch another therapy session, Mr. O'Malley," Tucker-Cannon said.

"It's not another session, it's the same one."

"I object," Mr. Hanson said.

"If the court doesn't see the relevance of this disk you can hold me in contempt," Stephen said.

"I will," the judge assured him.

Inserting the new disk, the screen showed the same therapy session but shot from a different angle. Daniel was there in profile, just at the edge of the image, Quigly sitting at the other side of the screen in her rocker. In the witness chair Quigly looked shocked, her mouth open, her eyes wide.

"That's a private recording, Your Honor," Quigly shouted frantically.

"What is this, Mr. O'Malley?" the judge asked.

"These recordings were made secretly by Ms. Quigly, Your Honor. They were delivered to me anonymously, probably by someone who works with Ms. Quigly and is concerned about her methods."

Now Hanson, the judge, and Rosa Quigly all exploded at once. Stephen waited while the judge shouted the others down, finally banging her gavel. When the hullaballoo had died down the judge turned back to Stephen.

"Let's put the question of how you came into possession of these tapes aside for a moment. Since we have already seen this session, what is the point of seeing it again?"

"Ms. Quigly testified the first recording we saw was a complete record of her sessions with the children. If you will let me play the end of the session, you will see that the therapy does not end with the cookie."

Judge Tucker-Cannon looked as if she wanted to say no, but then her eyes flicked toward the court camera.

"We will watch only the relevant parts."

"These are private," Quigly protested.

"They will be returned to you," the judge said, then silenced her.

Stephen fast forwarded to the end of the therapy. Daniel was back on the screen, sitting before grandmotherly Quigly, rocking in her chair. The scene unfolded as before.

"You can come and play again, Daniel, but right now it's time to leave."

"Can I go home?" Daniel asked.

"Not today."

"But I talked to you."

"You did very well but we need to talk some more."

"I don't want to go back there."

"It won't be much longer, I promise. We'll get you a family to stay with."

"I want to go home."

"Would you like a cookie to take with you?"

Where the police recording had ended, the conversation continued.

"You can take two if you want," Quigly said.

Daniel took one in each hand.

"Daniel, I know you want to go home and there is a way you can."

"How?"

"You've got to remember the bad things."

"What bad things?" he said.

"The bad things your daddy did to you."

Floyd slammed his fist on the table. This time the judge didn't warn him, engrossed in the playback.

Now Daniel dropped a cookie and his fingers went into his mouth.

"I know they're hard to remember, Daniel, but if you want to go home you have to. You have to remember the bad things your father did to you."

"He spanked me."

"Good, Daniel. But even badder things."

"Like what?"

"Like touching your private places."

"My privacy?"

"Yes, touching your privacy. He touched you there, didn't he?"

"He helps me zip my pants when I go to the bathroom."

"He touches your penis too, doesn't he?"

Daniel shrugged.

"Try to remember him touching you, Daniel, and next time when I ask you about it, you tell me and then maybe you can go home."

Quigly picked up Daniel's cookie and put it in his shirt pocket, then took him off camera, the audio still picking up their voices.

"When you remember your father touching you, then you can go home. Do you understand? Good boy, Daniel."

Stephen stopped the recording with the remote, then sat silently. Rosa Quigly hung her head. Hanson doodled on a legal pad and the judge fumed. The remote camera panned back and forth catching all reactions. Finally, the judge spoke in slow, measured words.

"Ms. Quigly, you perjured yourself here today," the judge said.

Quigly recovered her composure, straightened, and said, "Assertive therapy is the best way to uncover repressed memories. I did what was best for Daniel."

"Virtually every session ends like this, Your Honor," Stephen said. "She coerced Ruth too. Your Honor, the charges against my clients are supported only by the testimony of the children, and that testimony has been tainted if not out and out fabricated."

The camera whirred back to the judge, who was stunned into silence, her show trial coming apart at the seams.

"Mr. Hanson, Mr. O'Malley, I will see you in chambers," the judge said.

"What about us?" Floyd asked.

"You're not free yet, but have faith," Stephen said.

Mark did have faith—in God—not the justice system.

CHAPTER 54   **FREEDOM**

> In my entire career as counselor and mediator,
> I've never yet seen a case where a child has come
> through the conflict unscathed.
>
> — *UNDERSTANDING CONFLICT,*
> CHRISTINE MAITLAND

SAN FRANCISCO, CALIFORNIA

Tearing open the manila envelope, Mark spilled the contents onto the counter. He hadn't seen his personal possessions in six months and he felt like a kid on Christmas morning. His keys were there and he grabbed them first. Keys meant freedom—a car, a home of his own—and keys meant privacy—doors he could lock and unlock at will. He didn't bother to count the money, scribbling his signature on the receipt and stuffing his pockets with the rest of his belongings.

Two guards escorted Mark to the elevator. Remembering his first trip in the elevator Mark kept quiet. The guards never looked at Mark, but just before they reached the main floor one of the guards said, "There's a difference between getting off on a technicality and being found innocent." Mark's heart began pounding and when the elevator stopped Mark hurried out.

Stephen and Floyd were waiting for him and they hugged, laughed, and cried at the same time.

"Now I know how Paul felt," Mark said.

Stephen laughed, but Floyd shook his head solemnly.

"I never would have lasted as long as you did, Mark."

Stephen pulled them both by the arm to the stairs.

"The vultures are waiting out front. We're going to disappoint them."

Stephen led them to a parking garage, cracking the door, peeking inside. "They've staked out the garages too." Stephen pulled out a cellular phone and punched a number.

"We're ready," Stephen said. "Bring the van around."

Stephen kept his eye to the crack in the door until they heard the sound of a van.

"Now, we have to hurry."

Stephen led them through the door, Mark taking up the rear. A paneled van was waiting for them, the doors open. George Proctor was there motioning them to hurry. Mark could see reporters and cameramen running down the parking ramp. Proctor helped him into the van with a shove and then climbed in, slamming the door.

"Let's go, Guy!" Proctor shouted.

The man at the wheel accelerated with a squeal and they were off. Mark and the others sat in the windowless back. Through the front windshield he could see reporters and cameramen jumping out of the path of the accelerating van. Guy slowed as they reached the street, moving through the sea of photographers. Then they were on the street, media vans falling into pursuit. At the second light Guy turned right onto a one-way street, slowing and then accelerating quickly, leaving a space between their van and those following. As he did, two more vans driven by Proctor's men pulled out from the curb on either side, cutting off the media. Guy made the next light, but Proctor's men made sure the media didn't.

"Thanks for getting those recordings," Mark said.

Stephen hummed loudly, saying, "I'm not hearing this. Those tapes arrived anonymously and I want it to remain that way."

"Sorry," Mark said. "George, if you ever find out who got those disks would you thank them for me?"

Proctor smiled, taking his hand.

"I'm sure they don't need to be thanked, they were just doing the Lord's work." Then he turned solemn. "You know the attacks on you won't stop. Satan is behind this. His agents are attacking you on every side and they will do anything to stop you. If you are going to finish the Lord's work you better be about it."

Mark turned to Stephen, who looked as solemn as Proctor.

"Well, Stephen, can we be about the Lord's work?" Mark asked.

Now Stephen broke into a smile.

"Ira says the heavens are open to us."

"Not without my children," Floyd said.

"We pick them up this afternoon," Stephen said solemnly.

Floyd was relieved, smiling in anticipation of the coming reunion, but Mark noticed Stephen wasn't sharing the joy.

"Mark, George is right about your enemies," Stephen said. "They've taken your reputation from you and when they realize you can't be stopped by smearing you, they'll take your life."

"I've had plenty of time to think about this, Stephen," Mark said. "I'll move up to the New Hope."

Stephen looked relieved, but Mark knew removing himself as a target would only intensify attacks on other

members of the Fellowship. His security would come at
the cost of others and he intended to repay them for that
by completing God's plan.

A church parking lot was to be the transfer point for
the children, since the cult did not want the social workers on their property and the social workers did not want
Floyd and Evelyn to have contact with the foster parents.
Evelyn and Floyd waited with arms around each other,
their long agony soon to be over. Ruth arrived first, struggling to get out of her seat belt as soon as she saw her parents. Evelyn rushed forward and opened her door, pulling
her little girl into her arms. Floyd wrapped his arms
around the pair and they rocked together in a big family
hug. Mark and Stephen rejoiced with them.

Ruth was talkative and friendly, happy to be with her
parents again. She asked about her stuffed animals, her
friends, and what they were having for dinner, without
waiting for replies. Then Floyd took her in his arms, tossing her high in the air and then catching her. She giggled
and begged for more. While the family play went on the
social worker watched suspiciously, as if she expected
Floyd to molest Ruth at any time. The social worker was
plump, gray-haired, and overdressed for the warm
weather in a long wool coat. Stephen noticed the social
worker and stepped forward, saying abruptly, "You can
go now." She glared at him but took Ruth's suitcase out of
the trunk and left. Ruth was describing her new clothes
when Daniel arrived.

Floyd put Ruth down, ready to hug his son, but Daniel
sat in the car refusing to look at them. His social worker
got out and came around the car, opening the door. She
was young, wore her hair above her ears, and dressed in
slacks and a blue blouse. She frowned at Floyd and Ruth,
then smiled at Daniel, asking him to get out. Daniel remained in the car, staring straight ahead.

"Daniel?" Evelyn said, stepping forward. "What's
wrong, Daniel?"

When he didn't reply the social worker tried coaxing
him from the car. Again, Stephen intervened. "Stay out of

this," he warned. The social worker backed up, her eyes flashing.

"It's time to go home, Daniel," Floyd said.

"I don't want to go home," Daniel said.

"I'm not mad at you, Daniel," Floyd said. "I know they made you say those things about me and Mark."

Now Daniel turned on his father, spitting out his words.

"You did do those things. You made me have sex with you."

"I never did, Daniel," Floyd protested, his heart broken. "It never happened. I never touched you."

"I remember."

Floyd stepped forward and Daniel cringed in the car.

"If you strike the boy I'll report you to the police," the social worker said.

"No one is going to hurt Daniel," Stephen said. "However, if you say anything that further alienates the boy from his parents, I will bring suit against you personally and against your agency."

The social worker glared defiantly but kept her distance, saying nothing more.

"Let's go home, Daniel," Evelyn said, stepping in front of Floyd. "We can talk about it at home."

Seeing the social worker would not help, Daniel had little choice but to get out of the car, but he walked past his mother and father and climbed into their van, sitting in the backseat.

"How about a hug, Daniel?" his mother asked, leaning into the car.

"No. You let him do those things to me. I hate you and I hate him even more."

Evelyn pulled back, tears running down her face. Mark and Stephen could find no words to comfort the Remples. Their son had been returned to them but without the love he had once had for them. Unaffected by her brother's anger, and happy to be reunited with her parents, Ruth was bubbling over, talking incessantly, but the joy of her return was muted by Daniel's declaration of hate.

> In the end the therapist must not expect any
> gratitude. Uncovering the hidden truth is an
> ugly business, but very necessary. Only clients
> will benefit from exposing hidden abuse, and by
> the close of therapy even they may hate the ther-
> apist for forcing them to face that truth.
>
> — *HIDDEN TERRORS: WOMEN IN THERAPY,*
> ROSA QUIGLY

SAN FRANCISCO, CALIFORNIA

Rosa made sure there were no reporters lurking in the shadows before she parked and entered her office. The debacle on national television had put her in the middle of the media spotlight. She had been interviewed many times before about her analysis of other people, but never had she been the focus of the media—it was a special kind of hell. She had no privacy left; her picture was snapped by camerapersons at every turn, and even through gaps in her shades. Half of her clients canceled their appointments with her the day after the trial. The rest of her clients were scared away when they found her waiting room filled with reporters. Her professional life was in ruins and her privacy gone. Therapy—being a therapist—was who she had been for a decade. Without her work she didn't know who she was. She had to begin again.

She would move to another city; maybe on the East Coast. Tonight she would begin the process, sorting her papers, shifting her few remaining clients to other therapists. Ironically, the controversy had fueled sales of her book and she would have income, at least for a while.

Leaving the lights off, she let herself in and went to her office, locking the door behind her. She closed the blinds before turning the desk lamp on. The light was bright enough to read by, but it didn't have the power to drive the shadows from the corners of the room. Opening a desk drawer she pulled out a stack of patient files to review, starting with the top folder. She was leafing through the pages when she felt a presence. Then a form separated from the shadows—a man. Her heart pounded and she reached for her left desk drawer.

"It's not there," the man said.

Opening it anyway, Rosa ran her hand through the empty drawer.

"I thought you were a liberal," the man said. "What would you be doing with a gun?"

The man pulled Rosa's gun from his pocket, handling it casually, as if it were a tool, not a weapon.

"Get out of here or I'll call the police," Rosa said.

"If you had any faith in the police you wouldn't own the gun."

Rosa reached for her phone, then paused, watching for his reaction. He merely waved her on, pulling up a chair and sitting down.

Finding the line dead Rosa put the phone down and eyed the door, estimating her chances of making a run for it.

"Do you support mass transit?" he asked.

"What? Get out of here."

The man had strange bright blue eyes and in the dim light they seemed to glow.

"I said, do you support mass transit?" he repeated angrily.

"Yes, of course," she stammered, eyes flicking to the door.

"Do you ride mass transit?"

"Whenever I can. What's this about?"

"Don't lie to me. We know you drive a white Lexus to work every day."

The mention of others had Rosa searching the shadows again, but she saw no one. While he rambled on about mass transit she noticed he would close his eyes in a slow blink. At times his eyelids remained closed for ten sec-

onds or more. Hope swelled—she could be through the
door in that amount of time.

"Typical liberal. You vote to spend other people's
money for buses and subways instead of highways, then
raise gas taxes to force other people to ride them, leaving
the highway free for you. You pass gun control laws to
keep honest people from protecting themselves, then
keep one for yourself. By the way, is this gun registered?"

Now he sounded angry and she answered carefully.

"I'm not sure."

"Is it, or isn't it?"

"It's not my gun. A friend loaned it to me. I work a lot
at night and she thought I should have protection."

The man's eyes closed again, this time remaining
closed as he lectured her.

"It's illegal for you to have an unregistered handgun in
the city limits. That's a law people of your ilk created. If
you fire it in self-defense you're guilty of using a firearm in
the city limits. If you hit the person you are firing at you
better hope they are carrying a loaded weapon in their hand
or you're guilty of assault with a deadly weapon. If you
wound the person you will be sued for damages to cover
medical bills, loss of income, and pain and suffering.
You'll be in court for years and even if you win you lose,
because your lawyer will own you."

"Gun crimes are out of control in this country," she
said, baiting him.

With his eyes still closed he said, "Disarming victims
is a poor solution."

She bolted for the door but his hand shot out, grabbing
her arm, his eyes still closed. When she swung at his face
he grabbed her other arm, standing to face her. He was
powerful and she had no hope of breaking free. She
swung her knee at his groin but he was prepared and protected himself by swinging a leg across, absorbing the
blow. Then he turned her, pulling her right arm behind
her back and releasing her left.

"You're not a pacifist, are you?"

Now she screamed until she had no breath left.

"Finished?" he asked.

"Please don't hurt me!" she begged.

"If I was in the revenge business there would be no pain great enough to punish you for what you did to the Remples."

"You're one of them. If you kill me the police will find out. You'll all go to jail."

"I can't let you go on destroying families."

A chemical-soaked cloth was clamped over her mouth. She struggled vainly until she lost consciousness.

CHAPTER 56   **LIGHT IN THE SKY**

Developing a low cost method of delivering a payload to orbit is a difficult technical challenge. Once orbit is achieved, however, propulsion through the vacuum of space presents fewer technical obstacles.

— *ALTERNATE PATHWAYS TO SPACE*,
EDWARD NORTON

SAN FRANCISCO, CALIFORNIA

Crow reclined in his desk chair, feet on his mahogany desk, as comfortable in his funeral home office as he was in his own bed. This office was where he did his best thinking, and where he made the decisions that built his empire. Below him in the Master's temple, the plaster-of-paris deity resided, the avatar for the Master, the source of Crow's power.

Crow crossed his legs, the full weight of his legs now resting on the heel of one shoe. As usual, most of his thinking focused on the Fellowship. Shepherd had beaten the molestation charge but polls showed a third of America still believed he had abused children in his cult. That combined with the general dislike of fundamentalists would keep the heat of negative public opinion on the Fellowship. The Venus satellite was still a worry, but he hoped the Fellowship had been distracted from its technological goals by Shepherd's woes.

Rachel entered, wearing a leather skirt, walking directly to a mahogany cabinet, opening it to reveal an entertainment unit with the latest video technology. Rachel inserted a disk and pushed PLAY. Irritated, Crow rocked forward waiting for an explanation.

"The cult is flying again," Rachel said, settling onto the corner of Crow's massive desk. Her leather skirt was slit up the side, exposing most of her thigh. "They're lifting out of both the California and Mexico compounds." Rachel fast-forwarded through the digitized video and then hit PLAY. "Look at the size of the pieces they are lifting to orbit."

On-screen Crow saw the California compound viewed from the Gilroy Ranch, which was east of the launch facility. The launch pad was obscured by buildings, but rising over the rooftops were two of the lifting spheres. Normally speedy, the spheres crept skyward. When they cleared the building Crow could see they were attached to a large cylinder. The circumference of the cylinder was much larger than the *God's Love,* which was the size of a space shuttle. Clearly different from any of the spaceships the cult had been flying, the cylinder was also different from the modules used to assemble the cult's space station.

"What is it?" Crow asked.

"I don't know, but look at this." Rachel stopped the video, then tuned the tuner to cable news. There on the screen was another cylinder being lifted by two more spheres.

"This is the second cylinder to be launched from Mexico."

"Three of them? They must be building another space station," Crow said.

"I don't think so," Rachel said. "Look here and here," Rachel said, while pointing at the flat wall screen.

Crow could see what looked to be hatchways located in three places along the length of the cylinders.

"The cylinders appear identical. I believe these hatches will match up and the three cylinders will join to form a single ship."

"A new class of spaceship."

"It's the next generation of ships—larger than the *God's Love*. Their innovation rate puts Intel to shame."

Crow studied the ship until it shrank to a dot in the sky.

"It must be the Mars ship. They'll give it some religious name of course."

"Something insipid," Rachel agreed.

"We've got to find a way to stop them," Crow said, desperate but with no idea of what to do.

Now the screen showed only a small glowing light in the Mexican sky. Staring at the dot Crow despaired. With every new technological leap the cult moved another step off the planet. Without a means of following them they would soon be out of his reach. He felt powerless. After a moment Crow said, "Rachel, gather the coven. We're going to worship tonight."

"Do you want to sacrifice a dog?"

"No, something special."

Rachel raised her eyebrows, waiting for direction.

"It's time for a human sacrifice."

Crow had expected a reaction from Rachel, but the resulting smile was so cold even he shivered.

> In Roman mythology, Mars was the god of war.
> March was named for Mars and marked the
> beginning of the military campaign season
> which ended with a festival in October. Today
> we don't limit our conflicts to a single season.
>
> — *UNDERSTANDING CONFLICT,*
> CHRISTINE MAITLAND

NEARING MARS

The Fellowship's deep-space cruiser, *Genesis,* was made up of three parallel cylinders, each capable of supporting the crew if the other two were damaged. The bulbous main drive joined the three cylinders at one end and provided the primary propulsion for the ship. Electrical power and artificial gravity were provided by secondary drives located in each cylinder. Two lifting spheres, the *Rising Savior* and *Lamb of God,* were attached to the *Genesis*, one each to two of the cylinders. Riding piggyback on the third cylinder was the *God's Love*. Attached to the forward ends of the three cylinders was the rectangular-shaped Mars Habitat.

NASA had contracted with the Fellowship to deliver the Mars Habitat to the Martian surface where seven scientists would spend three months. Since there were no seas on Mars, and so no sea level, elevations were measured differently. Mean surface level was the artificial datum used as the standard for elevation. The Mars Habitat would be delivered near the Martian equator, three kilometers above the datum. Positioned between an ancient seabed and a small mountain range, the astronauts could explore diverse Martian features.

Micah settled into the pilot's seat of the primary flight deck and plugged in the earphones. Breaking into the telemetry that was broadcast to Earth when they weren't using the voice frequencies, he contacted his new wife on New Hope.

"New Hope station, this is *Genesis.* Do you read me, New Hope?"

Micah repeated the message several times, then sat back to wait. Mars was 130 million miles from Earth at this time of year, and it took nearly twelve minutes for a radio signal to transmit to Earth. Studying the looming red planet, Micah tried to imagine living on the arid surface with its wispy atmosphere. Except for a few lichen, life from Earth could not live here. Could the planet be terraformed? Possibly, but the result would always be a poor imitation of Earth, with one-third gravity and a thin atmosphere. The Fellowship had no interest in Mars but Earth governments were terrified the Fellowship was going to claim the planet for themselves. The Mars Habitat project was the U.S. government's effort to make its own claim to Mars, so NASA had been surprised when the Fellowship agreed to deliver the habitat.

"*Genesis,* this is New Hope. It's Shelly, Micah. I was at the doctor yesterday and everything looks normal with the pregnancy. No major problems here, although our friends in Congress are keeping the heat on. Stoop filed another suit, this one in the World Court trying to get us to adhere to the International Law of the Sea. Stoop's lawyers are claiming provisions of the treaty can be extrapolated to any undeveloped natural resources— including Mars. Our friends in the U.N. also voted to extend the moon treaty to the rest of the solar system and now claim jurisdiction over Mars. Emissaries from the U.N. delivered a copy of the treaty to Stephen. He tore it up after they left. I miss you, Micah, and I love you. This message will repeat."

The computer automatically repeated the message while it waited for the confirmation signal from the *Genesis.* It was impossible to converse over distances measured in light-minutes, so they had learned to anticipate questions and tightly pack their messages.

"I love you too, Shelly," Micah responded when her

message finished repeating. "We'll achieve orbit within the hour and land the habitat shortly after. Shuttling down the supplies will take another few days. Let Stephen worry about the lawsuits and Floyd manage the properties. I know it's hard for you, but let them pick up some of the load. How's Junior? Is he still climbing out of his crib? How is Daniel doing?"

Impatiently he waited for the message to repeat and then for the reply. Finally, he heard his wife's voice again.

"Stephen's people have filed countersuits and have restraining orders against Stoop's kooks in two states. I finally gave up and put Junior into a bed. He loves it. The Remples are still having a tough time. Daniel ran away again yesterday. The police picked him up hitchhiking to San Francisco. By the way, I've decided the baby's room should be yellow, that way it won't matter if we get a boy or girl. How about Abraham and Judith for names?"

Ira entered, climbing into the copilot's seat, ignoring Micah. Lowering his voice, Micah sent his final message.

"Time to go to work, Shelly. No on Abraham, yes on Judith. Wish I could be there to coach you through the delivery. Bye for now."

Micah wanted to be with Shelly, knowing he was missing a once-in-a-lifetime experience. A baby has only one birth and one first smile, and he wouldn't be there for either.

"Are you working or not, Micah?" Ira groused.

Jerked out of his reverie Micah focused on the task at hand. The complexities of the landing soon absorbed him, his loneliness temporarily forgotten.

> *Mariner 4*'s cameras were trained on the planet
> Mars, and the pictures were radioed back to
> Earth. They revealed something unexpected and
> disappointing: a cratered surface that looked
> more like that of the Moon than that of Earth.
> Of the "canals"—and of life—there was no sign.
>
> — *UNEXPLAINED:*
> *MYSTERIES OF MIND, SPACE AND TIME,*
> PETER BROOKESMITH (ED.)

ORBITING MARS

Having Mark Shepherd and Ira Breitling on board vexed Micah. He revered the leaders of the Fellowship and wanted to please them, so their presence distracted him. Mark kept out of the way during landing operations, but Ira was copiloting the ship and Micah found him difficult to work with. "I wouldn't do it that way," he would mumble, or "That's one way to do it," implying he had a better way.

Despite Ira's constant second-guessing, Micah was successful in directing the landing of the Mars Habitat. The research station was now safely settled on the Martian surface, tucked behind the lee side of a ridge to help protect it from winds that could reach 200 miles per hour. Once the habitat was down, half the astronauts stayed on the surface to anchor their new home while the remainder helped the *Genesis* crew land the supply modules that were maneuvered out of the hatches in zero gravity. It was three full days before the habitat was fully functional and they were able to shuttle down the last of the astronauts. Once the lifting spheres and the *God's Love* were again secured to the *Genesis,* Micah contacted Commander Grady in the habitat.

"We're ready to leave orbit, Craig. Do you have any last-minute needs?"

"Let's see," Craig Grady's voice crackled from the surface. "We've got the hot tub, the pizza oven, the pool table. Nope, it looks like we have everything we need. Just don't forget to come back for us."

"Remember, if you move, please leave a forwarding address. Good luck, Craig."

"Bring me a piece of an asteroid, Micah."

Signing off, Micah turned to look at Mark, who was standing behind the pilot's seats. "Well, Mark, do we proceed?"

Mark looked at Ira.

"The main drive performed as designed on the trip out," Ira said.

Now they both looked at Mark, waiting for the decision.

"Let's go," Mark said.

"Next stop the asteroid belt," Micah said, then punched commands into the computer that would take them deeper into space than any human had ever been.

The distance from the sun to the Earth is designated as one astronautical unit (AU). Mars is 1.5AUs from the sun and the asteroid belt another AU beyond that. The *Genesis* made the voyage to Mars in ninety days. The voyage from Mars to the asteroid belt took only forty days.

Over five thousand asteroids carry numbers or names in the belt, many more drift in an endless orbit, content to carry no human designation. The *Genesis* was now approaching one of the largest asteroids, Vesta, an irregular rock 336 miles long.

With Micah at the controls, the *Genesis* was within a mile of the asteroid, the ship's lights illuminating the oblong rock so cameras could record the encounter. But the crew of the *Genesis* had little interest in the asteroids and made perfunctory studies, gathering samples and taking special care to get high-quality recordings—a network television deal was awaiting their return.

Micah maneuvered the *Genesis* around the asteroid until it shielded them from the Earth. When the cameras had thoroughly scanned the surface the lights were turned off and the *Genesis* pulled back twenty miles from the asteroid. Then the internal gravity was reactivated. Once they could move about comfortably again, Ira, Micah, and Mark gathered on the flight deck. Bob and the rest of the Fellowship crew were crowded in behind. Ira spoke first.

"The flight from Mars was nearly problem free. We had six technical failures, all in minor systems. The engines performed to specs and at only seven percent of capacity. I see no reason we shouldn't proceed with the test."

"Micah, what about the flight systems?" Mark asked.

"Functioning as designed and all backups are in working order," Micah said.

"Life-support systems are operating normally," Mark said. Then turning, "Bob, or anyone else back there, do you have any reason we shouldn't proceed?" A chorus of "No's" followed. "Then let's pray for protection and get under way."

Bob squeezed into the front as they joined hands and the others formed a chain down into the depths of the ship. When they were linked physically they joined in prayer, praising their maker and savior, then praying for guidance and protection. They prayed to be worthy in the sight of God and for success in their mission. Then each turned to their tasks. Ira and Micah settled into the pilot's seats with Bob and Mark into the engineering stations behind.

The next hour was spent running through extensive checklists for every system and every backup. There was an environmental-control subsystem, food-and-water-management subsystems, and a waste-management subsystem in addition to redundant flight systems.

Like the New Hope station, the *Genesis* used a two-gas atmosphere, oxygen and nitrogen, maintained at 14.13 Newtons/sq cm (14.7 lb/sq in). The environmental-control subsystem stored, distributed, purified, and conditioned the ship's atmosphere, while maintaining atmospheric pressure. Each cylinder had its own duct system complete with heat pumps and fans, all connected through the bridges linking the cylinders. To remove carbon dioxide, excess heat, water vapor, and dust, each cylinder was equipped with particle screens, activated charcoal filters, and beds of zeolite (aluminum silicate). Except for the microchip control circuits, the technology had changed little since the 1980s.

Computers monitored all critical components, but Ira preferred to have human eyes in key positions. Once the checklists were complete the navigational computer was calibrated using Earth, Mars, and Polaris as anchors for three axes. There was no communication with the New Hope station.

With everyone secured at their station, the gravity was discontinued, their stomachs fluttering as they quickly reached zero gee. With a last look at the stars, Micah closed the shields over the ports. Accelerating at one gee, Micah took them a safe distance from Vesta before increasing power to the drive and accelerating to two gees. In an endless rotation, Ira demanded reports from all stations despite the all-green indicator board before him, and the lack of warning beeps from the computer. A significant portion of the Fellowship's assets were invested in the *Genesis*. The loss of the ship would impoverish the Fellowship, but the loss of their leaders would be the end of their movement.

"We've just passed point three c," Micah said, his words heard all over the ship.

The satellite they had used to test the capacity of their drive had reached only a tenth the speed of light. Now three times faster than they had ever achieved, they continued to accelerate at two gees. The computer controlled their flight, preprogrammed to achieve speed greater than subatomic particles.

"Point four c," Micah announced, and then, "point five c."

The ship was silent now, the crew monitoring all indicators.

"Point six c," Micah said. Then, "Mark, it's not too late

to stop this. We don't know what will happen as we approach the speed of light. According to the theory of general relativity we shouldn't be able to reach it at all. As we near light speed we should acquire mass. If we compensate by increasing drive we will only acquire more mass. In other words we can never achieve light speed."

"We've been through this, Micah," Mark said. "It's not possible to achieve light speed, but then it isn't possible to defy gravity either. All things are possible in Him, Micah."

"I know. I just wish you and Ira would have waited at Vesta. Point eight c," Micah said. "Acceleration is slowing."

The invisible hand pressing Micah to his seat let up slightly.

"Point nine c."

"Incredible," Mark said.

Now Micah's eyes were glued to the digital display, watching their speed continue to climb, inching toward the speed of light. He expected disaster at any moment.

"Point nine two c," Micah said.

Still they accelerated. Because it was considered impossible to reach the speed of light, little was known about the effect on passengers. Time would slow, relative to Earth, but what other effects? Some believed mass accelerated to light speed would become charged particles—a cosmic wave. Others speculated travel at light speed through the space-time curve would return you to your point of origin at the same moment you reached light speed—you could go nowhere fast.

"Point nine seven c," Micah said.

Their biggest concern with travel at these speeds had been collision with objects. As they accelerated, the energy of collisions increased proportionately, until even a microscopic particle could tear through the *Genesis*. Encountering a small boulder would release energy equivalent to a fusion bomb. Though experiments with the Venus satellite, as well as their own ship, reassured them. As they accelerated, the drive field funneled particles around the path of the ship. With enough speed, nothing could collide with the ship. Unless the object encountered was large, there was little danger of collision.

"Point nine nine c."

Now the crew collectively held their breath. Breaking the sound barrier created shock waves that could tear airplanes apart. They worried there might be unknown parallel phenomena to breaking the speed of light. Watching the display he saw the moment of truth arrive.

"One c," Micah said.

A warning beep from the computer was accompanied by a red warning indicator. Reflexively Micah and Ira checked the displays locating the problem while they continued with the flight plan.

"What is it?" Mark asked.

"We've lost navigational lock," Ira said. "It's not serious. The computer switched to gyroscopic."

Without stellar reference points the computer used internal sensors to measure variations and compute course and speed. It was a temporary solution with much greater potential for error. A few seconds of eternity passed and then the speed indicator was back. Micah gasped. "One point two c," he said.

"Micah, Ira, switch to the external camera," Mark said.

Ira turned on the monitor and switched to the camera mounted in the nose of the command cylinder—the image was black. Thinking the camera was damaged, Micah switched to a camera mounted just forward of the main drive. Now he could see the cylinders making up the ship, but still the sky was black.

"Where are the stars?" Ira asked.

"Maybe we better shut it down, Mark?" Micah said.

"No," Mark said. "We're nearly to the end of the flight."

The next few minutes were tense, the entire crew alternating between scanning their instruments and staring at their monitors, searching for stars. Then the program reached the deceleration phase and the ship was rotated so that the crew would once again be pushed back into their seats. Deceleration began and Mark watched the speed indicator as it crept backward from one point three times the speed of light. When they dropped below light speed the navigation computer came to life at the same time the stars reappeared. Cheers erupted from deep in the ship and relief spread among the flight crew. Ira and Micah remained focused as the computer struggled to identify the bright dots in the blackness. Then the computer signaled success and began computing position. A few seconds later they knew where they were. As if one they turned to the monitor to see a bright dot growing in the middle of the screen, a smaller dot to one side. Ira's hand came up, shaking noticeably. Touching the dot with one finger he said, "Pluto."

"And Charon," Micah added, touching the other dot.

Then they clasped hands and for the first time since meeting Ira, Micah saw the one-eyed man smile.

CHAPTER 59 **RESIDUE**

$$E = mc^2$$

—ALBERT EINSTEIN

ORBITING PLUTO

"**B**ob, can you see it?" Mark asked.

"Stand by. I'm inching forward."

"He should see it," Ira complained, tapping on the monitor.

Mark studied the image broadcast from Bob's lifting sphere as he approached the main drive of the *Genesis*. They were orbiting Pluto, the icy world at the farthest edge of the solar system, but instead of recording images of Pluto, they were inspecting the ship—at Ira's insistence. Ira had spotted something nestled against the bulbous main drive. It was nothing but a shadow to the others.

"I can see it now," Bob said from the *Lamb of God*.

The camera showed a black streak running along the joint between the drive sphere and the three cylinders it was attached to. Closing slowly, Bob extended the grapplers on the sphere and then inched forward until he could touch the black material with a probe. He scratched a line and the substance parted, showing the white paint of the *Genesis*'s hull below.

"It appears powdery," Bob said.

"It looks like soot," Micah said.

"It's granular," Ira corrected. "Collect a sample, Bob."

Bob scribed another couple of lines through the material, then delicately scraped the surface, pushing a sample into a container held in the other grappler.

"I've got some," Bob said. "Is that enough?"

"Yes," Ira said. "Now probe nearer the engine. I want to see the depth."

With great care Bob moved toward the engine and then scraped the material in two or three places.

"It's just a thin coat," Bob said.

"Drop the sample in the lock and then get back in here," Ira ordered.

Bob flew the *Lamb of God* to the cargo bay and dropped the sample inside, then backed out to dock the sphere. Ira hurried into the hold as soon as the pressure equalized, retrieving the container and hurrying off.

With Ira occupied, they set out to film the ninth planet. Bob reboarded the *Lamb of God* and Alex Montgomery took the *Rising Savior*. Micah, Mark, and Wally Martin—the quietist man on the ship—took the *God's Love*. Mark took the copilot's seat with Wally monitoring the engineering station. Micah piloted the ship away from the *Genesis,* rotating around to face the blue ball of ice below. Charon, the only moon and nearly half the size of tiny Pluto, was on the far side.

The spheres led the way down, cameras recording the encounter. Wally monitored the images broadcast from the spheres as well as those from the cameras mounted on the *God's Love.* The spheres would make the close passes while the *God's Love* filmed from a distance, catching the spheres in spectacular shots as they crossed below. Two miles above the surface the crafts entered Pluto's at-

mosphere, a thin mix of methane and neon. Built to negotiate the thick oxygen/nitrogen atmosphere of Earth, the
crafts felt little resistance.

"The surface is ice but it's no skating rink," Bob said
from the *Lamb of God*. "It's as rugged as the moon down
here."

Mark studied the video feed from Bob's sphere. There
were some plains of deep blue ice, but most of the surface
was made up of jagged spears and broken towers of blue
and green crystal jutting into the black sky.

"There's some kind of haze below me," Alex said from
the *Rising Savior*.

Mark saw a green mist in the valley below. "It's probably methane," Mark said.

"I wouldn't think the sun could generate enough heat
to melt that ice at this distance," Micah said.

"I'm dropping down to get a better shot," Bob said.

Alex followed in the *Rising Savior*, keeping his sphere
on a parallel course but staying above, his cameras focused on the *Lamb of God*. Micah brought the *God's Love*
over the two smaller craft, recording the silvery spheres
against the milky blues and greens of the frozen surface.

"There's virtually no gravity here," Micah said. "It
takes only a touch to maneuver."

To Mark, Pluto didn't seem much bigger than the asteroid Vesta, although the tiny planet had an unearthly
beauty no asteroid could ever approach. As they circled
the planet, Charon rose ahead of them, looming much
larger and brighter in the black sky than Earth's moon.
Now spiraling south they cut across Pluto's equator. The
muted blues and greens changed, deepening in hue, the
surface now mottled. Bob in the *Lamb of God* veered to
the right, then called over the speaker.

"Hey, it's red over here. I'm going down to get a better
shot."

Micah rolled the *God's Love* into a bank, although
there was little atmosphere to push against. The banks
and turns of the craft were programmed to mimic that of
travel in an airplane. Now Mark could see the red streak

running along the surface like a rust river, tributaries joining it along its length.

"What causes the red?" Micah asked. "Iron oxides?"

"Seems unlikely in a planet of this type," Mark said.

Mark was as curious as Micah about the distinct red sash wrapping the planet, but neither suggested taking a sample. They weren't explorers, they were missionaries. Someday scientists would come to the planet, the mysteries still here, untouched by the Fellowship.

"I don't believe it!" Alex exclaimed. "You've got to take a look at this."

Micah checked the radar displaying the position of both spheres, then banked the *God's Love*. Mark saw the *Lamb of God* race by below them in the same direction. Soon Bob was shouting too.

"I see it, Alex. It can't be. It's incredible."

Eyes glued to the monitors, they watched for the *Lamb of God*'s cameras to broadcast what the men in the spheres were seeing.

"Get your cameras on it, Alex," Micah said impatiently.

Then it came into view on the monitor. As if carved from a ridge of methane ice, a giant hand was lying flat on the surface.

"Here it comes," Micah said.

Looking up through the front port Mark could see the spheres hovering ahead. Micah tilted the nose of the *God's Love* so they could see the surface feature. The tiny image on the monitor couldn't do justice to the spectacle below them. Lying in the middle of a flat green plain was a blue hand, three of the fingers curled under, the thumb flat against the extended index finger.

"It can't be natural, can it?" Alex asked.

"It's got to be a sign from God," Bob said.

The others babbled excitedly, but Mark kept silent, unsure of what to think.

"*God's Love* to *Genesis*," Mark called. "Ira, are you watching this?"

"I see it, Mark," Ira said.

"What do you make of it?"

"It looks like a hand," Ira said simply.

Ira was holding back.

"I know that, Ira. Is that all you have to say?"

After a long pause Ira added, "It's pointing."

Ira was right. The extended finger was pointing across the plain into the void.

"It's a natural phenomenon, Mark," Micah said.

"What makes you say so?"

"Look closely at it. The fingernails are just a different color of ice."

Micah had them lower now and Mark could see that Micah was right.

"The knuckles look like a broken ridge. I bet there's debris on the other side. I'll bring us around."

Maneuvering the craft to the other side until they could see beneath the knuckles, Mark spotted rubble below in the shadow of the hand. From this angle there was no resemblance to a hand. The features weren't perfect, the edges rough, the detail incomplete. If they had approached the feature from the surface they would have passed by unimpressed.

"Remember the face on Mars?" Micah said. "One of the Mariner satellites photographed it. The tabloids claimed that the photo proved there was life on Mars. In the right light that region does look like a face, but from different angles it's nothing but ridges and boulders."

Micah was persuasive but still Mark was captivated by the hand. Calling Ira again Mark asked, "What do you think, Ira?"

"I think Micah's right. It's just an unusual formation."

Mark agreed and was ready to let it go when Ira chimed in again.

"But just in case, make sure you know which way that finger is pointing."

Ira was waiting when they climbed down from the *God's Love* into the *Genesis*.

"Look at this," he said, holding up a small bottle. "It's the sample Bob scraped from the exterior."

Mark took the bottle and shook the sample. The granular material was flat black and swirled like sand.

"It looks like graphite," Mark said.

"It's that and more. There are a dozen elements in that mix, perhaps more, all in proportion to those found in the universe."

Failing to understand the significance, Mark looked perplexed, Micah just as silent. Red-faced from excitement, Ira dribbled out his discovery.

"What we have here are the building blocks of the universe—only in trace amounts—but if we collected enough of this I think we would find all known elements and perhaps more."

"Is it some kind of residue from overheating," Mark asked. "Something we didn't shield for?"

"No. There was no overheating," Ira insisted.

Mark waited for Ira to explain.

"Remember, it was theoretically impossible to exceed light speed, since as you approach the speed of light you acquire mass," Ira explained. "But we did exceed the speed of light and we didn't acquire mass." Then holding the sample to the light he said, "Instead of adding mass, we created mass. That's what this is. We probably left a trail of it in our wake. The lighter elements would disperse easily—we probably left a hydrogen trail that stretches halfway back to the asteroid belt."

"You're saying we created matter from nothing by traveling faster than light?" Mark asked, incredulous.

"It's the secret of creation," Ira said reverently. "Imagine the beginning, God moving through the void, traveling faster than light, creating matter as He passes."

Now Micah took the sample from Ira, swirling the contents around in the jar.

"So this is the stuff of creation," Micah said. "But this time we are the creators."

> Only the elite travel to space now, the astronaut
> core a handful of highly trained professionals.
> The mark of a permanent presence in space will
> be when ordinary men and women
> leave the planet.
>
> — *ALTERNATE PATHWAYS TO SPACE,*
> EDWARD NORTON

CHICAGO, ILLINOIS

They were dealing drugs in the courtyard again. Huddled in a corner, four teens exchanged money for small plastic bags of crack. They dealt in daylight, knowing there was little danger. The police never came into the projects. The mailman only made half of his rounds and the UPS man was mugged the last two times he tried to deliver.

The drug deal was over and the boys split up, scurrying to dark recesses to get high and dream away the rest of the daylight. Tomorrow they would hunt their own kind again, stealing what little money their neighbors had to buy themselves two hours of oblivion.

Life had aged Selma Jones well beyond her years. The gray in her hair and the bags under her eyes came from a lifetime of worry and grief. Barely forty, nevertheless everyone called her "Grandma." She didn't mind, as long as she was treated with respect. She made sure of that. She was a strong woman and more than one purse snatcher had been run off with a bloody nose or broken teeth.

Now Grandma Jones looked for the brown stain her oldest boy left on the courtyard tile. He died four floors below her when a drug deal went bad. Dealing to a junky short of cash, her boy was murdered when he refused to cut his price—shot dead for forty dollars of crack cocaine. She was past her hate for the boy who killed Sal—it was her son who got his killer hooked in the first place. In the good book God warned that sin can come back and bite you, and people got bit every day here. A dozen years of Sunday school should have taught Sal about sin, but instead he bled to death on the courtyard tile. Witnesses said he died whispering Jesus' name.

Now her granddaughter and two friends skipped into the courtyard. They stretched out two ropes and Jasmine's friends began twirling. Jasmine timed a run into the blur of ropes. Then she was in, her legs pumping up and down in perfect synchrony. Her friends twirled expertly, while Jasmine danced, changing styles, spinning, and mouthing a chant Selma couldn't hear. Jasmine was gifted and if she hadn't been born poor and black she might be training to be an Olympic gymnast instead of jumping ropes m Chicago.

Too young to understand all that was denied to her, Jasmine played and giggled with her friends contentedly, blissfully ignorant of the squalor surrounding her. Like her mother, Francine—Fancy to her friends and family—Jasmine would soon come to understand her position in the world and that knowledge would destroy her self-esteem, so that even if a chance for a better life came to her, she wouldn't have the courage to take it. Selma had seen three generations lost that way.

It wasn't that Jasmine's mother hadn't tried to make a better life for herself. Fancy was one of the few who finished high school but was pregnant at graduation. Selma never knew for sure who Jasmine's father was, but there were two likely possibilities, one now in prison and the other dead from a drive-by shooting. Watching pretty little Jasmine dance among the twirling ropes, Selma despaired. Neither she nor her children had been able to break the cycle of poverty and now Jasmine would be the third generation of the Jones family to live and die in the projects. Already Selma had outlived her boy, and her daughter Fancy was nearly at the end of that same road. There was still hope for Jasmine, but precious little. In this world, nine-year-olds were at the end of childhood. There was a fifty-fifty chance she would be pregnant by age fifteen.

Settling back into her rocker, Grandma picked up her Bible looking for comfort. Deeply religious, she was the backbone of the choir at Christ the King Baptist Church. Not that church had done her children much good. They'd been regulars, she'd seen to that, and earned attendance awards, but still the wickedness of the streets called them and they answered. Why hadn't her prayers for them been answered? What sin was God punishing her for?

Angry at God she set the Bible aside—it wasn't good to delve into God's word when your heart was dark. Turning on the TV she flipped channels until Mark Shepherd's face caught her attention. He was broadcasting from the spaceship *Genesis,* which had picked up the astronauts who had been living on Mars. Selma had little interest in space, her problems were all outside her door and it angered her that the government wasted good money flying off into space. Worse, was the money Reverend Shepherd was spending doing the same thing when there were poor who could use it. Just a drop of the money they spent flying into space would get her and Fancy to the suburbs where there were good jobs and good schools.

Another man came on, the commander of the astronauts who had lived on Mars. Commander Grady talked of life there—living on Mars sounded worse than living in a desert—but Commander Grady was excited and talked of the possibility of building a colony on Mars. Life would be difficult for colonists, like life on the frontier. Everyone living in a colony would have to work together and depend on one another. The more she listened, the more she came to understand how hard such a life would be—hard and busy. If you lived on Mars there wouldn't be pushers and pimps on every corner, no drive-by shootings—no cars. Every minute of the day would be filled with chores just to stay alive. People would work hard, go to bed early, and get up with the dawn. It was the kind of life where people were too exhausted to get into trouble. It was the kind of life that could save Jasmine.

For a brief moment Grandma Jones dreamed Fancy and Jasmine could go to Mars and start a new life, but it was just a dream. Only the best and the brightest were astronauts—only the select few would ever go to Mars to live. Certainly poor black people would never be part of such a project—NASA wasn't a welfare program.

Then Mark Shepherd's face was on the screen. He was asked about a colony on Mars. "The Fellowship would be willing to contract with NASA to transport equipment and people to Mars for a colony," he said. But when asked whether his church would start their own colony he said, "The Light in the Darkness Fellowship has no plans to colonize Mars." Maybe Shepherd's church didn't want to move to Mars, Selma thought, but he had the power to take people there, even poor black people. She knew Shepherd's church was all white, but he claimed to love the baby Jesus. Maybe God would take his heart in His hands and make him see her need—Jasmine's need.

Selma raised her face to heaven and prayed to God to touch Mark Shepherd's heart. As she prayed hope swelled in her, then great joy. Knowing God helps those who help themselves, she set her mind to the problem of getting Shepherd to take them to Mars. He wouldn't take one raggedy black family to Mars and leave them. It would take a community to survive there, believers willing to work hard.

Grandma Jones left her apartment, crossing the hall to her friend Teresa's. Standing in front of the door she steeled herself for what was to come. Teresa would think she had lost her mind—everyone would—but every temple is built one stone at a time. Whispering one last prayer she knocked on the door, still unsure of how to tell her best friend that they were moving to Mars.

> Cloning the IBM personal computer was a simple matter because it was developed through a systematic, step by step process. Reinventing technology discovered through serendipity is a far more difficult matter because the intervening steps are missing.
>
> — *ACCIDENTAL GENIUS*,
> MALCOLM REYNOLDS

SAN FRANCISCO, CALIFORNIA

Kent Thorpe worked with only two assistants, who openly loathed and feared him. He didn't care, deliberately abusing them to keep them emotionally distant. With no natural interpersonal skills, he had been friendless as a child. He had hoped adulthood would be different but the same grating personality that alienated children alienated adults. Only his brilliance gave him a career as a physical chemist and even then he was perpetually lonely, even in a crowded lab.

His was a miserable existence made even worse by the knowledge that his life could have taken another path. He had been loved once. Not an attractive man, he had a bald spot on the crown of his head that had expanded over the years, leaving only a fringe of hair that he let grow over his ears. His head slightly misshapen, his neck nearly nonexistent, but with a fully developed ego, he was unwilling to settle for women at his own attractiveness level. Instead, he spent his evenings drinking and mourning the loss of the one beautiful woman who had loved him—Constance, who had been murdered by an incompetent.

Thorpe's assistants were in the next room, watching

through glass, waiting for him to beckon. He liked their subservience, their fear of him. The assistants were competent, but unremarkable, and in the years they had worked together on the project never once had any of them made a valuable suggestion—at least nothing he would credit to them. In Thorpe's worldview, he had single-handedly reverse-engineered the Fellowship's sphere, rebuilding the electronics from scrap.

Fry arrived with another man. Tall and dark, with a prominent nose, he looked familiar. He was as menacing as Fry but not in a physical way. His was an inner menace, projecting a disquieting aura. Mr. Fry smiled at Thorpe.

"Good morning, Kent," Fry said. "I've brought someone to witness the demonstration."

"Must he be here?" Thorpe asked.

"Yes," Fry said coldly.

The dark man's eyes narrowed, his gaze piercing. Shivers ran down Thorpe's spine.

"Let's start in the sphere," Thorpe said quickly, avoiding the dark man's eyes.

Retrieving a manila envelope from a file drawer, he led his visitors to the sphere and onto a platform so they could peer in. As they climbed the stairs to the platform the dark man lingered below, running his fingers over the nearly obliterated name "Rising Savior," then joined them. Opening the envelope, Thorpe passed them pictures as he spoke.

"This is the mess we started with."

The pictures showed the blackened interior of the sphere.

"The rocket exhaust pierced the porthole of the sphere and incinerated the forward controls. During reentry the heat build-up melted most of the other two control systems. The shock when the sphere hit the water splattered the softened circuit boards all over the interior. Then the whole mess was soaked in salt water for months. Rebuilding the controls from that mess was nearly impossible."

"But you did it," Fry said.

"No one else could have," Thorpe bragged.

"No one except Ira Breitling," the dark man said.

Temper flaring, Thorpe said, "Ira Breitling was a second-rate graduate student who stumbled onto his discovery." Pointing into the sphere he said, "He could never have accomplished this."

Seventy percent rebuilt, the interior had little resemblance to the blackened mess in the photos.

"Very nice," the dark man said, "but does it work?"

Thorpe disliked the dark man.

"Just watch," Thorpe said. "Notice the cabling running from the sphere to the consoles. I've slaved each gauge to my console so I can read them remotely." Leading the way he took them to the console. "As you can see, we are reading current flow through the restored circuits."

"And these circuits control the ship?" Fry asked.

"They regulate power to the antigravity drive built into the base of the sphere."

"You never opened the drive?" the dark man asked.

"No. It appeared to be intact and Mr. Fry and I decided it was best to leave it that way and try to rebuild the control systems. Like Pandora's box, we don't know what's inside and opening it could be unpleasant."

The dark man seemed displeased but let Thorpe continue.

"The circuits control three magnetic fields that are created within the drive. The intense magnetic fields overlap and can be varied in strength. Control of the fields is directly linked to the stick and foot controls inside the sphere."

"Very interesting, Kent, but does it work?" Fry asked impatiently.

Thorpe ignored Fry, enjoying the moment.

"In addition to the magnetic fields, power flows into the drive—what happens there I don't know—but watch this."

Increasing power equally to the three magnetic fields, Thorpe then slowly increased power to the drive. His visitors turned to watch the sphere. Particles began dancing around the room, swirls embracing them, particles pelting them, their skin prickling. Then there was light, bright blinding light that quickly faded. A few seconds later the sphere lifted from the floor, inching up until the cables it trailed became taut.

"You did it, Kent," Fry exclaimed.

"Of course I did it. Now if you'll let me open the drive I'll reverse-engineer it."

"I agree," the dark man said. "Dr. Thorpe has proved himself."

"We're not opening the drive," Fry said firmly.

"It's time, Fry. One working sphere does us no good. The antigravity drive is the prize that will break the cult."

Shaking his head, Fry said, "If we open it, and it's booby-trapped, we don't even have one."

"Leaving it sealed gets us nowhere," the dark man argued.

"How can you say that when Dr. Thorpe here has accomplished so much?"

"But there are limits," Thorpe said softly.

"What limits?" Fry demanded.

"The ship is levitating, but the system power is coming from an external source."

"What are you saying?" Fry said.

"He's saying you'll need a two-hundred-mile-long extension cord to fly that sphere into orbit."

"For now," Thorpe said quickly. "I'll figure it out."

"How long?" Fry demanded.

"I've probed the drive in every way I can, but I need more time," Thorpe said.

"What he's not saying, Fry," the dark man said, "is that he'll never figure it out until he can look inside one of those drives."

Thorpe squirmed under Fry's stare.

"We don't open it until we have a second," Fry said.

"A second?" the dark man prodded.

"Exactly. Thorpe, can this sphere be rigged with enough external power to reach the space station?"

"Yes, with enough time."

"Good. We can reach them—surprise them."

"You're going to hijack another sphere?" the dark man asked.

"I'm more ambitious than that. Sometimes there are two or three spheres docked at their space station and if we time it right we can get a shuttle."

"The public would never put up with piracy," the dark man argued.

"Not in this atmosphere," Fry said. "Somehow we've got to turn the public against them. The country has to want us to take their technology."

"They're child molesters," Thorpe said.

"They beat those charges," the dark man replied.

"They're hypocrites," Thorpe said bitterly. "They claim to be pro-life but the Breitlings didn't hesitate to abort their way out of a jam."

"Ruth Breitling had an abortion?" the dark man asked, surprised.

"She was Ruth Majors then," Thorpe said. "It was the same day of the accident. My girlfriend knew about it and told me."

"Can you use that information?" Fry asked.

"There's still residue from the child molesting charges," the dark man said. "It won't be enough to turn the tide of public opinion, but it's a help."

One of Thorpe's assistants came out of the control room and interrupted, speaking to Fry, his voice low and deferential.

"Mr. Fry, Dr. Thorpe, you might want to see this. It's about the Fellowship."

Following the assistant into the next room they found a monitor tuned to a news channel. A helicopter was providing shots of a submarine sandwiched between several tugboats. Seven of the Fellowship's spheres were spread along the length of the submarine's hull, and two of the shuttle-sized craft were parked at either end. Men were huddled around each sphere and around four more round structures that resembled the base of the spheres. The flash of welding torches could be seen along the length of the hull. A network logo and "Live from Groton, Connecticut" was in the corner of the screen.

"What's going on?" Fry demanded.

"The Fellowship bought a submarine and they're getting ready to lift it into space."

"That's a nuclear sub," Fry said.

"It's a Seawolf," the dark man added. "One was left incomplete when Congress cut off funding for the program. As part of the deal to close down the project, General Dynamics was given the hull of an unfinished sub as scrap."

The mention of Congress was the clue Thorpe needed. The visitor was Congressman Crow. Knowing someone as powerful as Crow was working with Fry boosted his confidence.

"It can't be more than a shell," Fry said. "What would the Fellowship want with it?"

"Submarines aren't much different than spaceships," Thorpe said. "If they can get it into orbit . . ."

"It looks like they're going to try," Fry said. "They could transport an army inside something that big."

Now the men on the hull boarded the shuttles and lifted off. Next the tugs cut loose their lines, backing away from the huge ship that floated rock still, waves washing up its sides and over its bow. Now minutes passed, nothing happening, except the chatter of the newswoman became more frenetic as she tried to pump life into her dying story. Then it happened—the ship began to move—but forward, cutting through the waves as if it was propelling itself.

"It's coming up," Fry said.

Thorpe studied the water line along the hull. The ship was rising, more and more of the hull appearing. Three-quarters of the ship rode below the waterline and as she came out of the water her true size could be seen.

"It gives us some idea of the power of those spheres," Fry said. "She must displace fifteen thousand tons."

With the helicopter paralleling the course of the submarine, they were receiving spectacular images of the great submarine rising from the waves, water cascading down its sides. As the huge bulk of the ship was pulled from the sea, water rushed in to fill the void, creating frothy swirl beneath the ship and spreading out to rock the tugs that were still moving away.

Now the ship was completely free—there were no propellers, the openings for the drive shafts plugged with welded steel caps. Picking up speed, the shell of the warship lifted toward the heavens, the news helicopter capturing the dramatic moment. Slowly falling behind, the helicopter kept its parallel course, trying to match the rate of climb. The submarine continued to outdistance the news copter and the image of the submarine began to shrink. Without another object to give it scale, soon the ship looked like a toy, not the behemoth it was. The image of the Seawolf shrank to a dot. Then it was gone, the ship well on its way to its new life in space.

CHAPTER 62

THE LONGEST JOURNEY

> On old maps of the Earth large regions were desig-
> nated *terra incognita*—unknown lands, beyond
> the frontiers of exploration. Until very recently,
> all of space beyond our planet was *terra incog-
> nita*. During the past two decades of solar sys-
> tem exploration the frontier has been pushed out
> to a distance of about 10 astronomical units
> (AU) from the Sun, beyond which no planets
> have been visited by spacecraft and even the
> largest telescopes can see only dimly. There, in a
> region of perpetual dusk, where the Sun is so
> small it would appear as a starlike point to the
> naked eye, lies still a *terra incognita*.
>
> — *THE NEW SOLAR SYSTEM*,
> J. KELLY BEATTY, BRIAN O'LEARY
> AND ANDREW CHAIKIN (EDS.)

NEW HOPE STATION, EARTH'S ORBIT

The *Genesis* was docked at New Hope station, umbili-
cals connecting the ship to the station at two points. The
shuttle *Rock of Ages* was mated to one of *Genesis*'s cylinders and each of the other two cylinders carried a lifting
sphere. Frozen and dehydrated fruits, meats and vegetables, and staples of every kind filled nearly a third of each
cylinder. Stored water added as much mass, despite the
presence of an efficient recycling system. The remaining
storage was devoted to spare parts—enough to rebuild all
the ship's systems. What little personal space the crew
was allowed was filled with family photos, books and
Bibles, toiletries, and clothes.

Inside the New Hope the crew, their families, and selected members of the Fellowship were gathered for worship. It was silent worship, each person meditating,

opening themselves to God, to see if He would move them to speak. Everyone knew the danger, everyone feared the *Genesis* would never be seen again, but no one spoke aloud of their fears. This was a day to praise God.

Micah Strong commanded the mission with Bob Morton as copilot and Gus Sampson as the first engineer. Ten others rounded out the all male crew, including Paul Swenson, who had been with Micah on the moon, and Floyd Remple, who would be the oldest man on board. All but two left family behind.

The worshipers were spread through two modules and the connecting tunnels. The constant roar of the air-handling equipment made for poor acoustics, and the speaker system was inadequate, so the silent worship style was well suited to the conditions.

Shelly was there with John Jr. and three-month-old Judith slept peacefully, her belly full of mother's milk. Restless, Junior scribbled noisily in a coloring book. Church-trained, he could sit through hour-long services, but today worship was pushing the limits of his ability to be good. Mercifully, Mark finally stood, his back to the hatch of the *Genesis,* and closed the service with a prayer.

"Great God of the universe, maker of all things, creator and sustainer of life, we ask Your protection for our travelers. God, we ask that You bless their journey, and extend Your protection to them during their long separation from the fellowship of believers. Once again we recognize the covenant You have made with us and seek to honor You by fulfilling the mission You have given us. Through our savior Jesus Christ we ask Your blessing on their journey. Amen."

Silence followed, then slowly the voices of the congregation rose as they sought out the crew, shaking hands, saying good-byes. Shelly waited while Micah talked with Junior, telling him to be good, and to take care of his mother.

"Bring me a present?" John Jr. asked.

"There aren't any stores where I'm going," Micah said. Then when Junior's face fell, "But maybe I can find something—it won't be store-bought."

"Okay, Daddy."

Then with a final hug and a kiss, Junior stepped aside for his mother. Holding Judith on her hip Shelly pulled Micah tight, enjoying the warmth of his body one last time. A full minute passed and still she would not release him.

"You've got to let me go sometime, Shelly," he said.

"Please come back, Micah, I couldn't stand to lose you too."

"If it's God's will, I'll be back."

"It is, I know it is. I'll pray every day for your return."

"I know. Now let me hold Judith."

Passing the still sleeping little girl over, Shelly said, "By the time you get back, she won't remember you, but I'll tell her about you every day."

"Wait until she can understand. If you tell her that her daddy is in the heavens she might think I'm God."

"Daddies *are* gods to their little girls."

"Micah, are you working or not?" Ira shouted from the hatch of the *Genesis*.

Micah kissed Judith on the forehead, then passed her back to Shelly.

"It's time to go," Micah said.

Shelly hugged and kissed him one more time, then let him go down the connecting tunnel to the hatch. Pausing, he waved from the door, Shelly and Junior waving back. Then he shook Mark's and Ira's hands and stepped into the hatch and was gone.

Shelly waited by the tunnel, hugging each of the crewmen as they passed, their wives and children gathering with her in the module. Then Floyd passed, carrying five-year-old Ruth, his other arm wrapped around Evelyn. Daniel trailed reluctantly, scowling. The Remples paused by the tunnel, Floyd hugging and kissing Evelyn and then Ruth, who clearly loved her daddy. But when Floyd reached out to Daniel the boy slapped his father's hand away.

"I told you to never touch me again!" Daniel said.

"I just wanted to shake your hand, son. I'll be gone for a long time."

"Good," Daniel said.

No one in the module was shocked by the scene, they all knew about Daniel. In the three years since he had been returned to the Remples he had never returned to the boy he once was. He still believed his father had molested him and spoke openly of it to other children and adults. Hostile to his parents and teachers, Daniel was a behavior problem at home and school. Only eight years old, he had run away six times, each time to his foster home in San Francisco.

Floyd was the last of the crew to enter and he closed and sealed the hatch. Now the crowd moved back into the module, gathering around monitors to watch the *Genesis* depart. Shelly noticed Daniel sat apart from the others, his nose in a book. Daniel had taken to reading, even in worship, losing himself in books, hiding from his family. Daniel's grades in school were abominable and he sought out classmates like himself—disgruntled troublemakers. A natural leader, he led even older boys into trouble.

A spray of particles announced the separation, the great ship drifting away from the station. Then the name "Genesis" came into view and above it Christian and American flags painted on the hull. More of the ship could be seen now—the *Rock of Ages* riding one cylinder. Only one sphere could be seen from this angle, the *Lamb of God*. Then the ship turned, the bulbous drive that joined the three cylinders rotating toward them. Now the ship picked up speed, shrinking to a dot and disappearing into the speckled void.

Shelly remained, staring at the stars, letting Junior wander off to play with friends. Only when Judith woke, fussing to be changed, did she move. Changing the baby on the floor she thought of the wives of the great world explorers who must have shared what she was feeling now. How did they manage to live for years without their husbands? There were so many things she would miss—his listening ear, his help with the children, his warm body in bed. Worst of all was the fear she would never see him again. Columbus had come home, but Magellan had died half a world away. Which had she married?

There were reporters waiting at the Christ's Home compound when they returned and Shelly waited in the stands by the launch pad to hear how Mark would handle them. Ira sat by Shelly. Mark began with a prayer. Few of the reporters bowed their heads. Two whispered to each other through the prayer. Next Mark gave a brief statement.

"Today the Light in the Darkness Fellowship deep-space explorer *Genesis* departed with ten crew members to explore new regions of space. The *Genesis* is capable of sustaining the crew for an extended period of time and we expect this to be our longest mission so far. Micah Strong is commanding the mission and is an experienced pilot who flew the Mars mission as well as to the moon. I will now take questions."

The first hand recognized was a woman.

"Are there no women on this mission, and if not, why not?"

"None of our women pilots wanted to leave their children for the amount of time this mission will take," Mark said.

"Did you give them the option?" the reporter persisted.

"The most experienced people were assigned to the mission."

The woman spoke again but Mark ignored her, pointing at another reporter.

"Which planets will the *Genesis* visit?"

"Our ships are not ground-controlled and the crew of the *Genesis* has wide latitude in deciding what will be explored."

"There has to be a mission plan," the reporter persisted. "Will they visit all nine planets? Six? Only the outer planets?"

"Only the first part of the mission has been planned in detail; for the rest of the mission the crew will make decisions within parameters we've set out."

"What parameters?" two or three reporters shouted, frustrated.

Shelly nudged Ira. They both enjoyed it when the reporters were exasperated with Mark, who never ran out of patience, and never let himself be backed into a corner. Deftly he answered their questions without lying to them.

"Will the *Genesis* visit Jupiter?" another reporter asked, fishing for details.

"I'm not going to discuss mission specifics."

"Why the secrecy?" the reporter persisted.

"Security concerns," Mark said.

Shelly smiled. If the real mission of the *Genesis* were known, members of the Fellowship might be in danger.

Another reporter was acknowledged. This one stood.

"Isn't it true that the *Genesis* is traveling to Mars to begin a colony and that the Fellowship is planning to claim Mars for itself? Isn't it also true that the *Genesis* is actually carrying one hundred colonists who will begin to terraform Mars?"

"No, none of that is true," Mark said.

Mark's simple answer infuriated the reporters and they zeroed in on the Mars colony theory. Having created a story where there hadn't been one, the reporters now circled the wagons, defending their theory against Mark's persistent denials.

"If the *Genesis* isn't going to Mars, then why not tell us where it is going?"

"Those hundred colonists couldn't live on any other planet than Mars, isn't that right?" another asked, lending credence to the colonists idea and the number of them at the same time.

"Humans can't live on Mars or any of the other seven planets," Mark said.

Each statement fueled more speculation.

"Doesn't the *Genesis* have the capacity to carry the necessary environmental equipment for colonists to survive?"

"If there weren't too many," Mark replied truthfully.

"So the *Genesis* could transport colonists and the equipment needed to keep them alive?"

"Yes. If we wanted to."

Now the reporters wrote furiously, creating the story

they weren't getting from Mark. Then Wyatt Powder stepped forward, a cameraman by his side.

"Reverend Shepherd, is it true that before Ira and Ruth Breitling were married they conceived a child and then to protect their reputation aborted the baby?"

Ira stiffened and Shelly instantly knew it was true.

"No comment," Mark said, caught off guard.

"Then we'll ask Mr. Breitling himself."

Walking toward Ira, his cameraman focusing on Ira's face, Wyatt Powder fixed his interview smile. Photographers surrounded Ira, flashes strobing, blinding Shelly. She reached for Ira's hand to comfort him, but he suddenly stood, pushing through the throng, hurrying toward the hangar. Powder shouted after him as he hurried away.

"Afraid of the truth, Mr. Breitling? Don't you consider abortion murder?" Then to his crew Powder said, "Looks like we've finally got them on the run."

CHAPTER 63   **RECONCILIATION**

> Destruction or loss of a fetus before the end of normal term is called an abortion. Abortions can be spontaneous or induced. For some people, induced abortions may have ethical implications.
>
> — *THE NEW WORLD DICTIONARY*

CHRIST'S HOME, CALIFORNIA

The location and mission of the Fellowship's deep-space cruiser *Genesis* was forgotten for a week while the press used the Breitlings as poster children for hypocrisy. Weekend talk shows were filled with pro-choice advocates excoriating the Fellowship and every other pro-life group. The members of the Fellowship kept to their compounds, avoiding the media, keeping their active flight schedule. The abortion battle was left to other pro-lifers who fought to keep from being tarred with the Breitling brush.

Ira and Ruth withdrew from the public view, hiding in their house in Christ's Home. Even Mark was refused entry at the door, always by a red-eyed Ruth—Ira was never seen. The Fellowship was rocked by the revelation and the Breitlings were the talk of the town. Most in the Fellowship were dismayed, some were angered, but only a few left the Fellowship because of disillusionment.

For the first time since moving to Christ's Home, the Breitlings missed Sunday morning worship. Mark led the congregation in prayer for the Breitlings, then preached on forgiveness. The normally jubilant church was abnormally silent and Mark felt his sermon had fallen on deaf ears.

On Monday Ruth stood on her porch explaining to Mark that she and Ira might be leaving the Fellowship.

"God's work isn't done, Ruth," Mark argued, "and there isn't anything that God can't forgive."

No matter what Mark said, it had no impact on Ruth. Mark called Christy that day and she arrived Wednesday afternoon.

Mark waited in the car while Christy knocked on the door. Ruth was slow to answer, her face haggard. Before Christy could speak, Ruth reached out for her.

"Thank God, you've come," Ruth said, pulling her inside and hugging her close. "He might talk to you. I'm so worried about him."

"How are you, Ruth?" Christy asked.

"Ashamed."

"It happened a long time ago, Ruth."

"But I've lied about it every day since."

"Has anyone ever asked you if you've had an abortion? Of course not. You didn't lie to your friends, Ruth."

"God calls us to confess our sins."

"To God, Ruth. You confess your sins to God, not to everyone you meet. Have you asked God to forgive you?"

"Yes."

"Then you are forgiven."

"No, I'm not. God has stopped up my womb."

"Many women can't have children. It's not because of sin."

"The doctors can't find anything wrong with me. I just can't get pregnant, and I'm getting too old," Ruth said.

"Perhaps Ira is the one—"

"It's not me," Ira said, coming from the back bedroom. Ira's eye patch contrasted sharply with his pale skin. Ira had aged a decade in only a few days, his face now gaunt, his clothes hanging loosely. His gait unsteady, he kept his hand on the wall as he entered.

"Ira, you don't look well."

"He won't eat," Ruth said. "It's all I can do to get him to drink."

"I'm fasting," he said.

"He's starving himself to death," Ruth said.

"Ira, you can't fast when you're not well."

"I'm fine—fine in all departments. Ruth can't get pregnant because of what I did. I made her get that abortion. I killed our baby. Ruth didn't want to do it but I insisted. Then God punished me by taking my eye," he said, touching his eye patch. "And he's been punishing us ever since."

"We should have confessed to the Fellowship, Ira. They are our family."

Ruth began to cry. Christy comforted her until Ira walked over and took his wife in his arms, leading her to the couch where she sat, head on his shoulder. Never had Christy seen two people with so little life left in them.

At a loss for words, Christy let them cry together, comforting each other. Christy had counseled Christians who experienced guilt over abortions many times, and the approach she took depended on their beliefs. With some, she could take the tack that a fetus isn't really a baby, but the Breitlings were solidly pro-life. Christy knew that the healing path for the Breitlings was through their beliefs.

"Ira, Ruth, God isn't punishing you, you're punishing yourselves."

Still wrapped in each other's arms, they looked up.

"We deserve to be punished for what we did," Ruth said.

"I deserve to be punished, Ruth. Not you. I'd give my other eye if it could bring our baby back."

"God forgives, only people can't forgive," Christy said. "Not without God's help, and the hardest person to forgive is yourself." Now they were listening. "Jesus went to the cross for our sins to spare us our own cross. If we don't accept God's forgiveness, then we are denying Jesus' sacrifice."

"But God is denying us children," Ruth said.

"Many people can't have children."

"But I was pregnant once, and the doctors say there is nothing wrong with either of us."

"My aunt's children are fifteen years apart," Christy said.

Christy saw Ruth's face soften, she was coming around, but Ira's jaw was set. He wasn't ready to forgive himself.

"Maybe God did take your eye, Ira, but the Deuteronomy passage says 'life for life, eye for eye, tooth for tooth, hand for hand, foot for foot.' If God was punishing you, Ira, wouldn't it be life for life."

Now Ira's good eye brightened, his temper flaring.

"I know the Scripture. God's punishment wasn't just my eye. He gave me a mission—His purpose is my purpose and I will repay Him for the mercy He has shown me."

"Is hiding in this house part of God's plan for your life?"

Ira's good eye suddenly went blank as he considered the paradox he'd argued himself into. He believed part of his punishment for the abortion was to be God's slave, but he couldn't fulfill that mission sitting in his house.

"How can we face our friends? Return to worship?" Ruth asked.

"Some will welcome you with open arms. Some will be angry. Most will be confused. All of this will be worked through eventually."

"It will be hard," Ruth said. "I don't know if I can."

A knock at the door interrupted them and Christy left them on the couch to think about their future. They were forgiving themselves, and now needed to work up the courage to reenter their society. Christy expected to see Mark at the door, but instead of just Mark she opened it to find the porch crowded with women and men all carrying candles. The sun had set and the candle flames flickered all the way down the block. Evelyn stepped forward, passing her candle to Mark.

"I'd like to speak to Ruth and Ira," she said.

"I don't know if they're ready," Christy said.

"Please."

Reluctant, because she feared setting the Breitlings back, she hesitated, but Evelyn was a friend.

The Breitlings stood when Evelyn entered, Ruth supporting Ira.

"Ira, Ruth, we would like to hold a memorial service for the baby you lost."

Ruth's eyes teared and Ira swallowed hard.

"Your baby never had a proper funeral," Evelyn said.

"I prayed for my baby, I did."

"Me too," Ira said.

"Would you join us in the service?" Evelyn asked.

Ira and Ruth looked at each other, relief spreading across their faces. Then Ira smiled a sad smile.

"Thank you, Evelyn."

"Evelyn, don't call it the baby," Ruth said. "If it was a girl I would have named it Melinda, after my mother."

Evelyn's eyes teared, her lip quivered. "All right, Ruth. We'll pray for the soul of Melinda Breitling."

Stepping between the Breitlings, Evelyn slipped her arms around them and walked them to the door. On the porch they gasped at the sea of candle flames filling their yard and street. Then they walked down the steps and were enveloped by the Fellowship. Christy watched from the porch as the procession headed to the church. She wouldn't attend. She was pro-choice and the conservative practice of holding funerals for fetal tissue made her uncomfortable.

She sat in one of the porch rockers, enjoying the evening. It was clear and the stars were thick. She knew some of the bright points of light were planets but she couldn't pick them out. She wondered which of those bright dots the *Genesis* was heading to. Was it really Mars?

Laughter echoed out of the dark from somewhere down the street. Three boys emerged from the shadows to stand under the streetlight. Giggling, they began throwing rocks at the light. A rock ricocheted off the light, but it didn't break. More giggling, then they began throwing again. Then the globe exploded, showering glass into the street, the boys scattering. As they raced past, Christy recognized the boy in the lead—it was Daniel Remple.

The next morning Mark took her to breakfast at the Pig and Pancake, its once bright pink exterior scoured by the winds, leaving only pale pink smears. The interior was as worn as the exterior, every vinyl booth patched, the carpet ragged, the plates chipped. The menu was the same, although the prices had moderated—the media no longer at their mercy. Josephine greeted Christy warmly, then winked at Mark.

"Seems like I've seen you two in here before. She's a pretty lady, Mark, or hadn't you noticed?"

Mark glared and Christy blushed; Josephine rolled her eyes, then showed them to a booth. Josephine wasn't the only member of the Fellowship who liked to hint that she and Mark should get married, and yet Christy knew others—like Ira—who didn't trust anyone who didn't profess to be "born again." Still, she connected with Mark like she had with no other man.

Josephine came and took their orders and while they waited for omelettes Christy asked about the condition of the restaurant.

"Such as it is, the Pig and Pancake is an asset, Mark. I'm surprised the Fellowship doesn't take better care of it."

"We put our resources where they are needed most."

"Like going to Mars?" Christy asked.

"NASA paid for the Mars mission."

"Many people think you're going to colonize Mars."

"Do they?"

Mark's smile wrinkles were showing and she knew he was playing with her.

"Don't be coy," Christy said.

"Coy? Do people still use that word?"

"Educated people do," she said. "Let me put it in a way you can understand. Don't be a jerk!"

"Me?" he said, his smile wrinkles deepening.

The omelettes arrived and they waited until Josephine had the plates down and the coffee cups refilled.

"Mark, why did you buy the Seawolf submarine if not to haul people to Mars?"

"It's big enough to be a space station, Christy. The welding on that hull is superb. The workmanship is better than anything we've produced ourselves."

"But it could be used as a spaceship, right? Everyone knows you've been working on it in orbit. That plus the fact you won't say where the *Genesis* is—well, you can see why people think you might be thinking of colonizing Mars."

"What if we were planning to go to Mars?" he said. "God has given us the means of getting there, not the government. Doesn't that give us the right?"

"Divine right?"

"If God has made it possible for us to do something, what right has the world to stop us?"

"God didn't withhold his love from the gentiles, why would God withhold this technology? Think of what it could mean if people from Earth did colonize Mars. A presence on another world would help us think globally. Nations would fade in importance. Without flags to fight for, peace would be possible. Mars could even act as a safety valve, giving displaced peoples a place to call their own."

"Always reconciling, aren't you?" he said kindly. "You believe every conflict can be resolved because you think there is a cause at the root of every conflict."

"There is always a cause, Mark, a fundamental dispute that can be resolved. Sometimes it's a border dispute, or a food shortage, or disagreement over how to divide up re-sources, but there is always a cause."

"The cause is sin, Christy. We are fallen creatures living in a fallen world. The only reconciliation that matters is with God. If unredeemed people moved to Mars they would form groups, then nations, and then border conflicts would begin all over again. The only peace is through Christ."

"Are you saying there are no conflicts within the Fellowship?"

"We don't always agree."

"But if all of you have accepted Jesus then why is there conflict?"

"Only Jesus was sinless. We're still sinners struggling with our sin nature."

"The world is the same, Mark. I work with people every day struggling with their natures, trying to get along."

Now Mark looked out the window, his serious wrinkles returning, thinking about what she had said. She respected the silence. There was no anger in their words. They disagreed, but the disagreement would strengthen their relationship, because they would learn that they could disagree and still love one another.

Christy poked at her omelette, then slowly buttered a piece of toast. Clearly Mark had thought of establishing a colony, his answers were well thought out and practiced. Knowing they were going to Mars worried her. History was replete with conflicts over new territory. The Europeans had fought over dividing up the new world and judging by the rhetoric in the U.N. there was no less passion today.

"Mark, sometimes by winning you can lose. Claiming Mars for yourselves will infuriate the nations of the world. Congress has passed a resolution asserting that only governments have a right to claim territory. You know the U.N. has made even stronger statements. The Muslim governments are particularly hostile to Christians claiming part of the heavens. Do you want to go to war with the whole world?"

Happy wrinkles returned and Mark looked peaceful.

"I will fight the whole world for His sake if I have to.

I feel like I've been fighting that battle most of my life."
Then he looked serious again. "I understand you have
our best interests at heart, Christy, and in fact, Mars
isn't where we want to draw the line. Would you inter-
cede for us?"

"What could I do?"

"Approach our own government, and the U.N. Propose
a treaty. We'll agree not to place an exclusive claim on
Mars if they agree not to interfere with our right to travel
into space."

"I'll contact Congressman Crow. He's been the main-
stay of the financial support for my reconciliation center.
I'm sure he'll take your proposal to the president."

"Didn't I hear he's running for the Senate?"

"That's the rumor. He's supposed to announce next
month."

Christy finished her meal, satisfied her trip had been a
success. Ira and Ruth were once again part of the Fellowship, and they had agreed to share Mars with the world.
Knowing Mark and his followers could be reasoned with
would go a long way to dispelling the suspicion people
felt for the Fellowship. With those issues resolved, her
mind was left with only one burning question. As if reading her mind he looked up at her and smiled, his eyes
fixed on hers.

"Christy, why aren't you married?"

"I've never been asked," she said evasively.

"Everyone in the Fellowship thinks I should get married. It's not that I don't want to—actually I've thought
about it a lot, especially lately."

Christy suppressed a smile.

"It's just that every time I think we've reached a point
where I can put some energy into a family some new crisis comes along."

"My work interferes with my relationships too. It takes
someone special to understand why you might be called
away at a moment's notice to mediate some crisis."

"I thought you'd understand. Christy, we'll be reaching a crossroads soon—the Fellowship I mean—and

when we're past that point I think . . . well, things will be different."

Now Mark looked uncomfortable and confused, like he didn't think he was making himself clear.

"I understand what you're saying, Mark." He looked relieved so she continued. "My work is satisfying, but recently it hasn't been enough. I guess I want more out of life than I've been getting."

"When the *Genesis* comes back things will be different," Mark said.

His feelings were still veiled, and his time line vague, but Christy could see it was a commitment. Surprisingly, she felt as warm inside as if he had proposed. Now she could only hope that someday the *Genesis* would return from wherever it had gone.

THE
NEW CHRISTIAN AGE

CHAPTER 64   **JOURNEY'S END**

> Because the goal I sought lay far
> In cloud-hid heights, today my soul
> Goes unaccompanied of its own;
> Yet this shall comfort me alone,
> I did not seek a nearer goal.

— THEODOSIA GARRISON

NEW HOPE STATION, EARTH'S ORBIT

Six months after the departure of the *Genesis,* the tabloid press pronounced the ship destroyed. Reasoning that the family men on board could not go six months without communicating with their wives and children, the media concluded the ship would never return. Over the next few months the tabloids ran stories about aliens capturing the *Genesis,* a collision with an asteroid, and that they were secretly building a base on Mars. When Mark Shepherd signed the U.N. Mars treaty in New York, he was peppered with questions about the location of *Genesis*. He answered none. The story in the weeks following was speculation about when the Fellowship would honor the Mars treaty and announce the existence of their colony. Instead, the Fellowship signed a contract to provide transportation for a joint Europe-U.S. project to build the first permanent base on Mars.

Judith took her first steps at eleven months, and said "mama" by her first birthday. Shelly encouraged "daddy" as her second word, but it was "cookie." Each month John

Jr. talked less and less of Micah, although they prayed for
his safe return every night.

On the anniversary of the *Genesis*'s departure they
held a worship service in Christ's Home. The media photographed them filing into the church and ran footage of
the *Genesis* departing on news broadcasts as Wyatt Powder intoned about "loved ones lost in the void."

Genesis was gone eighteen months when its twin, *Exodus,* delivered the Euro-American colony to Mars. With a
dozen huge supply modules stacked on its nose, the fully
loaded *Exodus* had transported enough equipment and
materials to build a self-contained station that could run
for a year. The media gave the fledgling colony big play,
running live broadcasts from the Martian surface—a red
desert—showing what the inhabitants would be up
against as they tried to tame the hostile planet.

Six months later the *Exodus* returned with more cargo,
doubling the number of residents and extending the reserve supplies by another year. By now the colonists had
bored under the surface of Mars, burying their homes to
protect them from the ultraviolet radiation passing nearly
unimpeded through Mars's wispy atmosphere.

As the luster of settling a new world wore off, concerns about the cost of the project began to be heard. The
billions being spent on maintaining a handful of people
on Mars could be better spent on the poor at home, the argument went. Chief defender of the Mars colony was
Senator Crow, who staunchly reproved those whom he
called "shortsighted." The future was in space, he argued
forcefully, successfully blocking efforts to end the project. Only if you listened carefully, did you also hear his
concerns about the monopoly the Fellowship maintained
on the space technology. "After all," he said one Sunday
morning on *Meet the Press*, "can we really trust the lives
of the brave Americans and Europeans living on Mars to
religious fundamentalists?"

Junior's first day of kindergarten came and went without Micah. Shelly cried herself to sleep that night. Two
months later Daniel Remple ran away. He had marijuana

in his pocket when the police picked him up in San José. Stephen got him off with probation.

Unlike the first two anniversaries of the *Genesis* mission, the third was not joyous. Knowing your loved ones could be gone for years didn't prepare the families for the agony of actually living without them. Seeds of doubt sprouted and grew. After the anniversary worship they held an open meeting and there were calls to send the *Exodus* after the *Genesis*. Mark did not send *Exodus*.

Daniel ran away again in June and they didn't find him until August, living with Josh in San Francisco. There was a brief court battle over the boy because Daniel claimed continued abuse. But with his father lost in space, and Mark careful to never be alone with him, his claims could not be supported. Even so, with help from a lawyer hired by Josh, Daniel petitioned to be emancipated from his family. The story created a brief tempest and the press revived the old stories of sexual abuse. Surprisingly, the judge ruled that Daniel was to be returned to his family. There were rumors that George Proctor had visited the judge before his ruling.

A month later Shelly received a call from the New Hope station—a message had been received from the *Genesis*. There were messages for all of the *Genesis*'s crew's families. Micah's message was a short "I love you, Shelly, and miss you. Tell Junior and Judith that Daddy is coming home." Shelly cried long and hard, frightening Junior and Judith into tears themselves. When she could control herself, she explained they were tears of joy. During the month it took the *Genesis* to reach the New Hope, Micah spoke often with Shelly and the children. Junior warmed up quickly, building on memories he still had of Micah playing with him. Judith was nearly mute when speaking over the radio, not knowing what to make of the voice that was supposed to be her daddy.

Communication from the *Genesis* was coded, but Micah's carefully worded messages made it clear the mission was a success. Shelly visited both the Christ's

Home and Mexico sites during that month, finding spirits high and great excitement about what news *Genesis* might bring.

New Hope station could not accommodate the number of people who wanted to be there, so it was limited to families and the leadership. Fearful a broadcast would be intercepted, the thousands of other Fellowship members spread across the country would have to wait impatiently for a representative to bring the news to their churches in person.

Shelly was on New Hope, waiting with Judith and Junior, the children nervous about who this "daddy" might turn out to be. Evelyn was there with Faith, now nine, tall and slender. Daniel stood apart as usual; just hitting puberty he was already taller than his mother and his physique muscular—Evelyn was afraid of him, as were all but the biggest children in the Fellowship. Daniel's face was tanned and weathered from running the streets day and night, and his pale blue eyes glowed from deep sockets. He was a good-looking boy, well on the way to being a handsome man, but the gentle, loving boy he had once been was buried under a mountain of anger and false memories.

Mark and Ira waited by the hatch to the connecting tunnel while the controllers directed the *Genesis* in. Shelly listened to the commands and Micah's clipped replies piped over the loudspeaker. Micah's voice excited her to the point of giggling and then crying.

"Oh, Mom!" Junior said. "Not again."

Judith took her mother's hand, squeezing it tight. Shelly picked her up and hugged her, realizing Micah had missed more than three years of these hugs.

The vibrations of the docking could be felt through the floor and the crowd hushed in anticipation. The few minutes it took to dock and pressurize the tunnel were interminable, but then Mark and Ira cranked the wheel, releasing the hatch, and their men were back. Jim, Steve, and Jason rushed out, hugging their wives and children, exclaiming over how big they had grown. They were the youngest men on the voyage, barely out of their teens

when they left and the three years in space barely showed
in their faces—but time for them had been different. Others followed, adding to the cacophony of laughing and
crying. Then Floyd Remple pushed his way through to
Evelyn, hugging her tight, then swinging her around. He
wore a full beard now, reddish like his hair. If the monkish bare spot on his head had expanded, Shelly couldn't
tell. Kissing Evelyn passionately, he then squatted before
Faith and held open his arms.

"Do you remember your daddy, little girl?"

Faith answered by throwing herself into his arms and
knocking him over. They rolled on the deck, arms
wrapped around each other, laughing with joy. Shelly
looked for Daniel and found he had retreated down a connecting tunnel, glaring malevolently at his father. Bob
Morton, Micah's copilot, and Gus Sampson, the first engineer, appeared, looking for their wives. Then Micah was
there, pushing through the mob, carrying something in
each hand. He barely managed to set his load down before
Shelly pinned him against the wall, kissing him inde-
cently. Then, she broke her embrace, letting him get a look
at the children he hadn't seen in more than three years.

"This can't be Junior, can it?" he said. "And you're not
my little Judith?"

They both nodded dumbly, letting him pull them into
his arms. Shelly studied him as he kissed and hugged his
children, who took the attention of a virtual stranger well.
Had he aged? There were wisps of gray in his hair, but
maybe they were there before. There were creases around
his eyes, but were they new? The only thing she was sure
of was that he was paler and thinner than when he left.
Now she wondered what she must look like to him?
Would he be disappointed? As if in answer he left the
children and hugged her again, kissing her passionately.

"What's this . . . Daddy?" Junior said, stumbling over
the unfamiliar word, and pointing at Micah's two bundles.

"You asked me to bring you a present, didn't you?"

"For me?" Junior said. "Can I open it?"

"This one is for Judith," he said, holding up a cloth-
covered dome.

When Micah sat it on a table, the crowd quieted and all the families gathered to see. Ira and Mark were pushed to the front.

"Just lift the cloth off, Judith," Micah said.

Like opening a birthday present, Judith lifted slowly, peeking underneath.

"Oh, boy, it's just what I wanted," she squealed, lifting the cover to reveal a homemade bird cage, woven out of reeds.

Inside was an orange bird that hopped nervously from perch to perch. As it fluttered back and forth it revealed a black underside to its wings and yellow streaks down its sides. Instead of featherless bird legs, this bird was feathered down to its toes. Most striking of all was its head. Instead of a beak, the bird had lips and a tongue that slithered in and out. Instead of flat eyes, they protruded, looking like halves of a cat's-eye marble.

"What is it?" Mark asked, uncomfortable with the creature's oddities.

"We've been calling it a bird, but that's only for convenience," Micah said. "It eats more like a frog, and its chicks are born alive—no eggs."

"Incredible," Ira said. "There are more, I presume?" he said dumbly.

"A whole planet full."

Cheers reverberated through the small enclosure, painfully loud to the children, who covered their ears. Then Micah felt Junior tug on his arm.

"What about my present?" he asked.

"It's right here," Micah said, lifting the other bundle to the table. This one was square, and again covered with a cloth.

Impatiently, Junior threw the cloth off revealing another cage, this one made of wire. Inside, the floor was covered with wood chips and in one corner was a hollow chunk of wood.

"There's nothing here," Junior said, disappointed.

"He's just shy," Micah said. Reaching into his pocket he took out something that looked like small seed pods. Holding the pod through the bars, he pursed his lips and sucked air, making a squeaking sound. The piece of wood rocked briefly, then an animal ran out, skittering up the side of the cage to take the pod in its mouth. It then retreated to the top of the wood to eat.

It was the size of a mouse and milky white in color. It had a long furry tail that forked on the end, ending in two puffs of dark fur. It had round ears that stood erect, listening, rotating nearly 360 degrees. Its nose was black and its eyes the same protruding marble shape as the bird's. It had two even rows of flat teeth, bright white. Its two back legs were larger than the front, and there was a noticeable pouch on its stomach. Most striking were its front legs that functioned as arms when it sat on its haunches to eat. The arms forked, giving it two paws on each arm. Again the children squealed with delight, but the adults stared in uncomfortable silence.

"It has four paws," Ira said. "What on Earth for?"

"Not on Earth, Ira," Micah said. "It's a common feature on his world. Instead of a prehensile thumb, many of the animals have two paws on each arm. It gives them incredible grip and they are very agile, especially the tree dwellers."

"I must study it," Ira said.

"This one is Junior's," Micah said. "But we've got specimens for you too, Ira."

"The planet," Mark said, taking Micah by the shoulder. "People can live there?"

Now the cabin was silent, even the children sensing the importance of the question.

"We did for six months," Micah said.

Shelly wanted Micah alone, but those waiting at the Christ's Home compound deserved to hear the news. The hangar was packed with members—most of Christ's Home was there. Two large wall screens were set up in front.

The crew and their families had reserved seats in front with Ira and Mark, and the standing room only crowd applauded as they came in, waving and thanking God for their safe return. Then they took their seats while Mark led them in a prayer of thanksgiving. Instead of "Amens" the prayer's end was greeted with loud cheering. When Mark had them quieted again he turned the meeting over to Micah.

"As you all know by now, we found what we were looking for."

Cheering erupted again. When Micah held up his hands to quiet the crowd they cheered louder. Finally, Mark and Ira had to stand to quiet them.

"The planet is like Earth in many ways. It has oceans and lakes, it has blue sky and mountains. There are forests and plains, deserts and tundra. Animals roam its forests, swim in its seas, and fly across its sky. There are trees for lumber, meadows of grass for pasture, and fruit hanging from trees. We breathed that air for six months, fed the grass to our goats, ate the fruit, and lived to tell about it. Although," Micah said, rubbing his stomach, "I wouldn't recommend eating the things that look like purple grapes."

Laughter and cheering erupted at the same time. Except Shelly, who now understood the risk they had taken and why Micah was pale and thin.

"It's a good world, friends, but it's not the Earth. The equatorial region is too hot for humans, but there are habitable regions in both the northern and southern hemispheres. Most of the seeds we planted sprouted and grew, but not all, and there are insects to deal with like nothing on Earth. The day is more than twenty-seven hours long, and the gravity is a bit stronger than Earth's. You need to remember that it's a planet of unknowns. We saw only a small percentage of the animal life. There will be predators to deal with and beasts in the oceans we can only imagine. Worst of all will be dealing with disease and infection. Except for an intestinal bug, we caught only colds, but there will be more terrible diseases. It's not the Garden of Eden, friends."

"Can our children pray in school there?" someone asked.

"Can we put up nativity scenes in the town square on this planet?" asked another.

"Will there be drug pushers selling poison to our children?"

The shouting continued, every member voicing their frustrations with being Christian in a secular nation. When all had been vented, they quieted, letting Micah speak.

"There will be nothing on this world except what we bring to it," he said.

"Then let's go," came a shout from the back. Others echoed his call and then cheering drowned every sound.

Smiling at their courage—perhaps foolishness— Micah waved them to silence.

"All right, Floyd. Let's show them what their new home looks like."

The lights went off, the wall screens turned blue. Abruptly a planet appeared on the screens, shot from a port of the *Genesis*—a blue-green marble in space, nearly indistinguishable from Earth. Clouds obscured large sections of the planet, but seas could be seen and unfamiliar land masses, mottled green and brown.

"There's a small moon, too, but not on this recording," Floyd said. "It's only a third the size of our moon. At night it looks like a baseball."

The image changed, shot from one of the spheres descending into the atmosphere. The audience leaned forward, anticipating their first view of a new world. Then they were through the clouds and land could be seen below. Missing from the scene were the sharp angles marking civilization where forests were cleared, the cities laid out, the roads paved. The coloration below was uneven and unpredictable, the shapes free-form, created by wind, fire, and flood.

The land rushed up to meet them. They could see mountains in the distance, and distinguish forests below. The land was lush, unspoiled, ready for the discipline of man.

"This is the region where we think we should build," Floyd said.

Murmurings of "how beautiful" sprinkled the hangar.

A lake flashed by, then two more, eliciting more excited murmuring.

"This region is well watered and the topsoil is deep."

"What about winter?" someone shouted.

"It was late winter in the north when we arrived but there was no snow on the ground," Floyd said. "We got dusted only once. We've got weather stations monitoring the climate there and six other places."

As they slowed and dropped lower, a distant bright green patch appeared—a meadow in the forest. A herd of animals stood in the center staring up at them, then as if of one mind, they bolted for the cover of the forest. Shorter than deer, with thicker necks and brown striping, the animals were graceful in flight, galloping rather than leaping to safety. Zooming in on a retreating trio, they could see it appeared to be a family unit with a larger male carrying forked horns, a smaller female marked by a dark mane, and a fawn, all tan without the brown striping. Then they disappeared under the thick overhang of the forest, the crowd excitedly jabbering.

"That's a common animal," Floyd explained. "We found them up and down the western end of the continent."

Micah nudged Shelly and whispered, "And they taste good too."

"You ate one?" she said in surprise. "But they're so beautiful."

"So are deer, dear."

Shelly was uncomfortable with her husband's pioneer sensibilities.

Another mountain range loomed and the sphere climbed to clear it, picking up speed with altitude. Occasionally there were editing jumps in the scene, the mountains coming closer by leaps. Then, passing close to the mountaintop, they shot over the peak, revealing an ocean on the other side. Again the crowd quieted, only the fidgety children could be heard. They crossed more lakes, then a range of hills, traveling through a pass, the ocean now only a short distance away. The coast was rocky, and as they approached they could see large formations jutting from the ocean, as if this end of the continent had broken off in large junks. Slowing again, they turned, following the coast that was cluttered with similar large formations offshore. There was no beach, the continent ending in a cliff. The waves beat against the cliff wall, sending spouts of spray into the air. Ahead a beach appeared with two large dome-shaped rocks, their crowns white as if covered with snow. Suddenly the crowns erupted in a fury of flapping as hundreds of birds lifted from the rocks. The screen was filled with snow-white birds, wings flapping fiercely as they fled from the sphere. Except for the fleshy lips and bulbous eyes, the birds could have been from Earth.

The beach broadened, the sandy expanse running into the distance. Occasional birds were scared from hiding, crossing in front of them. The beach ended at an outcropping and the sphere lifted up and over. On the other side was a sheltered cove with a crescent-shaped beach. High cliffs extended into the ocean, completely isolating the cove. Stretched out on the beach were animals—black bulbous bodies, long, thin necks, and long tails ending in a fork. Four flippers were spaced along the body and as the sphere passed a dozen animals bolted for the water, laboriously pushing themselves through the sand. Awkward and slow on land, as soon as they hit the water they rocketed beneath the waves. Dozens of necks protruded from the water as they stared at the camera. The heads were round but hardly distinguishable from the black necks that held them. With one more pass over the bobbing animals the sphere was off again, out to sea.

It was cloudy now and the sea gray. The monotonous expanse of gray suddenly ended, the picture jumping to an island. The sphere dropped to near wave-top level. Tall trees lined the shore, long slim trunks covered in green leaves, topped with an explosion of yellow. Nearly perfectly round, they resembled giant dandelions.

Filling in between the trunks was thick leafy vegetation. Suddenly out of that vegetation something shot toward the sky, flapping furiously. It was featherless like a bat, with bright green skin on top and dark skin underneath, but much larger and trailing a long whiplike tail. Four smaller limbs could be seen pulled up tight against the body. The sphere turned, following it as it headed out to sea. This animal was the strangest they had seen yet and Shelly shivered at the thought of the countless species yet to be discovered.

Suddenly the image veered away from the retreating creature, the screen now a blur of sky and sea. Then the camera focused on the sea below. Bright blue, the surface was calm and shades of blue and green could be made out in the depths. Then someone gasped and pointed and Shelly saw it. One of the shapes was moving. Shaped like a submarine, there was an animal moving beneath the surface. Scale was impossible to judge, but Shelly sensed it was big, maybe as big as a whale. Smaller shapes swam past it, moving much faster, seemingly unafraid of the monster nearby. The camera followed it for several minutes, but the shape never surfaced and finally disappeared into deeper waters.

Turning back to the island the sphere approached again and settled onto the white sand, panning the beach first— there were no crabs or birds in sight, just acres of white sand, sprinkled with unidentifiable seaweeds. Then the camera rotated inland and they could see detail. It could have been a tropical island on Earth, waist-high plants filling the space between the trees. A botanist would quickly see the unique qualities of the unclassified plants, but to the layman it was all vegetation. Occasionally, large insects buzzed through their field of view, but too quickly for details. Then something skittered around the trunk of a near tree. Shaped like a squirrel, but tailless and yellow in color, it resembled a chipmunk with bulbous eyes. Then it ran headfirst down the tree and across the ground toward the sphere, disappearing from the screen. The camera panned down until the curve of the sphere could be seen but the creature was gone. After panning back up, the camera again focused on the vegetation. Then suddenly the creature was crawling on the camera, its body blurred, its face looking in the lens. Laughter erupted in the hangar as the cute yellow creature wiggled its nose and seemingly studied the Earthlings who had visited its home. Then the image froze, the fuzzy yellow face on the large screens. Micah stood.

"That's a quick view of the new world, friends. It's wild, untamed, created by God and held in trust for His people's future. We know very little about it, but we know not all of the animals there will be as friendly as this little guy."

"Let's go!" someone shouted, and a chorus of amens followed. Now Mark stood and the crowd quieted, waiting for their leader to give the final word.

"From this moment on, all our resources will be devoted to moving God's chosen people to their new home," he said, pointing at the screen.

The wild celebration that followed lasted until late in the evening and ended only when Mark called them to worship.

CHAPTER 65   **REACTION**

> For life as we know it to exist, it must have
> water in liquid form, an atmosphere, and moder-
> ate temperatures. Around each star, whether a
> large red or a twin of our sun, is a small zone
> called the "ecosphere" where these conditions
> can exist.
>
> — *ALONE IN THE VOID?*, WILLIAM JEFFERS

SAN FRANCISCO, CALIFORNIA

Copies were made of the digital video that Floyd had produced on the *Genesis* during the voyage home, and meetings were called in churches, barns, and hangars at all Fellowship properties, timed so all would see the recording at the same hour. Unlike those at the California and the Mexico sites, few of the others in the Fellowship were privy to the visions given to Mark and Ira. They had been faithful followers who trusted God and the men whom they believed had been anointed to lead. Most trusted the leadership enough to turn their lives over to the Fellowship—income, property, decisions about where to live—but would they follow them to a planet full of unknown dangers? Would they leave television, radio, movies, shopping malls, hospitals, cars, and all the other modern conveniences behind to live a pioneer life?

At nine A.M. West Coast time the videos were set to run. Before the showing the congregations were admonished not to share what they were about to see with anyone outside the Fellowship. Mark and Ira knew they couldn't keep the secret for long, but they wanted government and media kept at bay as long as possible. The return of the *Genesis* had been front page news, but during the month that it took *Genesis* to reach the New Hope, the public had tired of the story and the Fellowship had done nothing to reheat it.

An hour after the video was run at a Fellowship church in San Francisco, Roland Symes received a call at the *Journal.* Over the years he had cultivated contacts within the Fellowship, never asking them to betray their leaders or friends, but rather asking them only to "share anything that might actually help the Fellowship." By pretending friendship and concern for their well-being, Roland could usually find a few people willing to supply information anonymously. It gave them a sense of importance, and Roland a pipeline.

"This is Rhonda Carter," the voice said. "Do you remember me?"

"Of course, Rhonda," Roland said, calling up his source database. He spoke as he was scanning her file. "Did your little girl get her braces?"

"Yes, she did."

"The kids haven't been teasing her, have they?"

"No. Half her friends have them too."

"Sure. That's the way it was in my school too."

Now Roland paused. He'd made her feel special—remembered. Now she would tell him what she knew, and maybe more than she originally intended.

"I'm calling because we've gotten some really good news and . . . well, I don't know why they're keeping it secret."

"I suppose sometimes secrets are necessary," Roland said, "but usually they do more harm than good."

"I feel the same way," Rhonda said.

"Besides, most secrets come out in the end anyway," Roland said, encouraging her.

"That's right, and this is so incredible."

Again he paused, waiting for her to get her words in order. When she spoke he could hardly believe what he heard.

"Our spaceship the *Genesis*—the one that just returned? Well, it found another planet, a planet where we're all going to move to live. Isn't that amazing? Everyone's so excited."

"Rhonda, do you mean Mars? The Fellowship is going to move to Mars?"

"No, not Mars. This isn't one of our planets. The *Genesis* flew to another star and found a planet there, and that's where we're going to live."

Roland's pen was flying across a yellow pad, one part of his mind recording Rhonda's incredible story, another part of his mind lining up questions.

"Rhonda, it would take at least twenty years to get to the nearest star and that's if you could travel at the speed of light, and it's impossible to travel at the speed of light."

"I don't understand any of that stuff, but they got there somehow."

"Are you sure the planet was orbiting another star? Maybe it was Mars, or perhaps the moon?"

"I've seen videos of those and this planet isn't anything like that."

"Tell me about the pictures."

"Oh, they were marvelous. It's a beautiful planet, and the animals are so strange."

"There were animals on this planet?"

"Oh, sure. We saw birds, some deer things, and a little yellow chipmunk."

Roland wrote furiously, filling in details inferred from

her brief descriptions. If there were animals, he knew there had to be vegetation. If there were animals and vegetation then there was a complete ecosystem with everything from bacteria to top predators. He could be getting the scoop of the century but still he couldn't shake the nagging feeling he was being suckered.

"Rhonda, don't take this wrong, but I'm still having trouble believing this."

"I know the feeling," she said.

"Is it possible the pictures were faked? You know what they can do with special effects. It could be they are trying to increase giving by making you think they can take you someplace they really can't. Did they ask for more money?"

"They already have all our money," Rhonda said. "If we had anything more to give we would do it gladly."

"There's no chance the pictures are fake?"

"There's no way to fake the animals they brought back."

"They have specimens? They brought back live animals from this planet?"

"The birds are the strangest-looking things. They don't have beaks."

Again Roland's hand recorded Rhonda's words while another part of his mind was struck by the importance of what she was saying. The crew of the *Genesis* had traveled to another world—something thought impossible. As exciting as that was, he was appalled at their carelessness. They had contaminated the Earth's ecosystem with life-forms from another world. Even if the alien animals were contained, they carried microbiotic life-forms that could be devastating—plague with no cure.

Roland thanked Rhonda profusely, assuring her she had done the right thing. Then he said good-bye and punched in Cindi Winslow's number. It would be twelve hours before the next edition of the *Journal* and lives were at stake. The receptionist recognized his name and transferred him immediately.

"Hi, sugar," she said. "Are you in town?"

"The Fellowship did the impossible," he blurted. "They left the solar system and traveled to another star."

"What?"

"There was life there, Cindi, and they brought it back with them."

CHAPTER 66   **SACRIFICE**

> Who are those who will eventually be damned?
> Oh, the others, the others, the others!
>
> — *THE ROYCROFT DICTIONARY AND BOOK OF EPIGRAMS,* ELBERT HUBBARD

SAN FRANCISCO, CALIFORNIA

The little devil statue that Crow bought at a gas station and then painted red was on its pedestal overlooking the ceremony chamber. Thirteen figures in black robes surrounded the man on the altar. He was stretched taut, hands and feet bound by leather thongs, his chest heaving, his face tear-streaked. The man's head rocked back and forth as he watched the figures around him, terrified of what was coming and helpless to stop it.

The chanting was low, but building, Crow leading the others who echoed replies. Eyes wild with fear, mouth taped, the man on the altar watched Crow hold up the knife, caked black with the blood of dozens of sacrifices. Bringing the knife down slowly he touched it to the man's pounding chest. The man began to weep.

Now the coven chanted while he traced a pentagram on the man's chest, at the same time planning the incision. He was well practiced now, and could remove the heart whole before it stopped beating. He liked the feel of a warm, wet, pulsating organ. The chanting built, Rachel and the others working themselves up to the moment, voices joined in praise of the master of the underworld.

The sacrifice would not be missed by society. His body ravaged by alcohol and drug abuse, he looked much older than his thirty years. His skin was gray, his hair sparse and brittle, his face and body covered with open sores. Rachel had lured their victim into her van with the promise of liquor. Only when sobered up for the sacrifice did he finally understand what was happening. There was little satisfaction in sacrificing drunks. The best sacrifice so far had been a teenager Rachel found passed out in an alley. Hollow cheeks, track marks on her arms and legs, she was an addict, but her body still retained some of its youthful vigor and her heart pulsed in Crow's hand nearly twice as long as any other.

It was time and he raised the knife high above his head, aiming below the heart so that he wouldn't damage it when he made the first incision. The intercom buzzed before he could plunge the knife into the man's chest.

Frustrated, he looked to Rachel, who stepped to the wall to respond. Then she was back, whispering to him.

"It's Simon. He says it's urgent."

"It better be," Crow growled, "or he'll be on the altar next month." Silencing the others with a wave, Crow punched the intercom. "What is it, Ash?" he growled.

"I'm terribly sorry to disturb you, Senator, but I thought you would want to know the news about the cult."

"Well, what is it?" he demanded.

"CNN just reported that they've discovered another planet with life on it. That's where the *Genesis* was, and they've brought back specimens."

Unlike the rest of the world, Crow's shock wasn't over the news of travel to another star, nor over the discovery of life on another planet. Crow's shock was over his inability to stop them. Hadn't he been called by the Master to this purpose? Yet even the human sacrifices hadn't brought him the favor he needed—the power. He looked back at the man tied to the altar and saw him for the first time for what he was—human filth. He'd been sacrificing human garbage to his Master. Winos, drug addicts, and prostitutes were insults, not offerings. Suddenly he knew what he had to do. Striding across the room, the victim's eyes widening with each step, Crow plunged the knife into the man's heart. Severed nearly in half, the heart's contractions finished tearing the chambers apart and with a spasm of pain the man lost consciousness, his blood ceased to circulate, and the brain began the four-minute dying process.

Crow was back on the intercom shouting orders at Ash.

"Get my office staff on the phone. I want the public health aspect of this looked into. Contact the Centers for Disease Control in Atlanta, and the Surgeon General's Office. Also get me the names and phone numbers of every department of health in every state where the Fellowship has property."

With a quick "Yes sir," Simon hung up.

Rachel was awaiting orders.

"Get rid of that filth," he said. "We're not insulting the Master anymore. You don't sacrifice the worst of the flock, you sacrifice the best."

"Or the young," she said, her black eyes shining. "But remember, no one searches for the street people, but they do for their children."

Crow knew the more connections one of their sacrificial lambs had, the more questions that would be asked. Kill a bum, and they look for the killer for a day. Kill a workingman and they look for a month. Kill a child and they'll look for a year.

"There's a way to kill two birds with one stone," Rachel suggested. Now she ran her tongue across her lower lip as if tasting her delicious plan. "Ira Breitling is behind the Fellowship's technology."

"You want to sacrifice him?" Crow asked.

"No, not until we have his secrets."

"He would never talk."

"To save his wife's life he might."

Rachel had long advocated kidnapping Ruth Breitling, but Crow had resisted, thinking it too risky. Even now he doubted Ira Breitling would betray the Fellowship to save his wife. Still, the thought of a terrified Ruth Breitling stretched across his altar pleased him.

"There's another purpose she can serve," Rachel said, a cruel smile on her lips.

When Crow heard Rachel's plan for Ruth Breitling, he knew it would please both him and his Master.

CHAPTER 67   **QUARANTINE**

> It wasn't the white man that wiped out the
> Native American nations, it was white man's
> disease. Given that the most likely life form to
> find on another planet is a microbe, care must
> be taken not to bring alien diseases to Earth
> or we could suffer the same fate as
> the Native Americans.
>
> —*ALONE IN THE VOID?*, WILLIAM JEFFERS

FELLOWSHIP COMPOUND, CALIFORNIA

The Council met as soon as the word of the discovery had been shared with the rest of the Fellowship. Gathered in the Christ's Home compound were Sally Roper, financial manager, Shelly Strong, Floyd and Evelyn Remple, Ira Breitling, Mark Shepherd, and Micah Strong.

"The first leg of the flight was based on the direction of the marker we found on Pluto," Micah said.

Mark shifted in his seat, uncomfortable with the word "marker."

"Basing direction on a pointing rock is inaccurate over short distances," Micah said, "and over stellar distances the error margin approaches infinity. Still, we identified five stars similar in magnitude to our own and mapped our course to move from nearest to farthest star. The first had only three planets, all gas giants."

Floyd turned on a wall screen and the blue screen flickered, a planet filling the screen. It was a swirling mass of clouds, red the dominant color.

"As you can see, the planet is a near twin of Jupiter, although we couldn't find anything similar to Jupiter's giant red spot. We have no idea what that means."

A fuzzy image of another planet appeared, a green gas giant.

"We took this video long-range as we were leaving orbit. This is the second planet in the system, nothing particularly remarkable about it."

Mark was struck by how easily Micah dismissed his astounding discovery. Now a third planet appeared, it too dominated by green coloration.

"We detoured to get a closer look at this one when we noticed something peculiar. It's pretty much like the last one except its moons are interesting."

The video changed and a large bright dot appeared in the middle of the screen, with several smaller dots nearby.

"You can see its moon is a mini solar system. The moon has several smaller moons itself. What you can't tell from this tape is that there are nine smaller moons circling the large one."

"Just like our solar system," Sally said. "It's another sign."

"Let's not jump to conclusions," Mark cautioned. "I'm still not convinced the hand on Pluto was a sign, and if it wasn't a sign then this is just a coincidence."

The faces of the others told him he was preaching to deaf ears.

"The second star is coming up next," Micah continued. "We're eight months into the voyage at this point—eight months your time."

A new planet appeared; this one filled the screen like the others, but it was an airless body, its surface pockmarked from meteor collisions.

"This system had six planets. This one is the nearest to its sun—about fifty million miles away when we encountered it, although we suspect its orbit is eccentric and it's much closer at perihelion. The planet doesn't rotate and the far side has been liquified recently. It's only about half the size of the Earth."

Another planet appeared, similar to the first.

"This is the second planet. It orbits at about the same distance as Earth but has no atmosphere." Micah paused, waiting for the next planet to appear. "We were pretty frustrated at this point. Ten months in space, claustrophobic, and our second disappointment."

Now the next planet appeared. This one was blue.

"This one seemed possible at first," Micah explained. "It has an atmosphere, but the blue you see is carbon dioxide ice. There's no free water on the planet and the atmosphere isn't much thicker than Mars'. There's another gas giant in this system with double rings . . . here it is."

Micah paused to let the others take in the beauty of the ringed planet. It was a green giant surrounded with two Saturn-like rings. Breathtakingly beautiful, the planet was a jewel in God's creation but not what the *Genesis* was looking for.

"We didn't visit the other two planets since they were on the far side of the star and too distant from the sun to be livable."

"So there was no sign in this system," Mark prodded.

"None that we found," Micah conceded.

Mark studied Micah's face—he was holding something back.

"Of course, we had to deviate quite a distance from the direction of the pointing finger to get here." Then the image on the screens changed. "Here comes the winner," Micah said. "The third star had what we were looking for."

The screen showed the now familiar planet from the original video.

"It has one small moon, breathable atmosphere, and is teeming with life. There are four other planets in the system. Two gas giants and two planets very similar in size and shape to this one. One of the other planets orbits nearer the star and is hot like Venus—not habitable. The other planet is the most interesting—here it is."

White clouds covered most of this planet, but patches of blue and brown could be seen through breaks in the clouds.

"The orbit of this planet would put it somewhere between the Earth's orbit and Mars'. It would be cooler than Earth but there are wide temperate zones. The atmosphere is nitrogen-oxygen—about the right mix—there is soil, water, and plenty of sunlight. Yet the planet has no life. Not even microscopic forms."

"It's like a garden waiting to be planted," Sally said.

"Our thought exactly," Micah said. "With enough time we could virtually duplicate Earth's ecosystem on that world. Moving to its neighbor means struggling to fit into an ecosystem that has no niche for people. On this world we could build it to fit us."

"If we had the time," Mark said, "but these aren't mutually exclusive ideas. We can work with this world and live on the other. Perhaps both were meant for us."

Now Micah and Floyd exchanged looks.

"There are two more things you need to know," Micah said. Then turning to Ira he said, "Ira, tell us again about your vision."

Ira looked startled, then leaned forward, putting his elbows on the table, his head resting in his hands. Then his good eye stared at the tabletop and he talked as if he were seeing the vision as vividly as he had the first time.

"There was a white dot that got bigger and bigger, turning yellow as it did. Then there were more bright dots, circling the larger yellow dot—six of these. The three outer dots turned green. The three inner dots changed color too. The one closest to the center became silver, the next green, and the third red."

Blinking his good eye, Ira broke his stare and looked up at Micah.

"This solar system doesn't match your vision, Ira," Micah said. "There are only five planets and only two gas giants. In your vision there are three gas giants."

"It could be interpreted other ways," Evelyn said. "God gave us the ability to go into space, and pointed the way. We followed God's direction and found a planet we can live on. It couldn't be much clearer," she said. Others at the table nodded in agreement.

"There's one more thing you need to see," Micah said.

Floyd changed digital recordings and soon a new image was on the screen—an airless body, its surface heavily cratered. Soon the image filled the screen as the sphere that did the recording raced toward the surface.

"This is the moon orbiting the planet," Micah said. "It resembles some of the big asteroids we visited in our own system, although it is nearly perfectly round—unusual for an asteroid. It also has huge crevices that cut nearly to its core. We shot this next footage just before we left orbit. We wanted to make sure the moon wasn't unstable and would create havoc on the planet it orbits. Then we found this," Micah said.

The surface of the alien moon was indistinguishable from the lunar surface—craters, boulders, a bright reflection and deep shadows. Those at the table strained to pick out what Micah referred to. Then Shelly gasped.

"Did you see it?" Shelly said.

The image changed as the sphere shooting the video banked and then climbed, rotating to reverse course. From the higher altitude they could all make out the feature below—it was another pointing hand.

Now everyone was mumbling and praising God, and Mark moved quickly to control the meeting.

"Let's not jump to conclusions," Mark said. "Yes it looks something like the formation on Pluto, but not exactly. Freeze the image, will you, Floyd?"

The pointing hand was fixed on the screen.

"It's imperfect," Mark pointed out. "It's not proportioned correctly. I can make out only four fingers. It may be we see a pointing hand because we want to see one. If we flew over the Earth's surface looking for hands it's likely we'd find one here too."

"But we haven't," Sally pointed out. "Not on the Earth, not on the moon."

"But we weren't looking for one," Mark pointed out.

"We weren't looking for it on Pluto," Shelly said. "And we weren't looking for it here either."

"I'm not saying we can ignore it, but let's not abandon the planet we have—maybe two—just because of a rock formation." The others looked skeptical so he turned to Ira for support. "What do you think, Ira?"

Ira had always been the practical one, the rational counterpart to Mark's emotional impulses. Together they had managed to keep the Fellowship focused on its mission. He needed that rational half now. Ira spoke without hesitating.

"I think we should find out what it's pointing at," Ira said.

The others were nodding in agreement when the door burst open and Paul rushed in, breathless.

"It's on CNN," Paul blurted. "They know we've been to another planet and we brought animals back. The governor has declared a state of emergency. We're going to be quarantined."

Mark sighed. They had hoped to keep it secret a little longer, knowing it would get out eventually, and when it did, they knew government interest would increase. Several branches of government had already been used against them, but the real power of the government had been kept in reserve. Now Mark worried that reserve of power would be released.

CHAPTER 68   **RUNAWAY**

> Family conflict is almost always a result of poor
> communication. Frequently the parents are poor
> listeners and the children incapable of express-
> ing complex and conflicting thoughts and emo-
> tions. While improving communication·can be
> extremely difficult, it is virtually the only way
> to keep some families intact.
>
> — *UNDERSTANDING CONFLICT,*
> CHRISTINE MAITLAND

CHRIST'S HOME, CALIFORNIA

Daniel threw his pack over the chain-link fence, then
climbed over after it. Staying in the underbrush, he kept
low until he was out of sight of the school. Then he cut
through town, sticking to alleys and backyards, acting
nonchalant when forced to pass someone on the street.
Once through town he avoided the road, taking the trails
through the waist-high brush.

He'd packed an extra large lunch that morning and had
smuggled out a change of clothes the day before. He'd
been stealing money for months and had enough stashed
away to get him a bus ticket. They would expect him to
go to San Francisco, but this time he would fool them. He
was going to Seattle this time. Josh had a friend there,
Syd, who would take him in and hide him until it was
safe. When would that be? Not until he was eighteen, he
guessed, but living in hiding for ten years was better than
living with his parents.

It wasn't just his father he hated anymore, but his
mother too. She kept defending his father, punishing
Daniel when he tried to get his sister, Faith, to talk about
what had been done to her. Soon the conflicts with his
mother were as great as with his father and he ran away.

He was coming to the last fence between him and free-dom and he angled toward the spot where he had dug a hollow underneath. When he got there he found that someone had filled it in, but the ground was still soft and he dog-paddled the dirt out of the hole. He was pushing his pack under the fence when he heard sirens. Pulling his pack back, he retreated into the brush to hide and watch. He could see the dust from cars drifting above the trees about a quarter of a mile away. Suddenly three state police cars came around the corner. Two raced past him, but the third pulled over just down the road. Four officers got out, three walking down the road, the fourth remaining. All of them carried shotguns.

They couldn't be after him. Something else was going on—but what? With his escape tunnel in full view of the trooper, he retreated deeper into the brush and turned away, walking in the direction the cars had come from. When he was out of sight of the trooper, he snuck to the fence and walked along looking for a way under. The ground was baked hard from the California sun and he didn't have a shovel.

Putting his pack on his back, he found toeholds in the chain link and then pulled himself up the wire. His feet were still small enough to fit in the spaces and he made good progress, quickly reaching the barbed wire at the top. Carefully, he gripped the wire between barbs and pulled it down, pushing himself up at the same time. Next he would pin the wire to the top of the fence with his foot and then swing over to the other side. He was poised on the top when he heard the trooper.

"Freeze right where you are!"

"I'm just taking a shortcut," Daniel said. "I do this all the time."

Not wanting to give the trooper a chance to argue, Daniel started to swing over the top. Once on the other side he was sure he could outrun the trooper, or talk himself to freedom.

"Freeze or I'll shoot!"

At the sound of a shotgun shell being jacked into the gun's chamber, Daniel froze.

"It's okay. I live here."

"Get back over that fence or I'll shoot."

"But—"

"Now!" the trooper growled.

Frightened, Daniel dropped back. Would the trooper actually shoot him for running away?

"What's the big deal? I'll just go through the gate," he lied.

"Not anymore you won't. This whole town is quarantined."

"What does that mean?"

"It means that nobody gets in and nobody gets out."

Daniel didn't believe the trooper so he began walking the perimeter of the fence, looking for a way out. Police and National Guard troops guarded every possible exit. As the afternoon wore on, and he walked the perimeter of the town, it became clear his days of running away were over.

CHAPTER 69   RUTH

> Sin . . . has been made not only ugly but passé.
> People are no longer sinful, they are immature or
> underprivileged or frightened or, more
> particularly, sick.
>
> — *THE PROVINCE OF THE HEART,*
> PHYLLIS MCGINLEY

CHRIST'S HOME, CALIFORNIA

Ruth Breitling liked children and worked as a teacher's assistant at the Christ's Home school. The classes were blended, so in the same room she worked with first through third graders, enjoying the developmental differences. With no children of her own she parented vicariously, teaching, baby-sitting, and foster grandparenting a half-dozen families. She was known as loving but firm, and well liked by both children and parents.

They were about to go to afternoon recess when the principal announced over the intercom that all classes were to stay in their rooms. A few minutes later the teacher was called to the office, leaving Ruth in charge of the class. The students were rambunctious now, since they were missing recess, and she decided to play games with them. Seven-up was popular, so she picked seven kids to go first and had the others put their heads down on their desks. While the seven snuck around and each touched another child, she looked out the window. The playground was empty—nothing to be learned from that. Then the speaker came on again.

"Would Ruth Breitling please report to the office?"

Worried that something had happened to Ira, Ruth started for the door and then remembered the class. There was no one to watch the students.

"Continue playing the game, please," Ruth told the class. "Mrs. Carmichael will be here shortly. Martha, you're in charge until then."

Martha, a mature, bossy student, beamed with pride. Happy to keep playing, the rest of the children picked the game up where they left off and Ruth hurried toward the office. The office was by the front entrance and waiting there was a tall dark woman with the blackest eyes she had ever seen. She was dressed in yellow coveralls, a plastic hood hanging over her shoulders. Two similarly dressed men waited with her.

"Ruth Breitling?" the woman asked. "We must hurry. Something's happened to Ira."

They weren't part of the Fellowship, she knew, but their clothes told her they worked with hazardous materials— like Ira often did. She let the woman take her by the arm, noticing the office staff watching through the glass. Outside they hurried her toward a large van marked "HAZMAT."

"Is Ira all right?"

"We're taking you to him."

Then they helped her in the back of the van. There were benches along the sides and she moved toward one but suddenly was grabbed by both arms and slammed to the floor. The doors closed behind her and a needle was jammed into her buttocks. She screamed, but a hand silenced her, and she was held down while the drugs circulated through her system, reaching her brain. As she sank into blackness, the last thing she remembered was the vibrations of the vehicle as it drove her away.

CHAPTER 70   **KIDNAPPED**

American astronomer Dr. Carl Sagan, one of the leading investigators in the field, has suggested that there may be as many as a billion Earth-like (and therefore habitable) planets in our Galaxy.

—*UNEXPLAINED:*
MYSTERIES OF MIND, SPACE AND TIME,
PETER BROOKESMITH [ED.]

CHRIST'S HOME, CALIFORNIA

When Mark heard that the state police had sealed off the roads leading to Christ's Home and the compound, he ordered an evacuation—not of people, but of their technology. Computers were wiped clean of technical data and all spare parts for spacecraft were loaded into sealed cargo containers and lifted into orbit. Key people were sent to the New Hope and other smaller orbital stations. Since the Mexican compound was still open, Mark ordered the evacuation of sensitive material from all foreign sites too. By dark all the Fellowship compounds and churches in the U.S. were sealed off, police or National Guard troops controlling access. Even those who had no connection to their space activities were confined to their homes under threat of arrest.

Stephen O'Malley called Mark at the Christ's Home compound.

"They're afraid you might have brought back a dangerous disease, Mark."

"It's nonsense," Mark said. "Micah and the others lived on the new world for months. They survived."

"As soon as someone dies from an unidentified disease, we'll be hit with a lawsuit," Stephen said. "Copycats will follow. It won't matter if the symptoms are different from person to person, their lawyers will convince sympathetic juries that we are responsible. Remember the lawsuits over silicon breast implants? The scientific evidence proved that the implants were harmless, yet jury after jury awarded millions to women desperate to blame someone else for their illness."

Now Mark regretted his decision to bring the animals down from orbit. He wanted everyone who had sacrificed to support the mission to see the fruits of the mission for themselves but his shortsightedness had put everything at risk.

"You're being charged with endangering the public health and violating laws regulating the importation of exotic and dangerous animals. However, they have banned contact with anyone who has been exposed to these animals, so until their anger at you exceeds their fear of an epidemic, you and the others are safe from prosecution."

The implications of the quarantine were devastating. While their communications stations in orbit would continue to be profitable, all tourist business would end, as would burials in space. They could shift operations to other countries—Mexico probably—but that would be costly. There was no risk to the people on Earth but their enemies could keep the fear alive for years. Mark made a decision. He called Micah and Floyd in to hear it first.

"It's time to move to the new planet."

Expecting elation, Mark was surprised by their subdued reaction.

"Mark, we don't even have full data on the planet," Micah said. "We need to study the climate and geology so we can select the best location."

"If we wait, lawsuits, government legal action, and

fines will drain our resources—within a year we could be bankrupt, all of our assets attached or impounded. We need to get as many of our people to the new world and as quickly as we can."

"What about the other marker?" Micah asked.

"First chance we get we'll see where it leads, but we're quickly becoming unwelcome on this world. We must move, now!"

Mark was their leader and even with doubts they followed orders.

"I'll tell Sally to begin liquidating some of our assets," Floyd said. "We only have a fraction of the supplies we'll need and we'll be cut off from U.S. suppliers—probably all western sources. As long as Mexico stays open to us we can get what we need shipped south. It will raise the costs some, but it can't be helped."

"*Covenant* is nearly ready, but we need a test run," Micah said.

"While Floyd organizes people and supplies we'll run the *Covenant* to Mars to test the drive. We can resupply the Mars colony at the same time and charge the run to the government."

Establishing a home on a new world would be their most complex undertaking and tax their resources to the maximum. The first step would be the most dangerous but the one they could most easily afford. For every person on the new world, there would be twenty-five people working on Earth to support them. As the new world colony grew the number of supporters would shrink, until it became prohibitively expensive to move any more off-planet. To make the enterprise feasible they needed to keep all Earth enterprises generating revenue long after the colony was established. Mark was about to turn to the finance issue when Ira rushed in, closely followed by Evelyn.

"Ira, you should be on the New Hope," Mark said.

"Ruth's been kidnapped," Ira said.

"What? Who took her?" Mark stammered.

"We've got to get her back, Mark," Ira said. "I need her."

Ira was dissolving into grief, so Mark turned to Evelyn.

"People came to the school dressed in protective clothing, like they were doctors or scientists. They paged Ruth and when she came to the office they told her Ira had been hurt and that they would take her to him. They put her in the back of a van and drove off. No one's heard from her since. We called the local fire district and the state but no one sent a HAZMAT team."

"She's suffered so much for my sins," Ira moaned.

Evelyn snaked her arm around Ira, comforting him.

"They took her to get to you, Ira," Mark said. "They'll call, and they'll want to trade her for you, or for our technology."

Now Ira looked hopeful but it was Mark who had to decide whether one life was worth the secret God had entrusted to them. He desperately wanted to avoid that decision.

"Evelyn, get George Proctor on the phone."

CHAPTER 71   **PRISONERS**

> For you created my inmost being; you knit me
> together in my mother's womb.
>
> —PSALM 139:13

PROCTOR'S COMPOUND, NEAR CALDWELL, IDAHO

Proctor had long known he was called to protect Mark Shepherd and his people, but until he heard they had traveled to another star he had not fully understood why. He had enjoyed the world's humiliation at each of their successes, but now he saw God's people could escape the world—live separately as they were called to do in the Bible. It was God's plan for His people and he would do everything in his power to see that it happened.

Every terrorist group in the world was suspected in

Ruth Breitling's kidnapping, as well as organized crime, although Proctor put them low on his list—they would have tried threatening Mark or Ira first. It was a long list, but the best place to start was with those who had tried to hurt the Fellowship before.

Proctor flew to his compound in Idaho. It was a fortress really, surrounded by barbed wire and stone fences that masked reinforced concrete designed to slow down tanks. The main building had once been a farmhouse, but there were so many additions the original structure was indistinguishable from the others.

His men patrolled the perimeter on all-terrain vehicles, rifles slung over their shoulders. The land had been cleared of native pine trees for a half mile in all directions, making it hard on government snipers. Nothing would stop artillery of course, but Proctor had plans for that contingency too.

More guards watched from windows on the third floor of the building—the windows bullet-resistant. Children played on the grounds, most swarming around the play structure near the barn they had converted to a school. The main building was filled with the smell of baking bread. Saturday nights they shared a common meal, the women coming together to create a weekly feast, including fresh breads. Only a third of his people lived in the compound, the rest spread out among the working farms in the area. Every farm was self-sufficient, donating from its profits for the common good.

Proctor climbed to the third-floor guard station. Brett McKenna was there, binoculars hanging from his neck. With sandy hair, a farmer's tan, and a red neck, Brett was a young man, energetic, fearless, and like most young men, thought he was invincible. Four years in the army had nurtured his love of country and patriotism, so when the government he swore to protect shut down his farm because of an endangered butterfly, Brett joined Proctor's army.

"Hello, sir, I didn't expect you this weekend," Brett said.

"Are they out there?" Proctor asked.

"Yes. In the usual spot."

Brett handed his binoculars over and Proctor focused them on a clump of trees perched on a small rise a mile away, just outside Proctor's property. He could see two men standing in the trees, one looking back at him with his own binoculars.

His compound was constantly watched by ATF agents, although they had yet to try to execute a search warrant. Federal agents weren't popular in rural Idaho where many of the residents had "Remember Waco" bumper stickers on their pickups. George knew the backlash over the Branch Davidian fiasco would keep the government out of his compound unless there was a clear danger to the public and he had no intention of becoming a danger. All their weapons were legal, all their bills and taxes paid on time.

He left Brett and went down to the basement and then through a hidden door into a room built dead center of the house. There under a rug was a trapdoor leading to a sub-basement. He climbed down to the room below that led to the cells. There were a dozen small cells built in the sub-basement, each with its own plumbing, plus two interrogation rooms. Eight of the cells were currently occupied. The man he wanted to talk to was in the last.

He switched off the lights to the cell block, then opened and entered, closing the door behind. As he walked the other prisoners were silent, familiar with his slow gait. They used to beg him when he passed, saying, "Please let me go home. I won't tell anyone. I have a family," or just as often cursed and threatened him. Nothing moved him, however, their sentences were for life and they had slowly come to accept that. All except the man in the last cell.

The cell block was pitch-black, but it made no difference to Proctor, who could see each of the prisoners as he passed. Lichter was the most pitiful, now wasted away to a stick figure. He sat on his bunk, head in his hands, no hope left in him. The other NASA engineers had fared better, eating well, exercising in their cells, reading the Bibles and Christian books they were provided. Both claimed to have accepted Christ, but neither was particularly convincing.

Rosa Quigly was standing at her cell door, and when he passed she spat at him. Still defiant, she rejected all of the books they gave her, tearing her Bible into tiny pieces, cursing the guards who brought her meals. Intellectually, she was the most gifted of the prisoners, a master of secular humanism who argued theology with Proctor's people. Ironically, her dogmatic defense of humanism kept her more alive than the others, but kept her from life everlasting.

Next to Rosa was the man who had fired the missile at the *Rising Savior*. He was a large man who kept himself strong with a daily regimen of exercise. He never turned down food, and never asked for any special favors. He read the materials they provided, but never asked questions, never discussed the Bible with the other prisoners or the guards, and rarely spoke. He was the most dangerous of the prisoners. Two months ago he had stolen a fork and now spent his nights under his bunk chipping away at the concrete. The hidden video camera recorded his slow progress every night. Early on they decided there was little danger since it would take him a year to get through the concrete and there was no way for him to cut through the steel reinforcing. They decided to study his techniques in order to learn how to improve their security. Right now his biggest problem was disposing of the pieces of concrete he was chipping away. Some of it was hidden in his mattress, and some had gone down the toilet. They were pretty sure he was eating the smaller pieces and it amused them.

He was sitting on the bunk staring defiantly into the dark when Proctor stopped in front of his cell.

"There may be a way out of here for you," Proctor said.

The man's expression remained blank.

"You'll never let me out of here alive. I know too much. Besides, if I get out of here I will kill you!"

Through his eyelids Proctor could see the man's eyes blaze with hatred.

"Things have changed since you've been in here."

Now the man looked intrigued.

"What things?"

"It may be possible to release you in such a way that you could not harm us."

The man walked to the bars, moving confidently in the dark, the sign of someone who has lived years in an enclosed space.

"I don't believe you."

Despite his words, Proctor could hear his interest.

"I'm a Christian. If I swear on a Bible will you believe me?"

The man laughed, cursing softly to himself. "You torture me—and the others here—imprison us without a trial, and keep us locked up in cells not fit for animals and you call yourself a Christian and ask me to trust you?"

"For what you did you should have been killed. When you went to war against us you warred against God. The only reason you're alive is because God is merciful—I'm not. You have a warm dry place to sleep and plenty of food. There are millions who have less."

"Less food, but more freedom. I'll gladly trade with them."

"That's what I'm offering. I'll trade you freedom for information."

"And my only guarantee is your claim to believe in an invisible being? There is no God. Your promise is worthless."

"It doesn't matter what you believe. What matters is what I believe."

Now the man looked thoughtful, finally understanding that the promise of freedom depended on Proctor's faith, not his own.

"I want you to swear on your family Bible!" the man said.

"I've got a New Testament with me."

"It's the whole thing or no deal, and I want two witnesses—not prisoners. It's got to be your people and they have to swear on a Bible too. One more thing. I want to look you in the eye when you swear, so turn the lights on!"

The prisoner was making demands to cover up the fact he was going to betray his employer. His simple conditions were easy to meet. More problematic was arranging to set him free. For that he would need Mark Shepherd.

> I think there are innumerable gods. What we on
> Earth call God is a little tribal god who has made
> an awful mess.
>
> — *PARIS REVIEW*, WILLIAM S. BURROUGHS

SAN FRANCISCO, CALIFORNIA

Ruth Breitling was tied hand and foot, lying on a soft
surface—a bed? She couldn't tell in the dark. The drug-
induced fog was clearing slowly. She remembered the
school and the people who said Ira was hurt. It was fuzzy
after that. She moved, rolling onto her back, realizing she
was naked. Now her terror completely cleared her mind
and all her senses came alive. She felt every bruise and
scratch on her body. Panicking, she struggled at the ropes
until her wrists and ankles burned.

Concentrating on her right wrist she wriggled until the
pain brought tears to her eyes. When the stinging subsided, she felt something wet running across her wrist—
blood—it might lubricate the rope. Suddenly there was
light.

Just a glow, it was like a beacon to her dark-adapted
eyes. Lifting her head she could see the outline of a door,
the light coming from underneath. Then she heard footsteps, a faint echo following each thump.

The footsteps stopped and then a small window in the
door slid open, letting the hallway light in. Then a face
blocked the light, but she could see no details. A bank of
fluorescent lights winked on and now she could see the
horror around her. The walls were covered with hideous
pictures of demons, bloodred, painted against a black
background. There were pictures of torture, men and
women, naked as she was, being dismembered by grin-

ning demons. Other people were being roasted on spits, their flesh blackened by flames, their faces sheer agony. Others were impaled, their bodies pierced by great stakes. From high on one wall was one form of the devil: cloven-hooved, horned, watching with glee the evil his minions performed.

More footsteps, this time heavier. The door opened. A tall, dark man entered. He had sharp features, his black eyes sparkled, his mouth a cruel smile. A woman stood in the doorway behind him—tall and beautiful. The man was familiar, but her mind was too cloudy from the drugs to recognize him.

Terrified and humiliated she closed her eyes, searching for a Scripture verse to meditate on. Nothing came so she recited the Psalms.

" 'Blessed is the man who does not walk in the counsel of the wicked or stand in the way of sinners or sit in the seat of mockers. But his delight is in the law of the Lord—' "

"Praying are we?" the man observed.

" '—and on his law he meditates day and night. He is like a tree planted by streams of water, which yields its fruit in season and whose leaf does not wither.' "

The man came forward, bending, slapping her across the face. Ruth gasped, the man smiled.

" 'Whatever he does prospers. Not so the wicked!' " She nearly shouted the word "wicked." " 'They are like chaff that the wind blows away. Therefore the wicked will not stand in judgment, nor sinners in the assembly of the righteous.' "

He slapped her again, then leaned over, his breath on her cheek.

"Is that what you are? One of the righteous?"

" 'For the Lord watches over the way of the righteous, but the way of the wicked will perish.' "

"It won't do you any good," the man hissed in her ear. "All this praying to a God that is past His prime. Gods age too, you know? Your god was in His prime six thousand years ago and even for a god six thousand years is a long time. He's been losing His power, bit by bit, year by year. He may already be dead. If He isn't, He soon will be."

His voice was seductive, his words crafty, selected to have a ring of truth when there is only one Truth. She began Psalm 2, trying to shut out the serpent.

" 'Why do the nations conspire and the peoples plot in vain? The kings of the earth take their stand and the rulers gather together against the Lord and against His Anointed One.' "

"That's from the Bible, isn't it? A very dangerous book. People shouldn't be allowed to read it."

He was baiting her.

"The problem is that it's history. It has no relevance today. The god with no name who turned rivers to blood, visited plagues upon nations, destroyed cities with a rain of fire and brimstone, isn't up to it anymore. You don't see much of that kind of thing now, do you? Know why? Because there's a new god in town. It's a world of sex and violence now. The word 'adultery' has no meaning, men have sex with men, women with women, and adults with children. Our streets are a war zone, robbery, murder, and rape are the backdrop of our lives."

" 'Let us break their chains,' they say, 'and throw off their fetters,' " she continued, struggling to resist his words. " 'The One enthroned in heaven laughs, the Lord scoffs at them. Then he rebukes them in his anger and terrifies them in his wrath, saying, "I have installed my King on Zion, my holy hill." ' "

"Your god doesn't terrify anyone anymore, Ruth. He's impotent. If He wants obedience He needs to do something spectacular, something supernatural—destroy a city or two. Destroy a city? He can't even save you."

" 'I will proclaim the decree of the Lord: He said to me, "You are my Son; today I have become your Father. Ask of me, and I will make the nations your inheritance, the ends of the earth your possession. You will rule them with an iron scepter; you will dash them to pieces like pottery." ' "

"That's tough Old Testament talk, but that was then and this is now. Sure, He was powerful when He was helping the Israelites but by the time poor Jesus came along He wasn't the god He used to be. Ruth, He changed water to wine—that's the best He could do. It's embarrassing, Ruth. Your God couldn't even muster a simple plague let alone save Jesus on that cross. He duped him, Ruth, and all those who followed him. I'm not saying He didn't make the most of what He had—a few card tricks, a stroll on water, multiply some kid's lunch—nothing you can't see in Las Vegas five nights a week and twice on Saturday. It was a good show and He attracted a few fanatics, put them in charge, promised them streets of gold after they died—that's the key, you've got to die to collect on the promise—and presto, you have a new religion."

His twisted history hurt her more than anything he could do to her body.

"It's blasphemy," Ruth retorted. "God sent His son to us to save us from our sins."

Eyes open now, she saw him smile at her outburst.

"God became human and sacrificed Himself for our sins," Ruth argued.

"Gods don't do that sort of thing, Ruth. Your God used that poor demented fool Jesus in a last desperate gambit to keep control of the world."

"Jesus changed the world."

"I'm not saying it wasn't a good move. Let's give credit where credit is due. It was well played and kept Him in control for another twenty centuries. But that hand has played out. He's losing control of the world. Can't you feel it, Ruth?"

Even knowing it was useless to argue, she couldn't help but defend her faith.

"God is still with us. He gave us the means to escape this evil world."

"Cutting and running doesn't say much about your God's power, now does it, Ruth?"

"God is fulfilling His promise to His people. We're going to cross the Jordan and occupy the land He has prepared for us."

"That's a pretty loose interpretation of Scripture, Ruth.

They teach you to play fast and loose with the Bible like that in Sunday school?"

"God's revelation didn't end with the Bible. He reveals Himself to us every day if we only listen."

"Has your God revealed to you what's going to happen to you here, Ruth?"

Terrified of torture—she collapsed in tears, then quickly fought to control herself, to deny him the pleasure of her suffering.

"I can see you have thought about your future."

Again she searched her mind for the Psalms, finding her place.

" 'Therefore, you kings, be wise; be warned, you rulers of the earth. Serve the Lord with fear and rejoice with trembling. Kiss the son, lest he be angry and you be destroyed in your way, for his wrath can flare up in a moment.' "

"Despite what you see here on the walls, Ruth, we're not going to torture you."

A wave of relief swept her.

" 'Blessed are all who take refuge in him,' " she continued.

"Actually, Ruth, you're going to be our first breeder."

Now she stopped reciting, her eyes opening, her heart threatening to pound its way through her chest.

"You see my god is very powerful, Ruth. In fact, he's running the world now. That's why your God is clearing out. Except of course we're not going to let you get away. You see my god demands sacrifice too—not nickels and dimes like yours—but blood. Human sacrifice—no, not you. Not for a long time, anyway. My god likes his sacrifices young and innocent. The younger the better. And that's what you're going to give us, Ruth. You're going to give us a baby to sacrifice to my god."

The horror of what he was planning was almost too much for her.

"No! I won't," Ruth said.

He came close again, whispering in her ear.

"You'll do whatever I want."

"But I can't have children," she said. "My husband and I have tried."

"If you can't, then you're of no use to us. But I think you can with the right man. Then when we get your baby we're going to take it on the day of its birth and cut its heart out. I'll hold that tiny heart in my hand and feel it beating like a rabbit's—newborn hearts do that, you know—and I'll hold it up to my god as a perfect sacrifice. Then my lord will give me the power to destroy the Fellowship once and for all."

Cringing with the horror, Ruth searched for her place in the Psalms, but the image of a knife plunging into a crying baby crowded out all other thoughts.

"No one could be so cruel," Ruth said.

"You'll give us our first sacrificial lamb, Ruth, and then another, and another, and another, until the end of your reproductive life. Then you'll join your babies in hell."

"I won't . . ."

"Won't what? Won't be a breeder? I'll take you anytime I want, Ruth, and when your babies are born we'll take them from you. You'll never cuddle them, or suckle them. The only memory you'll have is of them in your belly."

He walked to the door, then turned back.

"You could kill yourself, Ruth, but you won't. Suicide is a sin, isn't it, Ruth, and killing your own baby at the same time would be even worse, wouldn't it? Of course you have had some experience in killing your unborn babies, haven't you? I don't think you have the courage to murder another one. No, you'll live in hope that the god with no name will save you. Even as your belly swells larger you will pray for a deliverance that will never come. Then we'll take your baby and the process will start again. The only way out for you and your babies is to admit your God is as good as dead and kill yourself. Can you do it, Ruth? Can you curse your God and die?"

"Without God I am nothing."

"I thought so. By the way, don't bother struggling to get free. I'll have someone cut you loose. There's no reason to keep you tied down all the time."

"I'll fight you," she said.

"Oh, please do," he said, smiling. "By the way, you may already be with child."

Shocked at the implication, she stared at him wide-eyed.

"I didn't see any reason to wait until you woke up."

Laughing, he slammed and bolted the door, then turned off the light, leaving her in darkness and despair.

CHAPTER 73   **COUNCIL**

> Throughout the New Testament from the words of Jesus Christ, Paul, and James we are told to expect trouble (John 15:18–20; James 1:2–12). As Christians, we need to be aware of these influences and prepared to respond. But in recent years, drawing the battle lines has become more difficult because the attacks appear to be coming not only from the front but also from the rear.
>
> — *CHRISTIANS IN THE CROSSFIRE*,
> MARK MCMINN AND JAMES D. FOSTER

CHRIST'S HOME, CALIFORNIA

Ira's absence from the Council cast a pall over what should have been a glorious day. Sally Roper, Floyd Remple, Mark Shepherd, Micah Strong, and Shelly Strong had gathered to assess their progress toward moving off-world. Soon the first of their people would move off the planet, but they would do it without Ira. Ira had retreated to his home, fasting and praying for his wife, blaming himself for what had happened to Ruth.

In the month since Ruth had been kidnapped, Mark had only heard from George Proctor once, and that was a simple report that he was trying to find Ruth. It was frustrating that Proctor wouldn't share more, but Mark knew it was best that he didn't know more about Proctor's methods.

It was all Mark could do to keep Ira eating and alive. The hard truth was that the Fellowship didn't need Ruth to complete the mission, but Ira was essential. While he had well-trained people assembling drive units, he had kept the full secret of how they worked from any one of them. Without Ira the secret of faster-than-light travel would be secret once more.

Micah's report on the shakedown cruise of the converted Seawolf submarine, *Covenant,* was encouraging. They stopped three times on the way to Mars to realign the drive fields, but the return trip had been smooth. Equipped with the biggest drive they had ever produced the *Covenant* had used only a fraction of its potential speed in cruising to Mars.

Adding to the concern over Ruth's kidnapping, Sally Roper had a disturbing financial report. The resources of the Fellowship were being drained by the massive purchases Floyd was making to equip a colony on the new planet. A new world is nothing but raw material. It takes the products of a well-developed industrial plant to harvest those virgin materials, to process them into usable forms and turn them into finished products. Also missing from the new world was the infrastructure they took for granted—the roads, the railroads, the telephone and computer networks. Ultimately, their new home would have to be self-sufficient, manufacturing everything for themselves, but for now everything had to be purchased.

"We're liquidating our resources at an alarming rate," Sally said. "This is a fantastically expensive undertaking."

"We knew it would be, Sally," Mark said. "Will we have enough?"

"It's more expensive than we planned, because everything has to be transshipped through friendly countries. We could cut costs twenty percent if we could pick up in the U.S. and western Europe. And we need those tourist dollars—we've got to get the New Hope visitors' platform back in operation."

"That's not going to happen soon," Mark said. "Congress is going to hold hearings to assess the threat to Earth's ecosystem—the environmental lobby is in a frenzy. They'll drag it out for months, even years."

"Can't we take tourists up from Mexico?" Micah suggested.

"We're negotiating with the Mexican government now," Sally said, "but our government is threatening to close the border if they allow us to operate there."

"There's another way to get those tourist dollars back," Micah said. "Floyd has edited together a couple of hours of video of the new planet and Sonrise Productions in Atlanta has agreed to distribute it as a feature-length film. We'll transmit the video to Sonrise and they'll produce prints."

"The box office potential is tremendous," Sally said, brightening. "It could easily bring in a hundred million dollars in a few months."

The others laughed at her avarice.

"We won't put all the good footage in the first film," Micah said. "There's enough spectacular footage for three films. We'll release the second when the first one has run its course."

"Don't forget pay-per-view and cable," Sally said, triggering more laughter as she scribbled figures on a yellow pad. "Well, Floyd, you can buy your sawmill, your cellular phone system, your machine shop, your steel mill, your combines and tractors, your—"

"We get the idea, Sally," Mark said, cutting her off. "Get the video in theaters as soon as possible, Micah. Now what about the Ukrainians?"

"The deal for the submarine is still on but we've got to move fast," Floyd said. "They're getting nervous, and not just about relations with our government. If their Russian neighbors find out—"

"Are they worried it will trigger a war?" Mark asked.

"They're worried the Russians will try to get a piece of the action."

Everyone laughed again, making Mark wonder how joyful the meeting could have been without their concern about Ruth.

"What's holding up the deal?" Mark asked.

"They want the full price in hard currency," Sally said. "It's a cash-flow problem. If the movie deal works out we'll have the cash in a few months, but we can't make the purchases Floyd wants for the new planet and pay the Ukrainians."

"I have another idea," Micah said.

Mark marveled at the never-ending creativity of the people God had sent him.

"The Ukrainians like gold as much as hard currency. Some of the asteroids are loaded with gold. We could send the *Exodus* out to get one and make up the cash shortage with a few tons of gold."

The plan was accepted immediately, and the next few minutes were spent discussing logistics. Then Mark brought the meeting to a close with one final task.

"I'm tired of calling the new planet 'the new planet.' It's time to give it a name."

Naming the ships and space stations had been a function of the Council, but now no one spoke. Naming a whole new world was too important to do quickly.

"We don't have to decide today," Mark said after a long silence.

"I have a suggestion," Micah said. "It's not a biblical name, but it represents what we want our new world to be—a place where people are free to worship God in their own way without persecution. A place where we can escape from a repressive government that insists on regulating more and more of our lives and a place where we can raise our children to believe what we believe."

When they heard his suggestion, they sobered, thinking of the implications. One by one those around the table agreed, Mark making it unanimous, but wondering how the world would react to the name.

> The world's unmined gold reserves have dwin-
> dled to less than a billion troy ounces, half of
> which are in the Republic of South Africa. Still
> essential to commerce, and increasingly impor-
> tant in the manufacture of electronics, the world
> will soon be facing a gold shortage.
>
> — *STRATEGIC METALS,* RON WOLINSKI

ASTEROID BELT

The swarm of objects orbiting between Mars and Jupiter is called the asteroid belt. Too numerous to ever count, more than five thousand of these objects have been catalogued, a few named. Long-range spectroscopic analysis from Earth orbit suggested some of the asteroids consisted of heavy metals, like gold. On its trips to the asteroid belt, the Fellowship had confirmed the presence of heavy metals in the field. They were looking for one of these special asteroids now.

The *Exodus* found a promising candidate after ten days. Core samples confirmed the gold content of the asteroid. Unfortunately, the asteroid was huge, nearly ten miles long. Changing its orbit would be like moving a moon. However, the asteroid had been battered from numerous collisions, so they searched for fragments.

Space was the perfect medium for radar, since there was nothing to interfere with the broadcast of electromagnetic radiation, and their Israeli-built radar could detect even small objects at great distance. The nearest fragment of the asteroid took a day to reach, the requirements of acceleration and deceleration taking the bulk of the travel time.

Primarily silicate, the fragment was a disappointment. A day and a half later they were disappointed again with a second fragment. Two days later they found what they were looking for, a chunk of gold ore about twice the size of one of their spheres. Bob Morton estimated it would produce more than five tons of refined gold.

Micah and Bob took turns in the spheres, boring into the rock, then blasting away chunks, preparing a flat surface. Then steel beams were attached to the rock with expansion bolts, explosively driven deep into the asteroid. More bolts in the beams matched a modified cargo module that was bolted to the asteroid. Finally, the nose of the *Exodus* nested against one wall of the cargo module. It took a week to get the little space-train ready, then with Micah at the controls, the *Exodus* began to push. The mass wasn't any greater than when the *Exodus* was fully loaded, but the physics were different, since concentrating the mass on the nose of the ship changed the center of gravity, making it difficult for Micah to shape a drive field that would propel the ship. After a few false starts, the *Exodus* began picking up speed, pushing the asteroid like a tug pushing a luxury liner. The gold asteroid was on its way to Earth.

CHAPTER 75　　**INTRUSION**

> The Bible and the American Constitution: that's
> all the government anyone needs.
>
> —GEORGE PROCTOR

SAN FRANCISCO, CALIFORNIA

The Autumn Rest Cemetery sprawled over two hills northwest of downtown San Francisco. Crow owned the surrounding property and every year cleared another parcel to sell off as burial plots. Proctor and his people were hidden in one of those wooded areas across the main road from the facility, watching through night glasses. Based on information from the man who fired the missile at *Rising Savior,* Crow had become their number one suspect in the disappearance of Ruth Breitling and Autumn Rest was the property he visited the most.

It was nearly midnight and conditions were favorable. The grounds were patrolled by a private security company but they were predictable and easily avoided. Rachel Waters was not there, having left Autumn Rest four hours earlier. They were waiting only because she frequently worked evenings too.

"If she isn't back by midnight, she's not coming," Proctor said. "We'll wait fifteen more minutes, then we go."

Rich nodded, then whispered orders to the three men behind him. Ten minutes passed and then a car approached—a Porsche.

"That's her," Rich whispered.

Proctor had never seen Crow's assistant, although he had heard his men talk about how attractive she was. Training the glasses on her sports car he watched her pull up in front of the building. Leaving her headlights on, she stepped out and walked toward the door as if she was going to dash in to pick up something she had forgotten. When she did, Proctor closed his eyes, looking at her through his lids. What he saw horrified him.

"We go now!" he said loudly.

"What?" Rich said. "Let's wait until she leaves."

"I don't want her to get away," Proctor said fiercely.

Rich looked like he wanted to argue but he turned to the others. Signaling his men to follow, Rich led them through the trees and down a slight rise to the cemetery fence. They hopped a short decorative fence and spread out, ducking behind tombstones, circling around to a rear entrance.

They carried automatic rifles or nine-millimeter pistols with silencers. Guy also carried a .357 Magnum in a shoulder holster—he called it his "security blanket." Normally cautious, now Proctor urged the others on, moving them faster than prudent. They reached the back door undetected. With all of them flattened against the wall, Jim picked the lock, then on a count of three he pulled the door open and Rich and Nick entered, each pointing their automatic weapons a different direction. Now Guy hurried in, racing for the alarm panel. He had only seconds to disarm it. Well practiced, he quickly opened the panel, bypassing the timed switch just before the solenoid clicked, closing the circuit. Next he disarmed the system.

They had entered through a receiving area where several crated coffins were stacked in the middle of the floor. Jim and Nick led the way down the hall, moving slowly, noiselessly. The hallway branched and they started left but Proctor stopped them.

"Which way is the lobby?" he whispered.

"Sir, we want to avoid the lobby. There are windows there."

"She can't get away," he said without explanation.

"That way," Rich said, Proctor moving off at a noisy pace.

Proctor hurried down the hall and through another doorway. Now the walls were paneled with mahogany and he hurried on. Another corner and then he burst into the lobby—she wasn't there. Hurrying to the door he saw her pull away.

"We should have come in the front," he said, cursing himself.

"Why did you want her so bad?"

"Because she's not human," Proctor said, then turned away.

With his special sight, he had seen her for what she really was—leathery skin, wings folded against her back, horns, and tail. He had never seen anything like her—it terrified him.

The others were whispering behind him, startled by his words.

"Search the building," Proctor said.

Starting back down the hall he was grabbed and held from behind.

"She rearmed the alarm when she left," Guy whispered in his ear.

Down the hall Proctor could see the winking red eye of the motion sensors.

"We've already triggered the silent alarm," Guy said. "The security car will be here in minutes."

"Guy and Jim, you wait for the guards and neutralize them. Rich and Nick, come with me."

He led the way down the hall, opening and closing doors recklessly, gambling there was no one else in the building. There were offices, storerooms, a print shop, embalming room, gaudy chapels, and a crematorium, but no sign of Ruth Breitling. Finally, Proctor found himself in the storeroom, where he met Rich and Nick.

"If she's here, we're missing something," Rich said.

Thinking of the presence of the demon, Proctor was convinced Ruth Breitling was nearby. By taking Ruth, they had devastated Ira and weakened the Fellowship. The demon wouldn't leave such an important lever unattended.

Closing his eyes, Crow started back through the building. Working through the rooms systematically again, he studied the walls through his eyelids, looking for a sign. Room after room was clean, nothing to indicate a hidden passage or door.

"Here comes security," Jim shouted from down the hall.

Frustrated, Proctor hurried toward the lobby, Rich and Nick following closely. Halfway down the hall he saw one of the panels was outlined in red. Proctor tapped on the panel and then on the one next to it. Stepping back, Proctor kicked the panel with all his might, splitting the panel in the middle.

"Quiet down there," Jim shouted. "The security guards are here."

Ignoring the warning, Proctor kicked the panel again and again, shattering the wood and revealing a stairway.

"Freeze!" came the shout of one of the security guards.

Proctor turned slowly, watching two guards through his eyelids. They were side by side at the end of the hall, walking slowly forward, guns pointed at Proctor. Then

Guy and Jim stepped up behind them, pressing pistols against their heads. The guards surrendered immediately and his men ordered them to the floor to be cuffed, gagged, and blindfolded.

With the guards secured, Proctor stepped through the wall and headed down the stairs. There was a faint glow in the basement that suddenly went out. Proctor closed his eyes, seeing in the dark. Halfway down the stairs he slowed, gun in hand, studying the bottom. The stairs ended in a large space with three connecting rooms. Flashlights shone behind him, his men trying to light his way.

"Turn off those lights!" Proctor ordered.

Suddenly three shots were fired, the slugs hitting just below Proctor's feet.

Keeping his back to one wall, he inched down the stairs, his men feeling their way behind him. At the bottom Proctor stopped, studying the three doors at the bottom. All three were closed. Through his eyelids, Proctor could see that one glowed in a red outline, the other two were dark. He could see the outlined door was open a crack. Proctor passed his .38 automatic to Rich.

"Give me Guy's Magnum," Proctor said.

There was whispering, then Guy's .357 was passed to Proctor.

"Come out of that room or I'll shoot," Proctor shouted.

Proctor waited thirty seconds, then repeated the warning.

Taking aim at the door, Proctor fired three rounds in quick succession, stitching a line waist high from where the crack in the door began to the far edge. There was no scream, just a loud thud as a body hit the floor. Boldly, Proctor walked across the open space, seeing through his eyelids. Magnum still in his hand, he kicked the door open. The door rebounded when he did and he wedged it with his foot. Leaning in, he saw a body on the floor, blocking the door. He shoved the door hard, the body moving aside as he did. There was a large gaping wound above the man's right eye, gore sprayed across the floor.

Proctor's men pushed in around him, fanning out, looking for more guards and for Ruth. Proctor scanned the room with his closed eyes, horrified by what he saw. Then he reached for a light switch and turned on the lights so his men could see what Crow really was.

When the lights came on Proctor's men froze in disbelief. The walls were painted with scenes that could only be from hell. Naked men and women being tortured— eyes gouged out, limbs chopped off, people being burned alive, some skinned, many crucified. In the middle of the chamber was a large stone table, stained dark brown. The stain continued down the sides to the floor, where it spread out like frozen flames. Every man there was a hunter and knew what dried blood looked like.

Sitting high on a pedestal was a small statue of Satan, standing on cloven hooves, watching them with painted red eyes. Slowly, every man in the room turned to the statue, locked in a stare with the master of the underworld. In the light of day the statue would have been a laughable object of ridicule, nothing more than a childlike representation of the Devil. But here, in this den of horrors, it wasn't just a statue, it was Satan in all his terrible majesty, reigning over his basement kingdom. George Proctor felt the same evil, and the same nearly paralyzing presence. Then he closed his eyes, seeing the statue's head turn slightly, so that it was face-to-face with Proctor, Satan's lips curling into a cruel smile. Proctor returned the smile, then blew the statue into a hundred pieces with the .357.

The boom of the gun in the small basement temple sent every man to the floor, cringing in shock. With a deep feeling of satisfaction, Proctor turned and left the room, studying the other two doors. Now one of them glowed red. Walking to the door, he could see it was sealed with a large steel bolt. Sliding the bolt out, Proctor pulled the door open, flipping a light switch as he did.

The interior was lit by a single bulb, the walls painted with the garish horrors of the chamber with the statue. There was a cot along one side. Huddled on the cot was a woman, cowering against the wall, blanket wrapped tightly around her. It was Ruth Breitling.

"Ruth, I've come to take you home," Proctor said.

Ruth stared at Proctor, eyes blank, her body trembling in fear. Then slowly, her eyes brightened and her mouth began to move.

"George Proctor," she whispered in a hoarse voice. "God answered my prayer."

Then she ran to him, holding the blanket to her body as she did, nearly tripping over it until she wrapped her arms around him, crying on his shoulder. Rich came around behind Ruth, pulling the blanket the rest of the way around her, covering her back. After a minute Proctor pulled her arms from his neck. Sobbing uncontrollably from joy, weak from the abuse she had suffered, she let Proctor support her and lead her from her cell and up the stairs through the shattered mahogany panel.

"Someone's coming," a voice called. "It's a Porsche."

Proctor stiffened and pushed Ruth toward Rich. Ruth clung to Proctor.

"This is Rich," Proctor said softly. "He's a God-fearing man."

Ruth hesitated, then accepted Rich as her new guardian.

"Take her home, Rich," Proctor said.

"No!" Ruth said suddenly. "I can't go home."

"Ira is waiting for you, Ruth," he said.

"I can't face him. Please don't take me home—not yet. Please."

"All right," he said, again pushing her to Rich. "Get her to the airport. We'll take her to the compound."

With Ruth safely on her way, Proctor turned, whispering a prayer as he prepared to meet the demon.

Rachel Waters hadn't bothered to turn the lights on and was hurrying down the hall toward the hidden stairway when Proctor stepped out, blocking her path. She froze, sizing him up, eyeing the .357 in his hand—seeing in the dark as well as he did. Closing his eyes, Proctor could see the demon again, like a hologram surrounding the human form inside. Was she possessed, or had the demon taken human form? Would it die if he shot it? Could a demon die?

He blocked her view with his body, letting the others

retreat behind him, hurrying to the rear exit. The demon looked past him, her red eyes looking for Ruth. Realizing that Ruth was getting away, the demon stepped toward him.

"Don't move, demon!" Proctor warned.

Stopping midstep, she looked at Proctor with new interest, her eyes like molten rock.

"My name is Rachel Waters, George Proctor," the demon said.

Opening his eyes he said, "I know your human name. What's your real name? Or don't demons have names?"

The Rachel Waters form smiled at him; a patronizing smile.

"You fundamentalists see demons everywhere. Everyone who doesn't share your narrow-minded view of the world must be demon-possessed."

Closing his eyes again Proctor said, "I can see your true form, demon—your tail, horns, wings, the claws on your hands."

Now the demon lost its smirk, studying Proctor's closed eyes. Then she stepped left and forward, the demon aura mimicking every move of her human body in perfect synchrony. He followed her movement with his gun. Still watching his closed eyes, she stepped back and right, and again he followed her with the gun. Now the demon looked perplexed.

"You're imagining things, Mr. Proctor," the Rachel demon said. "You're hallucinating."

Opening his eyes and pointing the gun at her head he asked, "If I shoot you, will you die?"

"Of course I will, I'm human."

She remained calm, but there was a touch of concern in her voice. Whatever a bullet would do to her, she wanted to avoid it.

Sirens sounded and once again the human form of the demon became confident.

"The police are coming," Rachel said. "You won't get away now."

Proctor had rushed to face the demon, now he didn't know how to deal with it. He had prepared all his life for a showdown with human oppressors, not spiritual foes. Should he kill the demon's host? Would that send the demon back to hell or free it to occupy another host? Or should the demon be excised from the innocent host by the power of the Holy Spirit? The time wasn't right for this, but he was here and the demon was afraid of the gun. Deciding he might not get another chance, he closed his eyes to see the evil he was trying to excise, aimed the gun at Rachel Water's head, and pulled the trigger.

With inhuman speed the demon twisted, the bullet merely creasing the human scalp. Then the thing leapt at him, kicking him in the chest, sending him sprawling. When he brought the pistol up to shoot again, she grasped his wrist in her hand—her powerful hand. Wrenching the gun free, she threw it down the hall behind her. Her fingers couldn't completely circle his wrist, yet she held him tight. Then an inch beyond each of her fingers his flesh was pierced. Closing his eyes he could see the demon fingers extended beyond hers, the nails buried in his flesh. Wincing with pain he threw a wild punch at her face, but her free hand shot out, grasping his other wrist. Then she lifted him to his feet. Closing his eyes he could see the demon image, floating in front of the human face. Every orifice glowed red, the eyes brightest of all. Grinning, she slammed his gun hand against the wood paneling twice, breaking his wrist. His pain delighted her and she dragged him to the other wall, prepared to break his other wrist. Then the police came up behind her. She dropped him and stepped aside as two policemen with guns drawn came down the hall.

"If I'm arrested, I'll tell the police everything. How will you explain that chamber of horrors in the basement?"

She smiled and so did the demon.

"These men are part of our little worship group. You're not going to jail, you're going to take Ruth Breitling's place."

Realizing he was doomed to be spread-eagled on the altar in the hidden basement, he struggled to his feet. As he did, she punched him in the face, knocking him to the ground again.

"You're stronger than you look, Ms. Waters," one policeman said.

"Take him, please," she said, feigning fear.

Pointing their guns, they ordered him to freeze and roll onto his stomach.

"Take him to the basement and tie him to the bed," she ordered.

Deciding to die in an escape attempt, Proctor tensed, ready to jump the closest officer. Suddenly a hail of bullets ripped through the ceiling over their heads.

"Drop your guns!" Rich shouted.

Briefly eyeing the automatic rifle in Rich's hands, the policemen dropped their weapons. Proctor crawled down the hall toward Rich, careful to stay below the line of fire. Then he stood next to him, holding his broken wrist.

"Back up," Rich ordered Rachel and the policemen.

Proctor watched the demon through his eyelids. It snarled and glared, but obeyed Rich. It does fear the gun, Proctor realized. It must need the host.

Ordering them into a conference room, Rich ripped out the phone wires, then pulled the door closed and tied the phone wire to the knob, then stretched it across the hall, tying it to another doorknob. Cinching it tight, they collected the weapons in the hall, then hurried toward the back. They heard the door splinter as they fled.

> Sacredness of human life! The world has never
> believed it! It has been with life that we settled
> our quarrels, won wives, gold and land, defended
> ideas, imposed religions. We have held that a
> death toll was a necessary part of every human
> achievement, whether sport, war, or industry. A
> moment's rage over the horror of it, and we have
> sunk into indifference.
>
> — *NEW IDEALS IN BUSINESS*, IDA TARBELL

WASHINGTON, D.C.

Crow was in his Washington apartment sound asleep when Rachel's call on his private line woke him.

"Ruth Breitling has escaped," Rachel said bluntly.

Still groggy, Crow struggled to understand.

"Impossible," he said, his mind shaking off sleep cobwebs. "She was locked in and there was a guard."

"She had help," Rachel explained. "George Proctor led a raid. They killed the guard and broke Ruth out."

Crow fumed. Proctor had interfered with his plans before and could again in the future. Proctor had to be taken out of the game.

"What do the police know?" Crow asked.

"Nothing yet," Rachel said. "The two officers who responded to the security alarm were our people. They'll report what we tell them to report, but we can't sit on it much longer if we're going to use the police."

"Get some of our people over to Christ's Home," Crow said. "She'll probably try to get through the quarantine."

"George Proctor's too smart for that," Rachel said.

Rachel was right. The way to keep Ruth safe was to get her off the planet; take her to the New Hope. But because of the quarantine, the Fellowship fleet was grounded within the United States—would they violate that ban? No, once Ruth was free there wouldn't be enough reason to risk a flight. They would hide her until they could find a way to get her off the planet.

"I'll call Simon," Crow decided. "He'll know where Proctor might take her."

A few minutes later a sleepy Simon Ash was on the phone.

"Simon, what do you know about George Proctor?" Crow demanded.

Knowing his boss rarely answered questions, Ash didn't bother to ask what was going on.

"I know everything," Simon Ash said. "He's a dangerous religious fanatic, and a self-anointed bodyguard for Mark Shepherd and his people."

"Where would he go if he wanted to hide out?"

"Several places. He can disappear into San Francisco, Los Angeles, or Portland, but he hates cities, so he might run to Alaska. He's been buying property there—very remote property—but it's undeveloped. In a few years it'll be bigger and better equipped than his Idaho facility."

"What Idaho facility?" Crow asked.

"He has a farm in Idaho, north of Caldwell—a fortress, really. Barbed-wire fences, concrete walls. But Proctor wouldn't go there to hide. That's the first place police would look."

Crow thought for a moment and then realized Proctor wasn't trying to hide. He thought of himself as a hero for rescuing Ruth Breitling. To Proctor it was Crow who should be hiding, and Crow had to change that. After ordering Ash to gather as much information as he could about Proctor's Idaho property, he called Rachel back, giving her the location.

"If he doesn't show up in Christ's Home, he'll most likely run to Idaho."

"I'll contact Fry," she said. "He might have contacts with ATF. If Proctor takes Ruth Breitling there, we can quarantine his compound."

"That's not good enough," Crow said. "We can't have them telling their story."

"I doubt your friend Ruth will want to talk about her relationship with you."

"Proctor might, though," Crow said. "We need to discredit him."

"I'm listening," she said.

"Burn Autumn Rest. Blame the death of the guard on Proctor. Spread the word that George Proctor suspected a New Age group was worshiping on the property and destroyed it."

"I understand," she said. "I better go now, I smell smoke."

Thirty minutes later an angry Mr. Fry called.

"Kidnapping Ruth Breitling was stupid. You've jeopardized everything."

"By the time your Thorpe gets that sphere working the cult will be twenty light-years away," Crow shot back.

"Thorpe's closer to flying that sphere than you know. Besides, I've taken steps to slow the cult down. This fiasco with Ruth Breitling is blowing up in your face. If you go down, Crow, don't even think of implicating us."

"Don't threaten me, Fry," Crow grumbled. "This situation can work for us if we spin it the right way."

"I'm listening."

"I'll tell the press that as a community service I had been letting a New Age Christian group use the facilities at Autumn Rest. Self-proclaimed protector of the faith, George Proctor learned about it and set fire to the facility to teach the heretics a lesson. He murdered a security guard in the process. Proctor flees to his compound in Idaho where a federal warrant will be served for his arrest. He and his people will resist arrest, a firefight ensues, and he and Ruth Breitling die in the battle. It will be rumored that Ruth was pregnant with George Proctor's baby and that she hadn't been kidnapped, she had run away with her lover."

Fry chuckled at the audacity of the plan.

"It won't work if she gets a chance to tell her story," Fry pointed out.

"That's why you have to make sure she doesn't. Once she and Proctor are in Idaho, see that all communication with the compound is cut off."

"I can make it happen," Fry said confidently.

"This can't become a siege, Fry. The FBI and ATF need to go in soon."

"What we need is for them to start the fight. I can arrange that too, Crow, but from now on you don't make any moves on the cult without checking with me. You're an amateur. In a few days you'll see what a professional can do."

Fry's insults were hard to take, but Crow listened silently, knowing he needed his help, for now. But Crow had no intention of reporting to Fry, or to anyone but his Master.

CHAPTER 77 **SIEGE**

Remember Waco. Remember and learn.

—GEORGE PROCTOR

PROCTOR'S COMPOUND, IDAHO

They reached the Idaho compound by midday. Guy's wife, Marilyn, took charge of Ruth, drawing her a bath and rounding up clothes. A local doctor came and set Proctor's wrist, X rays would have to wait. Ruth refused any medical attention and when the doctor insisted, Marilyn ordered all the men to stay away from her. As details of Ruth's experience leaked out, the women felt empathy, the men collective guilt. Ruth adamantly refused to let Ira be contacted and again, Marilyn and the other women defended Ruth's right to make that decision.

By evening the police buildup began. Proctor ordered

the compound secured. Gates were locked, guard posts were manned, children were kept inside, provisions were inventoried. Semi-automatic weapons were converted to full automatic. The buildup around the compound continued through the night, helicopters landing just over the nearest hill. From the watch towers, Proctor's guards could see lights moving through the woods toward the perimeter.

FBI and ATF agents came to the gate in the morning, brandishing warrants for Proctor's arrest and to search the property. Proctor made the agents wait at the gate while he finished his breakfast, then two cups of coffee. When he finally sauntered out the agents were furious. Flanked by four armed men, Proctor opened the gate, letting the agents inside. Each agent wore a jacket with large yellow letters spelling either FBI or ATF. The agents reflected the affirmative action policies of the federal government. The FBI was represented by a black woman, a Hispanic male, and a white male. The ATF sent a white woman, an Asian male, and a white male.

"We have a warrant for your arrest," FBI agent Hernandez said.

"On what charge?" Proctor asked.

"We'll explain it to you on the way."

"You'll explain it to me now," Proctor said.

Hernandez locked angry eyes on Proctor but didn't try to take him prisoner, knowing Proctor's men were ready to defend their leader.

"You're charged with arson and murder," the white FBI agent said.

Proctor turned to the agent who spoke.

"Who was murdered and what was burned?" Proctor asked in a slow even tone.

Now the agent stepped toward Proctor, reaching inside his coat. Snapping their rifles to their shoulders, Proctor's men froze him midmotion. The agent slowly pulled his hand from his coat holding a pair of handcuffs.

"You're under arrest, Proctor," the agent said. "You know the routine, turn around and put your hands behind you."

Proctor smiled while his men laughed.

"Take it easy, Smith," Hernandez said.

"Back off!" the female ATF agent said to Smith.

Smith hesitated, wanting to defy the order, but stepped back.

"I'm Agent Crosby," the female ATF agent said. "We have witnesses who saw you break into Autumn Rest Cemetery and set fire to it. An unarmed security guard by the name of Harlan Kimble was murdered during the break-in."

"You have your facts mixed up," Proctor said, his bright blue eyes animated. "I broke into Autumn Rest Cemetery to rescue Ruth Breitling who was being held there against her will. In the process of rescuing her we subdued two people, tied them up, and locked three others in a room. When the man who was guarding Ruth fired on us, and then refused to surrender, I defended myself and my people. The man who died must be this Kimble. There was no fire."

Now the agents looked at each other, surprised by Proctor's willingness to confirm parts of the story and confused by his addition of details they had not heard. Crosby and Hernandez stepped back to confer. Now Smith turned to Proctor.

"Turn around, Proctor, I'm going to cuff you," Smith ordered.

"No," Proctor said, eyes twinkling, the hint of a smile on his lips.

Smith flushed, unnerved by a man who didn't defer to his position of power.

Smith stepped toward Proctor, Hernandez hurrying back to step between them.

"We don't know anything about Ruth Breitling being involved in this," Hernandez said. "But come with us and we'll listen to your story."

"In a democracy you do the investigation before you make arrests, not after."

Now Hernandez flushed, angry at being lectured.

"We've got a burned-out building and a body," Hernandez said. "We have five witnesses who have identified you as one of the men who broke in. That's probable cause,

Proctor. You'll have a chance to defend yourself in court."

"I'll never make it to court if I go with you," he said, looking at Smith.

"I guarantee your safety," Hernandez said. "You'll be under FBI protection."

Proctor's men laughed, the agents glowering.

"Here's what I'll do," Proctor said. "I'll agree to be interviewed about the incident at Autumn Rest. I want a panel of judges that we mutually agree on. At the hearing I'll provide witnesses and evidence. If at the end of that hearing the judges issue a warrant for my arrest, I will surrender."

"How dare you dictate to us!" Smith spat, Hernandez holding him back with a hand on his chest.

"You're resisting arrest," Agent Crosby said.

"I'm giving you a chance to avoid embarrassment and do your jobs properly," Proctor said. "And I'm keeping myself alive," he added, staring at Agent Smith.

"You religious fanatics are all alike—paranoid!" Smith snapped. "The only enemies you have are in your own twisted mind."

"That's what they told Custer at Little Bighorn," Proctor said.

More laughter from Proctor's men infuriated Smith.

"All right, Mr. Proctor," Hernandez said. "We'll go back and talk over your offer, but I'm not making any promises."

" 'Kings take pleasure in honest lips; they value a man who speaks the truth.' Proverbs 16:13," Proctor said.

As the agents turned to go, Agent Crosby's head exploded, the sharp crack of a rifle firing following a half second later. Brains and blood showered Hernandez, and he flinched reflexively, reaching out to catch Crosby as she fell. All dead weight, she slipped from Hernandez's grasp, collapsing into a limp pile of limbs and torso.

Everyone was shocked by the agent's sudden death. Proctor reacted first, ordering his men to back toward their building. Now the agents pulled pistols and dropped to the ground. Smith opened fire immediately, his first slug hitting Proctor in the chest, knocking him to the ground.

Now Proctor's men opened fire, their M-16s on full automatic, spraying the air, pinning the agents to the ground.

Rich snaked an arm around Proctor, helping him up, while Jim and the others covered their retreat with automatic weapons fire. Now the federal snipers opened up. A slug ripped through Jim's leg, and he collapsed to the ground. The wound spurted blood, the artery severed. More men raced from the farmhouse, helping Proctor and Jim. Guy threw Jim over his shoulder in a fireman's carry, hurrying toward the open farmhouse door. Proctor was through first, hurrying away from the door so the others could enter. As Guy stepped through, a bullet passed through his neck. Collapsing to his knees, Guy was pulled inside and Jim was lifted from his shoulder. Two bullets whizzed through the door, smacking into the wall on the far side of the room. The two men still outside dove in, the steel door slammed and bolted. From the second story and roof, Proctor's riflemen targeted the federal snipers. Using high-powered binoculars, spotters directed the return fire, driving the federal agents to cover.

Shutters on all sides of the house were closed and at every hidden gun port was a man armed with a rifle. Ineffective gunfire continued inside and outside the house for another minute until Proctor ordered his men to save their ammunition. Turning to the wounded, they found Guy had bled to death where he had fallen and Jim was unconscious from blood loss. Karla Simms was summoned, the only nurse in the compound. She applied a tourniquet to Jim's leg, then ordered him taken to the infirmary. A few minutes later she sent her son Tommy running through the complex to find men with Jim's blood type.

The children were frightened but well drilled and filed down to the basement where only a bomb—or fire— could reach them. Proctor pried the slug out of his Kevlar vest, then thanked God for sparing him.

After sending Rich off to check the defenses, Proctor went looking for Marilyn. He hadn't delegated the job of telling her that her husband was dead, but someone had taken the initiative. He found her in Ruth Breitling's arms, sobbing.

"I'm sorry, Marilyn," he said. "He died saving Jim's life."

Nodding, she controlled her crying, wiping her eyes with her hands.

"Why did they shoot? Why?" she asked.

"One of their agents was killed."

"We started it?" she said, incredulous. "You said we would never shoot first."

"It wasn't us. The bullet hit the agent at an angle. The shot came from outside the compound."

"They wanted a war," she said.

"Someone did," Proctor said.

"It's because of me, isn't it?" Ruth asked, drying her own eyes.

"They would have come after us eventually, Ruth. They've been looking for an excuse."

"If only I had gone home," Ruth said. "I should have told the police what happened."

"There were police there last night," Proctor said. "They were working for Crow."

Eyes wide she said, "He's a Satan worshiper. He's evil."

"I know. His assistant is no prize either."

Proctor didn't explain what he knew about Rachel Waters.

"I can tell people what happened," Ruth said. "I can tell them about what he did to me." Then resting her hand on her stomach, "But I must tell Ira first."

Seeing the gesture and the pain in her eyes, Proctor and Marilyn understood. Marilyn hugged Ruth tighter.

"It's your baby too, Ruth. Don't forget that. With you and Ira as parents it will grow up to love the Lord."

Rich came in, telling Proctor Agent Smith was on the line.

"I thought I'd killed you, Proctor," Smith said. "They'll sell those bulletproof vests to anyone. Next time I'll aim a little higher."

"The next shot is mine," Proctor said.

"You don't scare me, Proctor!" Smith said.

Proctor could hear a slight tremble in his voice.

"What do you want, Smith?" Proctor demanded.

"You have one hour to surrender."

"I gave you my conditions."

"That was before you murdered an FBI agent, Proctor. Now you'll surrender unconditionally or we'll come in and take you."

"The shot that killed your agent came from outside the compound. One of your own people killed her."

"You're a liar, Proctor. One of your trigger-happy farmers squeezed off that round. But I'll still make you a deal. If you surrender now, I'll recommend a charge of second-degree murder."

"I'll see your men answer for the murder of Guy Francis," Proctor said.

"Crosby had a little boy, Proctor."

"Guy Francis had a wife and two kids."

"I'm going to give you an hour, Proctor, but just so you know we're serious . . ."

The line went dead in midsentence. Proctor turned to see Rich and the others waiting to hear what was said.

"It looks like we're in for a siege. That will work for us. The television crews will be here soon. Once the world is watching we'll contact the Fellowship on New Hope station. Mark Shepherd will make sure our message gets out. Then we'll have Reverend Maitland brought in to negotiate. We've got video of what happened to Agent Crosby at the gate. We can prove we didn't shoot her, and with Ruth Breitling to tell her story, we'll be all right."

Suddenly Proctor heard shouting from deep in the building. Hurrying to the sound, he found Mark Carter stretched out on the floor, his chest soaked with blood—he was eighteen. Mark's parents were wheat farmers in eastern Oregon and financial supporters of Proctor's movement. A weekend warrior himself, Mark's father was proud when his son asked permission to join the movement full-time, and prouder still when Proctor accepted him.

Fingers on the boy's neck, Rich shook his head. Other men were hurriedly covering the bullet-resistant Plexiglas with plywood. Proctor could see a bullet hole in the plastic.

"What happened?" he asked.

"He was standing lookout," Rich explained. "He stepped across the window and the round came right through."

In the distance Proctor heard the phone ringing. He knew who was calling before he answered.

"Get the message, Proctor?" Smith said.

"You murdered a teenage boy!" Proctor said angrily.

"Teflon-coated bullets, Proctor. Your bulletproof glass isn't any good, and neither is your Kevlar. You have one hour to come out with your hands up."

"We have women and children in here, Smith."

"You should have thought of that before you started this."

The line went dead. Rich and the others were looking at him, but all Proctor could see was a dead teenage boy whose mother and father had entrusted him to his care.

Pushing past the others he climbed to the top level of the farmhouse. The original house had a third level that they had expanded so there were four dormers along each side. The windows in the dormers attracted enemy fire, but steel shutters stopped even the Teflon bullets. Instead of using the windows, they had built gun ports high on the wall, just below the eave. While the dormers attracted the fire, their snipers fired from hidden positions. Climbing up onto the gun platform he held out his hand, demanding a rifle. Handing over the weapon without a question, Cobb McGriff stepped aside.

"Where's the communications center, McGriff?" Proctor asked.

"It's the blue van across the road behind the state police cars."

Proctor looked through the scope, scanning the vehicles gathered on the edge of their property.

"I see it."

"What are you doing, sir?" Rich asked, climbing the platform to stand next to him.

"They sent us a message, Rich. I'm sending a reply."

"Are you sure about this, sir?"

"It's justice, Rich. An eye for an eye."

Proctor leveled the rifle, the barrel hidden by the shadow of the eave. The Magnum load would give him the distance, but if the target was moving, estimating lead would be difficult.

"Remember the sixth commandment, sir," Rich said.

"Smith should have remembered it."

Proctor rested the rifle on the ledge, since his broken wrist made it hard to hold. He studied the van through the scope. Two men were standing on the far side—one of them could be Smith but he couldn't be sure which.

"We've committed no crimes," Rich said. "We've only acted in self-defense."

Through the scope, Proctor saw a third man approach the other two, disappearing behind the van. Then two men appeared, walking toward a police car—they were standing in the open, believing they were out of range. When they paused at the car he got a good look at the men—one of them was Smith. Now he steadied the crosshairs on Smith's neck. Over that distance the bullet would drop. By aiming at his neck he should get a hit in the torso.

"If you do this there's no turning back, sir."

"I know," he said.

"Are you with me, Rich?"

"All the way," Rich said after a brief pause.

Proctor squeezed the trigger. The report of the rifle was like the crack of thunder. When he steadied the scope again, all the men were down behind the squad car. He could see their heads huddled around someone on the ground. Then the federal snipers opened fire again, pelting all sides of the house. He hunkered down, facing Rich for the first time.

Like so many of his generation, Rich revered the New Testament, relegating the Old Testament to history and prophecy. It was the kind of Christianity that made for pacifists, Christians who refused to defend the faith, letting their culture slip away bit by bit rather than fight for its soul.

Rich and the others looked grim, understanding their situation. They had two dead, and one injured, but they were ready to fight for their freedom, ready to die for God and for what their country had once been. Then the building began to vibrate.

Careful to stay out of sight, they peeked out windows and peepholes. Rumbling up the road was a tank. When every man had a look, they again turned to their leader. Closing his eyes, Proctor scanned the forces gathering outside the walls. Now he understood—there would be no siege and there would be no survivors.

"There will be no negotiations and they won't let us get our side of the story out to the world. They'll wait until dark. Then they'll be coming in force."

His men knew what to do, but first each went to his family, reassuring them, making plans in case they were separated, praying for God's protection. Proctor tried to pray, but his thoughts kept coming back to the demon. He'd never seen evil in a purer form. It was clear that Satan and God had gone to war and Proctor had faith that God would eventually win the war. What Proctor didn't know was who would win this battle.

CHAPTER 78 **ASSAULT**

> The pounding [of the Branch Davidian Compound] began a few minutes after 6 A.M., when an armored combat engineer vehicle with a long, insistent steel nose started prodding a corner of the building. Shots rang out from the windows the moment agents began pumping in tear gas. A second CEV joined in, buckling walls, breaking windows, nudging, nudging, as though moving the building would move those inside.
>
> — *TIME* MAGAZINE, MAY 3, 1993

FELLOWSHIP COMPOUND, CALIFORNIA

Mark was in the underground hangar, studying the plans for their next space transport. After Ruth's disappearance, Ira had become a hermit, barely eating, losing weight, refusing to work, leaving Mark to pick up his load.

"Mark, George Proctor called," Shelly said. "He found Ruth!"

"Put him through."

"We were cut off," Shelly said. "Mark, you better come to the communications center, there's something you need to see on TV."

The communications center was a large room filled with computers and monitors, transmitters and receivers. Designed for only a handful of workers, it was now filled with a crowd that had gathered to watch the monitors. The crowd parted to let him pass and stand behind Shelly at one of the consoles. The monitors showed an aerial view of a tank parked outside a large building—a farmhouse that had been added onto haphazardly. Suddenly a puff of smoke erupted from the barrel of the tank and a rock wall in front of the house exploded.

"That's George Proctor's place," Shelly said. "That's where Ruth is."

"What?"

Suddenly Ira pushed through those gathered in the communications center, spinning Shelly in her chair to look her in the face.

"Ruth? They said you found Ruth!" Ira said.

"Calm down, Ira," Shelly said. "George Proctor radioed the New Hope station that he had found Ruth. Before we could find out where she was the signal was lost." Pointing to the monitors she said, "That's George Proctor's place, Ira. There's been shooting. Some FBI agents have been killed. Ruth may be inside."

Now video showed a stretcher loaded into an ambulance, the body covered, one end soaked with blood. Another image cut in, another stretcher, this time a man writhing in pain, clutching his blood-soaked stomach.

"But what about Ruth? They can't break in, they could kill her."

Evelyn appeared, wrapping her arm around Ira, comforting him.

"Shelly, are we relaying communications for the FBI?" Mark asked.

"I'll call Sandy."

While Shelly contacted Sandy aboard New Hope, Mark watched the tank systematically destroying the fence in front of Proctor's refuge. The helicopter providing the images was at some distance, the image unsteady. Panning back, they could see activity all around the main complex, men taking cover behind cars, rocks, trees—anything that would stop a bullet. Proctor's military savvy led him to clear a wide killing field around his building. Infantry crossing the open spaces would be subject to murderous fire. So would anyone escaping from the building.

"Sandy has localized the FBI signal. We're relaying for them between Idaho and Washington, D.C."

"Tell her to break in, Shelly," Mark ordered. "They need to know that Ruth may be inside."

The drama on the screen continued, the tank finishing its work on the fence. Then the turret of the tank rotated, pointing toward one end of the building. A puff of smoke and the corner of the building exploded, debris erupting from the explosion like the spout of a whale.

"Shelly, has Sandy gotten through to the FBI?"

"They won't talk to you," Shelly said.

"Then cut off the relay until they do," Mark ordered.

The barrel of the tank's cannon now pointed at the opposite end of the building, and it too exploded, collapsing in on itself.

"Shelly?"

"We cut them off, Mark. But they refuse to talk with us."

"Oh, sweet Jesus, protect my Ruth," Ira prayed, while on the screen the battle continued.

The only thing better than the honor of dying
for my country would be the glory of
dying for my God.

—GEORGE PROCTOR

PROCTOR'S COMPOUND, IDAHO

Proctor's ears were still ringing from the explosion of the second shell when they called again.

"The hour is up, Proctor," Hernandez said. "The men come out first, hands in the air. Then the women and children."

"We won't be taken alive," Proctor said solemnly.

"Don't be a fool, Proctor," Hernandez said. "We don't want a massacre."

"I gave you my terms. I'll testify to a neutral panel of judges."

"You come out now and you'll get your day in court. That's all I can promise."

"Any deaths will be on your head, Hernandez."

"At least send out the women and children."

Hanging up, Proctor signaled to Rich. Every gun opened fire on the tank, peppering it with small arms fire. Ricochets whined in every direction, the hidden FBI and ATF agents hugging their protective cover. Then the tank started forward, rumbling toward the center of the complex.

"It's time, Rich," Proctor said.

Rich pulled half the men from their positions, sending them to the basement, while the remaining men increased their rate of fire. Proctor followed his men down to the well-protected room in the center of the complex, where the women and children huddled, then down to the lowest level. There he directed three men with sledgehammers to bust through a thin section of concrete wall. The burly men made short work of the temporary wall, revealing a tunnel. When the rubble was cleared he called to Marilyn to bring the children down. Just as they had practiced in numerous drills, the children came down single file, following Marilyn and Ruth. Proctor threw a toggle switch and the tunnel lit up, one of his men leading the way into the tunnel, Marilyn and the others following.

After making sure the evacuation was under way, Proctor and two men entered the prison wing, not bothering to turn off the lights. For most of the prisoners it was their first look at the man who visited in the dark; a middle-aged man, muscular in build, with icy blue eyes. No less terrifying.

"What's happening?" Lichter asked. "I heard an explosion."

The others shouted too, frightened by the commotion above them. Proctor ignored them, going directly to the end cell. The man who had attacked the *Rising Savior* with a missile was sitting on his bunk, calm.

Pointing his gun, Proctor said, "Turn around."

The man obeyed and Proctor unlocked the cell. Two guards cuffed him.

"I knew you'd come," the man said.

"Keep your mouth shut or I may change my mind."

Ignoring the pleas of the others, they left the cell block, pausing while the last of the women and children filed down the stairs and into the tunnel. Proctor ordered two of his men to take charge of the mercenary. The prisoner was pushed into the tunnel, a guard in front and behind.

"You can't let him go," Rich said.

"I swore before God that I would set him free, and I will."

"He's killed before and he'll kill again," Rich said.

"There is a way, Rich."

Leaving the basement, Proctor climbed into the din above, reaching the main hall just as the tank crashed through the porch and into the front wall, the door frame splintering, the steel door knocked back into the room. With a roar of turbine engines the tank backed away, turned, and aimed for another section. Sending Rich to the upper floors of the opposite wing, they raced to the top levels ordering the riflemen to withdraw in stages, sending half down immediately. Manning a gun port himself, Proctor looked for the tank but the angle was poor, the tank punching a hole in the wall at the other end of the building. Instead he sighted on the communications van and put rounds into its already peppered side. His first round drew fire, the federal snipers having located the gun ports.

When the tank rolled around to the other side, Proctor sent half the remaining men to the basement, while he and the few left fired their weapons as fast as they could, trying to mimic a larger force. Then he saw a flash and the wall next to him exploded, knocking him off the platform. Dazed he held his head in both hands, head aching, one ear bleeding. When the pain subsided he rolled over to see a gaping hole. Someone grabbed his arms, pulling him toward the stairs just as bullets rained in the opening. Helped to his feet at the staircase, he stumbled down while another explosion rocked the building.

When he reached the bottom, Rich and four men came running from the opposite wing, joining them in the center room.

"They're opening holes in the second story," Rich said, then, "You're hurt!"

Proctor looked at his side where three large slivers of wood protruded, his shirt shredded and blood-soaked.

"It's not bad," Proctor said. "Pull them out!"

Without hesitation Rich yanked the three slivers in quick succession.

"There's a lot of little ones that will have to wait," Rich said.

"Is everyone accounted for?" Proctor asked.

"We're the last," Rich said.

Just as they turned to go the clink of a tear-gas canister sounded in the next room, followed by the hiss of gas. More clinking and hissing, as canisters entered from all sides. Then a new sound, a muffled explosion, then a flash.

"Incendiary grenade," Rich said. "They're burning us out."

"They never planned on taking prisoners," Proctor said.

Called paranoid their entire lives, there was no satisfaction in having your worst fears about your own government confirmed.

The smoke from the fires was thick and dark, the flames spreading along the ceiling, creeping toward them. Suddenly the wall behind them caved in, the tank having punched through to the center of the building. The tank backed out, revealing a clear path to daylight.

Hurrying down the stairs and through the hatch below, they pulled it closed behind them. Rich started for the tunnel but Proctor deviated, entering the cell block. Holding his bleeding side, he hurried to the far end and began unlocking each cell, working back to the door. Then he paused, looking back as the prisoners began to emerge, fearful of him and of the sounds they could hear above them.

"There's still time for you," Proctor said. "Go up two flights of stairs and then out the back."

Then he ran to the tunnel, pausing inside to throw another switch. Then counting slowly to ten he ran down the tunnel to Rich. There was a muffled explosion at the count of ten, followed by the collapse of the opening, the end of the tunnel filling with rubble.

"Will the prisoners make it?" Rich asked.

"They put their faith in the world instead of God. Now their fate depends on that world."

CHAPTER 80

CONFLAGRATION

> Buzzards circled overhead and the wind blew
> hard on the day the Branch Davidians died.
>
> — *TIME* MAGAZINE, MAY 3, 1993

FELLOWSHIP COMPOUND, CALIFORNIA

Smoke poured from every window in the building where Ira's beloved wife had taken sanctuary. Flames had eaten through the roof on one end and licked at the holes blown in the walls by the tank shells. Helpless, Ira could only cry, eyes fixed on the battle being played out on national television. The FBI steadfastly refused to talk with Mark, even though he had ordered New Hope station to cut off the communications relay. The FBI was furious about the loss of communications and threatened legal action against Mark and the Fellowship for breaking in on official communications and for obstruction of justice. All Mark's pleadings fell on deaf ears, and he was reduced to watching passively with the rest of the world, their technology useless to help Ruth.

Now flames burned through the roof in the front of the building, bright orange tongues licking through black smoke. Both ends of the building were on fire now, the flames spreading quickly through the wood-frame structure.

"How many children are inside?" Mark asked, afraid of the answer.

None of Mark's people knew, but as if in answer to the question, the television reporter covering the conflict said, "We understand there are fifteen or twenty children inside. That's from the ATF agents who have had the fundamentalist cult under surveillance."

Suddenly Wyatt Powder broke in from the network studio in New York. He had nothing to add, since he was nearly three thousand miles away, but this was the latest "story of the decade" and Wyatt Powder wasn't going to let a third-rate reporter from a network affiliate in Idaho get the credit.

"How sure are they on the number of children, Cliff?" Powder asked.

"It's their best estimate, Wyatt," the reporter replied, responding as if he and the network anchor were friends. "They were running a school on the property and that estimate of the number of children would be based on normal attendance. However, I must reiterate that it is just an estimate."

"Have they let any of the women or children come out, Cliff? Or are they determined to sacrifice innocent children for their cause?"

"We've seen no one come out, Wyatt. As you know there is precedent for self-immolation among right-wing extremists like these. The agents here say the fire has spread much faster than would be typical of a wooden structure like this one. They believe the cult may have used gasoline to spread the fire to prevent any of their members from changing their minds and escaping."

"Fundamentalists have been known to do that, Cliff," Wyatt agreed. "Can you see—"

"Sorry to cut you off, Wyatt, but something is happening in the back," Cliff said, interrupting the network anchorman.

The aerial camera zoomed in on a body lying behind the building. As the camera came around they could see another body lying just outside a gaping hole in the back of the building where black smoke was billowing out. Suddenly a man ran out of the smoke, only to be peppered with bullets two steps later.

"It looks like some of the cult members have been shot, Wyatt."

The reporter ignored the fact there were no weapons with the bodies.

"Do you see any children, Cliff?"

"Negative, Wyatt."

Next a woman broke from the building, her hair and

clothes on fire. Now holding their gunfire, they saw her make it halfway across the clearing before she collapsed, rolling on the ground, a ball of flames. An ATF agent broke from cover, removing his jacket as he ran, throwing it over the burning woman, then beating out the remaining flames with his hands.

"Ruth?" Ira said mournfully. "Is that Ruth?"

"I'm sure it's not," Evelyn said, not sure at all.

"That's right," Shelly said. "She was a very short woman."

The agent who had extinguished the woman now stood, holding his hands out, turning them over as if he was in pain. Just as others were emerging from hiding to assist him, the agent collapsed, clutching his leg.

"He's been shot," Cliff shouted over the air waves. "He tried to save that woman's life and they shot him."

Every hidden agent fired on the opening now, killing anyone else who might have tried to escape the flames. The wounded ATF agent was dragged back to cover, the burned woman left in the grass, her clothes still smoldering. The helicopter moved on, circling the structure, looking for more drama. It was a fire story now, the images all of flickering flames and billowing smoke. Soon the third floor collapsed, sending a shower of sparks into the sky, and one by one the walls collapsed inward, feeding the central fire that burned white-hot. Ammunition and explosives detonated, blowing debris as far as the road and the woods outside the compound, and there was brief pandemonium as small grass fires were extinguished. From a wisp of smoke, to conflagration, to dying embers, it was all captured on digital video, a permanent record of the end of George Proctor and his movement.

The Lord God is subtle, but malicious He is not.

— ALBERT EINSTEIN

FELLOWSHIP COMPOUND, CALIFORNIA

Three days later the ashes of Proctor's compound were cool enough to be searched. Only nine bodies were found and the FBI concluded either there weren't as many inside as they thought, or the fire had been hot enough to completely consume the rest. The FBI also reported that the estimate of the number of women and children in the compound had been in error, since most of those thought to be in the compound later turned up at nearby farms. Only one body was identified as female, that of the woman who ran from the building on fire. Burned too badly to identify visually, dental patterns proved it was not Ruth Breitling. Dental records for other cult women were not made available, and the woman, and the other unclaimed bodies, were buried in a collective grave. George Proctor's remains were never identified. Sightings of Proctor began shortly thereafter with witnesses claiming they had seen him in a restaurant in Boston, in a brothel in Brownsville, Texas, in a gas station in Montreal, and windsurfing in Hood River, Oregon.

Five days after the destruction of Proctor's ranch, reports of a new "gay plague" surfaced in San Francisco. Beginning in the gay and lesbian community, it quickly spread to the heterosexual population. Transmission of the disease was respiratory, and its course horrific. Beginning with sudden fever reaching 104 degrees, weakness and disorientation followed, then bleeding from the eyes. Slowly the tissues liquified, the arteries and veins eventually bursting, the victims drowning in their own blood. Ebola was suspected, but early identification of the virus responsible showed it differed significantly in structure, suggesting a mutation—that is, until the disease appeared in three other towns surrounding the Fellowship's California compound, and then Christ's Home itself.

"Cult Brings Alien Plague," read the headline in the *San Francisco Journal*. The disease was dubbed "IT," by the press, the name quickly popularized as the plague spread through the infected towns. Quarantines were imposed on the stricken towns, but San Francisco was impossibly large with undefined borders. When the death rate reached two hundred, the tourism rate in San Francisco dropped to zero, and in Los Angeles, half of normal. Few in San Francisco could find relatives to take them in, since they were deathly afraid of IT. The lack of hospitality by relatives and friends had the unintended consequence of slowing spread of the plague. Soon the Centers for Disease Control had efficient procedures in place and each new patient was quickly isolated.

Even as IT came under control, the media whipped up the public anger until only fear of the plague kept mobs from storming Fellowship properties and lynching whomever they found. The fact that none of those who had traveled to the stars were infected by IT was explained away by saying they likely acquired immunity during their stay on the planet where the disease evolved. Op-ed pages filled with editorials comparing the deaths from IT to those in the gas chambers of the Nazis, and the Fellowship with totalitarian regimes that practiced ethnic cleansing.

Senator Crow led the attack on the Fellowship in Congress, railing about their flagrant disregard for human life and their responsibility to the victims and to society as a whole. With key congressional leaders behind him he introduced two bipartisan bills, one to eliminate compensatory caps in lawsuits against the Fellowship, and the second to declare their technology essential to national security and to allow the Defense Department to acquire any and all technologies related to antigravity and faster-than-light travel. The bill was moving swiftly through the Congress toward a president poised to sign it when Mark Shepherd made a pivotal decision.

Mark gathered the Fellowship Council after hearing of Crow's proposed legislation. Ira was holed up in his house in Christ's Home, refusing all but minimal nourishment and incapable of working. Mark feared he would never recover from Ruth's death. Micah was missing too, nearing Earth with the gold asteroid.

"Floyd, the *Covenant* must leave for the new planet immediately," Mark announced.

"Impossible," Floyd said. "We don't have all the supplies we need."

"We have enough for two years. If we grow crops we can survive indefinitely."

"It takes more than food," Floyd said. "Fuel, electricity, heat. We hoped to send an advance team to build shelters."

"Floyd, if we don't go now, we may never get away. They're blaming IT on us. The country is turning against us. We've always had enemies, but now the common man is turning on us. Any day now our own government will storm through our fences and take God's gift from us."

"Who will go? We're restricted from flying anywhere but in and out of this compound, and only then because they need us to keep the communications platforms running. There's no way to get our pioneers here or to Mexico and we can't pick them up where they are without risking attack."

"The pioneers will be the residents of Christ's Home," Mark said.

The others at the table looked concerned. A subcommittee appointed by Mark had spent five years deciding on the criteria for the first group to move to another world. Carefully selected to be spiritually mature, physically fit, adaptable, and adventuresome, the first group was made up of married couples ranging from twenty to forty-five, many with children. Now Mark was proposing abandoning years of work and planning, and taking potluck.

"Is that wise, Mark?" Sally said. "Most of those in Christ's Home aren't farmers or craftsmen. Frankly, I thought there would be a town waiting when I got there. I don't know if I can live like Robin Hood in Sherwood Forest."

"I know we didn't plan for this, but it has advantages," Mark argued. "We know each other, we've worked together, worshiped together—we're a community, and there is strength in community."

Looking thoughtful, Floyd said, "It might do my family some good. It would give Daniel a chance to start over. Get him away from some bad influences."

Mark knew Daniel had few friends because of his influence on the other children, not their influence on him.

"Sally, you would have to stay behind to handle our financial affairs," Mark said, "and Stephen to take care of legal matters."

Sally looked relieved and then asked, "What about Ira?"

"The move may be the only way to save him."

Many questions followed, details discussed, and plans made. Excitement grew with each decision, as did anxiety. They would be the first humans to emigrate to another planet.

CHAPTER 82　**NEXT MOVE**

I have second thoughts. Maybe God is malicious.

—ALBERT EINSTEIN

WASHINGTON, D.C.

It had been two weeks since the identification of the plague called IT, and Crow had effectively manipulated public fear of the disease into fear of the Fellowship. So he was in no mood for Fry to take all the credit for the damage done to the Fellowship. The two of them were walking along the Washington, D.C. Tidal Basin.

"We've got them where we want them now, Senator, despite your clumsy kidnapping of Ruth Breitling."

Fry used Crow's title, but in a mocking tone.

"We had Ruth Breitling in our hands," Crow said, still frustrated by the loss of his prize. "In another month or so, Ira would have been begging us to trade the cult's technological secrets for his wife."

"But now she's dead and you've lost your only leverage over Breitling. Every one of your little schemes has failed, Senator. That reminds me, they found William Lichter, your NASA saboteur."

"Found him?" Crow asked, worried.

"Relax, he's dead. He was one of the bodies recovered at Proctor's compound."

"I thought they never identified the bodies."

"The FBI didn't, we made sure of that. Rosa Quigly was one of the dead, too. All of the dead were somehow linked to plots against the Fellowship."

"We could use this. Give it to the media. Proctor was a kidnapper."

"There wasn't a single Fellowship bullet in any of those bodies. How would we explain killing innocent people? Besides, if the bodies had been identified they might have made connections to you and others we're working with. We'll have to settle for Proctor being dead. He won't be around to protect Shepherd anymore."

Frustrated by his inability to stop the Fellowship, Crow's anger grew.

"We wouldn't have needed to kidnap her if you'd let Thorpe open that drive."

"A functioning sphere is a secret weapon we can use against them."

"But you don't even have that," Crow pointed out.

"Thorpe's obsessed with discovering their secret. He'll get it working. Besides, we may not need it. We now have the excuse we needed to take their technology."

"You're responsible for IT, I take it," Crow said.

"We borrowed it from one of our germ warfare labs. It's a genetically altered form of Ebola. We spread it through the communities around Christ's Home. That's where they built their ships, that's the facility we want."

"Their ships are assembled in space now," Crow pointed out. "They have an orbital manufacturing plant for building drives."

"They want you to think everything is being built in orbit, but we've been monitoring their Christ's Home compound and they're still building there. Maybe not the big ships, but if we can get a look at components, machinery, even residue from construction, you'd be surprised what our people can learn."

"Eventually someone will identify your Ebola variant for what it is," Crow pointed out.

"Any day now, I would guess. That's why we have to take the compound soon. When will the president have the National Technologies legislation on his desk?"

"The House will vote tomorrow, the Senate within two days after that," Crow said. "It will pass."

"We'll be ready to move on their Christ's Home compound in three days."

CHAPTER 83

DANIEL'S SANCTUARY

> Natural law gives parents the right to raise their
> children according to their personal beliefs.
> However, for the sake of the children, society
> has the right to limit parental freedom.
>
> — *UNDERSTANDING CONFLICT,*
> CHRISTINE MAITLAND

CHRIST'S HOME, CALIFORNIA

Headphones on, rock music cranked up to shut out the world, Daniel lay on his bed, staring at the poster on his ceiling. The poster was of bubbling mud pots in Yellowstone Park. His mother had removed the posters of rock stars or models in swimsuits that he preferred, so he picked the mud pots, ugly like his mood, and fantasized pushing his father into the steaming mud, picturing him dying in agony as every square inch of his body received third-degree burns.

The CD he was listening to was forbidden music, smuggled to him by the daughter of another member of the Fellowship, who had a cousin outside the faith. Lisa liked Daniel, he knew, and as his body changed he was beginning to think of her a lot. She would smoke with him and would share a drink on those rare occasions one of them could get their hands on alcohol. She told him about going to a kegger once, when she visited an older cousin in San Francisco. She had gotten drunk at the party, throwing up when she got home. Furious with her, her parents grounded her for a month, but she claimed it was worth it. Daniel made her tell the story of the party over and over, knowing that was the kind of life he wanted. He hated the straitjacket his parents kept him in, and the boring town they forced him to live in. Like Daniel, Lisa hated life in

Christ's Home and she offered to run away with him. He had refused the first time she asked, knowing it would be harder for two to get away, but the more he thought about her, the more he wanted her with him. Next time—when the quarantine ended—he would take her with him. Knowing it would add to his father's hurt made it all the sweeter.

The door opened, his father and mother entering. His eyes went cold, losing the heat they had held when he thought of Lisa.

"Daniel, we're going to be moving," his father said.

Daniel never spoke to his father, except to curse him, and he made a show of turning up the volume on his CD player. Angry, his father reached for his earphones, which Daniel protected with both hands. Instead, his father grabbed the cord, ripping it from the player.

"I said we're going to move, Daniel."

Pulling his earphones off, Daniel ignored his father, turning to his mother.

"We're not quarantined anymore?" Daniel asked hopefully.

"There's been no change in the quarantine," she said.

"Then what's the point?" he asked. "What are we going to do, move across town to some other dump?"

"We're moving to the new planet, Daniel," his father said.

Like a wild animal, caged and destined to live out its life in a zoo, Daniel understood the horror of the life that awaited him. Moving to a different planet meant that sneaking away for smokes and drinks would be over and there would be no more contraband CDs smuggled to him. Running away would be impossible and there would be no child abuse laws to keep his father at bay. He would be at his father's mercy, and his father had no mercy.

"I won't go!" he said, finally locking eyes with his father.

"It's a wonderful opportunity," his mother said.

"You can't make me go," Daniel said, still staring at his father.

"It's for your own good," his father said.

"It's for *your* own good," he said. "You want to make me do those things with you again. I won't! I'll fight you."

Now Daniel stood, backing to the wall, earphones

hanging from his neck. His father was powerful, but each day brought Daniel closer to adult strength and size. He might be able to break away, to run for the quarantine line, make them arrest him. Before he could fight past his parents, two more men came through the door, advancing on him. Daniel bolted past his father, but the other men caught him, wrestling him to the ground. Flailing and kicking he tried to hurt them, but they were big and strong, and he was flipped onto his stomach, his hands taped behind his back. Kicking did little good, they simply sat on him until he tired. Screaming obscenities was the only course left to him, but they stopped that with another piece of tape. Then loaded into a wheelchair, he left his room—his sanctuary—for the last time.

CHAPTER 84   **EVACUATION**

> Space, room, expanse—that is America; green
> space, fertile land; and man, migrant man, only
> the traveler there.
>
> —HAL BORLAND

CHRIST'S HOME, CALIFORNIA

The residents of Christ's Home greeted Mark's decision to move to the new planet with mixed reactions. Many were reluctant—especially older people—but their commitment to the Fellowship was such that they would follow Mark Shepherd, even if it took them to a new star.

Within twelve hours of the decision, shuttles were lifting residents to New Hope station, which quickly filled to capacity. The converted Seawolf submarine, *Covenant*, was opened and the former residents of Christ's Home began moving in, setting up housekeeping in the vast ship, trying to adapt to the closed spaces. Not all residents of the town of Christ's Home were Fellowship members, many people choosing to live there because they enjoyed the friendly atmosphere created by the Fellowship. The sudden evacuation by the Fellowship planted the seeds of panic among the nonmembers.

When it was clear all three thousand Fellowship members were leaving, the remaining residents panicked. Trapped inside Christ's Home by the quarantine, terrified by IT, which had infected thirty of the residents, they organized, approaching Mark, demanding to know what was happening. He told them the truth—they were leaving the planet. He tried to assure them it wasn't because of IT, but they wouldn't be comforted. Next the residents went to the barricades, talking with men in yellow environment suits. There was no sympathy there, and they ended up back in their homes, caught in a war between the sacred and the secular.

When news of the evacuation of Christ's Home reached Washington, D.C., the House moved up the scheduled vote on the National Technologies Act. Even former friends of the Fellowship dared not speak in their defense, not with IT ravaging the bodies of innocent citizens. The National Technologies Act passed nearly unanimously. In a rare all-night session, the Senate honored its tradition of open debate and then passed the legislation with no amendments. It was signed by the president only two days after Mark's decision. The Fellowship's technology was now claimed by the United States of America. Troops were moved to the quarantine line. Fry's release of the Ebola variant had succeeded, but only to a point. Now the same fear of alien plague that brought the troops to the door kept them outside.

As the troops gathered around Christ's Home and the compound, the remaining members of the Fellowship scrambled to gather their belongings and get off-planet. Priority was given to getting their people out of Christ's Home, which meant equipment had to be left for last. Mark couldn't let any of their technology fall into government hands. Devising a plan, he radioed Micah, who was still guiding the massive gold asteroid to Earth, using a fresh code that he hoped hadn't been cracked yet.

"This is *Exodus,*" Micah responded. "What is it, Mark?"

"They're massing troops, Micah."

"We knew this was coming," Micah said.

"We're getting our people out, Micah. We're evacuating Christ's Home. We're transporting night and day."

"If we abandon the asteroid we can be back within twelve hours."

"No, we can evacuate with the ships we have. We'll get our people out, but we've had to make choices—people or equipment."

Micah understood. Sensitive equipment was being left behind in order to save people. But the choice bought their people only temporary security if the secret of their technology fell into the hands of their enemies.

"We've destroyed what we can't move, but that may not be good enough," Mark said. "They can learn a lot from what remains."

"I understand," Micah came back. "What can I do?"

"I want you to complete the delivery of the asteroid, but to a different destination."

Troops broke through the quarantine line the morning after the president signed the National Technologies Act. Equipped with chemical warfare suits they moved into Christ's Home, occupying the town and herding the remaining residents into the school gymnasium. Only eighteen of those residents who had been infected with IT were still alive, and they were transported out in helicopters, none ever seen again.

When the troops moved into town, the remaining Fellowship members fled to the launch compound, those previously reluctant to leave now anxious to be transported. Ira was carried from his home and shuttled to New Hope station, weak from fasting, emotionally dead. If captured he would die before revealing any secrets, but Mark wanted to make sure if he died it would be on the new world. By noon troops had secured the town and searched the buildings, confirming no residents were left. The sky highway was now a freeway with spheres and shuttles moving up and down, lifting a hundred people an hour.

Once the town was secured, the troops advanced to the fences of the Fellowship's launch facility, pausing there, sending in a negotiating team to meet with Mark. Many of Mark's men were armed, but they would quickly be brushed aside by professional troops.

Mark and Floyd met with Colonel Watson and two other officers a mile from the launch compound. The *God's Love* lifted off just as they stepped out of their cars, Colonel Watson watching the spaceship disappear into the bright blue sky. He wasn't wearing an environment suit, and neither were his aides.

"You are to stop all orbital flights immediately," Colonel Watson said. "Your ships and launch facilities are confiscated."

"Our lawyers have filed a suit to overturn the National Technologies Act," Mark said. "We've asked for a restraining order to keep you off our properties, and expect it any minute."

"Until you do, we've got orders to occupy your facilities."

"That's illegal search and seizure," Floyd said.

"It became legal last night."

"Why aren't you wearing protection, Colonel?" Mark asked suddenly. "Aren't you afraid of IT?"

Uncomfortable now, Watson looked at the other officers, then back to Mark.

"We now understand that the bacteria known as IT had a terrestrial origin."

"Fear of IT was the main reason for the National Technologies Act. Now it turns out that fear was groundless and the act unnecessary," Mark argued.

"It's still the law."

"Colonel, when we're done evacuating our people to orbit, we'll surrender the complex to you," Mark offered.

"You'll surrender now."

"Be reasonable, Colonel. If my people are infected with alien diseases, then getting them off the planet is the best solution."

"My orders are to seize your facilities, and secure all technologies and alien contraband. Then I am to sterilize the premises. In two hours my men will be in place to take the facility. Remove as many people as you can in that time. Those remaining will be relocated to internment camps until we are sure they are not infected with hostile organisms."

Without another word Colonel Watson returned to his truck, leaving Mark and Floyd in the road.

"How many people do we have left to lift, Floyd?" Mark asked.

"Over five hundred. If we overloaded the shuttles we might get half of them out, but that would be tops."

"We've got to get them all out at one time," Mark said.

"There's no way."

"*Genesis* could hold them."

"It's not built to land, Mark. The drive is designed to push, not lift."

"To exceed light speed the field has to envelope the ship just like the spheres. It could work."

"I don't know, Mark. Ira or Micah are the ones to talk to."

"But Ira's in no shape and Micah's commanding *Exodus*."

"The *Exodus* is nearing orbit, let's wait."

"*Genesis* has to come down now if we're to have a chance of loading it before the deadline. Who do we have who can fly *Genesis* for us?"

"All the pilots are flying shuttles or spheres. We'll have to divert someone."

"There must be someone."

"Shelly," Floyd said. "Shelly could fly *Genesis*."

> . . . perhaps men should think twice before mak-
> ing widowhood our only path to power.
>
> —GLORIA STEINEM

NEW HOPE STATION, EARTH'S ORBIT

Shelly was in the communications center helping coordinate the steady flow of shuttles and spheres to the surface when the call from Mark came.

"Shelly, we need the *Genesis* brought to the surface.
We've got only two hours to get everyone out. Can you
pilot *Genesis*?"

Suddenly filled with doubt, nevertheless she said, "Yes.
I'll get it down within an hour," not as confident as she
sounded.

She had Sandy open the speaker in Ira's room.

"Ira, this is Shelly. I'm taking *Genesis* to the surface to
rescue the rest of our people. I want you in the copilot's
seat. We're leaving immediately."

Whispering a prayer that God would restore his spirit,
she hurried to *Genesis*'s dock. Others were already
aboard, powering up the systems, checking seals and life-
support systems. Shelly slid into the pilot's seat, familiar
with the controls even though she had never attempted
what she was about to do—no one had. Once the control
systems were all activated and she had all green indicators, she switched to the engineering station, powering up
the drive. When flying a sphere the pilot monitored the
field that allowed the globes to defy gravity and fly
through space. On the larger craft gravity fields were
monitored by other crew. The *Genesis* was driven by
three overlapping fields, far different in power and frequency from those used in the spheres, and little of her
experience applied here. As the drives came up to full

power the computer configured the drives for flight in
space. She would have to override the computer, recon-
figuring the fields to insulate the *Genesis* from Earth's
gravity. It had never been done, so she was making an educated guess—then a bony hand rested on her shoulder.

Turning to see an emaciated Ira, his good eye dull, lifeless, Shelly's heart leapt for joy.

"You're the pilot, Shelly," Ira said. "I'll handle engineering."

"We're taking her down to the surface—"

"Just do your job and I'll do mine."

Shelly smiled. A semblance of the old Ira was there—
he was crabby again.

"Take her away from the station, Shelly. I'll make ad-
justments on the way."

At the last second, Gus Sampson slid into the copilot's
chair.

"Thought you could use some help. Rob Walker's
standing by the hatches, Shelly."

"Call Christ's Home," Shelly said, "tell Mark we're on
our way."

Sandy cleared them, then Ira cut the ship's gravity,
turning control over to Shelly, who moved them away
from the station, angling toward the blue planet below.

> I think you know that I believe we must be
> strong militarily, but beyond a certain point mil-
> itary strength can become a national weakness.
>
> —DWIGHT D. EISENHOWER

OUTSIDE THE FELLOWSHIP COMPOUND, CALIFORNIA

Colonel Watson left his captains to coordinate troop placement around the Fellowship's launch compound, separating to meet with a muscular man with a scar on his cheek.

"I delivered the ultimatum, Mr. Fry."

"Good, Colonel. Then they'll stop flying?"

"I gave them two hours to finish evacuating their people."

Fry's brown eyes smoldered, putting Watson on the defensive.

"You don't want those cultists," Colonel Watson said defensively. "You want their facilities."

"Some of them might be of help in understanding their technology."

"The ones you want left long ago. The deadwood will go up last. Let them take their old and crippled. They'll be a burden and slow them down, drain their resources."

"What of their ships? If we move now we might catch one on the ground."

"We'd never get one intact. They've got pilots in every ship. If we tried to capture one they'll either take them to orbit or blow them up. My way is the best way. By putting a tight deadline on them they'll have to use their ships to evacuate their people and that will force them to leave the rest of their equipment behind. You'll have to make do with that."

"There better be something left, Colonel," Fry grumbled.

Colonel Watson understood the threat, modifying his plan on the spot.

"To make sure, we'll take the facility in an hour and a half, not two."

Now Fry smiled, the colonel relaxing.

"Now you're thinking, Colonel. But do we have to wait quite that long?"

CHAPTER 87   **RESCUE**

> The sleek, aerodynamic design of rockets and
> other launch vehicles is a function of the need to
> reach escape velocity while traveling through
> Earth's thick atmosphere. If orbit could be
> achieved at a slower speed, friction would
> be reduced, and launch vehicles could be of more
> functional designs.
>
> —*ALTERNATE PATHWAYS TO SPACE,*
> EDWARD NORTON

FELLOWSHIP COMPOUND, CALIFORNIA

Even if Shelly managed to get *Genesis* through the atmosphere and down to the surface, boarding the spaceship would be a problem, since *Genesis* wasn't designed to land. The ship was essentially three cylinders joined at one end by a large bulbous drive. Shelly planned to settle *Genesis* down on two of her cylinders, but the docking and cargo hatches would be unreachable, eight feet off the ground. Under Mark's orders, three makeshift ramps were being hammered together so the passengers could board. Meanwhile, spheres and shuttles continued to pick up people as quickly as they could. Only the most prized possessions went with them: family photos, legal papers, family Bibles, family heirlooms. Members of the Fellowship had few material possessions, everything long since donated for the greater good. Nevertheless, there had been no time to prepare, no time to say good-bye to the town their children had been born in, the church where they had worshiped, or family members in the cemetery.

Evelyn's voice came over the hangar loudspeaker. "*Genesis* is fifteen minutes away. Mark Shepherd, come to the control center."

Mark hurried through the crowd, patting backs, giving hugs, passing out reassurance where needed.

"It's Micah," Evelyn said. "He needs to talk to you."

"I'm here, Micah," Mark said. "Go ahead."

"You've got to decide now, Mark. We can either deliver the asteroid or orbit it, but once we do it'll be at least two hours before we can deliver it again."

"The timing is tight, Micah. If you deliver it now, when does it arrive?"

"Sixty-five minutes, give or take five. It depends on how hard you want it to come down. We've never calculated anything like this before."

"Bring it down, Micah. Your best estimate will have to do on how hard."

"Don't be anywhere near, Mark. I'm just guessing, and once we let it go there's no stopping it."

"We'll be gone, Micah."

Shouts from the hangar drew Mark back. *Genesis* had been spotted. Outside he could see a black dot in the sky.

"Clear the field," he shouted, pulling and pushing people toward the hangar. Those near the doors cheered *Genesis* down, those inside taking their cues from those who could see. Mark felt enormous relief—they were going to get away.

"Mark, come back to the control room," Evelyn said over the loudspeakers.

Now the cheering stopped, the crowd looking worried.

Inside the control room Evelyn said, "It's David, Mark. He's on the radio."

David Wayne commanded the Fellowship's security force in position around the perimeter of the compound.

Hurrying to the control center Mark found a grim-looking staff.

"This is Mark, go ahead, David."

"Troops have crashed through the front gate, Mark. They're coming."

"It's too soon. They said we'd have more time."

David was silent, waiting for orders.

"Fall back, David. Let them advance, but delay them. Act like you're going to put up a fight, but don't get into a battle."

"We'll do our best."

"Evelyn, the *God's Love* is coming down for you and the others in the control room. Stay in touch with Micah and when he breaks off from the asteroid let me know, then clear out."

"What about you, Mark?"

"I'll board *Genesis*."

Taking a walkie-talkie so he could communicate with David, Mark hurried back outside. The *Genesis* was near the ground, dust outlining the patterns of the gravity fields that made the ship fly. Mark had seen the ship many times, but never with terrestrial cues in the background, and it looked immense, three large cylinders welded together, the large drive on the end, larger in diameter than the combined cylinders. The name "Genesis" painted on its side, above it the American and Christian flags, below it a Scripture verse. Studying the dust patterns, he could see the fields configured in an unfamiliar way—by God's grace the ship remained intact. But now its mass would be increased sharply as it packed in nearly five hundred passengers. As the fields were shut down, tractors dragged the loading ramps toward the great ship, crowds following each platform.

Forward hatches in each cylinder opened, the ramps pushed against the ship. Then like the children of Israel hurrying across the Red Sea, the members of the Light in the Darkness Fellowship climbed the ramps, disappearing into the bowels of the ship. Men and women, old and young, children by the dozens, some carried, some pulled along by parents and older siblings. Most every-

one carried luggage—boxes, suitcases, duffel bags.
Many children wore backpacks, used to carry books to
school, now they held stuffed animals, favorite toys, or
prized collections of baseball cards, shells, or stickers.
Some children cried, unable to understand but sensitive
to the anxiety of the adults around them.

The hatches were large but the ramps small and rick-
ety, unable to handle the crush of people climbing
aboard. Soon Floyd gave orders to limit the number of
people on the ramp and loading slowed.

"Mark, come in, Mark," David's voice crackled over
the walkie-talkie.

"This is Mark. What is it, David?"

"They're coming fast, Mark. Request permission to
fire on them."

"No!" Mark shouted.

"Then they'll be at the compound in ten minutes."

Mark looked at the long line of people filing into the ship.

"All right, David," Mark said into his radio. "Fire over
their heads and then retreat back here."

The popping of small arms fire sounded in the distance, coming from every direction. Then the air was
filled with the sounds of a full-fledged battle. The crowd
panicked, forgetting the weight limit on the ramps, surg-
ing forward. Floyd ordered beams brought and jimmied
them under the ramps, for support.

Urging the people aboard, Mark helped where he could,
lifting children, helping older people with heavy bags.
Slowly the crush diminished, the flow reduced to a trickle.
The perimeter guards arrived, joining the last of his people
crowding up the ramps. Three of his men were wounded,
one with a head wound. David rushed up breathless.

"They returned fire, Mark. We took casualties."

Now Mark's walkie-talkie crackled to life again—
Evelyn.

"Micah says the asteroid has been released."

"How long until impact?"

"Twenty minutes."

"Get your people to the *God's Love,* Evelyn."

David went to make sure his men got on board while

Mark made sure Evelyn and the others made it to the *God's Love*. Once Evelyn and the others were safely on the ship, Mark ordered the *God's Love* to take off. As he ran back to the *Genesis,* Mark saw the *God's Love* lift safely away and head for space. Then Mark hurried back to the *Genesis* and climbed the ramp to the open cargo hatch where the last of his people were entering the ship. As Mark reached the top of the ramp, a bullet ricocheted off the hull in front of him. Mark froze, then turned to see Colonel Watson and a squad of soldiers approaching from around the corner of the hangar.

"You're under arrest, Shepherd, and your ship is confiscated," Watson shouted. "If you try to leave we'll shoot you down." Two of Watson's men raised their weapons. One aimed a laser at *Genesis* to illuminate it for the guided missile to be released by the second man.

"You agreed to give us two hours to get our people out, Colonel," Mark shouted.

"Come down off that ramp, Shepherd, or I'll have you shot."

At the colonel's words, a half-dozen soldiers aimed their weapons at Mark.

"I've got five hundred people in here, Colonel," Mark pleaded. "Honest citizens who have committed no crimes."

"No one will be harmed if you come down now. Your people will be cared for and, in time, released back into society. You have my word on it."

Mark looked at his watch, knowing there was little time left.

"Colonel, you and your men have to clear out of this area. Remember what you told me about the danger of infection and the need to sterilize the compound? Well, I've arranged to sterilize the grounds for you. An asteroid the size of a house is going to land right here. It will obliterate everything within a half mile."

Colonel Watson glanced at the sky, then said, "You're bluffing."

"It's a heavy metal asteroid being guided to this spot by one of our spheres. They won't miss by more than a hundred yards. Do you know how much kinetic energy will be released by an object of that size, dropped from miles in the sky? It will be like an atom bomb, Colonel." Then Mark leaned back, looking at the sky as if he were trying to spot the meteor. Suddenly he froze and pointed at the sky.

"There it is."

Colonel Watson and his men followed his point and when they did Mark dove into the hatch, Floyd hitting the close switch. Staying low to avoid the bullets ricocheting off the walls, they hunkered down until the hatch was closed tight, families near the hatch screaming and crying with each round. Finding the nearest wall speaker, he called to Shelly in the cockpit.

"Get us out of here. Micah's asteroid is going to land where we're sitting."

"Quit shouting, Mark! We're working in here," Ira replied.

Joyous over hearing his old friend's voice, Mark wasn't ready when the ship lifted off the ground. Knocked to the floor, his stomach flip-flopped as the gravity fields enveloped the ship. Then he remembered the soldier with the missile and prayed it wouldn't be a short flight.

> Meteor Crater, near Flagstaff, Arizona, is one of
> the youngest impact craters found on the
> Earth. . . . Between 5 and 20 megatons of kinetic
> energy were released during the impact, which
> left a bowl-shaped crater roughly 1.2km in
> diameter and 200m deep, surrounded by an
> extensive blanket of ejecta.
>
> — *THE NEW SOLAR SYSTEM*,
> J. KELLY BEATTY, BRIAN O'LEARY
> AND ANDREW CHAIKIN (EDS.)

FELLOWSHIP COMPOUND, CALIFORNIA

Colonel Watson felt like a fool for falling for Mark Shepherd's "Look over there" trick, but for a moment he had believed Shepherd's threat to drop an asteroid on him and his men. Now Watson realized it was all deception and he was furious with himself for falling for it. He hadn't expected to capture one of their ships, but now he had a chance.

"Shoot it down," Watson ordered.

The *Genesis* was illuminated with a laser by one soldier, the second holding the missile. A few seconds later a tone indicated a tracking lock.

"Aim for the power plant," Watson ordered. "That should disable it and bring it down."

The private shifted his weapon from the center of the rising ship toward the drive unit, but still didn't fire.

"Fire, Private, before it gets too high. We want it intact." When the soldier didn't respond Colonel Watson turned on him. "Soldier, I'm ordering you to fire that weapon."

Then the young man lowered the weapon, turning to face his commander.

"I can't fire, sir. There's innocent people inside."

Watson's humiliation grew. Brow-beaten by Fry, tricked by Shepherd, and now his own men disobeying him. Watson was desperate to regain the respect a colonel deserved. Yanking the weapon away from the soldier, Colonel Watson put the missile launcher to his shoulder.

"I'm going to court-martial you," Watson said, reaiming the weapon as the *Genesis* climbed toward orbit.

"Keep the laser on the power plant, soldier," Watson ordered.

"I can't, sir. It's rotating away from us."

"Then aim dead center. It's not getting away."

As his head tilted up with the weapon, tracking the ship, Watson noticed a bright dot in the sky above him. Suddenly he realized that Shepherd hadn't lied about sterilizing the compound. Watson fired the missile, then dropped the launcher, shouting to his men to run for cover. Confused by their commander's retreat, the soldiers hesitated until they too saw the bright dot swelling above them. Dropping weapons as they ran, they scattered in all directions, running for their lives.

Seconds later the missile caught the fleeing ship, exploding on contact. Pieces of the hull sprayed from one of the cylinders, black dots against the bright sky. Then more dots fell from the *Genesis*—they were people, dripping like blood from the wounded ship. Some of the falling drops were children.

CHAPTER 89   **DELIVERY**

> If a projectile is large enough, it can survive pas-
> sage through the Earth's atmosphere, more or
> less intact and strike the ground or the ocean at
> high velocity. The threshold size for survival
> depends on the material strength and density of
> the body and on its velocity at the time of
> encounter; for a stony body, this size appears to
> be about 150m . . .
>
> — *THE NEW SOLAR SYSTEM*,
> J. KELLY BEATTY, BRIAN O'LEARY
> AND ANDREW CHAIKIN (EDS.)

EARTH'S ATMOSPHERE

Micah followed the asteroid deep into the atmosphere,
paralleling it rather than trailing it. As it fell, the asteroid's surface would heat, vaporizing volatile metals on
the surface, and if hot enough, the entire mass. Micah's
goal was to bring it through the upper atmosphere intact
and then allow it to pick up enough speed to annihilate
the complex without endangering the troops occupying
the town. Once the *Exodus* had released the asteroid, controlling the fall became more difficult. With its asymmet-
rical mass and constant rotation, the gold asteroid
sheared out of every gravity field that Micah tried to envelope it with. The best he could do was repeatedly re-
form the field, slowing the asteroid in fits and starts,
keeping it from accelerating to speeds where it would vaporize.

Before evacuating the launch complex, Mark had
arranged for a homing signal to be broadcast, and
Micah's navigational computer was keeping his ship on
track. Micah concentrated on the asteroid, keeping it on a

parallel course, at the same rate of descent. A chirping sound from the computer indicated he was a mile over the complex; taking manual control of the sphere, he let the asteroid go. Now in free-fall, gravity took over, accelerating the asteroid, building up the kinetic energy that would be released when contact with the ground converted it to heat.

As he watched the asteroid turn into a meteor, Shelly called from the *Genesis*.

"Micah, this is Shelly. Are you there, Micah?"

"I'm here, Shelly," Micah said, happy to hear his wife's voice.

"We've been hit by a missile. We can't pressurize one of the cylinders and the drive has been damaged. We've lost one of our fields and we're barely maintaining lift."

Instantly Micah rotated the sphere, scanning for the *Genesis*.

"Give me a beacon, Shelly."

Micah's computer picked up the signal and fed the coordinates to navigation. Accelerating as fast as his body could stand, Micah angled into the sky, breaking the sound barrier as he passed into a cloud bank. Closing rapidly, he slowed, his radar picking up the ship, ahead and above.

"I see you, Shelly."

"We've lost a second drive, Micah. We're going down."

Wobbling, the *Genesis* dropped, picking up speed as the remaining power plant struggled to keep the ship in the sky.

Rolling the sphere violently, Micah's head smacked the headrest, his ear painfully crushed. Diving, he chased the *Genesis* down, coming in above and upside down, looking for the docking ring.

"I'm above you, Shelly. Lóck the ring as soon as I've docked."

"It's too late, Micah," Ira said. "There's not enough time."

In the background Micah could hear people crying. They had packed everyone into the two intact cylinders, using every available space including the flight deck.

"Shut up, Ira," Micah said. "I'm working."

Warning lights winked on, the skin of the sphere over-heating. Recklessly, Micah chased the falling ship, bring-ing himself over the docking ring, trying to match the movements of the wobbling ship. Feeling he had the rhythm of the *Genesis,* he took the sphere down, trying to insert the docking probe into the docking ring, but the ship rocked unexpectedly, and he hit the ring at an angle, bouncing off the ship in a scream of tearing metal. As he steadied his gyrating ship, the indicator lights on his docking board all went red, the docking probe hopelessly damaged.

"It's over, Micah," Ira said. "We'll see you in Glory."

Micah could see the ground rushing up at them. *Gene-sis* wasn't in free fall but it was accelerating and the im-pact would destroy the ship and kill everyone on board.

"Shelly, open the loading bay in the damaged cylinder."

"What?"

"Open it, Shelly!" Micah shouted.

The hatch cracked, then slowly opened, the doors open-ing out, the winds buffeting them, threatening to rip them off. Micah flew the sphere in front of the falling ship, again watching the roll of the *Genesis,* timing his move.

"Micah, don't do it!" Shelly shouted. "We can't both die—the children, Micah."

"I'm working here, Shelly," Micah said, then his sphere shot forward, and with a scream of metal jammed itself into the cargo bay.

Stunned from the impact, Micah hung limp in his har-ness until the pain from a broken arm roused him. Using his good arm, he checked the indicator board for his drive—the drive wasn't damaged. Powering up the drive to levels never used, he extended the field, enveloping as much of the ship as he could. Within the gravity field of the sphere he had no sensation of up and down, and he waited for impact, not knowing whether his little sphere could add enough lift to save the *Genesis.* Just when he thought it had worked the ship hit, slamming his broken arm against the chair, consciousness briefly dissipating, the sphere nearly disgorged from the gullet of the ship—

but he lived, and the ship was still whole. After a brief eternity Shelly's voice was in his aching head.

"Micah, you did it," Shelly said.

"But we hit."

"Not hard. We bounced. We're rising slowly, but the *Rock of Ages* is on the way. Are you all right in there? We can't get you out until we dock at New Hope."

"Pressure's still good but the controls aren't responding," Micah said. "What about you?"

"We lost nine people, Micah. Four children."

"Who, Shelly?"

"Mrs. Robeson and her baby. The Samms lost both their twins, Sydney and Taylor. Rob and Erin Kenton and their oldest boy, Jeff. Betty Lambert and Kelly Young."

Micah knew them all, and the pain was more than he could bear. He began to weep.

CHAPTER 90   **IMPACT**

> No man is a Christian who cheats his fellows,
> perverts the truth, or speaks of a "clean bomb,"
> yet he will be the first to make public
> his faith in God.
>
> — *MORE IN ANGER*, MARYA MANNES

GILROY RANCH, CALIFORNIA

The Gilroys lost their ranch to the military once the quarantine on the Fellowship was imposed. Now media access to the hill overlooking the Fellowship's compound was restricted. Roland Symes had been invited to witness the take-over of the Fellowship compound, as were Bill Towers and Wyatt Powder and their news crews. Roland knew they had been selected because they had shown no love for the Fellowship, although hid it behind a thin veneer of objectivity.

Video cameras had captured the brief firefight and the retreat of the cultists to the launch facilities. Even more spectacular was the escape attempt of the *Genesis* and the subsequent missile attack. The explosion was recorded, but they were too distant to assess the damage. Then came the most dramatic video; the fall of the *Genesis,* the chase by the sphere, and finally the sphere's collision. Somehow the pilot of the *Genesis* had regained control in the nick of time, plowing a furrow in the earth and then caroming into the air again.

Thinking the action was over, Roland, Powder, and Towers watched as trucks rumbled toward the launch compound, loaded with equipment and engineers ready to occupy the facility and uncover the secrets of the cult's technology.

"Looks like it's over," Towers said. "I want to get a look inside their facility. You've been in there, haven't you, Symes?"

"Once, but there were lower levels I never saw," Roland said. "I wouldn't get my hopes up. Everything of value will be gone or destroyed."

"The military has techno-wizards that can reconstruct what went on in their factory from the microscopic residue on the walls," Towers said. "It's the end of their monopoly on space."

"Look down there," Powder said suddenly. "It looks like the army is retreating."

Grabbing his binoculars, Roland could see soldiers running in all directions.

"In the sky," Powder shouted.

Streaking above was a bright object trailing flame. Roland backed away, fighting the instinct to run, fascinated by what was to come. Towers stumbled back into his cameraman and they went down in a heap. Powder turned tail and ran, his cameraman holding his ground, camera tracking the asteroid all the way down.

The explosion was spectacular. Blinding flash like a nuclear bomb, an earsplitting boom, then the shock wave of pressurized air knocking lawn chairs and people to the ground. Both cameramen were on the ground now, steadying their cameras on the orange ball that had been the launch compound. Hot wind warmed their faces even at this distance. The fireball was dissipating now into a roiling mass of dust and debris, towering high into the air, forming a mushroom cloud, symbol of the nuclear age.

"Radiation," Towers said. "We have to get away from here."

"It wasn't a nuclear bomb," Roland said.

"If it wasn't a bomb—" Towers started.

"It was a rock—a man-made meteorite," Roland said. "I hope those techno-wizards you were talking about are good at the atomic level, because the cult's secrets have just been atomized."

CHAPTER 91 **DISCOVERY**

In humankind's conception of God, the supreme being is supposed to be omniscient. Yet a reading of the Bible shows that each of God's plans is ultimately thwarted by Satan. If God has the intellectual advantage, how is this possible?

— *A HISTORY OF GOOD AND EVIL*, ROBERT WINSTON, PH.D.

SAN FRANCISCO, CALIFORNIA

Fry filled every one of Thorpe's demands quickly and without question. Thorpe had the latest equipment, endless supplies, even a popcorn machine in the lounge—fresh popped corn one of the many weaknesses he indulged. Sitting with his feet up on his desk, he munched popcorn and drank a Diet Coke, watching video of the raid on the cult compound. Like watching a theatrical film, he cheered when the soldiers attacked, screaming at the cultists to run like the cowards he knew they were. His assistants stayed on the other side of the wall, working at meaningless tasks he assigned them. Behind him the rebuilt sphere sat waiting—it could float, but control of the ship eluded him.

He now knew the drive functioned when particles were fired into a chamber from three particle guns. What happened to the particles once inside he could only guess. He also knew the drive chamber was polarized and the magnetic field intensified exponentially when the particles were fired. Faster firing meant a stronger field, but only to a point, then more rapid fire seemed to have no effect. He also knew that the by-product of the firing was a reduction in gravity immediately surrounding the sphere—he could float it. He assumed the chamber held a vacuum, but firing metallic particles through a magnetic field into a vacuum did not neutralize gravity, at least not in his lab where he had tried it a hundred times.

The secret was in the drive chamber itself, but he couldn't crack the casing until they had additional ships, and they couldn't get those until he could fly this one.

The video came to his favorite part, the *Genesis* taking off, the missile seeking its target, then the explosion and the bodies falling from the ship. Stopping the action after the last of the bodies hit the ground, he rewound, stuffing another handful of popcorn in his mouth, then soaking the mass in his mouth with a swig of Diet Coke. As the picture ran backward he noticed the dust clouds below the ship. Reversing, then freezing the picture, he leaned forward studying the dust, seeing patterns. Tracing them with his finger he could see three clearly overlapping lines. Pushing PLAY he watched the dust, picking out the lines that changed subtly. Understanding dawning, he set the player to run a loop, watching the dust clouds over and over. Eventually, he rifled through boxes until he found a recording of the cult on the moon. Watching the powdery moon dust dance, he could see three lines again—three fields, three particle guns. Scrounging through his cabinet again, he found recordings of the earliest launches of the cult—there was little dust to watch, since they always launched off the concrete pad.

It was a clue, but when he fired the particle guns he saw no evidence of multiple fields. Still, if he fired them simultaneously—no, not simultaneously, but in series? Shouting to his assistants, he rousted them from their hiding place, putting them to work. Stuffing his mouth with the last of his popcorn he thought of Ira Breitling and the murder of Constance.

"I'm coming, Ira Breitling, I'm coming after you."

Then he turned to his anxious assistants, shouting orders with renewed vigor.

CHAPTER 92   **BACK FROM THE DEAD**

> "Teacher," said John, "we saw a man driving out
> demons in your name and we told him to stop,
> because he was not one of us." "Do not stop
> him," Jesus said. "No one who does a miracle
> in my name can in the next moment say
> anything bad about me, for whoever
> is not against us is for us."
>
> —MARK 9:38–39

NEW HOPE STATION, EARTH'S ORBIT

Covenant's departure was delayed so that *Exodus* could be outfitted to accompany *Covenant* to the new planet. *Covenant* would carry three shuttle-class ships remora style and three spheres. *Exodus* would carry another shuttle and two more spheres, leaving only three shuttles working in Earth orbit and *Genesis* undergoing repairs. On her first voyage, *Covenant* would carry three thousand passengers with another one hundred aboard *Exodus*. The remaining residents were transferred to their compound in Mexico to relieve the crowding on New Hope station.

The Fellowship was excoriated by the press for the deaths of two soldiers and the injuries of fifteen more. Despite knowing the blast at their compound was the result of an asteroid impact, the press insisted on calling it a "nuclear-type explosion." The deaths of the nine Fellowship members were downplayed, the four children who died treated as victims of their parents' fanatical beliefs. When the press finished spinning the story, the parents of the children were villains, the soldiers who killed them heroes.

The government of the United States now put full pressure on the Mexican government, demanding extradition of any Fellowship members who escaped from the California compound, and claiming ownership of all Fellowship ships and facilities. Mark and the others on the government's "most wanted list" stayed in orbit out of the reach of authorities. Publicly, the Mexican government sympathized with the U.S. government's claims but no official actions were taken against the Fellowship. Privately, the Mexican government was pleased that Mexico was now the center for the most advanced technology on the planet. As the Fellowship's activities shifted to their Mexican compound, south of Tijuana, the local economy boomed and new tax dollars were pumped into the Mexican federal government. As long as Mexico profited, the Fellowship was welcome.

Under Senator Crow's sponsorship, a bill moved through both houses of Congress to strip citizenship from those who left Christ's Home to emigrate to another planet. Still reeling from the attack on *Genesis* by their own government, the loss of citizenship pushed them from gloom into depression. There was no going back now, they had crossed their Rubicon.

Less popular, but also likely to pass, was Crow's National Restitution Act, which required those planning to emigrate to repay their country for services provided. The repayment was indexed to benefits. Those with college educations from state-supported schools, or who used federally funded student loans, repaying more than those with high school degrees. Younger people had to repay less than older people. Of course, those in higher tax brackets were to repay more than those in lower brackets. "It is unfair for citizens to take from a culture—be nurtured, educated, protected—and then leave without ever repaying that debt," Crow argued on the Sunday morning talk shows, relayed across the country by Fellowship communications platforms. The schedule of repayment worked out in Crow's office would ensure most people would leave the planet penniless and many wouldn't be able to afford to leave at all.

The president and influential politicians, including Senator Crow, attended the funeral for what were called the "murdered soldiers." Many of those giving eulogies spoke of reconciliation in one breath and shook a verbal fist at the Fellowship with the next. Two hours after the funeral, Senator Crow held a news conference to denounce the president for letting the situation with the Fellowship get out of hand. Blaming him for the deaths on both sides he then surprised the reporters by announcing his intention to run for the presidency.

Through it all the Fellowship continued to honor its communications contracts, providing service for most of the U.S. and the rest of the world. As long as the U.S. government kept its account up-to-date, the Fellowship would put up with the rhetoric. One by one, the rest of the Fellowship compounds in the U.S. were invaded and searched, some residents arrested. Stephen worked night and day flying around the country, seeing that members of the Fellowship who were arrested were released on bail. A dozen families wanted by the FBI were smuggled to Mexico and then lifted to New Hope to join the pioneers.

The "Cult War," as one tabloid labeled it, knocked the IT plague off the front pages, and by the time the plague was rediscovered, IT had been identified as a variation of

Ebola, a terrestrial plague. Editorialists who had blamed the plague on the Fellowship now railed about the Fellowship's attack on "innocent soldiers doing their duty," never apologizing for earlier slander, and never considering that since they were wrong before they could be wrong again.

Twenty hours before the scheduled departure for the new planet, Stephen O'Malley took a shuttle to New Hope, surprising Mark.

"What are you doing here, Stephen? You'll be quarantined now."

"They've lifted most of the quarantine restrictions and they're not enforcing those still on the books. I came because I didn't want to risk transmitting even an encoded message. Christy Maitland wants to meet with you before you go—you and Ira. She insists on seeing you on Earth."

"Ira?" Mark asked, disappointed.

"Yes, but it's clear she has feelings for you, Mark."

"Why doesn't she come up to the station?"

"I thought that was peculiar, too. You don't think it's a trap, do you?"

"Of course not, Stephen."

"She's sympathetic to our beliefs, Mark, but she doesn't share all of them."

"She wouldn't betray me, Stephen."

Mark knew that loving someone outside your faith was dangerous, but if he couldn't trust Christy, he couldn't trust anyone.

"Where does she want to meet?"

"Alaska."

The meeting was set for the next day at noon, the location in southeastern Alaska near the Canadian border. The Fellowship was restricted from flying in U.S. airspace but Mark had little respect for his government left.

Ira was grumpy about going since he was supervising the flight testing of *Covenant* and repairs to *Genesis* at the same time. Ira left his work, only at Mark's insistence.

With Mark at the controls of a sphere, they dropped into Valdez-Cordova County, Alaska. Radar would have picked up their descent but Mark quickly dropped to tree-top level to make it impossible to pinpoint their exact position. Using directions provided by Stephen, Mark and Ira followed a gravel highway to a lake, and then over the hills behind it to a valley with another lake and seemingly no road access. A seaplane was tied to a dock at one end of the lake and three large log cabins sat in a small clearing. Landing in the meadow, Mark got out, leaving Ira at the controls in case they needed to get away fast.

Mark watched the cabins for Christy to emerge but it was George Proctor who came out the door. Surprised to see him alive, Mark hurried to the cabin, pumping his hand vigorously.

"Everyone thinks you're dead, George."

"Let's let them keep thinking that, Mark," Proctor replied.

"We saw your compound burn on television. How did you get out?"

"We learned a thing or two from the Branch Davidian massacre—we dug a tunnel before we moved to the property."

"What about Ruth?"

"She's alive."

"Wonderful!" Mark said, overjoyed. "Let me tell Ira. He's in the sphere."

"Wait!" Proctor said firmly. "Ruth's been through a terrible ordeal. She was held prisoner by Senator Crow at his Autumn Rest Cemetery."

"What? Senator Crow? Why?"

"He's a Satanist. He planned to use her as a breeder, then sacrifice her baby."

Incredulous, Mark slowly understood the full horror of what Ruth had gone through.

"Crow raped her, Mark. She's pregnant and ashamed to tell Ira."

"I can't believe—"

"He was behind the attack on the *Rising Savior* too, and I suspect he was behind the child abuse charges. He's guided by a demon, Mark. I've seen it."

"A demon? It's too much—"

"It's his aide, Rachel Waters. I've seen its true form."

Mark wasn't sure of what to believe. As a Christian he believed in a spiritual realm, and the Bible spoke of demons being cast out, but it was easier for Mark to believe in the evil of a man than a spiritual force taking human form. He didn't doubt George Proctor had seen something, but until Mark saw the demon with his own eyes he couldn't believe Rachel Waters was anything but another wretched sinner.

"Senator Crow will pay for this," Mark said. "I'll get Stephen to see that criminal charges are filed, then we'll sue him for everything he has."

"No. She doesn't want people to know what happened to her. It took me this long to convince her to speak to Ira."

"Crow can't get away with this—with everything. He should pay for his sins and his crimes."

"He will, trust me," Proctor said, his icy blue eyes locked on Mark's. "The timing isn't right, though. If you make charges, the media will take Crow's side and the public will believe him, not Ruth and you. As far as the public is concerned, you and Ira are fanatics and a menace, Mark."

"So we do nothing?"

"For now. Ruth wants to get as far away from her nightmare as possible and I need the world to think I'm dead. Take her to another star."

"Where is Ruth?"

"Inside. She's come this far but now she says she can't face Ira. She wants you to tell him. If he can't accept her—and her condition—then he's to fly away. I'll take care of her. He won't have to worry about that."

"She did nothing wrong, George. Ira will understand. He'll forgive her."

"Forgive her for what, Mark? For being kidnapped and abused? For not dying?"

"I didn't mean to make it sound like she had an affair."

"If you're thinking like this, what will Ira think?"

Now Mark understood Ruth's fear. Would what happened to her always be between her and Ira?

Ira was still in the pilot's seat when Mark returned.

"I didn't see Christy," Ira said.

"She's not here. That was George Proctor."

"George Proctor's not dead?" Ira said slowly, confused.

"Ruth is alive too."

Suddenly pale, Ira looked like his heart had stopped, his black eye patch in stark contrast with his white face.

"Where is she?"

"Ira, something terrible happened to her."

"You said she was alive."

"She is—"

"Was she burned? I don't care, I want to see her."

"She was raped, Ira."

Hesitating only briefly, he said, "Where is she?"

"She's pregnant, Ira."

Another brief pause, then softly, "Where is she?"

"In the cabin."

Ira ran from the shuttle past Proctor. Ira's love for Ruth was strong and even the scheming of a demon had been unable to break their bond.

CHAPTER 93 **GOOD-BYE**

> Mountains appear more lofty the nearer they are
> approached, but great men resemble them not
> in this particular.
>
> —THE COUNTESS OF BLESSINGTON

GULF OF CALIFORNIA, MEXICO

Mark had returned to Earth for only the second time since the evacuation of Christ's Home. Both visits were at the request of Reverend Christy Maitland. Christy would have come up to New Hope station this time, but Mark wanted to taste and smell his home world one more time. So it was Mark's suggestion that they meet on Earth before he left for the new planet. Mark was smuggled to Earth in a sphere, meeting Christy in a small Mexican village on the Gulf of California. The weather was hot, the air dry, and the skies blue, the only blemish an occasional wispy cloud. They walked the Mexican beach together, hand in hand, just above the surf line. Evelyn had packed them a picnic lunch and they had eaten on the beach, then decided to stroll until sunset.

"You were right, Mark," Christy said.

"About what?"

"You said that something always happens to keep us apart."

"I'm only moving to a different star, Christy, it's not like I'm moving to a new galaxy."

Christy laughed, then squeezed Mark's hand tighter.

"My best friend moved to Chicago when I was ten and I never saw her again. You're moving to a new planet."

"We're going to build a new society, Christy. It's a chance to rethink everything, to start a civilization from scratch. Come with us."

Turning to look at Mark, she took both his hands in hers.

"I don't know—"

"I love you, Christy."

She smiled but the smile faded when he didn't say more.

"You love me and you want me to run away into space with you," she said. "Is that all?"

She was asking about marriage and Mark knew it, but he wasn't ready for that, not until he had fulfilled the mission God had given him.

"I have a lot of responsibilities," he said. "When we're settled on the new planet I can commit myself to our relationship in a way I can't now."

"Your calling is getting in the way again," Christy said.

"I'm not ashamed to say I take God's call seriously."

"I do too, Mark. Right now my calling is here on Earth."

Uncomfortable silence followed, both wanting a compromise, neither able to think of one. Instead they paused, watching the sun dip below the surface, then sat in the sand until the glowing orb of Sol completely sank from view.

When Mark had seen his last sunset, he turned to

Christy and kissed her long and hard, then held her close, whispering in her ear.

"I'll come back to Earth, Christy. I'll come back for you."

"I know," Christy said.

They were still holding each other when they heard the familiar whoosh of a sphere, then saw it coming in low over the sea, coming to take Mark away.

CHAPTER 94 **DEPARTURE**

> Mercury is too near the sun, the atmosphere of Venus is poisonous, Mars is too dry and nearly airless, the gas giants are incompatible with any form of life, and the frozen outer planets of our solar system inhospitable to humans. Unless humanity is willing to radically alter its lifestyle, it will have to look elsewhere for a second home.
>
> — *THE NEXT GIANT LEAP*,
> ROGER CORNHILL

EARTH'S ORBIT

The departure of the colonists for a new world was carried by all the major broadcast and cable networks. The broadcasters described the adventure with a mix of awe and contempt—awe over the technology, contempt for right-wing Christians. Wyatt Powder jumped from comparisons of the Fellowship pioneers to the Pilgrims, to thinly veiled accusations of racism, sexism, and religious intolerance. What should have been humankind's next great adventure was described to the world with a mixture of fear, revulsion, and suspicion.

When it came time for the departure of the star ship, *Covenant,* virtually every television in the world tuned in. The Fellowship fed the planet extensive footage of the exterior of *Covenant,* but only small portions of the interior, since the living conditions were cramped and they didn't want allegations of inhumane treatment. Pioneers were interviewed, all of them thanking God for making the voyage to the new planet possible. Commentators followed these interviews by asking, "If God were really behind this, wouldn't there be some Catholics on board? Or Jews? Buddhists? Is God's flock really an exclusive club?"

Then it was time for departure and Mark appeared on-screen, broadcasting from the bridge of the *Covenant.* The Fellowship had promised the networks that Mark would announce the name of the planet they would inhabit. The anticipation for Mark's announcement was so great that even Wyatt Powder stopped his voice-over. Mark faced the camera, his tone earnest, his comments half prayer, half farewell.

"We leave you now, people of Earth, to become the people of a new planet. It's a virgin world, prepared by the creator of the universe, held in trust for His people from the beginning of time until this moment. We accept this gift from God and pledge ourselves to live lives that will glorify His name.

"We've been asked many times what the name of the new world will be, since the right to name something belongs to the discoverers. What would you call a world of promise, a world where people are free to live their lives as they see fit, to worship God in their own fashion? What would you call a place of unlimited potential, where the only limits on men and women are those they place on themselves, and the government serves the people, not the other way around. There once was such a place, a brief shining moment in Earth's history that we hope to rekindle. Our new world will share the name of that place—America."

With that dramatic moment, the broadcast from inside *Covenant* was replaced with a shot of the outside of the

ship. The name "Covenant" was seen, painted on the side
of the great ship. Below it was painted the Christian flag.
Next to it were the remains of the American flag, just recently scraped from the hull. As the converted submarine
pulled away from the station, the name rotated slowly out
of sight. Soon, the bulk of the ship could be seen, the
drive end rotating toward the camera. Then, picking up
speed, *Covenant,* packed with people, supplies, and hope,
sped off into space.

Two months into the voyage to planet America, Ruth
Breitling went into labor. The ship's doctor, Lacey Sutter,
was there for the delivery, with Ira, as was Evelyn who
held one hand, Ira the other. When Ruth's cervix dilated
to ten centimeters, Dr. Sutter gave the word that Ruth had
been waiting for.

"Push, Ruth."

With the next contraction Ruth bore down, the pain
making it hard to maintain her concentration. When the
contraction ended her breathing was out of control.

"Easy, Ruth," Evelyn said. "The baby's almost here."

"I can't help it," Ruth said. "It hurts."

Evelyn sponged Ruth's face, concerned about her
color. Ruth wasn't the oldest woman to ever have a baby,
but she was nearing the end of her child-bearing years.
The abuse she had suffered before the pregnancy had
done nothing to prepare her body for the ordeal it was going through.

"When the next contraction comes, push hard, Ruth,"
Dr. Sutter said.

"It's coming," Ruth said.

The contraction gripped her and she squeezed her eyes
tight, her face nearly purple with the effort.

"Good, Ruth. I can see the baby's head. If you push
hard, you might do it with the next contraction."

Pushing again, the baby's head appeared, then while
Dr. Sutter rotated the head, one shoulder emerged, then
an arm popped free, and the baby slid partially out in a
gush of red fluid. With the baby free to its waist, Dr. Sutter sucked the baby's nasal passages and mouth clean of

fluid. Then holding the baby up so Ruth could see it between her legs, she said, "Look, Ruth. Look down here."

Evelyn helped support her head so she could see her baby. Ruth had trouble focusing but when she did she smiled. Then Ruth gently lowered her head to the pillow. Sponging her forehead again, Evelyn noticed Ruth was breathing easier now as if she were asleep. With a final contraction the baby came free, the umbilical cord trailing inside Ruth. Laying the baby on her stomach, Dr. Sutter clamped and cut the cord.

"It's a boy, Ruth," Dr. Sutter said.

"He's beautiful," Evelyn said.

No one addressed Ira, who had been silent since Ruth's water had broken. No one was sure how he felt about the baby. He'd been irritable and sulky the entire voyage, but then he always was. During the pregnancy the baby had been carefully referred to as "Ruth's baby," since that was biologically true. Ira had been attentive to Ruth's needs but never talked of the coming birth with any excitement. Now he removed the mask covering his face and looked at the small form lying on his wife's stomach. Reaching out he took its tiny hand between his thumb and finger. Reflexively, the baby gripped his finger and Ira smiled.

"We have another baby, Ruth," he said.

Ruth didn't respond, her face drained of all color. Evelyn shook her gently, but her eyes didn't open. Dr. Suffer hurried to the head of the bed, checking Ruth's heartbeat with her stethoscope. A few seconds later she shook her head.

Eyes tearing, Ira reached for the baby, cradling it in his arms.

"His name is Luke Majors Breitling," he said. "Evelyn, would you take the baby? I want to pray for Ruth."

Evelyn left with the baby, meeting Shelly, Mark, and Micah in the corridor. Evelyn's face told them something terrible had happened. Then she smiled and held out the baby.

"This is Luke," she said, holding out the newborn. "The first baby born in space."

> If any of you has a dispute with another, dare he
> take it before the ungodly for judgment instead
> of before the saints? Do you not know that the
> saints will judge the world?
>
> — I CORINTHIANS 6:1–2

PLANET AMERICA

The shuttle angled down into the atmosphere of planet America, a white streak across the sky from west to east. Nameless animals looked up at the unfamiliar sight, then sensing no danger, returned to foraging or hunting. Beneath the shuttle the pristine wilderness flashed by, nothing but splotchy landscape at first, but as the shuttle lost altitude, details emerged. The gray of a desert crescent cutting deep into the continent behind a mountain range. Sparse vegetation bordering the desert, spreading across a plateau that ended in sheer cliffs that dropped away to lush vegetation below. The mismatched continental plates met at that ridge, a half-mile drop between the arid plateau and the fertile land below. Now it was thick forest spreading into the distance, occasional rivers cutting through verdant lands. The east coast of the continent appeared, the sea a deep gray under the overcast sky. The shuttle banked, flying north along the coast until it found ·a clearing; then coming around it settled gently into the middle of the grassy meadow, the rear cargo hatch opening slowly.

Rifle in hand Micah climbed out, standing guard. When he was sure there was no animal threat he shouted to Mark, who pushed a hand truck loaded with boxes down the ramp into the meadow. Two other men followed with more hand trucks, rifles over their shoulders. The unloading continued for fifteen minutes until there was a sizable

mound in the meadow. Then the men returned one last
time to the shuttle leading out a blindfolded man, hands
tied behind his back. They sat him on a crate, then untied
his hands, backing away, rifles trained on him. He ripped
off the blindfold, his eyes darting around, taking in the
situation. Four men faced him, only Mark was unarmed.

"Don't try anything," Mark warned.

"Where's Proctor?" the man demanded. "I want to see
George Proctor."

Micah and the men laughed, but Mark answered honestly.

"George Proctor is on Earth."

"But we had a deal. He swore on a Bible if I helped
him he'd let me go!"

"He kept his part of the bargain. You are free now."

Looking around at the wilderness surrounding him, the
man said, "Free? Free to go where? To do what?"

"There are enough supplies to keep you comfortable
for a year. By then you should be living off the land."

"I want to see Proctor. This wasn't the deal!"

"He agreed to set you free but he couldn't let you go on
hurting people—hurting us."

"I'll give you my word. Don't leave me here."

"You're too dangerous. We have no way to protect ourselves from you."

"This is a death sentence."

"There's a pistol and rifle in there. You'll be able to
protect yourself."

"A man has to have hope. Food and water aren't
enough. Come back for me. Come back in a few months.
You'll see you can trust me."

"There is a cabin, that way," Mark said, pointing.

"You can't leave me."

"There's a Bible."

"I'll use it to start my fires."

"It's the only book you have—use it any way you see fit."

His face red with anger, the man studied the rifles, estimating his chances.

Mark backed away, the men with rifles covering their
retreat up the shuttle ramp.

"Learn to live off the land. Don't be in a hurry, don't take unnecessary risks. In time, God will reveal Himself to you."

"Proctor lied to me. You all lied to me."

As the hatch closed Mark said, "God be with you."

The last Mark saw of the man, he was frantically digging through the pile of supplies looking for a weapon. As they flew away he could see the man hastily assembling his rifle. The shuffle was long gone before the rifle was loaded. With no one to kill he fired randomly into the forest, emptying the magazine. When the last echo died the forest was silent. Slowly the animal sounds returned. Standing in the middle of that clearing, on a planet not of his birth, he knew no man had ever been as alone as he.

SETTLING DOWN

In the 1990s the media suddenly discovered that black churches burn down. Charges of racism hit the headlines, President Clinton jumped on the bandwagon, proclaiming that racists were attacking black churches. When the hysteria died down, insurance statistics proved that white and black churches burned equally often and that the "far right" was not using fire as a terror weapon. No apologies were offered by the President, no corrections were run in the newspapers.

— *SOCIAL PSYCHOLOGY*, RAYMOND JAMES

CHICAGO, ILLINOIS

The only movie theater in Grandma Jones's Chicago neighborhood showed adult films now. The audience was all men, who came and went at odd hours by themselves. Thirty years ago the theater was called the "Chief," decorated in an Indian motif. She remembered two large, gilded Indian heads with full headdresses that decorated opposite walls. She often wondered if the heads were still there but was too embarrassed to go inside to see.

Grandma had to travel fifty minutes by bus to a white neighborhood where the Fellowship's film was showing. It was cold the night she went, her old coat so thin it offered little warmth. Grandma Jones hurried along, watching for patches of ice on the sidewalk. It was five blocks to the theater from the bus stop and she passed many people, but never once did she fear being mugged, or cross the street to avoid dark doorways and alleys. It wasn't like a walk in her neighborhood.

The Fellowship film was being shown in an old theater called the "Aladdin," the theater decorated with flying carpets carrying young men wearing turbans. There was a fresh coat of paint over the exterior and the flying carpets had been touched up and outlined in red neon. The major chains wouldn't run the films and risk offending the Hollywood community that was virtually unanimous in opposition to the Fellowship.

A long line trailed down the block from the ticket booth and she fell in at the end. It was a mostly white crowd, middle class, a mix of young and old. No one said anything to her, nor did they stare, but she saw the sidelong glances as she passed. This was their neighborhood, not hers.

The smell of popcorn greeted her as she came to the ticket window, bringing back memories of sitting in the Chief with her friends, sharing a box of popcorn, giggling and flirting with boys.

The interior of the Aladdin retained a semblance of what once had been splendor. A towering genie emanating from a lamp dominated the lobby, filling one wall. It too wore a fresh coat of paint but it made the genie look cheap instead of awesome. There was a balcony but the theater had been divided to make it a duplex; the balcony now showed a separate film.

The only seats left were down in front and Grandma feared getting a crick in her neck from sitting too close to the screen. She found an empty seat on the right aisle two rows from the front. A few latecomers hurried in as the lights went down, the curtain drawn dramatically. One last man came down the aisle in the dark, taking the empty seat next to her. He was all arms and legs and fit poorly into the seat. It was too dark to see him well but his face was gaunt. She knew the type, nervous and high-strung, he probably didn't eat well. In dogs they blamed that type on too much inbreeding, but in people she knew it was a sickness of the spirit. The man needed to make peace with God so his stomach would start working properly.

Planet America filled the screen as seen from space and the crowd quieted. Classical music filled the background. This was the fifth film from the Fellowship and titled *Settling Down*. Planet America faded, replaced by a flock of birds flying across the crown of a forest. The birds were huge with wingspans of five or six feet. Golden feathers shimmered as if each were gilded, so bright it was almost blinding.

Leaving the birds the camera dove toward the forest, rolling left, revealing a sparkling lake in the distance and beyond that a village. Dropping low the camera skimmed the surface of the lake, the shore looming ahead. A dock with a rowboat passed beneath them and then it was up over a grassy knoll into a meadow to the village on the other side. People dressed in work clothes waved as they passed over. Two dozen buildings sprinkled one end of the meadow, most set on either side of a road that continued through the meadow and into the woods on the far side. All of the buildings looked like log cabins with shake roofs. The roofs were a deep red, the logs a greenish tint, making the pioneer village a colorful sight set in the lush green meadow. Continuing to the far end the camera slowed, zeroing in on one structure set at the end of the street. The steeple marked it clearly as the church. Coming closer they could see a bell hanging in the steeple. Now the image moved into the meadow toward a group of children at play. Climbing, they could see the clear outlines of a baseball diamond cut in the meadow. As they passed a boy got a hit and ran for first base, a girl on second racing toward third.

After a short expanse of forest they came to another clearing, this one filled with stumps. As they passed a tree was felled, dropping silently to the forest floor as cymbals clashed over the theater sound system. In Grandma Jones's mind she heard the sounds of breaking limbs and snapping twigs as the forest giant smashed smaller trees in its path. A man with a chain saw stood at the new stump waving at the camera. A deep sigh came from the man sitting next to Grandma Jones and his hand began thumping his knee. She ignored the man, turning sideways in her seat.

At one edge of the clearing stood a large structure with

no sides, this one built of cut lumber. Coming in low they could see a sawmill operating inside. Lumber was stacked ceiling high at one end.

Another turn of the camera and they were off to another clearing, this one under cultivation. Half of the clearing was filled with shoulder-high corn, the rest of the clearing split among several crops, none of which she could identify. A tractor lumbered down one side of the field toward a barn, a man in a straw hat waving, a little girl in his lap. Passing the tractor they came to another set of buildings, a half dozen along the edge of the clearing. Four long tables sat in front of the buildings. Women came from one of the buildings carrying food, reminding Grandma of Thanksgiving. Children played to one side, and others swung from ropes hung in the trees.

Now the camera skimmed over the buildings to the other side, where there were corrals and two more barns. Animals milled around in the corrals, horses, cows, goats, and chickens that scurried everywhere, but the camera focused in on a pen of animals resembling sheep—but they weren't. Covered with thick wool, the animals had long spindly legs like a horse, and a noticeable hump on their backs. Their heads were larger than a sheep's, the face flat, the eyes round and protruding.

The animals kicked up their heels as the camera came down, prancing around the enclosure, then finally huddling in the corner. Several babies were mixed in the herd, one small enough to stand beneath its mother, peeking out around her spindly legs, its head pushing through the hanging wool. "Ooohs," erupted from the crowd. The animals of planet America were what the crowds came to see and that is what the films of the Fellowship delivered.

Suddenly the man next to her jumped up, pushing past her to the aisle. His manner was brusque, angry.

Now the film centered on the animals, showing children playing with the sheeplike creatures, trying to ride them, and clipping the wool of the protesting animals. None of the animals in the herd carried horns, but the film showed another pen of similar animals, bigger and more powerful-looking, with two sharp spikes protruding from their heads.

The focus of this film was the domestication of animals, the previous films focusing on the exotic wildlife. Glimpses of life on the planet were seen through the interaction with the native animal life that they were trying to domesticate. The theme of the film was how hard work paid off in crops, better shelter, churches to worship in, and schools for their children. The Fellowship settlers who were interviewed spoke of working twelve hours a day, six days a week, then in the next breath spoke of the deep satisfaction with their lives. They were building their own society from the ground up. Every building, every law, and every social structure would be their creation, designed to complement their beliefs and values. There was no need to compromise your own values in order to make room for someone else's, since everyone shared the same beliefs. It wasn't Eden and the colonists laughed when the the interviewer suggested it. There were squabbles, debates, and minor conflicts, but no more than back on Earth and counterbalanced by the quality of life they were living.

Grandma knew that some of that quality of life depended on support from Earth. The colony didn't build the tractor she saw being used or even the simple tools like saws and hammers. All the manufactured goods were brought in from Earth and it would take tons of imports before the colony could produce their own. Still, life there was everything she hoped it would be. She was convinced that this is where her people needed to go.

> My reverence for human life is inversely proportional to the environmental damage caused by human civilization.
>
> —TOBIAS STOOP,
> FOUNDER OF THE EARTH'S AVENGERS

CHICAGO, ILLINOIS

Tobias Stoop left the Aladdin with murder in his heart. Seeing the environmental damage the cult was doing to a virgin planet boiled his blood. Clearing the forests not only killed trees that were centuries old, but also untold number of species that depended on those trees. Birds with restricted nesting needs, like Earth's spotted owl, could be wiped out on planet America just like the passenger pigeon, the dodo bird, and a thousand other species on planet Earth. It was as if the Fellowship colonists had learned nothing from the ecological rape of the mother world. The ravaging of the new planet had just begun, but with modern equipment—chain saws and bulldozers—they would match the damage the pioneers did to North America in a fraction of the time. Worst of all, they filmed their atrocities and used the revenue from ticket sales to expand the ecological holocaust under way on planet America. Every person who paid for a seat was an enabler and shared the responsibility.

Four blocks from the theater he paused by a van, making sure no one was watching. A quick nod of his head and the side door slid open, Tobias jumping in. The van was moving almost immediately. Janine was there, his latest lover. He took Janine when his last lover balked at escalating the battle against the cult. Seven members of his Earth's Avengers left with her, but he quickly replaced them with committed allies.

"They're clear-cutting the forests and domesticating native animals," Tobias reported.

The four men and two women in the van exclaimed in anger, now resolved to do whatever Tobias asked.

Tapping on the wooden crates in the van he said, "Those cultists are like a wildfire that keeps on burning until it runs out of fuel. Money is what is fueling that fire. It's time to cut off the supply."

Totally committed to protecting the ecosystem, they were ready to make the human sacrifices necessary for the greater good.

They split up in a parking lot, half switching to another van, lugging one of the wooden crates with them. Janine took charge of the second van, Tobias remaining in the first. The vans were nondescript, purchased secondhand by sympathizers who sold them to friends, who sold them to different dealers, where they were purchased again. With duplicate keys to the vans, Tobias and his friends had then stolen them from their suburban owners and would abandon them after they were done. Janine's van turned down the alley, giving their position by walkie-talkie to Tobias, who was now across the street from the theater. Wedges and hammers in their gloved hands, their faces covered by ski masks, they stopped behind the theater, hurrying to the exits and driving shims under the doors. When the doors were firmly wedged, Janine radioed Tobias they were ready.

Tobias and his people pulled their ski masks down, then the driver pulled away from the curb, drove a short distance, and then did a U-turn, driving just past the theater entrance. Then he stopped, put it in reverse, and backed up onto the curb, stopping just short of the glass doors at the entrance. The back doors flew open and two jumped out pulling the theater doors wide. Tobias and the rest grabbed glass jugs of gasoline, lighting the rags stuffed in the tops, and ran into the lobby.

A half-dozen people were in line at the snack bar when the ecoterrorists rushed in. Confused and afraid, the theater patrons backed up against the counter.

Tobias lobbed his first gasoline bomb toward the auditorium doors, the glass jug shattering, its flammable contents creating a wall of flame in front of the doors. His second jug went toward the stairs, breaking at the base, adding to the conflagration. Most of the customers at the snack bar bolted for the doors behind Tobias, but a small boy stood alone, abandoned by an older sibling, wide-eyed, fingers in his mouth, eyes streaming tears. A woman escaping through the door turned back, seeing the boy, and raced to him just as a jug of gasoline flew over the snack bar. A teenage boy and girl behind the counter ducked when the jug sailed their way, smashing into a popcorn machine and exploding in flame. Running below the counter the woman took the boy by the hand and escaped out the door. Then the teenage girl sprinted from behind the counter, her body engulfed in flames. She collapsed a few feet away, writhing on the lobby floor in a vain attempt to put out the flames.

Jugs of gasoline were flung in every direction, the great wall genie doused and engulfed in the cleansing fire, the dowdy interior being purified by the all-consuming flames. Retreating to the doors, Tobias and his people pulled the rest of their jugs from the van, flinging them into the lobby. Driving away, they radioed Janine and her team went into action.

Both of the rear emergency exits were already secured, but as a finishing touch Janine and the others set the doors on fire with jugs of gasoline, then they raced from the alley, slowing when they reached the street, carefully blending into traffic.

> Many complicated devices have been designed to
> inflict agony. Although the simple methods are
> still the best. Fire, for example, terrifies every-
> one except the rare pyromaniac. However, apply
> a flame to a few square inches of a pyromaniac's
> skin, and the pyromaniac quickly comes around
> to the common point of view.
>
> — *THE ART OF TORTURE*, COLIN MILLS

CHICAGO, ILLINOIS

Grandma Jones was enthralled by the snapshots of life projected onto the Aladdin's stained and patched screen. It was a rural life, composed mostly of working the land, harvesting crops, preserving food, and tending to animals. It was a simple life, and her heart longed to be part of it. She was watching two small Fellowship girls gathering eggs laid by alien hens when she heard the first person scream. The crowd panicked before Grandma Jones even smelled the smoke.

Instinct got Grandma Jones to her feet and into the aisle, the rush of the terrified crowd pushing her along. The nearest exit was through a curtained arch at the front of the theater, and she was pushed through the arch just before the crush of terrified people jammed up in the opening. Someone fell, the others tripping over them, and then stacking on top. There was a small alcove on the other side of the curtain where Grandma Jones had been pushed and it was packed with panicked people, those in front pushing on the breaker bars of the exit doors, those behind crushing against them. Screams erupted from those trapped in the theater, behind a wall of bodies filling the entrance to the alcove—screams of pain. Pushed aside by men fighting to get to the door, Grandma Jones was pressed against the wall of the alcove. She looked back to the arch, the curtains now torn down, the opening packed nearly to the top with bodies. Through the small remaining space at the top of the arch she saw flames suddenly spread across the ceiling of the theater. A sudden gush of black smoke accompanied the flame and the air became unbreathable. Now coughing mixed with screams and cries, the cacophony softening as those in the back of the theater passed out from smoke inhalation and those who had fallen in the doorway were crushed to death.

A dozen panicky people were jammed in that small space with Grandma Jones, the men still fighting each other to get the exit open. Smoke poured in from the theater and she slid to her knees, arms and legs battering her. Several men were overcome with coughing spasms, lungs filled with toxic fumes. As men weakened they were pushed aside, creating space for others who organized now, three men hammering the door with their shoulders. Suddenly the door gave and the men tumbled out into flames. All three men caught fire, two got up running away, hair and clothes on fire. The third man died where he lay rolling back and forth in a hopeless effort to extinguish the flames.

The rest shrank back, the door frame on fire and threatening to spread into their enclosure. With the theater now vented, hot dense smoke flowed through the alcove to the cool air of the alley beyond. Now the flames raced toward the hopelessly blocked doors, people dying by the dozens. As the conflagration heated up and flames burst through the roof, the airflow reversed, the cool outer air being sucked into the building. The flames in the doorway flickered, dying down. Those trapped with Grandma Jones saw their chance and ran through the doorway, across the body of the fallen man. Like frightened deer they leapt through the flames, jumping to safety, falling on the other side and rolling to put out flames. The flames around the door flickered back to life again and a woman stumbled going over the body, falling sideways against the frame, her clothes catching fire. She fell back into the alcove, stampeding those remaining, and they fled through the door over her body, ignoring the flames around the opening—most of those rushing through were on fire when they reached the other side.

Grandma Jones could not ignore the agony of the burning woman and she crawled to her, throwing her coat on the fallen woman and beating out the flames. The woman died under Grandma Jones worn coat, her face nothing but blackened skin, her hair burned to the scalp.

Grandma Jones could hear no screaming in the theater behind her now, the roar of the fire so loud it drowned all sounds except the pounding of her heart in her chest. The stack of bodies blocking the theater side was smoldering, threatening to burst into flames. The heat was unbearable, the air unbreathable—she was dying. Coughing, she crawled toward the flaming exit knowing she didn't have the strength to stand, let alone the speed to get through the flames without catching fire. Given the choices she decided to die of smoke inhalation. Face pressed to the floor, she sucked in a hot lungful of air, using it to whisper a prayer to God, asking for forgiveness of her sins and that Jesus take her home quickly.

A blast of cold hit her in the face—was this what it was like to burn to death? Your senses confused? Another blast— it was wet and wonderful. Through tearing eyes she could see water shooting through the opening. Flames around the door were extinguished, and she crawled forward. The water pressure increased and she was pounded by a hard stream. Careful to keep her head down so she wouldn't drown she reached the opening, crawling over the burned man. A blast of water hit her again, driving her to the ground. Suddenly she was grabbed by the arms and pulled through the opening into the clear air on the other side. Coughing, eyes blinded by tears, she was picked up and carried over the shoulder of a man, then gently put down. Covered by a blanket, she was given oxygen. Someone irrigated her eyes and when she could see again there was a face—a white face. Pulling the oxygen mask away he said, "Are you all right?" When she nodded he said, "There are others that need the oxygen, but if you feel dizzy, give a yell!"

She was in a row of survivors across the street from the burning theater. Fire engines were everywhere, the street filled with hose spaghetti. Flames were shooting twenty feet into the air from the roof of the building—the Aladdin would be a total loss. Looking left and right she could see only two dozen survivors. There had been hundreds of people in the theater.

The roof fell in, sending a shower of sparks into the sky. Lifted by the heat of the fire, glowing embers floated ever upward as if on the way to heaven—no, not to heaven—into the heavens, and that's where her people were to go. God had spared her from the flames to make it possible and now she had to fulfill her dream. To do that she needed Mark Shepherd, but he had traveled to the stars and not returned. God would bring him back, of that she was sure, and then they would meet.

CHAPTER 99   **MARKER**

> Dreams are the most common means of communicating with spiritual beings. Occasionally, a god will write on the wall or carve instructions in stone, but for the most part there is never any concrete evidence that the revelation came from anywhere but the messenger's imagination.
>
> — *A HISTORY OF GOOD AND EVIL,*
> ROBERT WINSTON, PH.D.

PLANET AMERICA'S MOON

Like Earth's moon, planet America's moon was pockmarked by meteorites, but unlike Earth's moon it also had deep crescent-shaped crevices that cut nearly to its core. Geologists on Earth would have coveted the opportunity to study the crevices, to understand the cosmic force that created them, but members of the Fellowship weren't explorers, they were settlers. One look at the topography of the moon and Ira simply said, "Interesting, now where's that hand?"

The first eighteen months on the planet had been all work, and Mark had kept his focus on meeting the basic needs of his people: housing, sanitation, food. Only when he was certain that the fledgling colony was firmly established did he give in to Micah's persistent request that he visit America's moon.

Micah took them to the dark side, coming up on the rock formation from above and behind. Like the formation on Pluto, under the shuttle's lights, a pointing finger could be distinguished on the pockmarked surface. Passing over the formation, Micah brought the shuttle around, coming back at it lower. Now it looked like an elongated pile of rocks. Only when they came from high and behind the hand, as Micah and his crew had the first time, did it look like a pointing finger.

"What do you think?" Micah asked.

"It's a rock formation," Mark said.

"It's a hand," Floyd exclaimed. "It's a sign from God."

"It may be, Floyd," Mark said, "but it's also a rock formation. I'm not saying it's not created by design, I'm just not sure."

"The coincidences keep piling up," Floyd said.

"We followed the hand on Pluto and found America," Ira said. "It makes me wonder what we might find if we follow this hand."

"What could we find if we headed in any direction?" Mark asked. "There's a universe of stars and planets out there."

"But nothing is pointing to them," Micah said.

Increasingly, Mark the leader felt like a follower. His flock of sheep were becoming rams, less willing to be led.

"Who will go?" Mark asked, giving in.

"I will," Micah volunteered.

"You've been away from your family too much, Micah."

"Shelly and I talked it over and she supports me. Junior too. Besides, we push the speed envelope with each passage. We can cover twice the distance in half the time of the initial voyage of *Genesis*."

"Is there anything nearby in the direction the finger is pointing?"

"We noted the time and position at discovery," Micah said. "There are several possible stars along the line of the point."

"Thousands, if you follow that path infinitely," Mark pointed out. "All right, see where it leads you, but don't take chances. Come back to us."

"I have reason to come back. Shelly's pregnant again."

CHAPTER 100 **PRESIDENT CROW**

> In every community there is a class of people profoundly dangerous to the rest. I don't mean the criminals. For them we have punitive sanctions. I mean the leaders. Invariably the most dangerous people seek the power.
>
> — *HERZOG*, SAUL BELLOW

WASHINGTON, D.C.

In October of the election year, Senator Crow was seven points behind in the presidential polls. Crow had trailed his opponent by between five and nine points since being nominated at the Democratic convention and nothing his consultants and media specialists could devise closed the gap. Then Crow's opponent caught "IT" and became the last victim of the Ebola variant. The Republican Party spent heavily, asking voters to vote for the dead man, thus making his running mate president, but to no avail. Crow won forty-seven percent to forty-five percent. Rachel Waters became chief of staff, Simon Ash her assistant. Crow's running mate, Carson Wheeler, governor of California, did his job and delivered California, and then Crow reneged on his pre-election promise to share power, assigning Wheeler the usual vice presidential functions of fund-raising and attending state funerals.

There were five balls on inauguration day, Crow attending them all, Congresswoman Sylvia Swanson at his side. With a bachelor president the media had a field day speculating on his sex life, the opposition spreading rumors that he and Rachel Waters were lovers. Gay activists countered by outing Rachel, revealing her relationship with Meaghan Slater, director of the National Womyn's Congress. Crow knew Rachel's sexual tastes were eclectic, but letting the public think she was exclusively lesbian ended the rumors he was having an affair with her. After the revelations about Rachel, speculation about his love life continued unabated, with every single woman who visited the White House named as a possible first mistress. The image of Crow as a playboy president caught the fancy of the public, and Crow's approval ratings began to climb as those who had voted for a dead man instead of Crow were slowly won over.

The first months of his administration were spent appointing his people to key positions, many of whom had shared blood rituals with him. Once Crow had settled into the White House, Fry came calling.

Crow met Fry in the Oval Office, sun shining through the window behind him, roses in the garden below in bloom. Fry was full of himself, feeling powerful, feeling like he controlled Crow. Hating the man he was partnered with, the new president was impatient to find out what he wanted and get rid of him.

"Mr. President," Fry said mockingly, "how does it feel to be the most powerful man in the world?"

"It feels like it was meant to be," Crow said evenly.

"Don't let it go to your head, Crow. You're here because I wanted you here."

"You overestimate your contribution, Mr. Fry."

"Your opponent didn't get IT by accident," Fry said.

"There are other ways for a man to die," Crow said.

"And who would arrange that? You? Rachel?"

Eyes fixed and cold, Crow stared at Fry, wondering if it was time to send him to the Master.

"When are you going to give up on Thorpe?" Crow asked. "I've got all the resources of NASA and the Defense Department at my command now."

Plopping in a chair, Fry put his feet up on Crow's desk. "Thorpe's got that sphere flying."

Crow masked his surprise.

"Floating?"

"Flying! He can maneuver it."

"Why haven't you used it? You could have taken their space station when one of the Ark-class ships was docked. That former Soviet sub, *Crucifixion,* would have made a great prize."

"It'll be back. They're making regular runs to that planet of theirs. Besides, the more runs they make, the fewer members they have left on Earth. Where would you prefer to deal with that cult? Here, or deep in space where there are no witnesses? Besides, one sphere won't carry enough men to take the space station and the ships."

"What choice do you have?"

"A lot more than I did when you were just a senator."

Fry took his feet down, then leaned on the desk, looking Crow in the eye.

"The military is still flying shuttles. You will turn one over to the CIA—my CIA. Then we're going to mount the sphere inside, load it with as many men as it can carry, and launch it. Once in orbit, the sphere can take the shuttle to their space station. The cult will never know what hit them."

Crow couldn't help but smile in admiration. He liked the plan. Pleased with himself, Fry put his feet back on Crow's desk. Crow took two Cuban cigars from his desk drawer, tossing one to Fry. He lit up, then leaned back in his chair, putting his own feet up. Dreaming of the power they would have with the cult's technology and the presidency, they puffed their cigars in silence.

CHAPTER 101

RETURN FROM AMERICA

> Love generates power, but power without love
> can only destroy.
>
> —MARK SHEPHERD

PLANET AMERICA

On the voyage from Earth to America, *Covenant* had been a crowded, noisy, busy vessel. The recycled air a thick mix of smells, the charcoal scrubbers never able to get it all. In every corridor, in every compartment, there was life and that meant noise, movement, and emotion. One birth had occurred on the voyage and six deaths, the *Covenant* arriving with fewer lives than it had left with. For a people commanded to be fruitful and multiply it seemed a poor beginning, but sixty-three women were pregnant when they arrived. Even in the cramped over-crowded spaces of the *Covenant,* love found a way. There were six marriages during the voyage, shared throughout the ship over the speakers. There were fights too, minor conflicts, water shortages, breakdowns, nightmares, claustrophobia, disease, and a host of other problems that are part and parcel of being human.

It was early spring in the northern hemisphere of planet America when *Covenant* arrived. New growth was everywhere, the grays and browns of winter sprinkled with the bright greens of new leaves and swelling buds. Escaping the confines of *Covenant* for the open spaces and clean air of America added to their joy at arrival, and they took the hardships of living in the open in good spirit. It took weeks to shuttle everyone down, the weather steadily improving, and on the day the last of the settlers landed the sun shone, the grass was lush, the meadow a riot of flowers in color combinations no one had ever seen. The community worshiped that day, building an altar in the meadow and decorating it with alien blooms. Then three thousand thankful people bowed their heads, thanking God for bringing them to this promised land.

Covenant left a month later for Earth and seventeen months after that it returned with another full complement. It was winter on America now and the new arrivals were met with a cold persistent drizzle and gray skies. The climate was mild, but everyone was permanently wet and damp; the only alternatives to the rain were the overcrowded dormitories, most of which leaked.

Covenant's third arrival came in the fall, just as the last of the harvest was being gathered. There had been much building in the two and a half years since the first arrivals and there was a town now with a church that doubled as a school, weather-tight housing, and dormitories waiting for the new arrivals. They celebrated Thanksgiving once all the new arrivals were down. With no dining facility to hold them all, community gatherings could only be held outdoors. The weather cooperated and they gathered around long wooden tables, new arrivals mixed with the seasoned to help them identify the foods they were eating.

To everyone's surprise, the *Crucifixion* arrived six weeks after *Covenant* left. The converted former Soviet sub was a monster ship carrying four thousand tightly packed people. Improvements in her drive allowed her to make the transit in five months, but conditions in the ship were nearly unbearable. The situation on Earth made it necessary to move as many people as possible and they endured the conditions to seek a better life for their children. The early arrival of *Crucifixion* taxed their resources and every building became housing, every blanket used, and food rationed.

Crucifixion's crew brought detailed reports to Mark of what was taking place on Earth and it was clear he needed to return. When Floyd offered to return with him, Mark accepted, but turned down Ira since he had a two-year-old son to raise. The day of departure, the community came together to say good-bye, feasting and worshiping. After the service Mark and Floyd shook as many hands as they could, then took a shuttle up to *Crucifixion*.

Hard work was a way of life on America. Up at dawn, work until dusk, in bed a few hours later to sleep deeper than anyone had on Earth. In contrast, on *Crucifixion* there was little to do. The computer flew the ship and the crew performed maintenance. To keep busy, Mark wandered through the great ship, cleaning, picking up, polishing, finding a nearly empty *Crucifixion* eerie. Floyd helped, working the lower deck. When each compartment had been policed they hauled the bins to the forward cargo compartment for disposal when they reached Earth. Then it was time to sweep and mop.

Mark found the simple labor refreshing. No decisions had to be made, no conflicts resolved. Free of the anxiety of being in charge, he found his mind sharper than it had been for years. Scripture touched him more deeply, he centered more easily during prayer, and his worship was more fulfilling. Acoustically, the empty corridors were perfect for hymn singing and he swept and mopped in rhythm with the songs that poured from his heart. Immersed in people's lives for two decades, the time alone on *Crucifixion* was a sabbatical, a time of renewal, and he relished it. It was no surprise then that when the *Crucifixion* docked with New Hope station Mark was disappointed.

Sally Roper and Stephen O'Malley were anxious to shift their loads to Mark, and he and Floyd were in a meeting within three hours of docking.

"How is the cash flow, Sally?" Mark asked. "Floyd brought another long shopping list with him."

"We've lost twenty-two percent of the revenue from our communications division. The military and government have been launching their own satellites. They're subsidizing costs to compete with us. We keep matching their price, but we're losing significant amounts of our business."

"What about the asteroid search?" Mark asked.

"We located four additional asteroids with significant gold content and sold them to the Russians. The smallest netted three hundred million, the largest five hundred."

"How have the films done?"

Now Stephen and Sally looked uncomfortable.

"The first film earned three hundred million domestically and we almost doubled that worldwide," Sally said. "The second did nearly as well, but *Alien Predators* exceeded all the others. It's still running in some theaters and the DVD will hit the stores in a couple of weeks. Our licensing agreements have generated revenue nearly equal to the box office receipts. Stuffed animals have done well, lunch boxes, T-shirts, toys—we're in Happy Meals this month. We're negotiating a cartoon series."

"We have more carnivore footage, so we can get *Alien Predators Two* into theaters when *Settling Down* runs its course," Floyd said.

"*Settling Down* hasn't done as well as we'd hoped," Sally said.

"Too domestic? I wondered about that," Floyd said.

"No, it's not that. Terrorists firebombed one of our theaters," Sally said. "Four hundred people were killed."

"What? Why?" Mark stammered.

"Six groups claimed responsibility. Some were anti-Christian, some environmental radicals," Stephen said. "After the firebombing there were two extortion attempts. They threatened to burn more of our theaters unless we paid them off. One wanted ten million, the other one hundred million. I turned both over to the FBI."

"Since then we've had two more firebombing attempts," Sally continued. "The police say they were copycat crimes and not well planned. One set a fire in a rest room, another threw a jar of gasoline on the screen. Neither did much damage. We increased security but the crowds haven't come back. To compensate we're going to shorten the theater runs so we can get to pay-per-view and digital sooner."

"Twenty lawsuits have been filed against us representing six hundred claimants—more than died in the theater," Stephen said. "There's over ten billion dollars in claims."

"But we're not responsible," Mark argued vainly.

"Their lawyers claim we were negligent in not providing adequate security and for not having a sprinkler system in the theater. Survivors and family members have been all over the morning news shows. The networks are exploiting the tragedy to the fullest."

"What about our insurance?"

"It won't cover ten billion dollars. Premiums have been quintupled and we've had to limit our showings to theaters with sprinkler systems."

Mark considered ending the film business, but their enemies would just come after the Fellowship in some other way.

"How are negotiations with the Russians coming?"

"They aren't as anxious to sell us another submarine as we thought they would be," Sally said. "We took possession of one of their submarine hulls six months ago, but since then they haven't responded to our inquiries. I have information that our government is negotiating to buy their moth-balled subs out from under us."

"Cancel negotiations," Mark said. "Complete the conversion of the third submarine but then all available revenue goes to moving our people to planet America. We can get by without a fourth Ark ship for now."

"We could section New Hope and move it to America," Stephen suggested.

"That will cut expenses, Mark," Sally said. "What about increasing revenues?"

"Show them, Floyd."

Floyd pulled a leather pouch from his pocket, untied the top, and poured out a pile of raw uncut diamonds.

"We dropped Dieter Bröck and his sons off on one of the southern continents," Floyd said. "Six months later they found a rich deposit. He says diamond mining hasn't been this easy since South Africa at the turn of the century. You scuff your feet, then just pick them up."

Avarice in her eyes, Sally poured the diamonds from one hand to the other. "How much did you bring back?" she asked.

"Dieter estimated we have about one hundred million in quality stones. If there's snob appeal in alien gems we might get much more."

Sally scribbled furiously on a yellow pad, then paused.

"This will help," Sally said, fingering the stones again, "but we'll have to limit how much we import. I'll make the necessary connections and find out how many we can sell a year and not drive prices down."

"We have another potential source of revenue," Mark said.

Now Floyd pulled a leather wallet from his pocket and revealed a dozen small glass vials. Floyd removed one filled with a yellowish liquid. Pulling the small cork he held it out for Sally to smell. Cautiously, she sniffed the vial.

"Mmmmm. Smells wonderful."

Passing it to Stephen, Floyd said, "We extracted it from a flower growing around the lakes near our settlement. We think there might be a market for planet America perfumes."

Stephen looked skeptical but Sally jumped on the idea.

"Have you seen what women pay for a half an ounce of perfume? Perfumes have snob value too. No woman wants to wear the same scent as others. What would a woman pay to wear a scent no woman on Earth has worn?"

"There's a dozen different scents here," Mark said.

"I'll file patents on the scents but we may run into Law of the Sea conflicts—other countries may not recognize our claim to discoveries we bring from America," Stephen said. Wrinkling his nose at a new vial he said, "Very unique."

"It doesn't matter," Mark said. "We'll demand the lion's share of payments up front and when the knockoffs hit the market we'll introduce new scents—we have a planet full of them."

"There's a ban on alien organic material," Stephen said. "Most Western nations have been pressured by our government to go along."

"We'll sell it where we can and duplicate the chemistry where we can't sell genuine planet America perfumes."

Stephen and Sally nodded appreciatively. Mark sensed his presence lifted their burden and his optimism and quick solutions energized them. Was it immodest of him to feel pride in God's gift of leadership ability?

"There are other problems, Mark," Stephen said. "There are warrants for you, Micah, and others because of the deaths at Christ's Home. Six wrongful death suits have been filed by the families of the men who died, and we're enjoined from selling our properties there. Other assets have been attached. We've been lifting our people out of Mexico but it's getting harder to get them out of the United States. They are enforcing the National Restitution Act. Anyone wanting to emigrate must pay up to two hundred thousand dollars to reimburse the government for services provided. When they can identify which of our people have gone to planet America they seize whatever property they can locate. Fortunately, our people own almost nothing of value; it all belongs to the Fellowship. They can't touch a church—not yet, anyway."

"God will get us through this, Stephen—somehow," Mark said, but wondered how much more tragedy lay before them.

Moving into prayer they turned their burdens over to the Lord, relief spreading through each of them, renewing them for when they would again pick up their loads. After an hour Mark closed the meeting.

"Christy wants to see you, Mark," Stephen said. "She began calling when *Crucifixion*'s return hit the news."

He thanked Stephen for the message, then hurried off to place a call. The others smiled knowingly as he left.

Christy kissed him on the cheek when they met, holding his body at bay, gently deflecting his hug. He wasn't offended. Running off into space and leaving the woman you love alone for more than two years was reason enough for her to be a bit distant. They met in a Mexican café since he was a wanted man in his own country. The café was across from a large tourist hotel in Tijuana, and half filled with Americans eating breakfast. Christy was dressed casually, light slacks, yellow polo shirt, hair pulled back and tied in a bun. Had she always been this beautiful? he wondered.

"I missed you, Christy."

She smiled, but didn't share her feelings.

"How is life on another world?"

"It's a good life. The air is clean, the soil rich, the forests full of wildlife. Everywhere you turn is a new experience. There are plenty of challenges, Christy. You'd be welcome there."

"Would I? I'm not a fundamentalist and I never could be."

Mark had always been unsure about Christy's relationship with God. She never talked of being born again or having Jesus in her heart. When he was honest with himself, he knew his feelings for her closed his eyes to questions he should ask.

"Everyone respects you, Christy. They might argue with your theology occasionally, but you would be part of the community."

"I'd be a heretic."

"It's different there. Here Christians—real believing Christians—are the minority. On planet America believers are the majority. We can tolerate a heretic or two."

He meant it as a joke but she wasn't smiling.

"No one wants to be just tolerated, Mark. People want to be valued, to have their views respected."

Against his will he found himself being sucked into an argument.

"How can you respect those who have no respect for your views? It was tolerance for other views that lost our country. Instead of a nation of Christians we became a nation of hedonists pursuing personal pleasure, and when Christians objected to the depravity we were called narrow-minded and bigots. Now the streets belong to the criminals and our children can't play in the parks because they belong to the gangs and the drug dealers."

"Yes, there are problems—" Christy said, but Mark cut her off.

"Television is a cesspool, Christy. Nudity, profanity, violence. It permeates every hour of every day."

"It makes me uncomfortable too," Christy said, "but we must accept we live in a diverse world."

"There's no such thing as moral diversity. Either it's sin or it's not."

Then Christy's face relaxed and she smiled.

"So what you're saying, Mark, is that you could accept someone into your community who was different than you as long as they shared your religious beliefs."

"We're not bigots, Christy," Mark said, relieved they seemed to be moving toward common ground. "All we've ever wanted is to be left alone to worship God, to live a moral life, and to be free to raise our children to share our beliefs."

"There are other people who would like that chance for their children too. When will you give them a chance to share that dream?"

"We've already taken some who weren't part of the Fellowship, but we have to be selective if we're going to maintain Christian community."

"I know of a group that would like to join you on planet America. Would you be willing to meet their leader?"

"Of course."

Smiling now she said, "Good, I thought you would."

Then Christy stood and waved at someone across the room. An old black woman holding a cup of coffee stood and waved back, then walked toward them.

"You set me up," Mark said, hurt that Christy had lured him to the café with ulterior motives.

"You'll only be here a few weeks. I had to get you two together."

"I thought you came to see me?"

Taking his hand she said, "I did want to see you, I just wasn't sure you would want to see me."

Before he could assure her of his feelings, the woman was there, hugging Christy.

"Mark Shepherd, this is Selma Jones."

"I'm so glad to meet you, Mark Shepherd," the woman said loudly. "Thank you, sweet Jesus, for making this possible."

"I'm pleased to meet you too, Mrs. Jones."

"Call me Grandma. Everyone does."

Inviting her to sit down, Mark could see she wasn't as

old as he first thought and her face nearly glowed from her obvious joy.

"Grandma Jones is the leader of a group of people who want to move to planet America," Christy said.

"That's right, Mark Shepherd. God has called me to gather some of his flock and take them to a place where the wolves can't prey on them."

Mark didn't know what to make of the woman. Hair halfway to gray, overweight, and her skin well wrinkled, she had aged beyond her years, but she had the energy of a young woman.

"We're God-fearing people, Reverend. We love Jesus, every one of us."

"I'm sure you do, but—"

"Our children are dying, Reverend. If the drug dealers aren't hooking them on poison, they run with the gangs or run from the gangs. A boy a week dies on my street, Reverend. And the girls, what choice do they have? There's lots of babies born, but I haven't been to a wedding in three years. There just ain't no choice—no good choices."

"They want a better life, Mark. Isn't that why you wanted to leave too?" Christy asked, keeping Mark on the defensive.

"Yes, but—"

"You got to save my grandchildren, Reverend. I already lost one of my boys and my girl . . . well . . . she's as good as dead."

"Grandma was in the theater that burned, Mark," Christy explained. "She was one of the few survivors."

"I took that as a sign that God still had some use for me," Grandma said.

Mark found himself warming to Grandma Jones. He could feel her love for the Lord. Still, he worried about the impact of adding inner-city families to their community.

"Tell me about your group," he said.

"We're all black folk if that's what you're asking," she said.

"I was asking that," he said honestly. "What kind of skills do the people in your church have?"

"They're working-class people, good with their hands. Carpenters, machinists, plumbers, electricians, all kinds of laborers. We got one doctor, two lawyers, and a dozen or more teachers, but mostly we're just poor working people."

"Any farmers in your group?"

"We've got farmers, of course they're ten years off the land. It'll come back quick though."

"Don't take this wrong," Mark said, "but do you have many intact families? It takes a mother and father working hard to support a family in the wilderness."

"We're missing some daddies, I'll admit that, but it won't be that way in the next generation. Give our sons work to do, some way to make their children proud of them, and they'll stick around." Then with a smile she said, "Besides, where would they go?"

Perhaps the Holy Spirit was leading him, perhaps he felt guilt since she had nearly been killed in the terror bombing of the theater. Whatever was moving him, he found himself considering taking her and her people to planet America.

"We're being crushed by this world, Reverend Mark. We want a better life for our children, a chance for them to live."

Christy was watching him intently and he suspected she was looking for signs of racism, but was it racism to know that diversity created factions, and factions become suspicious and eventually hostile? Homogenous communities were stable, and flooding their new world with inner-city poor of any color could destroy the harmony.

"I'd like to help, but I don't think it would work out," he said.

"It's because they're black, isn't it?" Christy accused.

Hurt because she should have known better, Mark's face fell.

"It's not that, Christy," Grandma said. "Reverend Mark's not a racist. He's thinking a bunch of welfare mamas and their babies aren't going to fit in too good."

There was no anger, shame, or apology in her voice.

"But we don't want to fit in. We want our own land, our own town, our own community. We'd always be second class compared to your people—I told you we're not educated folk. Our children would grow up feeling inferior just like happens here and it would start all over. Our children need to know what it's like to be on top for a change. It's an entire planet, surely there's got to be room for a few people like us."

Grandma Jones had tasted life as a minority and had seen the harm it caused. She and her people had learned the lessons of history. Feeling the Lord tug at his heart, he knew it was right to take them to America.

"All right, we'll transport you to America."

Christy squeezed his hand, then held it firmly, sending warm waves through his body.

"We'll pay you everything we have," Grandma Jones said.

"You'll need your money to buy supplies," he said, knowing they would have to heavily subsidize Grandma Jones and her people if they were to survive. Thinking of the costs he realized he had never asked how many people were in her flock.

"Grandma, how many people will be going to America with you?"

"Three thousand," she said.

Stunned by the number and feeling foolish for making a blind commitment, he stared straight ahead, wondering how he would explain to Ira and Floyd that they would be transporting three thousand black people who couldn't pay but a fraction of the cost. Then Christy hugged him and nothing else mattered.

"It's an honest offer," Stephen said. "I think we should consider it. It's perfect timing since we'll be transporting Grandma Jones and her people."

The Fellowship Council was meeting again on New Hope station. Sally Roper and Stephen O'Malley had nearly fainted when Mark had announced his decision to transport Grandma Jones and her people to planet America. Floyd was dismayed as well, worried about the reaction of the Fellowship members who would have to be bumped to make room.

After Mark's surprise, Stephen had one of his own. Simon Ash had called on behalf of the president with an offer. If the Fellowship would agree to a fact-finding mission to America, Crow would support lifting the National Restitution Act. Representatives of the United States government would visit the planet to assess environmental impact, and the condition of its citizens—the media were reporting that many were being held against their will. There was no mention of having the charges against Mark and the other leaders dropped. Still, it was tempting. It would cost so little to transport the fact-finders and it could result in significant gain.

"You can't trust him," Floyd argued. "After what he did to Ruth—he killed her."

"I'm not suggesting we trust him, I'm saying we should use him," Stephen said. "If we can get the National Restitution Act repealed, cash flow will improve."

"We can do without," Floyd said.

"Maybe we can sweeten the deal," Sally said. "They've frozen half of the social security accounts of our people on America and some pensions. They're demanding we prove the recipients are alive. If they agreed to free those accounts . . ."

Argument continued and Mark listened, wary of Crow's offer. George Proctor had filled Mark in on details of Crow's activities and his belief that Crow was supported by a demon. Whether Mark believed in the demon or not didn't matter. It was clear that Crow would do anything to destroy the Fellowship. Was this offer part of a trap? If it was, he couldn't see it.

"We won't do it under his conditions," Mark began.

"Under no conditions," Floyd cut in.

"Under the following conditions," Mark said firmly. "The National Restitution Act is to be repealed pending the outcome of the investigation. All social security accounts, pensions, and other frozen assets are to be freed and transferred to escrow before we leave, to be released upon proof that the beneficiaries are still alive. Charges against Fellowship members are to be dropped."

Clearly unhappy, Floyd mumbled to Sally but offered no more public protests. Stephen and Sally looked thoughtful, neither willing to be the first to put the Fellowship into the hands of Manuel Crow. Meditating in silence now, they waited on the Lord, listening for the still small voice. When Floyd could see they were nearing consensus he spoke.

"If we're going to walk into the lair of the beast we should be sure the door doesn't lock behind us."

"What are you suggesting, Floyd?" Mark asked.

"If Crow double-crosses us, then we need to be prepared with a response. A way to protect our people. I think Scripture shows us a way."

Then Floyd explained his plan and they were horrified by it. Heated discussion followed and then prayer and meditation. Four hours later the "Daniel Option" had been devised.

CHAPTER 102   **PROTOHUMAN**

Perhaps there is some evolutionary flaw that
makes all intelligent species seek self-
destruction. The very basis of evolutionary
advance is competition, the struggle for survival,
but to an intelligent being competition is more
than a battle for the next scrap of food; it is also
a fight for long-term advantage, which inevitably
provokes confrontation.

— *UNEXPLAINED:*
MYSTERIES OF MIND, SPACE AND TIME,
PETER BROOKESMITH (ED.)

WASHINGTON, D.C.

Tobias Stoop's pirated copy of the Fellowship film *Alien Predators* was of poor quality, since one of his minions had secretly recorded the film during a showing in Los Angeles. Stoop was in the living quarters of the White

House, his copy projected on President Crow's wall screen.

"Here it comes," Stoop said, intently watching the screen. "Watch the tree behind the lion."

What Stoop called a lion had little resemblance to its earthly counterpart. It had fur but its chest was thicker and its front legs longer than a lion's. The creature's back was humped and sloped down to a tailless rump perched on two short legs. With a thick tawny mane and whiskered snout, only its face resembled a lion. It moved like a gorilla, although it never made an effort to stand on its back legs.

The lion-thing was crouched in tall grass, watching a small clearing in a jungle. Two dozen dog-sized animals crowded around a pond. Hornless, with plump brown bodies and short legs, they looked like hairless sheep and just as defenseless.

The camera focused again on the lion-thing, ready to pounce. Then in the tree behind it Crow saw what Stoop was excited about. Peeking around the trunk of the tree was a brown face. Suddenly the lion-thing bounded forward, the camera following the action as it pounced on one of the little animals, clamping powerful jaws on the neck of one beast, the others scattering in all directions—showing no herd instinct.

"I'll run it back so you can see it better," Stoop said. "It looks human."

They watched the scene again, this time Stoop freezing the face on the screen. Details were fuzzy, but the furry face had two bulging eyes, a nose, and a mouth and lips. To Crow, it looked like a peculiar monkey. But something about the creature had intrigued Stoop.

"It's a protohuman," Stoop said.

"It's hard to see," Crow said. "You know this film is available in digital, don't you?"

Crow was needling Stoop, but the ecoterrorist ignored the jab.

"Those cultists won't ever get a dime of my money," Stoop said angrily.

"They had to resort to DVD sales after that unfortunate fire."

Crow watched Stoop's face for reaction but he stared back blankly. Crow knew Stoop's people were behind the fire, but Stoop was smart enough not to admit it, even to him.

"If you can't see that being in the tree, then I'll steal a better copy for you."

"I can see it. What's your point?"

"The planet the cultists have invaded belongs to that creature in the tree and his or her descendants."

"You think the creature is intelligent?"

"It doesn't matter what it is now, there's every reason to believe it's following the same evolutionary path as humans. In a few million years it will have as much intelligence as human beings—maybe more. Those Fellowship settlers are interrupting their evolution, stealing their future."

"I see," Crow said, playing dumb. "That monkey-thing will someday discover oil, invent the car, and then pave the planet so they have somewhere to drive those cars."

"It might be smarter than that," Stoop said. "It might choose instead to live in harmony with nature, balancing the needs of the plant and animal world with their own. The point is it has to have the right to make its own choices."

"I understand and sympathize, Tobias, but I'm not sure what I can do."

"You're the president. You've got every imaginable resource including the military. You can stop them."

"I could attack them here, but how would I reach them on planet America?"

Red-faced with anger, Tobias stammered; having no plan of his own to stop the cult he had no focus for his rage.

"But there is something . . ." Crow said, letting his words trail off, teasing Stoop.

Now Stoop's eyes brightened, the ecoterrorist desperate for some way to act.

"What is it?" Stoop said anxiously.

"Mark Shepherd has agreed to transport a fact-finding committee to planet America. Part of that mission will be to assess environmental damage. Perhaps you would be willing to join the mission?"

"Go to the planet? Yes, that's perfect. How many of my people can go with me?"

"None. Only you."

Disappointed, Stoop hesitated. "That limits my ability to act."

"It's a fact-finding mission, not a military operation."

"Then what's the point?"

"Bring back your own recordings—evidence of the damage the Fellowship is doing to planet America. Find those protohumans and demonstrate that they are intelligent. A majority of Americans distrust the cult now. You could add to that consensus."

"I don't care about what most people think. I act on what is right."

"Yes, but if a president is to use those resources you were talking about, he needs to have the country behind him."

"Will the cult accept me as one of the committee members?"

"As part of the agreement I select the fact-finding team. I'm selecting a range of people from openly hostile to openly sympathetic. To get the sympathetic ones they'll have to accept those they see as hostile. They won't like it, but they'll take you."

"Then I'll go to planet America," Stoop said, "and I'll find the native species that rightfully owns that planet."

CHAPTER 103

FACT-FINDERS

Man evolved on this planet over 50,000 years
ago, but only in the last decade or so has his
technology advanced to the point at which he
can communicate with the stars. Time will tell
if his faltering technological civilization will
destroy itself or allow him to live out his
full time on Earth.

— *UNEXPLAINED:*
MYSTERIES OF MIND, SPACE AND TIME,
PETER BROOKESMITH (ED.)

APPROACHING NEW HOPE STATION

Christy had flown in Fellowship shuttles many times,
but only Roland Symes, sitting next to her, had some experience. Simon Ash, in the aisle seat in their row, was
ashen. Meaghan Slater, president of the Womyn's Congress, was across the aisle. With her closely cropped hair,
work boots, jeans, and flannel shirt, she looked like she
was ready to farm, not journey to another world. Ms.
Slater's jaw was set and she worked at showing no emotion. Next to her, Senator Peng exuded nervous excitement. Archie Cox was seated next to the window on the
other side of Peng, eyes glued to the glass. As the representative from NASA, Cox had helped others to fly into
space; now his turn had come.

"Thanks for getting me on the team, Christy," Roland
said. "After some of the columns I've written I didn't
think I'd ever get this chance."

Christy had recommended Roland as media representative when President Crow called and asked her to be part
of the team. Mark had not been pleased, finally agreeing
only because Christy asked. While Mark was uncomfortable with Symes, he was furious over Crow's selection of

Tobias Stoop. Stoop and his extremist friends had kept up a steady barrage of lawsuits against the Fellowship, single-handedly soaking up millions of dollars needed to support the fledgling colony. Only when the deal looked like it might fall apart had Mark agreed. Tall and wiry, Stoop was a bundle of nervous energy, his face as tightly drawn as his nerves. With sharp features and no body fat, Stoop was a walking skeleton.

"It was either a muckraker or a yellow journalist," Christy said.

"Which am I?" Roland asked.

"You capture the essence of both," she said, smiling.

The loudspeaker system announced their arrival at New Hope station and the pending loss of internal gravity. Christy took the sudden lightness of her stomach in stride, but most of the others fought back a rising gorge. Simon was white, perspiring. Roland leaned toward him.

"Simon, if you have to use the barf bag be real careful," Roland said. "In zero gravity the vomit can bounce off the end of the bag and come right back at you."

"Please stop talking," Simon said.

"The vomit forms into globs—little barf balls," Roland added.

"Stop!" Simon said, bringing the bag to his face.

Christy elbowed Roland to shut him up. She wasn't seasoned enough to control her own stomach if Simon's puke started floating around the compartment.

A bump announced docking, a minute later the gravity came back, stomachs gratefully settling. When the hatch was opened they shuffled into New Hope, carrying one suitcase each. The severe limitations imposed by the Fellowship forced Christy to pack as if she were leaving for a long weekend, not a five-month voyage.

Floyd met them at the hatch and led the fact-finders through the corridors of New Hope directly to *Crucifixion*. The ship was fully loaded and would depart as soon as they were aboard. Christy knew some of those in the side corridors and they smiled or waved to her, ignored the others and glared at Tobias.

Once through the airlock, *Crucifixion*'s exterior hatch

was closed, the clang reverberating through the ship. Roland took Simon by the arm.

"That sound gives me the creeps," Roland said.

"Why?" Simon asked innocently.

"That hatch won't be opened again for five months. There's no way out of this steel coffin."

Trembling now, Simon followed the others into the bowels of the ship.

"Why are you tormenting that poor man?" Christy asked.

"He's the president's toady and I don't like toadies."

"I'm not fond of him either, but if you turn him into a raving lunatic you'll have to put up with it for five months."

"Good point. But he's such an easy mark."

The atmosphere in *Crucifixion* was thick with human smells. Few people could be seen in the corridor, most were in their compartments preparing for departure. Everything inside was steel, the walls, the ceiling, the floor steel grating covered with rubber mats. The sounds of life reverberated off the hard surfaces, the thousands of voices merging into one voice, the voice of the ship. To Christy that voice was a song, to Roland it was a whisper of secrets, to paranoid Simon the voice was speaking of him.

The ceiling was a maze of pipes and cables, each color-coded, and through the floor grating more pipes and wires could be seen. Large ventilation ducts ran the length, with occasional grates pumping out cool air. Light fixtures were nothing but fluorescent bulbs in aluminum holders, with plastic covers. The interior of *Crucifixion* had all the warmth of a water treatment plant.

The faces peering out of doorways were black. Smiling and nodding at those they passed, most smiled back. Christy, Meaghan Slater, and Congresswoman Swanson were assigned to a compartment near the drive end of the ship. Grandma Jones was there and fourteen other women. Bunks were stacked three high, six racks to a compartment, with only a few feet between the bunks. Every other available space was storage—cabinets, barrels, steel tanks. Netting hung between bunks holding personal belongings. One stack of three bunks was empty.

"Take the one on the bottom, Christy," Grandma Jones said. "That way we can talk."

Meaghan Slater took the top, climbing up in her work boots, banging her head on the ceiling.

"There's not much room," Meaghan complained.

"That's for sure," Grandma Jones said. "They call them racks. It's a submarine term. They're only eighteen inches wide."

Christy dropped her bag, then sat on her bed. She couldn't sit up straight. Instead, she lay down, the bunk above her a foot from her face.

"Zero gravity in two minutes," the loudspeaker announced.

"Better buckle in," Grandma said to Christy. "We'll have plenty of time to talk later."

Another woman took their bags and stowed them in a compartment. Congresswoman Swanson climbed into the middle bunk, her weight pushing it even closer to Christy's face. Pulling the straps across her middle, Christy buckled it like a seat belt. Feeling distinctly claustrophobic, Christy looked around. On the wall next to her was a long thin cabinet, like something from a bathroom. There was a mirrored door that slid open to reveal an empty space with a toothbrush holder. On the other side she discovered a curtain that she could pull, closing off her bunk, creating a tiny bit of privacy, something she knew would become precious as the weeks rolled by. There was a light above her head, hanging from the bunk above. They were allowed only one book besides a Bible, but she knew that meant there would be thousands of books on the ship to be circulated.

Suddenly Christy felt as if she were in an elevator, her stomach unsure of up or down. When gravity was gone the great ship vibrated and groaned, put into motion by the invisible forces that drove it. Now there was forward thrust and she was pushed toward the edge of her bed. The combined voices of the ship became anxious; children were crying.

"How long will this go on?" Congresswoman Swanson asked.

"Weeks," Grandma Jones said. "But they'll give us breaks. It'll be another hour or so before we get the first break."

"Weeks?" the congresswoman said anxiously.

"They'll just keep pushing the ship faster and faster until we're going faster than light itself. Once we get up to speed we'll have a few months when they can leave the gravity on all the time."

Lying in that tiny space the word "months" made Christy's heart pound. She wondered if she could go that long without a look at the sky, without the sun warming her face. Spring was coming to her home on Earth and she had been looking forward to a break in the Oregon rains, an end to the gray winter skies. There would be no garden in her yard this year, no petunias planted along her walk, no fresh strawberries from her patch. Her journey was off to a poor start.

Simon Ash was sedated two weeks into the voyage. In the mornings when the vitamin cart came around there would be two pills in his Dixie cup; one a vitamin, the other a tranquilizer. Additional pills were brought twice a day. Simon spent much of his day pacing the corridors, the constant motion helping to exhaust him so he could sleep. But his sleep was restless and unsatisfying. Simon wasn't the only one receiving the two-pill treatment.

Crucifixion's crew mimicked day and night in the ship with lighting, and that helped with sleeping. Christy developed her own routine, lining up for the bathroom early to avoid the rush, although on many nights the early bathroom trip necessitated another middle of the night trip. After her turn in the bathroom, while most of the women waited in the long lines for their turn, Christy would lie in bed reading, her curtain pulled, her reading light on. Informal rules of courtesy had developed and when a person's curtain was pulled no one spoke to them and no one peeked inside. Privacy was protected jealously.

The monotony of life on the ship wore on everyone.

Most of their food needed only to be microwaved, so little time was spent in food preparation and there was little to clean up. Clothing could be washed, but seldom since water was rationed. Bathing was limited, hair washed but once a week, and sponge baths replaced showers. Rooms were cleaned incessantly since there was little else to do. The corridors were used for walking during morning and evening hours—walking clockwise mornings, counterclockwise in evenings. Joggers hit the corridors between five and six A.M. The rest of the days the corridors served as the community square, people meeting to gossip and plan their new life.

Strangely, what Christy missed most on *Crucifixion* were chairs—there were none. The mess had the only seating, tables with benches and precious few of these. There wasn't enough space to sit up on the bunks and only occasionally could you sit on the floor without blocking someone's path. Days were spent standing or lying down and nights only lying. Sometimes Christy would get up in the middle of the night and sit on the floor of the corridor, back against the wall, trying to get the feel of sitting in a chair—the corridor wall was a poor substitute.

As the weeks passed Christy became obsessed with thoughts of chairs, much like a starving man obsesses about food, planning the meals he would have when food was available again. Christy thought of chairs often. There was a wooden rocker on her porch that held a special place in her thoughts—and her kitchen chairs, how could she forget those? They had rollers and you could move around the kitchen without ever getting up. Her chair fantasies were silly, she knew, but satisfying.

Her relationship with Mark got her special privileges and one day he took her to the flight deck where she sat in a pilot's chair, the feel almost a forgotten sensation. She would have enjoyed seeing the stars but the naked eye could not see them at the speed they traveled, the ship navigating by the gravitational signatures of the stars. Most evenings Mark would come for her and they would do the evening walk, counterclockwise, with the rest of *Crucifixion*'s passengers. Round and round they would go until bedtime, then with a hug or a brief kiss, they would part, always with commentary by those nearby.

Sundays and Wednesday nights were exciting and anticipated because of worship. The song of the ship on those days was gospel, and the ship rocked with thousands of voices raised in song. Senator Peng attended services with Christy in the dining room when it was their turn, but the other fact-finders refused to participate in "superstitious rituals." If they had participated they would have seen a people alive with faith, unafraid to show the joy their religious beliefs brought them.

Long hours with nothing to do brought out the ingenuity in people and they organized themselves into groups. Chess was popular since it was absorbing and time-consuming. Card games were played widely but Grandma Jones strictly forbade gambling, even for matchsticks. "New habits start now," she said when she stopped the first poker game. Instead, games were played for points and tournaments held. Christy learned to play bridge, partnering with Roland. They held their own in the tournaments, placing as high as fifth in the first month.

Bible studies were common and there was an approach for every type. Some groups engaged in raucous debates, others were like-minded believers who agreed on every interpretation. One ambitious group set out to memorize the entire Bible using visual images as mnemonics and was making good progress.

Children went to school, classes taught in the dining hall, children rotating in and out every hour. Christy volunteered as a teacher and worked in compartments with children on assignments, correcting papers, tutoring, testing, encouraging. Children were best able to adapt to space travel. Few were claustrophobic, most playful and mischievous like children everywhere. They made up games, playing tag in the corridors, hide and seek in compartments, and blind man's bluff. Paper was a rare commodity, but chalk was plentiful and the children decorated the walls continuously, driving some of the adult passengers to complain about the chalk dust. It was allowed to continue, however, after the children agreed to clean the walls regularly, and admiring the drawings was part of daily walks.

At the end of the sixth week of the voyage there was a wedding. Claris and Tom, sixteen and seventeen, were married in the dining room, a ship-wide party following. After the ceremony, the bride and groom circulated through the ship, the bride wearing one of four wedding dresses brought on the voyage. Worried that they were too young for marriage, Christy felt obligated to warn Grandma Jones about the poor success rate of teen marriages.

"You're still thinking Earth-think, honey," Grandma Jones said. "Where we're going he can be the man of the family, working the fields all day, bringing home the bacon, and there won't be no government money to seduce her away from her man. They'll make it together or they won't make it at all."

"They're still awfully young for marriage," Christy persisted. "Has anyone discussed the facts of life with them?" she asked delicately.

"Experimenting with the facts of life is why they're getting married in the first place," Grandma Jones said with a laugh. "Anything they don't already know they'll just have to learn by trial and error, but that's half the fun, isn't it?"

Grandma Jones laughed but when Christy didn't join in she sobered, fearing she had insulted Christy.

"I'm sorry, honey, I forgot you're still a virgin."

Embarrassed, Christy reddened.

"What's a matter with that Pastor Shepherd, anyway? I'm going to talk some sense into him."

"Please don't."

"He needs a good talking to."

"It's not just him, it's me too. I just don't . . . I'm not ready."

"Says you, but I says you're past ready." After a sigh she said, "I'll stay out of it if you say so, but you're ripe for the picking and if the good pastor isn't harvesting then it's time to open the field for U-pick."

A small compartment on the lower deck was designated the honeymoon compartment and the regular occupants vacated for three nights, rotating through bunks throughout the ship. After that the couple was separated again. There was no family space, all compartments gender segregated. The newlyweds walked the ship together after that, hand in hand, clockwise in the morning, counterclockwise in the evening.

Teresa White, Grandma Jones's neighbor in Chicago, shared their cabin along with two of her children. Teresa was open to a fault, sharing freely about her life before she had asked Jesus into her heart. Not an ounce of pretense, a hearty laugh, and a ribald sense of humor, Teresa was the life of the compartment and a sought-after companion. Her girls, Nashville and Fayette, shared the compartment, and her son Wheaton was at the other end of the ship staying with the men. When Christy asked about their unusual names Teresa answered in characteristic fashion.

"I named my children after the places where they were conceived. Although, if truth be known, Fayette should have been named Drive-in," she said, laughing at her own joke.

"Or Cadillac," Grandma Jones added.

"I never did like him that much," Teresa said, "but I sure loved that car—it was yellow. That was Fayetteville, then I had that little adventure in Nashville—always thought that was the prettiest name for a girl. I fudged on naming my boy Wheaton since the motel wasn't technically in the city limits, but it's a good name. I got two older boys too. York turned out as rotten as the city he was named after. He's in prison now and he'll be an old man before he gets out."

The compartment was quiet then, Teresa's normally booming voice had trailed off, sadness creeping in. Then life came back to her voice, her face animated.

"But Harlem, he turned out good. Never could figure that. They grew up together, only a year apart, and Harlem worshiped York, but when York turned down the wrong path Harlem didn't follow. He stayed out of the gangs and never got himself hooked on the drugs. Only boy in his neighborhood without a rap sheet—kind of embarrassed him," she said, laughing again. "He's apprenticed himself as a plumber. Got himself two kids of his own. I cried an ocean when I said good-bye to them babies. He thought about coming but his wife's not the country type. She's assistant manager of a Safeway and the pay's good. Those two are going somewhere, but then so are we," she said, banging on the steel wall.

Nashville was a quiet girl who liked to read and spent hours in her bunk, curtain closed, churning through book after book. Christy discussed some of those books with her in the corridors at night, their backs against the wall trying to fool their bodies into thinking they were sitting in chairs.

Fayette had a wild side and spent the days in the corridors, parading up and down, flirting with boys. Occasionally Fayette would slip out at night, ostensibly to use the bathroom, but twice Teresa went after her when she didn't come back in ten minutes. A shouting match erupted after the second incident, everyone staying inside their curtained racks, pretending not to hear the scolding Teresa gave her girl.

"Boys only want one thing and they won't buy the cow if they can get the milk for free," she said.

Grandma Jones's daughter Fancy was a drug addict and spent the first few weeks in withdrawal, irritable, sweaty, a bad case of the shakes. Without even tobacco to feed her addiction, she turned to her fingernails, chewing them to nubs, cuticles bleeding. Accepting no comfort, she was a psychological mess and the only person on board refused medication when she requested it.

"She's got to get through this sometime," Grandma Jones said. "This is as good a time as any."

Fancy's misery infected whatever part of the ship she occupied, dampening even Teresa's spirits when she was around. But by the fourth week Fancy was improving, smiling occasionally, joining in card games, helping with school. Slowly a new Fancy emerged, intelligent, attentive to detail, artistic. Fancy's skills were crude, undeveloped, so Christy sought out an art group and they adopted Fancy. Two of the men in the art group were single and became very attentive. When they asked her to model for the class one day, she beamed, posing for three sessions while the class immortalized her in chalk on the walls of the ship.

The young men created near caricatures of her face, highly fanciful etchings showing high cheekbones and glowing skin—she loved them for it.

Grandma Jones's granddaughter, Jasmine, was halfway through puberty and unsure of her body and her self. A pretty girl, lithe in form, athletic and with high energy, she played with boys as easily as the girls. Her changing form was affecting her relationships though, older boys noticing the woman emerging from the girl and vying for her attention. Enjoying her new status, Jasmine played one suitor against another. She would never be lonely.

Meaghan Slater spent the voyage evangelizing, showing up wherever young women were gathered, preaching feminist philosophy and promoting gender warfare. Many listened respectfully, there was little else to do, but "equal pay for equal work" meant little where they were going, and the concept of a "glass ceiling," even less. Warning the women on the ship to be self-sufficient and not dependent on men, to not become slaves to their families, fell on deaf ears, since the women had self-selected a life where family would be their primary focus.

Knowing she was merely humored infuriated the radical feminist, spurring her on, redoubling her efforts to convert someone. Using feminist theology, and quoting scripture, she referred to God as "Goddess," and suggested the Bible was a culture-bound anachronism. In her rewrite of Scriptures, the Bible was gender neutral. References to "father" were replaced by "parent," and instead of "son of God," it was "child of God." One day, Meaghan gathered together some of the more patient women for worship, but when she opened with the Lord's Prayer, saying, "Our Parent who art in heaven," the women began giggling and never recovered their composure.

After her religious period, Meaghan withdrew briefly, then reemerged, once again trumpeting her theology but with a new tactic. Now, instead of meeting with small groups of women she concentrated on cornering one at a time, whispering with them in shadows.

One day Christy returned to her compartment to see a young woman crying, head in the lap of Grandma Jones.

Their conversation ended abruptly and the girl hurried out. That night the compartment was cleared and Ms. Slater met with Grandma Jones alone. When Christy was allowed back in, Meaghan was in her bunk, privacy curtain drawn. After that Meaghan was never left alone with any of the young people, male or female.

Senator Peng moved easily among various groups and was often invited into card games, discussion groups, and Bible studies. Archie Cox, the representative from NASA, spent his time with the crew, pumping them for as much information as he could, or wandering the ship, peeking into everything that wasn't locked. He kept a journal and spent hours in his bunk, recording information. Tobias was nearly a ghost, unseen during the days, wandering the ship at night when most of the others were asleep. Roland and Congresswoman Swanson struck up a friendship, spending hours talking, the congresswoman a rich source of insider political stories. Roland filled a notebook with her stories.

The third month of the voyage found Grandma Jones busy settling arguments, breaking up fights, and encouraging reconciliation. Children still played in the corridors but they were also affected by the growing depression of the adults, and quarreled over rules and turns. The fourth month found the voice of the ship angry. When two fistfights broke out in a single day, Grandma Jones called the congregation to ten days of prayer, asking the Holy Spirit to cleanse the ship of the discontent that now permeated her people. After the evening prayer hour on the tenth day Mark made a ship-wide announcement.

"We are pleased to announce that *Crucifixion*'s transit to planet America will set a new record. We will arrive in three weeks and two days, nearly two weeks ahead of schedule. We will begin deceleration in thirty minutes. Everyone is to be strapped into their bunks."

"It's a miracle," Grandma Jones said as they prepared their bunks. "God heard our prayers and made this miracle."

It wasn't a miracle, Christy knew, each ship making the transit took less time than previous ships. Christy let her believe what she wanted to believe. There were weeks of deceleration ahead, but Christy knew they would be joyous ones, the tensions of the last month forgotten. Grandma's people were almost home.

Mark invited Christy to the flight deck as they approached orbit. Planet America resembled Earth—hues of blue and green, white clouds. Orbiting nearby was a smaller version of New Hope, and beyond that Christy could see rafts of cargo modules circling America like the rings of Saturn.

"What's all this?" she asked.

"Our future," Mark said. "Every ship that comes to America brings more than it needs to supply its settlers—most of it pushed ahead of the ship."

Christy had seen the cargo modules parked on the nose of *Crucifixion*.

"We don't need everything on the surface right now and it's easier to handle and store the modules in space. As we build the infrastructure of our society we'll bring down the appropriate materials."

Looking at the orbital storehouse, Christy realized how committed Mark and his people were to making America their new home. Every asset they owned on Earth was being liquidated, the money used to purchase a future for themselves and their children.

A day after orbiting planet America, Christy was seated in a shuttle, headed for her first look at an alien world.

> They crossed the wide desert, they climbed the tall peaks.
> They camped on the prairie for weeks upon weeks.
> They fought off the Indians with musket and ball.
> And reached California in spite of it all.
>
> —"SWEET BETSY FROM PIKE,"
> AMERICAN FOLK SONG

PLANET AMERICA

Christy studied the frost that framed the cabin window, the ice crystals as intricate on this world as they were on Earth. Did Jack Frost have a cousin, Christy wondered, or did he frost every window in the universe? Scratching at the frost, she discovered that it curled up under her fingernail just like on Earth.

The sun was a bright crescent on the horizon now and she could see a few people outside, most heading toward the outhouses. Slipping out from the layers of blankets, she dressed quietly, shivering in the chill room. Moving through the bunks she was careful in the dim light not to trip over shoes and boxes of belongings. The beds were filled with strangers, Grandma's group delivered to another settlement. She missed them. Becoming intimate with another group was draining. Pausing at the cold stove she remembered that the custom was the first person up in the morning built the fire.

"I'll do the fire," a voice said.

A middle-aged woman smiled at her from under a pile of blankets.

"You get out to the privy before a line forms."

"You're kind," Christy said, then left, closing the door quickly, keeping as much of the chill air out as she could. Her step disturbed the dogs asleep under the porch and two heads poked out, studying her. One was big and black like a Labrador, but huskier, the other a golden retriever. Neither dog looked anxious to be up and about yet. She left the privy shaking with cold, finding the golden retriever waiting for her. It looked pleased to see her although she couldn't remember it from the day before when they landed. There had been many dogs—dogs and children—everywhere in the town.

With the retriever following along, Christy left the privy and walked between the buildings to the front of the barracks and strolled toward the church, hands buried deep in the pockets of her fleece-lined coat. The dining hall was next to the church and she hoped there would be coffee.

A dozen people were gathered in the hall, all with steaming mugs of coffee. The kitchen was bustling with activity, the air smelling of fresh bread and frying bacon. Greeting those gathered near the coffee urn, she poured herself a cup, not bothering to look for sugar or creamer—everyone drank it black. The hall was filled with round picnic tables, centered on each were salt and pepper shakers. Four wood-burning stoves heated the hall and Christy picked an empty table near a stove, sitting with her back to the heat. Soon her chills were gone and her coat hot against her skin. Moving to the other side of the table, she took out her New Testament, turning to Second Corinthians. Other early risers were also engaged in devotionals, sitting by themselves at tables.

"Come here often?" Mark asked a few minutes later.

"Excuse me, do I know you?" Christy replied. "You look familiar but I can't place the face."

"We spent nearly five months together," Mark said, sitting across from her.

"And I haven't seen you since."

Christy was only mildly irritated by Mark's absence. Mostly she enjoyed his discomfort and the advantage it gave her.

"Arrivals are always a busy time, but I'm ready to make it up to you. Tomorrow's the Sabbath. After church we can picnic by the lake. Some early flowers are already blooming."

It was the equivalent of March on planet America with frost in the mornings but warm afternoons. Rain was typical in this latitude at this time of year, but they had arrived during fair weather.

"If I don't get a better offer between now and then I'll go."

"I'll tell the kitchen to pack us a lunch. Sorry, but I'll be in meetings the rest of the day."

Mark looked worried she might be angry about being left again.

"I've got a whole new world to explore," she said. "I'll keep busy."

Mark left and a half hour later Christy joined the line to get breakfast. There wasn't a low-fat option on planet America. Fried potatoes, bacon, scrambled eggs, and fresh bread were the only offerings. There was apple juice, coffee, or milk, Christy refilling her coffee mug. Taking her tray back to her table she whispered a blessing, then smeared a thick slice of bread with the freshly churned butter. A bran muffin and orange juice were Christy's breakfast at home.

Evelyn slid in next to her, Floyd taking the seat nearest the fire. Holding hands they prayed together, then Floyd reached for the salt and pepper, generously spicing his potatoes.

"Take it easy, Floyd," Evelyn scolded. "The nearest heart surgeon is five months away."

"I wouldn't need as much salt if there was ketchup," Floyd complained. "Who eats eggs without ketchup?"

"Everyone," Evelyn said. "I brought something for you, Christy."

Evelyn pulled a small jar from her coat pocket.

"It's jam," Evelyn said. "It's made from local berries—something like blackberries but easier to pick—they don't have thorns. It's not poisonous or anything. We've been eating it since last fall."

There was a purplish paste in the jar and Christy spread a small amount on the corner of her bread, then took a tiny bite. The sweet fruity flavor was nothing she had ever experienced. Truly alien, but similar enough to the berries of Earth to be palatable.

"It's good," Christy said, surprised.

"It makes a good cobbler too," Evelyn said.

"You could sell this on Earth," Christy said. "Fellowship Jams."

"You know we can't bring anything organic to Earth," Evelyn said.

"Those laws aren't about public health," Floyd said, his mouth half full of potatoes. "They're trying to strangle us financially. But Mark's too smart for them."

A young woman took the seat next to Floyd, bowing her head in prayer. It took a minute to recognize Faith Remple. She was a teenager now, caught in the awkward stage between childhood and adulthood. An inch taller than her mother, long brown hair, brown eyes, cheeks rosy from the cold. Like most of the Fellowship children, she had a rugged outdoors look.

"Hello, Faith. Do you remember me?"

"Sure. You're Reverend Maitland."

"Christy."

Faith's plate was filled with the calorie-loaded foods but she looked fit, not fat. The active lifestyle of the colonists allowed them to eat like longshoremen.

"How do you like living on planet America?" Christy asked.

Washing a mouthful down with a swig of whole milk, Faith said, "It's pretty neat. I miss TV, I guess, but they show movies on Saturday nights."

"We've got a radio station too," Floyd said. "We've been running old radio shows—*Fibber Magee, The Lone Ranger, Jack Benny.* Everyone listens."

"I'd like to be on radio," Faith said. "My friends and I are putting a show together. Pastor Shepherd said if we were good enough he'd put us on."

"Sounds like fun. I hope I'm here when you do your show."

Faith looked confused and said, "I thought you were gonna stay forever."

Evelyn and Floyd looked startled, then quickly stared into their food.

"I'm only here for a visit, Faith. Why did you think I would stay forever?"

Evelyn cut Faith off before she could answer.

"You better check over your algebra before class starts, Faith."

"I'm still hungry," Faith protested.

"Take some bread with you," Evelyn said, shooing her daughter from the table, glass of milk in one hand, slice of bread in the other.

Christy made a mental note to catch Faith alone sometime for a talk.

"How is Daniel doing?" Christy asked.

Both Remples frowned, then Floyd left to get seconds.

"He hates it here, Christy," Evelyn said when Floyd was gone. "He skips school, never shows up for work detail—we don't know where he is half the time. He's been called in front of the community three times."

"Is that like going to court?"

"Yes. When someone is a problem, a community meeting is called and they must come and explain their behavior. I'm afraid of what will happen if he gets called up again."

"He could be punished?"

"He has been punished. For not showing up for work detail he was put on rations for a month—that means he can't come into the dining hall and has to pick up his meals at the kitchen window. It didn't do any good so they cut him to half rations. He showed up for work after that, but was nothing but trouble and they stopped caring if he showed up at all. They've been lenient because he's our boy, but they can't keep looking the other way."

Floyd came back with another heaping plate, salting heavily.

"What will happen to him if he doesn't cooperate?" Christy asked.

"We don't have much of a range of punishments," Evelyn said.

"They ought to introduce public whipping," Floyd

said, then shoveled another forkful of eggs into his mouth.

"You ought to be ashamed of yourself, Floyd. No boy ought to be whipped, especially not your own son."

Floyd said nothing, concentrating on his eating.

"We're afraid they'll banish him, Christy," Evelyn said.

"Banish?"

"They had to do it once already. Ian Castles kept beating his wife and kids. He wouldn't stop no matter what the community did so they flew him to an island somewhere. He can't come back for at least five years."

"Would they do that to Daniel?" Christy asked.

"There has been talk," she said.

After breakfast Evelyn guided her to her work assignment, the golden retriever that had followed her from the privy trailing after her. A knot of people was gathered in front of the church by a tractor and a trailer, a pack of dogs milling about. Gus was there giving orders, a cup of coffee in his hand, his breath steaming with each word. Hands buried in her pockets, Christy shuffled her feet keeping warm. Sylvia and Meaghan joined them, Meaghan finishing her bread as she came up the street. Suddenly Gus called Christy's name and told her to get on the trailer. Evelyn joined her and they sat on bales of hay. Someone passed a blanket and they spread it over their laps. Meaghan climbed on with the last group, but Sylvia left with a group heading back into town. Then Gus climbed on the tractor and with a jerk they were off, taking the road out of town, the pack of dogs following—Christy's golden retriever with them.

The road was nothing but graded dirt, the bulldozer that created it parked at the edge of the clearing, ready to bulldoze more of the forest into submission. Once into the forest the road was lined with stumps and debris pushed out of the way by the brute force of the Earth-built machine.

The forest was wild like few places on Earth. American forests were second or third growth for the most part, cultivated and harvested like a farmer's crops. Experiencing planet America's forests was like traveling back in time. Leaving the clearing they plunged into a tangle of growth where new trees fought for light, spindly trunks stretching toward the life-giving orb in the sky. The trees resembled evergreens, but the hues were wrong, the trees often splotchy as if they were camouflaged. Plants that could pass for ferns were thick wherever larger trees cast shadows. Unidentifiable bushes filled every other space, just now beginning to bloom. Vines tied the whole mass together, as if the forest would fall apart without the encircling ropes. The forest was nearly impenetrable, and after a few more weeks of spring, traveling the road would be like passing through a green tunnel.

After a short bumpy ride the forest changed, the undergrowth thinning, the trees now towering. Soon the average tree matched the largest old-growth Douglas firs. Some matched the girth of the giant redwoods, their tops lost in the crown far above where tiny shards of blue were the only sky to be seen.

"Look at the size of those trees," Evelyn said. "Half of them are too big for our mills. Can you imagine that, trees too big to be cut down?"

North America had been like that. Christy had seen pictures of loggers perched on boards, high up on the trunks of trees where their saws could manage the diameter of the girth. Those trees were gone now. Would the same thing happen to planet America? Was it wrong to harvest these magnificent giants even for a good purpose?

They passed through two more clearings, one with a small lake, both prepared for crops, men and women busy in the fields or near the buildings built along the forest's edge. After they rocked an hour in the back of the trailer, the forest thinned again and they entered another clearing and cut across the meadow grasses toward two buildings on the far end. A gully ran along one side, the growth thick along the sides indicating a stream in the bottom. Abruptly the tractor stopped and they all scrambled off, stretching to wake sleeping muscles. Christy walked away from the others into the meadow, studying the early blooming flowers—small, purple, with white centers, tiny bits of yellow sprinkling the core.

"They're going to plow all this beauty under, you know?" Meaghan said.

Meaghan and Evelyn stood behind her, Christy's golden retriever and two other dogs trailing behind them.

"We've got to have farmland and the meadows are ready-made for farming," Evelyn said. "Even with chain saws, bulldozers, and dynamite it would take months to clear this much acreage."

Meaghan picked one of the purple flowers and asked, "How do you know that this isn't the only meadow on the planet where this particular species grows? If you plow it under it could be lost forever. Your children's children will never see it."

"It grows in every meadow I've ever seen," Evelyn said evenly. "Besides, if it's that fragile a species, then it would be wiped out by fire or disease sooner or later anyway, leaving a niche for something else to evolve."

Christy was amused by the way the Fellowship used evolution to defend their actions. Every one of them was a creationist.

"If given the chance even the most fragile species can adapt, find a way to survive," Meaghan argued. "But adaptation takes generations—your plows won't wait for that."

Tension was rising so Christy stepped in.

"That golden retriever keeps following me," Christy said. "What's his name?"

"Squeaky," Evelyn said. "*She* got the name as a pup."

"She," Christy repeated. "Whose dog is she?"

"She's a community dog. No one owns her."

"Who sees she gets her shots, gets her spayed, feeds her?" Meaghan asked.

"The dogs mostly feed themselves, but there are scraps behind the dining hall most nights. As for shots—"

The sound of breaking limbs came from the forest on the far side of the clearing, Squeaky and the other dogs freezing, one of the dogs assuming the classic stance of a pointer, although he looked half German shepherd. Then, as if of one mind, the dogs bolted for the forest, barking as they went. A few seconds later the rest of the dogs thundered by.

"What's out there?" Christy asked.

"Let the dogs handle it," Evelyn said, steering her back toward the buildings.

"They could hurt whatever it is," Meaghan said.

"Maybe," Evelyn said. "Usually they just run them off."

"Them what?" Christy persisted.

Enjoying her discomfort Evelyn said, "Just them."

Evelyn left, Christy right behind her. With another look in the direction of the yapping dogs Meaghan hurried to catch up.

Their work turned out to be assembling bunks in new communal living quarters. Pieces were cut and drilled in the yard, then carried inside where they were assembled. Christy and Meaghan worked with Evelyn, who acted as if she had assembled many of the three high bunks. By lunch they had a room full of bunks, ready for mattresses and bedding.

A tractor pulling another trailer brought them food—raw milk, coffee, tea, egg salad sandwiches, slices of salami, boiled eggs, three apple pies, and vitamin tablets for all. Four hours of high calorie work with no break and no snack left her famished and she ate enthusiastically, forgetting her dislike for egg salad. When the meal was over there were precious few scraps for the dogs, who snarled warnings at other dogs that approached some scrap they had snagged.

After eating, most of the crew rested, some cat-napping, backs against the barn wall, sun warming their bodies. Christy walked around the barn studying the flowers and grasses in the meadow. Squeaky followed her, Christy rewarding her companion with the crust off her pie.

Christy was no botanist, she couldn't identify fine morphological details, but plants on America were truly alien. What they called grass, for example, was green, it was fine, and there were seed stalks, but the green was tinged with blue, the blades diamond-shaped, the seed stalks hung with tiny balls. Flowers were the same mix of familiar and unfamiliar. The purples were too deep, blues too pale, petals in unfamiliar shapes. A sharp sting on her arm and she slapped reflexively, finding a bloody splotch, a crushed insect in the middle of the red blob. It had broad wings like a fly but the needle nose of a mosquito. Now she worried about malaria or its alien equivalent. Rolling her sleeves down to protect her arms she rounded the corner of the barn. Squeaky suddenly darted ahead, then froze. On the edge of the meadow was an animal. The size of a moose, its head was down in the grass, an enormous rack all you could see. Unlike the ungainly looking moose, this animal was sleek, with a powerful chest covered in a mat of gray fur, the rest of the body tapering to muscular haunches, its body covered in a shimmering tawny fur. The legs were thicker than an elk's and it sported a long tail that switched back and forth driving insects away. Then the head came up eyeing her and Squeaky. The antlers branched a half-dozen times on each side, all branches curling toward the front and ending in points. The head looked more like a horse than a moose, with the characteristic bulging eyes. Finishing its mouthful of meadow greenery, it bent again, ripping up more of the vegetation. Then Squeaky barked, growled, then barked again. Christy didn't want to drive the animal off—it was too beautiful—but she didn't want to scold Squeaky, discouraging her from protecting people. The animal looked warily at Squeaky, but continued eating, confident the lone dog was no threat. Then half the pack came round the corner, breaking into a run when they spotted the animal. Squeaky bolted after the attacking pack, the animal now turning in flight, bellowing an angry mule sound as it bolted into the forest, the pack following.

Christy had mixed feelings about the dogs. They offered protection, but also drove off animals she dearly wanted to see.

Soon Christy was back to work assembling bunks. There was a "you bend it, you straighten it" rule, to preserve the precious nails. Christy was given a hammer in the afternoon as they attacked the second dormitory and Christy found herself straightening many nails. Thus motivated, she quickly learned to drive straight and true, and by the end of the day rarely bent a nail.

She fell asleep on the way back to town, her head lolling from side to side, her right arm tired, her muscles sore. The sun was low when they reached camp, Evelyn shaking her awake. Christy returned to her dormitory, washing in cold water, then lying on her bunk waiting for dinner. Meaghan was there too, snoring in the bunk next to hers.

The dinner bell rang and she shook Meaghan awake; they walked to the dining hall together. Sylvia Swanson was there looking ragged, her gray hair falling out of the bun on the back of her head. They lined up together.

"What was your job?" Christy asked Sylvia.

"It was wash day," she said. "I haven't worked that hard since . . . I've never worked that hard."

"Did they have you washing clothes on a rock in a stream?" Christy asked.

"No, there's a shed over there full of washing machines and dryers—big industrial types. We loaded and unloaded all day long. We hung most of the sheets on lines to dry." Reaching into her pocket she pulled out a clothespin. "I hadn't seen one of these in twenty years."

"Were there any men working in the laundry?" Meaghan asked.

"Two old men. They were running steam presses."

"Figures," Meaghan said. "It's women's work unless there's a machine to run."

"What was your assignment?" Sylvia asked.

"We built bunk beds. They're starting a new farm."

"Destroying another meadow, you mean," Meaghan said.

Sylvia pursed her lips, preferring to hear it the way Meaghan told it.

"We passed a couple of other farms on the way, more meadows plowed under, more wildlife destroyed," Meaghan said, her severe face red with anger.

"That's the kind of tragedy we feared," Sylvia said. "Tobias should know about this," she added.

Now they were inside and to the food line. Each of them was handed a plate with meat loaf, a large pile of potatoes, and a mound of corn. The only choice was whether or not to smother the potatoes and meat loaf with gravy—Christy passed on the gravy. A tray of warm rolls was at the end of the line and Christy took two, following Sylvia and Meaghan to a table in the corner. Only she thanked God for the food, the others eating ravenously through her prayer.

She tasted everything before pausing to butter one of her rolls; bland as food prepared in large quantities always is, it still tasted good. On Earth she rarely ate butter since it was loaded with fat. Here she spread a thick layer over half a roll, her bite leaving a groove in the thick butter. Faith circulated among the tables with coffee and filled their cups. Only boiled water was safe for drinking, and there was little of that, so tea and coffee were popular even among children.

Roland Symes joined them, then Charlie Peng and Archie Cox. The men looked as tired as the women. Only Peng prayed before they ate. Christy waited until their forks slowed.

"Hard day at the salt mines?" Christy asked.

"Salt mining would have been easier," Roland said.

"Look at my hands," Archie said, holding them out.

Blisters lined each palm.

"And I was wearing gloves," he complained. "I'm an engineer, not a logger."

"They had us splitting wood," Roland explained. "Eight hours of splitting wood. We got so tired it was dangerous. I almost cut my foot off. Here, look."

Roland pulled his leg from under the table, holding it up. There was a wedge cut out of the toe of his boot.

Christy cleaned her plate, then broke the other roll in half.

"Try this, Christy," Charlie said, pushing her a container from the middle of the table.

It was filled with a reddish brown substance. Christy spooned some onto her bread and tasted it.

"It's good. It tastes familiar."

"It's apple butter," the congressman said.

"We've only been here a day and I'm already getting sick of apples," Sylvia complained. "Apples, apple juice, apple pie, apple butter."

Finishing her roll, Christy found she was still hungry. Faith appeared, refilling her coffee cup.

"Would you like dessert?" Faith asked.

Everyone asked for dessert and Faith left to wait on them.

"Where's Tobias?" Christy asked, noticing the man's absence.

"He refused to split wood," Roland said. "It's tough for tree huggers to chop wood. It's like dismembering your grandmother."

Senator Peng chuckled, but then sobered quickly under glares from Meaghan and Sylvia.

"He's probably gathering data," Sylvia said. "All this work is designed to keep us from doing our real job."

"Seeing how they live is part of our job," Christy said.

"We won't see much from here," Sylvia argued. "How come we weren't allowed to see where Grandma Jones and her people are living? I suspect the conditions are substandard."

"I'll bet they're not living at the Ritz like us," Roland said sarcastically.

"We've only been here one day," Christy argued, but then Faith interrupted, returning with a tray of small dishes, passing them out, then putting a pitcher of cream on the table. The dishes were filled with warm apple crisp.

"Oh, boy, more apples," Sylvia said sarcastically.

Everyone but Meaghan laughed. Christy poured cream over her crisp, enjoying the spicy sweetness, but worrying about Tobias. He wasn't just an activist, she knew, he was an ecoterrorist and she didn't like having him on the loose.

CHAPTER 105

DANIEL'S RATION

In a healthy home, parents and children communicate openly and freely so discipline is rarely required. On those rare occasions when it is appropriate, the punishment should not deprive the child of their dignity, self-esteem, nor harm the child physically in any way.

— *UNDERSTANDING CONFLICT,*
CHRISTINE MAITLAND

PLANET AMERICA

Daniel was passed two meat loaf sandwiches, an apple, and a bottle of milk, then the kitchen window was closed. It was nearly dark when he headed to his eating spot, his dog Sam following. There was a screened porch on the back of the church and he settled onto the porch swing to eat. Sam sat at his feet, staring at the sandwich, waiting for scraps. There would be few scraps, since Daniel's punishment kept him hungry most of the time. The first sandwich was gone before he opened the milk, draining half of it. Partially satiated, now he could afford some compassion and he tore off the crust, dropping it to Sam who snatched it in midair. Halfway through the second sandwich he saw a man come out of the woods.

It was a scarecrow of a man, skinny, bony. He passed the porch, glancing briefly at Daniel, showing no reaction. Daniel ate as the man passed and then gave the last bit of sandwich to Sam. Next he polished up the apple on his dirty shirt and took a big bite. He missed candy. Sweets were rare on America. Sugar was saved for baking, but because of his punishment he couldn't get desserts—no pie, no cobblers, no jams. He savored the apple, but having to settle for it angered him. There was so much he was missing. Television, radio, rock music, candy, pop, Hostess

Twinkies were all light-years away, as were his friends. Most of all he missed driving. Cars meant freedom. On Earth they would never have been able to keep him at home once he could drive. By now he would have his learner's permit, and he could be saving to buy his own car. That wasn't possible here. A few kids his age drove now—tractors mostly, some trucks—but only the best students or the best workers got to drive. He refused to play the game.

Worst of all, one boy his age—Rob Evans—was an apprentice pilot, learning to fly a sphere. Daniel hated him for that and more. Robert never skipped class, turned in a late assignment, or even spoke out of turn. On Sundays he actually wore the medal he earned for Scripture verse memorization—he was a nerd, but on this world nerds ruled.

Sam's ears came up and a second later Daniel heard the sound of footsteps. Melody Crane appeared, long blond hair in a french braid, blue jeans, and a corduroy coat. Checking first to see if anyone was watching, she slipped in the screen door making sure it closed quietly behind her. Then she stood looking at him, too shy to sit next to him on the swing. Eyes blue, small delicate features with freckles across her nose, she was the prettiest girl on the planet. Best of all, Robert Evans thought she was his girlfriend.

"I brought you something," she said, pulling her hand from behind her back. It was a dish of apple crisp.

"All right," Daniel said.

"I forgot a spoon," she said. "I can go get one if you want."

"That's okay. I'll eat it like a dog," he said, lapping his tongue.

She laughed.

"Come sit down," he said.

Handing him the dish, she sat next to him, not quite touching. He put the dish on the floor, knowing Sam would eat it, but not caring.

"You coming to church tomorrow?" she asked.

He sat back, stretching his arm around her shoulders, then scooting over so their hips and legs touched.

"I might go just so I can see you," he said smoothly.

She smiled, her teeth bright in the twilight.

"You're the prettiest girl on the whole planet."

"You skip so much church and school, it's no wonder you're always in trouble."

"I refuse to kiss-up like Robert. You can't tell where his lips end and Mrs. Tompkins's rear begins."

Melody giggled and Daniel pulled her closer, rubbing her shoulder. She turned slightly toward him, snuggling under his arm. When she stopped giggling he leaned over and kissed her, lightly at first, then a little harder. She was inexperienced, not knowing what to do, merely pressing her lips to his, but it was exciting and she would learn—he would teach her. He broke away for a second, touching her cheek lightly. Her eyes closed at his touch, her head bending back. Pulling her tight against him they kissed long and hard, hearts pounding. When they paused Daniel saw a man in the woods, watching them—the skinny visitor. When he realized Daniel had spotted him he backed into the shadows of the trees. He could still be there, Daniel knew, hidden, watching, but when Melody pressed against him again, lifting her head to be kissed, he forgot about the skinny visitor.

> In almost every marriage there is a selfish and an
> unselfish partner. A pattern is set up and soon
> becomes inflexible, of one person always making
> the demands and one person always giving way.
>
> —IRIS MURDOCH

PLANET AMERICA

Mark pulled Christy along the shore of the lake. The sky was blue, the meadow green, the air warm—maybe sixty-five. It was a beautiful spring day, no matter what planet you were on. New life began in the spring and it seemed fitting for her and Mark to be together on a new world. This wild world was invigorating, intensifying every feeling. She hungered more, slept more soundly, and yes, loved more deeply. Holding hands with Mark she felt like a teenager again, giddy, silly, and slightly aroused. The electricity in his touch told her he felt the same.

Squeaky followed behind them, encouraged by a few scraps of meat from Christy. Mark carried a picnic basket in one hand and a rifle strapped over his shoulder. The gun made Christy nervous but also secure.

Mark spread a blanket on the far side of the lake, the town visible across the still water. Squeaky settled into the grass next to the blanket, waiting for scraps. The picnic was meat loaf sandwiches, deviled eggs, pickles, and apples. There was a Thermos of coffee and two cups. Praying together first, they ate, making small talk, Christy joking about her work on the bunk beds. When they were down to eating apples, Christy reclined, feeling the warmth on her face.

"I was going to say the sun feels good," she said. "But it isn't the sun, is it?"

"Technically no, but that's what we call it."

"If you close your eyes you feel just like you're on Earth," she said.

"The gravity isn't quite the same, and there are other differences, but I know what you mean. It's alien but not as much as I thought it would be. We're comfortable here because this planet is one of God's creations, and so are we, so we shouldn't be surprised that we're compatible. It confirms what we believed all along, Christy. God created all this for humanity."

"But it's still alien, Mark. I saw an animal yesterday as big as a moose, but with antlers more like an elk's. There's nothing like it on Earth."

"I know the animal. We don't have a name for it. Most people call them Bulls."

"I think I'm beginning to see what Adam must have felt like when God brought all the animals to him to be named."

"Want to take a walk? See what's out there?"

"Won't Squeaky just scare them away?"

"I brought a leash," Mark said.

They packed the picnic supplies and left them to be picked up on the return. Squeaky accepted the loop of rope around her neck but wasn't leash-trained and Mark's arm was pulled to and fro whenever an attractive scent was just out of sniffing range.

They reached the woods, the undergrowth soft, easily pushed aside. The forest was primarily evergreens, although the foliage was leafy instead of needles. They came to a trail, the walking easier now.

"It's an animal trail," Mark said. "Bulls and green deer make these."

"Green deer?"

"Yeah, they look sort of like deer and they're . . . well, green. We aren't very sophisticated about naming animals."

Christy studied the forest but saw nothing but an occasional bird flitting between branches above them.

"Look there," Mark said, stopping suddenly.

Following his point Christy saw a small mound of

leaves rustle just off the trail. Squeaky froze, then whined softly. The small pile of leaves moved at turtle speed.

"I think I know what that is," Mark said.

Handing her Squeaky's rope, Mark knelt by the mound, plucking leaves off the top. The mound continued moving, unaware of Mark's efforts. When he had the leaves off he stepped back, taking Squeaky. Then Christy knelt, seeing a gray creature shaped like a flounder and just as flat.

"Their backs are tacky so the leaves stick, making perfect cover."

Christy touched the back of the fleshy creature with a finger, pulling it away with some difficulty, her finger now sticky.

"Look at their legs," he said.

Gingerly, she picked up one edge of the creature. Like a centipede, there were hundreds of tiny legs moving in waves along the bottom of the animal. She was repulsed and engrossed at the same time. Pulling off a few more leaves she looked at the triangular-shaped head. It was the same fleshy gray as the rest of the body. If there were eyes and a mouth they were underneath. No shell to protect it, slow moving without any defenses, stealth was its only hope. Sprinkling it with leaves again she rejoined Mark and Squeaky.

"It's so helpless-looking. I'm surprised they survive."

"The dogs don't eat them," Mark said. "They'll dig them up and play with them, but that's all. I suspect they taste pretty bad."

After a half mile Mark led them off the path toward the sound of running water. Another quarter mile and they came to a stream. The bank was a steep slope. A small furry animal ran along the stream, disappearing into a hole in the bank.

"If we're quiet, he'll come back out," Mark said.

Squeaky was agitated, having trouble sitting still, whining softly.

"The dogs think these things are pretty tasty," he explained.

Christy wrinkled her brow, squeamish at the thought of

a beautiful dog like Squeaky eating the little creature. Dog food came from cans in Christy's experience, not burrows.

A minute later a head popped out, looking around, then ducking inside again. A second later another head popped out of a hole a few feet away. Now she realized the bank was honeycombed with holes, heads occasionally appearing and disappearing. Finally one of the fuzzy little animals risked a step outside, squatting, head high, nose sampling the air. Shaped like a prairie dog, it was about the same size, with thick fur that shimmered in the sunlight. Its hind paws were webbed, each front leg ended in a branch with two paws. An otterlike tail was held out taut. Unlike other animals on America, the eyes were recessed, protected by a bushy brow.

Satisfied Squeaky wasn't hunting them, the animal thumped its tail rhythmically. Three more animals appeared, taking up the erect posture, sniffing, one eye always on them. Squeaky whined, leaning forward, held firmly by Mark's rope. Now all four thumped their tails and a half-dozen more animals emerged, watching, but also beginning their routines. Working along the bank they sniffed the mud, occasionally pausing and digging furiously until suddenly they would jam their heads into the mud, and then jerk back, a wiggling animal in their teeth. With three quick snaps of the jaws the meal would be swallowed. Alternating guard duty and feeding, the group moved slowly down the shore of the river away from where they stood.

"Do you know what they're eating?" Christy whispered.

"No. We can go dig one up if you like."

"No thanks," she said quickly.

"I know how you feel," he said. "Even furry little beasts like those gave me the creeps at first. They're very Earth-like, except for their paws. At first I felt like I was living on a planet full of freaks."

"If the animals here were horrifying monsters they would have . . . well, horrified us," Christy said, "but these animals don't terrify, they just make you uneasy."

"It's not permanent," he said. "Some animals still give

me the creeps, but not many anymore. The children don't seem to notice at all. A raccoon would scare them more than one of those," he said, pointing to the retreating cluster of animals. "We better head back," he said, then pulled Squeaky away from the bank.

Disappointed at watching dinner scurrying away, Squeaky barked in protest. A dozen animals disappeared into holes.

"The whole bank is Swiss cheese," Mark said. "Their territory runs a mile downstream and there are holes the entire length."

The details of the forest were odd: the birds, the insects, the leaves on the evergreens, the buds of the trees and bushes, but when the unfamiliar details were added together it felt like early spring in a forest, a good time for a walk with someone you loved. She was sorry when it was time to return for supper and evening worship.

She saw little of Mark the rest of that week, although she was so tired from the work it would have made little difference. All the core structures were up and weather-tight and it was time to plumb the buildings. Unskilled workers like Christy dug ditches, carried lengths of pipe, and assisted real plumbers who cut, fitted, and soldered. Two days later the weather returned to normal, the skies clouded up, and the rain began. It was light but steady; they worked in rain gear in a constant drizzle.

Roland, Charlie, and Archie worked as ditch diggers, Tobias still refusing to "rape the new world." Meaghan worked side by side with the men, refusing easier duties. Sylvia, however, was grateful for kitchen duties since she wasn't fit for harder labor. They ate together at meals, talking about what they'd observed of the Fellowship and their impact on the planet. Tobias joined them occasionally, skipping half his meals but showing no ill effects. Disliked on the voyage out, he was even more unpleasant now, dominating dinner conversations with rants about the environmental atrocities he had witnessed.

When they finally had one working shower, the community drew numbers to determine order, Christy getting 102. The boilers were fired up, the water pumps turned on, and everyone applauded as a woman named Inga Molton paraded past in her robe, waving the slip of paper with number one on it. Fifteen minutes later she emerged, hair wrapped in a towel, skin scrubbed pink, the crowd applauding even more loudly. The line to use the first flush toilet was just as long.

Two days later their work group was shuttled back to another community, leaving the fact-finders behind. Then they were picked up by a shuttle, Mark riding with them on the passenger deck.

"We're going to our first settlement," Mark said. "It's the most developed."

"Is Grandma Jones's community on the way?" Christy asked. "It would be nice to see her again."

"She doesn't want visitors right now," Mark said.

Sylvia eyed Mark suspiciously.

"She doesn't want visitors, or you don't want her to have visitors?" Sylvia asked.

"Why would I care?" Mark responded defensively.

"Historically, white males prefer to keep their race pure," Sylvia said.

"Grandma Jones asked for a separate community," Mark said.

"Because she wouldn't be welcome with your people," Meaghan said.

"We didn't have to transport those people," Mark said.

"'Those people'?" Roland said. "I'm one of *those people.*"

"You're deliberately twisting my words."

"We're reading the meaning behind your words," Tobias said.

"Think whatever you want," Mark said, exasperated.

Mark left them then, riding the rest of the way with the pilots.

The first settlement on America was named New Jerusalem, but it bore little resemblance to a Middle Eastern city. Two dozen buildings lined the only paved street on the planet. Two blocks long, the little strip of concrete looked out of place among the unpainted log and frame structures. There were dormitories, a dining hall, and a church of course, but also homes—individual family dwellings. Shelly and Micah lived in one, on the far edge of the community near one of the farms. Meaghan and Christy were assigned to stay with the Strongs.

Shelly greeted them at the door, her new baby in her arms. Squeaky was there too, brought by Mark on an earlier shuttle. Squeaky separated from a half-dozen dogs gathered in the yard. Christy scratched her ears and then fed her a scrap she had saved, happy to see her adopted pet.

Shelly's house was a cabin, with unfinished bare wood inside and out, but it was wired for electricity and was plumbed. There was a bathroom with a tub and a toilet and an electric hot-water heater and stove. The house was heated with wood and a couple of cords were stacked against one outside wall. There were two bedrooms and the kids had vacated one to make room for Meaghan and her. Judith moved in with her mother, while Junior moved out to a shed behind the house, excited about living in his own place. Baby Zachariah slept in a bassinet next to her mother's bed.

Shelly was excited to see Christy, hugging her and asking how she had been. She was cordial to Meaghan, but Meaghan was cool, clearly disapproving of a woman who chose to be a housewife. Shelly had prepared a stew for their dinner, serving it with corn bread and applesauce.

"Applesauce, apple crisp, dried apples, apple jelly. Why so many apples?" Meaghan asked at dinner.

"Apple trees have done well here. They're hardy, take to the soil, and the native insects don't like them much. Peaches haven't done as well but they're trying a new insecticide that seems to be working."

"Poison," Meaghan said. "Call it what it is."

"We're guests here," Christy said. "It wouldn't hurt to be polite."

Meaghan couldn't manage an apology but did keep quiet.

"When's Micah due back?" Christy asked.

Worry lines appeared and Shelly momentarily lost her smile.

"Whenever the Lord releases him, I guess."

"Is he on planet America?" Meaghan asked.

"No," Shelly said. "More stew?"

Shaking her head, Meaghan said, "Is he on Earth?"

"He's exploring," Shelly said, now passing the plate with the corn bread.

"Exploring where?" Meaghan said.

"In space. Ready for dessert? It's apple dumplings," Shelly said.

Meaghan's face fell and Christy laughed, relieving the tension at the table. She was as curious about Micah's whereabouts as Meaghan, but would respect the privacy of the Fellowship.

It was planting season and their work assignment was to help plant corn, fix meals for workers, laundry duties, and sometimes chopping wood. Mark came to see Christy frequently over the next week, taking her for walks and for picnics. Christy loved those times, the two of them alone, walking hand in hand, searching out planet America's wildlife that came in as much variety as Earth's. They kissed on those walks, more often as time went on, feelings for each other growing.

Meaghan Slater was crabby much of the time they spent in New Jerusalem, while Congresswoman Sylvia Swanson managed to be civil but disapproving of everything the Fellowship did. Simon Ash was perpetually sick, afraid that every sniffle was a symptom of the next IT, every breath loaded with microbes that ate away at his intestines. He was of little use on work details, constantly complaining of muscle aches, scratches, and cuts, and starting every time the dogs chased off into the woods after an animal. Eventually, the Fellowship gave up on Simon, leaving him on the screened porch where he spent the day writing in his notebooks, working as secretary for the fact-finders.

Archie Cox and Charlie Peng seemed to be enjoying themselves and the work. Archie was drafted to work with other engineers, helping to design a dam being built upriver. Although it was not exactly his field of expertise, he made many valuable contributions and many friends. The senator, who insisted he be called Charlie, was as popular with the members of the Fellowship as he was with Grandma Jones's people, spending most nights on someone's porch playing cards, laughing, and telling stories.

Roland Symes also enjoyed life on America, learning to drive a tractor, plowing, and planting. He called a few of the acres "his" and openly regretted they would be leaving before he had a chance to bring his crop in. Nights would find Roland sitting on a porch or under a tree, writing in his notebook or speaking into his recorder, preparing stories to run when he returned to Earth.

The weather improved each week and was pleasant by the end of their second month on the planet. It warmed to the low seventies on most days, the nights cool but not cold. Rain showers rolled through occasionally, but the long gray days of rain were behind them.

One night Christy came back to find Mark, Floyd, and Shelly bent over aerial photographs spread on the kitchen table. When she asked about them they quickly put them away, telling her nothing. They were secretive that night, whispering together out on the porch after she had gone to bed. It hurt her that Mark continued to leave her out of important matters.

Early the next morning Floyd and Mark returned to Shelly's home, joining them for a breakfast of pancakes and sausages. The sausages were made of an unknown meat and tasted gamy. There was fresh-churned butter for the pancakes, a jar of Evelyn's jelly, and two syrups, one they called honey. It was brown, and thinner than any Earth honey. What little flavor it had was overwhelmed by sweetness. The other syrup was made from tree sap. It was sweet but with a smoky flavor she had trouble liking. She ate her pancakes plain.

After breakfast they told Meaghan and Christy they were taking them on a hike. Outside they found Roland waiting, just as curious as the women about where they were going. Without explanation, Mark called for Junior who was going with them, and then Floyd whistled for dogs, five separating from the pack to follow. Squeaky appeared around the corner of the house and Christy called for her, tossing her a piece of sausage.

Mark and Floyd led them across a field of ankle-high corn and then along a road bulldozed through the trees. The dogs ranged from side to side, sniffing, males marking randomly with their urine, chasing off any small animals and birds that crossed their path. Spring was in full bloom now and the forest lush with new growth. The air was fragrant, a potpourri of strange organic smells, the songs and screeches of birds constant.

They passed two farms, then the road ended abruptly at a pile of debris bulldozed into a mound. They skirted the pile and continued on an animal trail, climbing a hill. Soon they were breathing hard and removed their light jackets. Mark, Floyd, and Junior carried rifles and Mark and Floyd carried packs. They stopped occasionally to sip water from plastic bottles. After an hour of walking they paused and Mark offered Christy a trail mix made up of native foods. She spread a small amount across her palm trying to identify what she was about to eat. The mix was made up of pea-shaped nuts, a toasted grain that looked like breakfast cereal, large red raisins, green twigs, and yellow flakes. Roland put his nose close to her hand and sniffed.

"It's all good," Mark said.

"Would you like to label the various parts?" Christy suggested.

"The red things are dried fruit—they grow on vines along riverbanks. Those round nuts taste like walnuts. They're soft unless you toast them." Holding up the grain he said, "We're trying to cultivate this like wheat," he said. "It's a large grain and makes a pretty good flour—has a fruity flavor."

"What about the yellow flakes?" Roland asked.

"It's some sort of mutation," Mark said, watching their faces. "The first season we planted corn, we found one stalk with flakes like these instead of kernels. We've planted a field of this kind of corn now."

"Does it pop?" Roland asked.

"No, it doesn't."

"And the twigs?" Christy asked.

"Tastes something like nutmeg," Mark said.

Everything identified, Christy tossed the handful into her mouth, finding the mix of unusual flavors surprising, but not unpleasant.

"Well," Roland prodded. "Are you going to throw up? Die?"

"It's good," she said.

Roland dropped a pinch in his mouth, screwing up his face anticipating dislike. Instead, his face relaxed.

"Needs sugar," he said, then took a handful.

They walked another half hour, then broke into two groups. Floyd and Junior took Roland and Meaghan and cut into the woods, leaving the trail behind. Squeaky stayed with Christy, and Mark kept a rottweiler named Max. Refusing to say why they split up, Mark and Christy followed the trail, the dogs now tired, staying close, letting small animals get away with showing themselves. After a mile the trail leveled and they came to a clearing. Several of the large "bulls" were at the far end and the dogs gave chase, driving them into the woods. While they waited for the dogs to tire of the chase, Mark took an aerial photo from his pack and studied it, then whistled to the dogs and led off again

"Where are you taking me?" she asked.

"You'll see," he said mysteriously.

A short distance on the other side of the clearing, they came to a stream. Mark turned and followed the bank, the walking difficult since the underbrush was thick. After another quarter mile Mark stopped.

"You go the rest of the way by yourself," Mark said.

"Go where?" Christy asked, surprised.

"There's a lake through there," Mark said, pointing into the woods.

"Let's go together," she said.

"This is your lake."

"My lake?"

"No one has ever seen that lake, Christy. You'll be the first."

A sense of awe grew in her.

"Someone must have been here before."

"No," he said firmly. "We know the lake is here because of the aerial photos, but no one has had time to come up here to explore. This isn't like Earth, Christy. The mountains haven't been climbed, the lakes haven't been named. The sources of the rivers have yet to be discovered, the poles haven't been visited. Your footprints will be the first on the shore of this lake."

Thinking of the footprints she had left on the moon, Christy now felt joy as well as awe. These opportunities came to her because of Mark, her life richer because of him.

Mark held Max back so she and Squeaky could go alone. After just ten yards through the underbrush, Mark was screened from her view. Suddenly she felt vulnerable, but Squeaky was with her, staying close in the dense brush. Then they climbed a fallen log and came to a trail running roughly in the direction Mark had indicated. Nose down, Squeaky followed the trail, Christy hesitating—trails were made by animals. Trusting Squeaky to scare off the wildlife, she followed the dog down the narrow path. It sloped gently, then curved left through rocky ground where it almost disappeared. Skirting a large boulder she looked ahead to see blue through the foliage. Squeaky trotted ahead, disappearing when the trail turned again. Following, she came out of the trees onto the shore of the lake—a breathtaking sight.

The lake was a half mile across, towering evergreens bordering its oblong shore. At one end was a cliff so flat and smooth that it looked man-made. In the middle of the cliff was a small waterfall that fed the lake. The lake was a shiny blue jewel in a forest-green setting. The water was crystal clear and she could see pebbles and sticks on the bottom of the lake. A school of tiny fish swam along the shore—at least they looked something like fish. Farther out in the lake, Christy could see ripples, something larger skimming the surface. At the end of the lake opposite the waterfall there were white birds floating on the surface, occasionally ducking under.

Christy's eyes ate up the scene, wanting to be the first to consume it all—the first to see the waterfall, the first to see that particular species of bird, the first to skip a stone across the surface of the lake. Christy looked along the shore for flat pebbles, picking up three. Taking the first stone she bent to get a flat trajectory and sent it skipping across the surface. One, two, three skips, then just before it hit again something leapt out of the water, snagging the stone in midair. It happened so fast she got only a glimpse, but the animal was covered with fur, not scales. She dropped the other pebbles.

A few more steps along the shore and the insects found her, buzzing her head. Her long sleeves protected her arms and she kept her hands moving. Some of the flying annoyances were bloodsuckers—she'd had experience with them—others she didn't know about.

Christy walked toward the waterfall but found it difficult going. The shore was littered with broken limbs and fallen trees. Squeaky found the going rough too and kept ranging into the woods to find an easier way. She came to a log that extended from inside the forest to deep in the lake. On the far side it looked like a marsh and smelled sour like a bog. When she climbed the log something splashed in the water to her left. She froze, then called for Squeaky who jumped up on the log next to her. Three more splashes followed, Squeaky barking at the movement. Tall reeds filled this part of the shore, growing from gray mud and spread from the shallows to the tree line. Where the reeds ended there were clumps of yellow and green plants floating on the water and shaped like bunches of bananas. She walked on the log into the lake and three more splashes followed, Squeaky whining, acting like she wanted to jump in after them. Studying the banana bunches, Christy spotted one of the animals. Shaped like a torpedo, the green and yellow animal had four legs, but no eyes she could see at this distance. She stepped along the log and the animal she was watching dove off the flower clump, disappearing into the lake. Squeaky tried passing her on the log, nearly knocking her off. There were such things as piranha on Earth, she knew, and she wasn't going to risk a dip in an alien lake that no one had ever seen before. Shooing Squeaky ahead of her, Christy walked back to the shore. With the bog blocking her way, the only way to get to the waterfall was to cut into the woods, which looked dark and forbidding, compared to the sunny openness of the lake. She decided that seeing the waterfall first was enough for her, and that she would walk back up the hill and invite Mark to go with her the rest of the way.

When Christy turned to retrace her steps, she saw something large disappear into the trees. Oblivious, Squeaky moved down the log, then jumped to solid ground. Christy studied the spot in the trees where the animal had disappeared, then climbed off the log, keeping an eye on the woods. Ahead of her, Squeaky froze, eyes riveted on the forest. Christy could see nothing, wishing she had gotten a better look at the animal, but all she had seen was a tailless rump. Suddenly a shape separated from the trunk of a tree twenty feet off the ground. Bark-colored and the size of a mountain lion, the animal hit the ground charging toward them—no screeching, no roars, just the sound of rustling leaves. With an angry bark, Squeaky charged. Terrified and helpless, Christy could only yell for help, screaming Mark's name.

The animal was reddish brown now, but changing color as it came, becoming the color of the grass. It had no tail and seemed furless, its skin smooth, shimmery. Its rear legs were larger than the front ones, and it used them almost exclusively, front legs more for balance. It had the jaws of a bulldog and bulging eyes, the head covered with the same shimmery skin. There were no ears, only symmetrical holes on either side of its head.

Squeaky's charge surprised the predator, which was used to having to chase down its food. When the two met, the animal leapt into the air, over Squeaky. With hardly any loss of motion, it turned and jumped on Squeaky. The first sound Christy heard from the animal was its jaws snapping closed, just short of Squeaky's neck. The jaws missed, but the front paws slashed Squeaky's sides, the dog squealing in pain. Recovering quickly, snarling and snapping, Squeaky jockeyed for position, but every charge was answered by a leap in the air and a slash.

Squeaky was bleeding badly now, but the dog had heart and would not run.

Christy found a waterlogged branch and advanced on the fight, screaming, "Leave her alone, get off of her." Another blow from the animal and one of Squeaky's front legs collapsed, nearly severed by the beast's claws. When the dog fell, the animal's jaws clamped on her neck, Squeaky's squeal cut off by the strangling jaws. Running forward, Christy swung with all her might, cracking the beast across its spine. It made no sound, but with a powerful shake of its head threw Squeaky to the side and turned on Christy. Christy held the stick menacingly, but the animal had no experience with clubs, no basis for fear. Its back legs bunched, its eyes riveted on her, a tongue slithered out, tasting Earth blood for the first time. Satisfied, it crouched. Christy braced herself for the attack. Then she heard something thundering through the grass—it was Max.

With a snarl, the rottweiler crashed into the beast, Max's jaws angling for a death hold. The beast tumbled, Max on top, and jaw to jaw the animals struggled for dominance. Without the catlike claws of the predator, Max was losing the toe-to-toe struggle, his underside raked by the predator's claws. Sensing this, Max backed off, letting the animal up. Once on its feet the predator hesitated, now unsure of itself. The rottweiler wasn't as vulnerable as the golden retriever, with a powerful body and massive head and jaws. Max jumped just as the animal turned to leap away, knocking it down, then struggling to get a grip on the predator's neck.

Then Mark came from the woods, rifle at his shoulder, pointed at the struggling animals, looking for a clear shot. Finding none, Mark held his fire, calling for Max to break away. Max was in it to the death, however, which came suddenly. The predator broke free and tried to run but one leg was crippled and it stumbled. Max was on the escaping animal instantly, jaws clamping on its neck, the snap of the vertebrae heard above Max's snarls.

While Max repeatedly shook his dead trophy, Christy ran to Squeaky, who lay whimpering in the grass, bleeding profusely. One leg hung limp, bloody slashes all along her sides. Mark knelt next to her.

"We've got to stop the bleeding," she said.

"It's no use, Christy."

"We can stop the bleeding and get her to a veterinarian."

"Even if she lived that long there's nothing a vet could do."

"She saved me, Mark."

"I know. Dogs are one of the best helpmates God provides us, Christy. There was never any question of coming to America without them."

Irritated by his sermon, Christy said, "She's not just a used-up part ready to be thrown away, Mark."

"I know. Squeaky was a good dog."

"Can't we do something?"

"We can stop her suffering."

Mark stood with his rifle. Christy wanted desperately to think of another solution, knowing there was none. Stroking Squeaky's head, she repeated over and over, "Good dog, Squeaky. Good dog." Still whimpering, the dog quieted, those simple words the best reward a dog could hope for. With a last stroke of the head, Christy walked away, startled by the rifle shot even knowing it was coming.

At the shot, Max came bounding through the grass, ready for trouble, jaws still red with blood. Prancing in a wide circle he searched and sniffed. Finding no danger he followed his nose to Squeaky, sniffing at her body, nudging her. After several tries he walked away and settled into the grass, licking his wounds.

Christy followed Mark to the carcass of the creature. Unlike other animals she had seen on the planet, this one resembled nothing on Earth. The shimmery skin looked slick, but like a snake was dry to the touch. The claws were three inches long, on both front and rear paws, an even row of fangs lined the upper and lower jaw.

"It changed color," Christy said. "It was reddish brown when it was against the bark, but was green when it came through the grass."

"Like a chameleon," Mark said.

"It changed faster than that," Christy said. "It was very hard to see it."

"I've never seen one of these," Mark admitted. "You were the first to see the lake, and the first to see this."

At Christy's request, Mark gathered rocks, covering Squeaky, then they left the lake, calling to Max. The big dog bounded through the grass, tongue lolling, as enthusiastic as ever, seemingly unaware of its fight for life a few minutes before, or of its fallen comrade. Christy envied the shallowness of its memory. When they reached the animal trail, Mark took her hand.

"I wanted today to be special, Christy. I wanted you and the others to feel what it's like to be an explorer. There's no feeling like being the first to see something, the first to understand something."

"I felt it, Mark," she said. "It was special to me."

"God meant for us to explore, Christy, to push outward. There is no boundary for the Christian—not physical or spiritual."

On another day she might have argued with him, pointing out that pushing outward often meant running over others—ask the Native Americans.

"You get to name the lake, Christy. It's your right as discoverer."

"Can we call it 'Squeaky's Lake'?"

"Sure," Mark said. "On Saturday night I'll have you tell Squeaky's story in the dining hall. It will become part of the history of this land and generations will know about you, Squeaky, and Max, and what happened here."

"I'm not good at telling stories."

"You'll tell it with feeling. That's what makes a good story." After a few yards he said, "You should name the animal that killed her too."

"Shouldn't it be named according to some sort of taxonomy?"

"We haven't had much time for working out genus and species. Just give it a common name; let the scientists give it an unpronounceable name later."

A good name would inform, she thought. It would tell

those who heard the name something about the animal and what to look for.

"Call it a 'leaper,'" she said.

When they rejoined the others, they immediately wanted to know what happened. Max was still bloody and Junior asked about Squeaky right off. The others sobered as Mark told them what happened, calling the creature a leaper as he told the story. All of them expressed concern for Christy, and remorse over Squeaky's death—except Meaghan who said, "Maybe if you'd given her the rifle it wouldn't have happened."

Mark reddened but Christy quickly stepped in, pointing out she had never fired a gun in her life. Roland took her side, pointing out that he'd had no problem getting to his hot springs and back, and there was no reason to believe Christy would either.

"What did you name it?" Christy asked to defuse the tension.

"Symes Springs," Roland said. "I liked the alliteration."

"What about you, Meaghan?" Christy asked. "What did you see and what did you name it?"

"I refused to participate in the exploitation of this planet," she said.

"We think there's a waterfall back there," Junior explained.

"You should have gone," Roland said. "You could have named it Feminist Falls."

Mark snickered, while Meaghan stomped off.

"Feminist Falls," Mark said. "You know, I bet that sticks."

Micah was home when they got back to Shelly's. Shelly's eyes were red from tears of joy, the kids were still hanging on him, Judith in his lap, Junior at his side. He put Judith down when he saw Mark and Floyd, hugging each warmly. Then something peculiar happened. Holding Micah by the shoulders, Mark stared into his eyes and said, "Well?" As if to tease him, Micah waited a few seconds, then said, "Yes!" Then Floyd and Mark started pounding each other's backs, hugging each other again.

"Why are you so excited?" Roland asked.

"Oh, Micah's safe return, of course," Mark said.

It was more than that, Christy knew, but they were entitled to their secrets, and even Roland didn't pursue it. Micah's return meant they would have to move. Shelly and Micah needed privacy and there was precious little with three children. Guests made the small living space intolerable.

They were packing to leave when they heard the sound of a shuttle landing. Junior opened the door and ran out with Judith. A minute later he came back with Ira Breitling, black eye patch and all. He was as severe-looking as ever, shaking hands with Micah, but not smiling. Christy hadn't seen or heard of him since they had arrived on planet America. They were told only that Ira was at "the lab." Then Judith came in, leading a little boy—three-year-old Luke Majors Breitling.

His eyes were black, his hair dark, his skin pale. He was a thin boy, bright-looking, eyes busy, taking in everyone and everything. He stayed with Judith, letting her mother him as if she did it often. Christy studied him, seeing his mother in his features, but not Ira. Ira came to her and shook her hand.

"Thanks for what you did for Ruth," Ira said.

"I wish I could have done more," Christy said.

Then Ira left with Mark, Micah, and Floyd, walking outside to stand by the shuttle and talk. Micah did most of the talking, his hands waving around excitedly. The others enjoyed the spectacle, even Ira managing a slight grin.

They used the shuttle to fly her and Meaghan to town, where they moved into an empty dormitory ready for new arrivals. They took bottom bunks in opposite corners, privacy being a rare commodity. Christy took the opportunity to shower and wash her things, hanging them in the bathroom to dry.

With time before dinner, she took a walk, tossing scraps to a couple of dogs so they would follow her. She walked toward the lake, keeping well away from the forest that ringed the clearing. Clouds were moving in, the temperature dropping. Too nervous to wander far, she was about to turn back when she saw a dog come out of the woods followed by two people who turned toward town. It was Tobias and Daniel and they were talking like old friends, Daniel laughing occasionally at comments Tobias made. Shelly had never seen Tobias in a jocular mood. After five months of living together on the voyage to planet America, Tobias had not become that close to anyone. Now here he was looking like Daniel's best friend.

Tobias and Daniel spotted her and suddenly the laughing stopped, the pair disappearing into the woods. The dinner bell rang and she turned toward the dining hall, worrying about the company Daniel was keeping.

Roland was at a table in the corner, pushing lamb stew around on his plate, trying to identify one of the local vegetables.

"It's called yellow stuff," Christy said, sitting opposite him. "Seriously. I asked the server what it was called and she said, 'Yellow stuff.' "

"It tastes like hominy," he said. Turning serious he said, "How are you doing? You had a terrible experience today."

"It turned out that way, but until that leaper attacked, it was one of the best days of my life."

"In what way?"

Embarrassed, she said, "I enjoyed being the first to see that lake. I felt like Columbus."

"A poor choice to compare yourself to," he said. "He discovered land that was already inhabited."

"But this place isn't like that. There are no Native Americans here."

"That's not what Tobias says. He's got evidence there are sentient beings on America."

"What?" Christy had never heard this from Tobias.

"They live in the equatorial region, but the Fellowship won't take us there."

"I could ask," Christy offered.

"Would you? They might do it for you."

Christy doubted Mark would have hidden the existence of an intelligent species, but knew the fact-finders wouldn't be satisfied until they had seen for themselves. Changing the subject she asked, "Didn't you enjoy discovering your hot springs?"

"Sure, but I'm not counting on it being called Symes Springs any longer than my stay here."

"Mark meant it when he said we had the right to name them."

"I think it will be Squeaky's Lake forever, Christy, because you named it. You're their kind of people."

"And you're not because you're African-American?"

"There's not a whole lot of color in this community, or hadn't you noticed?"

"They brought Grandma Jones and her people."

"And Grandma was smart to keep her people away from the Fellowship."

Christy preferred diversity to the homogenous community of the Fellowship, but knew—perhaps hoped—it wasn't racism that kept it mostly white. It was a commitment to a style of worship and cultural preferences.

"Are you going to stay, Christy?" Roland asked, buttering his corn bread.

"What? Here?"

"It's an open secret that Mark wants you to stay."

"He hasn't asked me."

"Will you stay if he does?"

Christy stirred her stew, sipped her coffee, thinking.

"It's a good life," she said. "I like the simplicity of the work and the food. The problems here are basic; problems of survival—resolvable problems. I sleep better at night. Everything is new here, fresh, unspoiled. I could enjoy shaping the direction of this culture."

"I see," Roland said, then went back to eating.

"I take it you see it differently."

"I do," he said. "I see a racist society sprouting on this world. Dogmatic, rigid, fundamentalist, they and their ideas will spread across the planet. They'll cut down the forests, strip mine for ore, pollute the atmosphere until they lose the ozone layer around this planet too. If they're not stopped they'll do the same to planet after planet." Then after a pause he added, "They'll overrun Grandma

Jones's enclave eventually. If she and her people are lucky their land will be set aside as a reservation, if they're not lucky slavery will be reintroduced."

"Slavery? You can't be serious."

"It will happen," Roland said. "History foretells it. Could you be a part of that kind of society, Christy?"

"It won't be that kind of society."

"Maybe so, Christy. Maybe."

They ate in silence after that, Christy considering her answer before Mark asked the question.

The first wedding of spring was the following Sunday. Asserting a level of control unacceptable on Earth, young people waited until spring to marry. Then, like an assembly line, the marriages took place one a week on Sunday afternoons. This spring there would be twenty-three marriages in New Jerusalem, the ceremonies continuing into fall. There were only ten wedding dresses and these were used week after week, chosen by the bride for size and style. Creativity went into accenting the dresses, hairstyle, and choice of flowers. A wedding banquet followed each marriage, so spring and summer were a constant celebration.

The fact-finders were invited to the ceremony that would unite Mitchell Wilson and Karla Kincaid. Only Tobias Stoop refused to attend. Mark Shepherd performed the ceremony, the music and vows traditional. After Mark pronounced the couple Mr. and Mrs. Wilson, he instructed the groom to kiss the bride. The church was packed with friends and family who cheered loudly at the newlywed kiss. Then the teenage couple left the church, pelted with a local grain, rice being in short supply. The weather was good and the reception was held outdoors. After the receiving line greeted every guest, the newlyweds were surrounded by other couples waiting their turn to be married. The brides-to-be were half of Christy's age, and in Christy's judgment too young to be married.

Meaghan Slater was irritated by paternalistic traditions that filled the ceremony and vows. After filling a plate from the buffet table, she stormed off to eat alone.

Roland and Charlie Peng circulated, Roland asking questions, taking notes. After the cake had been cut, the bride and groom disappeared to prepare for the honeymoon. Mark found Christy then, inviting her to go along on the honeymoon. Mark laughed at her confusion, promising that he would explain on the way.

When the shuttle lifted off, it was half filled with family, still celebrating the wedding. The newlyweds sat in back of the shuttle, holding hands, whispering to each other, giggling. Mark sat with Christy, explaining the custom that had developed on planet America.

"We could have marriages without honeymoons," Mark explained, "but it was a custom we didn't want to give up. Our young people don't live together before they marry so they need the time to adjust to each other. Besides, many of them will return home to live in their parents' houses. A week of privacy is important to get the marriage off on the right foot."

"So where are you taking them?" Christy asked.

"Honeymoon Valley. We built a cottage there and the couple gets to use it for a week. It's completely private. We're building two more honeymoon cabins, since the number of marriages is increasing, but the one we're going to was the first."

Mark took her to the flight deck when they neared the valley, then had Floyd, who was piloting the shuttle, circle. The valley was small, surrounded on all sides by sheer cliffs, dense forest beyond that. A small pond could be seen at one end of the valley and a creek that ran the whole length from the lake to where it disappeared against one of the cliffs. A cabin sat at one end of the valley near the pond on a carpet of bright green vegetation, sprinkled with flower color spots. Floyd put the shuttle down near the cabin, the young couple's family unloading supplies the couple would need during their week in the valley. While family members unpacked and cleaned up the dusty cabin, Mark took Christy on a tour of the little valley.

"There's no way into the valley except by air," Mark explained. "There are no predators in here and only a few small animals and birds."

"No leapers?" she said.

"No leapers. We've used it for three summers now and never had a problem. You can see we didn't even bring a dog."

Leading her to the creek, Mark showed her a pool created by shoveling a depression in the sandy bank.

"Feel the water," he said.

It was bathwater warm.

"A hot springs?"

"It bubbles up along the bank here," Mark explained. "It makes a natural hot tub. We think this valley is the bowl of a nearly extinct volcano that collapsed in on itself. The remaining thermal activity is what produces the hot springs."

The grass was lush, the air clean, the sky blue with puffs of white clouds, planet America birds providing a musical backdrop. Christy couldn't imagine a better way for a couple to start a life together. When they walked away from the pool into the meadow, the newlyweds walked over and looked at it, Karla giggling at something Mitchell said.

Next they toured the cabin that had been swept and cleaned, a dozen hands completing the work in a few minutes. There was a screened front porch, with a swing built for two, hung from the rafters by chain. It was only one room, a large bed dominating the space. There was a stove—wood fired—shelves for storage and electric lights. A generator behind the cabin provided power. There was a fireplace built of rock, and the floors and walls were a polished knotty wood, the bed and kitchen table made of the same. The bed was covered in a handmade quilt, sky-blue dominating the pattern, the curtains matching. The tablecloth brought out more of the blue, as did the braided rug. The shelves had been stocked with food, dishes, and silverware for two. There was a radio hooked to an antenna high on one of the cliffs. The Wilsons would check in twice a day. A large piece of their wedding cake was in the middle of the table next to a new Bible, the Fellowship's gift to the newlyweds.

When the cabin was clean and stocked, the newlywed

Wilsons were called from the meadow, their family lay- ing hands on them, praying God would bless their mar- riage. Then as the family climbed aboard the shuttle to leave, Karla was given a package by her father. Then Floyd lifted the shuttle into the air, and they flew off, leaving the couple to begin their honeymoon. Once in the air Christy asked Mark about the last-minute package.

"It's a white nightgown—actually negligee would be a better word."

"From her father?"

"It's from her mother and father. It's another custom that's developed here. We ask our children not to have sex before marriage; it's only right we tell them when it is the right time."

"The white symbolizes virginity?" Christy asked.

"I suppose," he said. "No one decided they should be white, they just are."

"And by giving the bride a negligee it's the father's way of giving her permission to have sex."

"Something like that."

"What is given to the groom?" she asked, pointing out the double standard in assuming the woman was solely responsible for sexual restraint.

"He gets to see the bride wear it," he said, smiling, his checks turning pink. "He's the only one she'll ever wear it for."

Christy smiled too, but more at his naivete.

Mark leaned out, looking down the aisle of the shuttle, making sure no one else was within earshot, then took Christy's hand.

"I was going to talk to you at the lake, but then the leaper attacked. Then I kept putting it off waiting for just the right moment, but it never came. I guess there isn't a wrong time to tell someone how you feel. Christy, I don't want you to go back to Earth. I want you to stay here with me."

She knew this moment was coming, but still felt unpre- pared.

"I love you, Christy. Will you marry me?"

Her eyes teared, and she nodded her head yes. She didn't have to think about it, she responded instinctively.

"Yes, I will," she said. "But I have to go back to Earth, one more time. I have family."

"If you must," he said. "But that world has a way of keeping us apart."

"It won't this time," she said. "Can we honeymoon in the meadow?" she asked.

"I think I can get us at the top of the list," he said. Then he kissed her.

She hugged him tight, only now fully understanding how much she wanted this. When she released him he pulled a ring from his pocket. There were three stones, blue, red, and white—the white clearly a diamond, at least a carat in size.

"A ruby, a sapphire, and a diamond," he said. "I didn't know what kind of stone you liked."

"I'm eclectic," she said. "It's beautiful, but I can't take it, not yet."

Puzzled and hurt, he asked why.

"If the other fact-finders know we're engaged they won't trust me. I need to be seen as neutral to make sure they make the fairest report possible."

"I don't care what they report."

"It matters, Mark. Keep the ring for now, just until after they file their report."

"I can't tell anyone?"

"No."

"Do you know what pressure I'm under? Evelyn and Shelly lecture me about marrying you constantly. Every mother on the planet with a single daughter has tried to match me up—most of their daughters are teenagers."

"I'm flattered you picked me," she said. "I'm no spring chicken."

"I think God picked you for me, Christy."

He meant it as a compliment, but his tendency to spiritualize everything was the one trait of his that she disliked the most. Still, they snuggled together like the newlyweds had, and she fantasized about what their honeymoon would be like. Snuggling under the sky-blue quilt, skinny-dipping in the hot springs, sitting on the porch at night watching the stars come out. Could such a dream really come true?

> In 1 Samuel we read that God had David
> anointed in secret, knowing that Saul would kill
> David if he found out. God could have chosen to
> strike Saul dead, or make David invincible,
> but instead, He used secrecy to protect David
> from violence. Clearly, violence is a
> part of God's world.
>
> — *THE CASE FOR CHRISTIAN VIOLENCE*,
> JAMES D. FOSTER

PLANET AMERICA, SOUTHERN CONTINENT

Tobias was tense as they descended into the jungle where the video with the "protohuman" in the background had been shot.

Tobias had nagged Mark daily to search for the protohumans seen in the video. After repeatedly accusing Mark of hiding the "First Peoples of America," Mark had finally agreed to take him to look for them.

"What about those gorilla-lion things in the video?" Simon asked nervously, eyes glued to the window. "They looked dangerous."

"Don't worry, Simon," Roland assured him. "The dogs will keep them away."

"But we didn't bring any dogs," Simon pointed out.

Roland's face fell, his eyes grew wide.

"Then we're done for," he said.

Charlie Peng laughed, Christy repressed a smile.

When the hatch opened, Mark and Floyd exited first, rifles ready. They had landed in a clearing, keeping as much open ground as possible between them and the jungle. The air was humid and the temperature near one hundred. They wore long-sleeved shirts and pants to protect their limbs from insects, their clothes instantly plastered to their bodies. Tobias had to be held at the door until Mark and Floyd signaled it was safe, then he hurried out, digital video camera in hand, turning around and around, studying the dense jungle.

"This is the place," Tobias announced. "The protohuman was right over there."

Recklessly, Tobias ran to the edge of the jungle, studying the trees. Mark and Floyd spread out, rifles ready. Head tilted back, Tobias searched the treetops.

"They're not here, but I'm sure they're territorial. They won't have gone far. We have to look for them."

Mark and Floyd exchanged looks, neither excited about leaving the clearing.

"It's dangerous to leave the clearing without dogs," Mark said.

"Dogs would just drive the creatures away," Tobias said. "There's no danger if we don't harass the animal citizens."

"We know of at least two dangerous predators that live in these regions," Floyd said. "You've seen one of them in our movie. The other looks like a furry alligator—long legs, very fast."

The remaining color drained from Simon's face.

"Maybe we should wait here for the protohumans," Simon said, wiping sweat from his brow.

"They'd like that," Tobias said. "They don't want us to know the truth."

"We'll take Tobias to look for his monkeys," Mark said, reluctant to leave the clearing. "The rest of you can stay here."

Only Simon wanted to stay, so they shut him in the shuttle and he waved through a porthole as they set off through the jungle single file. Mark walked in front, rifle ready, Floyd took up the rear. Tobias followed directly behind Mark, impatient with the pace and periodically shushing those who followed. The jungle was hot and steamy and everyone but Tobias soon tired, the energy sweated out of them. After an hour, Tobias's repeated shushings were as irritating as the insects.

When something scampered through the brush ahead,

Tobias snapped his camera to his eye, recording rustling leaves. During the pause, Mark looked over his little safari, seeing that the heat and humidity were quickly taking their toll.

"Another fifteen minutes and we're turning back, Tobias," Mark said.

"Then move faster," Tobias said, pushing ahead of Mark.

Mark reached for him but he was gone.

"Don't get too far ahead!"

Tobias ignored Mark's shout, and was soon out of sight. Sylvia and Charlie had trouble keeping up as it was, and could not move any faster, so Tobias was on his own. Ten minutes later they came to a river, the banks thick with vegetation, thick swarms of insects hovering over the water in shadows cast by the towering canopy. The river was the color of pea soup. A rank odor emanated from the water and the smell of rot was overpowering.

"I can't go on," Sylvia said, collapsing into the grass, Charlie joining her.

Christy and the rest weren't in much better shape. Soaked in sweat, faces and hands covered in red welts, no one wanted to continue. Mark and Floyd passed around plastic water bottles and trail mix. Everyone drank but no one ate. After a few minutes of rest, Mark decided to leave Tobias and return to the shuttle. Then Tobias returned, holding his camera and waving for them to follow.

"I found them," Tobias said softly.

Red-faced with anger, Mark reluctantly followed, the others wearily falling in. Tobias led them along the bank for a quarter mile, then bent down, creeping forward until he paused and pointed up. One by one they crept up to kneel next to Tobias, looking into the trees.

The animals resembled chimps—tailless, hair covered, half the size of an adult human. Their faces differed, though, facial fur being light blond, not the deep brown of the body. The bulge of their eyes was not as great as other species on America, and they had a flat nose, not a snout. There were ears too, half-moon–shaped and covered in the same blond fur. They were too far from the animals to see their hands and feet well but they were able to climb from limb to limb with ease.

"Tree dwellers, just like our ancestors," Tobias said to Mark. "Notice the family groupings?" Tobias asked. "The large ones are most likely males. See that one? It's female. It's carrying a baby."

"Maybe it's carrying a midget," Roland suggested.

Meaghan and Sylvia withered him with glares.

"I mean maybe it's carrying a vertically challenged person-thing."

"These are the rightful heirs to this planet," Tobias said to Mark. "You're stealing their future."

"They're monkeys, Tobias," Mark said. "They eat, they poop, they procreate. Nothing more."

"Just because they live in harmony with nature doesn't mean they aren't intelligent. Besides, it doesn't matter what they are now, it matters what they'll evolve into."

"We're not going to wait around to see, are we?" Roland asked, slapping at an unnamed biting insect.

"They'll always be monkeys," Mark said flatly.

"We'll see who owns this planet after the U.N. gets a look at my recording," Tobias said. "I'm going to get a better shot."

"We'll wait five minutes, then we leave with or without you," Mark said.

Christy crawled over and took Tobias's space beside Mark.

"He's an idiot," Mark said.

"He's an activist," Christy said.

Tobias crept through the grass, pausing every few yards to make sure the animals were still in the trees. Christy saw no change in their behavior, although three or four were watching Tobias approach. When he was below the animals, one of the largest climbed limb to limb toward Tobias. Mark lifted his rifle, sighting along the barrel, tracking the animal. Tobias kept still, the camera on the creature moving above him. Finally, the animal stopped directly above Tobias and stared down. Tobias kept his eye to the recorder, the creature perched only fifteen feet above him.

"He's taking a big risk," Mark whispered, the rifle aimed and ready.

After a long slow look, its curiosity was satisfied and the big animal lifted his head, turned, and defecated on Tobias. Cursing, Tobias stood, wiping feces off his face and then his camera. While Tobias cleaned himself and his camera, the animal turned again and urinated on him. Floyd, Mark, Charlie, and Roland erupted in loud guffaws, startling the creatures in the treetops. They were still laughing when Tobias came back, wiping his face and hands with leaves.

"Like I said, Tobias," Mark said, trying to control his laughing. "They eat, they procreate, and they poop. Oh, and they pee too."

Floyd, Charlie, and Roland guffawed again and Mark shook with mirth.

Controlling himself, Mark said, "As discoverer of this species you have the right to name it."

Trying to clean his hair of the brown feces, Tobias said, "No one has the right to name them. They will name themselves when the time is right."

"You're refusing the right to name them?" Mark asked seriously.

"Absolutely."

"Then I'll name them," Mark said. "From this moment forward these creatures shall be known as 'poopers.'"

Laughter erupted again and this time Christy let slip a giggle.

Tobias stewed in the back of the shuttle on the trip back to New Jerusalem. He smelled like fresh manure and the rest of the fact-finders were content to let him sulk. Christy took advantage of her connection with Mark and was on the flight deck when Shelly radioed, asking Mark and Floyd to come to the Remples'. Then she added, "Bring Christy, we have a situation here."

The Remples lived just on the outskirts of New Jerusalem. They were the organizational heart of the Fellowship, planning for the development of the infrastructure of an entire planet, assessing needs, setting priorities, placing orders. Their house was like most

Christy had seen, with a kitchen, a small living room, two bedrooms on the main floor, and a loft. When Mark and Christy entered, they found Daniel sitting at the kitchen table, angry and defiant. Shelly and Micah were standing by the kitchen stove sipping coffee, Evelyn was at the table with Daniel, her eyes puffy and red. Faith was not in the room.

"What's wrong, Evelyn?" Floyd asked, glaring at Daniel.

Floyd and his son exchanged hateful looks. There was no love left between them. Christy remembered the first time she'd seen Floyd and his son, Daniel sitting on his daddy's lap, while they watched news about the *Rising Savior*. Now Daniel was nearly as big as his father, more defiant with every pound he put on.

"Tell your father, Daniel," Evelyn said, eyes red, voice firm.

Daniel turned his back on his father.

"Someone tell me," Floyd roared.

"Daniel's got a girl in trouble," Evelyn said. "Melody is pregnant."

Face flushed, hands clenched, Floyd was so angry it made it hard for him to speak.

"Little Melody Crane?" Floyd said. "The Cranes are good people, Daniel, and you did this to their little girl."

Now Daniel turned to face his father.

"She's almost as old as I am. Besides, she wanted it."

Floyd slapped Daniel across the face, Daniel jumping to his feet, squaring off with his father.

"Don't ever hit me again!" he said. "I won't let you touch me anymore, not that way, not any way. You can't make me do things anymore."

"You'll marry her," Floyd said. "You'll do the right thing and marry her."

"I won't," Daniel said. "Besides, how do I know I'm even the father?"

Floyd's arm flinched, as if he stifled the urge to slap his son again. Daniel saw the movement and smirked, feeling like an equal now.

"It was over between me and Melody anyway," Daniel said. "I've got my eye on a new girl."

Floyd trembled with rage and tears dripped from Evelyn's eyes.

"The Cranes asked for a community meeting," Shelly said. "They're demanding biblical justice."

"I won't go to court again," Daniel said.

"You will, and you'll abide by the decision," Floyd said.

"Or what? Stop feeding me at all? My girlfriends sneak me food anyway."

Each of Daniel's needles struck home, hurting his father as he intended, but also his mother. This nuclear family was in meltdown, Christy knew, and she could think of only one way to save it.

The court met the following Saturday night, the church filled to standing room only. It was raining hard when they gathered, and everyone came in wet, exacerbating a gloomy atmosphere. The fact-finders were all there, eager to see how the cult's justice system worked. Daniel was escorted in by four men, each larger than he. Now Daniel sat in the front row on the right, his family beside him. The Cranes were on the left, father, mother, and four children, Melody the oldest. Melody kept her head down, blond hair hanging loose, covering her face.

Five chairs were lined up across the front, Mark sitting in the middle, Micah on his right, Ira on his left. Two men Christy didn't know sat on either end. Mark opened with silence, letting everyone clear their minds and seek the leading of the Lord. Daniel shuffled his feet, rocked in his squeaky chair, being deliberately annoying. After twenty minutes Mark prayed this meeting would find God's justice. Then Mark asked the Cranes to present their case. Mr. Crane rose, facing the crowd, not the judges. A tall, thin man, hair brown; his daughter clearly favored her mother.

"Everyone knows my Melody. She's a good girl. Always in church, always placed high in the Bible verse competition. A good student in school. Maybe not the best, but a hard worker. She asked Jesus into her heart when she was five. She grew up in the Fellowship—well, you all know that. She never gave her mother or me any reason not to trust her. Never got into a lick of trouble, until she started hanging around with that boy."

Mr. Crane pointed at Daniel, who winked at him. Mr. Crane reddened, his eyes narrowed, and he trembled with rage. When he could speak again, his words were carefully selected, his tone venomous.

"He took advantage of her," Mr. Crane continued. "He seduced her. I don't like saying this, Floyd and Evelyn, but you know he hasn't been the same since they took him from you. He's got an evil streak. He's been a bad influence on everyone who's tried to befriend him. Now he's got my Melody in trouble. We demand biblical justice."

"What would that be?" Mark asked.

"We want Daniel Remple to marry Melody."

The crowd erupted in "Amens," and shouted agreement. Mark let them vent, then said, "Floyd and Evelyn, do you have something you'd like to say."

Floyd started to rise, but Daniel jumped up.

"I'll speak for myself!" Daniel said.

Floyd sat, relieved not to have to defend his son's actions. Now that he had the floor, Daniel didn't have anything to say. He turned toward the crowd behind him, looking around the room. Christy followed Daniel's gaze. When Daniel found Tobias in the back of the church, he stopped his search. Tobias began working through the crowd along the left wall, moving to the front. When he was close he nodded, Daniel getting confidence from his presence.

"You can't force me to marry her," Daniel said.

"Her name is Melody," Mark said. "Call her by her name."

"Fine," Daniel said. "You can't make me marry Melody, or Clovia, or Sharon, or Nancy, or Lily, or any of the other girls I've been with."

Gasps filled the church, then angry shouts and crying mothers and daughters. Daniel's shotgun blast of names hurt the girls and their families. Melody was staring at him now, incredulous. He studiously ignored her. Pleased with the pain he had dished out, Daniel smiled.

"You want the rest of the names?" Daniel asked.

"No," Mark said. "This is about you and Melody."

"I don't even think it's my baby," Daniel said.

Mr. Crane jumped to his feet, the man behind him restraining him, his wife holding his arm, begging him to be calm. Christy saw Tobias smile at that, then say something to Daniel she couldn't hear.

"You don't deny you engaged in premarital sex with her?" Mark asked.

"It was sex, but it wasn't premarital. I never intended to marry her."

Now Melody sobbed, publicly humiliated by the boy she loved. Glancing at Melody, Daniel's face fell. Then Tobias leaned toward Daniel, whispering again. Noticing this time, Mark turned to him.

"If you've got something to say, Mr. Stoop, then say it to everyone."

"I told Daniel that he has nothing to be ashamed about. Sex is a part of nature. Animals aren't embarrassed by their instincts and the human animal shouldn't be either."

Roland was against a wall, pen poised over his notepad, scribbling notes. Then Sylvia Swanson spoke from a pew.

"Tobias is right, you know. We all have sexual urges and teenagers feel it strongest of all. Since you can't stop them from having sex, you need to educate them. You need to teach your children to practice sex in a safe manner. Passing out condoms in school is a good way to reduce the risk of pregnancy."

"Shut up," someone shouted from the back, others joining in.

"We'll be polite to our visitors, or I'll close the meeting," Mark said firmly. Then to Sylvia he said, "Passing out condoms never reduced the pregnancy rate anywhere it was tried," he said. "If we did that we would condone behavior that is immoral." Then before she could respond he said, "Let's stay focused on the problem at hand. Melody is pregnant, Daniel is the father."

"You don't know that," Daniel said.

"You are, Daniel," Melody said. "You're the only one I was ever with."

Looking unsure of himself, Daniel turned to her to respond, but Mark silenced him with a point of his finger.

"The Cranes have asked that Daniel marry Melody. I see no other option," Mark said, looking at the other judges. Micah, Ira, and the others nodded agreement.

"There is another option," Daniel said. "Melody could have an abortion."

Angry shouts filled the hall and again Mark let his people vent. When they were calmer, he asked for silence.

"We won't punish the baby for your sin," he said to Daniel. Looking sad now, he turned back to the Cranes. "I'm having second thoughts about this," he said. "Do you think Daniel would be a good father and husband?"

Both Cranes shook their heads, and now Melody looked afraid. She loved Daniel, and hoped that if he was forced to marry her he would be a good husband and a loving father. But Christy knew that if Daniel was trapped in a marriage he resented, he would grow abusive, punishing his wife and children for his own mistakes. What the Cranes wanted could ultimately be the death of their daughter.

"Mark, may I speak?" Christy asked. "For Melody's sake, and her baby's, you can't force Daniel to marry her. A marriage needs to be based on love. A shotgun wedding is a poor foundation for the supportive, loving environment a child needs to be raised in."

"But he does love me," Melody protested. "He told me he did."

"Even if that is true," Christy said, "he will resent you and the baby for taking away his freedom."

"You can't make me marry her," Daniel said.

"If we decide that's the best course, then you will marry her," Mark said sternly, eyes locked on Daniel.

"I'll marry her," a voice called from the back of the church.

Those in front turned to see a teenage boy standing three rows from the back. Christy recognized him as Robert

Evans. He didn't have Daniel's good looks, his face ordinary, his skin sprinkled with pimples. He was shorter than Daniel by an inch, and thinner. Christy knew he was polite and mature for his age. He was one of a handful of boys that were apprentice pilots, learning to fly the Fellowship spacecraft. Melody was half standing; looking at Robert, her tear-streaked face showed uncertainty.

"Do you mean what you said, Robert?" Mark asked.

"Yes, sir."

"Could you raise the baby as your own and not resent it?"

"Yes, sir, I could."

"Can you accept the fact you weren't the first man in Melody's life?"

"I love her, sir. It doesn't make any difference to me."

"She doesn't want you!" Daniel shouted. "You don't deserve her."

Now Melody looked to Daniel, hopeful that he would fight for her.

"Will you marry her, Daniel?" Mark asked.

Daniel hesitated until Tobias whispered to him.

"No, I'm not ready to get married."

"Then sit down and shut up," Mark said.

Daniel hesitated, so Mark nodded to a man behind Daniel who grabbed him by the shoulders and forced him into his seat. The church rang with applause.

"Mr. and Mrs. Evans, could you accept Melody as your daughter-in-law, and love her even knowing her past?"

Robert's parents looked into each other's eyes, then turned to Mark and both said yes.

"Could you love Melody's baby as your own, even knowing the circumstances of its conception?"

"Yes," they replied immediately.

"I always wanted grandchildren, I just didn't expect it this soon," Mrs. Evans said.

Nervous laughter spread through the church, people around the Evanses hugged them and whispered encouraging words.

Turning to the Cranes, Mark said, "Daniel would make a poor match for Melody, and a poor father. Are your hearts clear to accept Robert Evans as your son-in-law?"

Mrs. Crane began to cry, but she nodded yes, Mr. Crane adding, "Yes, and God bless you, Robert."

Others shouted "Amen," and again Mark waited for the congregation to express their gratitude to the Evans family. Now Mark looked at Melody, who was watching Daniel, who still refused to make eye contact with her.

"Melody, Daniel won't marry you, and I'm not sure we'd permit it now even if he changed his mind. You know Robert, you know he's a good person. Many of us thought you and he would end up together someday anyway."

Others in the hall shouted out agreement.

"Robert says he loves you and I believe he'd treat you and your baby right. But it's up to you, Melody. Will you marry Robert so your baby will have a father?"

The church was silent again, the only sound the patter of rain on the roof. All waited for her answer, but it came hard for Melody. Melody stared at the floor, then closed her eyes as if in prayer. Finally, she raised her head and glanced at Daniel, hoping for any sign that he wanted her. Daniel avoided Melody's eyes.

"I'll marry Rob," Melody said softly.

Loud, long applause followed, those gathered feeling that the Lord had led them to a satisfactory resolution of a problem. The Cranes and the Evanses were congratulated on the pending marriage of their daughter and son and they all looked pleased. Robert beamed too, engaged to the prettiest girl on the planet and a hero to the community. But Christy noticed that Melody wasn't celebrating. Her parents were congratulated, but most people ignored her, not sure of what to say. The pregnant teenager kept her head down, glancing furtively at Daniel. When the commotion finally waned, Mark took control again.

"We're not finished yet," Mark said. "Congregation, if this marriage is to work, then we need to put the sin that brought us here behind us. God has forgiven Melody for her sin and we must do the same. We must agree not to gossip about Melody and Robert, or about their child. We must agree to treat them as equals in everything we say and do. If there is anyone here who cannot agree to this, speak now or nevermore."

Mark waited a full minute before continuing.

"Robert Evans and Melody Crane will be married this Saturday. I apologize to the other couples who will be bumped back a week."

Again those gathered applauded. As the din died, Christy heard Melody's mother say, "We'll have to start on the dress right away." Melody nodded, solemn.

"We have one last matter before us," Mark said, quieting the crowd. "Daniel, you have refused to become part of this community. You've repeatedly violated our standards and the biblical principles on which they were founded. We've run out of punishments, I'm afraid. We can't let you continue to prey on our daughters, and we can't let you continue to poison our community."

"Banish him," someone shouted. Others agreed, and Christy knew that would be the outcome unless she could convince them there was another option. She waved at Mark to get the floor and then stood.

"You have another choice. Daniel can return to Earth," Christy said. "Perhaps in time he could come back to you."

More murmuring behind her, all negative.

"Banishment isn't permanent," Mark explained. "We would check on him. Perhaps with time alone, time with his thoughts and with God, he could come back to the community. If he goes to Earth he'll be immersed in the secular culture that did this to him."

"I never want to come back," Daniel said. "I hate this place, I hate not being able to drive or see a movie. I want to watch TV, buy Slurpees, drink a Coke once in a while. I'd kill for a Big Mac."

"You'd never see your family again," Mark said.

"I'll never forgive my father for molesting me. If I never see him again it's all the same to me."

"And your mother and sister?" Mark asked.

Pausing a few seconds, he said, "I want to go to Earth."

"Floyd and Evelyn, it's your decision, not Daniel's."

The Remples whispered together for a time, then Mark said, "Would you like to take a day or two?"

"No," Floyd said. "Daniel will never be happy here. If he's ever going to find happiness it's back on Earth. Christy, will you try to find him a good home?"

Christy nodded, the Remples nodded, and Daniel beamed.

"It's decided then," Mark said. "Daniel Remple, you are to return to Earth."

Only Daniel applauded, others expressing condolences to Floyd and Evelyn. Faith was tearful, but Daniel ignored her and his family, shaking hands with Tobias. Others of the fact-finders came forward, talking with Daniel. Charlie Peng tried reassuring the Remples, telling them that he too would look in on him. They accepted the offer graciously but acted as if Daniel had died that night.

Melody's wedding was identical to all the others Christy had attended, except there was a forced quality to the happiness. Melody was beautiful in her dress, choosing to wear yellow flowers in her braided hair and carry a large bouquet of yellow and white. Robert wore a yellow flower in his lapel. Even the cake was decorated with yellow accents. Upon instruction, Robert lifted the veil and gave Melody a quick peck as if he had never kissed a girl before. Christy suspected it would be an awkward honeymoon. Melody smiled at everyone in the receiving line, accepting kisses on the cheeks and warm handshakes. Unlike her parents' smiles, Melody's was forced, hiding her sadness. She loved Daniel but had married another man—married for life on planet America.

Daniel watched the wedding from a distance, eyes on Melody the whole time. Everyone knew he was there but ignored him, counting the days until he left their community. He came closer when it came time for the couple to leave for their honeymoon. Melody was smiling as she stood in the door of the shuttle to throw her bouquet, but as she threw it she made eye contact with Daniel. As soon as their eyes met her smile faded. Her new husband saw her looking at Daniel and quickly pulled Melody inside.

That was the last time she would see Daniel and Christy could see the pain on her face.

Departure for the fact-finders was moved up when the new Fellowship Ark-class ship, *Prophet,* arrived. *Crucifixion* had been expected and not *Prophet.* The change in ships was not explained.

The next week Mark and the others claimed they were busy shuttling down settlers, however none came to New Jerusalem. Christy never saw any of the new arrivals and no new supplies were landed. Christy didn't mind, she enjoyed her privacy in the dormitory and the unlimited access to the bathroom.

Melody and Robert did not return after the honeymoon week, having flown instead to stay with relatives on a farm. They would stay away until Daniel was gone. When the day of departure came, only Christy was sorry to go. Roland had notebooks and recordings full of material for articles or a book. Tobias had his recordings of stumps, plowed meadows, trash dumps, slaughtered native animals, and smoke from chimneys. Each of the others carried their common experiences filtered through their worldview. Meaghan was filled with righteous rage at the subjugation of women she witnessed on the new world. Congress-woman Swanson and Senator Peng saw a world in need of government, secular control that would bring educational standards to their schools and choice to their curriculum. Charlie Peng at least could accept the right of the Fellow-ship to raise their children in their beliefs, but even he agreed with Swanson that the children needed to be exposed to other belief systems, other views of religion, history, and science, so they could make informed choices. Archie Cox had learned the least, since he was to discover the secrets of their antigravity drive. The voyage home was his last chance. Nervous about the claustrophobic quarters of the return flight, nevertheless Simon was the most anxious to leave. His fear of everything new meant that planet America was slowly killing him and he needed to get home just to survive.

Christy left reluctantly, thinking ahead to living on

576 ЖAMES F. DAVID

planet America with Mark and to their week in Honey-moon Valley. It would be next spring, she knew—spring on America. She found she regretted missing the harvest. The corn was high, the wheat green in the fields. Apples would need picking, corn shucking, and there would be beans to pickle. Canning had already started with early crops, but by fall anyone who wasn't harvesting would can. Christy wanted closure, she wanted to bring in the crops she helped to plant. She couldn't help this year, but she would be back for the next harvest, and the next, and every one after that. That was, if the world didn't find another way to come between her and Mark.

FINAL SOLUTION

> He said to me: "It is done. I am the Alpha and
> the Omega, the Beginning and the End. To him
> who is thirsty I will give to drink without cost
> from the spring of the water of life. He who over-
> comes will inherit all this, and I will be his God
> and he will be my son. But the cowardly,
> the unbelieving, the vile, the murderers,
> the sexually immoral, those who practice
> magic arts, the idolaters and all liars—their
> place will be in the fiery lake of burning sulfur.
> This is the second death.
>
> —REVELATION 21:6–8

PLANET AMERICA

Tobias disappeared the day they were to shuttle up to *Prophet*. Meaghan had his recordings and instructions of whom to give them to. "He's going to stay and defend the planet," was the only explanation she shared. They delayed leaving for three days while they searched for Tobias, but on an undeveloped world it was impossible to find someone who didn't want to be found. Mark and the other leaders met to consider what to do, but had little choice but to leave him. Then for the first time on planet America, guards were posted at key facilities.

The voyage to Earth was pleasant but odd. To Christy's surprise not only did Mark accompany them, but so did Floyd and Evelyn, Micah and Shelly and their children. Mark explained that Micah was needed back at Earth and he and Shelly refused to be separated anymore, choosing instead to take the family on the voyage. Then once in orbit they docked with the space station orbiting planet America spending a day while members of the Fellowship worked at unexplained tasks. Then when they departed, Christy discovered that Ira had boarded for the voyage to Earth. After what had happened to Ruth, she thought he would never return to his home planet. Something unusual was going on. Roland sensed it too, asking her if she knew. To satisfy her own curiosity, not Roland's, she asked Mark, who said, "After we're married there won't be any secrets." The answer irritated her, but she was the one who had insisted they wait to marry, so she didn't press for answers.

On the voyage to Earth she found the members of the Fellowship better company than the fact-finders, and spent most of her time with them, helping to clean the vast ship. Daniel hid from his mother and father the entire voyage, spending his time with Meaghan Slater and the other fact-finders, sharing every scandal, bit of gossip, and secret he was privy to. Using Daniel's information, they fleshed out their reports, ready for the congressional hearings.

The ark-class ship *Prophet,* another converted Soviet-era submarine, made the voyage to Earth in less than four months. Christy was so excited by seeing New Hope station again that she didn't think it odd that *Covenant* was docked at the station. Anxious to get to Earth, the fact-finders were pleased to learn there would be no quarantine period, and that they were free to return immediately. All did, only Roland and Senator Peng taking time to find Christy and Mark and say good-bye.

Sally Roper and Stephen O'Malley had arranged meetings with Mark and Floyd since there were always a myriad of problems to deal with, and for once they had all of the leaders together. Christy was actually glad to be separated from Mark, needing to see friends, settle her business affairs, and sell her home. Her time on Earth was going to be a time of personal good-byes.

Despite his protests, Christy kept Daniel on New Hope

station an extra day, making sure Meaghan and the others had shuttled down before her and Daniel. She worried about how close Daniel and Meaghan had become on the voyage. She planned on taking Daniel home with her, then contacting friends about finding a home for him— Daniel had other plans.

The day they shuttled down, Daniel refused to say good-bye to his parents. Floyd and Evelyn were deeply hurt, tears in their eyes, watching their son turn his back on them and walk out of their lives forever. Then when Christy walked Daniel out the gate of the Mexican compound, she saw Meaghan in the crowd of vendors. Standing next to her was Josh, Daniel's former foster parent. He ran to them as soon as he saw them, hugging both long and hard. Daniel had a place to stay, and people to love him, but they would take Daniel down a different road than Floyd and Evelyn.

"They've been training marines to assault this compound," Stephen said when the Fellowship Council met. "Proctor has a contact inside one of the squads that is training, but he isn't sure he can give us a warning. They're stationed in San Diego and when they decide to come after us they'll be here within an hour."

Stephen and Sally were full of bad news. All of their U.S. facilities had been seized, property confiscated, and many members arrested. President Crow had supported suspension of the National Restitution Act as promised, but no Fellowship properties had been released. As Crow had promised, some social security accounts and pensions had been transferred to escrow, but not all, and Stephen doubted even the digital video of those Crow claimed were dead would satisfy him. Worse, two of those receiving social security benefits had died two months before Mark could record their statements, and now there was no way to prove they had been alive and eligible for the social security checks Stephen had collected in their name. Stephen and Sally could be arrested once the deaths were reported, and if neither of them could return to the United States to conduct business, they would be severely hamstrung.

Mark sympathized with their problems. They had carried the burden while he had been building a new world; now it was time for him to pick up the burden again.

"Sally, are all our assets liquid?"

"Mostly, and all can be within a month," Sally said.

"Good, liquidate everything. Floyd has a long list of purchases."

"Of course he does," Sally said.

Everyone snickered. Sally was perpetually perturbed by what she saw as Floyd's profligate spending.

"We've got gems to help with the purchases," Mark said and Sally looked relieved. "We won't get a positive report from our fact-finders. It's time to move all our operations."

"New Hope too?" Stephen asked.

"We'll have to break it up, take it in pieces," Floyd said. "What we can't take we'll move to lunar orbit and pick up later."

"We're leaving Earth for good, aren't we?" Stephen asked.

"Yes," Mark said.

"They'll try to stop us," Stephen said.

"That's why we've got to go before they know we're going," Mark said.

> Quantum mechanics is very worthy of regard.
> But an inner voice tells me that this is not the
> true Jacob. The theory yields much, but it hardly
> brings us close to the secrets of the Ancient One.
> In any case, I am convinced that
> He does not play dice.
>
> —ALBERT EINSTEIN

WASHINGTON, D.C.

Fry was as insufferable as ever, but Crow tolerated his arrogance since Crow knew that soon his usefulness would decline significantly. Once Fellowship spacecraft were under military control, the rogue CIA agent and his colleagues would be eliminated.

They were in the Oval Office, Rachel leaning against Fry while he described plans for the assault on New Hope station. Kent Thorpe was there, awed by being part of the inner circle.

"The timing is perfect," Fry said. "The Ark-size ships *Prophet* and *Covenant* are both docked at the station. *Covenant* is about half loaded, ready for another run. Best of all, both their deep-space cruisers are there: *Genesis* and *Exodus*."

"What about the smaller ships?" Thorpe asked.

"There's a shuttle attached to each cruiser and two more making runs between Earth and the station. We count six lifting spheres bringing cargo up."

"There should be more," Thorpe said.

"I know," Fry said testily. "They've shifted some of their fleet to planet America. It doesn't matter. There are more than enough targets at the station."

"Is Ira Breitling on the station?" Thorpe asked.

"He is," Fry said. "They're all there. All the leaders. They've made a major mistake by gathering in one place."

"Is the shuttle ready?" Crow asked.

"The sphere is installed in the bay and it's operational," Thorpe said. "The weapon I designed is also ready."

Crow looked at Rachel, who smiled appreciatively. Everything was in place. Soon the cult would be destroyed and the technology their god had given them would serve Crow's Master.

"The next step is yours," Fry said.

Smiling, Crow said, "I'll call Goldwyn and put it in motion."

Kent Thorpe left the White House in his Lexus, turning onto Pennsylvania Avenue. Heady with power, imagining Ira Breitling dead, he didn't notice the blue Caravan behind him. Driving directly to his lab, he now decided he wanted Breitling captured alive. He wanted Ira Breitling to suffer for killing his Constance, and know that Kent Thorpe was the reason for his suffering.

By the time he turned into the industrial park housing his lab, the car following him was a red Focus. The Focus continued, but the car behind, a green Honda, turned, following Thorpe past the modern facilities to a ramshackle warehouse in the oldest portion of the industrial park. As Thorpe typed in his access code to enter his lab, the Honda passed again, in the other direction.

CHAPTER 110

PROCTOR'S NEWS

> God led the people of Israel to the Promised
> Land, which was already occupied. What God
> had promised them wasn't just land, it was culti-
> vated land, vineyards, farms, and villages. It was
> up to Joshua and his army to evict the occupants
> of the land. I'm so thankful that planet America
> was unoccupied.
>
> —MARK SHEPHERD

NEW HOPE STATION

"I came to say good-bye," Proctor said.

Mark shook his hand and motioned him toward a chair. Proctor had come to New Hope station to see Mark, and he never called unless it was important.

"That sounds so final."

"The signs are all around us, Mark. You and I know we've nearly reached the goal God gave us."

Mark had come to respect George Proctor over the years and he had been invaluable to the Fellowship.

"George, I haven't always understood the mission God gave you, but I know your heart is for the Lord. Come with us to the new world. You could live with us, or if you'd rather, we'll give you your own continent."

Proctor smiled at that thought.

"A whole continent of our own? Tempting, but we're soldiers for Jesus, and there's no war to be fought where you're going."

"Maybe it's time for peace?" Mark suggested.

"Not yet. Your people aren't the only Christians here," he said. "Others will need our help, especially in the dark days coming."

Mark didn't ask what the "dark days" were. All Proctor's thoughts were apocalyptic.

"I came to tell you something else. Crow has one of your spheres."

"Impossible," Mark exclaimed.

"They salvaged the one that crashed into the ocean. We believe they've got it working again."

Mark was stunned.

"It can't be true! How do you know this?"

"We've been watching Crow's inner circle. There's one man that comes and goes regularly. We picked up one of his associates. After a little persuasion, he told us they had a sphere."

Shocked by what Proctor told him, Mark worried out loud.

"If they have our technology, we'll never be safe from them."

"They have the sphere flying but they don't know how it works. At least not yet. We know where they have it, but the security is good. We can make only one entry. We won't know if the sphere is inside before we hit the lab."

"If they have a working sphere, why haven't they flown it?" Mark asked.

"Good question," Proctor said. "The National Technologies Act gives them the right to it but they've kept it secret. It's strange."

Mark thought of the pending move, wondering if that would be sufficient now that Crow had access to the technology.

"George, this technology wasn't meant for the secular world—it's too soon. It's not in God's plan for them to follow us to the stars so soon."

"I know. They need to be stopped," Proctor said.

"When?"

"The sooner we do, the better."

Knowing the secular world would follow them to the stars someday made the quality of the parting important. Mark had intended to make separation from his home world amicable but now wondered if President Crow would let that happen.

> The only way to effect change is to use the
> power in hand. The power I wield is the
> power of the press.
>
> —GRAYSON GOLDWYN,
> EDITOR OF THE *SAN FRANCISCO JOURNAL*

◆

SAN FRANCISCO, CALIFORNIA

Like the catacombs in Paris, the offices of the *San Francisco Journal* were a dark maze of rooms. Walls had been added, others taken out, the plumbing replaced, the whole building rewired, first for electric typewriters and then for computers, and painted, repainted, and repainted. The furniture was multigenerational, every space cluttered with desks, chairs, bookcases, printers, computers, and innumerable stacks of paper. If ever there had been a planned decor for the interior, it couldn't be discerned now. There were plans for a new building, if the paper ever became profitable again.

Roland greeted Christy warmly at the reception desk, noting the navy skirt and white blouse—Goldwyn would approve. Because of Christy's visit, Roland had upgraded from jeans to khakis. He led her to the third floor, then through a large open area divided into cubicles to a conference room with a glass wall. Grayson Goldwyn was there, unlit cigar in hand, red tie, blue suit.

"Nice to meet you, Reverend Maitland," Goldwyn said graciously in his loud voice. "I've long admired your work."

Christy thanked him, complimenting him on his philanthropy. Goldwyn asked an assistant to bring coffee, then they settled at one end of the conference table. Goldwyn took the seat with his back to the outer office and signaled Christy to sit at the end of the table. They made small talk, waiting for the coffee. Goldwyn asked for her impressions of the Fellowship and the society they were building on planet America.

"It's a bold experiment," she said. "Like the Pilgrims who came to our America, they sought out a new world where they can practice their faith without persecution and raise their children to do the same."

"You called it an experiment," Goldwyn said. "Do you think they can succeed?"

"They can," she said, "but you have to define succeed narrowly. In my judgment they have the resources to survive on planet America, but not the resources for a sustained industrial society. Without trade with Earth I don't see how they could sustain the limited industry they have."

"You might be underestimating them," Roland said. "I snooped around some while we were there and they have a lot in storage. They've purchased a lot of older equipment, one or two generations behind. You can buy that equipment at nearly scrap value and it's still functional."

The coffee came and they spent a minute opening packets of sweeteners, adding creamer, and stirring. When everyone was ready Goldwyn continued.

"Getting back to this experiment of theirs, Christy. Do you approve of it?"

"I support their right to worship according to their beliefs."

"Yes, yes," Goldwyn said impatiently. "Everyone supports that right. I'm asking whether you like the fact it's an all-white colony—I know there are some token Asians and African-Americans."

"Grandma Jones and her people are there, too," Christy reminded him.

"But segregated. They're re-creating South Africa, not America."

"I wouldn't populate a new world the way they have," she said honestly.

Putting the unlit cigar in his lips, Goldwyn leaned back looking satisfied.

"I would be more inclusive, wouldn't you?" Goldwyn said.

"Mr. Goldwyn and I are bothered that so many people are excluded from the opportunity planet America represents," Roland said. "Do you have to be a fundamentalist to want a better life for your children? If you think it's possible God used evolution as a tool of creation should you be condemned to live out your life in a ghetto where the role models are drug dealers and pimps? Mothers who have never heard of the god the Fellowship worships weep when their children starve to death."

"Of course that's true, but—"

"Reverend Maitland," Goldwyn cut in. "Don't you agree that children of all colors and creeds deserve a chance for a better life?"

"I do, yes."

"Of course you do. I feel the same, so I'm prepared to set up a foundation to pay the way for diverse peoples to travel to planet America to start new lives."

"That's very generous, sir," Christy said.

Waving away her praise with his hand he took the cigar from his lips.

"I'm not doing this for me, it's for the children. It's about the future of the whole human race, not just a sliver of it. We've got the backing we need to do this, Reverend Maitland, but of course we can't get these people to planet America. Not without the help of the Fellowship."

"You want me to talk to Mark?"

"Would you? Actually I'd like to meet with him myself," Goldwyn said.

"Maybe I should talk with him first," Christy said.

"It's important that he sees how serious we are," Goldwyn said. "Perhaps you could arrange a meeting between Reverend Shepherd and Roland. Roland speaks my mind on this. He can share what's in my heart."

"I think I can get him to agree. We can shuttle up to New Hope," she said.

Roland held up his hands in protest. "I never want to leave mother Earth ever again. I'll meet him in Mexico."

"I'll see what I can do," she said.

Thinking about the idea as she left the *Journal* building, she warmed to it. If she could mediate one last agreement, this one between Mark and Grayson Goldwyn, she could leave her birth world a lasting legacy and leave for planet America with a feeling of closure.

CHAPTER 112   STS *ATLANTIS*

> The development of the Space Delivery System,
> or space shuttles, was a tremendous step in
> reducing the cost of delivering a payload to orbit.
> However, the shuttle depended on disposable
> parts. Rejecting designs for an STS that did not
> have disposable components set the space program back twenty years.
>
> —*ALTERNATE PATHWAYS TO SPACE*,
> EDWARD NORTON

EARTH'S ORBIT

The launch of shuttle *Atlantis* was flawless, the ship reaching low Earth orbit with no problems. The launch attracted a minor amount of press coverage because shuttle launches were unusual. The space plane delivered most U.S. government payloads to orbit now, the Fellowship performing most of the rest of the orbital lifting. There was little concern expressed over the secrecy surrounding the payload, since shuttles and rockets were still used for sensitive military payloads.

Once in orbit, *Atlantis* made the first of two scheduled orbital corrections. The first happened to match its trajectory with New Hope station. With the station high in geosynchronous orbit, *Atlantis* passed beneath the Fellowship's space station. The second maneuver was scheduled for the second orbit and would move *Atlantis* to a higher orbit.

Inside the cargo hold of STS *Atlantis* rode the rebuilt *Rising Savior*. At the controls, waiting for the second orbit, was Kent Thorpe.

CHAPTER 113 **SECRET LAB**

> There is no security on this earth;
> there is only opportunity.
>
> —*MACARTHUR: HIS RENDEZVOUS WITH HISTORY*, DOUGLAS MACARTHUR

SAN FRANCISCO, CALIFORNIA

Guy Francis had died at the siege of their compound and they missed his technical skills. Cobb "Scarecrow" Mc-Griff had stepped up, younger than Guy, but with an aptitude for disabling security systems. Unfortunately, he was untested in the field. Surveillance told Proctor and his men that the security guard left the reception area every two hours to patrol the perimeter of the building, patrolling the interior every hour. There were checkpoints on his rounds and unless he punched in his code at every point, the central office was notified. They would call then, and if he didn't answer the phone, the police would be notified and a patrol car diverted. Once he began his exterior patrol he could be overdue at a checkpoint by no more than five minutes. Depending on the location of the nearest patrol car, Proctor estimated they would have ten minutes, at the most, from the moment they took out the guard. Proctor, however, had worked out a plan to give them more time.

They waited in the shadows for the guard to start his two A.M. rounds. As soon as the guard was around the corner of the building, they hurried to the front, each man wearing a pack and carrying two five-gallon cans of gasoline. They then split up. Nick Lawson and Sandy Singleton followed the guard, staying in the shadows. Every station he checked in at gave them a few more minutes inside. Only when he became suspicious would they secure him.

Scarecrow McGriff led the way to the front door. He was tall, almost six feet, with hair the color of straw and a slight frame. Growing up on a wheat farm in eastern Washington, he frequently wore the overalls that earned him his nickname. Scarecrow quickly opened the door, then moved to the alarm control box behind the reception desk and disarmed the proximity alarm. Proctor and Jim Nelson entered at Scarecrow's signal, carrying the gasoline. After they carried in the cans and packs left by Nick and Sandy, they followed Scarecrow down the hall. He moved carefully, checking for alarms, but found none. At the end of the hall they went down the stairs. The doors at the bottom were locked and rigged with an alarm system. Cobb traced the wires, then rigged a bypass so when they opened the door the circuit wouldn't be triggered. Inside was a two-story space with a third of it divided into smaller rooms, all filled with electronic gear. The walls of the largest space were lined with equipment, but in the middle of the space was a platform built to sit against a curved object.

"This is it," Proctor said, "but the sphere is gone."

"What now?" Scarecrow asked.

"See if there's a safe," Proctor ordered.

They found one in a back room. Scarecrow was drilling into the safe when Sandy Singleton hurried in.

"The guard's taped and stored," Singleton said.

"Plant the explosives and spread the gasoline," Proctor said.

Cobb finished drilling and packed the holes in the safe with plastic explosives. Then he pressed a detonator into place and attached a radio receiver. They set the explosives off from the next room. The lock was blown out, but the door was still closed. Looking through the jagged hole Proctor could see file folders and equipment. Handing the light to Scarecrow, he had his young safecracker look inside.

"It's part of a backup system for their computer network," Cobb said. "They might have more copies at another location."

"I doubt it," Proctor said. "Control this technology and you control the world. They wouldn't leave multiple copies lying around. Make sure the contents of this safe burn."

When the lab was rigged, they spread the rest of the gasoline in the upstairs offices, planting the remainder of their explosives. Then they set a timer and left the building. They were on the highway when they passed the police car coming to investigate. A few seconds later the building exploded, instantly engulfed in flames.

They changed cars three miles away, and again ten miles later. After the last car change the others celebrated, but Proctor knew the job wasn't finished. There was one more place where the information discovered in that lab was stored—in Dr. Thorpe's head. Where was Thorpe? he wondered. And where was the sphere?

CHAPTER 114

THE TRAP

> The foundation of a relationship is communica-
> tion. Communication is built on honesty.
> Honesty on trust. Without trust,
> the relationship crumbles.
>
> —CHRISTY MAITLAND

FELLOWSHIP COMPOUND, MEXICO

Mark stepped off the Fellowship shuttle just before
sunset. Micah and Floyd were with him, both there to
make sure he didn't leave the compound with Christy.
They had argued with Mark for a half an hour trying to
convince him to remain in orbit. When they were this
close to completing the mission God had given them,
they didn't want Mark to take any unnecessary risks. It
amused Mark the way they treated him, as if he were
Adam and Christy Eve.

As Mark walked through their Mexico compound, he
shook hands with a dozen friends he hadn't seen in over a
year. Others were members of the Fellowship whom Mark
had never met, but faithful workers nevertheless. Mark
greeted all, even though he was anxious to move on. Christy
would be here soon, with Roland, and he planned to use his
last trip to Earth well. There was much to do, and little time.

He met Christy and Roland at the gate, kissing Christy
and shaking hands with Roland. Despite their months together on the return voyage, Mark had never warmed up
to Roland—too many editorials critical of the Fellowship, too many irreverent remarks. Visiting America had
done nothing to change Roland's views. His first editorial
upon returning focused on the lack of diversity on planet
America, his second on the environmental impact of the
Fellowship colonists. Tobias Stoop could have written the
second article, Mark thought bitterly.

The three of them walked together to the compound canteen, filling coffee cups and settling at a small table in the corner of the cafeteria. Regular shuttle runs were taking emigrants to *Covenant* and *Prophet,* and lifting spheres shuttled back and forth to orbit, hauling tons of cargo with each lift. *Covenant* was nearly full and *Prophet* would be within a week. On the ground, trucks rumbled in and out of the compound night and day, the ground crews divided into shifts and working around the clock.

"Isn't this an unusual amount of activity?" Roland asked.

"We don't usually have two Ark ships in orbit at the same time," Mark said.

"I suppose that explains it," Roland said.

A bad start, Christy thought. Roland was digging for information and Mark's answer was taken as evasive.

"Grayson Goldwyn asked Roland to meet with you, Mark, as his representative," Christy said. "Mr. Goldwyn has a very generous proposal."

"I'm listening," Mark said.

"I mean really listen," Christy said, squeezing his arm.

"I'll really listen," Mark said, letting Christy open his heart to Roland.

"Mr. Goldwyn is prepared to set up a foundation to sponsor families who want to move to planet America. This new foundation would pay for passage, supplies, and provide financial support while the colonists get themselves established."

"We're doing that now," Mark said. "We would be happy to accept his donation."

"You're not listening," Roland said, imitating Christy. "You're moving your people to America, but there are so many more who would like the same opportunity. The Goldwyn Foundation would select these colonists and the Fellowship would provide transportation. You would be reimbursed for the costs, of course."

"You would select non-Christians," Mark said.

"The Foundation would support people of diverse faiths."

"It would upset the balance on planet America," Mark said.

"You don't have balance," Roland argued. "All your people are sitting on the same side of a scale. A healthy society needs people to sit on both ends so that there is balance. It's diversity that makes a society great."

"Diversity brings divisiveness," Mark argued. "Our new society isn't well enough established yet to introduce radically different points of view. Harmony and cooperation depend on common values and shared beliefs."

"It's diversity that made this country great."

"Is it diversity that made Japan great?" Mark countered.

Christy had heard these arguments before and knew it was time to intervene. Before she could speak, she heard a distant rhythmic thumping. As it grew louder the canteen quieted, the two dozen people gathered for meals now listening. Suddenly Mark stood, panicked. Then he reached out, grabbing Roland by the front of his shirt, dragging him from his chair.

"They won't hurt you, Mark," Roland said. "They just want to make sure that everyone has the same opportunity that your people have."

Mark's reply was drowned in the roar of turbine engines and thumping rotors.

CHAPTER 115

LIGHTNING RAID

War is not a parlor game in which the players
obediently stick to the rules. Where life and
death are at stake, rules and obligations
go by the board.

—ALBERT EINSTEIN

APPROACHING THE FELLOWSHIP
COMPOUND, MEXICO

Seldom do you get a second chance in the military, but
Colonel Watson had his. Mr. Fry had pulled strings to get
him the assignment of taking the Mexican compound,
Colonel Watson understanding he would be in debt to Fry
if he succeeded, and his career over if he didn't.

The Apache gunships led the way toward the compound, flying over, making sure there were no missile defenses. Colonel Watson's troop transports followed,
trained to spread out, overcome any resistance, and occupy the compound. The spacecraft were to be secured
first, technical facilities second, and finally the rest of the
compound. Acquiring technology was the primary mission, the secondary goal was Mark Shepherd. He'd made
a fool of Watson once before, but this time it was Watson
who planned on doing the laughing.

The Apaches completed their pass and began orbiting,
looking for signs of resistance—there were none. Civil-
ians scattered in every direction, but there was no small
arms fire, missile radar, or heavy weapons. Watson
looked out the door of his transport, seeing the well-lit facility ahead. There were three large launch pads used by
the shuttles—concrete rings—and four other paved areas
used by the lifting spheres. Cargo containers were
stacked around the launch sites, and sitting near the cargo

were two spheres. He could see one of the shuttle pads from his helicopter, and there was a shuttle parked there. According to their intelligence, there should be two shuttles and three spheres on the ground.

The first helicopters were dropping into the compound, an anthill now, people running aimlessly. Then Watson noticed three men running directly from a warehouse toward one of the Fellowship's shuttles. Watson's stomach knotted. Then, from just out of his sight, came the sound of a thirty-millimeter cannon as an Apache helicopter stitched a line toward the men, then through them. Two of the men were shredded by the large-caliber shells, the third turning and running back toward the warehouse. The shuttle safe, Watson smiled. The mission was going as planned.

The fact that God had David anointed in secret
to protect him from Saul leads some to conclude
that there is no God. If there was a God, they
argue, why would an omnipotent God need to
use secrecy to protect a man? It seems to be a
very ineffectual response. On the contrary, it
takes great strength to put someone you love at
risk for their own sake. I've watched my daughters hammering a nail, knowing the risk to their
fingers, but I loved them too much to interfere
with the valuable lesson that was soon to follow.

— *THE CASE FOR CHRISTIAN VIOLENCE*,
JAMES D. FOSTER

FELLOWSHIP COMPOUND, MEXICO

Mark left the canteen at a dead run heading for the
nearest shuttle. The Fellowship couldn't risk letting their
ships be captured. As he ran, Mark heard machine-gun
fire. Turning the corner of a warehouse, the sounds of
gunfire became louder and he saw troops ahead. Mark
continued along the wall of the warehouse, then ducked
in an open door. Micah was inside, with Bob Morton and
an apprentice pilot—a teenager who had never soloed.

"We've got to get to the shuttle," Mark said breathlessly.

"Too late," Micah said, pointing.

Two bodies lay on the landing pad and on the far side
two helicopters were landing, troops spilling out, surrounding the shuttle. Mark's heart broke at the sight of
the dead, but he didn't have time to grieve for them.

"We've got to destroy that ship," Mark said.

"I can damage it," Bob offered. "Make sure it won't fly."

Mark looked into Bob's face. The man had been a long

and faithful servant of the Lord, and Mark didn't want to lose him when they were this close to living free.

"Be careful," Mark said, giving his blessing.

"I'm not ready for glory yet," Bob assured Mark, then ran deep into the warehouse.

Mark led Micah and the teen pilot through the warehouse and out the other side. The second shuttle was there, the landing pad protected from the helicopters by a crane, left inadvertently hanging over the pad. They sprinted to the shuttle's open aft cargo hold just as they saw helicopters landing a short distance away, disgorging troops. Suddenly a sphere appeared over a building, shooting into the sky.

"That's one safely away," Mark said. "Two more to go."

"You take the shuttle, Micah," Mark said. "I'm going to help get the spheres away."

Mark ran toward the sphere pads, ignoring Micah's shouts to come back. Running through stacked cargo modules recklessly, Mark popped out onto a pad just as troops came through the other side, quickly surrounding one of their spheres. Bullets whined past his head, puncturing the metal containers behind him. Without breaking stride he turned, cutting back into the protection of the cargo modules heading for the next sphere—that sphere was lost. A shuttle and a sphere in the hands of the enemy, Mark realized, knowing everything they had worked for was now at risk.

Turning toward where the last sphere was parked, Mark found he was ahead of the troops this time, breaking into the clear. Floyd was there, climbing up the side of the sphere. After Floyd dropped inside, another member of the Fellowship closed and sealed the hatch.

"Take off, Floyd," Mark shouted, even knowing he couldn't be heard.

Then an assault rifle fired from his left and the man who had sealed the hatch fell, knocked back by the bullets piercing his chest. Mark ran toward the fallen man, but bullets ricocheted off the concrete pad around him, turning him back into the stacks of cargo where he hid, watching for Floyd to get away.

Cautiously, troops emerged, circling the sphere. Just as their circle was completed, the whoosh of a takeoff sounded. Mark saw that Micah's shuttle was up and away. Troops fired small arms at the ship, but it continued toward space, unaffected. Then Mark saw one of the Apache helicopters circle low over the launch pad, hovering over Floyd's sphere. Then more troops came, and another circle was formed around the lifting sphere, the inner circle pointing their weapons at the sphere, the outer circle ready for a counterattack—something Mark knew would not happen.

Mark looked back at the sphere Floyd was in; the Apache helicopter was hovering low, trapping it. Other troops were aiming rocket launchers at the sphere. It was effective containment and now they not only had the sphere, but they also had Floyd.

CHAPTER 117 **NO REGRETS**

The psychological break from the unrepentant family is the next to the last step in healing. Only when the client cuts the emotional strings to those that abused her can the last stage of healing begin.

— *HIDDEN TERRORS: WOMEN IN THERAPY,*
ROSA QUIGLY

SAN FRANCISCO, CALIFORNIA

Daniel was home—his adopted home—sitting on the couch, watching television with Josh. They were eating ice cream, watching a television show that Daniel's parents would not have approved of. Daniel was free of his parents, free of the cult, free to do what he wanted, when he wanted, and with whom he wanted. Sure, Josh wanted Daniel to go back to school, but that was okay with Daniel. He knew there would be kids there that knew how to have a good time—and girls. He thought of Melody briefly, and then of her with Rob Evans—it hurt. Melody had been special to Daniel, but he wouldn't let them force him to do anything, not marry Melody, not stay on planet America. It was all worth it, but the image of Melody in the arms of Rob Evans haunted him.

Daniel scooped out a big spoonful of ice cream, tasting it again as if for the first time—cookies and cream, his favorite. They made ice cream occasionally on America, but always vanilla. That was another thing he hated about planet America, the sameness. Did everyone have to go to bed at the same time, worship the same way, and eat vanilla ice cream? Couldn't they crumble up a cookie and put it in the ice cream once in a while?

Tomorrow would help him forget his old life. Josh was going to pick up a driver's manual for Daniel so he could study for his permit. He had traveled light-years to gain his freedom, and a driver's license would complete his journey.

A news bulletin suddenly appeared on the screen.

"We interrupt our regularly scheduled program to bring you this special report."

Pictures of helicopters flying in circles around brightly lit buildings appeared, a voice explaining they were joining a cable news broadcast. Then the announcer identified the pictures as coming from the Fellowship launch compound in Mexico. A woman reporter could be heard now, describing the action below, saying over and over, "There has been gunfire, and we believe there have been casualties."

"You want to turn this off?" Josh asked.

"No," Daniel said.

"I'm sure your parents are safe on the space station," Josh said.

"I don't care about them, anyway."

"I don't care," Daniel repeated to himself, but he

couldn't help but wonder if one of the running figures was his mother, or even his father. Now the picture swung wildly while the helicopter came about. Then the image stabilized on a sphere surrounded by two rings of soldiers—a helicopter hovering above. Daniel could see a body lying next to the sphere. He leaned close to the screen.

"There are a lot of men in the Fellowship, Daniel," Josh said.

"I know. I don't care anyway," Daniel said, even while he studied the screen closely.

CHAPTER 118 **NO ESCAPE**

> When I hear people say that they worship many gods, I imagine myself telling my wife that I love other women as much as I love her. I don't think Evelyn would tolerate that and I don't think God would either.
>
> —FLOYD REMPLE

FELLOWSHIP COMPOUND, MEXICO

Troops were pounding on the hull of his sphere with rifle butts. Floyd looked through the porthole to see a rifle pointed at him. Reflexively, he shifted so the rifle couldn't be angled at him. He was lucky this model had only one porthole. There was more pounding on the hull. Floyd risked a glance and saw a face mouthing, "Open the hatch." Floyd ignored the command. He could hear and feel the thump of the helicopter overhead and knew weapons were aimed at the sphere.

Keeping away from the porthole, Floyd slid along the

hull until he reached the flight controls and flipped the toggles to fire the particle guns, the gravity waves building. With power, the control panels lit up, Floyd scanning them quickly. The sphere was pressurized, the gravity field was surrounding the ship, all control circuits were functioning, their indicators glowing green. Now the pounding on the hull became intense, and he heard someone scrambling up on top of the sphere, trying to open the hatch, which was secured from inside.

Floyd couldn't fly the shuttle while squatting against the wall, but if he climbed into the pilot's chair he would expose himself to the porthole. Still, if he could give the sphere a little power, then he could maneuver out from under the helicopter and shoot into the air where he could safely strap into a chair and fly the sphere—it was a risky plan.

He chanced another peek at the porthole and saw the face mouthing something. The man put a hand over his ear, then held it in front of his lips. Floyd understood and put the earphones on. He turned on the power to the radio and heard someone speaking.

"Do not attempt to fly your sphere. We have a helicopter hovering overhead, and if you move horizontally we will shoot you down. We have armor-piercing weapons."

Floyd was afraid. He had nowhere to run, his fate certain, but he would not let the world get the sphere. Floyd prayed for deliverance, but couldn't concentrate, instead he thought of his family, and thought of Daniel. Evelyn knew he loved her, as did Faith, but there was unfinished business with Daniel.

"Shut down your engines," the voice said in his earphones, "and open the hatch. This is your last warning."

Floyd decided to risk taking off. If they had murder on their minds nothing he could do would change that. With the helicopter overhead he would have to angle his flight, but to do that he would have to expose himself to the porthole. It would take a few seconds to adjust the field and apply power. He visualized each move he would make, moving his hands and feet in rehearsal. When he felt ready to make his move, he counted down from ten. When he got to three the porthole exploded. Penetrated by a bullet, the slug fragmented when it hit the far wall, two pieces piercing Floyd's abdomen. Now his stomach felt on fire and he clutched it, feeling his shirt wet with his blood.

CHAPTER 119   **SABOTAGE**

> Men will kill to get something they want, and
> they'll die to protect something they have.
>
> —GEORGE PROCTOR

FELLOWSHIP COMPOUND, MEXICO

Colonel Watson ran his hand along the steel side of the Fellowship shuttle and across the name "Rock of Ages" stenciled on the hull. A Christian flag was painted below the name, and you could still see the faint red, white, and blue where the American flag had been removed.

"Lieutenant, have that flag scraped off and repaint the stars and stripes," he said. "Scrape the name off too."

In the midst of battle, Watson was already preparing to display his trophy. Then rifle fire sounded behind him. Watson's men were firing toward the warehouse, seeing something Watson could not. Suddenly a forklift raced out of the open warehouse door, toward the shuttle, sheets of steel held in the forks, protecting the driver. Bullets whined in all directions, the steel deflecting the small arms fire. Watson called for heavier weapons, but it would be too late, the forklift was going to ram the shuttle.

"Stop it," Watson shouted uselessly.

Then a man jumped from the forklift, running toward the warehouse. Half a dozen guns swung toward the running man and his back was peppered with small arms fire. The driver collapsed, facedown on the concrete. Now troops scattered, running from the path of the onrushing forklift. Watson backed away, firing at the machine, bullets ricocheting off the steel frame, watching in horror as the yellow forklift hit the shuttle dead center, arms piercing the wall with the sound of screaming metal. The bullet-riddled steel plates the forklift was carrying slammed into the wall of the shuttle, the lift coming to a sudden jolting stop, the engine stalling. Fearing explosion, his men ran from the shuttle, looking for cover, but there was only the sound of distant gunfire.

When he was sure the shuttle wouldn't explode, Watson picked himself up and studied the damage to his prize. The raised arms of the lift had punctured the shuttle at the cargo level, leaving the precious drive intact. Colonel Watson ordered the forklift started, and then backed out, leaving two holes. The damage didn't look too bad, although the shuttle would take some repair before it could fly into space again. Relieved, Watson ordered a barrier be erected around the shuttle to protect it from more sabotage.

With one prize in hand, Watson took a squad of men and headed for the sphere pads. As he walked, he checked in with the other units. One sphere and one shuttle had gotten away, but Watson had control of one shuttle and one sphere, and another sphere had been trapped on the ground, although the pilot refused to come out. Watson hurried toward the pad with the last prize, anxious to be there when the pilot surrendered the sphere. Three ships, surely Fry and the president would see that as a success, Watson thought, and promotion couldn't be far behind.

CHAPTER 120

COURSE CORRECTION

> All progress has resulted from people who took
> unpopular positions.
>
> —ADLAI STEVENSON

NEW HOPE STATION

Ira and Shelly were crowded in the control center on New Hope, watching the news. New Hope was filled with settlers being transferred to *Covenant* for the voyage to the new world. All were watching monitors, the only noise restless children.

"Maybe we should cut off their broadcast," Shelly suggested.

"Let the world see what their government has come to," Ira said.

"I've got Micah on the radio," Cynthia said excitedly.

"Are you all right?" Shelly asked.

"Yes," Micah said. "Bobby Johnson's with me. Tell his family."

"Is Mark with you?" Ira asked.

"No. He went after the spheres, but only one has managed to lift off—Don Pell's flying it. He's rendezvoused with me. We're orbiting over the compound in case we can help. If Mark calls, contact us and we'll go after him."

There was one unsecured sphere left, and the drama on the screen told them someone was inside, refusing to come out—it could be Mark.

Worry about Mark's fate, and watching the drama on the screen, held their attention. It was at that moment the shuttle *Atlantis* carrying the recovered sphere made its second course correction, climbing toward New Hope station.

CHAPTER 121

IN THE HANDS OF THE ENEMY

> Then she called, "Samson, the Philistines are
> upon you!" He awoke from his sleep and
> thought, "I'll go out as before and shake myself
> free." But he did not know that the Lord had left
> him. Then the Philistines seized him, gouged
> out his eyes, and took him down to Gaza. Bind-
> ing him with bronze shackles, they set him to
> grinding in the prison.
>
> —JUDGES 16:20—22

FELLOWSHIP COMPOUND, MEXICO

Mark watched in horror when the soldier fired a round
into the sphere's porthole. Mark prayed Floyd was safe—
a steel sphere wasn't the place to be if bullets were ricocheting around. Floyd had to surrender or die, and the
world would have a sphere—another sphere, he reminded
himself. President Crow was committing murder to get
hold of the Fellowship's technology. Then Mark realized
that there was another place where Crow could acquire
Fellowship technology, and that the attack might not be
limited to Earth. Reluctantly, he left Floyd trapped in the
sphere, promising himself to free his friend somehow,
someday.

Keeping low, Mark hurried through the stacks of cargo
toward the control center on the second story of the warehouse. New Hope station needed to be warned and the
ships docked there moved to lunar orbit, safely out of
reach. Ahead of him a soldier stepped into his path, M-16
pointed at Mark. Turning back, Mark ran to an intersection and turned left, now running head up, full speed. Another soldier appeared and he dodged down another aisle,
now moving away from the warehouse. Another soldier

appeared and he had to stop, and turn, only to face another. He was surrounded. Like a trapped animal he
looked around wildly. There was no way to go but up and
he jumped, grabbing the top of a steel container, then
pushing himself up with his hands. His knee was over the
top of the container when hands grabbed his other leg
and he was pulled down into the hands of his enemies.

CHAPTER 122   **FLOYD'S DECISION**

> According to Soviet reports, he [Colonel
> Vladimir M. Komarov] died when the Soyuz
> plunged through the atmosphere and, parachute
> lines hopelessly tangled, crashed into the
> ground. Tass declared that the Soyuz had per-
> formed normally in orbit and had been success-
> fully braked with retro-rockets. [Komarov was
> dead, the Space Age's first casualty in flight.]
>
> — *WE REACH THE MOON,* JOHN N. WILFORD

FELLOWSHIP COMPOUND, MEXICO

The fire burned in Floyd's belly and his legs were growing numb. His shirt and pants were soaked with blood. He
was dying. If he surrendered to the troops outside the
sphere, he might be saved. They would have medics and
he could be airlifted to a hospital in one of their helicopters. To save his life he would have to give them the
sphere—the technology God had revealed to Ira to fulfill
his vision. Floyd desperately wanted to live, to see his
wife and children again, and especially Daniel—he hated
the thought of dying without reconciling with his son. But
as desperate as he was to hold his son in his arms again,
he could not betray God's trust.

"Open the hatch or we'll fire," a soldier shouted through the porthole over the roar of the helicopter's turbine engine.

Asking Jesus to give him the strength, Floyd chose to be a faithful servant.

"I'm shot," he said, pushing himself to his feet.

When there was no response, he forced himself to shout, pain radiating out from his gut to his limbs and head with each word.

"Open the hatch, we have a medic," a soldier shouted back.

"I'm bleeding," Floyd shouted, stepping to the center of the sphere.

Floyd could see the soldier's face in the open porthole, dust swirling behind the soldier from the backwash of the helicopter. As soon as Floyd exposed himself, the soldier aimed a pistol at him. Noting his blood-soaked clothes, the soldier said, "Open the hatch and we'll get you a medic."

Nodding, Floyd tried to straighten up, as if to reach the hatch release above him, then he buckled over in pain, falling over the back of the pilot's seat. Spears of fire shot through his body when he hit the seat. The arm with the gun poked deeper into the sphere, turning toward him.

"Open the hatch or I'll shoot," the soldier shouted.

"I'm trying. It hurts," Floyd said.

"Open the hatch now!"

Summoning his remaining strength, Floyd lunged toward the controls, shoving the joystick and the power lever at the same time. A bullet tore into his side but there was only so much pain a person can feel. The sphere shot upward; Floyd slammed to the deck of the sphere, unconscious.

> The alternative to the belief that some people
> will be consigned to hell is the teaching called
> universalism, that everyone will be saved in the
> end. I find universalism to be a very pleasing
> doctrine. I wish it were true.
>
> — *UNCOMMON DECENCY*, RICHARD J. MOUW

FELLOWSHIP COMPOUND, MEXICO

Ready to take command of the troops surrounding the occupied sphere, Colonel Watson stepped out from the cargo modules onto the landing pad just as the sphere shot into the air, triggering a deadly chain of events. One of his men had been leaning into the porthole when the sphere took off, and he went with it. The sphere tore through the Apache helicopter, impacting just behind the cockpit. The Apache's fuel tanks ruptured, and two dozen men below were drenched in gasoline, waves of the flammable liquid washing across the concrete toward the cargo containers. Continuing skyward, the sphere split the ship in two, the tail section spinning out of control, the tail rotor tearing into the men gathered below. Then the primary rotors came apart, metal fragments flung in all directions, slicing and dicing everything in their path. The bulk of the copter tilted when the tail section was lost, then dropped, crushing three men before exploding in flames, igniting spilled fuel. Flames engulfed the survivors, human torches scattering like chimney sparks in the night. Licking across the landing pad, the flames spread to the cargo containers, finding new abundant fuel in the packing debris scattered around the containers.

The sphere continued to rocket skyward breaking the sound barrier, the sonic boom vibrating through the compound. Air friction heated the shell of the sphere and the interior through the open porthole, but it could not harm Floyd. What little life he had left was crushed out of him in the uncontrolled takeoff. The interior temperature climbed to four hundred degrees before the atmosphere thinned to the point of little resistance. The heat now radiated into space, the sphere leaving the gravity well of Earth on a trajectory taking it past the moon and into space, its cargo, one dead human being.

Shouting orders no one heard, Watson fled the inferno, seeking shelter in the stacks of cargo. Soon these too were on fire and he continued to retreat. A dozen of his men lay dead back on the pad, a dozen more badly burned. The fire was spreading through the cargo, burning toward the hangar. If it caught fire they could lose spare parts, records, and computer files. Prepared for a firefight, not to fight fire, Colonel Watson had no choice but to save what he could.

CHAPTER 124 **WORRY**

A wise man heeds his father's instruction . . .

—PROVERBS 13:1

SAN FRANCISCO, CALIFORNIA

The television went blank, Josh turning it off with the remote. Staring at the blank screen, Daniel could still see the last scene. The wrecked helicopter, men sliced to pieces, soldiers burned to death. The images of the bodies of members of the Fellowship were fixed in his mind too.

"Are you all right?" Josh asked. "I shouldn't have let you watch that."

"I'm okay. I told you I don't care," Daniel said, trying to convince himself. "You can turn it back on."

"No."

Daniel got up, carrying his melted ice cream toward his room.

"You can watch it, I know you want to. I don't mind," Daniel said.

Closing his bedroom door, Daniel pressed his ear to the door, hearing the TV come back on. Grabbing his Walkman, he put his headphones on and searched the AM dial until he found a station broadcasting the assault. Despite denying it for years, he found he did care what happened to his mother and sister and, to his surprise, his father.

CHAPTER 125 **PANIC**

> Then I saw the beast and the kings of the earth
> and their armies gathered together to make war
> against the rider on the horse and his army.
>
> —REVELATION 19:19

NEW HOPE STATION

"**I**ra, you better look at this," Cynthia said, pulling Ira toward the radar screen.

One of Cynthia's assignments was monitoring the space around New Hope, tracking satellites, approaching and departing spheres, Fellowship shuttles, space cruisers, and Ark-class ships. Normally, a U.S. space shuttle launch wouldn't attract much attention because the U.S. shuttles weren't capable of reaching New Hope station. It was a warning buzzer that called for Cynthia's attention.

Ira came to Cynthia's station and studied the radar with his one good eye.

"This can't be right," Ira said. "A shuttle can't fly this high."

"It's accelerating, Ira," Sandy said.

Then before their eyes the trajectory changed sharply, shuttle *Atlantis* now on a collision course with the station.

"Evacuate everyone to the ships," Ira said. "Now!" Then turning to Shelly he said, "Where are your children, Shelly?"

"They're on *Covenant,*" Shelly said. "Rollerblading."

Empty Ark-size ships were used as dormitories and for other activities. Rollerblading in an empty cargo hold was popular with the children.

Cynthia, Sandy, and others began shouting, clearing the control room, then returned to their consoles, broadcasting to the entire station. Hundreds of settlers gathered around monitors throughout the station listened dumbly, then confused and fearful, they began to move. The resulting confusion clogged corridors and hatchways. Within a minute there was gridlock on the station.

Shelly remained in the control room, watching the radar as *Atlantis* came. Shelly turned on the exterior cameras, rotating them toward Earth and the approaching shuttle. She found it, centering *Atlantis* in the middle of the screen. It was coming fast. To avoid colliding it would have to slow soon, and to do that it must either rotate and fire the main engines, or fire the maneuvering jets to alter course. It did neither.

Coming straight on, the shuttle slowed with no visible exhaust. Then the cargo bay doors began to open. Something came out of the shuttle on an arm, pointing at the station. It was long, nearly the length of the hatch. Without a flash or any sign of a mechanism, objects streamed from the end of the device. Shouting a useless warning, Shelly instinctively braced for an explosion. Instead she felt the station shudder, then suddenly they were in a hurricane—the hull had been breached and the station's atmosphere was rushing to the vacuum of space. Triggered by explosive decompression, automatic doors on the station closed, temporarily stemming the air loss. Each module had emergency air supplies and now their pressure valves blew, the tanks venting, replenishing the lost air. When the roar of the emergency tanks faded, Shelly joined Ira at the engineering station. Module three was showing zero pressure. Anyone inside that module was dead.

Then the station vibrated again, the monitor showing the strange gun firing at module nine.

"They're isolating us," Ira said. "We're cut off from *Prophet* and *Genesis*."

More violent vibration sent loose objects clattering to the deck as the attack continued.

"There are people in those sections," Cynthia said. "They're killing them."

"Sandy, contact our ships," Ira ordered. "Find out if they have pilots on board."

Internal lines were jammed with panicked people begging for help, screams in the background. Switching to radio, Sandy called the ships one at a time. Only *Exodus* responded—the ship had a pilot who was powering up the drive. Ira ordered him to get away as soon as possible.

"Look at the monitor," Cynthia shouted.

The attacking shuttle had nudged against the station. The nose of *Atlantis* was open, the blue arc from cutting metal could be seen where the shuttle touched the station. At this angle they could now see into the bay of the shuttle and there in the back was one of their spheres.

"It has to be the *Rising Savior*," Ira said.

"John's ship," Shelly said. "They killed John to get it and now they're killing us with it."

Movement in the shuttle bay caught her attention. Men in silver environment suits were packed into the front, ready to assault the station.

"Why couldn't they just let us go?" Shelly said. "Why?"

"Because God and Satan are at war, Shelly," Ira said. "And neither will settle for a tie."

> You looked, O king, and there before you stood a
> large statue—an enormous, dazzling statue, awe-
> some in appearance. The head of the statue was
> made of pure gold, its chest and arms of silver, its
> belly and thighs of bronze, its legs of iron, its feet
> partly of iron and partly of baked clay. While you
> were watching, a rock was cut out, but not by
> human hands. It struck the statue on its feet of
> iron and clay and smashed them. Then the iron,
> the clay, the bronze, the silver and the gold were
> broken to pieces at the same time and became
> like chaff on a threshing floor in the summer.
>
> —DANIEL 2:31–35

EARTH'S ORBIT

With his part done, Kent Thorpe relaxed in the sphere. The troops in space suits were moving into the station now, securing New Hope station. Was Ira in that damaged module, he wondered, lying dead, his lungs frozen, his body swollen from the gases released from solution by the instant vacuum? He would know soon. One of his monitors came to life, the picture broadcast from the helmet of a soldier. The picture bounced, impossible to follow, as the man climbed into the station. Once inside, the artificial gravity of the station made it possible to walk, the picture stabilizing. Thorpe was shocked by what he saw. The module was full of bodies. Men, women, and children—many in their parents' arms—lay against the wall, sucked there by the explosive decompression. The horrific sight sickened him, but he quickly rationalized it, blaming the cultists for not sharing their technology. Warming to his rationalization, he now blamed Ira for the deaths since it was his selfishness that had caused all this, and the death of Thorpe's one love. No, it wasn't Thorpe's fault those people had died, it was Ira's, and he would pay for their deaths, and the other deaths he had caused.

Tuning to the cult's radio frequencies, Thorpe picked up a transmission.

"Daniel, Daniel, Daniel," someone was shouting. "Implement the Daniel Option."

Thorpe recognized the voice as Ira Breitling's. Pressing the transmit button he broke in on the broadcast.

"You're a murderer, Ira Breitling. You murdered Constance Wong," Thorpe said.

"Who is this?" Ira radioed back.

"This is Kent Thorpe."

Silence, and Thorpe fantasized Ira trembling at the mention of his name.

"Kent, is that really you? Where are you?"

"I'm in your *Rising Savior*. I rebuilt it. I've discovered your secret."

"You blame me for the death of Constance?" Ira asked.

"Your carelessness killed her."

"It was an accident, Kent. Constance was a friend of mine."

Breitling sounded contrite, but not afraid, and that wasn't good enough.

"There are troops coming to get you right now, Breitling. Resist and they'll kill you. Surrender and you'll spend the rest of your life in jail. I hope you resist."

"How could you carry so much hate for so long?" Ira asked.

Thorpe didn't answer because he couldn't admit the truth to himself. His hate would have faded if there had been someone to take Contance's place, but he was a difficult man to love. Rejected by his peers all his life, he had grown up lonely, watching the other kids play, date, go to dances, marry. Constance had been the one exception in a solitary life, a glimpse into what life could be. When that life was snatched away from him, he longed for the lost companionship like an addict for heroin. With another fix, he might have had the strength to forgive Ira, but his life had been one of loneliness and hurt. The only way to survive those emotions was to channel them into hate. His hate gave him reason to live.

"They're coming for you, Ira. Do you hear me? They're coming."

"I forgive you, Kent," Ira said.

Ira stopped speaking after that, and Kent never heard his voice again. A minute later the shuttle *Atlantis* shook violently. Switching to the military frequency, Thorpe heard, "They just blew the station in half." Switching to the external camera he saw debris flying into space around the joint connecting the module the shuttle was attached to and the rest of the station. Slowly, a gap appeared between two modules—the station was coming apart.

CHAPTER 127   **SEPARATION**

> What about dealing with Nazis and Satanists
> and people who advocate legalized incest and the
> heretics in our churches? What does it mean
> to treat *such* persons with gentleness
> and reverence?
>
> — *UNCOMMON DECENCY,* RICHARD J. MOUW

NEW HOPE STATION

New Hope had once been sixteen modules, two rows of eight joined together with connecting corridors. Four of those modules had been moved to orbit around planet America, leaving twelve cylinders connected by four corridors, the cylinders numbered one through six along the space side, and then seven through twelve on the Earth side. The control centers were located in modules two and eight. The Ark-class ship *Prophet* was docked at module six and *Covenant* at module one. Their cruisers *Exodus* and *Genesis* were docked at modules four and ten. Shuttles were docked at modules seven and twelve and one on *Prophet*. Four spheres were at the station, one docked to *Prophet* and one each on the three shuttles.

The U.S. space shuttle *Atlantis* had attacked modules three and nine, perforating the modules, making them uninhabitable. After *Atlantis* attached itself to module nine, troops in pressure suits occupied that module, and crossed over into module three. They were now forcing the doors into connecting modules that were packed with panicky settlers trying to get to *Prophet* and *Covenant*. Ira, Shelly, and the other leaders were isolated at one end of the station, unable to help those trying to get to the Ark ships.

Keeping the station between his ship and the attacking shuttle, Micah nosed the shuttle *Jacob's Ladder* against module three, young Bobby Johnson sitting beside him in the copilot's seat. More connecting seals blew, this time between modules two and three. The station separated in a spray of ice particles and debris. He could see one of the attacking soldiers in a silver suit in the gap opening between modules, stumbling, trying to find a handhold. There were more explosions at the other joints, and now he heard Ira over the radio.

"We've blown all of the seals, Micah. We're cutting gravity in those modules."

Applying power, Micah gently pushed the module he was butted against. Module three was connected to module nine, and *Atlantis* was on the other side. With luck, some of the troops would still be inside. As the module finished tearing free, the soldier in the space suit drifted out of the gap, vainly trying to grab hold of something. Another soldier appeared, his legs floating out the opening.

"Micah, look!" Bobby shouted.

Micah followed the teenager's point to see the mechanical arm from *Atlantis* carrying the weapon, extending above the module, the weapon bending to point at them. Normally separating modules was delicate work but Micah had nothing to lose. Recklessly, he applied power, the modules sliding from the middle of the station. He had centered the *Jacob's Ladder* on module three, but missed the actual center of gravity. Bashing into the other modules, the segment bounced and twisted as it came free, the weapons arm attached to *Atlantis* swayed with each jolt. With one last shove, modules three and nine were pushed free, taking *Atlantis* and its weapon with them. Mission accomplished, Micah reconfigured the shuttle's fields just as the weapon fired, a stream of pellets passing noiselessly over the top of their ship. Bobby was breathing rapidly, eyes wide, face wet with perspiration.

"Are you all right?" Micah asked.

"It's not what I expected. It's so quiet."

"But people are still dying—our people."

The modules were rotating now, looking like a floating dumbbell, *Atlantis* stuck to one end. With *Atlantis* unable to aim accurately, the pilot of *Exodus* took the opportunity, breaking free of the station. Ira looked back to see the rotation of the freed modules bring the shuttle around toward *Exodus,* the weapon arm angling at the fleeing ship.

"*Exodus,* this is Micah," he shouted into the microphone. "They're going to fire."

Exodus suddenly accelerated, angling below the station and away from the attacking shuttle. *Atlantis* fired anyway, the stream of particles chasing *Exodus,* missing the fleeing ship, the stream continuing toward the space station and the shuttle docked there.

"Oh, no," Micah said. "They're going to strafe the station."

DECOMPRESSION

> "Doing good" is as easy as breathing. Doing the
> right thing doesn't prick your conscience, and you
> don't wrestle with your conscience later. "Doing
> evil" is altogether different. For most people,
> doing the "wrong" thing is difficult. It's not the
> weak who can override years of cultural condi-
> tioning, it is the strong. However, once the line
> has been crossed, doing evil gets easier and easier.
>
> — *A HISTORY OF GOOD AND EVIL,*
> ROBERT WINSTON, PH.D.

NEW HOPE STATION

Ira ordered the control room evacuated when the troops broke through the outer airlock door. Ira and Shelly herded the others from the module, Ira holding back, making sure everyone else got out first. Slowly, through narrow corridors, they herded men, women, and children into the next module and through it to shuttle *Redemption*. The shuttle was nearly full of staff and colonists, a pilot at the controls, waiting for orders to leave. Stephen O'Malley was at the door of the shuttle and yelled to Ira.

- "We're nearly full. We can squeeze you in but the rest will have to go on *Covenant.*"

"Take off," Ira shouted to Stephen. "We'll get away with the others."

Stephen hesitated, not wanting to leave his friend and leader in harm's way. Just then the stream of pellets from the *Atlantis*'s rail gun ripped into the shuttle. Made from depleted uranium, the steel-jacketed slugs stitched a pattern diagonally across shuttle *Redemption*. As the slugs tore through the flight deck, the pilot was nearly cut in half, the windshield blown out. The unharnessed copilot was ejected into space by the explosive decompression. While the atmosphere escaped through the flight deck, the slugs continued across the bow of the ship, puncturing each level of the shuttle and the attached sphere, killing some passengers and wounding many more.

As the shuttle *Redemption* decompressed, the atmosphere of New Hope station rushed to fill the vacuum created in the shuttle. The sudden hurricane strength blast of air knocked Stephen into the *Redemption*. The automatic airlock doors on New Hope slammed closed a few seconds later, cutting off the loss of atmosphere, trapping Stephen and the others in the crippled shuttle. Shelly and others rushed to the airlock door, trying to force it open, to save Stephen and the others, but the pressure differential was too great.

"It's no use," Ira said. "They're dead."

Shelly froze in shock, thinking of the men, women, and children on the other side of the door, gasping for breath, blood boiling, vessels in their brains bursting. Images of Jews packed into gas chambers came to Shelly's mind and the horror was too much for her. She sobbed in despair, then thought of her own children. The same thing could happen to them. With mounting panic, she hurried with the others toward *Covenant*.

In the New Testament we are told not to resist
an evil person. Jesus then gives examples to
illustrate what He means. His examples include
being struck on the cheek by the back of a hand,
sued, and being forced to carry a load for someone. Nowhere does He explain what to do in the
face of systematic extermination.

— *THE CASE FOR CHRISTIAN VIOLENCE,*
JAMES D. FOSTER

EARTH'S ORBIT

From his vantage point in the belly of shuttle *Atlantis,*
Kent Thorpe had witnessed the destruction of one of the
Fellowship shuttles. Furious, Thorpe screamed into his
microphone at the gunner who had fired at the *Exodus*
and hit the shuttle instead. On the monitor he had seen the
front end of the ship torn apart, the flight deck riddled,
the ship explosively decompressing.

"Get us free," Thorpe shouted as the module they were
welded to floated away from the station. From the radio
he knew they had captured *Genesis* intact, but a half
dozen of their men were trapped in the segment that had
been pushed free—three of them officers. Those men
were trying to get back into the shuttle but unfamiliar
with zero gravity they were having trouble.

He picked another call out of the cacophony in his
ears. They had reached module six where *Prophet* was
docked. Once through that module they would have the
biggest prize of all.

> Martyrdom does not end something,
> it is only a beginning.
>
> — INDIRA GANDHI

NEW HOPE STATION

Shelly nearly collapsed from relief when she saw Micah in the hatch of *Covenant,* helping people inside. As soon as he saw her and Ira, Micah pushed through to them, taking Shelly in his arms.

"Evelyn's watching the kids, Shelly," Micah said before she could ask.

"How did you get here?" Shelly asked, holding him tight.

"We docked *Jacob's Ladder* with *Covenant.*"

Still hugging each other, they were pried apart by Ira, who pushed them both toward the hatch.

"We've got work to do," Ira said.

"Bobby Johnson is preflighting *Covenant,*" Micah said.

"He's not even a pilot," Ira groused.

"Many of our pilots are dead. Some are trying to get to *Prophet* and the other ships."

Now inside the ship, Sandy directed two men to seal the hatch, getting the giant ship ready for flight. Climbing to the flight deck they found Bobby in the copilot's seat, Cynthia next to him holding the preflight checklist. Bobby looked relieved to see them.

"You and Ira fly *Covenant,* Shelly," Micah said. "*Atlantis* is out there somewhere. I'll run interference for you to make sure you get away, then rendezvous with *Exodus* to put the Daniel Option into effect."

"Let's just leave," Shelly said. "Leave together."

"They'll follow," Micah said. "They'll never leave us alone. We have to stop them now while we still can."

Ira rubbed under his eye patch, settling into the engineering station, checking to see if Bobby had the ship's fields properly aligned.

Shelly and Micah were hugging again, but soon broke, Micah kissing her long and hard.

"Kiss the kids for me," Micah whispered. "I'll see you in a few months."

"What about Mark?" Ira asked.

"I'll do what I can," Micah said.

With a last kiss on Shelly's cheek, Micah was gone. They had come to Earth as a family, unwilling to ever be separated again. Shelly understood that serving God meant putting yourself second, but it was a hard path to follow, especially when she felt she and her family were pawns in the war between God and Satan.

Shelly took the pilot's chair, much to Bobby's relief, Sandy sitting behind her at the communications console, announcing to the passengers they needed to secure themselves. A few minutes later Shelly felt the ship shudder when Micah's shuttle separated from *Covenant*. Ira confirmed that all the systems were ready and Shelly reduced internal gravity to zero and released the docking clamps. Reshaping the gravity fields, she moved away from the station. The ship's radar was cluttered with reflections from the pieces of New Hope, but cleared as they moved away. Soon the screen showed three distinct segments of the station, *Prophet* still docked to module six.

"What's happening with *Prophet*?" Shelly asked Sandy, who was trying to raise *Prophet* on the radio. When Sandy didn't answer, she turned to see tears in Sandy's eyes.

"They're begging for help, Shelly. They're killing our people and they're taking *Prophet*."

Powerless to help those on *Prophet,* Shelly determined not to lose *Covenant*'s refugees. *Covenant* had been loading settlers and was half full when the attack came. Hundreds of terrified families huddled in the bowels of the ship, praying for God to deliver them.

Ira searched space with radar and cameras, trying to spot *Atlantis*.

"I've got contact with *Jacob's Ladder*," Ira said. "He's below us, passing under the station."

"They've just broken into *Prophet*'s control room," Sandy said. "The radio just went dead."

"I've got the middle segment on radar," Ira said. "It's still moving away from the station." Then Ira switched back and forth from radar to the monitors, saying, "*Atlantis* is not there. It's broken away."

Shelly searched the tiny segment of space she could see through the front port, vainly looking for the enemy shuttle.

"I've found it," Ira said. "*Atlantis* was behind *Prophet*. It's coming up on us from behind and below."

"Warn the passengers," Shelly said, then without waiting she increased power, accelerating away from the pieces of New Hope. The Ark-class ship's engines were powerful, but its mass great. *Atlantis* had only a sphere to move it, but it was already up to speed, catching *Covenant,* passing on the starboard side.

"They're calling us," Sandy said. "If we don't return to New Hope they're going to fire."

Shelly ignored the threat, continuing the acceleration. If they could get enough speed, the slugs would warp around the ship. In response a stream of pellets traced across their path.

"Micah's coming in *Jacob's Ladder,* Shelly," Ira said. "Keep the faith."

Shelly checked the monitor and saw *Atlantis* slipping behind *Covenant,* its weapon swinging toward the ship. A stream of pellets spurted from the end, *Covenant* vibrating with the impact.

"We're losing air," Ira said. "We've lost pressure on the cargo deck."

"Let me speak to them," Shelly said.

A second later she heard ". . . return to New Hope immediately, or we will fire for effect."

"We've got families on board," Shelly said. "Women and children. My children are on this ship."

"Their lives are in your hands," the voice replied. "Return to New Hope or you will be destroyed."

Checking her monitors, Shelly could see *Atlantis* losing ground and she wondered what kind of range the weapon had. Then behind *Atlantis* she saw *Jacob's Ladder,* climbing, angling on a collision course. "No, Micah, no," she whispered to herself. Then *Atlantis* was firing again, the weapon tearing through the hull of *Covenant* just in front of the drive. *Covenant* shuddered as precious atmosphere blew out into space.

Shelly studied the shape of the fields on the computer monitor. Improperly aligned they could tear the ship apart. Then the ship shuddered again from another volley and her instrument panel lost power. They were now flying blind.

CHAPTER 131   **LAST CHANCE**

> *Homo sapiens* has already reached the point at
> which a full-scale nuclear war could end Earth's
> civilization—perhaps forever. And even if such a
> war does not take place, he stands a good chance
> of poisoning his planet with industrial or chemi-
> cal waste, of releasing a new plague created in
> the genetic engineering laboratories, or simply of
> succumbing to the strain of a fruitless attempt
> to meet the needs of an increasing population.
>
> — *UNEXPLAINED:*
> *MYSTERIES OF MIND, SPACE AND TIME,*
> PETER BROOKESMITH (ED.)

EARTH'S ORBIT

"**Y**ou're letting them get away," Thorpe shouted into his microphone.

"Give us more speed," the gunner replied.

Thorpe pounded the wall of the sphere. He knew the

628 ✠ JAMES F. DAVID

sphere had more power than it was showing, but he didn't
know how to align the fields to maximize acceleration.
Covenant's giant bulbous drive unit was showing on his
monitor now, the ship and Ira Breitling getting away. A
stream of crystallized atmosphere was venting from the
starboard side of the ship where they had torn open the
hull, but still the monster accelerated.

"Destroy the drive," he shouted into his microphone.

"Orders are to capture it intact," the gunner said.

"If possible!" he shouted. "It's getting away. Disable
the drive before it's too late."

Seconds passed as the gunner talked with his commanders.

"We're doing it on your authority," the gunner said.

"Yes. Just fire."

It was too late. As the gunner aligned the weapon a Fellowship shuttle appeared on the monitor, passing just
over *Atlantis,* shearing off their weapons arm, the scream
of the metal vibrating through *Atlantis*'s hull and into the
sphere. Then the shuttle was gone, into space. Thorpe
pounded the walls, bloodying his hands, oblivious to the
pain. Helpless without the weapon, he could only watch
as *Covenant* escaped into space, Ira Breitling out of his
reach.

CHAPTER 132 **UNCONTROLLED**

> McDonald's sells hamburgers. Ford sells cars. I
> sell news. The only difference between what I'm
> selling and what they're selling is . . .
> there is no difference.
>
> —GRAYSON GOLDWYN,
> EDITOR OF THE *SAN FRANCISCO JOURNAL*

SPACE

The Ark-class ship *Covenant* accelerated uncontrollably, instrument panels dark, monitors blank. The control systems were redundant, so the damage to the ship was extensive. Blind, Shelly and the others on the flight deck had no way of knowing whether *Atlantis* was preparing to fire again, or whether Micah had destroyed it. And what of Micah? With no radio, Shelly wouldn't know for months whether he had lived or died. Suppressing her anguish, Shelly refused to let the world make her cry again; besides, she had her children to worry about and *Covenant* was in trouble.

"Before we lost instrumentation I could see that the animal deck had depressurized," Ira said, "but most of the top two decks were still holding atmosphere. The aft compartments were breeched. We haven't felt more vibrations so I'm assuming they didn't hit us again. Either Micah stopped them or we've moved out of range."

Remembering the teenager who was helping to fly the ship, Shelly reached out, touching his arm. Bobby was white-faced, perspiring heavily.

"Stay calm. We need you to help us get control of the ship."

Bobby swallowed hard, then took a deep breath.

"Just tell me what to do," he said.

"Stay here and watch the panels. Let me know the instant we restore power." Then to Ira, Shelly said, "We've got to stop *Covenant*'s acceleration."

Nodding gravely, Ira said, "There is no deadman's switch," he said. "Until we tell it otherwise the drives will push us faster and faster." After a rub under his eye patch he asked, "What's our heading?"

Shelly shrugged and said, "I didn't have time to plot a course. Out there, somewhere," Shelly said vaguely.

"Let's find out how badly we're damaged," Ira said.

Ira looked grave and she understood why. The lower deck and aft portions of the ship were open to vacuum and the drive couldn't be shut down. The drives could also be controlled from an engineering station midships and from the aft compartment; however, the midships station was useless since the damage was between it and the drive. It was possible the third station was still functional but it was in one of the damaged compartments. The heavy acceleration made it even more difficult.

Ira released his harness, then let himself "fall" to the rear wall, fumbling with the backup controls that would turn the gravity on. Shelly touched Bobby's arm again and pointed out the window.

"Let me know when we reach light speed," Shelly said.

"When the stars go out," Bobby said. "Right?"

"Yes, when the stars go out," Shelly confirmed.

Then with the gravity coming on, she released her harness and pushed herself to her feet, at least two gees pushing her toward the bowels of the ship where the settlers were. With every step she took, dread of what she might find when she reached the settlers grew.

CHAPTER 133

ORBITAL DESTRUCTION

> However, if a spacecraft is launched with suffi-
> cient velocity (some 17,400 miles an hour), it
> will not plunge back to Earth but will go into
> orbit, where the pull of gravity balances the ten-
> dency to fly off straight into space . . . Inertia
> keeps gravity from winning, and gravity keeps in-
> ertia from winning . . . As long as the satellite
> maintains the same velocity, it will continue to
> orbit Earth at the same altitude.
>
> — *WE REACH THE MOON*, JOHN N. WILFORD

EARTH'S ORBIT

When the *Atlantis* turned back toward New Hope,
Micah set course to rendezvous with *Exodus* on the far
side of Earth. With *Covenant* safely away, he had time to
think about the next move. The Daniel Option had to be
put into effect, but Mark was somewhere on Earth, and
Micah had no idea of where. The Fellowship Council had
agreed that everyone in the Fellowship was expendable.
Even Moses never stepped foot in the promised land, but
the people he led prospered there. It would be a bitter pill
to swallow, but getting their people to the new world mattered more than any individual, even Mark. Still, Micah
wasn't ready to give up on finding him.

In the shuttle *Jacob's Ladder*, Micah found *Exodus* orbiting where planned. The sphere *Jesus Wept* was docked
with *Exodus,* and Micah maneuvered *Jacob's Ladder* into
position, docking on the dorsal side. Don Pell had flown
the sphere out of the compound, and Jared Carter was the
pilot of *Exodus*. A half-dozen other men were with them,
two of them pilots.

Micah explained what needed to be done, giving each
man and ship an assignment. Then they recharged the

life-support systems in the *Jesus Wept,* and inspected the damage *Jacob's Ladder* sustained in the collision with *Atlantis*. Working quickly, they soon separated the ships, Micah now flying *Jesus Wept,* Don Pell in *Jacob's Ladder,* and Jared Carter back in the pilot's chair of *Exodus.*

The communications platform they orbited near was automated, but regularly visited for service by the Fellowship. It carried a quarter of the Fellowship's contracted broadcast signals. With Micah directing, Don docked his shuttle with the platform, engaging the hatch locks. When anchored they began to push, moving the platform toward Earth. Computers on the station struggled to keep signal locks, but the station was designed to be stationary, and soon all signals were lost, knocking out network, cable satellite television, and long-distance telephone service from widespread parts of the world.

Following Don and the platform to the edges of Earth's atmosphere, Micah waited until Don released from the platform, then flew ahead, finding the next target, a U.S. military satellite. There was no docking ring in the satellite, it having been orbited by rocket, but Micah didn't need to dock to disable it. Angling his sphere for a near miss, he sheared off one solar panel, and sent the satellite into a spin. Turning, he could see spurts of gas as the satellite tried to stabilize itself. Making another pass, he took off the remaining solar panel, the satellite once again tumbling, its dish receiver bent and useless.

With *Exodus* following at a safe distance they worked their way around the Earth, selectively destroying every intelligence and communications satellite and station in orbit, except one—the original satellite orbited by the Fellowship. Military and civilian communications networks were systematically shredded, ground stations rerouting repeatedly, until the limited land lines were overloaded. They hesitated when they reached the international space station Freedom, but the abandoned station could be easily reoccupied and refitted, so they pushed it Earthward. There were almost three hundred satellites in orbit, Micah and the others ignoring weather and research satellites. Finally, they had disabled or destroyed all the pretargeted satellites, leaving only one of the Fellowship's orbital platforms. Now *Jacob's Ladder* docked with the last platform and began to push it, not toward the Earth, but along its orbital path toward New Hope station.

CHAPTER 134 **COLLISION**

> The third and best known of the Newtonian laws of motion states, simply, that for every action there is an equal and opposite reaction.
>
> — *WE REACH THE MOON,* JOHN N. WILFORD

EARTH'S ORBIT

Kent Thorpe was frustrated. New Hope station was captured because of his genius, but Ira Breitling had gotten away. Now Thorpe was stuck in the sphere, unable to pursue Breitling and reduced to a spectator while others examined the secrets of the station and captured ships.

Along with the Fellowship space station they had captured one of every kind of Fellowship craft. The Ark-class ship *Prophet* was the big prize, which came with two spheres and a shuttle. They also had *Genesis,* a deep-space cruiser, and one of the newest Fellowship shuttles, *Mary's Gift.* Communications from the action on the ground was confused, but as far as Thorpe could tell they had captured at least one more shuttle and another sphere.

Waiting for orders to take *Atlantis* to Earth, Thorpe could only listen passively to the calls over the radio and watch his monitors. His part of the operation was over. The station was in sections now, but they had troops in both sections. Once the damage to the connecting locks was repaired, the sections could be joined again. Perhaps, Thorpe thought, using Fellowship spacecraft, the segments pushed out of the middle of the station could be recovered.

As Thorpe monitored the transmissions between troop commanders, someone suddenly broke in, ordering radio silence. Then the troops were ordered to evacuate both segments of New Hope station, and get to the captured ships.

"What's happening?" Thorpe demanded. "Why are they abandoning the space station?"

"Houston has picked up something on radar. Something big and it's coming toward us."

"Us?" Thorpe said. "You mean the station?"

Thorpe typed instructions into his computer, calling up an echo of *Atlantis*'s radar. Now he could see the object Houston had spotted. It was in the same orbit as New Hope station and it was closing fast.

"Mr. Thorpe," the commander of *Atlantis* cut in. "We've been ordered to intercept the object."

"We have no weapon," Thorpe protested.

"Mr. Thorpe, move *Atlantis* to intercept, or be arrested when we land!"

Thorpe was insulted by the commander's tone, but he complied, making a mental note to mention the commander's insolence to Fry.

Reluctantly, Thorpe adjusted the fields around *Atlantis*, moving toward the onrushing object, the radar illumination indicating it was a quarter the size of New Hope. The object was accelerating, and *Atlantis*'s speed quickly cut the distance between them. It appeared on the monitor, three modules joined together, rows of antennae on the Earth side of the mini-station. Docked to the station was a shuttle and a sphere flew nearby. The intent was clear, they were going to ram New Hope station.

"There's another docking ring on the top of that communications platform," the captain said. "Dock with it and stop them from ramming New Hope."

"Yes, sir," Thorpe replied sarcastically, knowing it was useless. The sphere moving *Atlantis* didn't have the power of the shuttle moving the station. Turning, he brought the shuttle up behind the still accelerating platform. As he expected, the sphere changed course, putting itself between *Atlantis* and the communications platform.

Now chasing the platform, Thorpe could see New Hope ahead of them—collision was inevitable. Thorpe continued trying to catch the platform, but the sphere kept interfering until New Hope loomed dangerously close. Then the Fellowship shuttle dropped away from the communications platform, letting it coast the rest of the way. Not waiting for orders, Thorpe adjusted his gravity fields, and *Atlantis* veered off. As Thorpe flew *Atlantis* to a safe distance, he watched the pending collision with sick fascination.

The ship *Prophet* was free of the station and pulling away, as was *Genesis*, but the shuttle *Mary's Gift* had been docked at the end of the station where the communications platform was aimed, and was now caught between the platform and the station. The radio traffic was intense, orders shouted back and forth, men near panic.

The platform collided with *Mary's Gift,* driving it into the New Hope segment it had just separated from. In a classic example of Newton's laws, the shuttle was driven into New Hope, the platform wall crumpling, the hull of the *Mary's Gift* ruptured. The force of the collision put the New Hope segment into motion, sending it into its other segment, which still contained some of the men who had captured it. The collision ruptured joints and modules. Atmosphere exploded from the station in a spray of ice particles, spreading in every direction. Glinting in the sunlight, the escaping atmosphere turned space into a kaleidoscope of twinkling lights.

The speed of the communications platform more than made up for its lack of mass, and the chain reaction the collision created tore the station segments apart, modules separating, connecting tunnels twisting and coming apart from torque far beyond design specifications. Silently, in slow motion, the station tore itself to pieces, the state-of-the-art space station soon nothing more than tons of space junk. Mixed among the wreckage were the bodies of men, women, and children.

CHAPTER 135   **ASTEROID BOMBS**

Science magazine reported in July that Asteroid 1986DA, orbiting the sun, might just be composed of 10,000 tons of gold and 100,000 tons of platinum. The asteroid is about a mile wide and shaped like a canned ham. If the suspicion is true, the asteroid is worth $1.12 trillion.

— *THE OREGONIAN*

ASTEROID BELT

Micah flew the sphere *Jesus Wept* through the asteroid belt, taking direction from Don Pell in the *Exodus*. Carefully, the men on *Exodus* vectored Micah toward the target asteroid. Micah slowed, approaching carefully, the oblong asteroid rotating slowly. Matching the speed and rotation of the asteroid, Micah crept up to the space rock, until the lights of the *Jesus Wept* illuminated the surface.

The surface was flecked with crystals and twinkled under the bright lights of the *Jesus Wept*. Flying the sphere along the asteroid, Micah searched the surface for the drive they had attached to the asteroid over a year ago. Finally, he found the malfunctioning drive bolted into a crevice. Maneuvering over the unit, he paused the *Jesus Wept*, then extended the manipulator arm holding a particle gun. Having performed this operation a dozen times in the last few days, Micah expertly inserted the gun into the fitting of the drive, a green light and a chime indicating connection. Then Micah injected particles, hoping to activate the drive.

"That did it," Don Pell said over the radio. "The computer is shaping the field."

Acknowledging Pell, Micah removed the particle gun from the fitting, then backed the *Jesus Wept* away from the asteroid, letting Don and Jared finish running a diagnostic on the drive from *Exodus*.

"We're sending it now," Don said.

Of the hundred asteroids they had prepared for this day, nearly two dozen had failed to respond to remote commands. Of those malfunctioning units, they had managed to activate a dozen drives manually. They had destroyed the drives they could not repair lest the enemy find them someday. Now, with the last asteroid on its way toward Earth, Micah could think again of Mark.

Micah flew his sphere to the *Exodus* and docked. Then they set course for Earth, passing the still accelerating asteroid a few minutes later.

CHAPTER 136 **ECOTERRORIST**

> Until the masses overcome their addiction to
> materialism, someone must be the champion for
> our animal brothers and sisters.
>
> —PERSONAL DIARY, TOBIAS STOOP

PLANET AMERICA

So far Tobias had been little more than a nuisance to the Fellowship colony on planet America. Stealing food and sabotaging equipment, he had forced the Fellowship into posting guards and diverting precious resources to repair and replacement. However, for the most part, their rape of the planet continued unabated, frustrating Tobias. He needed to be more than a pinprick, he needed to wound them deeply.

He knew the terrain around the Fellowship colonies now, the gullies, ravines, and caves. He had created a cozy home for himself in one of the caves, furnished with stolen items. He had also experimented with local vegetation, discovering that some were edible. The price of that knowledge was severe stomach cramps and diarrhea. He knew how to prepare and preserve the fruits and roots of a half-dozen local plants and had a quantity hidden away in his cave. Most of his food supply was still stolen from Fellowship fields and storehouses, but within a year he expected to be self-sufficient. Hidden in his cave, Tobias had survived the winter on planet America, and had confidence that he could survive indefinitely on his own.

He was ready now for more drastic action—fire would be his weapon. The Fellowship structures were either log or wood-frame construction—vulnerable to fire. There was some risk to the environment, but stopping the Fellowship would more than compensate.

He'd left his cave the day before, traveling through the forest, avoiding the crude Fellowship roads. He spent the night in a tree, tied to the trunk so that he wouldn't fall out when he dozed off. Just after dawn, when the nocturnal carnivores had returned to their lairs, he climbed down and continued toward his target, an established farm. He had scouted the farm before. There were six buildings, three loaded with hay and animals brought from Earth, the other buildings living quarters. He would burn the barns and the dormitories tonight.

Reaching the farm, he found a place to hide, and settled in to watch the comings and goings until dark. Soon he realized that something was different. He'd scouted the farm many times, even stolen from the kitchen, so he knew it was normally a busy place. Now, however, the farm was quiet. There were no animals in the pens; no workers weeded the garden or chopped wood. No children played in the yard; no one carried garbage from the kitchen to the burn barrels. Most telling of all was that there were no dogs. He'd hidden near farms before, and dogs always found him but paid little attention, since they were community dogs, attached to any and all humans.

Curious now, Tobias crept through the fields, pausing every few yards to study the buildings, half expecting a trap. Close now, he could see the garden was overgrown with weeds and that part of the fence had been knocked over. Farmers would repair a fence immediately to protect their crop. Creeping to the edge of the garden, Tobias paused. Animals had been eating in the garden, the crop destroyed before it had a chance to mature.

Tobias studied the windows in the dormitory—no movement. Stealthily, he crept up to the nearest and peeked inside—no signs of life. With the same stealth, he checked each of the other two living quarters, finding nothing.

Now throwing caution to the wind, he entered the buildings one by one, finding no one, nor any personal belongings. There was no equipment in the barn, no tools in the sheds, no ax by the woodpile. The farm had been abandoned. Puzzled, Tobias walked through the empty buildings, seeing that every tool and piece of equipment had been removed. Even the toilets were gone. Puzzled, but pleased, Tobias gathered kindling and built fires in each of the buildings. This farm would never be reoccupied.

When each building was in flames he hurried back to his hiding place, watching the fire reclaim the land for the planet. Dusk came, and the flames still licked the darkening sky. He hoped the flames would last. Night fires were beautiful. As he watched, he heard a snuffling sound behind him. Tobias turned slowly. An animal the size of a badger stared at him from the top of a boulder, sniffing the air. The furry animal was a dusky gray, with faint white stripes. Its head was triangle-shaped, the eyes dark marbles. The back legs were longer than the front, and well muscled. Tobias guessed it could jump like a kangaroo. Tobias had never seen the animal before, but its coat was loose as if it had been hibernating and hadn't eaten in months.

Tobias heard movement behind him and he turned to see two more of the animals come around a tree, both smaller than the first. These too snuffled, perhaps smelling a human for the first time. Tobias looked back to the first animal, to see it had come off the rock and was now twenty feet away. Suddenly the animal hissed, baring a large set of fangs. Tobias had been to this farm many times before but never seen these animals. Too late, he understood the dogs were keeping the predators away.

The largest animal lunged as Tobias turned to flee. Needle-sharp teeth buried into the back of his leg, Tobias collapsing. Then the animal began shaking his head violently, tearing out a chunk of muscle from Tobias's calf. Tobias screamed as a second animal hit his other calf, shredding it as well. Pounding at the animals ripping at his legs, a third hit his shoulder, biting clear to the collar bone, snapping it. His legs useless, one arm crippled, he flailed at the beasts as they tore away chunks of his flesh. Tobias fainted briefly, then woke when his stomach was torn open and his intestines pulled from his body. Pain too intense to be comprehended wracked his body. Tobias lived a few minutes longer as his body became part of the food chain of the planet.

Men copied the realities of their hearts when they
built prisons.

— *THE OUTSIDER,* RICHARD WRIGHT

UNKNOWN LOCATION

There was no way for Mark to tell time in his cell. The
banks of neon lights were always on, the tiny room bright
as an operating theater twenty-four hours a day. They
took his watch when they took his clothes. Food was
shoved through a slot in his door but came at irregular in-
tervals. With no other cues he counted the days with his
sleep cycle. By his reckoning it had been forty-three days
since his capture. He wore blue hospital pajamas and
slept on a mattress on the floor. There was a steel toilet
and sink, but no toilet paper or towels. No charges had
been filed against him, no phone calls allowed, no questions asked. The rule of law no longer applied to him.

He had begged for a Bible until he realized it gave
them pleasure to deny him. Now he spent his days reciting Scripture from memory, meditating, and in prayer. He
had trouble clearing his mind, his thoughts drifting back
to the carnage he had witnessed. Many of his people had
died, including Floyd, who had been with him nearly as
long as Ira. Even worse than the memories of the slaugh-
ter was ignorance. Who had lived and who had died?
What had happened to his people? How many had escaped? But the question that ate away at his soul was
what was Christy's role in his betrayal? He had come
down from New Hope at her request and while he tried to
convince himself that she had been duped, he couldn't
shake his doubts about her.

Mark was praying when he heard footsteps in the
corridor—many footsteps. This was new. The footsteps

ended outside his door. The lock was turned, the door opened. Four uniformed men came in, cuffing him, leading him to the door of his cell without saying a word. Mark had been blindfolded when brought to his cell, so he had never seen the corridors.

With a hard shove he was pushed through the door, flanked by two armed men, the other two behind. The guards wore army fatigues but without insignia. There were other cells along the corridor, but all the doors were closed and there were no windows. Following the guards up the stairs at the end of the corridor, they climbed three flights, then walked down a long corridor. Guards were posted at intersections. Finally, they left the building to a courtyard. It was dusk, the sun just below the horizon, and in the dim light Mark could see one of the Fellowship's shuttles. Surprised, he stopped, hoping briefly it was a rescue. A shove from behind dashed his hopes. He was devastated—he had failed God.

The magnitude of his failure sapped his will to live and he shuffled now, plodding along only to avoid the painful prods from behind. They crossed the courtyard to another building. Finally, the guards pushed him down onto a chair. Then the guards left him alone. Like his cell, the room was bare except for a mirror that covered most of one wall—someone was watching. Now the door opened. It was Christy. She was smiling.

"How are you, Mark?" Christy asked.

"Did you betray me?" Mark blurted. "Did you set me up?"

"How could you think that?"

"You set up the meeting with Roland Symes."

"I didn't tell anyone about the meeting, please believe me."

"How many died?" Mark asked, ignoring her plea.

Averting her eyes Christy said, "I'm not supposed to talk about it."

"Floyd's dead, isn't he?"

"I had to agree to certain restrictions or they wouldn't let me see you."

"They have a shuttle, what else did they get?"

"I can't."

"Then what did you come for?"

"To see you. To know you were still alive."

He could see she still cared, but now he found he was uncertain. She had never been part of the Fellowship, at least not by belief. Perhaps he was meant to live life alone and by getting involved with Christy he had angered God.

"Did any of them get away?"

"If I violate the agreement I'll never get to come back."

Now they were both silent, Christy near tears, Mark withdrawn.

"Mark, they want to negotiate with you. They don't want anyone else to get hurt."

"After what they've done, how can you work for them?"

"I don't work for them—"

"They're manipulating you, Christy."

"It's what I do," she snapped. "I mediate. I try to find win-win solutions."

"Christy, sometimes there is no middle ground. Sometimes it is a matter of right and wrong and one side has to win and the other lose."

"I don't believe that. They're going to planet America, Mark. They're going to take control of the colony."

Now Mark understood how great his defeat had been. The world had the Fellowship's technology and enough ships to transport an invasion force.

"President Crow has assured me that your people can stay on America, Mark. They only want to establish a government presence so the planet can be opened up for other colonists."

"Will more of our people be allowed to emigrate to the planet?"

Now Christy looked uncomfortable.

"After diversity goals have been met, it may be possible." Hurrying on she added, "It's a chance to avoid more bloodshed, Mark. We can negotiate a better deal later."

"Later? When they control our technology?"

"They're afraid of you, Mark. You made a giant leap in technology and refused to share it. It put them in an inferior position. They weren't used to that, weren't prepared for it. Soon they'll feel like equals again and they won't fear you anymore. That's when we can get concessions."

"If they have the technology, what do they need me for?"

"They want you to go with them to America, to get your people to surrender. Micah and Ira will listen to you."

Micah and Ira were alive. The cause was not lost. He would not be a part of the final victory, but the war wasn't over.

"You can't negotiate with Satan, Christy. There is no middle ground between good and evil. They murdered our people and I won't help them kill any more."

"Thinking like that won't help us reach a solution," Christy said. Then more softly she added, "If you help them we can be together."

Taking her hand he said, "We were never meant to be together, Christy. I can see that now."

It hurt to say that, the pain in her eyes as great as his. Standing, he walked to the mirror, turning his back on Christy and confronting the world behind the mirror.

" 'You looked, O king, and there before you stood a large statue—an enormous, dazzling statue, awesome in appearance. The head of the statue was made of pure gold, its chest and arms of silver, its belly and thighs of bronze, its legs of iron, its feet partly of iron and partly of baked clay.' "

"What's he talking about?" a voice asked over a speaker.

"It's Scripture," Christy said. "It's from the book of Daniel. Mark, talk to me," she pleaded.

" 'While you were watching, a rock was cut out, but not by human hands. It struck the statue on its feet of iron and clay and smashed them. Then the iron, the clay, the bronze, the silver, and the gold were broken to pieces at the same time and became like chaff on the threshing floor in the summer.' "

"If he continues this rambling we'll have him returned to his cell," the voice threatened.

"Mark, please. Look at me. No one else has to be hurt. If you help them they'll let you move to planet America to be with your people."

" 'The wind swept them away without leaving a trace. But the rock that struck the statue became a huge mountain and filled the whole earth.' "

"Take him back to his cell!" the voice ordered.

"Mark, please," Christy begged.

Mark was dragged out by the guards and he left without looking at Christy. When they crossed the open space between the wings of the prison he fell to his knees so that the guards would have to stop and he could take a quick look up at the sky. Somewhere out there between Mars and Jupiter were the rocks, coming to smash those feet and topple the giant. A painful jab with a rifle butt and he was moving again, now whispering praise for his God.

CHAPTER 138   **POINTS OF LIGHT**

One day, 65 million years ago, a large asteroid
perhaps 10 km across may have collided with the
Earth. Luis and Walter Alvarez and their colleagues believe the effects of such an impact . . .
could have caused the extinction of numerous
life forms (including the dinosaurs) at the end of
the Cretaceous period.

— *THE NEW SOLAR SYSTEM,*
J. KELLY BEATTY, BRIAN O'LEARY
AND ANDREW CHAIKIN (EDS.)

WASHINGTON, D.C.

Kent Thorpe paced nervously outside the Oval Office. Crow had demanded to see Thorpe after his new lab had been destroyed. Thorpe had blamed the destruction of his original lab on the lack of proper security. Fry and Crow had argued violently then, each blaming the other, but thankfully, ignoring Thorpe. The loss of his notes and data had been a setback, but the capture of several Fellowship spacecraft meant they could afford to dissect a drive. So a second lab had been equipped for Thorpe and he was given a sphere. Now that lab was gone and the Fellowship sphere destroyed.

Rachel Waters came out of the Oval Office, smiling coolly, motioning Thorpe in, then closing the door behind him. President Crow was seated behind his mahogany desk, black eyes flashing with anger. Fry sat to the side, smiling smugly. No one asked Thorpe to sit down.

"Explain what happened," Crow said simply, his voice soft and deep.

"I didn't have time to analyze the . . . the wreckage."

"Tell me!" Crow demanded angrily.

"X rays, magnetic resonance, high frequency sound waves—we used every means possible to look inside that drive—it appeared hollow. So we started drilling. It happened just as we penetrated to the core of the drive. The explosion pulverized foot-thick concrete walls. There's a crater six feet deep where my lab used to be."

"Why aren't you dead?" Crow asked coolly.

"I was monitoring the procedure remotely," Thorpe said nervously.

Fry laughed. Thorpe's failure with the drive empowered Fry, since he had been opposed to opening it. Thorpe feared Crow and Fry equally, but until now Crow had supported his approach to analyzing the Fellowship's technology.

"I should have opened the drive in a vacuum instead of a nitrogen environment," Thorpe explained. "I know I can do it successfully next time."

"Next time you'll be standing by the drive when you open it," Crow said. "That should ensure your best effort."

Thorpe swallowed hard, knowing Crow meant what he said.

"We can't afford a next time," Fry said. "We need every ship we have to get us to planet America. That's where they moved their orbital manufacturing facilities. If we can capture that—"

"You failed here, what makes you think you can succeed there?"

"If we don't succeed, then I'll agree to let Thorpe blow up another lab. If we do capture the right facilities we'll be building our own drives."

Crow was considering that when Rachel returned.

"Simon Ash is here to see you with Archie Cox. They say it's urgent."

Thorpe welcomed the interruption—blending into the background.

Ash was white-faced and perspiring, Cox grim but with an air of self-importance.

"Well?" Crow demanded when they stood before his desk.

"Dr. Cox has brought news of an important discovery," Ash said.

"What is it?" Crow asked impatiently.

Cox opened the envelope he was carrying and withdrew several pictures. The photos were of bright dots against a black background.

"Before they left the solar system, the Fellowship stopped in the asteroid belt and moved some of the asteroids out of their orbits," Cox said.

Risking notice, Thorpe walked closer to the desk. Cox was pointing out clusters of bright dots.

"These are coming toward us?" Crow asked.

"They are moving to where Earth will be in its orbit six months from now. It's difficult to judge speed and trajectory, but computer projections show an eighty-seven percent probability of encountering some of the asteroids."

"So what?" Fry said, thumping the center photo with his finger. "Won't they just burn up in the atmosphere?"

"No, they won't. What we call falling stars are created by meteors the size of a marble. Meteors one kilogram in size—about two pounds—can actually survive to reach the surface of the Earth. It depends on iron content and—"

"Get to it, Cox," Crow snapped, cutting him off.

"The asteroids the Fellowship sent our way are much bigger than two pounds. Meteorites of up to sixty tons have been found intact on the surface. Hundred-ton meteorites will create craters, larger meteorites explode."

"Explode?" Fry said. "I thought you said they were made of iron? You can't get an explosive reaction from iron."

"Remember what they did to their compound near Christ's Home. When a moving object meets a stationary one, the velocity of the moving object is reduced to zero. The kinetic energy of the movement has to be released—usually as heat. A meteorite moving at a velocity of five kilometers per second relative to Earth—about ten thousand miles per hour—would have enough kinetic energy to make the mass as explosive as an equivalent amount of TNT. Move the mass faster than five kilometers per second and the kinetic energy increases exponentially. A tenfold acceleration gets you one hundred times the explosive potential."

"How big are these asteroids?" Fry asked, now concerned.

"Some are hundreds of tons; some are thousands of tons."

"They're going to bomb us," Fry said. "But we have six months to prepare. We'll have strategic facilities dispersed and in hardened sites by then."

"This isn't going to be like a cruise missile attack," Cox said. "There won't be pinpoint accuracy, but it won't matter. An asteroid detonated in the atmosphere near the Tunguska River in Siberia in 1908 destroyed several square miles of forest. The Wolf Creek Crater in Australia is half a mile wide. There's a two-hundred-mile-wide crater in the Czech Republic. If they impact in our oceans phenomenal tidal waves will be created. You should know that asteroid impacts have been linked to mass extinctions. An asteroid impact in the Yucatán peninsula sixty-five million years ago is widely believed to have wiped out the dinosaurs."

Fry was shaken by what he heard, but Crow looked calm, even happy.

"How many impacts will there be?" Crow asked.

"At least fifty asteroids are on the way."

"Any way to stop this?"

"Use the ships you've captured to deflect the asteroids," Cox said.

"We need those ships to capture planet America," Fry said.

"If you act soon, even a slight nudge will be enough for the asteroids to miss the Earth," Cox explained. "Each day you delay, it takes more time and more energy to alter the trajectory sufficiently to avoid Earth's orbit."

"Each day we delay means another day for that cult to prepare to defend their colony," Fry said.

Crow wasn't listening, he had already made up his mind.

"Fry, you take the bulk of the ships to planet America and bring back Ira Breitling and any other technicians on that planet. Do what you want with the rest of the cultists, just make sure they're never a threat again. Cox, I'll give you one of our captured shuttles and a sphere to deflect those asteroids."

"Two ships? That's not enough," Cox blurted. "And what about the Mars colony?"

"Deal with the asteroids first," Crow said.

Initially surprised that the president would allocate few resources to protecting the planet, Thorpe then understood. Crow wanted the asteroids to reach Earth.

"Deflect the biggest ones first," Crow said, as if it explained his decision.

Now Crow turned to Rachel who was by his side, waiting for orders.

"I want to see Shepherd," he said to her.

"I'll take care of it."

As Thorpe left with the others, he began making plans to survive what was coming. With only two ships, Cox had little chance of deflecting more than a handful of asteroids. In six months the Earth was in for a pounding unlike anything in human history.

CHAPTER 139

SHELLY'S CHOICE

> [To] blot out of every law book in the land, to
> sweep out of every dusty courtroom, to erase
> from every judge's mind that centuries-old prec-
> edent as to women's inferiority and dependence
> and need for protection; to substitute for it at
> one blow the simple new precedent of equality,
> that is a fight worth making if it takes ten years.
>
> — *THE NATION*, CRYSTAL EASTMAN, 1924

DEEP SPACE

Deep in unexplored space, Shelly set a cup of steaming tea in front of Ira, who was asleep, head resting on his folded arms. The computer terminal next to him dis-played his latest calculation of *Covenant*'s position—it confirmed what Shelly already knew.

"Ira, wake up. I brought you some tea."

Shelly would have brought food too, but Ira stopped eating days ago when he first understood their dire cir-cumstances.

"Thanks," Ira mumbled as he roused, his one good eye a web of red veins.

"You've confirmed our location?" Shelly asked.

"Yes. I prayed I was wrong, but I keep coming up with the same answer."

It took three months to finally shut down *Covenant*'s drive, and slow the ship to sublight speed. The damage to the control systems had been extensive, the drive running on full power with no way to control it. Before finally shut-ting the drive down, they had reached a speed unimagined even by Ira, traveling blindly into the void. Now *Covenant* was so distant from Earth, the constellations were too dis-torted for the navigation computer to identify them. Ira had resorted to triangulating their position using pulsars. The

unique signatures of the collapsed stars could be distinguished regardless of distance, although detecting them
was much more difficult than for normal stars. It took Ira a
week to identify three of them. During that time, Shelly directed repairs and inventoried their provisions. One thing
was obvious from the beginning of inventory, there were
too many survivors for the few supplies.

Ira was fully awake now, and sipped his tea, occasionally
rubbing his bad eye. Finally he was ready to face the truth.

"We're in a bad situation, Shelly," Ira said.

"I know."

"We've got 1600 people on board, but can't support
but half that number."

"Perhaps a few more than half," Shelly said.

"The drive core is eroded below specifications so I
don't know how long it will last, and we're so far from the
new planet that even if we push the drive to 110 percent
of design power, it will take us eight months to get there.
We can't risk more or the drive will surely fail and we
could end up marooned in space." Rubbing under his eye
patch Ira continued. "Even if we hold the power at 110
percent everyone will be dead when we arrive."

"It's true, we can't all make it," Shelly said.

A sip of his tea, then, "I don't know what to do."

"Yes you do," Shelly said. "There are nearly eight hundred children on board. They have to come first."

Ira's eyelids drooped, his head nodded, then he shook
his head violently.

"I can't make that decision," Ira said. "I need Mark,
Shelly. God gave him the gift of leadership."

"The adults are gathering in the lower hold now, Ira,"
Shelly said. "The older children will care for the younger
ones."

"No, Shelly. There must be another way."

Reaching for Shelly, Ira lost his balance, nearly falling
from his chair. Shelly helped Ira back into his seat. Ira
swayed and Shelly steadied him with a hand on his shoulder. Then Ira looked into his cup.

"You put something in my tea," he said, his words slur-
ring. "You had no right to make the decision."

"Someone had to," Shelly said, tears welling. "I knew you couldn't do it."

Ira was sagging now, unable to keep himself upright. Shelly helped him out of the chair and let him slide gently to the deck.

"It's the only way, Ira," Shelly said. "We would be killing each other over crumbs in a few months. Choices had to be made."

A thumping sound reverberated through the ship as the air was pumped from the lower hold where the adults huddled together, praying for God to take them quickly.

"No, Shelly," Ira said, then he lost his fight with consciousness, his eye slowly closing.

"It was the only way," Shelly said.

Holding Ira's head in her lap, Shelly listened to the pumps and cried, tears dripping on Ira's still form.

CHAPTER 140   **STALKING RACHEL**

> When Jesus got out of the boat, a man with an
> evil spirit came from the tombs to meet him.
> This man lived in the tombs, and no one could
> bind him any more, not even with a chain. For
> he had often been chained hand and foot, but he
> tore the chains apart and broke the irons on his
> feet. No one was strong enough to subdue him.
>
> —MARK 5:2–4

WASHINGTON, D.C.

Just after midnight, Rachel Waters left the White House in her black Lexus. Proctor knew she seldom used the government limousines and drivers. Most cabinet-level officials feared for their lives, but Proctor knew Rachel had no fear of death because he knew what she was.

He followed her at a distance. Normally, he would keep two or three cars between himself and the person he was tailing, but at this time of night there were few cars on the road. Taking her usual route toward her home in Georgetown, Proctor felt comfortable hanging back, knowing where she was going and where he would confront her. Unexpectedly, she took a different exit and Proctor had to race the Ford up the ramp to make sure he saw which way she turned. Her Lexus was sitting at the top waiting for him. Closing his eyes he could see her face in her rearview mirror, eyes glowing red. The demon wanted him to follow. Proctor stared back, whispering a prayer for courage. Then Rachel Waters turned, driving slowly, making sure Proctor was right behind.

CHAPTER 141 **INVESTIGATIVE REPORTER**

> Roland Symes is the best investigative reporter
> I've ever worked with. Getting the story is the
> only thing that matters to Symes, and woe to the
> person who gets between him and his story.
>
> —GRAYSON GOLDWYN,
> EDITOR OF THE *SAN FRANCISCO JOURNAL*

Roland Symes paused at the top of the freeway exit, looking for Proctor's car. He had spotted Proctor parked near the White House and watched him, seeing his interest in Rachel Waters. When Proctor followed Rachel Waters, Roland had followed him. Something was up.

Proctor was alone, and that seemed wrong to Roland.

If Proctor was going to kill or kidnap Rachel Waters he would have brought some of his men. And why go after the president's chief of staff? Why not the president? It wasn't like Proctor to play the Lone Ranger. In his long career selling weapons and promoting violence, he always kept in the background, letting his gullible followers take the fall for most of his crimes.

On the passenger seat rested Roland's cell phone and gun. Roland hesitated, wondering if it was time to call the police. So far he had an exclusive—once the cops were notified, the story would be out. He had no intention of letting that madman Proctor harm Ms. Waters, but there hadn't been any real danger to her yet. At least until he lost them.

Angry with himself, Roland guessed. Turning right he sped down the winding road. A mile later he spotted car lights ahead. They looked like Proctor's, so he turned off his lights and slowed.

Touching his cell phone, and then the gun, he hesitated again, promising himself that he would call the police just as soon as he found out what was going on.

CHAPTER 142

PROCTOR AND THE DEMON

> Then Jesus asked him, "What is your name?"
> "My name is Legion," he replied,
> "for we are many."
>
> —MARK 5:9

WASHINGTON, D.C.

Proctor didn't bother to hide from the demon, letting her lead him to some unknown destination. They drove through congested Georgetown to a new development, most of the land still covered by trees and brush. Waters parked by an empty lot, then got out and walked slowly through the brush. Dressed for work, she wore a gray skirt and jacket over a white blouse.

Proctor drove past, turned, and parked facing the opposite direction. Proctor studied the surroundings, looking for a trap. He doubted there was one. The demon wanted a confrontation. He wanted it too.

Proctor got out. It was overcast, early fall, the air cool, the ground still wet with that afternoon's rain. With his eyes closed, Proctor watched the demon moving through the field. A human would have stumbled through the brush in that darkness, but the demon moved comfortably, stepping over obstacles. Proctor followed as easily, eyes closed, seeing not only the obstacles but the glowing footprints left by the demon. She waited for him in a small clearing, hands on her hips, a smile on her face.

"I've been looking forward to this," the demon said, with a voice he hadn't heard before. It was still feminine, but it cut through him like a cleaver.

"Where is Mark Shepherd?" Proctor asked.

"Is that why you came here tonight?"

The government claimed that Mark had died in the

"police action" at the Fellowship's Mexican compound. Proctor knew better.

"Mark Shepherd is dead," the demon said, chuckling.

Proctor didn't believe the creature.

"Then where is his body?" Proctor said.

"Want to preserve it for the resurrection? Don't bother. Judgment day is coming, but it won't be your God who does the judging."

"Will you be the judge?"

"You flatter me."

Her eyes still glowed red, but now Proctor could see her whole body shone as with an inner light.

"Tell me where Mark Shepherd is," he said again.

She laughed, a hideous sound, now only faintly human.

Proctor took off his coat, pulling two knives from his belt. The blade of one was etched with a cross, the other with the symbol of the fish.

At the sight of the knives the demon laughed again, then she took off her own jacket, beckoning Proctor forward.

"Foolish man," she chuckled.

Cautiously, Proctor stepped toward the demon.

"What is your name, demon?" Proctor asked, inching forward.

"Call me Unis, for I am one," the demon said, laughing again.

Then, with a sudden leap she was in front of him, each of his wrists held tightly. She moved faster than humanly possible and now her face was inches from his. With his eyes open he saw the beautiful Rachel Waters, with his eyes closed he saw the glow of the demon within her. Proctor struggled with all his might, but couldn't free himself from the beast's grasp. Then she threw him aside, laughing as he tumbled into the brush. He lost one of the knives when he braced himself to absorb the fall, but came up quickly, rushing her. She knocked him aside with a powerful blow, but he managed to rake her side with his remaining knife. Quickly blood soaked her white blouse and she looked at the wound.

"Do you know how much I paid for this?" the demon asked, laughing uproariously.

The demon's voice had power and if he heard it much

more it would drive him insane. Again he charged, lunging for her belly. Deftly she dodged the blow, grabbing his knife arm and swinging him around. Holding his wrist, she tore the knife from his grip. Then pinning him with an arm across his chest, she held the knife high, ready to plunge it into his throat.

"That would be too quick," she said, then slashed him across the cheek and threw him aside. Gasping from the pain, he felt the wound. A deep cut ran from the corner of his mouth to his ear.

"Nice edge," she said. "Did you sharpen it yourself?" Running a thumb lightly over the blade it came away bleeding. "You could skin someone with a blade this sharp," she said. Then smiling, "Now there's a thought."

Lying on his back, hand pressed to his face to stop the bleeding, Proctor saw the demon step toward him. He didn't need to close his eyes now to see there was little human left. The shell that was Rachel Waters was dissolving, the form of the demon emerging—a hideous horned beast. Proctor crawled away, the demon coming slowly, feeding on Proctor's fear.

"God protect me," Proctor whispered. "I have failed you."

With that prayer he understood why the demon was winning. Proctor had made the mistake so many of God's servants had through the centuries. He had begun to attribute his successes to himself. He wasn't a remarkable man; he did remarkable things only when he let God work through him. He was only the vessel through which God's power flowed. Even as the demon picked him up with one hand, he prayed to God to forgive him for his conceit and then submitted to God's will, even if that will was for him to die. As he was lifted off the ground he felt the Holy Spirit fill him. His body trembled, sweat trickled down his back, and his flesh was covered with goose bumps. He had no control of his body now, but through his closed eyes he saw his hand snap up, reaching out just as the demon brought the knife toward his other cheek. With an unearthly strength, he stopped the demon's blow, her wrist gripped tightly in his hand. Now Proctor could see his own flesh glowing. Praying that God would forgive him a brief moment of pride, he looked the Rachel demon in the face and smiled.

With a screech that would terrify the dead—probably had terrified the dead—Proctor was thrown aside, tumbling across the ground. With no conscious thought, he came up into a crouch. Just in front of him he saw the other knife in the grass. Proctor picked it up, the knife glowing with the same light that now surrounded Proctor. Now they were equally armed, he with the knife etched with the cross, the demon with the fish blade.

Using the knife, the demon cut through the waist of Rachel's skirt, slitting it down to her crotch, then stepped out of it, kicking it aside. Now she crouched, jockeying for position, feigning attacks. A spiritual force had taken control of Proctor and he found he could match the demon's moves. With another screech, the demon in Rachel's body lunged, swiping at his chest.

Proctor jumped back to avoid the blow, slicing her across the forearm. Oblivious to the pain, she lunged again, her arm passing under his armpit, just missing his chest. He trapped her arm under his, burying his knife in her side. Rachel the human should have been finished, but the Rachel-demon twisted, the knife still buried in her, almost wrenching it from Proctor's hand. Concentrating on keeping his knife, Proctor relaxed his other arm and the demon jerked her arm free, the knife cutting nearly to his ribs.

Proctor jerked the knife from Rachel's side, blood flowing freely, streaming down her bare legs. It was a bleeding contest now, and he was winning. The demon knew that and came at Proctor again.

Proctor backed away, slashing at the Rachel-thing, slicing her arm every time she lunged. Rachel was soon bleeding from another dozen cuts. Proctor moved in a circle, keeping the demon in the middle, and soon came back to where he had started. Rachel collapsed to her knees at that point, the host body drained of life-giving fluid. There was little left for the demon to animate and the demon inside screamed in defeat. Proctor advanced, ready to strike again. Slumping into a bloody heap,

Rachel Waters died, releasing the demon that had possessed her. Now it came out of her body, Proctor seeing the winged beast free of Rachel Waters. With a venomous stare it stepped toward Proctor.

"It's not over," it said in a deep rumbling voice. "We've got your God on the run and it's not over until every one of His followers is dead."

Then it spread its wings and shot into the sky, disappearing in an orange flash. When it was gone, Proctor suddenly felt very human, weak, the strength of the Spirit ebbing. He hurt now, from his wounds and from bruises and sprains. He walked to Rachel Waters. Covered in blood, her limp form lay in the grass. Proctor felt sorry for the woman, wondering if she had invited the demon into her body by word or deed. Proctor knew many who had made choices like hers, leading to eternal death. With a final prayer that God would forgive her soul, he left, his last hope gone of finding Mark dead in the clearing.

CHAPTER 143

ROLAND'S REVELATION

Now Thomas (called Didymus), one of the
Twelve, was not with the disciples when Jesus
came. So the other disciples told him, "We have
seen the Lord!" But he said to them, "Unless I
see the nail marks in his hands and put my finger where the nails were, and put my hand into
his side, I will not believe it." A week later his
disciples were in the house again, and Thomas
was with them. Though the doors were locked,
Jesus came and stood among them and said,
"Peace be with you!" Then he said to Thomas,
"Put your finger here; see my hands. Reach out
your hand and put it into my side. Stop doubting
and believe." Thomas said to him, "My Lord and
my God!" Then Jesus told him, "Because you
have seen me, you have believed; blessed are
those who have not seen and yet have believed."

—JOHN 20:23–29

WASHINGTON, D.C.

Roland remained hidden until Proctor had gone, terrified by what he had witnessed. Roland had found Proctor's and Rachel Waters's cars empty and called 911
asking for police to be sent. Then, guilt-stricken because
he had put an exclusive ahead of Ms. Waters's safety,
Roland took his gun in hand and went looking for her.
Turning into the empty lot, he had followed the sound of
voices, creeping through the brush, ready to take Proctor
by surprise. When he found them, Proctor's back was to
Roland, Rachel opposite him, hands on her hips, laughing. The laugh was like nothing Roland had ever heard.
Studying the pair closely, he realized something was
wrong—something about Rachel. She was glowing. Then

when she leapt in front of Proctor, it was with inhuman speed, and when she threw him aside Roland had frozen in shock, gun in his hand. It wasn't Rachel Waters that needed protection, it was George Proctor.

Huddling in fear, Roland witnessed the fight, saw the unearthly glow surround Rachel Waters and then George Proctor. Then, when Proctor finally killed Waters, Roland had seen the spiritual being emerge from her body, heard it threaten Proctor and those who followed God, then shoot into the sky and disappear in a flash. At that moment Roland realized he'd chosen the wrong side.

Fearful that the spirit being would return and reanimate Rachel Waters, Roland remained hidden. After several minutes, when the being didn't return, he found the courage to walk up to the body, staining his shoes and pants with blood. Ms. Waters was there, motionless, in a patch of bloody grass. Roland looked to the sky where the being had disappeared—nothing there. In the distance he could hear the sirens of a police car. He should go, he knew. Standing next to a dead body, his clothes covered with her blood, his explanation would sound psychotic. Still, he didn't move; he couldn't move. He had lived his life betting there was no life after death—no judgment to come. He'd gambled with his eternal soul and lost. Remembering his role in the capture of Mark Shepherd, Roland felt like Judas holding his pieces of silver.

When the police arrived he was still standing in Rachel's blood, nearly catatonic from guilt.

CHAPTER 144

COURSE ALTERATION

> At the end of the twentieth century there was a
> move to outlaw land mines since they were
> indiscriminate killers, taking civilians as often
> as soldiers. Of course hidden bombs are too
> effective to be given up easily.
>
> — *A HISTORY OF GOOD AND EVIL*,
> ROBERT WINSTON, PH.D.

SPACE, BETWEEN EARTH AND MARS

The captured Fellowship shuttle *Rock of Ages* had been repaired and repainted, now carrying the U.S. flag and the name "American Eagle." *American Eagle* was deep in space, between the Earth and Mars, its mission to deflect the Fellowship asteroid bombs. Archie Cox was in command of the mission, although two air force pilots actually flew the ship. They were flying parallel to one of the leading asteroids now, their lone sphere circling.

"I've found something," the sphere pilot reported. "They've attached something to the asteroid."

"Is it a docking ring?" Cox asked.

"I don't think so. You better take a look at this."

Cox watched his monitor, the camera from the sphere panning the rugged surface of the asteroid coming to a stop, focused on a man-made object.

"It looks like one of their drives," Cox said.

Cox hadn't anticipated this, assuming that the Fellowship had sent the asteroids toward Earth with a simple push, letting gravity and orbital mechanics do the rest. The presence of a drive suggested the asteroids were guided missiles, not random bombs. Either way, the asteroids had to be diverted and President Crow had given him only one shuttle and a sphere to work with.

"Ignore the unit on the asteroid for now," Cox or-

JUDGMENT DAY ✠ 663

dered. "We'll deal with it if it interferes with the course alteration."

The sphere pilot acknowledged, then maneuvered his sphere in close, finding a flat surface along the oblong rock. Spreading the metal frame attached to the sphere, he pushed up against the asteroid until it was solidly set.

"Ready here," the pilot reported. "I'm elongating the field."

The sphere's electronics were echoed in the shuttle and Cox watched the sphere's gravity fields elongate and spread around the asteroid. The fields expanded normally at first but then a bulge appeared—near the drive.

"Hold it," Cox ordered, watching the readout.

"I see it," the sphere pilot responded. "It looks like the drive attached to the asteroid just powered up. It's creating its—"

Without warning the drive on the asteroid exploded, the asteroid splitting into three large pieces and hundreds of small ones, expanding in a ball of destruction. The transmission from the sphere was lost and Cox had only a second before the fragments from the shattered asteroid reached *American Eagle*.

The shuttle's hull was pierced, the ship losing power—lights and gravity gone. Geysers of precious atmosphere shot from a dozen holes. Other fragments pounded the hull of the shuttle, knocking the crew senseless. When the bombardment ended, Cox and the crew of the *American Eagle* roused themselves, ignoring injuries, and hurried through the ship with flashlights, patching leaks. It took two hours to find and seal the last leak. Power was still out and it took another hour to get the backup batteries running. By then they were working in environment suits, the oxygen-poor air unbreathable. With the life-support system functioning again, they stripped off their suits and took stock of what was left.

The sphere didn't answer radio calls and it wasn't visible in nearby space. If they could get radar working they could search for it, but without control of their own ship they couldn't rescue the pilot even if he was alive. Cox divided the crew into teams and they traced electrical systems, jury-rigging bypasses where they couldn't repair the systems. Twelve hours later, batteries nearly exhausted, they once again had the drive generator supplying power. With full instrumentation restored, they now fully understood their situation.

Environmental systems were severely damaged, oxygen reserves nearly exhausted. The shuttle's environmental recycling system was ninety percent efficient, but required supplemental oxygen and water. Worse, the drive control systems were malfunctioning. The drive was operating, they had restored gravity in the ship, but they couldn't manipulate the gravity fields for propulsion. In other words they would float in space for a couple of months, until the shuttle's recycling system finally shut down. The only other ships capable of rescuing them were on their way to planet America. Cox and his crew wouldn't give up hope, but there was none.

The end would be ugly, Cox knew. Madness and hostility would infect the crew before the end, as they fought over rationed resources. Some might even resort to murder, to stretch dwindling supplies. There was no realistic hope. The Fellowship's booby-trap had done its work.

Staring out at the stars, he ran over the inventory of the ship in his head, particularly the pharmaceuticals. Archie Cox was planning to die in his own way, in his own time.

> When it comes to slavery there's plenty of
> shame to go around. White folks should be
> ashamed of buying African people and making
> them slaves in America. African folks should be
> ashamed of selling their own brothers and sisters
> to the white folks.
>
> —SELMA (GRANDMA) JONES

APPROACHING PLANET AMERICA

Claustrophobic, Simon Ash would never have returned to space on his own accord. Only his dependence on Crow—and his fear of him—put him back in the converted submarine *Prophet,* which had been rechristened *Voyager.* Meaghan Slater was on board too. They were to act as guides for Colonel Watson's troops, who filled the passenger deck of the huge ship. Kent Thorpe was part of the mission too. The long voyage to planet America would give him time to study the Ark-class ship and perhaps winnow out more of the Fellowship's technological secrets.

Mr. Fry was in command of *Voyager,* carrying presidential authority to confiscate all Fellowship property and occupy planet America, which would be a U.S. protectorate. The occupying force carried by *Voyager* was a mixed group of men and women, prepared to occupy, pacify, and administer the new world. The Fellowship colonists were to be rounded up, identified, registered, and assigned an identity number. All guns would be confiscated. Men sixteen and over would be incarcerated while they pacified the population. Many of the Fellowship men would ultimately be deported, the women and children dispersed to new communities to keep them from organizing a resistance.

666 ✠ JAMES F. DAVID

The deep-space cruiser *Genesis,* renamed *Nova,* had flown to America attached to *Voyager.* When they reached planet America's system, Colonel Watson took *Nova* and separated from *Voyager,* taking one of their two spheres with him. They approached planet America slowly, searching space actively with radar and listening passively across the entire electromagnetic spectrum. No signals were coming from America, or anywhere in near space. *Voyager* stopped just outside the orbit of America's one moon, while *Nova* searched it, finding nothing. Colonel Watson then took *Nova* to the planet, orbiting America, searching for a Fellowship space station. They found nothing. Puzzled, Thorpe, Ash, and Slater were called to the flight deck.

"I thought there was a space station orbiting America," Fry said to Simon.

"There was, and there were cargo modules floating everywhere."

"Colonel Watson found nothing on the far side or anywhere in orbit. We're picking up nothing on radar," Fry said.

"He's right," Slater said. "Space was thick with cargo modules."

"They must have landed everything," Simon said.

Fry looked dubious.

"We need that space station," Thorpe said. "They manufactured drives there. Nothing else is important."

"Colonel Watson is bringing *Nova* back to dock," Fry said. "You three will accompany us to the surface in the shuttle to scout out the settlements. *Nova* will stand by with an assault force."

Simon knew cruisers weren't designed to land, although the Fellowship had done it once. He was glad to be in the shuttle.

They packed the shuttle with soldiers, Simon riding on the top deck with Meaghan Slater. They dropped through the atmosphere fast, clearly worried the Fellowship would attack. At the threshold of regurgitation, they leveled out and slowed. A few minutes later he and Meaghan were called to the flight deck.

"We're coming up on a farm. Do you recognize it?"

They were a hundred feet above the forest, moving

slowly. A sphere flew a parallel course, just below them. In a clearing ahead Simon could see a tilled field and buildings along one side. The shuttle accelerated and they shot over the buildings—no missiles were launched, no guns fired. Turning, they made another pass; the only response was a few flying mammals startled from trees.

"Put us down," Fry said, and Colonel Watson ordered the pilot to land the shuttle in the middle of the field. The sphere continued to circle, acting as lookout. As soon as the door of the shuttle was opened, fresh moist air flowed through the ship. The smells of planet America brought back memories of Simon's previous stay and he trembled.

Simon watched from the flight deck as soldiers poured from the belly of the shuttle, encircling the ship. Working across the field like waves approaching a shore, the heavily armed men and women reached a dormitory, kicking the door open and rushing inside. Another squad entered a barn. Soon both groups were back, signaling all clear. Ordering him and Meaghan to stay, Fry and Watson left the shuttle and inspected the buildings, then returned to the ship.

"Abandoned. No personal items inside, no bedding, no linens, no food," Watson said. "The layer of dust shows it's been empty for a while."

They left the farm traveling west. The three largest settlements were in a valley a hundred miles from the coast. They found another farm, but the buildings had burned to the ground and there were no signs of life. Next they found a sawmill, abandoned like the farm, the buildings standing but the equipment removed. Stacks of lumber still sat in the drying shed.

The sphere raced ahead now, bolder, scouting the large community west of them, the pilot reporting no sign of life. They approached the small town cautiously, landing near the outskirts, searching building by building, finding nothing. Again there was no food, no personal items.

"They must have dispersed into the country," Colonel Watson suggested. "Somehow they were tipped off that we were coming."

"Or they've retreated to a fortified position," Fry said.

At the next village they let Simon and the others off and they explored the buildings with the others. It wasn't the town Simon had lived in, but it was nearly identical—buildings lining both sides of a muddy street, a church with a steeple at one end.

Simon recognized the third town they dropped into as the one he had lived in—New Jerusalem—the paved street clearly distinguished even from the air. There were also more buildings than any other town they had surveyed, and more cleared land surrounding the town. The streets were empty, however, and no animals could be seen. This time they landed near the edge of town, the soldiers more casual now, searching the first few buildings, then signaling the town was empty. Simon and Meaghan Slater led Watson and Fry up the street, explaining what the buildings had been used for. Every window was dark and lifeless. Then a soldier shouted from a porch. Holding up an apple he shouted, "Someone's been living in this one—there's food."

Hurrying to that building, they found signs of life: personal belongings, beds made, food on the shelves. Next, Thorpe shouted from the porch of the dormitory he and Simon had lived in.

"The lights work," Thorpe said, flipping the switch, turning the lights on and off. "They use drives for generating electrical power. We need to find it."

"They took to the hills," Colonel Watson concluded as they walked up the street toward the church. "We'll take their town and their food. They'll come to us when they get hungry enough."

"There's someone at the church," Fry said, pointing.

A black woman sat in a rocker in front of the church. They paused long enough to let the soldiers check the buildings on either side, then walked slowly toward her. With soldiers on each side of him, rifles ready, Colonel Watson led them up to the old woman.

"Who are you?" Colonel Watson demanded.

"Selma Jones," she said, "but everyone calls me Grandma. You can too."

"Who's in charge here?" Colonel Watson said.

"You're looking at her," she said, with a touch of sadness.

"You're with the Fellowship?" Colonel Watson asked.

"No," Grandma Jones said.

"Where's Ira Breitling?" Thorpe demanded.

The old woman looked Thorpe in the eye and gently said, "He's not here, honey. He and his people are mostly gone. You should go too. Go and leave us in peace."

"Gone where?" Colonel Watson asked. Then when she didn't answer, "It would be better for you if you helped us."

"You don't understand," the old woman said. "They're not anywhere on this planet. God led them to a new home."

"She's lying," Fry said. "She would have gone with them if they left."

"It's the white people who left," Grandma Jones said. "They offered to take us, but God had a different destiny in mind for me and mine. There's just too much history between white and black folks for us to live together. This way we get this whole planet to ourselves. We're totally free now, free to become whatever it is God intends us to become. We can live in harmony with nature like our ancestors, kill each other in tribal warfare, or reach for the stars like our white brothers and sisters did. And we got nobody to blame for what happens now but ourselves."

"How many of you are there?" Colonel Watson asked.

"You should go while you still can," Grandma Jones repeated.

"We're here to stay," Fry said. "Planet America is now an official protectorate of the U.S. government."

The old woman looked genuinely sad and hung her head.

"You said they were mostly gone," Thorpe said. "There are still some around here?"

The rumble of thunder sounded in the distance. Simon looked at the sky, it was overcast but didn't look like rain.

"There are a few out there that couldn't bear another long journey in space. A few others had been shunned and couldn't be found when it was time to leave," Grandma said. "A few more had gone crazy and took to living in the hills like hermits. They don't bother us and we don't bother them."

Then Watson heard a radio crackle to life and his radioman stepped forward, face ashen.

"It's *Voyager,* sir. They're under attack."

CHAPTER 146　**ALONE IN THE VOID**

> I have never obtained any ethical values from
> my scientific work.
>
> —ALBERT EINSTEIN

ORBITING PLANET AMERICA

The first kamikaze sphere rocketed up from the surface, sonic booms in its wake. As the atmosphere thinned the sphere accelerated at a rate that would crush a human occupant. The crew of *Voyager* detected the sphere on radar, but precious seconds were lost as commanders were notified and confirmation received. By the time the collision course was confirmed, collision was inevitable. *Voyager's* mass was just too great to put into motion before the sphere reached it.

The sphere struck *Voyager* a glancing blow on the starboard side, just forward of the drive. A gaping hole was torn in the side of the converted submarine, the explosive decompression blowing soldiers and equipment into space. With hull integrity destroyed, the ship buckled at the point of the collision, the gravity fields distorting as the drive bent around the side of the ship. The multiple gravity fields now pulled the ship in different directions; its submarine hull had been originally designed for the even pressure of the ocean depths, and later modified for

JUDGMENT DAY ✠ 671

the even pressure of an internal atmosphere. Now the interior bulkheads buckled, seals broke, atmosphere rushed for the vacuum of space, and men and women died by the hundreds.

Docked aft of the flight deck, the deep-space cruiser *Nova* survived the initial collision, its crew radioing Colonel Watson they were in trouble. Realizing *Voyager* would never fly again, *Nova*'s pilot powered up the deep-space cruiser, ordering his crew to release the docking clamps. Once his own fields were in place they were protected from the gravity waves uncontrollably sweeping the ship below. Warped by the collision and the resulting gravity waves, the docking clamps wouldn't release *Nova*, and the pilot ordered they be cut loose. As the mother ship tore itself to pieces, a crewman in an environment suit was locked into the airlock with a cutting torch to free *Nova*. He had just begun cutting through the first latch when *Nova*'s radar picked up another sphere on a collision course.

Nova was still firmly latched to *Voyager* when the second sphere struck the Ark-class ship midships. The collision killed most of the surviving army. The soldier in the airlock, already in a space suit, survived the collision and the explosive decompression. The collision finished the soldier's job, tearing *Nova* free of *Voyager*, expelling him into space.

The soldier found himself floating between the two ships, *Nova* somersaulting through space toward planet America. *Nova*'s belly was split from bow to stern, leaking atmosphere and bodies. *Voyager*, just below him, was slowly crumpling its huge mass into a ball. He had no propulsion unit, but it didn't matter. He had no place to go. His gauges told him he had a two-hour life span. Then below him he saw something rising from the planet. A ship like *Nova*, followed by a shuttle. He called over his radio for help, but the ships angled away, picked up speed, and soon disappeared into deep space leaving him alone in the void.

> All who are under the yoke of slavery should
> consider their masters worthy of full respect, so
> that God's name and our teaching may not be
> slandered. Those who have believing masters are
> not to show less respect for them because they
> are brothers. Instead, they are to serve them
> even better, because those who benefit from
> their service are believers, and dear to them.
>
> — I TIMOTHY 6:1–2

PLANET AMERICA

Colonel Watson and the others listened to the garbled transmissions coming from orbit, periodically trying to break in, to get a coherent description of what was happening. Piecing together the bits and pieces they picked up created a picture of unmitigated disaster. Finally, all transmissions ceased. Watson was still numb from the magnitude of the destruction of his ships in orbit when there was a distant explosion, flames and then smoke visible over the trees. Watson's men hit the ground, rifles pointed in all directions. No attack came.

"That was your shuttle, I'm afraid," Grandma Jones explained. "'Course if they did it the way I told them we might still use the drive as a generator."

"I'll kill you," Fry said, getting to his knees, reaching for his pistol.

Suddenly a half-dozen black men came out of the church, rifles cocked and ready. The soldiers aimed at the men on the porch as more gun barrels appeared on the roof. Then rifles appeared on every rooftop along the street and from under every porch and every crawl space.

"Put your guns down," Grandma Jones said.

Colonel Watson looked around nervously.

"Don't you be figuring your chances, Colonel, 'cause you haven't got a one," Grandma Jones warned. "There are a couple hundred guns pointed at you and your men and most of the people holding them don't like white people much."

"There's no point in picking a fight," Simon counseled, nervously studying the dozens of rifle barrels he could see. "We're stuck here until help can come."

"Help? Help from where?" Thorpe asked. "We left only a shuttle and a sphere back on Earth. A shuttle doesn't have the range to get here."

"They'll learn how the drives work," Simon said. "They'll come for us."

Thorpe shook his head in disgust.

"Without me they don't have a chance," Thorpe said.

"We're stuck here," Fry said. "But this isn't the time to make our stand."

Watson looked around, trying to see if there were as many hidden guns as Grandma Jones claimed. Reluctantly, Watson gave the order to surrender. As his soldiers put their weapons down, women crawled out from under buildings and circulated, gathering rifles, handguns, and grenades. Knives and ammo belts were taken next. When the soldiers were disarmed they were ordered to sit in the middle of the street, surrounded by men with rifles.

Now women appeared with ropes and began tying the hands of the captives.

"What's the point?" Meaghan Slater protested. "We have no guns, we have nowhere to go. Why tie us up?"

"I told you," Grandma Jones said. "We want our own planet. We don't want to be competing with white people. We're not going to let it all happen again."

"We passed two empty towns," Meaghan said. "We'll go there to live."

"We'll be needing those towns soon enough," Grandma Jones said. "What we don't need is unhappy white soldiers marauding around the countryside. I decided there's only one thing to do."

"You're going to kill us?" Simon blurted.

"No, I wouldn't permit that," Grandma assured them.

"Of course, that may have been kinder than making you slaves."

"Slaves?" Colonel Watson said as his hands were tied. "You can't be serious."

"What else are we to do?" Grandma asked. "You're trained killers. We can't let you run loose and we don't want to kill you. Besides, we need laborers."

"I can help you keep the Fellowship's generators running," Thorpe said, trying to curry favor.

"We're done depending on white people," Grandma Jones said. "We'll either do for ourselves, or we'll do without."

Holding up his tied hands Fry said, "These will never hold me."

"We've got chains," Grandma Jones said. "The forge is heating up now. And don't forget what happens to runway slaves."

Fry paled at the threat, thinking of whipping, maiming, and gelding.

"We're not all white!" someone shouted from the back.

Simon looked around, finding a quarter of the soldiers people of color, although only ten were African-American.

"When we can trust you, we'll set you free," Grandma Jones said.

"You can trust me now," Simon said as his hands were tied. "I don't want to be a slave."

"No one ever wanted to be a slave," Grandma Jones said, standing and walking toward Simon. "It's a hard life—not just the work that puts you into an early grave. It's the spirit-breaking injustice of being owned. Having someone else decide when you eat, when you sleep, whether you live or die." Looking over the prisoners she said, "You've got women here, so there'll be children." Then looking at Meaghan she said, "I'll do my best to protect you, but you need to know, your children won't all be white."

Meaghan Slater paled at Grandma Jones's prediction.

"That's the hardest part, seeing your children born without hope of a better life. Worse yet, seeing your children sold at auction."

"You can't do this to us," Simon said, tears running down his face.

"I really am sorry," Grandma Jones said. "It will be hardest on you. Your children won't know any other life except what you tell them about. Your grandchildren won't know nothing about being free."

"Please, we can live in peace together," Simon pleaded.

"It'll be hard on you at first, but you'll adapt," Grandma said with compassion. "I know right now the future looks dark for your people, but they say the first hundred years are the hardest."

CHAPTER 148   **LAST LOOK**

> By the time Lot reached Zoar, the sun had risen over the land. Then the Lord rained down burning sulfur on Sodom and Gomorrah—from the Lord out of the heavens. Thus he overthrew those cities and the entire plain, including all the vegetation in the land.
>
> —GENESIS 19:23–25

UNKNOWN LOCATION

Hands tied behind his back, hood covering his head and cinched around the neck, Mark was pushed roughly into a chair. Mark landed sideways on the seat. Immediately the guards began kicking his legs, driving them to the front of the chair. Such petty abuse was common and he had learned to suffer it in silence. Mark could tell by the smell of the air they had taken him outside. As he sat in the chair, his back ramrod-straight, his shins aching and bleeding, he breathed deep and long, enjoying air that was free of human smells. He wore only hospital pajamas and the air was cool. He quickly chilled, goose bumps forming on his skin. He didn't mind. He would suffer a blizzard to be outside.

Shivering, Mark heard heavy military footsteps, stopping a few feet away. Then one man approached, his voice loud in Mark's ear as if he were inches away.

"We have your technology, your cult is destroyed, your people dead, imprisoned, or captured. Your God did not choose well."

It was Manuel Crow. Crow's career was built on lies, but if the Fellowship was destroyed it would be the one truth he would tell. Either way, Mark had failed God.

"We've sent a fleet to capture planet America," Crow hissed in his ear. "Everything that was yours is now mine."

Mark listened for Crow to mention the other world, but he spoke only of planet America. *He didn't know!* Mark's heart leapt with joy. Planet America had been a blessing, but it wasn't the planet of Ira's vision.

"Nothing to say, Shepherd?" Crow asked. "Then I've got something to show you."

His hood was torn off, Mark finding it was night. He looked up to see Crow towering above him, sharp features barely distinguishable in the dark.

"Look to the west," Crow ordered.

Mark looked at the stars above him, relishing his first view of the sky in months. Crow's hand slapped the side of his head, his eardrum ringing.

"To the west!" Crow repeated.

Mark followed his point, seeing nothing at first, then spotting a bright dot that wasn't a star.

"It's the first of your asteroid bombs," Crow said. "There are many more coming."

Now Mark suspected Crow's victory was not as complete as he claimed.

"There are others close behind that one," Crow continued. "This planet is in for quite a pummeling, thanks to you. The experts tell me thousands will die from the initial bombardment, and millions more from the starvation, disease, and war that will follow."

"You brought this on yourself," Mark said, refusing to be blamed. "Besides, if you have our technology, why didn't you stop them?"

"We tried, but you booby-trapped them."

"You can evacuate the target cities and installations. No one has to die."

"There won't be any warnings and no evacuations. Tomorrow, after the first strike, I'm going to declare martial law. In a month or so I'll suspend the Constitution and disband Congress. There will be some resistance, of course, but I have my people ready to take care of loose ends. Most people will be too busy worrying about survival—and cursing you—to worry about the loss of a few freedoms. I might even whip up a pogrom against fundamentalists like you, orchestrate some church burnings, maybe a few lynchings. That should break the back of the fundamentalist movement. Best of all, thanks to you, I don't have to worry about term limits. I'm president for life."

Mark knew it would happen just as Crow said. Inadvertently, Mark had given Crow what he wanted—power.

"Now look up above you, Shepherd. Look at those beautiful stars. You gave them all to me, and to my lord, Satan. Now say good-bye to the sky because you will never see it again."

Then Crow pulled the hood down over Mark's head, cutting him off from the heavens. Now he was lifted to his feet and dragged away.

"Thank you, Mark Shepherd," Crow called after him. "You've given me more than I ever dreamed of."

Inside the hood, tears flowed down Mark's cheeks.

> Go, assemble the elders of Israel and say to
> them, "The Lord, the God of your fathers—the
> God of Abraham, Isaac and Jacob—appeared to
> me and said: I have watched over you and have
> seen what has been done to you in Egypt. And
> I have promised to bring you up out of your
> misery in Egypt into . . . a land flowing with
> milk and honey."
>
> —EXODUS 3:16–17

SPACE STATION, ORBITING
PLANET PROMISE

Micah sat in the communications room of the space
station orbiting the planet named Promise, as he did
every day, watching for his family. Shelly and his children were months overdue and nothing short of catastro-
phe could have delayed them this long. He had seen
Covenant strafed, but escape into space. He thought the
ship had made it safely away, but now realized the damage to the ship was much greater than he first thought.

Sometimes Micah thought that God asked too much of
his people. So many had to die to reach the world God
had shown to Ira so many years ago. Now named
Promise, the new world floated in the void, the second
world in a six-planet system, just as Ira had seen in his vision. Promise's mass was similar to Earth's, the gravity
nearly identical. There was less tilt to the axis, and the
climate had fewer extremes. Two-thirds of the planet was
temperate, with mild winters, and summers where the
highs rarely exceeded eighty-five degrees Fahrenheit.
While leaving planet America had been painful—they
had invested so much in that world—most of those who
were building homes on the surface were ecstatic about

their new home—but not Micah. Shelly and the children never made it to planet Promise, nor did the sixteen hundred people on the ship with them.

Micah would give up his vigil once he decided whether to curse God and die, or accept God's will and go on with life. Until then he would continue to come to the space station control room day after day, refusing to step on the new world without his family.

"Micah," Sandy said, touching him gently on the arm. "It may be nothing, but we're picking up something on radar . . ."

Micah was out of his seat in a flash, studying the screen. There was something out there, but they were too new to the planet Promise's system to have mapped all the comets and asteroids. Then the radio crackled to life.

"This is *Covenant*. Can you hear us?"

It was Shelly. Micah lunged for the microphone, Sandy leaning aside.

"Shelly, it's Micah. Are you all right?"

"Micah . . . I'm fine. The children are here. We're okay."

Pinching his eyes tightly closed, Micah fought to keep his tears from flowing. Sandy hugged him, then keyed another microphone.

"This is Sandy, Shelly. Micah is a bit overcome. Welcome to Promise. How many are with you?"

A long silence followed.

"We had mechanical problems," Shelly said. "There were too many of us. We couldn't all survive. We had to make a choice."

Those in the control room now gathered around the speakers, hearing the sorrow in Shelly's voice.

"Only the children are left."

Gasps of horror filled the control room.

"We need food and water. The air is bad. Bring us oxygen and CO_2 scrubbers."

"We'll bring you supplies, *Covenant*," Sandy said. "We have everything you need."

The control room was silent now, each thinking of

those they knew on the ship. Then Micah remembered Ira was on the *Covenant* and that Shelly had said there were no adults left.

"What of Ira, Shelly?"

"He's here, Micah. He won't speak to me. I knew we needed him. I wouldn't let him die with the others."

The radio crackled again, then Ira was speaking.

"Is Luke there, Micah?" Ira asked.

"He's here, Ira. He's fine. He'll be glad to know his daddy is coming home."

"What of Mark? Did you find Mark?"

"No. I'm sorry, Ira." Then Micah said, "Ira, tell Shelly I'm coming. Talk to her. Forgive her. She did what she thought God wanted."

Then Micah sprinted from the control room to *Exodus*. It would be days before *Covenant* could be docked at the space station and he wouldn't wait that long to see his family. He would bring them the supplies they needed, and then bring his family safely to the station. Then they would make the final leg of the journey to the promised land, together.

THE NEXT TESTAMENT

CHRIST'S HOME

December 24, twenty years later

Without her bodyguards Christy felt vulnerable. People on the street were huddled in clumps, sharing bottles of Christmas cheer, many of them drunk. City power had been cut at nine even though it was Christmas Eve, federal law preventing special accommodation for religious holidays. Most of those on the street were men and they looked her over as she passed. Even at her age, and in the red robes that marked her as a licensed religionist, she was vulnerable. Walking steadily, but with forced confidence, Christy ignored the looks and comments of the men.

Christ's Home bore little resemblance to the town she had visited with Simon Ash so many years ago. She passed the Eternal Rest and Sandman Motels, both run down and now renting rooms by the hour. The Pig and Pancake had been burned to the ground when the military first took the town, but pink paint could still be seen on some of the concrete blocks in the rubble. Christy paused, remembering her breakfast with Mark the day he had given her a tour of the launch facility. There were so many possibilities then. They could have made different choices, lived different lives, but the choices were made, their lives lived.

She left the restaurant and walked past boarded-up houses toward the hill where the church still stood. Up ahead there was a fire in a barrel and a knot of soldiers around it, warming their hands. Christy was particularly wary of soldiers and police who hid their crimes behind uniforms and badges.

Approaching the group, she put on a show of confidence. As she came into the light of the fire they looked her over just as the men on the street had. She carried no purse but there were pockets in her scarlet robe designed for her identity papers. She handed them to a young lieutenant in a dirty uniform. He studied her papers long and hard.

"Where are you going at this time of night, Reverend Maitland?" he demanded finally.

"To the church on the hill," she said.

The lieutenant leafed through her internal passport, studying the pages of stamps recording her movements around the country, never having seen anyone who had traveled as much as she. The other men were ignoring her now, passing a bottle around—except one, who was staring. He looked vaguely familiar but Christy was unable to place his face.

"Why do you want to go to the church?" the lieutenant asked. "There's no one there but an old traitor."

"It's Christmas Eve. I'm going to celebrate the birth of our savior, Jesus Christ."

The lieutenant looked disgusted, rolled his eyes for the amusement of his men, then handed her papers back.

"Tell that old man if he rings the bell at midnight, I'll arrest him."

Nodding, Christy tucked her papers away and continued up the hill. The eyes of one soldier followed her into the dark.

Christy had never walked up the hill to the church before, only driven, and it was steeper and longer than she remembered. She was out of breath when she reached the top. The church stood as she remembered it, although the Fellowship hall was nothing but a skeleton, the siding torn off and burned for fuel by neighbors. The rest of the hill had never been developed and she could see the town below and the valley on the other side. The only lights were scattered fires. She knew that somewhere out there was where the *Rising Savior* had been launched.

A dim light shone from the church and she stepped inside, pausing in the back, looking around. A sputtering lantern lit the interior. He was there, moving chairs into rows, the pews ripped out years ago. He didn't hear her come in and continued working, moving slowly, slightly bent over, dragging one leg. Prison had been hard on him, aging him beyond her. Hair gray, he was balding on his crown. He was thin to the point of looking sickly, and he moved with pained difficulty. His Roman nose still stood out in profile, but it was crooked now. He had changed much over the years, but he was still alive.

"Hello, Mark," she said.

He turned, looking for her. Uncertain of how he would treat her, she hung back, letting him find her. When he did he smiled.

"Hello, Christy," Mark said.

An awkward silence followed, neither willing to say the wrong thing.

"Have you come for the service?" he asked. "It's going to be a candlelight service, there's no electricity."

"It's a conservation measure," she explained. "Christmas Eve services should be by candlelight anyway, don't you think?"

He moved another chair into place.

"Did you get me out of prison, Christy?"

"I negotiated your release," she said.

Moving another chair he said, "How did you do it? Crow hates me. After the asteroids fell he blamed me for the disaster. I became the number one enemy of the state. That's why I'm the fine figure of a man you see today."

"I'm sorry it was bad for you. I tried every year to get you released."

"What did you give Crow, Christy? What was the price of my release?"

"Oil. George Proctor agreed to renew sales to the U.S. if you were released."

"George Proctor? He's still alive?"

"He's president of the Alaskan Republic, Mark."

Mark shook his head, moving another chair.

"Alaska is a separate country now?"

"When Crow suspended the Constitution, George led a revolt. It was a bloody war but in the end Alaska seceded from the union."

Mark shook his head as if he couldn't believe what he was hearing.

"I got no news in prison. Nothing to read at all for the first three years. I never did get a Bible."

"I have something for you," Christy said, coming forward.

Fishing in her robes she pulled out a Bible, handing it to Mark.

"Thank you," he said.

"Look here," she said, opening the Bible to Revelation and then flipping to the end of the book. Turning the next page Mark saw there was another book there titled *The Fellowship*.

"What's this?" Mark asked, puzzled.

"It's an account of what happened to you and your people."

"My name's here," he said, reading the first paragraph.

"You're all in there. George Proctor wrote it. There's another version of your story after George's version. I don't know who wrote it, but it has intimate details only someone close to you could know."

"It's blasphemy to put this in a Bible."

"Is it? The Bible is a record of God's dealing with humankind. Your story is a part of that history.

"I'm writing my own version of the events, Mark. I'd like you to help me."

The door opened, a family coming in, each parent carrying a small child. They hesitated when they saw Christy's scarlet robes, fearing arrest. Mark's church was unlicensed and the Christmas Eve service illegal. Normally, no one would care enough to bust the service, but her presence made it look like a raid.

"Please come in," she said. "Join us for worship. Reverend Mark and I are old friends."

Relieved, the couple took seats toward the back, holding their children in their laps.

"Will many come?" Christy asked.

"A dozen, maybe as many as twenty. Being public enemy number one makes it difficult to build a congregation."

The door opened and more people came in; two more families and a young couple. All of them eyed Christy but were reassured by the first family.

Christy knew her official robe was the problem and took it off, even though it was illegal for her to be in public without it. Helping Mark with the last of the chairs, she then sat in the front, waiting for the service to begin. Mark passed out candles, which they lit, then the service began, the flickering candles splashing shadows around the walls. There were no hymnals, so they sang from memory—"The First Noel," "O Come, All Ye Faithful," "O Little Town of Bethlehem." Halfway through the last carol Christy's skin prickled, and dust bunnies danced around the room.

Mark opened a Bible—not the one Christy had given him—and began to read the story of the birth of Jesus. The wise men had just arrived to present their gifts when the door opened and a group came in. The worshipers turned in fear, expecting soldiers. Christy gasped when she recognized them—Micah was there, and Shelly, both well into middle age. There were younger ones too, she didn't know. Then pushing through the group came an old man with an eye patch—Ira Breitling.

Mark and Ira rushed each other, embracing and laughing. Shelly came to Christy, holding out a hand.

"Christy, is that you?" she said. "We never expected Mark, let alone you."

"Where did you come from?" Christy asked. "What are you doing here? You're in danger. You must go."

"We have a shuttle outside," Micah said. "We have a few minutes before the soldiers get here." To Mark he said, "We came for you, Mark. You're welcome to come too, Christy." Then to those seated in the church he said, "You're all welcome to come with us. It's a hard life on planet Promise, but it's a good life. You can worship God openly and you'll live in a community that shares your beliefs."

The tiny congregation whispered excitedly. They all knew the story of the Fellowship and of how God had led them to a new world.

Christy stepped back, letting the joyful reunion go on without her. She had never really been a part of the Fellowship, and the old feeling of being marginalized came back. Soon it was clear the entire congregation would be leaving for Promise. Shelly saw Christy hanging back and left Mark to join her.

"Please come, Christy," she said.

"I have a ministry here," Christy said. "You don't need me. Take George Proctor."

"He turned us down and sent us here. He's a warrior, and there are no wars to fight on Promise."

"You have no problems?"

"We've had disease, famine, natural disaster, and come through each stronger in community."

"I don't know, Shelly," Christy said.

"We have to leave, Christy," Shelly said. "They'll be here soon and we can't come back anymore. It's too dangerous, they're building orbital defenses."

Mark joined them, holding her hands.

"Please, Christy," he begged.

Then the door burst open, the soldiers that had checked Christy's papers rushed in. The six men fanned out, aiming their rifles.

"You're all under arrest," the lieutenant said. Then turning to a sergeant, he said, "Take two men and see if you can find their ship."

Before the sergeant could follow his orders, one soldier swung his rifle and shot the sergeant in the chest. The sergeant's last breath exploded from his lungs, his body collapsing in a heap. Then pointing his rifle at the head of the lieutenant he ordered the others to drop their weapons.

Christy and the others stood dumbly, unsure of what was happening.

"Pick up their weapons," the soldier ordered.

Still no one moved until Ira shouted a command.

"Get the guns, Luke," Ira ordered.

Christy watched Ira's son—Crow's seed—gather the weapons.

"On the floor," the soldier with the rifle ordered.

When the soldiers were down, Shelly walked over to the man, studying him. The face was weathered and scarred, the eyes pale blue.

"Daniel Remple!" Shelly announced. "It's Evelyn's boy."

Luke and the other man kept guns on the soldiers,

while the rest gathered around Daniel, hugging him, shaking his hand. Tears began to drip from Daniel's eyes.

"What about my mother and father?" Daniel asked.

"Floyd died when they raided the Mexican compound," Shelly said. "Your mother's still alive and so is your sister. You're an uncle, Daniel."

"I'm happy for Faith," Daniel said. Then sadly, "I have things I wanted to say to my father—to apologize."

"He never stopped loving you, Daniel," Shelly said.

"We go now, or we don't go at all," Micah cut in.

"He's right," Daniel said. "We reported in when we spotted the shuttle landing. There are more troops and gunships on the way."

"Everyone, get to the shuttle, now!" Micah shouted.

Pushing those nearest him, Micah soon had them moving through the door, into the night.

"Can you forgive me for what I did?" Daniel asked Shelly. "I said terrible things. The way I treated my mom and dad—"

"God will forgive you, Daniel. All you have to do is ask," Shelly said.

"You don't know what I've done—terrible things."

"God will forgive you, Daniel. Now can you forgive yourself?"

"I want to see my mother. I want to go home."

Taking his arm, Shelly pulled Daniel through the door. Now Mark faced Christy.

"Please come to the new world with me," Mark said.

"It was never meant to be," she said. "That's what you told me the last time I saw you."

"I was wrong, Christy. I've had twenty years to think about what happened and I know you never betrayed me. You wouldn't. I still love you. Come with me."

Christy's eyes welled with tears.

"I can't, Mark. I've had time to think too. I don't believe what you believe, Mark. I don't see the world the way you and your people do. You see black and white where I see shades of gray. I look for middle ground; you see nothing but clear dividing lines. I seek compromise while for you your way is the only way."

"We were good together," Mark said. "It could be that way again."

"Mark, I believe your colony is doomed. The people who left Earth with you are too homogeneous; there's almost no diversity. For an ecosystem to survive it takes diversity, and human civilizations are the same. You are trying to create a new world order built on social inbreeding. Without diversity each new generation will be weaker than the last."

"But God called us, Christy. God made it possible."

"We're going now," Micah said, coming back in the church, dragging Mark toward the door.

"Please, Christy," Mark begged.

"If you stick your heads out this door we'll blow them off," Luke said to the soldiers on the floor, then backed toward the door.

"Good-bye, Mark," Christy said, pushing him through the door and closing it. Her heart broke as she saw the pain on Mark's face.

The soldiers were up immediately, looking for another exit, disappearing through a back door. A few minutes later the dust bunnies danced again, and she heard the whoosh of a spaceship flying to the stars.